LONG PAST DUES

ALSO BY JAMES J. BUTCHER

The Unorthodox Chronicles
DEAD MAN'S HAND

LONG PAST DUES

JAMES J. BUTCHER

ACE
NEW YORK

ACE
Published by Berkley
An imprint of Penguin Random House LLC
penguinrandomhouse.com

Copyright © 2023 by James J. Butcher
Penguin Random House supports copyright. Copyright fuels creativity, encourages diverse
voices, promotes free speech, and creates a vibrant culture. Thank you for buying an authorized
edition of this book and for complying with copyright laws by not reproducing, scanning, or
distributing any part of it in any form without permission. You are supporting writers and
allowing Penguin Random House to continue to publish books for every reader.

ACE is a registered trademark and the A colophon is a trademark of Penguin Random House LLC.

Library of Congress Cataloging-in-Publication Data

Names: Butcher, James J., author.
Title: Long past dues / James J. Butcher.
Description: New York: Ace, [2023] | Series: The Unorthodox Chronicles; 2
Identifiers: LCCN 2023003646 (print) | LCCN 2023003647 (ebook) |
ISBN 9780593440438 (hardcover) | ISBN 9780593440445 (ebook)
Subjects: LCGFT: Fantasy fiction. | Thrillers (Fiction) | Paranormal fiction. | Novels.
Classification: LCC PS3602.U848 L66 2023 (print) |
LCC PS3602.U848 (ebook) | DDC 813/.6—dc23/eng/20230130
LC record available at https://lccn.loc.gov/2023003646
LC ebook record available at https://lccn.loc.gov/2023003647

Printed in the United States of America
1st Printing

Book design by Daniel Brount

This is a work of fiction. Names, characters, places, and incidents either are the product
of the author's imagination or are used fictitiously, and any resemblance to actual persons,
living or dead, business establishments, events, or locales is entirely coincidental.

*This book is dedicated to good mothers,
both those who understand why their children
do the things they do, and those who don't need to.*

May their patience with us never run out.

LONG PAST DUES

ONE

GRIMSHAW GRISWALD GRIMSBY SLID HIS ENCHANTED bicycle to a stop on the cracked pavement leading up to the house's sun-scoured door. Green sparks crackled from the rear gears as his *Torque* spell tried nudging the wheel forward, but he held it in place with the handbrakes as he gauged the neighborhood. This particular street was worn, relative to the quaint standards of Hyde Park. The pavement was pitted and faded to a bleached gray, while the homes on either side of the street were long, narrow collections of chipped brick, cracked timber, and rusted fixtures. However, even compared to its neighbors, this house seemed ill kept, or maybe just abandoned.

Grimsby wiped at the sweat on his brow with the loose sleeve of his oversize suit jacket before pulling a folded paper from his pocket. He double-checked the address, then leaned his bike against the short chain-link fence that guarded the small yard of wild, overgrown grass, propping the ever-spinning wheel up off the ground, where it spun in the still afternoon air like a windmill. Even from the broken-hinged gate, he could smell that the warm spring air was dampened by the odor of mold and something wet and pungent.

His steps ground over sun-cracked concrete and creaked on the old porch as he approached the door, and all the way he couldn't help but feel eyes on him. It made a shiver crawl through the gnarled burn scars along his left side, like ice-water veins from his fingertips all the way up the side of his neck. He scratched at the sensation and shook away the nervous feeling, forcing himself to remain as rigid and professional as he could.

He was an Auditor now, after all.

Though it didn't exactly feel like he had always imagined it would.

He rapped his knuckles on the weathered door, the rough surface stripped clean of paint by sunsets and neglect. His knock sounded meek, almost shallow, and no reply came from within.

He scowled and knocked more firmly, making his knuckles ache, until he was sure the occupant must have heard. It was the last name on his list, and he wouldn't return to the Department before checking it off. Menial task or not, he'd do his job.

Footsteps creaked inside the house, drawing slowly closer. Grimsby saw the peephole in the door darken as someone on the other side peered through, then heard the clatter and clack of multiple dead bolts and locks unwind and recede.

The door opened a crack, and a portly face with reddened eyes and lanky locks of dark, stringy hair peered out from within. "Yeah?"

"Samuel Goode?" Grimsby asked, trying to look imposing yet respectable as he imitated Auditors he had met in the past, though he had chosen to forgo their traditional white masks in favor of his glasses. The masks were for when things got ugly, and he expected today to be as banal as any other. Besides, he didn't care for the way he looked in one.

The man's face was smooth and shiny with sweat, but the circles around his eyes were deep and dark, cracked with more sleepless lines than the pavement outside. "Tentatively. Who's asking?"

"I am Auditor Grimsby," he said, still feeling a thrill of excitement at that particular pair of words, though it had slightly dulled over the last few weeks. Making house calls and riding his bike wasn't exactly what he'd had in mind a few months ago, when he received his badge, although it had been much more than he had expected before that.

Goode eyed Grimsby's outfit and scoffed. "A while to go until Halloween, kid. Come back when you fit in Daddy's suit."

He began to close the door, but Grimsby slid his foot in its path. He instantly regretted the decision as the man's idle strength nearly twisted his foot against the door's frame. Samuel Goode was a lot stronger than he looked, though Grimsby supposed most Therians must be.

He managed to choke his yelp into a more respectable grunt and drew his Department badge, a bifold of leather with a pentacle embedded in a silver shield within and his name below. "I'm afraid I'm a real Auditor, Mr. Goode," he said, trying to keep his voice straight over the pain of a likely stubbed toe. "I just need a moment of your time."

Goode looked at the badge in disbelief, then back at Grimsby. "If you're a real Auditor, where's your partner? I thought you guys never fly solo . . ."

Grimsby felt his stomach drop at the mention of a partner and bit back an unprofessional reply. Before he could come up with an appropriate substitute, however, Goode glanced past him and an unpleasant grin curled his face.

"Wait," he said, his smile wolfish, "did you ride a *bike* here?"

Grimsby tried to keep his face even but felt his fingers squeeze tight around the badge as he put it away. He half expected it to crumple in his hand like cheap plastic. "May I come in?"

Goode sighed, though a smirk still littered his face. "Fine, whatever, *Mr.* Auditor."

He opened the door wider and stepped aside. He wore a pair

of stained cargo shorts and a T-shirt that had a sloppy, indecipherable logo on it, though it was of a style that looked to be for a heavy metal band. Now close to him, Grimsby could tell the odor he'd smelled outside had come from Goode himself—and was even more pungent up close. Grimsby clenched his jaw but managed to keep his face straight and avoid wrinkling his nose.

Who said he wasn't a professional?

He entered, though the house was so dark it took his eyes a moment to adjust. Clutter was collected against the baseboards to either side of the short hall before him. Discarded wrappers, old shoes, dirty laundry, all of it with the settled manner of having been left in place for quite a while. The wall to his right fell off to an arched doorway, with a darkened living room beyond filled with scattered cardboard boxes and piles of who knew what.

Grimsby felt a brief flare of disgust before remembering his own apartment had looked quite similar not too long ago.

What was quite different from his own abode, however, were the windows. Every pane of glass had been covered with layers of curtains, bedsheets held up by thumbtacks, and even glued-on tinfoil. The few threads of light that managed to stray their way inside shone in the drifting dust like crossbeams.

Goode must have noticed Grimsby examining the source of the dimness. "The light gives me a headache. It's part of my . . . condition," he said, "and no, I'm not a psychopath."

"Oh good, because that's exactly what a non-psychopath would say," Grimsby said, managing a smile. "No, Mr. Goode, I'm here because—"

"You're my new zookeeper?" he asked.

"Well—I wouldn't call it that. As you are a registered Therian, I'm here to ensure you're prepared for your coming period of mandatory asylum. I need to—"

Goode interrupted him in a stuffy voice. "'Make certain I am ready for a period of stay lasting no less than three days, beginning no later than twenty-four hours before the apex of the lunar cycle,' blah blah blah." He sighed bitterly, using his hand to mimic a sock puppet talking. "Yeah, kid, I've heard the speech before. Every month, actually, so yeah, I know why you're here. So, which is it?"

Grimsby frowned, uncertain if he had missed some context. "I'm sorry?"

"If you're here, that means you're on Department house-call duty. Which means you're either the new guy or you drew the short straw. So, which is it?"

"Well, I—" he began, standing up a little straighter.

"New guy, of course," Goode scoffed. "Listen up, new guy. I know the deal, okay? I've been going to the cage since I was thirteen. I haven't missed it once, and I'm not going to miss it this time."

Grimsby felt annoyance crawl into his jaw and prickle his scalp. He supposed he shouldn't have been surprised at the flippant attitude. Goode was a Therian with a spotless record of Asylum attendance; it was why the task to make sure he was prepared for the coming full moon was one of Grimsby's many dully routine duties. He would be annoyed, too, if someone with a badge showed up every night to remind him to brush his teeth.

Though the attitude wasn't what bothered him.

What bothered him was that Goode had been completely correct in his assumption.

Grimsby was the new guy.

It had been six months since he got his badge, and he had been doing nothing but busywork since. House calls, recording complaints, writing citations for minor magical offenses, like kids hexing their tutor's hair to fall out. His most exciting moment to date was when he had to corral a rogue familiar, though it had only been a rabbit, much more manageable than some of the others he had faced in the past.

Much more.

He had dreamed of being an Auditor all his life, imagining what it would be like during his early years of training and then while working long shifts as a minimum-wage children's magician. He had concocted every scenario and image in his head.

But he'd never once dreamed it would be boring.

So when it was, he hadn't known whether he should be relieved or disappointed. It only took a few more weeks for him to settle on the latter.

Half a sigh slipped from his lips before he caught himself, but his chest deflated and his shoulders slumped lower all the same. He had promised himself he wouldn't stray back toward what he had been before he became an Auditor. Deflated, defeated, and content to stay that way.

Turned out, that was easier said than done.

He shook his head, bringing his mind back to the job at hand.

Then something caught his eye. A scrap of paper with a string attached, like the kind used as a price tag at a yard sale. It sat on the dusty table beside the door.

He picked it up and raised a brow as he read the handwritten text. "*Eye, newt. Three ounces,*" he said. "Is this yours, Mr. Goode?"

The Therian balked for a moment, then regained his flippant demeanor. "It's just a ritual reagent," he said. "Civilian-grade. I— I have a permit, if that's what you mean."

"A seller's permit?"

He shrugged. "Gotta make a living somehow. The Department stipend barely covers rent, and no one's going to hire me when they see *Therian* on every ID I own. They probably think I'm as likely to eat customers as help them."

Grimsby frowned. If Goode was on the up-and-up with his little business, he likely wouldn't have been so nervous when the tag was found.

"You mind if I take a look around?" he asked, feeling cautious excitement rise in him. Maybe he could find a case here after all. His first case.

Goode's lank hair seemed to bristle in agitation; his expression went as cold and hard as concrete in winter. "You have a warrant?"

Grimsby opened his mouth, then closed it again. He took a deep breath and shook his head. "No, Mr. Goode, I don't. Just thought I'd ask."

"Well, as long as we're asking." He stepped to the door and opened it. The fingernails on his hand were unclipped near to the point of talons. "I'd like to ask you to leave."

"Of course," he said, trying to ignore the nervous tenseness in Goode's motions. He was hiding something, but it wasn't as though Grimsby could snoop around until he found out what it was.

He was an Auditor, and that meant he had rules.

Though that didn't mean he couldn't come back. Especially if he could convince his director it was worth investigating. Even if it ended up only being a citation for wrongful possession of Unorthodox paraphernalia, it would still be his first real case.

Maybe it would even be enough to prove he was ready for something more than milk runs.

He drew his gaze over the sullen, dark interior of Goode's home one more time and suddenly wondered if he wanted to press the issue. Whatever he was selling, the Therian didn't seem to be living large by any stretch of the imagination.

He hardly seemed to be living at all.

Then again, perhaps it was his Department-given responsibility to press the matter.

He shook his head, setting his conflicted thoughts aside for the time being. Either way, it would have to wait. Goode was his last stop, but the Assessor would be expecting him at the Department headquarters soon. He had no time to waste agonizing over whether to chase a hunch or let it go.

He walked out the door and felt Goode's eyes on his back the whole way. Primitive instinct made the hairs rise on his neck. It was the feeling of being stalked by a predator.

He didn't look back until he reached his bike, and when he did he saw the afternoon daylight flash green off Goode's eyes in the darkened doorway for an instant. Then it was gone.

"Have a nice day, Mr. Goode," Grimsby called, ignoring the chills that brushed over the back of his neck. "I expect to see you at the Asylum by tomorrow afternoon."

"And I expect to see you for many months to come, *new guy*."

Goode said the words like a curse, and Grimsby felt it keenly.

But even as he rode away and the feeling of being watched faded, the real worry pressed in on him, gnawing at his stomach like he'd swallowed a live rat.

How much longer would his dream job remain a disappointment?

TWO ✳

LESLIE MAYFLOWER STOOD HIS USUAL WATCH AT HIS window, glaring out between the dusty blinds of his darkened living room, studying the street. He wasn't certain of the time—it was hard to keep track of time when he had been sleeping only every three days or so. So he glanced at the wall. The sun shone through the slats in thin lines, reflecting through the bottles of whiskey that lined his coffee table. Judging from the angle, it was early afternoon.

The time was near.

In front of the familiar house across the street, Sarah was pruning her garden. The kids were off to school for the day, leaving the street quiet. She usually spent her days off in her garden, enjoying the calm and tending to her lilies until her children came home from school in the afternoon. He sometimes watched her live out her tranquil morning peacefully, and found something like peace in that for himself.

But today, Mayflower wasn't watching Sarah.

He was watching for the mailman who had been recently assigned to his street. Mayflower didn't like the look of him, and he didn't like the way he lingered in front of Sarah's house. He had spent enough years hunting things that needed to be hunted to know one when he saw it.

Or at least he used to know.

He cursed and turned away from the window. The Huntsman, the man Mayflower used to be, would have known.

Now, he wasn't so sure.

He raised a hand to scratch the coarse gray scruff on his chin and found himself tracing the wrinkles under his eyes for a moment. Maybe his age was catching up to him. Maybe he was jumping at shadows. Maybe the mailman was just a slow driver.

But he wasn't slow, was he?

He usually raced briskly through his route. He stopped before Mayflower's mailbox for less than five seconds. But every day for the last month, he had stopped before Sarah's for nearly a minute. Sometimes he'd look through a stack of letters, others he'd be on his phone. And occasionally, just for a moment, he'd look up at Sarah, only when he thought she wasn't watching.

But Mayflower was watching.

He was always watching.

The lone sound of an engine approached in the distance. The type of engine and the time of day told Mayflower it was him.

The mailman.

He drained the last dregs of his bottle. He sat it alongside the others that lined his coffee table and opened the front door. He went outside, his passage disturbing countless days of dust, which swirled in the blinding beams that poured into his house.

The sun, apparently affronted that Mayflower had left his lair, stormed his head in an effort to split it from front to back.

He deepened his glare to keep his skull together, and made as though he was inspecting the stability of his peeling picket fence. He had been meaning to mend it for some time. In fact, he had been meaning to do a lot of things for some time. He glanced back to his house, and his mind wandered back for a moment to the time when it had been his home.

Now it was just where he lived.

He shook his head and turned his mind to the task at hand. The truck was close.

When it pulled up to stop before his mailbox, he pretended to meander over, struggling to scrub the scowl from his brow and instead don his most placating smile. It felt, and probably looked, closer to a grimace.

The man in the truck started as Mayflower reached the open doorway to his seat. He was wiry, with limbs that were lean and tan from days walking in the sun. His sandy hair was barely thinning with age. Mayflower judged him to be under thirty.

In other words, a punk

"Oh!" the man said. "Hello, sir. How're you today?" he asked, managing a smile that Mayflower found unconvincing. His teeth were too straight. Too white. His cheeks too clean-shaven.

He seemed too normal. Aggressively normal.

What was he hiding?

"Fine," Mayflower said. He had never had the chance to study the man up close until now, and he was doing so thoroughly. The name tag on his breast read *John*.

Mayflower had never met a John he liked.

In fact, he had killed the last John he'd met.

John was the name equivalent of unsweetened oatmeal. Bland to the point of suspicion. It could be the name of an average guy, an unidentified corpse, or someone who was trying too hard to appear unremarkable and unthreatening when they were anything but.

The question was, which was this John?

"Um, that's good," John said, squirming under his gaze. He hesitantly pulled out a handful of letters. "Here you go."

"Put them in the box, John," Mayflower said.

John's brow furrowed in confusion. "But aren't you just gonna take them after I—"

"In. The. Box. John," he repeated. Each punctuated syllable made his head pound.

"Oh—okay, then," John said, standing and climbing down from his seat to inch past Mayflower to get to his mailbox.

As John turned away, Mayflower leaned in the vehicle and looked around, searching for anything that might give him a reason to break the man's neck. Blood, ritual markings, a hidden tome or rune.

Disappointingly, he found none of the above.

He then scanned for more mundane reasons to snap John in two. Zip ties, razor blades, maybe a gun. God, he prayed to find a gun. Hell, even a roll of duct tape. Any of them would have been enough justification for his instinctual response to the man.

But there was nothing. It was clean, even neat.

Mayflower muttered a curse.

Some Huntsman, he thought.

Then he saw something under the seat. Something long and narrow, wrapped with paper to hide its true purpose.

Maybe he had been right after all.

Mayflower reached in and grabbed it, pulling it out.

"Hey!" John said as he turned from closing the mailbox. "What are you—"

Mayflower shot him a glare that silenced him. Then he withdrew the item.

It was a modest bouquet of lilies.

He stared for a long minute. "What are these?"

John's face turned bright red, and he stood on his tiptoes to glance over at Sarah, who was still working peacefully in her garden, tending to lilies of her own. "Look, it's personal, okay? Anyway, what are you doing in my truck?"

"Neighborhood watch," Mayflower said flatly.

"I don't think that gives you jurisdiction over federal property."

"You're in my neighborhood, aren't you?"

John frowned. "Mucking around in a mail truck is a federal offense, you know."

Mayflower locked down John's eyes for a long time. Long enough that John looked away, and then some more until the mailman coughed awkwardly.

"And are you going to report me, *John*?" he finally asked.

John stammered, "Well ... no ... I ... I don't think that's necessary, just—just stay out of my truck, okay?" He held out a shaky hand for the bouquet.

Mayflower scoffed. "Oatmeal," he muttered, shoving the lilies into his hand. He should have been relieved. Instead, he was only disappointed, and even he knew that was not a good sign.

What the hell is wrong with you? he asked himself.

He shook off the question like an old dog and stepped back, allowing John to pass and climb into his vehicle. Before he could put it in gear, however, Mayflower gripped the doorway's frame. "You know, John, this is a tight-knit neighborhood. We watch out for each other closely. Very closely. And we can be unreasonable when it comes to protecting our own."

John turned a couple of shades whiter as he nodded vigorously. "Yeah, Mr. Robinson told me something about that the other day, too. Though not quite so ... grimly."

"Who?"

"Your—your neighbor? I thought you said you were close-knit."

Mayflower curled an annoyed lip. "Drive, John."

"Yes, sir," John said, offering an uncertain smile before pulling up to the next box and hurriedly shoving its owners' mail inside, glancing back at Mayflower as he did.

Mayflower watched him until he left his sight, then he glanced across the street to see Sarah look up at him from her garden. She smiled and waved, as she always did. Mayflower pursed his lips in the closest thing to a real smile he could manage and waved back, as he always did. He ignored the sick feeling in his stomach. Then he retreated inside, resuming his post at the window.

So, the kid had some flowers. That doesn't say he's not a monster, he thought.

No, but it does say something about you, he thought back.

"Shut up," he growled, dropping into his old armchair and ripping a cigarette from the crumpled pack in his breast pocket. He began to light it, but through the open archway to the kitchen he saw the sticky note pinned to the icebox by a magnet. The top half he had tucked under the magnet, but the bottom half was clear.

He couldn't read it from this distance, but he didn't need to. He had spent too many hours staring at the words that had been penned by the gentlest of hands.

Take care of yourself.

He took a shaky breath and dropped the lighter on the coffee table, his teeth mashing the unlit cigarette's filter to pulp as he cradled his head in his hands.

What did that even mean anymore?

THREE

"Again," MRS. OX SAID, CROSSING HER BROAD ARMS over her squat frame. The familiar on her shoulder twitched and tilted its head, a gilded raven's skull with eyes of carved jet, at Grimsby, who lay panting on the shaded grass.

He managed to sit up, dabbing at his sweat-streaked brow with his ill-fitting sleeve. "I can't do it," he said, glaring at the tree Mrs. Ox had pointed him toward.

"Can or cannot, matters not," Mrs. Ox said, her Ukrainian accent almost as thick as her forearms, which looked like they could churn iron into butter. "I am Assessor. I say 'Again,' you again."

Grimsby groaned but staggered to his feet and toward the tree, which was a straight-trunked pine. Its lowest branches and chunks of its bark had been stripped bare by his previous spells, but the tree itself had not budged.

Of all the trees in the private reserve that surrounded the Department, he had quickly grown to despise this one the most. He had spent all afternoon trying to fell it with his spells, to no avail.

Blasted, stubborn shrub.

A soft breeze began to roll over the glade, bringing a small measure of respite from the unusually warm spring afternoon, carrying with it the smell of the nearby Mystic River. The sound of the highway on the far side, however, muddled any feeling of natural solitude. The reserve around the Department was sizable, especially being so close to central Boston, but it was still a small sliver of nature in the otherwise dense city.

Mrs. Ox snapped her fingers, drawing his wandering attention. "You have your trial, Auditor," she said. "Fell the tree." She withdrew a notepad and held up a hand to the raven familiar. It twitched its skull in an eerie semblance of the real creature before digging in its hollow scrapyard sculpture of a body as though preening itself, then withdrew a pencil that was worn to hardly a nub. Mrs. Ox took the pencil and made a note as she observed Grimsby.

He tried to focus his attention on the pine, and to not think about what she was writing, but concerns clung to his thoughts like dust to an old ceiling fan. This assessment was a test to evaluate his worth as an Auditor.

He was failing.

It didn't help that around him there were a dozen or more stumps of trees, some scorched black, others shattered, and one so smooth that a chain saw might have done it in. Each was a trial given to another Auditor, and each a badge of success.

He glared up at his own pine and ground his teeth in welling anger, trying to fill the pit of shame that had burrowed in his gut. The trial was absurd of him to even attempt, he knew. It was a test of strength.

But *Bind* wasn't a spell about strength; after all, it was Grimsby's spell, and strength wasn't something he had extra spades of, either magically or physically. He'd tried learning other spells from grimoires within the library at the Department, but he couldn't manage. It was like trying to learn to curl your tongue or have double joints. Some spells just didn't work for some witches.

And none of them worked for him, it seemed.

He knew only three, the first two taught to him by his mother from their old family grimoire. Those spells came as naturally to him as walking had, and so might have the others within the grimoire, but it had been lost in the same fire that took his mother. The last spell he had cobbled together himself. None of them were spells based on having a powerful Impetus, the inner force that shaped magic drawn in from the Elsewhere, but instead were flexible and efficient. They were more like pocketknives than chain saws.

But he couldn't fell a tree with a pocketknife.

Unfortunately, the scars on his left arm, which ran from his fingertips to his neck, also marked a much-deeper wound on his Impetus. One that he had never fully recovered from. He simply couldn't afford chain saw magic.

Though perhaps that's what being an Auditor required.

Oksanna—or Mrs. Ox, as she had come to be called—was right: she was a Department Assessor. It was her role to make certain Auditors were fit for service, both physically and mentally. Grimsby was never quite sure which of those two categories magic fell into. Ultimately, it was up to her to decide if he was ready.

And so, if she said "Again," he would again.

He had no other choice.

He just wished his mother had decided to teach him some kind of simple *Chop* or *Slice* spell, or whatever other verb might be useful for felling this twice-darned tree. Although perhaps that would not have been the best choice for a young Grimsby's first spell.

He suddenly remembered the first time he had sent a ball spinning without touching it, and his mother's proud smile, but her face was almost a blur. Even so, a warmth bloomed in his chest, though it burned into a hollow of ice within the briefest moment. He glanced down at his hand and the scars that marred it.

How different things might have been.

He shook his head, then his bad hand, as though whipping away something unpleasant.

He looked at the towering pine and felt his chest sink. "I don't think I have enough Impetus left for this."

Mrs. Ox scoffed. "Enough Impetus? Is like saying you don't have enough fingers to shape clay. Impetus does not go away—it is not like clay you have run out of. It is the hands that shape the clay of the Elsewhere. But even without clay, you have hands, yes?"

Grimsby glanced between his scarred and unscarred palms. "Sort of."

"And so also you have your Impetus."

"But what if I don't have the strength to use it?"

"Strength? Impetus is not about strength, fool boy. It is about will. It is about stubbornness." Her dark eyes glittered for a moment, mirroring those of her familiar. "And you are stubborn, are you not, Auditor?"

Grimsby managed a nod. He *was* stubborn. He had been for hours.

But he was also tired.

"Y-yes. I am," he said, as unconvinced as he sounded.

"Then you have your will." She flexed an arm in an exaggerated manner, the seams of her jacket protesting. "Stay stubborn long enough and you will be strong."

Grimsby replied only with an uncertain nod.

He summoned his waning Impetus. It rose, a churning warmth from the depths of him, almost defiant at his exhaustion. It pulled power from the Elsewhere into him, like a second pair of lungs drawing in a hot breath, and for a moment he let the heat brace his twitching muscles. He took care to direct the ambient energy away from the burn scars that ran all along his left shoulder and arm. He felt it tickle at the edge of the marred skin, and where it did, sparks snapped to life beneath his coat.

He directed the energy toward his right hand with practiced mental effort. Impetus might have felt like fire, but it flowed like water. He could vaguely direct it, though it wasn't easy. It was almost like shifting his own personal gravity or bailing out a boat with a teaspoon.

His hand grew warm, and he formed the idea of the spell in his mind, imagining it on the tip of his thumb. His fingertip began to spill forth ghostly, glowing blue ink, which quickly formed itself into a faintly shimmering rune for the spell. It wasn't from any language Grimsby knew of, but he had long since memorized its form from that old grimoire.

Often with his spells, necessity required him to place them in a hurried panic, but he took his time during this trial, trying to make certain the structure was precise. Every spell was almost like a vessel for the Impetus driven into it. Each subtle imperfection would be as a leak in a teapot, spilling out power as useless heat, making the spell weaker than it ought to be.

And he needed every edge he could find.

Though Mrs. Ox had declined to loan him an axe when he had asked.

He was unsatisfied by the first rune; it was misshapen and would falter quickly. He smudged it out of existence and replaced it, this time leaving a more pristine version. It would hold.

He hoped.

When he had finished, he went to another, neighboring tree and placed the rune's opposite number, a similar yet different symbol, then repeated the process a few more times, creating more pairs. Like positive and negative sides of an electric magnet that wasn't powered on.

He would have preferred a rock or solid concrete, anything

that wouldn't bend or sway; placement mattered most with *Bind*, but there was no other point to leverage the runes nearby. The nearest solid object was a boulder thirty yards away, and every bit of distance between the runes made for less efficient use of his limited Impetus.

He carefully placed as many sets of runes as he could muster the strength for. They crawled up the tree's height until he had to stand on tiptoes.

With each spell, his Impetus waned, growing colder, like a campfire hemorrhaging embers, until he could barely feel it. With it, he felt his muscles and breath exhaust in kind, the spells draining not only the power he could draw in from the Elsewhere, but whatever else he could muster as well. The warm spring air did little to ease the deepening chill that filled him as his Impetus receded, drawing a bone-deep shiver from the passing breeze. Even his breath fogged on his lips briefly in the afternoon sun. He shivered, pulled his jacket tightly around him, feeling the fabric slide roughly over his scars, and managed one final *Bind*.

Finally, with the spells in place, he staggered over to Oksanna and dropped onto the rocky grass, his teeth chattering.

Mrs. Ox let him take a moment, then nodded. "Begin."

Grimsby nodded and took a deep breath, silently hoping to finally succeed. He reached out a hand, sensing the bonds between the binds like invisible cobweb strands that radiated heat. He made certain to take a mental hold of each one, and then said the catalyst word.

"*Bind!*"

The blue runes flared to life, drawn to their partners by the spell. The strands became visible and began to glow, like heating wires made of cobalt. They pulled taut, making the trees tremble and timber groan. Pine cones and needles fell to the soft earth, and angry critters above vacated their nests to retreat to quieter, neighboring trees.

Grimsby stared, his chest tight. He had already sunk as much Impetus into the spells as he could; now it was a question of which was stronger: his magic or a tree.

Then, for a moment, the trees bowed toward each other, their tallest boughs crashing together.

Grimsby felt some swelling pride in him. Never before in Mrs. Ox's assessments had he made the two touch anything more than a few branches. Perhaps this time he would succeed. Perhaps this time he'd prove himself. Perhaps this time—

One blue-light tether grew to a blinding glow, then suddenly snapped in a dying flare of sparks. In a crescendo of disappointment, the others quickly followed, like ripping seams on a corset, until the last of them was gone.

The trees rocked back and forth for a moment before settling once more, as though shrugging off nothing more than a harmless breeze.

His hopes snapped to pieces just as quickly, and he let his head hang.

Another failed attempt.

Mrs. Ox said nothing, instead only scribbling on her clipboard as she took notes. "So be it," she said. "And says here your other spell—you still have only two?"

Grimsby gulped and nodded hurriedly, although it was a lie. His third spell, *Chute*, was of little use, but he had used it to get rid of something dangerous just before he had become an Auditor. Something the Department wanted quite badly. If they knew of the spell, they might be able to get it back, and so he had never told them.

Mrs. Ox glowered skeptically but continued. "Your other spell—*Tor-kay*?"

"*Torque*," he corrected.

"Ah, yes. *Tork*. It is also a spell you employ? What is its function?"

He felt his cheeks grow warm despite the bone-deep chill his spells had left him with. "It just—well, it turns stuff," he said.

She frowned and exchanged glances with her familiar quizzically before making a note. "Turns . . . stuff." The bird seemed equally unimpressed, or that was Grimsby's assumption as it cawed at him. The sound was strangely hollow, reverberating from the depths of the familiar's skull.

"It's really more useful than it sounds!" he said hurriedly. "Well, it's at least *as* useful as it sounds." His stomach twisted in shame. Auditors were some of the most powerful witches around. The others could probably turn invisible, implode buildings, or even drive a car.

And here he was . . . turning stuff.

"We will assess that spell"—she cut herself off, seeming to see Grimsby's shambled state for the first time—"tomorrow."

He let out a relieved sigh and fell back onto the cool grass, staring at the sky through the trees. His relief quickly drained away as a thought came to mind. "Mrs. Ox?" he asked.

"Hmm?"

"What happens if I fail your assessments?"

"I assess if you are able to be Auditor or no," she said. "If you fail, it means you are not ready."

He felt a wedge of fear cut into him. "But I'm already an Auditor!"

She nodded. "And Auditors, too, can be . . . What word did director use? Ah yes. Fired."

He gulped, and the sky seemed to start spinning before his eyes.

"No fear, Grimsby. I am sure 'turn stuff' will be just as impressive as . . ." She cast an eye to the pine that still stood strong. "As *Bind* was."

He looked over at her and saw some mirth in the wrinkles around her eyes, though it gave him no comfort.

"Now I must go. Director and I speak after he issues cases."

Grimsby shot up like he'd sat on a hot coal. "He's issuing cases today? I thought that was tomorrow!"

"It was. But is now today."

"Twin-tailed comet!" he cursed, scrambling numbly to his feet and looking around for the tree he had left his bicycle against. "I have to go, please excuse me!"

Oksanna dismissed him with a wave and turned her attention back to the pine he had failed to fell. She made another note on her clipboard.

Grimsby felt intense curiosity about whatever damning remark she was jotting, but he pushed it away. He quickly mounted his bike and pedaled through the grass to the nearest path, willing what little Impetus his short rest had recovered into the *Torque* enchantment in his rear wheel. He let the spell carry him at an almost reckless speed toward the Department.

With any luck, or perhaps only with a great deal of it, Grieves might be feeling generous enough to assign him a real case. Otherwise, he'd be stuck on *new guy* duties once again.

FOUR ✳

G
RIMSBY SLID HIS BIKE INTO THE RACK JUST BEYOND
the Department's entrance. He tried not to think about
the lot full of sleek black cars he'd just pedaled through, or how
all the other slots in the rack were empty.

He was still working on getting his license. After all, he'd
rarely had an opportunity to even sit in a car, let alone become
licensed. He had no family to speak of, mostly, and his former
position as a children's magician had barely afforded him rent, let
alone anything like a car. But even if he managed to get a license,
who knew how long it would be until he was issued a vehicle.

He held his badge to the dark square of mysterious electronics
beside the oiled oak doors. After a moment, the light flashed red
and an offended beep sounded. Grimsby grumbled and waited for
the light to reset before trying again. More offended beeps ensued.
It took three tries before the light finally flashed green and the
locked doors clicked open, allowing him inside the building.

The front entry was floored with cold concrete stained warm,
polished to a bright sheen. Broad pillars of deep, textured lumber
supported the walls, met between with bricks that had been taken

from the original Department headquarters in Salem. The walls were bare, save for a patterned molding and a single pair of black doors at the room's center. It made Grimsby feel like he was walking into a museum, though whether he was there to see the exhibits, or was one himself, was still up in the air.

A familiar face sat at the polished stone reception counter. Though there were enough spaces for ten receptionists, only one was on duty.

"Grimshaw." Stanwick nodded without looking away from the monitor in front of him. His gray frizz of hair stood out wide above each ear, leaving a shining bald field of sunburnt skin between. "Checking in?"

"Yes, sir," Grimsby said. "Is the director still here?"

Stanwick frowned at the word *sir* but tapped a few keys on the keyboard in front of him. "Yes, looks like. Better hurry, though. He's nearly done giving out assignments."

"Please tell me Mayflower is here, too?"

A few more clicks, then Stanwick shrugged his creaky shoulders beneath his plaid suit jacket. "Nope. He hasn't been in for three weeks. Guess you can call that Huntsman's privilege."

Grimsby bit back a sharp reply that Stanwick didn't deserve. "I had another name in mind for it," he said through gritted teeth. "Thanks, Stanwick."

The man bobbed his twin puffs of gray frizz in a nod, then pressed another button. The black doors beside the reception desk opened silently, allowing Grimsby inside.

He scuttled through them and down the long hall beyond. Unlike reception, this hall had tiled floors that looked much more dated and mismatched. Some looked like they belonged in ancient temples, others looked as though they had been dredged up from sunken cities, yet they had been fitted together with careful effort. Each had a symbol laid into it, though none of them matched, as they had been gathered from cultures across the globe. Some of the sigils even glowed to life as he passed and faded when he had gone. They were supposed to be protective spellwork from times long gone, but while most modern Auditors put little stock into the efficacy of such old magics, Grimsby was less certain.

At this end of the hall was a twin pair of oak doors, oiled and aged, starkly contrasting with the black steel at the opposite end. In his rush, Grimsby pulled them open hurriedly enough that they slammed into the walls, making him wince. Beyond was a large, elongated-dome room, with timbered support beams and hand-painted murals over the ceiling that were well aged and even better maintained.

The Department of Unorthodox Affairs had been born in Salem, but when it had outgrown its original building there, every brick and timber had been carefully moved to a new location, settled along the Mystic River. Of course, the original building had been too small for the modern era, and so it had been expanded into a muddled maze, half storied structure, half modern office, and all labyrinth.

Grimsby had been there for months, and he hadn't even gone beyond the primary level of the building, as the levels that had been delved below were beyond his pay grade. The only time he had been down there was when he had been arrested just before being hired.

As impressive as it was, the Boston Department wasn't sufficient for a whole country. Though while dozens of other branches had sprung up over the nation as the Department grew, with some larger or better staffed, especially New York, this had been the first.

This was where witches had stopped being hunted for the first time in recorded history.

Even in his hurry, Grimsby found himself skidding to a halt, eyes drawn upward to the murals painted on the domed ceiling:

Auditors, clad in colonial military uniforms, standing up against Therians, black dogs, and, in true revolutionary spirit, even a couple of British redcoats, not to mention a dozen other creatures long since dead from the world. They fought wielding nothing more than the strength of their Impetus.

And an occasional gun or sword.

Even now, though he'd seen the murals a hundred times, he still couldn't help but stand in awe. They seemed almost banal to the other staff, but to him they were incredible. He had once thought he would never have the chance to see them in person. That was, until the worst week of his life six months ago. He had somehow managed to survive and, on top of that, had miraculously come out of it with a job as an Auditor. A job he had been turned down for countless times.

And all it had taken was him nearly being killed almost as many times in a far fewer number of days.

Yet, after months of the most mundane tasks, he wondered— so deep down that it felt like he was hiding the thought from himself—if it was worth it.

He found his gaze had fallen from the murals to the tiled floor.

"Grimsby," a voice said suddenly, so close it made him jump.

He hurriedly pushed his glasses back into place and turned to see Rayne standing before him, her sharp teal eyes hard beneath stylish, thick-rimmed glasses, her nearly black hair tinged with red, a trait Grimsby's cheeks quickly adopted.

He felt his collar suddenly become tighter than he remembered, and he found himself straightening up to his full height. "Oh, Rayne—I didn't see you—" he began, but her eyes narrowed and his words faltered.

"Auditor Bathory," she corrected him, her temper seeming particularly short today. "You're—somehow—a professional now, Grimsby. Act like it."

His mouth hung open for a moment before he remembered

how to close it. "Right. Of course." He paused, noticing the dark rings of exhaustion around her eyes for the first time. "You look . . . tired."

She arched a dangerous, narrow eyebrow.

"Sorry, I meant you look tired, Auditor Bathory," he said, trying to suppress the small grin that curled the corner of his mouth.

Her statuesque expression might as well have been a mask for all it changed, but she let out a soft breath that could have been a scoff, which was about as close to a laugh as he'd heard from her in a long time. "I've been busy."

"Right, of course. I forgot. How's the search going?"

Her face hardened into glass, sharp and brittle, and a little more transparent to the concern beneath. "There's no sign of Auditor Hives anywhere. I checked Peters's old notes again and again, but they're useless, and none of them are recent enough to mention what he did with Hives anyway."

Grimsby shuddered at the mention of the former director's name. John Peters had nearly killed him in the frantic days just before he joined the Department, and Grimsby was still unsure if he had returned the favor or not. Either way, he had unintentionally left Peters a bloody mess before the end, though the thought still made him queasy. Mayflower had assured him that Peters was still alive when he put a bullet in him, but Grimsby wasn't so sure it mattered, even if it was true.

He shoved the memories down and focused on Rayne. "Do you think Hives is alive?"

"No," she said firmly. There was little emotion in her voice, though it seemed a result of effort. "But whatever he is, I need to know. We weren't partners for more than a few weeks, and he betrayed the Department. But"—her face grew distant for a moment—"we trained together for a long time. All of us did. You should know as well as I do that whatever he was at the end—that he wasn't always like that."

Grimsby bit back the first, sour reply that came to mind. "No, he used to settle for leaving me with bruises. Last time we chatted he tried to kill me."

Her lips pulled tight in a line for a moment, as though she held back a reply of her own. "Even so, I owe it to him to at least find out what happened."

Grimsby looked at Rayne's ringed eyes and realized what he saw.

She was worried—and any emotion from the enigmatic girl was rare enough a sight.

"So you're worried about him?" Grimsby asked. He felt some odd cold pit in his chest, one that he wasn't sure what to call, but he found himself hanging on her answer more than he expected.

"Well, of course. His disappearance could cause any number of troubles for the Department, if he is alive. He could leak sensitive information, slander us in public, maybe even use his magic to hurt someone." She paused, her somewhat distant expression growing focused on him. "Why wouldn't I be worried?" Her tone was exacting, sharp like a scalpel.

"No, I mean, you should be," Grimsby said, feeling like he was suddenly being dissected. Then he realized what that little pit had been.

It was envy.

Rayne hadn't always been this cold, this . . . professional. Like Hives, she had been different when they were young apprentice witches learning from a cycling group of Department mentors.

The teachers, and the trials, always changed, but Hives and Rayne had always been there, enduring both alongside him. There were others, too, but they had left a few at a time, either through elimination or simply dropping out to pursue more mundane lives. By the end, though, it had been only the three of them. They'd never exactly been friends, but still they had been the two people Grimsby was closest to. Hives, his rival and occasional bully, and Rayne . . . Well, he wasn't sure then, and he was somehow less sure now.

Regardless, the Auditor Bathory he'd come to know since joining the Department was indeed the perfect Auditor. Cold, collected, and professional.

And yet here she was, concerned for Hives, the guy who had spent a good portion of his life making Grimsby feel small and powerless.

Again he felt his face grow hot, but this time it was with welling anger.

Then he thought of what he would do if something similar had happened to Mayflower. The envy and anger both vanished, replaced with a shameful cluster of buzzing nerves in his stomach.

He suddenly felt keenly selfish.

"Well," he finally managed, his tone apologetic for words he hadn't said, "if there's anything I can do to help—"

"Of course there isn't," she said reflexively. She recoiled almost as soon as she let the words slip out, but they hung in the air like a plague haze.

Grimsby would have preferred it if she simply had sucker punched him in the stomach. At least then he could let himself react. Instead, he just tried to keep his face level, but it felt like a mask drawn thin, ready to tear.

Rayne took a short breath and looked away. "I'm sorry. That was uncalled-for."

"No, I understand," he said, managing a taut smile. "There's a hundred other Auditors with more experience and training. Without—" He unconsciously put his right hand over the scars on his left. "Without issues."

"Trust me." She managed a solemn smile, an expression he'd rarely seen from her, especially recently. "You're not the only one with issues, Grimsby."

He tucked away the lingering pain from her words, at least

enough to match her expression. "Well, if you need someone to vent to, I'm probably better at listening than I am at being an Auditor." He smiled again, though this time it was a bit more genuine. "It's not a high bar, after all."

She began to walk past him but put a cool hand on his shoulder, making him freeze. "Thank you. I might take you up on that."

He tried to act as though his heart hadn't just begun attempting to break free from the cage of his ribs. "Any time," he squeaked.

Her hand slipped away, and so did she, leaving him in the middle of the main hall. He shook himself, trying to think about anything other than her perfume or the missing weight of her hand on his arm.

Then his heat-addled brain remembered his rush to find Grieves, and he made his way as quick as he dared toward the director's office, trying to keep his head on straight through the whirlwind of mixed emotions.

His steps scuffed over the tiled ground, contrasting with the sharp clicks of the other passing Agents and Auditors. The Agents, in deep blue suits, largely ignored him. They weren't witches, most weren't even Unorthodox, but rather men and women trained to use more mundane methods of dealing with both. To them, he was just another unproven witch, as likely to go rogue as he was to actually help someone.

However, the other Auditors, all in dark suits from black to charcoal, weren't nearly so warm.

They regarded him coolly from behind the lenses of their glasses, making him feel like raw meat in front of hungry wolves. He tried to smile and offer casual nods, but the only replies he received were narrowed eyes and tightened jaws.

It was clear they didn't think he had earned his suit and badge.

Perhaps they were right.

Grimsby felt his shoulders fall and just tried to focus his gaze on his hurried feet, making his way to the director. He hastened through the long, echoing halls, passing dozens of darkened, empty offices. The operations wing was one of three at the Department, alongside research and logistics. Of the three, it was the smallest, as the Auditors and Agents were the fewest in number among Department personnel. It also had the most pieces of the original structure from Salem, while the other wings were expanded and modernized.

Director Damien Grieves's office was the last, situated just before the entrance to the main briefing hall. Broad, well-oiled doors of oak had been left open, originals rather than the imitations most other offices sported. As Grimsby approached, he saw a pair of Auditors file out of the room, each holding manila folders that carried their next assignments.

Director Grieves appeared in the doorway behind them, slight of frame and of average height. His perfectly groomed appearance hadn't wavered once since Grimsby had known him. At first, it had been a comfort, but it had become almost uncanny and disconcerting. Day or night, early or late, rain or shine, Grieves was always immaculate. It was as though the man was more machine than witch.

The director began to close the doors, and Grimsby let himself break into a full sprint. "Wait!" he called, skittering to a halt before him.

Grieves raised a brow at him. "Auditor Grimsby," he said, voice as smooth as his shaven cheeks, "I had thought you'd be on Asylum attendance patrol."

"I finished, sir," Grimsby panted.

"The Therians are accounted for?"

Grimsby nodded, happy to save the breath of uttering a word.

"Very well. Come in." He stepped back, allowing Grimsby to enter.

The director's office was an odd mixture of luxurious and

barren. His large desk shone with a perfect finish in the warm light of open windows, the hand-carved timber of impeccable taste and quality.

Yet the desk had no hint or trace of personal possessions. Even the notepads and pens were as neatly laid out as if an architect had been hired to do it. The only frame on the wall held an order stating that Grieves was the interim director, until Peters's replacement could be officially chosen.

Though Grimsby knew firsthand that nobody called Grieves the interim Department director.

The last item on his desk was a collection of manila folders in a neat stack. Some were as thick as Grimsby's thumb, while others were more modest, fewer than a dozen pages. He waited to see which Grieves would assign him.

Grieves said nothing, however, and instead only sat down in his chair, his hands steepled, and waited expectantly.

"Um . . . sir?" Grimsby asked.

"Your partner? Where is he?"

Grimsby felt his face grow red. "Oh, uh, Mayflower, sir? He's—he's occupied at the moment. But if you give me an assignment, I'll be sure to share the details with—"

"No."

The word felt like an anvil on the back of Grimsby's skull. "No? I don't understand."

Grieves took a breath and leaned back, moving his hands to cross in front of his mouth. "Auditor Grimsby, do you know why the Department operates in pairs?"

"Well, not specifically, sir."

"Accountability. A single Agent or Auditor can be easily subverted, defeated, or killed. I could name a half dozen creatures from around the globe that could kill most any single man or woman, just by their very nature. And ten times as many in the Elsewhere."

Grimsby felt his mouth open to retort, but he struggled to force it closed again.

"But it's more than just in the field," Grieves continued. "Accountability to another individual acts as check and balance for the actions of our people. Especially where Agents and Auditors are paired together. The Department began when Unorthodox and Usual individuals found common ground to work together, and we uphold that tradition whenever we can."

Grimsby could only nod. The director wasn't intending to have a conversation.

"And so, by allowing your partner to continuously shirk his duties, both to you and to the Department, you have shown you are not yet ready to be accountable for more serious responsibilities."

Grimsby felt his temper flare, sending stray sparks crackling off his scars. "And so who was it who was *accountable* for finding out it was Director Peters who had murdered another witch in cold blood, Director?"

Grieves's brow twitched by almost imperceptible measures. "Indeed. And in recognition for this, you were offered a position. Yet if you cannot handle the most basic responsibilities required of Auditors, how am I to entrust you with ones that might cost lives?"

"I've handled basic tasks for six months! Doing odd jobs and errands with no complaint."

Grieves raised a brow.

"Well, moderately quiet complaints," Grimsby admitted.

"I did not say 'tasks,' Auditor Grimsby. I said 'responsibilities.' Your foremost being to the Department, your second being to the people we are charged with protecting—"

"Well, obviously—"

Grieves's eyes narrowed, and suddenly one of the fluorescent tubes above their heads shattered, raining down glass shards.

Grimsby jumped back, shocked, but the director didn't seem to notice.

"Do not interrupt me again, Auditor Grimsby, or you'll be 'Mr. Grimsby' for the foreseeable future."

Grimsby felt his tongue shrivel in his mouth.

"Your third responsibility," he resumed, brushing broken glass from the shoulder of his tailored suit, "is to your partner. And you have been shirking your duty."

"My duty? What am I to do? Make him get out of his house? Write him up for an absence? He's the thrice-cursed Huntsman! I can't make him do anything! No one can!"

"Huntsman or not, if you can't convince one man to do his job, how can I expect you to do both yours and his? I'm sorry, Auditor Grimsby," he said, drawing the thinnest manila folder from the stack, "but until you *and* your partner are ready for serious work, you'll be handling more mundane tasks."

He handed the folder to Grimsby. It was scarcely three pages. A quick glance told him it was another list of names and addresses, this time for checking on individuals who had had incurable but endurable curses laid on them, like growing teeth instead of hair. More milk runs.

"Please, Director, give me a real case. I'll take anything!" He frantically looked at the pile and found the next-thinnest folder. "What about this one?"

Grieves's mouth tightened in annoyance at Grimsby's forwardness, but he seemed to allow it. "That is a RUIN case, one that Auditor Bathory has asked me to set aside for her."

Grimsby frowned. RUINs were rituals of unknown intent and nature, but that wasn't what made his jaw clench. He'd have taken such a case in an instant.

What bothered him was the apparent, immediate, and blatant hypocrisy.

"Does Auditor Bathory have a partner?" he asked.

Grieves's expression grew razor thin in apparent anticipation of Grimsby's line of questioning. "No."

"I thought cases were only for Auditors with partners. Is there a reason Auditor Bathory is the exception? Or was she promoted to become the first Super-Auditor and no one told me?"

The director pinched the bridge of his nose, appearing suddenly quite fatigued. "Because, Auditor Grimsby, she has proven she is competent. You have merely proven you are fortunate."

Grimsby halted mid-breath, like someone had just dropped a frozen lake on him. He felt his muscles grow heavy, and suddenly he felt like slumping to a heap on the ground.

So, Grieves thought he hadn't earned his position, just the same as the others.

If that was so, why ever offer him the position in the first place?

There was a knock on the open door, and they both turned to see one of Grieves's assistants, wearing a finely checkered tan suit jacket, her hands holding a scribbled note.

"In time, Auditor Grimsby, you will have your chance. But not yet. Please excuse me a moment." He walked to the woman and exchanged a few quiet words with her.

Grimsby could barely hear him. His whole body felt wracked with tension and fatigue, like a worn-down spring under a cinder block. What more could he do to prove himself? How could he ever show he was worth something if no one was willing to give him a chance?

His heart felt like it had fallen and begun boiling in his stomach, making his arms tense so hard with angry steam that his joints popped.

His eyes fell to the RUIN file, set aside from the stack.

He was done waiting for somebody to give him a chance.

It was time to take one.

He glanced over his shoulder to see the director distracted by the assistant. Quickly and quietly, he exchanged the contents of his folder with those of the RUIN folder. Then, seeing the folder was left too thin, he quickly took a handful of pages from one of the thicker files left in the stack and padded the contents.

He was fast and silent, and he quickly found himself thankful for the year of practice he'd gotten with sleight of hand at his last job. Performing real magic for kids all day was exhausting, but close-up fake magic was basically as good. And far less fatiguing.

He heard Grieves wrap up his conversation. Grimsby tried to appear casual, then remembered he should still be upset and quickly began to fake brood. It took all his acting chops not to let the terrifying thought of Grieves noticing his pilfering actions show in his face.

"Now then," Grieves said, picking up the former RUIN file and making Grimsby's heart skip. "Is there anything else?"

He felt his dry throat croak, "No, sir."

Grieves put the file on the stack and nodded. "Good. Now, return to your responsibilities, Auditor."

Grimsby shook himself, then smiled, gripping the folder in his hands tightly. "Yes, sir, Interim Director."

FIVE ✳

ELIZABETH "RAYNE" BATHORY RECOGNIZED GRIEVES'S knock even as it sounded on the door to her small office. His silhouette was clear through the frosted glass, crisp and steady. She found herself annoyed, only to instantly try to repress it. Weeks—no, months of restless nights had left her fuse shorter than she would have liked, and she already regretted snapping at Grimsby earlier. The last thing she needed to do was be flippant with the Department director, interim or otherwise.

She carefully set down her mug of cold coffee, the front of which read MAGIC BEANS, stood, and straightened her blouse before donning the Auditor jacket from the back of her chair. She found herself staring at Wilson Hives's empty desk as she had done countless times since he vanished, and felt her frustrations well once more. She pushed them away, forcing herself to remain calm and placid. She stepped over the circle of scattered notes and photos that filled the main space of her office, unlocking and opening the door.

"Director," she said, managing to sound accommodating, a feat that surprised even herself, "what can I do for you?"

Grieves tipped his graying head of dark hair in a gesture of moderate respect—a gesture that she'd noticed he reserved for few others. "I have the RUIN case you requested," he said, producing a slim manila folder, though he didn't extend it to her. "I must say, I was surprised to hear you request another case at all. You've been quite . . ." He trailed off and glanced at the disheveled office behind her, eyes lingering on the haphazard circle of papers on her floor. Each was a sliver of evidence or a potential lead she had managed to find.

All of them had led to nothing.

"Engaged?" she offered, suppressing the chill that ran across the scalp of her dark, tied-back hair. She had hoped Grieves would grant her request with little thought, though she should have known that was a castle in the sky. The director was a fine-toothed comb and a shark all in one. It was wiser to simply hope he had his attention on larger prey.

Grieves adjusted his well-fitted suit. "I think perhaps a more appropriate term would be 'consumed,'" he said. "Months you've been hunting for Auditor Hives, and yet suddenly you request a RUIN that I'd have to force most Auditors to look into? I must say, it was . . . unexpected."

Rayne tried to keep her composure; the director was suspicious already. That certainly was faster than she intended. Perhaps she should have asked another Auditor to take the case for her—but no. She couldn't risk them looking into it.

Not until she knew the truth herself.

She'd been so consumed with finding Wilson that she had forgotten how long she'd been looking. Months without wavering; of course Grieves would find her divergent behavior curious, if not downright suspicious.

She needed to subvert his questions, and quickly. The director was no fool, and every moment spent speaking to him risked him uncovering more than she could allow.

"I just needed a break," she said, "some menial case to put to rest so that I can get myself to focus again." It wasn't even wholly a lie. She could feel she needed to step back. She had been so close to the case for so long that she felt like things were lost in her periphery.

But there never seemed to be time.

Perhaps another pair of eyes would accomplish something similar, but there was no one else who was invested enough to look for him. Auditor Hives was abrasive, to say the least. He'd had few friends even before he had been revealed to be a criminal. Even Rayne didn't particularly care for him as a person, and she had known him for a long time, but he was still her partner.

At least, if he was alive.

Alive or the inevitable, she had to know what had happened to him.

Though she'd be lying if she said it was wholly charity.

The former, corrupt Department director, John Peters, was connected to Hives, and so was she. In fact, she doubted she'd still have a position at all if Grieves hadn't vouched for her character. Even his allowing her to pursue this case, or the new RUIN, was a sign of his confidence in her. Yet even with his support, she'd forever have a looming shadow of doubt over her trustworthiness until Hives was found. But if she managed to secure his confession, or at the very least figure out how he had died, she might have a chance of clearing herself of suspicion.

Grieves eyed her from behind his stylish half-rimmed glasses, making her feel like she was under a microscope. An ironic feeling, given that the lenses were flat, as were many Auditors' and witches'. Their glasses were more a means to shield them from unconsciously peering into the Elsewhere than a tool to correct vision.

And the director's vision was quite keen.

She knew he was well aware of her motives in regard to her search for Hives, but the RUIN case was another matter. Hopefully, he didn't yet know why she had asked for it. He might force the issue, however. After all, he was the acting director. If he did so, she would be hard-pressed to keep his curiosity at bay without incriminating herself.

She had to hope he let the matter rest—at least for the time being.

Grieves stared for a long moment, but she refused to let her gaze waver from his. He was a predator, and that meant he was excellent at spotting weakness.

He needed to know she was a predator, too.

Finally, he looked away to his watch. Whether it was because he believed her or because he had more pressing matters, he relented. He handed her the folder. "Be cautious, Bathory. As you've no partner at the moment, I want full, concurrent reports on your findings, and any fieldwork you do will require some form of backup."

"You don't think I can handle this alone?" she asked, more edge to her voice than she intended.

"No," he said, as cool and calm as snow-sloped mountains, "I don't think you should have to." He dipped his head again, not a bow or a nod, but something in between, and turned away to click briskly down the hall.

She closed the door behind him and dropped the folder on the desk, leaning over it on her hands. She felt them shaking and clenched them tight to make them stop. Still, even as her nails dug furrows into her desk, they refused.

She was frightened, and she hated it.

She wanted to run after Grieves and ask for his help, but she couldn't risk it. If he knew why she was truly interested in this case, she'd be lucky to stay out of a cell, let alone pursue answers.

She cast the thought aside. She needed to focus on the matter at hand: finding Hives. The RUIN case was hers now; she could pursue it at her leisure. More importantly, no one else could go meddling with it for the time being. At least not so long as she found answers before the Department grew impatient. She had bought herself a little time.

She moved to stand in the center of the ring of notes and photos. She needed to think—she needed to work. Most of all, she needed to find answers, if not to the RUIN case then at least to Hives's disappearance. She raised a hand and summoned a modicum of Impetus.

The papers began to tremble, as though a light breeze had coursed through the room.

"*Suspend.*"

Like newspaper on the street, the documents began to flutter around in a miniature slow-motion hurricane that followed her flowing gestures. Photos, notes, maps, and more all circled her like a whirlpool of information. She let her eyes unfocus, taking in the passing pages. With a simple motion, she conjured one that caught her eye to hover in front of her before sending it back into the swirling mass.

She wanted to focus on the words, the pictures, the clues she had spent months gathering, but her mind wavered, as scattered as the documents around her. She couldn't focus, as her attention constantly drifted to the folder on her desk.

She took a deep breath and approached it, the torrent of pages following her, slapping harmlessly against the sides of her desk as they did.

She picked up the folder and stared at the cover. She didn't need to look inside to know what she'd find.

She had seen it, even before the Department had been alerted to it.

Though she still didn't know how.

Another knock sounded at her door, making her start. She dropped the folder onto the desk, and the slow-motion hurricane of documents suddenly collapsed, sending every page to rain about the office in a chaotic mess.

She groaned in annoyance but felt a tremor of fear run through her at the same moment. She cast it aside along with the scattered pages. She had nothing to fear—not yet, at least. If Grieves wasn't aware of her secret, neither was the Department. This wasn't some covert task force sent to apprehend her.

But then, who was it?

The knock came again, though it wasn't Grieves's controlled meter, but rapid and pulsing. It rattled the frosted glass of her door and instantly made her brow twitch in annoyance. She left the folder and pages where they lay and opened the door.

Before her was an Auditor she didn't recognize, a woman perhaps a few years older than her. She was almost startlingly beautiful, with lips shaped expertly in soft red and sharp cheekbones, but her eyes were open too wide, showing too much white to contrast with their blue irises. She looked up as though not expecting to see Rayne and smiled with perfect teeth. "Auditor Bathory?" she asked, then paused and glanced behind Rayne into the office. "Did I come at a bad time?"

Rayne didn't answer for a moment. She knew every Auditor in Boston, if not by name then at least by face. After all, they all worked out of the same building.

So, who was this stranger?

"Can I help you?" she asked, the words more statement than question.

The stranger smiled wider and tucked a lock of her loose dark hair behind her ear. It was almost the same shade as Rayne's own. "Actually, I was hoping I could help you. I'm Auditor Defaux—from the New York Department branch."

Rayne suppressed a sneer. The only thing New York Auditors and Boston Auditors had in common was a mutual distaste for one another. The New York branch was larger and better funded, but Boston—specifically Salem—was still the heartland of the Department, where it had all begun.

She pushed aside the budding sense of rivalry within her. Despite the friction between them, Boston and New York often worked together when the need arose. "Help me with what?" she asked, careful to remain neutral.

Defaux said nothing at first, instead reaching into her pocket to withdraw her badge.

Rayne frowned. "Look, I believe you are who you say you are. You don't have to—"

She was interrupted when Defaux opened the badge.

It was the Department standard, a pentagram embedded onto a shield, but the name below it didn't read *Defaux*.

It read *Wilson Hives*.

SIX ※

GRIMSBY LOOKED ABOUT UNCERTAINLY AS THE BUS hissed to a halt. He double-checked the partially burnt-out sign at the front, but sure enough it read EMERALD HOLLOW, the neighborhood of Mayflower's address—at least according to the Department.

But surely this couldn't be where the Huntsman lived. It was so . . . suburban.

He made his way to the front, nodding thanks to the driver as he passed. She only rolled her eyes in reply. The doors nearly caught his suit jacket as they closed behind him, and the bus groaned and trundled down the road, flanked by lines of identical two-story houses with genuine white picket fences.

Grimsby pulled out the scribbled card in his pocket. On one side, it held the Huntsman's phone number, which he'd given to Grimsby after they were both nearly killed by a demoness. On the other side was an address, though this Grimsby had taken from the Department records.

Yet, when he pictured the place, he had expected some half-abandoned brick warehouse, or maybe a lodge in the woods. Perhaps even a fortress with panning spotlights and blaring sirens.

He never would have guessed he would find trimmed lawns, shaped hedges, and the distant laughing screeches of children.

He shook his head again. It didn't matter. He wasn't here to see how Mayflower's homelife was.

He was here to tell the Huntsman off.

He felt his stomach twist into a little ball of nervous anger, and a chill shiver of fear wrapped around his spine like frozen tinfoil. The Huntsman was without a doubt the deadliest man Grimsby knew, and though he would have liked nothing more than to wait for the bus to come back around and go home, that wouldn't fix his problem. Without Mayflower, he couldn't get a case from Grieves.

At least, not legitimately.

He still held the manila folder in his tight grip, too afraid to leave it anywhere for fear that someone would discover what he'd done. Taking the file was a stupid mistake, and he had regretted it almost immediately. Yet how could he return it without Grieves discovering his insubordination?

He folded the problem up in his mind and tucked it away. He had other issues to deal with.

Issues with a temper and a lifelong history of killing Unorthodox with a really, really big gun.

Grimsby took a deep breath and steadied his heart as best he could. He had to confront the Huntsman face-to-face.

But first, he needed to find his lair.

Grimsby looked around, realizing that the only real difference between the homes was what shade of neutral they were. Then, after some walking, he saw one on the opposite side of the street that stood out from the others.

The lawn was overgrown, and the fence creaked in the breeze, white paint peeling from its dried-out boards. The house had an oddly flat quality to it, like it was the only home in Emerald

Hollow that was actually hollow. Like a cardboard cutout of a home, made to blend with the others.

But, more than anything, it was the old, rusted jeep in the drive that told of the Huntsman's presence.

Grimsby forced himself to march down the street, toward his target, but he quickly found his stride beginning to slow. His knees grew tight and his palms were slick with sweat, dampening the folder in his grip.

He disliked arguing with people at the best of times, as if arguing could ever be part of the best of times, but Mayflower was one of the few friends Grimsby had. The thought of confronting him was terrifying, and more than simply because the Huntsman was dangerous.

He didn't want to lose a friend. He had few enough as it was.

He stopped across the road from Mayflower's place, feeling frozen on the warm sidewalk. He stood there for long minutes, his mind racing and yet coming up with nothing useful, like someone had put it on a hamster wheel.

Suddenly, he heard the clickity-clack of bicycle wheels, and a small voice cried, "Look out!"

He turned to see a boy on a bike who couldn't have been more than ten years old, hurtling toward him at uncontrolled speed.

Grimsby squeaked and managed to hop out of the way, feeling the handle clip his coat.

The kid sailed past but began to wobble and lose control, crashing into the trim green lawn of the house Grimsby stood before.

He began to hurry over as the child sat up and stared at his skinned palms. His T-shirt was stained with fresh grass. His face seemed like it might burst with tears if not for the tenuous, trembling lip that held them at bay like a failing levy.

Then a second bike slid past Grimsby without him even

realizing it. A girl, looking a year or two older than the kid, slid to a halt in the grass beside the fallen boy. Their twin sandy hair and gray-green eyes told Grimsby they were likely siblings.

The girl hauled the boy to his feet, muttering over and over, "You're fine, you're fine. Don't tell Mom. You're fine."

After a few moments of this, the boy finally seemed to calm down to merely a simmering cascade of sniffles, and his sister turned to see Grimsby for the first time. "Sorry, mister. We were just racing and didn't see you there."

Grimsby managed a smile and tried to convince himself the crash he had caused wasn't foretelling his conversation with May-flower. "Are you two all right?"

The boy held up dirty, skinned palms, as though to show a jury evidence that he was not in the least all right.

The girl only nodded. "Yeah. What are you doing here anyway, mister?"

"Oh, sorry. I'm just here to talk to your neighbor." He gestured to Mayflower's house.

The boy's eyes widened as he whispered, "The boogieman? Momma says don't bother the boogieman."

The girl huffed and smacked his palm lightly, drawing a yelp. "Momma also says don't call him the boogieman." She turned back to Grimsby. "That's just Mr. Mayflower. Momma says he's grouchy, but he's nice." She said the words like she was reciting the gospel of Momma.

"Yeah. He's definitely grouchy," Grimsby said, smiling despite the knots in his gut. "Try to take it slow, all right?"

"Says who?" the girl asked.

Grimsby pulled out his badge. "Says an Auditor."

The little boy's eyes went wide. "Whoa! That's so cool!"

Grimsby balked, not expecting the genuine awe in the boy's voice. "You—think so?"

The boy didn't manage whole words, but instead nodded

emphatically, the tears on his cheeks forgotten. Even his older sister seemed impressed.

And, just for a moment, Grimsby felt like a real Auditor.

He could face the Huntsman.

"Thank you," he said, clearing his throat. "Now, please excuse me, lady and gentleman."

He left the two children to continue their games and crossed the street to Mayflower's drive. He passed the old jeep, which still bore the bullet holes from their encounter at the Lounge, an Unorthodox-owned nightclub. He was surprised at the thin tinge of nostalgia he felt as he remembered that terrifying night.

He shook away the memory and stood tall before Mayflower's front door. Well, not tall, but precisely average, globally speaking, which was as tall as he was able to manage.

He tried to think of what he would say and felt his mouth go dry. Before he could give himself a chance to lose his nerve, he rapped his knuckles frantically on the door.

There was a bitter groan from inside the house, though whether from an old man or old timbers it was hard to tell. It was shortly followed by the muffled sound of shattering glass.

"Go away," Mayflower's gruff voice called from inside.

"Les," Grimsby called, "it's me. We need to talk."

Another groan. He heard a muttered, "Damn it, Grimsby," followed by heavy footfalls. A moment later, the door tore open, revealing the Huntsman.

He was wearing a threadbare flannel robe, sweatpants, and several weeks' worth of beard. His gray and black hair was more gray than Grimsby remembered, and his bloodshot eyes said it had been too long since he had last slept.

Grimsby couldn't help but stare, shocked. It had been less than a month since he'd last seen Mayflower, but he wouldn't have recognized him passing by on the street—if not for his unusual height.

In fact, the only part of Leslie Mayflower that felt like Grimsby's partner was the heavy revolver that hung from his grip at his side.

"What do you want?" Mayflower demanded, squinting bleary eyes at the setting evening sun. His breath smelled of whiskey and little else.

Grimsby cast a glance over his shoulder to the kids across the street, who had ducked behind their decidedly nonopaque picket fence to spy on the conversation. Following Grimsby's gaze to spot them, Mayflower slid his gun behind his back.

"Maybe we should talk inside," Grimsby said. "Can I come in?"

Mayflower grunted and retreated into his darkened living room, gesturing for Grimsby to follow. "Shut the damn door, would you? I have a headache."

Grimsby looked around at half a liquor store's worth of scattered whiskey bottles, all empty. "Can't imagine why."

Mayflower ignored him and crunched in his slippers over a patch of broken glass. It seemed a whiskey bottle had somehow recently and mysteriously shattered against the wall.

"So," Grimsby said, standing on the doormat. "This is what you've been up to?"

Mayflower dropped himself into an ancient armchair of sagging leather. "Yep." He pulled out a worn pack of cigarettes from the pocket of his robe and put one in his mouth without lighting it; he seemed content to only chew on the filter. "How did you find my place?"

"You work at the Department. You're in the records."

"Bah, I didn't give them my address when they hired us."

"Well, the one on file was from thirty years ago." He looked around, wondering if that was the last time the place had been dusted. "I half expected to find out you'd moved."

Mayflower's gaze seemed to hollow itself out right before Grimsby's eyes. "No," he said softly.

Grimsby made his way over to Mayflower, toward the chair beside his that matched his own, except it seemed almost new, or at least barely used. Before he could sit, however, the Huntsman shot him a dangerous look, and Grimsby quickly found his preference had become standing.

"So, what do you want?" Mayflower asked.

"What do I want?" Grimsby repeated, finding his voice quickly growing thready with emotion. "Well, for starters, a partner would be nice."

Mayflower said nothing.

Grimsby began pacing back and forth in front of the awkwardly leaning coffee table, kicking a path through the fallen bottles of whiskey. "Where the blue blazes have you been? When we first started together, I thought things were going to go great, and then you started showing up less and less. Do you know how long it's been since I even saw you last?"

"A week?" Mayflower muttered, his voice making it seem like a genuine guess.

"It's been almost a month!" Grimsby said, dropping his manila folder on the table in exasperation. "A month of checking practitioner permits, taking complaint calls, auditing restricted Unorthodox. A month of doing it all alone!" He felt his voice rising, and though he tried to calm it, he had little luck. "And come to find out I'm being passed over for real cases because my so-called partner isn't even around enough to do his job!"

Mayflower leaned forward, his elbows on his knees, his hands held limply in front of him. His eyes seemed locked on the gun in his grasp and the faint scratches on the wooden grip.

"We were supposed to be in this together, Les," Grimsby said, feeling his voice crack with anger. He forced his tone to become gentler. "Where have you been?"

"Here," the Huntsman answered.

"Here. Doing what? Drinking whiskey in your pajamas?"

"Evening robe," Mayflower corrected.

"It stops being an evening robe if you've worn it for a month. Look." He stopped pacing and tried to meet Mayflower's gaze, but the Huntsman didn't look up. "I didn't come here to chew you out—well, maybe I did, a little. But I also came here to find out what was going on, and where you've been. I came here to find out what's wrong."

Mayflower said nothing, but his posture slumped bare inches, like invisible weights had just been hung around his neck.

"I need someone to watch my back, Les."

"I agree," he said quietly.

Grimsby felt some measure of relief flood him. "So you'll come back to work?"

"I agree you need a partner. What about that Rayne girl you're always making eyes at?"

Grimsby's embarrassment was quickly drowned out with cold confusion. "What? No, I mean you, Les."

The Huntsman shook his head, raising it for the first time.

He looked so *tired*.

It wasn't the tiredness of a sleepless night, but that of a restless life.

"I can't, kid," he said.

"Can't?" Grimsby straightened, feeling anger budding in his field of confusion. "What do you mean *can't*?"

He said nothing, but only traced the engravings on his gun, his dark-ringed eyes distant.

"You and I fought monsters together, Les. I've seen you do things no other man would have the will to do. You're the dang Huntsman, Les. You can do anything."

Mayflower almost managed a smirk, but it collapsed instantly. "No. I've only ever been worth a damn at one thing."

"What?"

He didn't answer, though his body seemed to bear a sudden weight that Grimsby couldn't fathom.

"What is that supposed to mean?"

"It means I'm done. With the Department, with being a Huntsman." He turned hard eyes to Grimsby. "With you."

Grimsby felt like his skin had just frozen and shattered, all in an instant. He stood there, mouth open, his friend's words echoing in his head.

"How—how can you say that?" He barely managed to numbly fumble the words.

"Look. Six months ago, when all that shit happened and the dust finally settled, you became an Auditor. You got what you wanted, Grimsby. Not everyone else was so lucky."

"What do you mean?"

"What did I get?"

"What?"

"What the hell did I get, Grimsby?"

"I don't know—"

"I got pulled out of retirement. I got my gun put back in my hand. I—" He stopped. The growing, familiar, almost comforting anger in him suddenly drained away, leaving him as pale as a statue.

Grimsby didn't know what to say. Mayflower had always been so strong and indomitable. Yet here he seemed almost frail. Like somebody had taken the real man and replaced him with a glass replica.

"Well, what do you want, Les?" Grimsby said, trying to keep calm, though he felt frantic. "Let me help you."

"You can't."

Grimsby felt like the ground was crumbling beneath his feet. "Let me try, at least!"

Mayflower looked away, then his shoulders sank. "I'm—I'm

sorry. Just leave me alone, Grimsby. Get Grieves to assign you someone else. Anyone else."

Grimsby stood there, unable to move, his mind a broken blank. He felt like his whole consciousness was pressed up against his eyes, threatening to spill out of his skull.

"But—you're my partner."

"No," Mayflower said, gritting his teeth in a pained effort, "I was your goddamn babysitter, and I'm done with it."

Grimsby couldn't breathe.

He didn't know what to do. He needed to think. He needed to scream. He needed to say something.

But instead, he did the only thing he could do.

He left.

He fumbled with the folder on the table, but his shaking hands dropped it, scattering the pages all around. He let it lie and hurried to the door, numbly missing the handle before finally exiting into the darkening evening.

He left the door open behind him and trudged toward the bus stop, clenching his fists so hard that his nails bloodied his palms.

What had he done wrong?

SEVEN ✳

LESLIE MAYFLOWER QUIETLY SHUT HIS FRONT DOOR, TRY-
ing not to watch Grimsby depart as he did.

God, he felt sick.

He had sent the kid packing, and done it more harshly than he
needed to. But it was the right call.

Wasn't it?

He growled at his throbbing head and dropped back into his
old armchair. The thing practically had an outline of his skeletal
frame at this point. He sank into the cushions, which were so
worn they barely deserved the name.

Had it really been a month since he'd worn the suit? That
couldn't be right. Though after a brief counting of liquor bottles,
it seemed more plausible.

He shook his head and chewed on the filter of his unlit cigarette. He hadn't meant for things to go so far. He hadn't meant to
slip for so long. But he had broken a promise, and it was weighing
on him.

A promise to himself.

It was one of three he had made in his life. Though he had
managed to keep the other two, thank God.

But how long would it be until he broke those as well?

He twisted the ring on his finger and stared out the window for long minutes.

No, he was no use to anyone like this, especially not Grimsby. The kid needed someone who could watch his back, someone who could take the hits he wasn't yet ready to take. Before, it had been Mayflower. He had thought he was ready. He had thought he was strong enough.

He had been wrong.

He had thought himself the old soldier, coated in dust and rust, who just needed to get moving again to be what he once was.

He had been wrong about that, too.

He wasn't a soldier. He was a weapon. A relic better left buried.

At first, he had thought killing Peters a few months before had been the last straw, the one that had broken him, but it was more than that. He had been broken long before that; killing Peters had simply been a reminder. He had just thought all wounds could heal if you were tough enough.

He was wrong about that, too.

The wound was still there, torn open again each time he pulled the trigger, though it never truly healed. Whether that was because it couldn't, or because he wasn't tough enough, it hardly mattered anymore.

He held his old gun in his hands, his eyes tracing every nick and scratch, some left decades before he was born. Others well over a century.

He was just so *tired*.

But he had two promises left to keep. Maybe breaking the first had been necessary. Maybe keeping all three was only ever a pipe dream to begin with.

He caught a glimpse of his haggard reflection in the mirror beside the door.

"'You will not become a monster,'" he said, feeling his mouth grow bitter with each broken word. "Yeah, right."

With the body count he'd racked up in his time as a Huntsman, he was more monster than most any man or beast he'd gunned down. It hadn't bothered him when he was young. It had been the job, a duty his family had always carried. But that was before Mary; that was before—before everything changed.

Everything except you, he thought.

He scoffed bitterly and set the gun on the table, his slippered feet crinkling the papers Grimsby had left.

He glanced down at them, and old, beaten gears in his mind began turning despite his best effort. It looked like a RUIN case. Ritual of unknown intent and nature. Probably just some asshat toying with magic they shouldn't be. Though he doubted if there was a magic in existence that didn't fit that bill. He would be no use on such a case anyway. He didn't know a damned thing about magic that he didn't need to, and he liked it that way.

He reached for a fresh bottle of whiskey, but one of the photos, fallen from the folder, caught his eye. It was like he had spotted a familiar face in a crowd that suddenly vanished. He paused in his reaching for a new bottle, then growled and picked up the photo instead.

"As if you could ever change," he muttered to himself.

It looked like a plain enough scene. A ritual circle, outlined in some kind of special paint or something, with symbols Mayflower recognized as serious business. Anyone could pull off a ritual; it didn't even take a witch to do it. The magic was in all the crap you had to gather and set up. The real trick was knowing what you were doing enough to not get yourself killed.

He imagined it was a lot like being an electrician.

There were some rituals so basic that they were sold on the television. Some for as low as four installments of whatever you could afford. Those were simple enough that even if you screwed it up it wouldn't do much worse than give you a cold or make your hair fall out, and even if you got it right the results would be almost imperceptible.

This wasn't one of those rituals.

The primary symbol at the ritual's center had been smudged out, hiding its purpose, though the ring of supportive symbols around it remained at least partially legible. The five reagents that would determine the ritual's function were also missing, like bullets pulled from a revolver's chamber. Without those, sussing out what it was meant to do would be near impossible: hence it being a RUIN.

But there was something about the scene that gnawed at him. It was an uncomfortably familiar feeling, like déjà vu from a nightmare. He felt a cold pallor spread over his chest. He couldn't say for sure how he knew, but he was certain that he did indeed know: whatever the ritual was meant to do, it couldn't have been good.

It was smart to look into it. Smart, and also not his problem.

But even as he tried to shrug away the clutching feeling of responsibility that clung to him, he couldn't pull his gaze from the photo. *Something* had drawn his eye, but what? He shook his head and was about to set it down—when he paused.

It wasn't the ritual that he recognized. It wasn't even the marred runes that outlined it.

It was their arrangement.

More than that, the symbols might have been foreign to him, but the way they were drawn, with cool, elegant, yet sharp lines that were somehow both delicate and cruel . . .

He had seen this style before, like familiar handwriting.

Then, as he squinted his eyes, he found the muddled mess of the main symbol almost resembled something he knew—or had known. A single shape that echoed within buried memory.

Though he did not know what it meant, he knew he had seen it—but only ever once.

The trouble was: when?

It was smudged beyond recognition, but if he squinted his eyes, he could almost—

His grip tightened as he stared at the image, racking his brain to think of where or when he'd seen it. Suddenly, he wished he had taken it a bit easier on the whiskey. His head pounded and thrummed in defiance as the old gears turned, but he ignored the pain, combing his dusty memory for some shredded thread of information.

But it was no use.

There was too much rust. Too much dust. And no shortage of whiskey.

He growled, ready to give up and grab the bottle again, but the photo gnawed at him. He needed answers.

Or was it something else he needed?

He ground the cigarette to mash between his teeth, spitting it out into an empty bottle.

It didn't matter. He couldn't go down this road. Not again. He had already told the kid he was out. It was best he stay that way.

Yet a feeling loomed over him, one of responsibility and dread. His gut told him this was unfinished business. A loose end no one but him could tie up, and if he didn't, good people might get hurt.

The kid might get hurt.

And deep down, he knew he was right.

"Damn it, Grimsby," Mayflower growled.

EIGHT

RAYNE STARED AT THE BADGE IN DEFAUX'S GRASP. HER chest felt bound in an iron cage, her heart a furious inmate imprisoned within, rattling its bars. She had been searching for months but had found no trace or hint of what had happened to Hives after Peters had taken him. Yet here was his badge, which had almost certainly been with him when he vanished.

"Where did you get this?" she asked, reaching out with a shaking hand.

Defaux grinned and slipped it back into her jacket before Rayne could even touch it. "Are you hungry?" she asked.

Rayne paused, still shocked from the revelation of Hives's badge. "What?"

"Hungry. Food," Defaux said very slowly, as if teaching Rayne the pronunciation of the words. "I feel like I haven't eaten in *ages*! Where's your cafeteria around here?"

Without waiting for Rayne to answer, she wheeled on her heels and strode out into the hall, her sharp stilettos echoing their clicks down the empty tiled corridors.

Rayne shook herself and began to follow, then paused and

returned to her office long enough to collect the RUIN folder. She couldn't risk leaving it alone. She rushed to catch up and called, "Wait a minute!" But Defaux seemed not to hear her, instead looking around like any given door might lead to her next meal.

Though there were no windows, Rayne knew it was past hours. Most of the other personnel would have already clocked out for the evening, leaving the halls empty and echoing.

Where had the time gone?

She shook her head, focusing on the task at hand. Defaux didn't seem to be the hottest stick on the pyre, but any shred of information she knew could lead to a major breakthrough in the search for Hives.

So why wouldn't the blasted woman just stand still?

Rayne's temper flared, hot in her belly, eclipsing her shock. She needed answers, and now.

She hurried after Defaux and grabbed her shoulder, perhaps harder than was strictly necessary.

Defaux glanced first at her hand, then seemed to trail her eyes over her arm back to her face. "Yes?"

"Tell me where you found his badge," Rayne said. Then she felt her resolve falter and crack, supplanted by the whelming desperation of months of failure. "Please."

Defaux shrugged off her grip. "I will," she said, "on the way to the cafeteria."

Rayne drew in a deep breath, bracing her collapsing patience like shoring up a failing dam. "Fine. Follow me, and keep talking."

She walked briskly past Defaux, keeping her head half turned to listen as she led the way.

"A group of Agents found it in a bust in Newark," Defaux said.

"Like inside a sculpture?" she asked, frowning in mild confusion.

"Um, no. A bust of an illegal smuggling ring."

"Oh," Rayne said, suppressing the urge to slap her own fore-head. "That would make more sense."

Defaux suppressed a smile, though she seemed to put in considerably less effort than Rayne had. "When was the last time you slept, Bathory?"

"It's—it's not important." She waved the question away like a gnat. "Who'd you hit?"

Defaux shrugged. "A bunch of small-time Unorthodox that broke off from the Kindred clan out there and went rogue. A cyclops, a couple minotaurs. Oh! And a dryad. She was a mean one. All bark and nearly as much bite."

She smiled at her own remark and seemed to expect Rayne to at least loose a courtesy chuckle.

Rayne, however, was in no mood. Instead, she waited for Defaux to continue, but the seconds of silence seemed to drain on and on until her patience was dry. "And what did you find?" She hoped that Hives himself was among the contraband, but she also knew that hope was in vain. If he'd been recovered, she would have heard by now.

"Mostly we found illicit components, a couple illegal grimoires, and a handful of trafficking victims. But Auditor Hives's badge was among it all."

"What the hell was it doing there?" Rayne asked, mostly wondering aloud.

"The badge itself explains that, doesn't it?" Defaux said. "Probably some contraband shipped in from Boston. We get a lot of it," she added somewhat pointedly.

"We cover twice the area with half the people—" Rayne began, bristling instinctively at the jab before reining herself in. "It doesn't matter. The only thing I care about is finding out what happened to him. Was—" she began, though her voice caught for a moment. "Was there any other sign of him?"

Defaux shook her head. "No, and I doubt he was ever there.

Probably someone just pawning his stuff. There'd be good money in genuine Auditor badges." She halted as they reached the central foyer that connected the three wings of the Department. The cafeteria, used equally by all staff, was just beyond the entrance to the logistics wing.

It had become Department policy to keep a moderately stocked buffet for overnight work, as it was common enough that it had become a necessity, though the quality of the food was eternally suspect.

Defaux didn't seem to care. She dragged Rayne behind her and hurried through the banks of empty tables. Unlike the operations wing, logistics—and by extension the cafeteria—was nearly devoid of anything wood or stone. Stainless steel, plastic, and industrial carpet were the substitute standard, and it felt to Rayne uncomfortably like a prison.

Defaux looked over the smattering of overcooked, dry foods in the various bins as though they were a waiting feast and she couldn't decide where to begin.

Rayne tried to remain patient, but each time she did, the effort grew greater. "You're certain he wasn't there? Or at least some other sign of him?"

"What do you normally get?" Defaux asked, ignoring her question. "It all looks so good."

Rayne growled and snatched a tray, shoveling random food onto it. She piled on overcooked eggs, steam-split hot dogs, and bruised apples.

Defaux's eyes followed her all the while, oddly hungry.

Rayne found herself glaring in thought at each mediocre morsel, wishing she could use *Suspend* to help her collect all the stray threads of possibility that wrapped around her mind.

"There," she said, leading Defaux to the table and dropping the tray down for Defaux before setting the RUIN folder before herself. "If you want it, you're going to have to talk."

Defaux smiled. "Of course." She settled in beside the tray, but her eyes lingered on Rayne, waiting.

She took a deep breath. "Okay, if his badge was in New York, how did it get there?" She framed it as a question, but really she was simply tracing her thoughts aloud, hoping they might spark some insight from Defaux. "He'd never part from it willingly."

Defaux arched a brow. "Unless maybe he was trying to shed his identity? He'd been associated with Peters, after all."

"It's possible," she said, tracing invisible lines on the RUIN folder to orient her thoughts. "But if Hives was intact enough to try and lie low, that would mean that Peters hadn't abducted him; he had extracted him."

"Which, by extension, would mean he was as much a traitor as Peters, and is on the run."

Rayne shook her head, scratching out the lines as she tossed out the thought. "No, Hives was an ass, and probably a puppet—but he wasn't smart enough to outwit the whole Department. Peters couldn't trust him with anything incriminating. He probably manipulated him and then needed to dispose of him."

"So, logically, he's probably dead, right?" Defaux said.

Her words startled Rayne from her thoughts. She looked down, brow furrowed tightly. Her eyes bored into the folder's cover while her mind churned.

Defaux stared at her, her expression pressing. "Well? Isn't he?" she asked.

Rayne shot her a furious look, but it was undermined by her own shudder. The new evidence Defaux brought forth made the conclusion more and more unavoidable. And if he had perished, so, too, had her best shot to ever clear her name.

"I mean," Defaux continued, "if what you're saying is true, and Peters wanted to get rid of him, what better way to dispose of him than having him killed? And as quickly as possible to boot?"

Rayne's stomach twisted. The thought had of course occurred

to her, though she dared to hope otherwise. "Maybe. But if he had, we'd likely have found a body by now."

Or a familiar, she thought, failing to suppress a shiver. Peters had taught her the finer points of familiar-craft during her first year as an Auditor, but even in her nightmares she would never have dreamed he'd been making them out of *people*. They still didn't know how many he'd made, or who he had made into the things. Hell, they weren't completely certain *how* he did it.

Though Rayne had some theories she'd decided were better left unspoken.

Perhaps Hives had been made into one of those things before Peters was killed? A familiar could have been told to stay somewhere dark and hidden, and be unable to defy the orders of its master. It might wait there for days—years. If there was even a shred of the real Hives trapped inside such a creature, it would be the most horrible fate she could imagine.

Suddenly, she felt her own ambitions of clearing her name were quite selfish.

Either way, she needed to find him.

Her feelings must have been painted on her face despite her best effort, as Defaux gestured to the tray of food. "You should eat something," she said.

Rayne waved her away. "Why did you bring the badge to me? Shouldn't it be in an evidence locker in New York?"

"I'll tell you," Defaux said, "if you eat something."

"I don't care about eating!" she snapped, her voice sharper than she intended. A passing Analyst with multicolored hair paused outside the double doors and raised a brow at her, but after a hard glance from Rayne she quickly shuffled on.

Defaux shrugged. "Then I'm out of answers."

Rayne groaned. "Fine. Fine!" She dragged the tray over to herself and seized a fork, bitterly shoving some scrambled eggs into her mouth.

Defaux watched her for a moment, her eyes oddly focused, before she seemed appeased. "The badge has been in our evidence for a few weeks now," she said.

"What? Why haven't I been told about this?" Rayne said, her hand covering her mouthful of mashed eggs as she spoke.

Defaux shrugged again. "Classified? Look." She leaned in, but paused, gesturing expectantly at the tray of food.

Rayne seethed as she took a bite of rubbery hot dog.

"Look," she continued, her wide eyes intensely blue, "we all know about what Peters—and by extension Hives—did. The Department's a bit . . . paranoid right now. After all, if someone respected and powerful like Peters could do something so terrible, who's to say there aren't others like him, still hiding? Who can we trust? Especially"—she cleared her throat apologetically—"here."

Rayne near choked on the food in sputtering, wordless anger, but her face must have said enough, as Defaux made defusing gestures with her hands.

"Easy! The point is, we're making certain every *I* is spectacled and every *T* is sipped before we make any moves. But we don't have our heads in the sand down there. We've all heard about Hives's partner's search for him. We've . . . kept tabs."

"You mean you've been watching me? The Department's been spying on me?"

Defaux smiled. "Spying implies it's illegal. Being observed is in your contract." She tried to seem relaxed, but when Rayne's expression remained stone, she became apologetic. "We've just had people keeping an eye on you. Can you blame us? I mean, come on, if Peter's corruption extended past Hives, who's the next person that would be . . . infected?"

Rayne opened her mouth but then closed it again when no reply came out. So, the Department's unofficial investigation of her had already begun. She had suspected that. But how much did they know?

"So," Rayne said bitterly, "that doesn't answer my question. Why did you come to *me*?"

Defaux's smile totally fell away, perhaps for the first time since Rayne had opened her door to her. She withdrew the badge from her pocket and turned it in her hands for a moment. "Because I know you haven't had any help with this," she said. Then, more quietly: "And I know what it's like to be alone for so long."

Again, Rayne found herself without reply. She felt her ire and hostility falter, quickly replaced by guilt. Though Defaux hadn't exactly been forthcoming, she *was* here to help—and she was the first who had offered since Rayne had taken up the case of Hives's disappearance.

Aside from Grimsby, she supposed, though his good intentions were hollow through no fault of his own—or perhaps rather because of his own faults.

She felt the meager meal churn in her stomach. When had she become so coldly calculating? Grimsby was a good person and had come farther than most anyone else would with as little as he had. He didn't deserve an ounce of scorn—not even in her own mind.

She shook herself and turned her attention back to Defaux.

"I—" she began, before realizing she was overcomplicating something simple. "Thank you."

"Let's just keep this between us, for both our sakes," Defaux said, her smile returning. She made a small show of furtively slipping the badge into Rayne's jacket pocket and winked. "Besides, don't thank me yet. This doesn't exactly solve your problem."

Rayne shook her head, but Defaux was right. The badge alone was just a clue, but what was it telling her? Nothing besides theories.

"True, but it's a step in the right direction. I just wish I knew what the next step was."

"Well, how about a tracking spell?"

Rayne scoffed, trying to keep any scorn from her voice. "I already tried that. Wherever he is, either he's shielded or he's dead."

"That sounds like a pretty basic tracking spell," Defaux said. "I might have something a bit . . . stronger."

"I used every accessible spell in the library. Not one could find him."

"Sure, but what did you use as a focus? A toothpick? Some dandruff from a comb?"

Rayne felt her embarrassment rise. "A used water bottle from his desk."

"You were his partner for almost a year, and that was the only personal item you had of his?"

"His apartment had been destroyed after he was taken," Rayne said. "He hadn't been in contact with his family in months, and never kept much. Even his blood was missing from the reliquary. I'm guessing Peters didn't want him traced and had it removed. So, yes, a used water bottle was the closest thing to him I had."

"And you used a dowser?" Defaux asked.

Rayne held up her wrist. On it were two watches, the first digital and cheap, the second mechanical and—decidedly less so. It was old, much older than her, and though it was in fine condition, the hands were still. "No luck."

"Doesn't surprise me," Defaux said. "A good shield will keep you from linking a piece back to the whole. Even fresh blood wouldn't be enough to crack it. But even if you can't track his body, you could still track his Impetus."

"To do that I'd need something important to him, not just some junk he left behind."

Defaux tapped a manicured nail on the badge.

Rayne's eyes widened, her sleepless mind finally catching on. "Of course. If this focus doesn't work, nothing would!" Even if he had betrayed the Department knowingly, she'd never met an Auditor whose badge didn't mean a great deal to them.

"There she is," Defaux said with a smile. "But a regular tracking ritual still won't cut it. You'll need something stronger. Fortunately, I'm a bit of a specialist in that field."

Rayne felt her heart thrumming, though this time, for the first time she could remember, it was with excitement rather than dread.

Did she finally have the means to find the truth? Perhaps even get her life back to normal?

Then her eyes fell to the folder on the other side of the tray of food, and dread returned once more. Hives wasn't her only concern at the moment, though it was the older of the two. The RUIN case still loomed as well, and if she didn't figure it out before someone else did, it might damn her in the eyes of the Department, especially considering her alleged connection to Peters.

But there was time.

With Defaux's help, she could discover the truth about Hives and then turn her attention to the RUIN.

Maybe she could manage to find a way out of all this.

She idly opened the folder beside the tray, expecting to see photos of the scene, a scene she already knew all too intimately.

Instead, she was greeted with a list of names and addresses.

She stared in confusion, shuffling through the pages.

"What is it?" Defaux asked. "What's wrong?"

Rayne didn't reply, instead frantically sifting through the folder until she found a name, the name of the Auditor these foreign pages had been intended for, and the name of who almost certainly had the RUIN case that held her fate in its hands.

"Damn it, Grimsby," Rayne said.

NINE ✳

GRIMSBY GRUNTED AS HE HAULED HIS BIKE UP THE stairs to his apartment. The metal staircase rattled and groaned nervously, but the last time he had left his bike outside, a murderous black-skulled familiar had almost destroyed it, and without it he'd be considerably less mobile when it came to making house calls.

He paused to catch his breath, his eyes falling to the scarred brick wall across from his home. Etched into the graffiti-stricken wall by claws months ago, the jagged words still made cold tendrils of worry slither around his spine.

THIS ISN'T OVER

Of course, that was easy to say, or scrawl, before he blew up old Blackskull with a land mine to the chest. At first, it had been a relief that the Department had found no trace of the familiar's remains, save for a severed arm. It seemed a reasonable outcome to a point-blank encounter with explosives. Yet Grimsby had been nearly as close and he had survived largely intact. Over time, any relief he felt had putrefied into paranoid concern.

Perhaps Blackskull wasn't quite as over as Grimsby would have liked.

His prickling nerves gave him a burst of energy to quickly climb the remaining steps and pull his bike inside, bolting the reinforced deadlock behind him.

The studio apartment was dark, lit only by the flickering images of an old black-and-white Western playing on the nearly-as-old tube TV. Grimsby hung his coat in the closet, the door to which he had thrown out after the incident where a *different* familiar scribbled some hideous art project on the inside while waiting to ambush him in his home. He leaned his bike against the front door before grabbing a package of dried ramen from a pallet of the same, which he had bought from a warehouse with his first paycheck from the Department.

"Hungry?" he called toward the couch.

A nest of partially shredded blankets nestled in the cushions twitched but made no reply. A gray-green hand of knobby knuckles extended out, backlit by the television, and beckoned silently. The hand was half as wide as Grimsby's own, but the fingers were nearly twice as long.

Grimsby sighed. "Wudge, you know you can get up and take one whenever you want, right?"

Wudge only beckoned again, this time twisting to face him enough that Grimsby could see the yellows of his eyes, horizontal pupils almost goatlike, burrowed deep in the nest of blankets.

Grimsby sighed and took a step toward him in the darkness, but his ankle suddenly caught on some kind of tightened line suspended just above the ground. He flailed his arms wildly as he tried to regain his balance, but the trip line caught on the tongue of his shoe and he quickly fell forward to the ground.

When he tried to catch his fall, however, he found the wooden floors had been coated in some kind of oil, and his palms slipped out from under him, making him crack his head against the floorboards.

He lay there for a moment, hearing little besides his own groans and the ringing in his ears, but as those subsided, he began to hear Wudge's croaking cackle, like a nearly pubescent bullfrog's giggle.

"Half-witch should watch where it steps," Wudge said.

Grimsby struggled to get enough traction to sit up, glaring at Wudge from under the throbbing lump that was already sprouting from his forehead. "I swear, Wudge. These pranks are getting old. I could have gotten a concussion!"

"Wudge has no idea what half-witch talks about." He extended his hand. "Raw-men, please."

Grimsby wobbled precariously to his feet, his knees caving to keep balance like a baby deer. "How is it that I'm an Auditor now, and still a half-witch? That should make me a full witch at least."

Wudge waved his extended hand dismissively. "Other witches are twice as big."

Grimsby bit back a sour reply. "I'm serious, Wudge, no more pranks. I—" He glanced back at the trip line. "Are those my shoelaces?"

Wudge snorted, his eyes glinting from the mound of blankets.

Grimsby felt his hands curl tight around the ramen package, cracking the noodles in his grip. He tried to take a deep, calming breath as he usually did when Wudge was misbehaving, but after the disastrous meeting with Mayflower, his chest already felt too tight to breathe.

He felt sparks well up on his scarred arm, but he quickly remembered the oil he was standing in and forced his Impetus to subside. It was like trying to push a beach ball underwater with one hand, but he managed it with practiced effort.

He slipped out of his oily shoes and padded his way into the kitchenette to wash his hands. The hot water burned on his scars and stung the half-moons his fingernails had dug into his good palm.

He glared at Wudge, feeling anger clench around his throat and tongue, but something Mayflower had said came back to him.

You got what you wanted, Grimsby. Not everyone else was so lucky.

The Huntsman likely hadn't known it, but the words might have been more true than he realized.

Grimsby grabbed the half-crushed package of ramen and carefully trod over to the couch, looking out for any additional surprises Wudge might have constructed. He saw none, but that only made him more nervous.

"Wudge," he said, settling down on the small portion of the couch that wasn't buried in blankets or ramen wrappers. "You've barely gotten off this couch in months."

Wudge said nothing, but a darting hand snagged the package from Grimsby's grip, drawing it into the blankets. Tearing sounds and crunching noises quickly followed.

"What—what did you *do* before we found you in Mansgraf's lair?"

"Wudge did what he does here. Nothing. Except here Wudge has cowboys." His large yellow eyes were focused intently on the screen, watching a man in riding chaps wrestle a cougar.

"But, I mean, what did you *want* to do? You said Mansgraf had something you wanted, right?"

The yellow eyes scowled, and Grimsby caught a flash of dozens of needlelike teeth. "She-bitch lied to Wudge. Said she had door and would let Wudge through if he guarded her lair. But door was fake. Now she-bitch no more, Wudge no door. Now, Wudge just do as Wudge does."

"You can't just sit here forever, Wudge."

The tiny creature hunkered down in the blankets. "Wudge can, too."

"No, I mean, you can't just give up."

"Give up? Wudge has nothing to give. Especially not up. Too short, like half-witch."

Grimsby ignored the mocking moniker. "Well, what about this door you were looking for? Surely it's still out there somewhere."

The blankets trembled in what might have been a shake of Wudge's head. "Door lost. Wudge lost. Lost can't find, only be found."

"But why not try? Anything's better than moping around here for the rest of time."

The yellow eyes narrowed. "You just want to get rid of Wudge!"

Grimsby scoffed. "Wudge, as much as I love it when you put glue on the toilet seat or freeze my pillow solid—"

Wudge cackled.

"I don't care if you want to stay here for a while. Just—just try to find a way to make your life better while you do, you know?"

Wudge's cackle fell to silence. Then, in a voice unusually small, even for his size, he croaked, "But what if Wudge fails again?"

Grimsby found a small, sad smile on his lips. "Simple. You just try again." He neglected to mention that succeeding might not be so simple. "Trust me. I have a lot of experience in both areas."

There was a reluctant moment of silence, marred only by the quiet, low-definition sound of a cougar shrieking on the television. "Half-witch will help Wudge?"

Grimsby hesitated.

The last time he had agreed to help Wudge, the tiny creature had threatened to strangle him when he later refused to follow through. Though, in fairness, Grimsby had given his word and had tried to go back on it.

Even so, he had surmised that Wudge had some kind of supernatural power when it came to making promises, one that he didn't fully, or even partially, understand.

"I will help you as much as I can," Grimsby said, trying to pick his words carefully, "so long as it doesn't keep me from my obligations at the Department."

Wudge took a sharp breath, then nodded. "Okay, half-witch. Wudge will try."

He grumbled and kicked as he tried to unwind himself from the coil of blankets, revealing his cartoonishly thin legs and arms and bulbous stomach. He pulled his head free, shaking his dangling ears, which reminded Grimsby of a furless rabbit. He still wore his odd helmet that seemed to be made of a large, hollow onion, and though it had sprouted numerous white hairs, it hadn't begun to rot as Grimsby feared it would.

Finally, Wudge stood, free from his blanket asylum, to a towering eighteen inches in height, which he had assured Grimsby multiple times was tall for his kind—whatever that was.

"Wudge will look," he said, cracking his numerous joints as he stretched. He grinned at Grimsby with far too many needle teeth and said, "Thank you, half-witch."

Then he simply vanished.

No smoke, no fading from view. He simply existed one blink, and did not the next. If it wasn't for the mess he'd left, Grimsby would have never known he was there at all.

Grimsby tried to smile but found himself too tired to do so. More than that, suddenly the room felt a bit too cold, a bit too dark. How long had it been since he hadn't had Wudge's eccentric company?

He glanced at where the missing closet door had been and felt his skin prickle with beaded sweat.

He shook his head. "Ridiculous," he muttered. There was no monster in his closet, at least not this time. There was no door to hide behind anymore. Besides, he was a grown man—more or less. He should be fine by himself.

Then his mind wandered to Mayflower, and the words the

Huntsman had left him with. Perhaps he was more by himself now than he had been in a long time.

He tried not to think about it, but it was no use. The idea of being an Auditor but not Mayflower's partner—it somehow made the job feel more bleak, more . . . frightening. It seemed an insurmountable task to try to do it alone, and even if he was assigned a new partner, a stranger, it would never be the same as if he and Mayflower were side by side again.

The Huntsman had saved his life on multiple occasions, and he had returned the favor, though not quite as often. As far as Grimsby was concerned, Mayflower was about the only thing like family he had.

But Mayflower didn't seem to feel the same way, and that hurt more than Grimsby had ever imagined it would.

He stared at the television Wudge had left on, but as the hero drew a worn revolver to duel the villain, he found himself turning it off as quickly as he could, leaving him in the quiet dark.

He let himself sit for a time, the only sound coming from the clicking of the standing fan he had gotten to replace the one that had torn loose from the ceiling months before.

He took a deep breath and felt it tremble in his chest. If he let that breath have its way, it would have come out as a small, shuddering sob.

"No," he said to himself.

He exhaled quickly and stood, forcing himself to move. The old Grimsby would have cried in the dark. But that wasn't him anymore. He had been alone before, and if he would be again, so be it.

He was the only company he needed.

Though, as he bundled up and tucked away his undermining emotions, he realized he was alone in his apartment for the first time since he had been hunted by familiars.

And it was very dark.

He waved a hand to the floor lamp in the corner of the room and said, *"Bind,"* forcing himself to do so calmly and more slowly than the prickling hairs on the back of his neck wanted.

The lamp clicked on, spreading faint, warm light to shadow the studio apartment. Instinctively, he cast a quick glance to the open closet, but it was devoid of anything more threatening than a vacuum.

"Don't be a child," he chided himself, though he kept the closet in the corner of his eye.

He grumbled this to himself again and again as he cleaned up the oil from Wudge's prank. He told it to himself another time as he settled into the cot he'd purchased when Wudge had commandeered the couch that had once served as his bed. And he told it to himself a final time as he climbed restlessly from bed and cleaned the apartment of ramen wrappers and noodle crumbs, all the while keeping the closet in view.

Finally, more because he was too exhausted to be afraid than because his words had stuck, he face-planted back onto his cot and fell into fitful sleep, though he left the light on as he did. His dreams were full of skeletal figures, empty revolvers, and bloody Auditor badges. The ominous words of Blackskull rattled around in his mind.

This isn't over.

He awoke with a start when a finger prodded his shoulder. At first, he thought it was just another dream. The rag-clad form of the Blackskull and its kindred had sunk their claws into him frequently in his nightmares since their last encounter. But even as he stirred enough to dismiss the idea, the prodding came again. When he realized it wasn't in his head, the half of his brain that was conscious instantly panicked, while the remaining half refused to get out of his cot.

The result was him tipping the cot over, tumbling to the floor in a twist of blankets and confusion.

"Half-witch sleeps too hard," he heard Wudge say. "Anything could eat him up."

He cracked open his eyes to see the nuisance standing over him, poking him with one eerily long hand and scratching under his loincloth with the other.

"Wh— Wudge?" Grimsby mumbled, the gears of his mind feeling like they'd been caked with rust as they slowly groaned into motion.

"Wudge finds it," he said. "Now needs half-witch's help."

"Found what?" he asked.

Wudge only grinned toothily.

TEN

GRIMSBY SHIVERED IN THE COLD BREEZE THAT COURSED through the alley. The air was damp with chill mist that bloomed around every streetlight, and the only sound was that of wind and occasional tires over asphalt. He was only wearing his pajamas and a plush bathrobe, as Wudge had insisted time was of the essence. He scowled at the cracked mirror that was leaned up against the brick wall among other refuse. It was big enough to fit him, though only just.

"You're sure about this?" he asked Wudge, clenching his arms tight around himself against the cold. Dawn was still hours away, and with it Boston would begin to rouse from its midnight slumber.

Wudge nodded enthusiastically, making his flopping ears go wild. "Yes, yes! Wudge made sure. Found it and came straight to half-witch."

"And you found—what was it again? Your door?"

"No! Piece of the door. Very small, but Wudge can feel it! It might help Wudge find the real door."

"And you need my help . . . why?"

Wudge groaned in annoyance, like a toddler explaining to an adult why the sky should be purple instead of blue for the fifth time, slapping his onion-helm with one hand of knobby fingers. "Half-witch said he'd help Wudge. Did he lie?"

"No, no, I didn't lie. I just didn't think it would be so . . . soon. You've been gone, what"—he yawned so wide that he felt his jaw pop—"six, seven hours?"

"Wudge was gone for days!"

"In the Elsewhere."

Wudge nodded.

"And while you were searching for the door, did you keep going back and forth from our world to the Elsewhere?"

"Your world," Wudge corrected him. "But yes, Wudge did."

"You know time works weird in the Elsewhere, right? Just because it was days for you doesn't mean it was a full night's sleep for me."

Wudge waved away his words like annoying flies. "Bah! Half-witch wastes time. Go through. Wudge will be on other side waiting."

Grimsby glanced again at the mirror. The reflection was his own, but it was unlikely to remain that way for long. All mirrors were waiting portals to the Elsewhere. They just needed to be opened—which was why the only reasonably reflective surface in his own apartment was a polished steel mixing bowl mounted to his bathroom wall.

He had been through mirrors before, but even so, he was forced to suppress a shiver, though it wasn't easy in the cold air.

The Elsewhere wasn't a place a witch went without good reason. It was far too dangerous, and too bizarre. Besides, sometimes witches went through a mirror and didn't come back for seven years, if they came back at all. It was probably where the superstition about mirrors and bad luck had originated.

"Wudge, I don't know," he said. "This is serious stuff, I—"

He turned to see Wudge's beady eyes glaring at him. "You gave Wudge your word," he said, but there was something beneath the anger that welled in his gaze. The tiny creature stood taut as though in defiance of the emotion that lurked within, but Grimsby was all too familiar with that move.

Wudge was alone; he was frightened.

And he needed help.

Grimsby took a breath and shook his head. What kind of person would he be if he backed out now? Let alone what kind of friend? "All right, all right. I'll go. But we better be back before I need to go to work."

Wudge's scowl melted into a mischievous grin. "Wudge will make sure of it. Now, go!"

And with that, he vanished.

Grimsby stood there in his pajamas, alone in the alley.

"Odd's Bodkin," he cursed, then he reluctantly closed his eyes and peeled the large round glasses from his face. He braced himself, then opened his eyes once more.

His glasses were his mask—a kind of physical and mental trick that he and all other witches had to learn as children. It was a means of keeping your mind out of the Elsewhere while still being able to peer in when you needed to. Some witches, like Auditors prepared for dangerous fieldwork, used real masks, but most tended toward the more subtle glasses.

Without them, without his mask, to shield him, the world had changed.

Gone was the concrete and brick alleyway. Instead the ground had become grit-strewn cobblestones, slick with a fresh rain. The walls on either side of him seemed to tower much taller than before, though the gap between them felt more narrow. Vaulted buttresses arched between them high above, like he had fallen into a crack between two grand cathedrals, rather than a mini-mart and a laundromat.

Beyond them, the narrow strip of night sky had become scarlet. It glared down, making his eyes strain. Set in its center, surrounded by cracks that wove through the clouds like broken glass, was a black sun. Or, perhaps, moon. It seemed to absorb all light that dared wander too near, and Grimsby had the sinking feeling it would do the same to him if he strayed too close.

He tore his gaze from the sky and focused on the mirror. The longer he stayed without a mask, peering into the realm of the Elsewhere, the more likely it was for something to peer back at him. Unmasked, he would be like a beacon to some creatures on the other side, all eager to devour his Impetus like ethereal sharks.

He stood before the mirrored glass, but the reflection was odd. It showed the warped alley around him, but he himself was distinctly missing from the eerie image.

He pressed his palms against the glass and concentrated, willing his Impetus through his fingers and into the cool surface. It was more difficult with his left hand. The gnarled burn scars leaked power whenever he lost even the slightest measure of control. They glowed and smoldered, and he worried his robe might catch light if he pushed much further. But soon the glass shimmered, like the surface of standing water, and his hands pressed through, reaching in to join the reflection on the other side.

He swallowed the lump in his throat and began to push into the mirror. It felt like his skin was being slowly encased in cooled steel with every inch he moved. Within moments, he was up to his elbows. Moments after that, he pressed his head through.

As he did, he crossed the threshold. He felt like he was suddenly falling forward as the mirror pulled him in. Within a second, he was fully inside its grasp. Then, suddenly, he fell out into open air, like he had been pressed up against a door whose hinges had snapped.

He tumbled forward onto cobblestone, the mirror shattering behind and sending shards of glass falling with him. He landed in a heap in the same alley he had just left, except this time it was a little different.

Before, with his glasses gone, he had *seen* the Elsewhere, but it wasn't real. It was an image, like the kind staring at the sun leaves when you close your eyes, or when you look down into a still pool of water to see the surface world reflected and alien below.

Now, he was *in* it. The ground, the air, the sky—they were all fully real.

For whatever that was worth in this place.

He stood and brushed himself off, replacing his glasses before looking around for Wudge, but the creature was nowhere to be seen.

Then he heard a chilling, familiar sound. It was distant, but even so, goose bumps prickled over his skin, revealing the many faint scars he had been left with the first time he heard that same sound.

It was the keening wail of a Geist, drawn to the broken glass of the mirror. He wasn't sure if it was the shattering itself or something else that attracted them, but Geists flocked to broken glass like ducks to bread crumbs.

Squishy, Grimsby-shaped bread crumbs.

He cast his eye to the sky, but none of the clouds moved.

Yet.

He needed to get away. Now.

He took another desperate look around for Wudge but didn't see him anywhere. He couldn't wait. He had seen, and felt, what a Geist could do to a creature before, and he had no interest in being turned into red rain.

He moved quickly down the alley, rather than out onto the road where anything could see him. The corners were more twisting and labyrinthine than the real world's, and he quickly realized he had lost all measure of direction. The scale of this world to its waking counterpart was constantly in flux, appearing to be one way when he peered into the Elsewhere, while becoming something totally different when he took the plunge into it. The normally familiar neighborhood was completely foreign to him now, leaving him to wander and hope to find some recognizable landmark.

The black sun was directly above, like a single, leering eye, offering no clue to which way he should go.

He winced as a distant bell began to sound, like the toll of a clock tower. It tolled seven times for him, and him alone. Seven minutes had already passed, meaning he was in the second window. Whether he returned now or in just under seven hours, only seven minutes would have passed in the waking world. However, if he was just moments more, he'd return a full week after he had left.

"That's an easy way to get fired," he muttered to himself. Then again, he imagined the Department was not wholly unfamiliar with that unfortunate event. He was certainly not the only witch to visit the Elsewhere, though he doubted Grieves would have sanctioned this particular expedition.

He found an exit to the alleyway, the dark walls of stone looming tall over the empty street beyond, their slate-tiled rooftops adorned with broken, inhuman statues. Some seemed half sunk into the dark walls, while others were shattered and strewn about like fallen branches. He finally let his pace slow, reasonably sure the Geist would no longer be hunting him. The creatures were drawn to broken glass, but they seemed more like a swarm of insects than a living being, lacking any real intelligence.

He pressed against the alley wall and peered out into the street, uncertain what he was looking for. He had been to the Elsewhere a handful of times before, but only once had it been as reckless as this.

Far off in the distance, he spotted the broken skyline of towers that amassed near where downtown Boston would be. They seemed impossibly precarious; their damaged frames would have surely collapsed instantly in the waking world, but here they were still and steady. Between them, massive, skeletal figures strode with steps longer than most city blocks. They moved like titans of black bone, silhouetted against the red sky. The hollows in their skulls smoldered with green fire, though they felt closer to dying embers than open flames.

Grimsby shuddered and looked away from the figures, afraid they might somehow feel his gaze even from miles off.

"The big ones feed on folks," Wudge suddenly said from behind him. "Their fear, their nightmares. They like the dark-tall places in the city."

Grimsby whipped around to see the small creature sitting on a crenelation set into the wall, bouncing his long, rag-clad feet on the engraved stonework.

"Where the heck have you been?" he demanded in a harsh whisper. "You said you'd meet me on this side!"

Wudge frowned. "Is this not meeting, half-witch?"

"I was thinking something a little more prompt."

He shrugged bony shoulders and hopped down, idly picking at the navel of his potbelly. "Wudge didn't say *prompt*."

Grimsby felt his temper flare as his cheeks grew hot, but he forced the feeling away, taking a deep and calming breath. "No, I suppose you didn't. Let's get moving. I don't want to miss my return window."

Wudge grinned his too-many teeth. "Not far now. Wudge made sure mirror half-witch used came close."

"I thought that the mirrors were, like, paralleled with those from our world," Grimsby said, "like two ends of a tunnel."

Wudge made a retching noise. "Half-witch thinks too much like a human. Mirrors go where they go, unless they go elsewhere. That is why it is Elsewhere. See?"

"No." Grimsby was pretty sure that wasn't right.

But only *pretty* sure.

Wudge pondered for a moment, then nodded. "Probably for best. Especially for humans. Safer to not see, most times." He padded out onto the open street, heedless of the distant titans of bone, the Geists above, or anything else that lurked about.

"Wudge!" Grimsby hissed, but he was promptly ignored. He glanced around one last time, looking for anything lurking between shadowed gables, then hurriedly chased after his unreliable companion.

They walked for a short while, Wudge moving briskly forward with Grimsby on his heels, casting nervous gazes anywhere shadows fell, which was practically everywhere in the Elsewhere.

Slowly, figures began to emerge from the crowded structures all around, pouring forth like black mist from open maws. At first, Grimsby recoiled, then he slowly recognized them for what they were: Figments.

He had only seen them before while looking into the Elsewhere from the waking world. They were shadows of people, real people, though here they were barely more than a dimming of the light in the shape of a person. He cautiously extended a curious hand, touching one as it passed. It felt oddly warm, but the Figment paused and almost seemed to shiver before moving on in shuddering bursts of quick and slow motion, sometimes forward and sometimes in a way that looked like it was being rewound.

Grimsby thought back to all the times when unprovoked chills had crawled over his spine and suddenly wondered how many of them were from something in the Elsewhere actually crawling over him.

Another shiver struck him, though he hoped this one was natural.

Wudge didn't heed the Figments, ignoring them even when the street grew smoky and dim as more crowded in. His gaze was focused on something ahead, a structure of some kind. Grimsby tried to get a better look, but between the alien architecture of the

Elsewhere and dodging uncomfortable contact with Figments, he couldn't get a clear picture.

Finally, they drew close enough that Wudge grabbed Grimsby's pajama pants leg with a clammy hand and dragged him behind a cracked and broken pillar of black marble. Wudge pulled him down to hunker behind the cover while simultaneously using him as a ladder to climb up enough to see over it.

"There," he said, pointing a spidery finger to the building across the street.

For a moment, Grimsby didn't see anything unusual about the structure. It was oddly tall, with no truly straight lines to its stonework frame. It was just as the other buildings were, all arcades, archivolts, buttresses, and other terms he had learned in his studies but forgotten. But then he noticed the doorway. Where the other buildings had open gaps where doors and windows might normally be, this one had an actual door.

Actually, as he squinted through his thick glasses, he saw it wasn't a door at all. It was a barricade of wooden planks, packed with stained cloth in the gaps, sealing the entrance off. The windows were the same, their sightless gaze blocked by boards. Though the farther they rose from the ground, the more haphazard the barriers seemed. Like whoever had constructed them had grown tired of the effort as they ascended.

"So, your—what was it again?"

"Piece of the door."

"That's in there?"

Wudge pointed far into the sky, toward the looming tower at the structure's top. "Up there."

Grimsby followed his finger and caught sight of something moving behind the ramshackle shutters on the topmost set of windows, blotting out the candlelight illumination coming from within. Something very big.

"And what else is inside there?"

Wudge shrugged. "Does it matter? Big, small, few, or many, inside we go anyway."

"You're frighteningly practical about these kinds of things, Wudge."

Wudge grinned and winked one yellow eye. "This'll be fun, half-witch. You'll see." He darted across the street, leaving Grimsby crouched behind the broken pillar.

Doubts assailed him as to just how much *fun* he was about to have, but he was quite certain of one thing: he wasn't going to be bored.

ELEVEN

GRIMSBY FOLLOWED WUDGE AROUND THE BACK OF THE building, down a crooked alleyway of looming arches and twisting shadows. The building had few windows on the sides, and those few they found were totally blockaded by old boards of gnarled oak.

"How are we supposed to get in?" Grimsby asked. "Whatever is in there seems to have the place locked down. What is it, anyway?"

"Wudge found a way. A secret way," Wudge said, trailing his long fingers along the dark brick walls. "And what is inside is the thing that has what Wudge wants."

"I meant in a more specific sense." He began talking faster than he meant to, betraying his growing anxiety. "Is it a trans-dimensional squatter, or maybe an ancient guardian from forgotten times, or a thief with a dubious past who learns the only real treasure is the heart of gold he had all along? Is there just one of them? Is it a sinister cabal with a collection of golden hearts? What are we dealing with here?"

Wudge paused and frowned for a moment, honestly considering the question. Then he shrugged, casting it aside just as quickly. "Don't know. Don't care."

"Smoke and mirrors," Grimsby cursed, feeling his stomach tense with nerves. "Well, how are we supposed to beat *it* if we don't even know what *it* is?"

"Don't need to beat it. Just need to steal the piece of the door. Then leave. No get seen, no need beat." He continued to trail his fingers along the wall until one of the bricks grated under his touch. He stopped, grinned, and pressed harder. The brick receded, and with it so did many others in a cascade of dust and crumbling mortar, revealing a door of moldy wood.

Grimsby raised a brow. The door was just over Wudge's height, barely big enough for Grimsby to even crawl through. "What is that doing there?"

Wudge's grin widened, baring his countless teeth. "Wudge can always find a way into places where he isn't welcome." He didn't seem to care to offer any more explanation, and Grimsby was too nervous to press the issue.

"Do we even have a plan?"

Wudge groaned. "Plan plan plan." He flapped his fingers up and down in a mockery of speech. "Half-witch needs to have more fun fun fun."

"You'd have a different definition of *fun* if you were human."

"Fleh!" Wudge said with a fed-up flinging of his hands. "Fine! Half-witch sneak in, find the piece. Wudge will distract. Half-witch take piece and run. We live, we leave, we win."

"That still seems a little vague—" he began. "Where do I even find this 'piece'?"

Wudge didn't reply at first. He only opened the tiny door, rolled his goatlike eyes, and vanished. Finally, his faint words echoed from all around Grimsby. "Look for the ivy."

"The ivy? What does that even mean?" he demanded.

There was no reply.

"Puppy dogs' tails," Grimsby grumbled, kneeling down to crawl through the darkened opening. "I should have stayed in bed."

The rough ground bit into his palms and knees, cutting easily through the thin cloth of his pajama pants. He wriggled his head and shoulders through the narrow frame, his bathrobe tugging on the wood as he did. Finally, he pulled through, finding himself in a darkened tunnel. He began to crawl, his hands grating over the grit-strewn ground, and he was forced to ignore the bits of stone that stuck in his palms.

The tunnel was far longer than it should have been. The walls couldn't have been more than a foot thick, but the tunnel stretched on for far more. After a few feet, the door behind him creaked shut, leaving him stranded in dusty darkness. Then he saw a light at the end of the crawl space and began to worm forward, trying desperately not to think about becoming stuck in the cramped corridor.

He drew close enough to the light to see it was cracking through the seams of a second doorway, identical to the first. It was slightly ajar, and Grimsby could just hear the departing, padding steps of Wudge's flapping feet. He creaked open the door, wincing at the noise it made in the silence, but he heard neither shouts nor growls of alarm.

He wiggled through the portal, managing to squeeze himself between the miniature doorframe after some effort, to land in an unceremonious heap on the other side. Despite the light he had seen, the room was still dim. What little illumination there was came from the cracks between boarded windows and a few scattered candles. The flames on their wicks tottered and swayed, flickering briefly to look like tiny, dancing humans before fading to shapeless fire once more.

Grimsby climbed to his feet and brushed the dust from his pajamas and plush robe. He glanced around, but there was no movement. Then, above, the floorboards suddenly groaned and bowed as some great mass moved over them.

He took panicked cover behind a broken wardrobe leaning against the room's murkiest corner. It almost seemed like whatever was above might crack through the floor from its own weight, but after a moment of pacing the sound ceased.

He let himself take a strained sip of air in relief, but it was short-lived. He needed to find this *piece* that Wudge was so adamant about, whatever it might be. Was it a piece of wood? A key? An old doorknob? *Piece* was quite vague and not at all helpful. Though it was about what he should have expected from Wudge.

"Look for the ivy," he muttered. "Look for the ivy."

The room he was in looked almost like a cramped hostel room, with only a wardrobe and bed. Unfortunately, it seemed like it was meant for a single person to stay in for a short while, not a vault for storing precious things.

He glanced out the partially boarded window and realized Wudge's door had taken them not only inside, but somehow several stories up as well, leaving a long gap to the hard ground. He felt his head spin and gulped, shaking away the sickening intrusive thoughts to see firsthand how long it would take to hit the ground.

The only door in the room led to a hall.

A quick glance up and down its length told him there were more rooms like his own, but none of them seemed outstanding or of interest. He crept around for a few minutes, looking for ivy, but none revealed itself, and he quickly had the nauseating suspicion that he would not find the prize here, but rather upstairs, where that large mystery thing was roaming.

He spotted stairs at the far end and, after a brief session of minor hyperventilation, took those instead. With careful, toe-tipped movements, he climbed the steps, every creak and whine making him wince. Fortunately, the whole structure seemed all too happy to make noises of its own, hopefully masking his quiet ruckus.

Then he heard a voice from the room beyond the top of the stairs. It was like the low rumble of grating stones but had an oddly childlike quality to it, with slow and uncertain words.

"I'm bored," the voice said. "Ain't we waited our turn out yet?"

It was loud enough that Grimsby moved more quickly, letting the sound hide his footsteps. He reached the top of the steps to find a more open level, like a loft. It was packed to the ceiling with crates, shelves of mismatched clutter, and haphazard mounds of worthless antiques. The largest of the piles was somehow smoother, though, like it was covered with a tarp of rough, shaggy leather.

Then the whole thing twitched, and Grimsby realized it wasn't a heap of covered garbage, but rather some*thing*. "Echidna? You there?" the massive creature called, odd concern in its voice.

"Yes, yes, Lump," a second voice distractedly answered. It was smaller and feminine, though neither quality was hard to manage relative to Lump, but it was sharper and decisive as well. "Mother's still cross with us—I expect we'll be here three more days, just before our window ends."

Lump groaned, his massive form shuddering. "T'ree days? That's forever."

"Lump," the one he'd called Echidna said, leaning out from the crowded shelves of books. She held one propped open in a lithe hand, her arm idly flexing sinewed muscle. Her head was a wild mane of dark and curly hair that bobbed around her face. She looked almost oddly human, except when candlelight struck her olive skin at the right angle, it gained a sleek, iridescent sheen. She peered over the open tome in her hands at Lump. "You're how old?"

The indoor mountain raised a meaty paw that was vaguely human, or would have been if the fingers weren't as thick as Grimsby's wrists. "Uhm, err," Lump said, counting off on his fingers, "more than this many. Pretty sure."

The woman sighed, though when she did, it sounded like a hiss coming from multiple throats. "Yes. I'm pretty sure four centuries is more than that as well. You'll live. We'll be home before you know it."

"Okay, 'Idna . . ." Lump muttered, moments later groaning and letting his arm fall to the floor despondently, making the whole building tremble.

The woman shook her head, making her dark locks of hair shudder oddly. "Just go back to sleep. I'll wake you if I find anything good, or when it's time to go."

Lump sighed but relaxed, his mountainous body taking a steady rhythm of breath. The woman receded back into the shelves, humming quietly to herself in time with the flutter of turning pages.

Grimsby knelt behind the railing of the stairs, trying to get a better look at Lump in the dimness. The only things he could tell for certain were that Lump was massive, and he had hands that could crush Grimsby's slight frame with ease.

In fact, it was probably a safe bet to assume that was Lump's primary function.

He was likely some kind of guard. But the woman's role, Grimsby was less certain of. Perhaps she was also on watch? She had the look of someone who knew how to fight. Though she seemed much more interested in the shelves of books than potential intruders.

Either way, Grimsby was still more concerned with the massive Lump. He was quite certain the creature could crush him in his palm like a tin can of tomato soup.

Chunky tomato soup.

He felt his legs grow unsteady beneath him, and he had to grip the railing tight to keep his balance.

Why had he let Wudge rope him into this?

He gritted his teeth and glared hard at the ground, though he turned his glare inward. No, he hadn't been roped into anything. He had volunteered to help because Wudge was his friend. A very odd and annoying friend, but a friend all the same.

And it wasn't right to leave your friends when they needed you.

It wasn't *right*.

Grimsby didn't realize he was angry until he felt the heat flush in his cheeks. The words were suddenly as clear in his mind as they had been when Mayflower said them.

I was your goddamn babysitter, and I'm done with it.

His stomach twisted into knots. His knuckles cracked as they scratched into the scabs still left there. His eyes burned.

It wasn't right.

Mayflower wasn't right.

Grimsby was an Auditor. He didn't need a babysitter.

He needed a partner.

He needed a friend.

At the moment, he felt quite alone.

He tore his mind away from the Huntsman, though it felt like threads tearing from their eyelets in his mind. He needed to focus.

He was a professional.

There was no need to worry about just how easily Lump could crush him to paste. Neither he nor Echidna had seen Grimsby yet. He just needed to avoid them, find the piece of the door, and get out.

Unfortunately, finding the piece seemed like a task all too similar to finding a needle in a haystack. Except the hay was an entire floor of odd antiques, crates, and shelves. And the needle could be, well, anything.

It could also be anywhere, in any container, or just rolling around on the floor, for all he knew. He glanced around, looking for some sign from Wudge, but the creature was nowhere to be seen.

"Look for the ivy," he muttered, but even with the words echoing in his head, he saw no trace of greenery or vines, save for Lump's shaggy mane of hanging moss.

He desperately hoped it wasn't lodged somewhere in there.

He shook his head and took a breath to steel himself. He had little choice but to look around, though every second he spent doing so was another chance at being caught. Fortunately, with Lump slumbering and Echidna reading, he might have a shot.

He moved away from the stairs, keeping to the wall. Lump had situated himself in the room's center, while Echidna was in the far corner. There was a rough path through the gathered junk, though much of it had tumbled and fallen at some point. He watched where he put his feet, stepping over a rocking horse of oiled and weathered wood, slipping under a fallen armoire, moving through its contents, which hung like dusty curtains.

There was a strange heat in the room, but it wasn't pressing or ambient. It was almost like he was walking through banks of invisible steam, which seemed to swirl and sway, dissipating with his passing before beginning to build up again in his wake. It wasn't true heat, however, but rather something more ephemeral—like the memory of a hot breeze on the nape of his neck.

For an infrequent moment, Grimsby was glad he was smaller than most. He easily fit through gaps that someone like Mayflower would have struggled with, and his lighter weight barely made the floors creak. Even so, he was careful to keep his steps irregular, trying to blur his own noise with the structure's natural groans.

He peered around for anything of interest, but nothing stood out. He passed shelves of glass vessels filled with what looked like ritual reagents or potion ingredients. There were chests left ajar and filled with moth-eaten clothes. He even saw a stuffed creature that looked like a half beast, half man, though neither term seemed an accurate description.

He could still feel that heat pulsing all around, a warm sensation that made his scars itch and sweat tingle on his scalp. He paused, trying to locate the source of the sensation, but as he passed through cold and warm spots, he realized it wasn't one location, but rather many.

Yet that odd, shifting heat remained, like a looming titan's breath, and as his eyes combed the collection of mismatched miscellanea, he realized what it was.

It was ambient magic. Power radiating from the objects all around him.

He felt his mouth go dry. He had seen enchanted items in his time, even made a couple himself, but many of these looked *old*, and magic that didn't fade with time was often powerful—and, by extension, dangerous.

He looked around at the mounds of gathered junk: were they truly all enchanted, or even cursed?

The thought was a worrying one. Curses were simply enchantments that were bad for whoever possessed them, and it was far simpler to make a nasty curse than it was to make a moderately convenient enchantment. So, if he was right and he was really walking through a magical hoard, it was far more minefield than treasure trove.

He held out his hand, though he avoided touching anything. Faint heat radiated from almost every item in the room, but there were so many, and most were so weak, that it felt like background noise on his skin.

"Eyes aflame," he cursed, barely a whisper.

He briefly hoped maybe Wudge's trophy would stand out more than the rest, but nothing arose in the sea of shifting magic, and without time to examine and test the objects, finding the specific one Wudge was looking for had become even more impossible.

Then he spotted a wiggle of movement from an open cabinet that loomed at the peak of a pile of mismatched tomes, carved figurines, and other odd paraphernalia, directly above Lump's resting place. Sitting atop it, kicking his rag-clad feet in plain view of everything, was Wudge.

Grimsby froze, his eyes growing so wide he could almost see

around his massive glasses. He was simultaneously trapped and in the open, not to mention he had no idea where the piece was. If Wudge made his ruckus now, there was no chance he'd both find it and escape.

He waved a furtive hand at Wudge to get his attention, trying to tell him to stop and wait.

The little creature was staring at Lump with a grin that would have been mischievous if it had a third as many teeth involved, but he didn't seem to see Grimsby.

He watched as Wudge reached behind his back and pulled out an *actual* anvil. Though it was of a small variety, only the size of Grimsby's head. Wudge's trembling, twig-thin arms showed surprising strength as he lifted it over his body. He positioned himself directly above Lump and what looked like the top of the thing's head.

Grimsby suddenly wished he had never let Wudge watch television.

He felt his heart skip town and flee the country all in the span of a half second. Then, atop a leaning, two-legged chest between him and Lump, he saw a small and simple box of iron. On the front of it were imprinted two Roman numerals:

IV

"Ivy—" Grimsby breathed.

Just then, Wudge hurled the anvil straight down with all his tiny might.

Metal clunked. Bone cracked. Lump roared.

Meanwhile, Grimsby could only manage a panicked squeak.

TWELVE

GRIMSBY DIDN'T STOP TO LET HIMSELF THINK. HE WAS afraid that if he let any rational thought enter his brain, it would be the irrefutable suggestion to run away screaming.

That left only the irrational thoughts.

He ran toward the chest with the *IV* imprinted on it, grunting as his foot caught on the sharp edge of a fallen suit of empty armor, which pierced easily through his slipper and into his heel before tearing his footwear away. He ignored the pain and tried not to let himself limp. He needed to avoid touching anything he didn't have to. A bad curse might shrivel his arm to dust or turn his eyes to buttons, and he already had enough problems to deal with.

Lump roared, in furious pain. The anvil had stuck fast in the side of his head, held by his tangled, mossy mane of greasy hair. He shook his shaggy head from side to side, and the sound of ripping fibers filled the room. Finally, the anvil tore away, peeling hair and scalp with it, leaving gray bone, the color of slate, bare beneath. Lump rubbed his exposed skull with one massive paw, but even as he did, the skin began to crawl back into place, knitting itself together like living leather.

Grimsby gulped down the bile that welled in his throat, born of disgust and fear in equal measure.

The creature was even bigger than he had thought, his shaggy head the size of a small boulder. He had a large, drooping nose and a craggy, pitted face that looked like worn limestone. His mop of green hair draped over his twin eyes, which glinted like angry garnets.

The mountainous creature looked up, his face twisted in confused rage. There, standing atop the cabinet on the mountain of knickknacks beside him and wearing a jack-o'-lantern grin so wide it nearly split his face, was Wudge.

He stuck his thumbs under his drooping ears and wiggled his spidery digits at Lump, dancing back and forth on his rag-clad feet. *"Big dumb, big dumb, why don't you come and get some!"* he sang like a whiny bullfrog.

Lump roared and slammed his fist into the side of the piled objects, shattering many and causing an avalanche of miscellanea, but Wudge leapt nimbly away, sliding down a tapestry draped between two mounds of sealed crates. He landed in a scurrying sprint in a direction that was thankfully away from Grimsby.

Lump growled and set off after Wudge, not even bothering to stand. Instead, he clambered like a large toddler on all fours, desperately trying to crush the nuisance of Wudge under his palms.

Grimsby tore his eyes away from the duo and reached the iron box. He fumbled with the latch that held it shut but otherwise found it unlocked. He threw open the lid, expecting to find some knocker or doorknob, or whatever other piece of the door it was Wudge had been after.

Instead, all he found was dust and an old nail.

He stared in confusion, trying to process in his mind. Had he found the right ivy? Had Wudge's information been wrong? Had this whole absurd ordeal been for nothing?

He fished around in the box, desperately hoping he had missed something in the dim light, but his fingers found only the nail, its surface cold and rough with dark corrosion.

When he withdrew his hand, however, he found the nail came with it, dangling from the tip of his finger like he was magnetized.

He frowned and shook his hand, but the nail refused to break contact with his skin. He tried to pull it away with his other hand, and it came loose easily. Except it then remained stuck to *that* hand.

He was so distracted that he had forgotten that Lump wasn't the only occupant in the room.

A flicker of movement caught his eye, and he turned to see Echidna emerge from the stacked shelves of tomes not nearly far enough away. She looked surprised but focused, her keen eyes tracing Lump's lumbering movements. Then, in less than a breath, her venom-green gaze turned to Grimsby.

For a moment, they both froze, Grimsby doing so in some foolish, instinctive gambit that Echidna's vision was based on movement. Echidna doing so likely to process the whole scene.

Then she *moved*.

She emerged from the shadowed shelves not on legs, but on serpentine coils, her sinuous tail propelling her forward at shocking speed, seemingly uncaring of the debris in her path as she slid nimbly over it.

Grimsby was so shocked that he let loose a mouselike squeak, which would have been a full scream if he'd had the breath to spare. He stumbled back, but his bare heel struck a rusted black-iron cauldron. He fell onto his side, twisting around the pot painfully. He struggled to his feet to begin a stumbling run toward the stairs, but he had barely made it a few steps when something hard and sharp struck him between the shoulder blades.

He tried to cry out, but the blow whipped the air from his lungs, and instead he tripped and crashed into a stacked pallet of candles made of black wax. His eyes blurred with tears at the searing pain, and his hands desperately reached back to check the severity of his wound. His robe and pajama shirt proved to be poor armor, as both had been slashed away, leaving a long and ragged welt across his back. It was shallow, but the sheer pain that flared over his back felt like his spine had been suddenly transmuted to red-hot iron.

He managed to crawl to his hands and knees, sending candles rolling away, just in time to see Echidna slither before him. Her long locks of dark hair seemed to move and writhe of their own accord. This close, he could see the iridescent sheen of her skin was actually minuscule scales, as smooth as marble.

"Who are you?" Echidna demanded, her tail whipping back and forth like a hunting cat's. The tip had a metal barb on it that was speckled red with a splatter of his own blood.

Grimsby clambered to his feet. "Would you believe I'm a professional?" he asked, gritting his teeth through the pain of her strike. "And you're a what, a Medusa?"

Echidna's eyes flared in annoyance, her locks of hair freezing for a moment. "Medusa is—was—a woman, jerk. Not a species."

Grimsby glared, trying to look like he was recalling his history lessons, when really he was summoning his Impetus. He felt the heat grow in him and hoped Echidna would not notice his scars smoldering to life. "So you're a gorgon?"

Echidna glared and shook her head. "Idiot human," she muttered, then lunged at him, her coiled lower body tensing to encircle him like a python.

Grimsby raised his right hand and let his Impetus surge through him. "*Torque!*" he cried, expecting to send a twisting torrent of magical momentum.

Instead, a field of dim motes of light bloomed forth, like a swath of distant stars caught in the shimmering heat from blacktop in summer. It hovered in space like a tiny, suspended nebula. However, when Echidna struck it, it suddenly seemed as though she was trying to move through invisible molasses. She lagged to a glacial pace, from her coils to the slightest twitches of her furious expression. As she writhed in slow motion, the stars swelled and grew slowly brighter.

Grimsby stared in utter shock, his hand still limply raised.

He had used *Torque* since he could speak. He had cast the spell ten thousand times over, and though sometimes he could barely manage the slightest force, it had always done the same thing.

But this wasn't *Torque*.

It was alien to him. As much so as if he had tried to lower his left arm and instead started shouting obscenities. He was so stunned by the broken familiarity of his own magic that his focus wavered, and his spell shattered.

The shimmering field boomed like the thrum of a drum, dispersing in an explosion of metallic mist. Echidna regained her bearings almost instantly, lashing out at him before he could run.

He felt powerful muscle and sinew wrap around him so quickly that he could barely move. He managed to draw a breath and brace himself an instant before her serpentine coils drew taut, constricting his body from ankle to shoulder.

Echidna's lean frame curled around him like a snake around a tree branch. She came face-to-face with him, twisting in a way no human could ever replicate. From this close, he could see her split tongue and the thin-slitted pupils of her green eyes, whose piercing gaze made his skin itch.

"Who sent you?" she demanded. "The Bloodline? Department? Bastion?!"

Grimsby sputtered something that did not even remotely resemble words. He felt like his ribs were about to crack at any moment.

Echidna sighed in more annoyance than anger and let her coils loosen by thin degrees. "Who sent you?" she demanded again.

"W-Wudge," Grimsby sputtered.

Echidna frowned. "What the hell is Wudge?"

Grimsby gestured with his head toward the other side of the building, where Wudge was still leading Lump on a mad chase, cackling as he did. Every passing moment sounded like an avalanche of breaking wood and rending metal.

Echidna's angered eyes widened with sudden and genuine alarm as though she was noticing the rampage for the first time. "Lump!" she shrieked. "Lump! Stop! You're breaking everything!"

Lump didn't seem to hear her, instead only continued his crawling chase, roaring in frustration at every missed swipe of his quarry.

"Mother is going to kill me," she muttered to herself with genuine fear. Then, just as Grimsby was about to speak, her coils tightened and silenced him. She called out again, "Wudge! I have your witch! Surrender or I will crush him!"

The cackling ceased, and though Grimsby couldn't see Wudge, he saw Lump come to a skidding, confused halt.

Then, just feet away, Wudge appeared, perched on the helmet of the scattered suit of empty armor. He scratched his onion-helm, glaring with yellow eyes. "Why snake-lady think it is my witch?" he demanded, looking at Grimsby like he was a stray cat. "Could be anyone's witch."

The barbed tip of Echidna's tail whipped back and forth in agitation. "So you wouldn't mind if I simply"—her tail constricted, squeezing Grimsby until his bones creaked—"crushed him?"

Wudge shrugged. "Finders, squeezers," he said.

Grimsby tried to croak a desperate plea, but he had no air left in his lungs to speak. His vision was beginning to grow blurry, and his skin was quickly feeling as though it was freezing over as his circulation struggled to move his own blood.

Echidna said nothing, only continued to slowly strain the life out of him.

Finally, just as his vision was beginning to grow dim, he distantly heard Wudge speak.

"Fine. Fine! Is my half-witch. Let him go!"

The coils loosened enough that Grimsby felt breath seep into his crumpled lungs. He coughed and sputtered, trying to wriggle his arms free, but he was still too numb.

"Then tell me," Echidna said, "how did you two find this place? Who sent you?"

Wudge frowned at her through the eye gouges in his onion-helm. "Wudge found this place. And no one sent Wudge. Except maybe Wudge sent Wudge. Depends on who Wudge asks. Complicated question."

Grimsby managed to regain enough control to look around, though his head thundered so badly that it felt like it might shear in two at any motion—but only if his spine didn't beat it to the punch. Behind Wudge, Lump had climbed to his feet and wandered over, his head nearly eight feet off the ground despite his hunched posture.

Lump glowered at Wudge and raised a meaty paw to squish him, but Echidna stopped him with a wave of her hand. She mouthed something to him, and Lump growled before nodding.

He knelt down and wrapped one massive hand around Wudge, leaving only his head free. Then he gripped the wrist of his clenched hand with his free hand and, with a strained noise of pain, he simply tore his own hand off and let it fall to the floor. The severed paw didn't loosen its grip around Wudge, however, leaving him in a cage of detached meat and bone.

Grimsby stared in muted horror. It was like the small lizards he had seen on sidewalks when he was a boy, which could detach their tails at will. Except Lump did it with his hand, leaving a gray-blue stump of meat and exposed bone.

Then, in moments, the stump grew darker as flesh knit itself into existence. Tiny sprouts emerged, more like vines than anything human. They braided together, growing larger and thicker, until a new hand had grown where the stump once was.

At the same time, the hand around Wudge cracked and shrieked as the flesh desiccated to dull gray stone, like it was the hand of a statue rather than something that had once been alive.

Grimsby stared, almost forgetting the snake coils that confined him.

Wudge, for his part, looked more annoyed than anything else. He struggled a bit as the hand became a cage of stone, but seemed to find himself trapped.

"Wudge hates trolls," he muttered.

Echidna drew away from Grimsby, suspended by her tail still coiled around him, like a serpentine mooring. She paused just long enough to pick up the empty iron box Grimsby had dropped, then hung in the air before Wudge. She held out the iron box. "Tell me," she said, eyeing the empty container, "what did you come here to find, Wudge?"

Grimsby caught a glimpse of her face. It seemed too earnest, like she was asking the only question that mattered. He turned his attention to his wriggling arms. Echidna's split focus had let her coils slip. He could almost free his right hand.

Wudge wiggled in the stone hand, making it rattle on the floor. "That's none of snake-lady's business."

Echidna's expression widened in frustration before settling into a smile like a bear trap. "If you do not tell me in five seconds, I will crush your witch, and then Lump will crush you."

Lump giggled at the idea.

Grimsby, hoping the monsters were well enough distracted, managed to pry his arm loose just before Echidna's coils tightened alongside her threat. She didn't seem to notice he had managed to get one limb free. Or perhaps she simply didn't care.

"Five," she said, slowly squeezing.

Grimsby felt his joints begin to pop. It would be mere seconds before he was completely unable to breathe, let alone manage a spell. He needed to do something, anything, and he needed to do it *now*.

"Four."

Wudge yawned, his worming tongue rolling over his needle teeth.

Grimsby fumbled around for something in reach, but the only thing he got his hand on was the water-stained tome Echidna had dropped when she snagged him. It was thick and heavy, but even striking with the metal-bound spine, it would prove a poor weapon.

"Three." The metal box creaked in her tensed hands.

Then he saw it. A nearby shelf was stacked high with precarious curios, but at the top was a glass vase holding a remarkably preserved rose. The flower did not interest him.

The vase, however, was another matter.

"Two."

His legs grew numb as Echidna crushed him. His spine felt as though his hips might detach from it at any moment.

He summoned a mote of Impetus and thumbed it as a *Bind* rune on the book's spine. With it, he might recall the book back and get a second chance if he missed.

"One."

He whipped the book at the shelf, trying hard to hit the vase, or at least send the tome sailing behind the tottering cabinet to be pulled back to him.

But Echidna seemed to sense his struggles, and a shifting of her tail seized the motion of his throw. The book landed a few feet in front of the shelf in a mess of its own pages.

She turned to the sound, then glared at him and returned her attention to Wudge. She snapped the box closed in her hands, like jaws locking around prey.

"Enough. Last chance."

Grimsby placed a second rune on his palm with shaking fingers and only barely managed a whisper through the wrapping of serpentine sinew around his chest. "*Bind*," he wheezed.

There was no tether of blue light as *Bind* usually had. Instead, a faint blue arc emanated from the rune on his palm, like a partial sphere around his hand.

Something was wrong.

Meanwhile, the rune's opposite took on a soft red glow of its own. Both grew brighter, and he felt an odd weight against his palm, as though the book was in his hand despite its distance. It pressed against him, and he instinctively pushed back. The book skittered away from him, tearing pages loose, until it struck the shelf with the vase atop, sticking fast, like gravity had suddenly turned sideways.

Even more than it had with *Torque*, the misbehaving magic left Grimsby with a jarring sense of confusion.

Bind was the single most ingrained word in his mind. He was as familiar with it as he was with his own palm. It almost felt like reality itself was betraying him for his most defining spell to behave so oddly.

Yet he had no time to question or reason. If *Bind* had suddenly begun behaving this way, he had to adapt or be turned into human paste.

He forced more Impetus into the runes, making the connection stronger. Normally, this would have been like adding tension to a stretched rubber band, but now it seemed to be like adding pressure to a coiled spring. The blue and red arcs of light bloomed, and the tome pressed so hard into the shelf that Grimsby could feel it pushing back against him, like there was an invisible rod between them intent on extending further and further.

Even Echidna noticed, turning her attention from Wudge as the mass she was encircling began suddenly forcing her sideways. Her eyes grew wide as she realized what Grimsby was up to.

But it was too late.

The cabinet tilted back. The vase fell, and all eyes seemed to follow it.

It crashed to the ground, shattering into countless shards.

Everyone held their breath, though Grimsby did so only because he could not draw one in his confinement.

Then, the sky shrieked.

The thin light that pierced the boarded windows dimmed, then fell to blackness. The only remaining illumination was from the scattered candles. At the edge of their light, seeping between the boards that covered each window, was a chillingly familiar mist. As it drew nearer, Grimsby could see the clawing, twisted faces in its depths and hear their warbling keen.

They were Geists. Many Geists. And the room was being slowly flooded by them.

THIRTEEN

MIST SEEPED IN THROUGH THE CRACKS BETWEEN boards, drowning out the already sparse strands of light that found their way into the lofty chamber. The candles that were strewn all over winked out one by one as the gray clouds rolled over them, their tiny, humanlike flames withering with small gasps of agony.

"Damn it!" Echidna hissed. Her eyes darted around to the coming Geists, so formless and numerous that they looked like a haunting, hungry avalanche.

Pained faces swirled in the shadowed depths of the mist, twisting into existence and wailing before rending apart once more. Grimsby felt a chill shudder through him. His dozens of small, raking scars from his last encounter with a single Geist grew cold, like icy nails over his skin.

He struggled against Echidna's scaly coils, spurred on by adrenaline and fear. She was so distracted by her own, likely similar emotions that he managed to slip free and tumble from her grip.

Wudge wiggled in the petrified grasp of Lump's severed hand, his bald ears flapping madly, but he couldn't break loose.

Lump only stood, dumbfounded, though his gaze seemed dull and distant, not so much terrified as confused.

Grimsby took the opportunity to seize Wudge, stone hand-cage and all, though he was barely able to lift Lump's petrified palm. He grunted and managed to carry it using the index and pinky fingers as handles, though it felt like the weight would tear his arms from their sockets.

"Lump!" Echidna cried out, slithering back toward her companion, abandoning the empty iron box among the other massed curios.

The massive troll knelt over her, wrapping his bulky form around her like a hand covering a baby viper. Then his skin began to grow dull and craggy. Within a few moments, it had turned to the same gray stone as his former appendage had.

The Geists rolled over him; their invisible teeth and claws, or whatever it was they had, scraped and screeched against Lump's petrified form, but though they left shallow scratches, they could not harm the stone.

Unfortunately, Grimsby was not made of stone, but instead was primarily composed of much-squishier materials.

The Geists seemed all too aware of this.

They rolled toward him, keening cries almost deafening.

"Run, stupid half-witch!" Wudge shouted from Grimsby's grip.

All too happy to follow some kind of command, since his panicked brain offered none, Grimsby's body obliged. He ran, sprinting desperately toward the only exit, the stairs, though his gait was awkward and slowed by the weight of the stone hand.

Wudge shrieked as he bounced along, though whether it was in sickening glee or emphatic fear, Grimsby was uncertain.

He ignored the sound and ran with all his terrified might toward the stairs, hoping to descend quickly and find some shelter from the Geists. He might have been fast enough if he had been able to run normally, but with the added weight of the stone hand, he was too slow.

The boarded windows above the stairs seethed with more mist. It flowed through the gaps like cigarette smoke straining between gnarled teeth. The Geists quickly suffused the stairwell, making it impassable. If he tried to use it now, it would be like forcing his way through cotton candy made of razor wire.

He racked his brain for some way to use his magic to help, but nothing came to mind. Besides, he still was uncertain why it had been acting strangely to begin with. He couldn't take a risk in using it until he figured that out.

But his alternatives were running short. And while he didn't know what his magic might now do, he certainly knew what the Geists would do if they reached him.

He found himself trapped, standing in a single pool of light cast by a handful of candles. The mist drew closer, and he backed instinctually away. At least until his back hit another window. Unlike the others, this one's glass panes remained intact, and it had only two boards barricading it. Outside it was almost blindingly bright. The Geists must have ignored the sealed portal and used other means of entry instead.

Grimsby knew he was trapped. With nowhere to run, the Geists would close in on them, and within a few agonizing minutes, he and Wudge would be shredded into little more than red rain.

He felt a cold weight on his bare heel and looked down to see the strange nail from Wudge's box. Though he had dropped it in the chaos, it had stuck to his heel this whole time. It was a miracle it hadn't impaled his foot.

Whatever the thing was, he was sure it was cursed. After all, why else would it be stuck to him? You wouldn't go through the trouble of preventing people from dropping a magical nail that made you win every lottery you entered or made spinach taste like cake.

It would like as not do something far, far worse.

The only grisly silver lining he could see was that he wasn't going to live long enough to figure out what horrible things it would do to him. Although he also wouldn't be around long enough to figure out why his own magic had betrayed him—

Suddenly he suspected why his spells had been acting strangely—and that he might have another option.

It involved doing something dumb.

Very dumb.

But he was fresh out of smart things to try.

He turned to the window, dropped Wudge unceremoniously to the ground, and began to pry at the boards. He was lucky; whoever had hammered them into place had done so with only a single nail on each side, apparently unconcerned with burglars at this height. He managed to pull the side of the lower board free to dangle from the frame, leaving just enough space.

Hopefully.

"Half-witch!" Wudge shouted, his normally croaking voice closer to a squawk.

The Geists were nearing now, the mist reaching his exposed feet, shredding away the wrapped leather like an invisible sandblaster on their hunt for the soft flesh beneath.

He hauled Wudge away just before the Geists reached flesh. But Wudge's relieved expression turned wide-eyed when Grimsby heaved back the stone hand.

And then hurled it through the window.

Wudge's scream was drowned out by the shattering of glass and the renewed hunting keen of the Geists. The tiny creature's voice quickly fell away, but Grimsby was not far behind. He took a short, bracing breath and ran toward the shattered window, diving through.

He felt cloying, clawing cold bite into him as the Geists surged around him, but within a moment he was defenestrated and out of their grasp.

And he was falling.

He tumbled in the open air, trying desperately to figure out which way was up before it was too late. He managed to find the ground, approaching far too fast, and hoped against hope that he wasn't wrong.

He called forth as much Impetus as he could muster. It surged through him like a flare in his veins, causing his skin to grow fiery hot, while his scars burst into flame, burning away the sleeve of his cloth robe like the tail of a comet.

He fervently hoped he was right about his hunch and threw out his right hand toward the ground, seeing Wudge nearing impact.

"Torque!" he shouted, half expecting a spinning torrent of green energy to appear and then swiftly become the last thing he would ever see.

Instead, the air wavered, filling with the blue-green motes of light as it had before when he had used the spell against Echidna. It was as though someone had put a block of star-suspended glass directly between him and the cobblestone ground.

Wudge, still screaming, struck it first. The fist slowed nearly instantly, as though it had struck invisible gelatin. It still hit the ground, but did so at a fraction of the speed. The stone shattered, sending Wudge tumbling forward in a strangely slow-motion clamber.

Grimsby hit it next and felt the air squeeze out of his lungs like he had belly flopped onto a trampoline made of ice. He sank down deeper and deeper but slowed more and more with every inch, feeling like he might be smothered by the force over his face and chest. Finally, he came to an almost stationary drift about a foot over the ground. The stars had begun to burn brightly, trembling like eggs beginning to hatch.

When he dismissed the odd spell with a dull wave of his hand, a sudden boom nearly deafened him as the faltering field deto-nated into a wave of pressure and mist.

He fell the last foot face-first, cracking his forehead on the ground, embedding some gravel between his eyebrows, and muss-ing his glasses. Tiny slivers of glass fell around him, though for-tunately not large enough to shatter and reveal him to the Geists.

He rolled over onto his back to see the top of the building enshrouded in them, seething around the broken window he had left in his wake as though searching for him. But, like blind hounds without a scent, the creatures had lost their prey and be-gan to disperse.

With a small measure of relief, he saw they remained gray and were not hued red by the blood of a victim. Lump and Echidna must have stayed safe from the creatures.

And, somehow, so had he and Wudge.

He heard a scuffling of feet and turned to see Wudge standing over him, his long fingers balled up into fists and perched on his hips. He began to bat rapidly at Grimsby's face like an agitated cat.

"Half-witch so stupid! Now we never find door!"

"Wudge—" Grimsby began, trying to both sit up and shield his face, but the little creature persisted.

"Never should have asked half-witch help! Always do it own self, she always told Wudge, but no, Wudge ask help. Wudge stupid, Wudge deserve onion, Wudge—"

Grimsby held up the nail.

Wudge's frown vanished, replaced by a rare breed of smile: one completely untainted with mischief. "Half-witch did it!"

"One problem," Grimsby said. He turned his palm upside down to let the nail fall, but it only dangled against his skin, re-fusing to lose contact.

Wudge nodded. "Wudge thought maybe it was cursed."

"You knew?" Grimsby asked, his temper flaring despite his dissipating adrenaline.

"Wudge figured. Not the same as knowing," he said, then frowned in thought, placing one balled hand of knobby knuckles beneath his chin like he was imitating a sculpture. "But . . . maybe better this way!"

"Better how?"

"Well, this way Wudge isn't the one who is cursed."

"How is that better?"

He shrugged. "Better for Wudge."

"No, that's not better, Wudge! This curse messed with my spells and nearly got us killed up there! Fix it. Now."

"Can't fix. Not now, at least."

"What are you talking about?"

"Wudge figure find the piece of door first, fix curse second, find real door third. Still working on fixing curse part." His eyes widened in sudden realization. "Was that a plan? Did Wudge make a plan?" He seemed quite proud of himself.

"Wudge . . ." Grimsby began, though words were an exhaustive effort. "Is that why you asked me along? To get cursed for you?"

Wudge grinned but denied nothing. "Wudge will fix! But can't fix if it cursed and attached to Wudge. So have it stick to half-witch, then fix! Obviously."

"Obviously." Grimsby wanted to be angry, but he was too tired. He let the emotion slip away and just felt his whole body slump in exhaustion. He glared at the nail dangling from his palm and meekly shook his hand in one last attempt to remove it.

It stayed put, so instead he shook his head.

Maybe Mayflower had the right idea about helping friends.

"Let's just go home."

FOURTEEN ✳

I T DIDN'T TAKE LONG FOR WUDGE TO FIND A MIRROR FOR Grimsby to return through. Unfortunately, as he fell into the real world and the mirror shattered behind him, he realized he was in a gas station bathroom two blocks away from home. He glanced around, but Wudge was nowhere to be found. All he had to be sure his adventure had been real were a missing slipper and the nail in his pocket, which still refused to part from him. He sighed and hopped awkwardly over the grimy, glass-strewn floor, apologized to the confused clerk, and trudged home in the cool darkness, clenching what remained of his bathrobe around him.

His bare foot was numb and bleeding again by the time he reached his stairs. He limped up to his door and stumbled inside. The room was dark, so he instinctively muttered *"Bind"* to the runes that linked his standing lamp's drawstring to the ground. Instead of pulling together, however, they pushed apart, and his lamp fell over, shattering the bulb.

"Silent nights," he cursed in an exhausted mutter. He fumbled through the dark to his cot and fell into it, the numbness of the cold slowly departing to leave the dull aches of worn muscles and the sharp pains of his injured foot behind.

What was he supposed to do now? With this cursed nail in his pocket, he couldn't even manage the most minute magics of which he was normally capable. As if convincing Mrs. Ox, the Department Assessor, he was worth keeping on as an Auditor wasn't difficult enough already, now his magic was even more crippled than normal.

He tossed and turned, trying to find a comfortable position, but between his aching body, the swollen welt Echidna had left across his back, and the mounting concerns of his looming assessment, he failed. The breaking daylight began to assail his eyelids, and just as he was finally about to drift to restless sleep, his brass alarm clock started blaring. It rattled and rumbled until it fell from the coffee table and clattered to the ground.

He cracked open bloodshot eyes. His hours in the Elsewhere had passed as a mere seven minutes in the real world, but that didn't mean they were any less exhausting. He felt like someone had put boxing gloves on the blades of a giant blender and dropped him inside.

And now it was time to get up for work.

He creaked to his feet, wincing as his right foot touched the ground. It was already painfully swollen and would likely annoy him for a few days.

If it didn't get infected first.

He grumbled as he limped to the shower, stripping away his sweat-sodden pajamas and ruined robe. The robe stuck to him at first, frustrating him until he fished the nail from its pocket. Apparently it wasn't finicky about where it was touching him, so long as it was. He ended up just holding it in his hand as he let the water grow warm.

The hot water felt good, mostly. He instinctively recoiled from the warmth when it touched the gnarled burn scars that covered his left side, but eventually he let himself relax as it flowed over him. The scars weren't sensitive to heat—in fact, they were more tolerant than his unblemished skin—but they had left him with a reflex to draw away from sudden warmth that even physical therapy hadn't been able to cure.

He closed his eyes and leaned against the wall of the shower stall, tracing his fingers over the nail in his grip to keep awake.

There was some good news in all this. His usual Department work, such as checking on at-risk Unorthodox or looking for minor magical misconduct, rarely required any actual magic. Until now, that had been one of his greatest frustrations with it, but until he could rid himself of this cursed nail, it was an odd relief.

With any luck, Wudge would find a way to remove the curse, and he could go back to normal. Whatever that might look like.

Although, without Mayflower, normal was most likely going to be making house calls for the foreseeable future. Perhaps indefinitely. Not to mention doing it alone. He felt his stomach flip in place but tried to shove the feeling away.

Even if that was the sum of his career, it still beat being a magician at a children's theme restaurant.

Didn't it?

At least there he had made kids smile. He had yet to have anyone be happy to see him at his current job. Up until he had met the two children outside Mayflower's house, he had been mostly met with grimaces, glares, and an occasional guffaw. No one wanted an Auditor on their doorstep—or anywhere near them, for that matter. Unless it was the direst of circumstances, folks preferred to steer clear of the Department and pretend Auditors didn't exist. His mere presence seemed to shatter that comfortable illusion. Although maybe that wasn't a fault. Maybe that was what it was supposed to be like.

Perhaps that was the problem.

He didn't just want to be an Auditor.

He wanted to *help* people.

He had thought that was what being an Auditor was about.

Instead, he found it was just about making sure people obeyed the law.

The realization was hollow. And yet, he had waited his whole life to be an Auditor. He had bled for it. He had fought for it. Eyes aflame, he had almost died for it.

And even after all that, it wasn't what he hoped it would be.

But was that because he wasn't doing it right, or because he had never realized what it really was? He was uncertain, and neither option gave him any comfort.

The shower went cold as the hot water ran out, forcing him to peel open his eyes. He realized the water had pooled halfway up his shins in the tub. A quick glance at the drain revealed that it had vanished, leaving smooth plastic instead.

"Puppy dogs' tails, Wudge," he cursed. It hadn't been the first time his odd houseguest had pulled this particular trick. He'd have to get him to fix it the next time he came back for ramen.

He knelt and dipped one hand into the water, willing forth his Impetus as he began to trace a circle on the tub's bottom. After a few passes, a faint trail of dim light appeared where his finger touched, and soon there was the outline of a circle. He placed his palm on it and muttered.

"*Chute.*"

There was a muted boom as water suddenly blasted into his face as if from the end of a hose. It knocked him off his feet and out of the tub before he had enough wherewithal to sever his connection to the spell, dismissing it with a wave from the hard, damp floor.

He coughed and spat tepid water from his mouth and nose, wincing and grasping at the lash across his back as he rolled on the tile.

His confusion rose until he remembered the nail, still gripped in his left hand. He held it up and glared at it, pointed a threatening finger.

"You're lucky you're already dead as a doornail," he muttered.

He climbed to his feet and shook himself like a wet dog. At the edge of his vision he realized there was something in the standing water that hadn't been there before. A quick glance revealed it to be a . . . teapot?

He scooped it up, pouring discolored water from the spout. He then tilted his head, making water do the same from his ear.

Its surface was silvery metal, like finely polished steel, and it was elegantly engraved with a mixture of vines, roses, and other greenery that seemed odd in such monotone metallic shades.

"Huh," he said as the dripping water came to a halt. He looked at the nail, then back at the pot. "Did you do this?" he asked.

The nail did not reply.

He shook his head. "Talking to inanimate junk." He glanced over to the polished bowl that served as his mirror, seeing his steam-guised reflection. "Does that seem reasonable to you, Grimsby?"

He shook his head at himself. "Seems quite silly, Grimsby."

"Then I better quit it before they send me to the Asylum," he said.

"Most certainly," he replied.

He found a towel that was almost dry, padded out to his only other room, and put the teapot on a shelf in the doorless closet, right beside the wooden box he'd gotten from the Lounge. It seemed as good a place as any to put them. Both were things he didn't want to think about, and neither was a thing he had time for today.

He quickly dressed, shoved a snack bar into his mouth, and exited the apartment. He latched all three locks behind him and half stumbled down the stairs in his exhaustion, nearly choking on his breakfast. But, as he picked up his bike and willed some Impetus into the enchantment on its rear wheel, the air began to glimmer with dim sparks of light. He tried to pedal, but the nail's curse turned his *Torque* from a boon to a brake. He grumbled and had half a mind to hurl his bike at the wall, but it wasn't until he dismounted and turned to do so that he realized he wasn't alone.

He blearily realized it was Mayflower, dressed in his aged and worn suit, arms crossed as he brooded against the graffiti-stricken wall.

Grimsby wasn't sure what to do. He had half expected to never see Mayflower again after they had last spoken. He felt his face flush in anger and his stomach twist in unease, yet even so, he felt some great warmth of relief spread over his chest. He wanted to think of something to say, something cutting and poignant that could convey the sudden storm of mixed feelings.

He failed, and instead only managed a solitary "Hi." Through a mouthful of peanuts and chocolate.

Mayflower grunted, holding up the folder Grimsby had left in his hurry. "You forgot something," he said, then raised a brow. "You look like crap."

"Yeah, well." Grimsby swallowed his food and tried hard not to glare. "Crap looks twice as good as I feel," he said, taking the folder, uncertain what to do with his hands otherwise. "You dress up in uniform just to return the lost and found?"

Mayflower glowered over his shaded glasses. "I think there's something to that RUIN," he said, sounding like he was forcing professionalism. "It's worth checking out."

"Checking out?" Grimsby asked, failing to keep the bitterness from his tone. "Well, I hate to break it to you, Mayflower, but it's not my case—and certainly not *our* case. Those are reserved for people who show up to work." He felt his throat strain tight as he spoke. "People with partners."

The Huntsman looked away, staring at the clawed marks left on the wall by Blackskull months before. Grimsby knew the man had a few scars of his own from those claws. "I shouldn't have been so hard on you," he said.

"Is that an apology?"

"No. I meant what I said, just not how I said it. You need someone who can watch your back, someone to keep you safe. That's not me, not anymore."

"So why are you here?"

He said nothing for a long moment, then let loose a breath. "I think this case, this RUIN, has something to do with an old case of mine. Something I need to put to rest. And—" His gaze seemed ready to bore through the brick wall like a drill. "And I need your help to do that."

Grimsby felt hot anger rise in his chest, almost like his own Impetus. Mayflower had all but cast him aside, all but abandoned him, because of some self-destructive, masochistic guilt parade. He'd left Grimsby to twist in the wind for weeks, and now, *now* he wanted help?

Grimsby wanted to tell him to buzz off. To go and dig up old wounds on his own. He wanted to scream at him, to demand he apologize, or at least say anything that would make it feel like their friendship hadn't just been an illusion.

He felt himself almost swelling up, like a balloon about to burst forth with furious, justified tirades of why he was right and Mayflower was wrong.

Then he let himself take a breath, and as quick as it had filled him, all that anger waned to dull, thudding pain.

Mayflower needed help. The rest of it didn't much matter.

He said nothing for a moment, then sighed and forced a tight smile.

"All right."

Mayflower tore his eyes from the wall and glanced over at him, and though his expression quickly became stern and stoic, Grimsby thought he saw a flash of surprise in his partner's face.

The Huntsman nodded, and Grimsby knew it was about as much as he could expect in the way of thanks. "Good."

"But you do understand that it's still not our case, right?" he asked. "I stole it."

Mayflower raised a brow. "Stole? I go away for a few weeks, and you start stealing?" He shook his head. "Kids these days."

Grimsby scoffed, but halfway through it became a genuine chuckle.

"This case is ours," Mayflower asserted, turning and heading unceremoniously toward the street and the jeep he'd left there. "I told Grieves this morning."

"Told him?" Grimsby asked, following the Huntsman. "I bet he didn't like that much."

"He did not. It was a good way to start the day."

Mayflower climbed into the old, pitted jeep and idly unlatched the passenger door for Grimsby.

He got in, taking some comfort in the rough, sunbaked leather seat. "So what now?" he asked.

"Now we go to the Department to get the case materials. And you tell that Rayne girl of yours that we're taking her case."

Grimsby gulped. "What? *I'm* telling her?"

Mayflower nodded. "Grieves's condition was that he did not want to be the one to inform her. So, the polite thing for you to do is let her know."

"Me? Why don't you tell her?"

Mayflower shrugged. "Because I don't care about her enough to go out of my way. I'm guessing that's not the case for you."

Grimsby felt any relief fade away in an instant. "On second thought, maybe I'm not on board with being your partner again."

"Tough luck," Mayflower said, latching the locks shut and revving up the old beast. "You're stuck with me for now."

For now, Grimsby thought, his gut twisting into knots. He quickly shoved the dread down, deep down, and focused on the problem at hand: how would he avoid being throttled by Rayne?

FIFTEEN ✳

GRIMSBY STOOD IN FRONT OF RAYNE'S OFFICE, ADJUST-ing his ill-fitting coat and clearing his throat. "Rayne, I sort of messed up— No, no, I definitely messed up." He shook his head and tried to stand taller, keeping his voice low. Everything he could think to say just kept coming out worse. "Rayne, I'm sorry, I might have borrowed your case . . . And I'm not giving it back, because Mayflower wants it . . . Gah!" He threw up his hands. How was he supposed to tell her? He hadn't meant to take the case. Well, actually he supposed he had, but he hadn't thought it through. If he had, he would have—

"Grimsby!" a sharp voice said behind him.

He whirled around to see Rayne stalking toward him, her stride clipped and furious, her face disturbingly even aside from her eyes, which were wide enough to show the whites all around her teal irises.

"You!" she said, pointing one finger.

"Me?" He took a reflexive step to one side, and then to the other again, glancing back at the frosted office window in confusion.

She came to a halt over him, her hands on her hips. "Where is it?"

He gestured over his shoulder to the office, flustered. "You were supposed to be in there."

"Oh, I was?" she asked. "You know, I think you're right. I was supposed to be in there working on a case. *My* case. Now, where is it?"

He cleared his throat again, but his voice was barely above a whisper. "It's, um, well. It's not your case."

She froze, her head tilted a couple of degrees too far to one side, her eyes still dangerously wide. "Excuse me?"

"The case. It's, well, Grieves is giving it to me and Mayflower."

"He is what?"

"I'm sorry, I didn't mean to take it! I would have taken any of them. But on the bright side, you can focus on finding Hives, so really if you think about it—"

"Focus? You think I'm unfocused?"

"What? No! I just mean—"

"You know what? Forget it." She looked away, her face shadowed. "When you offered to help, I didn't realize this was what you had in mind."

"I didn't! I had nothing in mind, I swear. I rarely do!"

"Just—" She forced her way past him and unlocked her door. "Just go. I have work to do. And so do you."

"Rayne, I'm sorry, I—" He stopped as she looked back, her face a brittle mask.

"I thought we were friends."

Anything he was going to say withered in his throat. He tried to cobble together something, some desperate apology, but everything was so fragile that it fell apart before he could even try to say it.

"Rayne—"

She shut the door, leaving him in the echoing quiet.

He let his arms fall to his sides. He wanted to try knocking, he wanted to explain himself, but what would he even say?

He heard a gruff chuckle behind him and turned to see Mayflower leaning against the hallway corner.

"Was that entertaining?" Grimsby demanded, storming toward him. "Does my crumbling life amuse you?"

The Huntsman stifled his chuckle, though he took his time about it. "In a way."

"Have you been waiting there this whole time?"

"Long enough," he said. "You look like crap."

"You already told me that this morning."

He shrugged. "Needed to be said twice."

Grimsby balled up his hands to keep from clawing at his own hair or making an ill-advised attempt to strangle Mayflower. Then he took a deep breath and forced them back down to his sides. "I'd appreciate it if we could just get to work."

Mayflower nodded, though he seemed frustratingly smug. He revealed Grimsby's folder. "I had Finley print off some extra information that wasn't in the original file. Some extra photos, new angles, that sort of thing."

He handed the file over. The front still read OVERSIGHT TASKS, which were Grimsby's normal responsibilities, but the first page was instead labeled RUIN, an acronym for a ritual of unknown intent and nature.

Grimsby glanced through the pages, skimming the information.

"So there's no clue as to the ritual's intended function?" he asked.

"No."

"So why this case? What makes you think it's tied to something?" he asked, trying not to look like he was intent on Mayflower's reply.

"It's a hunch," the Huntsman said. "Probably nothing."

"Sure, but there've been dozens of other jobs, other RUINs, also probably nothing, and yet you stayed in your all-day robes. Why did this one lure the Huntsman out of his lair?"

Mayflower scowled. "It's a home, not a lair."

"Well . . ." Grimsby said with a shrug and a tilt of his head that implied it was most certainly a lair.

"I have a feeling about this one."

"A good feeling?" Grimsby asked.

The Huntsman was quiet for a moment, his gaze burning into the distance. "Trust me. Whatever this was meant to do, it wasn't good." His eyes were masked by his darkened glasses, but Grimsby could tell he was holding back.

"How can you be so sure?"

The Huntsman grunted. "It's a hunch. Let's just leave it at that for now."

Grimsby was just about to argue when something in the file caught his eye.

"What is it?" Mayflower asked.

"Well, usually RUINs are, well, ruins. Mostly heaps of magical ash and burnt-out symbols painted onto the ground, the innate magical energy of their components having been expended."

"So?"

Grimsby pointed to the photos. "But with this one, something must have gone wrong. It's too—well, clean. Maybe it was miscast, maybe it was interrupted. Either way, I don't think whoever started it finished it."

"You think they might try again?"

"Maybe. It would be impossible to know for sure without knowing what the ritual was meant to do."

"And what was it meant to do?"

"That's the thing; it's a RUIN. If it were obvious, it'd be filed away by now."

Mayflower glared in response. "Aren't you supposed to be the witch?"

Grimsby felt his face redden, and he bit back a sharp reply. The Huntsman was right; this was his job. He needed to do better.

He needed to *be* better.

"All major rituals have five main components—one for each section of the pentagram. Each is chosen and designed to help channel the magic in the right way, like digging a channel for water before opening a dam."

"Skip the lecture. Tell me the important crap."

"Without us knowing what those ingredients were, it'll stay a RUIN. Unknown. But if we can somehow figure out at least a few of them, we can narrow down an idea for what we're dealing with."

"And find who's behind it," the Huntsman said, his tone grim.

"Yeah, maybe that, too. But there's a chance this could be nothing."

"Nothing?"

"Well, we've got nothing to go on yet. It could be something small—like some kids trying to bind a spirit to prank their teacher, or a tracking spell to find someone's lost dog. That's why most Auditors hate RUINs; they're usually a waste of time."

Mayflower said nothing for a long moment, then pulled out a cigarette to chew. "So why did Rayne want it so badly?"

Grimsby opened his mouth, but no reply came out. It was a good question, though it still didn't assuage his guilt. He glanced over his shoulder to her office before turning his eye back to the photographs.

"So, what now?" he asked.

"We go to the scene," Mayflower said.

"What? Why?" He held up the folder. "The Department already swept the area. They'd have already collected the evidence and left nothing behind."

"You overestimate the Department's thoroughness. They always miss the most important leads."

"What? What leads?"

Mayflower said nothing; he only started toward the jeep. Grimsby was forced to hurry after him, trying not to think about Rayne and whether she might ever forgive him.

He did a poor job of the latter.

SIXTEEN

GRIMSBY CHECKED THE MAP IN THE RUIN FOLDER against the street signs, then gestured down a narrow side street. "It's down there, I think," he said, ducking the piercing gaze of a vagrant man beside the alley.

Mayflower grunted and turned off the main street, the jeep bouncing lightly as it hit the half curb that led into the alleyway. It was crowded with empty dumpsters and fire-escape ladders, but the jeep narrowly managed to fit between them.

"I don't see any tape or signs cordoning the site off," Grimsby said, "but it should have been around here somewhere."

Mayflower ground the jeep to a halt and held out his hand for the folder. Grimsby passed it over and the old Huntsman scanned the photos within. Then he scanned the alley. "Down there," he said. Without a pause, he unclipped his seat belt and hopped out, stalking down the alleyway with purpose.

Grimsby followed, barely managing to squeeze out of his door due to an adjacent dumpster. He hurried after Mayflower, glancing about with casual nervousness. He was glad it was broad daylight, as he had avoided alleys at night since his first encounter with Blackskull.

"Are you sure this is the place?" he asked, casting a glance back toward the main street. Pedestrians and cars passed by, as calm and busy as on any other street in the Mission Hill area. "It seems hard to believe that anyone would try an illegal ritual so close to so many people."

"I've seen men stabbed to death in crowds before, and no one noticed until someone started screaming," Mayflower said, half distracted as he referenced the pictures against a few alcoves in the alley.

Grimsby's stomach turned at the thought. "You— You weren't the one stabbing them, right?"

Mayflower shot him a glare that was disturbingly ambiguous. "Point is, people do terrible things right under other people's noses. Sometimes it's even the best way to hide it— Here, this is the one."

He pointed to a segment where an older structure had been renovated, leaving an alcove large enough for a pair of narrow parking spots. Yet there was nothing occult that Grimsby could see. No sigils or runes, no painted pentagrams, not even dusty footprints.

"How can you tell?" Grimsby asked. "I don't see anything."

"Don't look at what is here," the Huntsman said. "Look at what's not."

Grimsby frowned but didn't argue. There seemed to be a lot that wasn't there in the alley—almost everything in the universe, in fact. But as he looked closer, he realized the place seemed almost too clean, especially compared to the rest of the alley. Like a power washer had passed through, but only in a ten-foot radius.

"Looks like no leads were missed after all," he said, feeling a touch deflated. Despite his words, he had hoped there would have been something left behind. Some clue they could follow.

Mayflower nodded. "They're quick about it these days, I'll give them that. Pentagrams and strange symbols make folks nervous—though they'd be more so if they realized exactly how much bad a ritual can do."

Grimsby scuffed his foot on the ground in annoyance, hoping in vain to dig something up beneath his heel. "So this was a waste of time."

Mayflower glowered carefully around, then turned an eye back to the alley entrance. There, the idle vagrant man had shifted enough to watch them from beneath the brim of his street-worn baseball cap.

"Not yet," the Huntsman said, pressing the RUIN folder back into Grimsby's grip. "Look around. See if you can dig up anything." Then he took long, easy strides down the alley toward the vagrant.

Grimsby let out a short breath but decided it was better to be thorough. The Department had already swept the area, but maybe they'd missed . . . something.

Though what a team of professionals might miss that he wouldn't was beyond him.

He carefully traced the area around where the site would have been, using the photos to help him picture it in his mind. The pentagram was usually the primary shape of a ritual—it was one of the most fundamental symbols of complex magic. He scraped his heel across the concrete, leaving behind a vague streak to mark the circle the pentagram would have been within. At each point of the star, a symbol and a reagent would have been placed, each intended to shape the magic that was being conjured forth. Unfortunately, though a few minor components had been found when the Department arrived on the scene, they weren't helpful or conclusive. It was sort of like trying to tell what someone had been cooking by finding salt in their kitchen.

A breeze swept down the alley, kicking up grit into his face and carrying with it the thick scent of exhaust and damp trash.

He coughed the smell away, then paused, watching a loose plastic bag twist and dance as it was pulled deeper down the alleyway.

Someone had cleaned up the site after they had finished, or abandoned, the ritual, and the Department had further scrubbed the area when they found it. This place would hold no answers.

But what if something had been left behind that wasn't in this place?

He cast a glance to Mayflower, who was leaning on the wall beside the vagrant, tersely conversing, then turned to follow the dancing plastic bag as it drifted deeper into the alley.

It caught once or twice on chain-link fences and garbage bins, but he pulled it free and returned it to its course. The wind died down once or twice, and he waited patiently for the inevitable breeze to return and carry the bag once more. Eventually, he found himself in a vacant lot, which had been hastily filled with gravel and marked as a paid parking area. It was surrounded almost entirely by brick-faced buildings, but their shape channeled the breeze toward a dead-end corner, where he could see a gathered pile of trash had already found residence.

He examined the pile for a few minutes, at first finding nothing that wasn't sodden down by the recent rains, but then spotted a loose, dry scrap of paper that had found its way to the top of the stack. It looked somehow . . . familiar. It fluttered away from his grip once or twice before he managed to snag it.

It was a simple paper label, like one used at a yard sale. The ink had partially faded, bled away by either sun or rain, but he could still make out the words *Eye, newt. 3 oz.*

More importantly, he recognized the handwriting. It belonged to Samuel Goode.

He felt his heart begin to speed up. The odds of a reagent tag like this being unrelated to the ritual nearby seemed slight— though not so slight as the odds of him finding it in the first place, let alone recognizing it. Even so, Goode's home wasn't far from here; in fact, he might have been the closest reagent vendor in the area.

It wasn't anything conclusive, but it was a lead. And it was more than the Department professionals had managed to dig up.

He carefully stowed the tag in a baggie inside the RUIN folder and returned to the jeep, having to consciously command his legs not to run giddily. He needed to remain professional—except being professional was exactly what was making him so excited.

He had the first lead of his first case, and he had found it on his own.

He saw Mayflower leaning against the jeep, his eyes boring bullet holes into the pavement where the ritual had been.

"Find anything?" he asked without looking up as Grimsby approached.

Grimsby held up the baggie with the tag inside. "You could say that. Nearby vendor's price tag for some basic ritual components. It's not much, but— " He paused as Mayflower took the baggie and raised a brow.

"Told you they missed things," he said, handing the evidence back with a nod. "Not bad." The words didn't sound special, but Grimsby felt like there was some weight behind them. It made his face redden with awkward pride.

"What about you? Find anything the Department overlooked?" Perhaps it was more feasible than Grimsby had realized.

Mayflower nodded. "Same place as usual."

"As usual?"

"Witches are so worried about the strange and the Unorthodox that they forget the normal stuff—and the normal people." He paused, then shrugged. "No offense."

Grimsby hadn't felt a single inkling of offense until the Huntsman had said *no offense*, but he was too focused to let it bother him. "So what normal thing did they miss?"

"Clyde."

"Who?"

He jerked a thumb to the spot where the vagrant had been, though it was now vacant. "Clyde over there was the one that reported the site, though he didn't offer up his name when he did. Turns out there was something here that wasn't there anymore by the time the Department arrived."

Grimsby perked up. "Was it a reagent? If so, we can start to narrow down what this ritual was about!"

"I imagine it was. Silver chains etched with some symbols."

"Skies alight! That's fantastic news! The symbols might tell us even more. Where are they?"

"There's the rub. They're long gone by now. Clyde pawned them for a new coat."

Grimsby felt his chest deflate, though a small voice told him he shouldn't have expected it to be so easy. "Well, that's still something. Chains can be useful for all kinds of things, but it's almost always binding magic."

"Like trapping something?"

"Not necessarily. It can also be linking two things together. Connecting objects, which can be good or bad depending on how you do it."

"So basically that doesn't help us at all."

"Well, it's a start. We at least know the ritual probably wasn't some kind of magical bomb. And I know where to head next."

Mayflower gave him an odd look, then snorted and shook his head, gesturing to the jeep. "Then let's get moving."

SEVENTEEN

RAYNE TRIED TO KEEP HER RAGE CONTAINED AS SHE strode through the long corridors to her office. The only passersby were a scant few Agents and a passing flock of familiars that looked to have once been ravens. They fluttered by on paper wings, their bodies made of little more than hollow aluminum mounted to their bleached skulls. They held documents in their clutches, probably from one of the older Department witches who had yet to trust an email.

Her heels clicked sharply on the tiled floor despite her best efforts. After confronting Grimsby, she had planned to take the issue up with the director but had turned around before reaching his office. She couldn't risk him seeing how invested she had been in the case; it would lead him to asking questions she couldn't answer yet. Even so, giving away her case had been a betrayal—though perhaps not one as great as Grimsby taking it in the first place.

How could Grieves have simply given away her RUIN case? She chastised herself immediately for asking such a simple question. There was little the director wouldn't do to keep the Huntsman under heel—though whether that was because he was a valuable asset or because he was simply less dangerous that way, she wasn't sure.

Besides, it wasn't as though Grieves knew the import of the RUIN to her. She hadn't told him, nor could she. If he knew, she would at the very least be suspended until the case could be pursued further.

The worst part was she didn't know what such a pursuit might lead to, whether it be damnation, vindication, or something between. But that was why she had risked pursuing the case in the first place. She couldn't trust anybody else to handle what they found—only herself.

Not even Grimsby; though of all people, she thought he might have been her ally, not her enemy.

She told herself what she always had: she didn't need anybody else. She had come this far alone, and she wasn't going to stop for anyone or anything. She was strong.

She just wished being strong didn't mean being alone.

Deep within, she felt that old, grating rage begin to rise, like a caged beast stirring from hibernation. She hadn't felt it since she was a child—at least, not until recently. But it had begun troubling her a few months ago and had only worsened as her stress made her discipline fray.

She forced the feeling away and scolded herself, lashing down her welling emotions to make certain nothing broke loose. Now was neither the time nor the place—and it never would be.

Her frustration boiled in her belly, and she felt her cheeks grow hot as she contained her anger. It wasn't until she had unlocked and entered her office that she let herself lean against the wall and loose a constrained groan that gave a voice to what thrummed in her veins. Her calm slowly returned.

"Rough day?" Defaux asked.

Rayne jumped, knocking her glasses askew. She quickly righted them before they fell altogether, leaving her unmasked and exposed to the Elsewhere. She must have been so focused inward that she hadn't noticed Defaux, seated on the edge of Hives's desk.

"Where have you been?" she asked. "I haven't seen you all day."

Defaux leaned over her crossed legs. She had one high-heeled shoe dangling loose from her toes, bouncing in time with her knee. "I was looking into what it might take to create a tracking spell for the former Auditor Hives," she said.

Rayne's heart stalled. She had been so consumed with worries about the RUIN case that she hadn't thought of Hives for hours— there was so much to do. She suddenly felt like more weights had been placed upon her chest, making it difficult to breathe.

"And?" she asked, letting brevity hide her breathlessness.

Defaux shrugged and stood up, stretching until the seams in her jacket creaked. "I think we can do it but not without class-three approval."

Rayne groaned. "That would take weeks, even if it did get approved! I can't wait that long."

"Hives might not have that much time," Defaux agreed, "but it's the only way we can be sure to break through whatever shroud might be hiding him. Unfortunately," she said, gesturing to the badge on Rayne's desk, "every moment that passes makes his connection to our source all the weaker, and therefore makes the ritual less likely to work."

Rayne dropped into her chair, propped her elbows on the desk, and threaded her fingers through her tied-back hair. She stared down at the badge beneath her, her stomach twisting into knots like a Gordian snake.

Her RUIN case had been taken. Hives seemed to be growing farther from reach each passing second. And Grimsby, one of the few people she'd thought she might trust, had betrayed her.

She was alone.

There was so much to do, yet so little time to do it. Every

moment seemed to bring with it another fuse, each burning short in rapid order, and all trailing back to a Damoclean powder keg. If she missed extinguishing any single one, it would be disastrous. But she only had so much time, only had so many hands, and after so long bearing the burden alone, it was like she was being crushed beneath its growing weight.

She felt a hand on her shoulder and looked up to see Defaux seated on the edge of the desk, her languid curls of dark hair shadowing her face.

"There's something going on," Defaux said, her voice calm, even soothing. "Something besides Hives."

Rayne said nothing. What *could* she say? She had known Defaux for barely two days, and yet now, more than ever, she needed someone else to help her shoulder the load.

Yet she had no one.

Hives was gone.

Grieves was busy with his own schemes.

And Grimsby . . .

She felt the cloying despair in her chest sharpen into anger.

To hell with Grimsby.

It was Grimsby who had put her in this mess. Him taking the RUIN was just one more fuse for her to stomp out. But she couldn't do it alone. She needed help, or eventually a spark would find its way to that powder keg.

And when it did, her whole world would go to hell with it.

Though she had known Defaux only briefly, the stranger from New York had been the first to offer a tangible hope to find Hives, to make things how they were before. She had risked herself and her position to bring Rayne that faint chance at redemption. And she asked for nothing in return—no favors or payments. Nothing.

If Rayne hadn't been so desperate, she might have been suspicious.

But she was long past being able to afford suspicion.

She needed an ally.

She needed a friend.

And, aside from Defaux, she seemed to have run out.

"A few days ago," Rayne said, managing to keep her voice steady, "there was a RUIN—a ritual of unknown intent and nature."

Defaux raised a brow. "So? We get a dozen of those a week on Long Island alone."

"Yes, but I—I found the ritual. Before anyone else had reported it."

"What do you mean?"

She took a deep breath. "I *woke up* there. In the middle of the night. One second"—her voice shook despite her best efforts—"one second I was at work. The next, I was *there*."

"Did someone take you there?" Defaux asked, leaning forward intensely. "Or were you somehow transported?"

Rayne hesitated. The response wasn't what she'd expected. She had anticipated suspicion, apprehension, or even for Defaux to walk out and report her on the spot.

Instead, she had an odd fervor to her, like she had just received a puzzle to solve after years in solitary confinement.

"I don't know," she said. "I don't know if I was brought there or—or if I had some kind of part in it." She shuddered, anxious doubts clawing apart her insides. "I can't remember anything."

"What was the ritual?" Defaux asked. "Could you tell?"

Rayne shook her head. "No—most of the reagents were already burnt-out or gone, and I didn't recognize the sigil. I knew no one would believe me, so I scratched it out and ran."

"That's a shame; that sigil could tell us a lot."

Rayne arched a sharp, slightly prideful brow. "That's why I memorized it."

The New York Auditor smiled. "Impressive. What did it look like?"

Rayne grabbed for a pen and paper, her hands finding the

manila folder that had once held her now-pilfered assignment. She scribbled an imitation of the sigil on the cover. It wasn't perfect, but it was close enough. She slid it over to Defaux, who stared at it for a long moment.

"Hmm," she said, crossing her arms and standing a spare pace away from the symbol as though it might bite. "Interesting."

Rayne felt her heart begin to speed up. What would Defaux do? With this information alone, she could make certain every fear Rayne had about Grimsby's own investigation might come true. Defaux could have her suspended, investigated, and perhaps even disbarred, if not full-on arrested.

Perhaps an even worse fate awaited her, should the ritual's true purpose come to light and prove to be malevolent.

Regardless of what its intent was, when the Department was informed of the situation, Rayne would become an unknown quantity, a rogue asset, especially with the shadow cast over her by her relationship with Hives. She would be excised, one way or another.

Yet she could do nothing. She was powerless. She felt so foolish to have spilled her secret, all because she couldn't bear it alone anymore. She should have stayed silent. She should have shunned this stranger before—

"Well," Defaux said, nodding to herself, "it's not much to go on. But it's a start!"

Rayne said nothing for a moment, then slowly asked, "You'll help me?"

Defaux gave her a confused smile of perfectly white teeth. "Well . . . yes? Why wouldn't I?"

Rayne stared. Of all the outcomes she had imagined, this hadn't been one.

She had expected Defaux to turn on her, like the others. Instead, she seemed almost . . . excited. Eager, even, to help.

What could Rayne say? How could she voice the surge of un-expected relief that flowed over her?

For once, she wasn't alone.

The words didn't come, so instead she slowly reached out and grasped Defaux's arm. "Thank you."

Defaux tilted her head. "You—don't get help often, do you?"

She scoffed, but it came out more bitter than she meant. "I don't usually need it."

"What you *need* is some sleep. This place have a bunkhouse?"

"Yes, but I don't have time. I—"

"When was the last time you slept?"

Rayne opened her mouth to reply, then realized just how long it had been. She said nothing.

"Exactly," Defaux said. "You go get some sleep. When you wake up, you look into that symbol. Meanwhile, I'll see what I can scrounge together to find Hives."

Rayne wanted to argue, but she relented. It would be foolish of her to think she could go for days on end without rest and still perform at the level she needed to. "Fine. But—please, be discreet. I don't need any more eyes looking at me than there already are."

"I think I can manage that," she said, mouth twisting into an odd smirk. "You rest."

Rayne nodded and went to the door, pausing to look back. "Thank you, again. Just—thank you."

Defaux smiled serenely. "Of course."

EIGHTEEN

GRIMSBY FELT EVERY BUMP IN THE ROAD THROUGH THE worn cushions of the jeep's aged leather seat. The familiar whistle of wind whisked through the cabin, filtered in through numerous scars in the rust-mauled exterior.

He watched the highway go by, downtown Boston in the distance. The towering buildings caught the morning sun and scattered it across the city, creating light and shadow where they shouldn't be.

He remembered the cityscape's desolate visage in the Elsewhere, and the colossal titans of dark bone that stalked its ruins. He shuddered and forced the image from his mind, turning his attention to the plastic bag in his hand. Inside was the tag he had scrounged. Despite the Department having swept the area, no one had found the connection to Samuel Goode.

No one except Grimsby.

He felt a small thrill of satisfaction. It was most likely just luck that he had found it, but maybe it was more than that. Maybe he was actually cut out for the job after all.

He just had to convince Grieves of the idea.

And just maybe himself as well.

"Thanks," he said to the brooding Huntsman, bracing himself as Mayflower swerved around a slow lane of traffic.

"Eh?" he grunted, hunched over the wheel, hands diligently at ten and two.

"Thanks for coming back. I know we didn't leave on the best of terms when we last spoke, and we both said . . . things. But I'm glad you're back."

The Huntsman said nothing, though his eyes seemed to grow distant. He took another turn, this time an exit, cutting across three lanes. Horns blared, but no one was forced to speed up or slow down to make way. Somehow, the Huntsman navigated the road like it was an open river. An open river filled with a flotsam of annoyed bystanders.

The jeep caught a pothole as it slowed for the exit. The rune-engraved bars that separated the front and back seats rattled. Once, Grimsby had been back there instead of up front. Now, however, things were different.

He and Mayflower were partners again, and it felt right.

Grimsby hardly recognized Goode's neighborhood as it sailed by. The last time, he had ridden through it on a bike, feeling like a child in his big brother's suit. This time—well, at least he wasn't on a bike.

Mayflower glared around at the run-down town houses, cramped together with their narrow strips of yards. "These folks should take some pride in their homes."

"I don't know," Grimsby said. "Maybe they just don't have enough to spare at the moment."

"You don't need to have anything, not if you just do the work."

"Didn't I step over broken beer bottles when I came to your house?"

"Whiskey. Beer makes you soft."

"So what's whiskey good for?"

"Flesh wounds," he said, then more quietly: "And making you forget."

Before Grimsby could inquire further, he spotted Goode's home on their right. "There! The one with the tinfoiled windows."

Mayflower pulled up outside the half wall of collapsed bricks that outlined the dead yard. He got out of the jeep and walked around to the back. Grimsby quickly followed.

"What are you doing?" he asked as Mayflower opened the trunk.

He didn't answer for a moment, instead rummaging in the collection of boxes and cases until he found what he was looking for: a case about the size of a deck of cards. He opened it to reveal two rows of six rounds, their tips gleaming silver. He began to exchange them for the rounds in his gun with deft hands.

"I don't think we'll need those," Grimsby said, swallowing the nervous lump in his throat.

"That's a fool thing to say."

"What?"

"He's a Therian, Grimsby. Even outside of the lunar cycle he's faster and stronger than either of us. We'd need these to take him down."

"Who said anything about taking anyone down, out, up, or otherwise? We're just here to talk."

"Because talking always turns out so well for us."

Grimsby opened his mouth, then closed it again, not wanting to admit Mayflower was right. "We just need to know what he knows so we can find a lead. That's it."

"And does my having silver bullets prevent us from doing that?"

Grimsby frowned. "Well—no."

"And does my having silver bullets prevent him from deciding to fur-out and rip us to pieces?"

Grimsby felt a bad taste in his mouth as his imagination

supplied unfortunate images, and couldn't find room to argue. "I suppose maybe you're a little right. Wait—what do you mean *deciding* to? I thought Therians shifted involuntarily."

"That's what you're supposed to think. It makes people feel safer to think their neighbor can't eat them in broad daylight," he said. "Most can't choose to shift. But *most* is far from *all*."

Grimsby thought of having gone to Goode's home alone and unarmed and felt sweat prickle on his temples. "How come I wasn't told about that?"

"The Department slants information to suit what they need. People wouldn't let Therians live among them if they thought they might turn into monsters at any moment. And upsetting a group of Unorthodox that can occasionally turn into hungry murder-machines is a bad habit historically." He slotted silver slugs into his gun as he spoke. "So, you say they only shift during lunar cycles, which is mostly true, and stick them in the Asylum during that time. Keeps both groups grumbling but complacent so long as there's no accidents."

Grimsby did not care for the way Mayflower said *accidents*; it somehow sounded red and messy.

"Besides," the Huntsman said, pocketing the box of remaining rounds, "not bringing these goes against one of my core rules."

"Which is?"

He clicked shut the cylinder of his revolver and holstered it. "If you're going to talk to someone who can kill you, you better be damn sure you can kill them right back."

"That's psychotic."

"Maybe to you. Where I come from, it's called respect."

Grimsby's mouth was left agape, and though he was uncertain Mayflower's words were right, he couldn't help but feel there was at least something like wisdom in them.

But it was a dangerous, lonely kind of wisdom, one he wasn't sure he envied.

"So if that's one core rule, what are the others?" he asked.

"You're not ready," Mayflower said simply, straightening his haphazard jacket. In its shifting lining, Grimsby saw a glimmer of silver threads.

Before he could press the question, the Huntsman was moving, and he was forced to keep up.

They approached Goode's front door, Mayflower's heavy steps creaking on the old floorboards of the deck. He rapped his knuckles on the threshold. "Sam Goode," he called, sounding both at ease and demanding, "we'd like to speak with you."

There was a rustle and clatter of noise from inside, and a few moments later Goode's many dead bolts and chains began to click and rattle. The door opened a crack, revealing Goode's round and shiny face. His long, lank hair had been pulled back into a short tail at the top of his head. His reddened, dark eyes curled into a scowl as he saw them.

"Two suits this time? What do you want? My stint at the Asylum doesn't start until tonight."

Grimsby waited for Mayflower to speak, but the Huntsman remained silent. He glanced over expectantly, only to realize Mayflower was waiting for him to do the talking.

"We—uh, have a few questions for you," he said, clearing his throat to rid his voice of the squeaking noise it was making. "Regarding some reagents found at a crime scene."

Goode glowered. "And?"

"We think they were purchased from you," Grimsby said.

The Therian's eyes narrowed. "You don't know that. I don't sell anything you can't find a hundred other places. Why don't you go check with each of them first before bothering me?"

Grimsby pulled out the plastic bag with Goode's handwritten tag on it. "Because of this."

The Therian glared at it for a moment. "Oh. Well, I suppose that probably narrowed down the search a bit."

"Just a touch. Look, you're not in trouble—"

"Yet." Mayflower's grave voice tolled, his lone syllable a warning tone.

Grimsby tried to smile away the Huntsman's not-so-subtle threat. "We're just trying to identify what the ritual was intended to do. What can you tell us about it?"

Goode glanced at the tag. "About what? It's newt eye. Practically every ritual from bogus ones to regrow hair to the real deal needs it. Either way, it's not my job to ask. It's my job to sell. I've no idea what they would want to use it for, and I don't care."

"Do you remember who you sold it to? Maybe anything else they purchased?"

Goode's face was hard, but a sheen of sweat beaded on his brow. "I told you, it's common crap. I sell a dozen of those jars a week."

Grimsby couldn't quite tell what, but there was something beneath Goode's words, something he wasn't sharing.

"I think you're lying to us," Grimsby said, his words surprising both Goode and himself.

The Therian growled, and the sound was more literal than Grimsby had ever heard from a person before. "Well, why don't you go draw up a warrant to bring me in? Or you can find me tonight in my cell, though I wouldn't recommend it." His voice was bitter but had a note of defiance in it. "Meanwhile, I'll start thinking *real* hard about any details I missed, *new guy.*"

Grimsby opened his mouth but found no argument he could make. He couldn't officially interrogate Goode, even if he had been trained to do so, and so any information he divulged or withheld was up to him. He could get a warrant, as the Therian had so annoyingly described, but without any reason for urgency, it would take too long to get processed. Even if he could get one the same day, Goode would be in the Asylum before he could get back, and he'd likely be in no mood for talking when he had grown horns, claws, and who knew what else.

He was about to concede defeat when the Huntsman stepped forward.

Goode glanced over to him with dark eyes, sizing him up. His nostrils flared as though he were catching a scent, and shortly after, his skin grew a shade paler.

"I don't think a warrant is necessary," Mayflower said.

"Whatever, man," Goode said as he began to shut the door.

He was interrupted when Mayflower leaned back and kicked it open with a short, devastating blow.

Goode was knocked away, falling back into the darkened entry. His shocked expression became wide and furious in the light that dawned over him. Mayflower straightened his ill-knotted tie and stepped inside.

"Hey!" Goode barked. "You can't do that, you're—"

Mayflower crouched in front of him, conveniently pulling his jacket back enough to reveal the revolver at his side. "The only thing that should matter to you is that I'm asking a question. Right now, every other damned thing in this world is secondary. Understand me?"

Goode began to clamber to his feet, but Mayflower drew the gun from his coat, letting the business end dangle toward the floor.

Goode froze.

"I know you can smell the silver in here. Now, answer my partner's question: who did you sell the stuff to?"

Goode was pale even in the darkness, though Grimsby could see yellow flash in his eyes as he shook his head. "I can't, I can't! If people knew I'd spill to any suit that came asking, no one would ever buy from me again."

"You have a license, though," Grimsby said, fighting the discomfort of being so near Mayflower's foreboding presence. "Why would they not?"

"No one is *licensed* to sell anything worth a damn! You think

I keep this house peddling newt eye and cat bones? People can buy that crap online. They buy from me because they get what they need and can't be traced."

"And now we want to trace them," Mayflower said, standing to loom over Goode's rotund body. "Who were they, and what did you sell to them?"

The Therian groaned and shook his head, but his shoulders slumped in defeat. "I don't know who it was. A bald guy. He wore a scarf over his face and I never caught his name. He didn't even talk; he just gave me a list."

"What did he buy?"

"A bunch of stuff. More than I sell in a year."

"What for?"

"You think someone waves that kind of cash around and I'm going to start asking questions? No way. He bought. I sold. End of transaction."

Mayflower dug in his pocket and pulled out a pad of paper and a pen. He tossed them down to Goode. "Write it down. All of it."

Goode meekly took the implements and began scribbling.

Grimsby felt like he had become suddenly carsick, but he tried to keep a straight face until the Therian had finished.

He held up the paper and pen to Mayflower, and the Hunts-man took them, his eyes never leaving Goode's, as though he were watching for any ill motive or sign of movement. He must have found none. He backed away out the door and turned to the jeep.

Grimsby stayed where he was, his legs refusing to move.

Goode glared up at him, some of the fear having fled his eyes, leaving him looking hurt and ashamed. He glowered at Grimsby. "Get out of my house," he said, his voice cracking.

Grimsby stepped forward and offered a hand to help the man up. "I'm sorry, I—"

Goode slapped it away. "I said get the hell out!" he screamed.

Grimsby, stunned more than hurt by the blow, stumbled back out of the house and hurried to the jeep. He heard the door slam shut behind him, the clatter of locks quickly following.

Mayflower was waiting, his eyes scanning the paper he had extracted from Goode.

"This list has some serious stuff on it," he said. "I'm guessing whoever was interrupted managed to recover the more important reagents before they booked it."

Grimsby didn't hear him, not really. His mind was too busy replaying the shrillness in Goode's voice. He kept seeing the fear in his eyes again and again. It made him sick to his stomach.

This wasn't what being an Auditor was, was it?

No, it couldn't be. It *wouldn't* be.

"Grimsby? You listening?"

He shook his head and looked up at the Huntsman. For a moment, he didn't look like Mayflower. He looked like a stranger.

"That was wrong," Grimsby said, his words emerging of their own accord.

"Excuse me?" the Huntsman asked, his tone as level as the horizon, but his eyes guillotine sharp.

Grimsby felt a swell of panic under that executioner's gaze, but he tensed himself and made the words come out. "What you just did. It was wrong. You shouldn't have threatened him like that."

"He had the info we needed. I just got it out of him."

"By threatening his life."

"I didn't say anything. I just implied it."

"You of all people should know how much you can say without a word. You made him afraid for his life, and that's why he talked."

"Yes, yes I did," Mayflower said, turning to square with him. "You have an issue with that?"

Grimsby felt his reserve waning. The Huntsman's glare weighed on him, and more than just because of its intimidating nature. Mayflower was his partner. He wanted to do right by him. He wanted to be friends with him.

He wanted to make him proud.

But there was no pride in what the Huntsman had just done.

Grimsby took a sharp breath and raised himself up as much as possible. He met Mayflower's gaze and held as steady as he could. "Yes. I think I do."

They stood that way for longer than Grimsby was comfortable, and then some, but he didn't dare back down. He felt like he was staring down a train, and the only thing that kept it from running him over was his own stubbornness. His own will.

Then something in Mayflower's face cracked, like a hairline fissure in a mountainside. It was a razor-thin motion, but one Grimsby noticed. He couldn't dare guess at what was going on behind the Huntsman's eyes, but he knew enough to know it was difficult.

"Okay," Mayflower said, turning his eyes back to the list in his hand.

"O-okay?" Grimsby asked, feeling like someone had opened a trapdoor beneath him, yet he remained floating above the abyss solely due to disbelief.

"Yeah, okay," he repeated, "you're right. That was over the line. Now shut up about it, and let's make some good out of it."

"I'm . . . right?" Grimsby muttered, his voice deadened to a whisper by shock. What had just happened? He had never seen Mayflower back down like that. Not once. And yet he had just watched the Huntsman concede before his very eyes.

And to *him* no less.

"You want to explain how I'm right?" he asked with a nervous chuckle. He was only half joking.

"Don't push it," Mayflower said. "Just take a look at this."

He handed the list over, and Grimsby skimmed it, trying to focus, though his head was still reeling.

"I'm more of an expert at stopping rituals than performing them," Mayflower said, "but . . . a lot of this stuff seems pretty delicate. Living branch of a century oak, last tears of a virgin, and—what the heck is 'the sole of a *kurdaitcha*'?"

"Aboriginal shaman," Grimsby said, scanning the list, "or the shoes they wear. Depends on whether he spelled 'sole' right."

"Any of this make sense to you?"

Grimsby shook his head. "It's like puzzle pieces that don't fit. There's too much on here for any one ritual."

"So you think it's just the first of many?"

"Maybe. Though maybe not." He furrowed his brow in thought. "I think maybe our bald perp bought some red herrings to throw off anyone curious about his recipe."

"Makes sense. So we have no idea which of these might be part of the ritual—or if this is even the whole list. He could have other suppliers." Mayflower nodded. "But did you see the last one?"

"'A fallen stone during its first full moon.' What is that, like a meteor?"

"Meteorite."

"What?"

"Once it hits the ground, it's a meteorite," the Huntsman said distractedly. "Before that, it's a meteor, and before it hits the atmosphere it's a meteoroid."

"Oh. I didn't realize you were an astronomer."

"I'm not. My wife—" He paused, then let out a sudden breath, like he'd just moved a twinging muscle. He shook his head. "Point is, something like that is pricey and has a pretty short expiration date. Not something you're likely to throw on the list as a decoy."

"So you're thinking whoever is behind this is going to try again, before that meteorite's expiration date?"

He nodded. "Before the full moon's over."

"So we just need to find out where, and we can see for ourselves what they're up to."

"That's my thought."

"So, where do we start?"

"Not where. Who. Finley."

"Ah," Grimsby said, then paused. "Wait, who?"

NINETEEN ✳

GRIMSBY CLIMBED OUT OF THE JEEP AND GLANCED around at the lot of black, mirrorless cars. Mayflower's rusted-out vehicle stuck out like a mountain crag in the middle of a rolling black sea.

"Didn't they offer you a car when you came back?" he asked as they entered the building's concrete facade.

"They tried," Mayflower said, then scoffed. "Even insisted."

"And you said no?"

"That jeep has been with me since the start. I've rebuilt her from little more than scrap more than once. I know every sound she makes, every grind of every gear. You think I'd trade that for anything?"

"Okay, but have you ever thought about the ship of Theseus?"

"Yes." The Huntsman scowled. "But Theseus never had a jeep."

Grimsby shrugged. "You could at least get a radio installed," he said, suppressing a grin.

Mayflower's only reply was a growl. He nodded to Stanwick, who bobbed his frizzy mess of gray hair in return and opened the door to the runed hall.

Grimsby still felt nervous as the tiles twitched and hummed, occasionally glowing with soft light as they passed. The Huntsman ignored them, taking long strides that forced him to keep up.

They entered the main hall to find it mostly empty. A few assistants and Agents moved about or spoke in quiet tones, but the rest of the staff was likely at work in the library or reliquary, or in the field.

During his short period at the Department, Grimsby had spent most of his time in the operations wing, along with the other Agents and Auditors. Enough so that the odd mixture of old architecture and modern construction was familiar to him. He had occasionally visited the research wing as well.

But he had never been to logistics.

That was where Mayflower led him.

The hall branched off the main hub, where the domed roof and walls sported original murals. However, the hall quickly grew long and empty. It felt almost barren. The occasional art along the walls looked like modern efforts at old styles rather than the genuine articles, and the floor had shifted from hardwood to razor-thin carpeting that did nothing to cushion the concrete floor. The sound of Grimsby's shoes and Mayflower's boots scuffing on the ground seemed to echo more loudly than it did elsewhere, making the space feel endless and empty.

Mayflower stopped at a wooden door with a frosted-glass window. Painted letters on the glass read REMOTE ANALYSTS. He entered and Grimsby followed, though he balked as he did.

It was an *office*. A massive office.

Dozens of people muttered quietly and shuffled around off-white cubicles. Somewhere a phone rang endlessly. There were computers on practically every surface, and in front of each was someone dressed in a simple collared shirt, slacks, and usually a plaid jacket of some kind, though there were a few solid-colored variants; none, however, wore the gray-black of Auditors or the blue of Agents.

Grimsby had to regain control of his slackened jaw to shut his mouth. How had he not known about this place? So many people, so many computers, and yet he'd never heard of it?

"What is this place?" he asked.

"You think the Department runs on Agents and Auditors?" Mayflower scoffed. "They just do fieldwork. Analysts handle everything else, from research to acquisitions to PR. For every Agent or Auditor, there's likely twenty other personnel."

"I thought all the researchers were in the library or reliquary."

"You aren't going to learn everything stooping over a century-old tome. You can learn even more from the internet."

"I—" Grimsby said, sheepish. "I don't know how to use a computer."

"Me neither, and I'm too much of a bitter old bastard to learn. That's why we have Finley."

He looked around the office, then began walking, weaving through cubicles as Analysts scurried from his path like gazelles before an elephant.

Soon, Grimsby began to hear the tinny blare of rock music, as he often heard on the bus during his commute. They reached a cubicle that might have been off-white like the rest, but it was impossible to tell with the strange, shifting rainbow of colors that were projected by every device inside. It was a vomit of hues that instantly made his head hurt.

Seated in front of three screens, with her feet tucked up beneath her like a cherubic gargoyle, was a young woman perhaps a few years older than Grimsby. She bobbed her head under massive headphones, from which heavy guitar riffs leaked. Her hair had been dyed almost as many colors as had been projected on the walls, and it was currently bound back in a chaotic braid. She wore the relatively standard style of the other Analysts, though her jacket was a plaid of black and blue, rebelliously close to the colors reserved for Auditors and Agents. She also sported a collection of chains around one wrist and spikes on her heavy boots.

"Finley," Mayflower called, but she made no motion of having heard. She only glanced over at one of her monitors, which displayed a full-screen video of a very fit woman dancing under spotlights to the thrum of the music.

"Finley!" Mayflower roared, drawing a dozen nearby eyes. Grimsby was pretty certain people could see him from the farthest-flung cubicles in the office, like a haunted, looming lighthouse in an off-white sea.

Again, no reply from the woman.

Finally, Mayflower growled and reluctantly reached out to tap her on the shoulder.

She peeled off the headphones and whirled around with a scowl, her freckled brow charmingly dissonant with her hooded eyes, but the frown vanished when she saw the Huntsman.

"Les!" she cried, leaping out of her chair and wrapping her arms around him in a hybrid hug-tackle. As she did, the headphones around her neck stretched their cord tight before ripping it from the computer. The music began blaring painfully loudly from terrible speakers, making people around the office groan and glare at them.

Grimsby hardly noticed, as his jaw had dropped open so wide he could practically taste the chaotic rainbow of light.

Finley was *hugging* the Huntsman.

Mayflower, for his part, held his hands up like a gun was pointed at him, though he looked more uncomfortable than surprised. After an extended period, he lost his will to remain stoic and gently began prying her arms from him.

"Yes, hello, Finley," he muttered under the music. "Good to see you, too."

She allowed herself to be pried away, though her dark eyes remained bright. "I was starting to think you'd never drop by."

"Sorry. Things got . . . complicated."

"They always do with you," she said, a tinge of sadness beneath her mirth. She turned to Grimsby and raised a brow. "Who's the dweeb?"

"Dweeb?" Grimsby said, uncertain he had ever heard the word before, but very certain it was not a compliment.

"Grimshaw Grimsby, Miranda Finley. Miranda Finley, Grimshaw Grimsby. There. Introductions are done."

She rolled her eyes at him and grinned covertly at Grimsby. "I'm guessing he's always this much of a grump?"

"Only when he's around," Grimsby said, half shouting over the music.

"Enough!" Mayflower said, glowering. "We've got work to do."

"Let me guess," Finley said, plugging her headphones back in to stifle the blaring music. "You need my help."

Mayflower grumbled something unintelligible, but it was clearly an affirmative.

"Yay!" she said with genuine excitement. "Whatcha got?"

Mayflower handed her the list. "We've got a RUIN with a list of ingredients. We need to find out where it might take place again."

Finley skimmed the list. "If whoever got these was a real pro, there'll be decoys on here. Junk they didn't actually need, but that would throw off the scent of the ritual's true intent."

Grimsby nodded. "We thought so, too, but I figured with all that information and the location of the original attempt, we could still narrow down—"

"The viable locations where ley lines might intersect to perform the ritual again," Finley finished. "Makes sense. I have a few simulations I could run. If the heavy mojo here matches up with

the right flavors of ley lines, we might have a shot at finding a location."

"How long will it take?" Mayflower asked, glaring dubiously
at the triple screens of the computer behind her.

She shrugged. "Couple of hours, maybe."

He grunted, "Fine," and leaned against one of the cubicle's
wobbly walls.

"You're just going to wait here, huh?"

He nodded.

"All right, fair enough. And what about you, dweeb?"

"Me?" Grimsby said, stumbling. "Oh, I don't know—"

Mayflower grunted. "Go get some sleep, Grimshaw. I can tell
you're lacking."

"I'm a witch who lacks many things. What's one more?"

The Huntsman glowered.

"So you *do* care!"

"I just care that my witch being short a nap might cost me my
ass." His face was hard, but there was some genuine concern in
his voice. "There should be some spare cots in the operations barracks. Go on, I'll come find you when this is done."

Grimsby began to argue, but a yawn overtook and nearly unhinged his jaw. Maybe Mayflower was right. He had barely slept
after his escapade with Wudge, and he was no use to anyone half
awake.

"All right, all right. But don't go anywhere without me."

Mayflower grunted and waved him away. Finley had already
returned to her seat and had begun clicking away at the board of
keys in front of her.

Grimsby left them in the cubicle and made his way back toward the operations wing of the Department, feeling his eyes
grow heavier with each step.

TWENTY ✳

THE BARRACKS WAS DARK WHEN GRIMSBY ENTERED. THE room had a dozen double-bunked beds, and all but one of them were empty. Grimsby left the light off and maneuvered through the dark, using only the single band of illumination that spilled in from the crack beneath the door.

He took a bed on the opposite side of the room from the only other occupant, lying on the narrow mattress. As he did, he felt the soft surface almost envelop him. How long had it been since he had slept on anything other than his couch or a cot?

He couldn't remember, and he certainly hadn't remembered how much more comfortable a real mattress was. His exhausted body was all too happy to sink into the cushions and be forgotten, ready for sleep, but his mind yet wandered.

What would they do when they found whoever was behind the RUIN? Grimsby had never arrested anyone before, and his last real fight had been before he'd gotten his Auditor badge. Would the perpetrator come along quietly, answer to the law, and one day be released again?

After all, despite Mayflower's hunches, they still weren't sure what the ritual was intended to even do. The only facts they had were that the RUIN was unlicensed, that it was almost certainly more powerful than was allowed by the Department, and that it was binding magic. But such magic was amorphous and could be used for almost anything. Although, as far as Grimsby knew, little of it was used with good intentions. Trapping and imprisoning was often by its very nature a cruel act.

And yet, that was exactly what he was supposed to do to whoever was behind the spellwork.

His stomach twisted and thrashed with guilt from something he hadn't even done. But it was his job to do it. It was the job he had always wanted, and now it left him lying awake when he was otherwise exhausted.

He twisted and turned, the mattress now more confining than comfortable.

"Guilty conscience?" a familiar voice asked.

Grimsby sat up to see a figure seated on the edge of the bunk across from him. He readjusted his glasses and squinted his eyes before realizing who it was.

"Rayne?" he asked. "What are you doing here?"

She gestured to the bed she had left on the other side of the room. "Sleeping. Or, at least, I was."

"Oh," he said, awkwardly detangling his legs from the blankets. "I'm sorry. I didn't realize it was you."

"No, I should thank you. I had already overslept." Her tone was oddly smooth and relaxed. "There's too much work to do, you know?"

He nodded. "I know the feeling."

She leaned forward, her visage hidden in the shadows, but he could smell a waft of her familiar perfume. It was dark and sweet, like cloves and honey. "Have you made any progress on the RUIN case?"

"Uh, sorta," he said, scratching at the side of his face and turning away from her intense gaze. "I probably shouldn't talk about it yet."

"Shouldn't talk to me about my own case?" she asked. "How Department of you." She chuckled, the sound halfway between soft and bitter.

Grimsby balked. Even a half-hearted laugh had been more than he'd heard from Rayne in a long time, and suddenly he felt like he was holding something fragile. Something that might break if he said the wrong word.

"No, not like that!" he said. "I'm just not sure what we have, if anything, you know?"

He felt her hand rest on his, and the sudden heat there was enough to make him worry his scars might smolder in the dark.

"Grimsby—Grimshaw," she said, her voice growing soft. "I need to know what you know. It's important."

He felt his first reply stammer to its death in his throat, leaving him mumbling against the heat of her touch. The last time she had touched his hand like this had been years ago.

"Please," she said. The one word seemed to stretch on forever.

Instinct and procedure both told him to keep his mouth shut. Auditors were supposed to keep details between themselves, their partners, and their superiors, and Rayne was none of these. Yet even so, the touch of her hand on his brought him back to that sunny afternoon, years ago now, when she had played the piano for him.

When they had their first, and only, kiss.

It was the last day he would see her for a long time, as she would pass on to become an Auditor and he would not.

They had never spoken about that kiss since, not once, and it had been such a fevered moment in his memory that he'd begun to wonder if it ever happened at all. The sun, the piano, the kiss. It had been something too perfect for him to be a part of, and the long years since had been so dull and dark that the memory seemed less and less likely to be real.

Yet he had told himself again and again that it had to be, not because he believed it, but because on his coldest days, it was one of the few sparks of warmth he could conjure to keep him going.

He knew he should deny her. He should tell her nothing.

But he couldn't.

She had given him something wondrous.

And to deny her now would bring him closer to believing their shared moment so long ago was just a figment of his imagination.

It was one of the few truly beautiful moments of his life, and he couldn't bring himself to part with it.

His eyes found hers in the quiet dark, and the words poured forth. "The Department didn't look far enough beyond the ritual site. After some snooping, we came up with a list," he finally managed, voice almost desperate to tell her whatever she wanted. "Some reagents that were used for the ritual. With those, and some ley-line mapping, we're pretty sure we can figure out where they will try it again."

"Try it again?" she asked, her face placid. "You don't think they succeeded the first time?"

"No—at least, I doubt it. I think they messed up."

"Did they?" she asked, her gaze narrowing. "How?"

"Well, we discovered some etched silver chains were involved, but the guy who found them pawned them. If the ritual had gone to plan, that silver would probably have turned to ash or at least molten slag."

"Perhaps the ritual wasn't as dangerous as you thought."

"Mayflower says otherwise."

"Mayflower?"

Grimsby nodded. "He says he's seen it before. He isn't sure where, but he's sure it wasn't good."

"Interesting," Rayne said. Her eyes grew distant, like she was dwelling on memories of her own.

"Whatever the case, based on the components involved, this ritual was something serious and time-sensitive. And, if our list is right, whoever's behind this invested a lot into it. If they failed, they'll try again."

She thought for a moment, then finally nodded. "I imagine they will. Thank you, Grimshaw." She smiled. "Now, shouldn't you get some sleep?"

He balked, hoping he might find some way to drag on their conversation, to delay long enough until he found the words to apologize for taking her case.

And maybe to ask if she remembered that sunny day, long ago.

Whatever those words might have been, they eluded him.

Instead, he only nodded numbly.

Rayne withdrew her hand, leaving him feeling all the colder for its absence. She stood and stretched before heading toward the door.

Grimsby stared anywhere except for the silhouette of her lean figure as she did, and he could almost hear that piano's somber tune.

Rayne shouldered on her jacket and glanced back at him, a curious and foreign gleam in her eyes.

Then she was gone.

He lay back down, trying to force his eyes closed, but though his exhausted limbs felt weighed down with irons, his mind felt like it was spinning inside his skull. The heat of Rayne's touch still lingered, and her fading perfume made him dizzy.

He wanted to go after her, to ask her if she remembered that sunny afternoon. But he didn't, and it was for the same reason he hadn't since he had become an Auditor.

He was too frightened.

Because if she didn't remember, then maybe it really only ever had been a dream after all.

And somewhere, deep down, he needed it to be real. Even now.

Though if it was, that only made his betrayal of her all the worse.

He groaned and shoved his face into the pillow until his closed eyes flared with distorted color. "Sleep, idiot!" he chided, though the odds of that seemed to only grow more distant.

Despite his knowing he needed to rest, no position felt comfortable, felt right, and as a result he found himself tossing for long minutes, his mind as disobedient as his body. His stomach twisted with anxious guilt for what he had done to Rayne. Whatever her interest in this case was, he had never meant to pry it from her—heck, he would have been happy to help her with it if he had ever been given the chance.

He finally tossed away the blanket and climbed to his feet. He needed to go after her; he needed to apologize.

But most of all, he needed to ask her if she remembered.

Perhaps he could still make things right. He could speak to Grieves and bring her in on the case alongside himself and Mayflower, though he doubted the Huntsman would be pleased at the idea. Even so, it felt like the right thing to do, and it was the only amends he could think of that loosened the growing coil of guilt in his gut.

He went to the hall, eyes glaring against the bright, fluorescent lights, and hoped to see Rayne, but it was in vain. His minutes of tossing and turning had given her ample time to go wherever she was going.

"Eyes aflame," he cursed, regretting his indecision.

Perhaps she had returned to her office? It seemed the most logical place.

He hurried that way, hoping to find her, determined to mend their relationship—whatever it might have been.

He found her office with little trouble; each frosted glass window was marked with the names of the office's occupants, though many were blank. He supposed that must have meant they were empty, although he found that made him wonder why he still didn't have an office of his own, and that led to a whole slew of thoughts that he simply didn't have time to reason with.

He felt a jolt of mixed dread and jealousy when he spotted Rayne's office, as the door read: AUDITOR ELIZABETH BATHORY and, just beneath it, AUDITOR WILSON HIVES.

There was no love lost between him and Hives, especially after their last few encounters—during which Hives had nearly killed him several times. But even so, Grimsby couldn't help but feel regret for what had happened. It had been he who turned over Hives to Peters, after all. He had thought he had been bringing the Auditor to justice; instead he might have condemned Hives to a terrible fate. Or perhaps helped him escape.

Grimsby shook his head; it hardly seemed fair that he felt responsible for both extremes simultaneously, especially given they were mutually exclusive. The guilt was like black ink on his palms; the more he wiped it away, the more it coated him.

He raised a shaking hand and knocked on the glass, though the sound was fainter than he intended.

He growled at himself and stood a little straighter, knocking more forcefully.

At his touch, the door creaked open, apparently having not been fully latched.

"Rayne?" he called, peering through the dimly lit crack. He could just see Rayne's desk, with a haphazard pile of photos and notes scattered around it in a loose circle, but she was nowhere to be seen.

She must have gone somewhere other than her office.

He grabbed the handle, intending to close the door, but as he did, his eyes fell to the wastebasket just inside the doorway. Within was the manila folder that had originally held the RUIN case, and now likely held Grimsby's original assignment.

He hesitated a moment. The contents were still, technically, his responsibility, though they weren't as pressing as the other items currently on his agenda, like a cursed artifact or rogue ritualist. Even so, they would need to be dealt with.

Yet he knew how—well, *weird* it would be to go rifling through Rayne's garbage.

He shook his head; he was a professional. He had a job to do, and if that meant digging through trash, so be it.

It wasn't creepy if he was a professional.

Right?

He quickly fished the folder out of the bin, glad it was full of only paper and nothing more foul. It was then he noticed the odd symbol scribbled on the folder's face, just below the assignment number printed on the front. It seemed almost frantically drawn, and immediately put him into a strange unease.

"Auditor Grimsby!" a rough voice called, somehow already short of patience.

He yelped and jumped, feeling like a child caught with his hands in a jar of unappetizing cookies. He slammed shut Rayne's door and turned to see Oksanna, the Assessor, glaring at him over her crossed forearms, which looked like twin oak logs sticking out of the rolled-up sleeves of her charcoal jacket.

He froze in his tracks, clutching the folder to his chest. "Oh, Mrs. Ox! H-hello."

"No 'hello, Mrs. Ox' me, Grimsby! I wait for you this morning for assessing, and no Grimsby! I think, 'Surely he would not miss appointment, is good boy,' and wait longer, and still no Grimsby!" The familiar on her shoulder bristled its paper wings and cawed from its hollow skull, sharing its mistress's distemper.

"I—"

"No! You want be termin—terminat— " She groaned in annoyance at her own words. "Fired? You want to be fired?"

"N-no, ma'am."

"Then come. We make assessment now." She whirled on her heel and began to storm away.

Grimsby's mouth went dry, and his hand unconsciously found the nail in his pocket. With its strange effect on his magic, there was no way he'd pass an assessment. Not to mention that he would much prefer the Department not find out about the item altogether. They might demand he turn it over, which would be troublesome to begin with, and even if it were possible, it would be a betrayal of Wudge's trust in him.

He had hurt enough of his friends already.

"Maybe we can do this another time?" he offered.

Mrs. Ox whipped around on her heels again. "I know you did not just say this. I know, after graciously giving you not one, not two, but third chance, you did not just ask for fourth. It surely cannot be!"

"It's just— Now's not the best time, you know?"

"Not the best time is exactly best time for assessment. Is it best time when you are wrangling gargoyle before it tear down building? Is it best time when you must go into Elsewhere to destroy evil spirit? Is it best time when bad man in alley pulls gun on you for being witch? No! Is bad time. And if it is bad time now, it is good time to assess. Now, come."

Once more, she turned to stalk down the halls, the raven on her shoulder fluttering its wings to keep balance, her broad form perhaps a bit less brooding than it had been a moment before.

Grimsby sighed, unable to argue. He couldn't talk his way out of the assessment altogether, but neither could he pass.

What could he do?

He could only hope he came up with a plan before Mrs. Ox began his trial.

TWENTY-ONE

I F IT HADN'T BEEN FOR THE GROWING BALL OF TWISTED nerves in his belly, Grimsby might have fallen asleep on the short drive to the testing ground. Mrs. Ox had refused to let him out of her sight, as though he might somehow disappear, and so had firmly offered to give him a lift to the nearby glade where he had failed his first test.

The Assessor crunched the Department-issued black sedan to a halt, its shiny black paint already marred by dust and dirt from the gravel road. She climbed gruffly out, giving Grimsby a stern gaze to ensure he followed. She approached the tree that had bested him, which he immediately recognized by the trunk, its bark stripped away by his spells. He tried to ignore the dozens of stumps nearby, each of which marked a successful trial, but found it impossible. It felt like they were all spectators, whether cut, scorched, or shattered, and had come to watch him fail once more.

He began to trudge glumly toward the victorious tree, but found Mrs. Ox had instead moved to a lone stump nearby.

She propped one foot up on the smooth wood, her heels at

odds with the thickness of her calves, and waited for him to approach.

"Mrs. Ox, I really don't think I can—"

She hushed him with a glower, producing her dreaded clipboard. "Auditor Grimsby, as you have failed to fell tree for first trial, I have had to find other means to begin second trial." She stomped on the stump, which looked to have been cleaved apart by a single strike from the sharpest blade. "This is tree felled by Auditor Bathory for her trial. Since I had intended to find her, but found you instead, you shall continue where she left off."

Grimsby eyed the stump warily. "What, you want me to put it back together again?" he asked, before realizing that, without the warping magic of the nail, his *Bind* spell might actually do a decent job of it.

Oksanna shook her shawled head. "No. You will now remove stump, so we can plant new tree for Auditors in future."

He felt his jaw tighten even as his eyes went wide. The stump itself was almost two feet across; the roots beneath likely went down dozens of feet.

"A bulldozer would barely get this thing out!" he said. "How in blue blazes would I do it?"

Oksanna glanced to the familiar on her shoulder, then they both shrugged. "With *Torque*?" she offered. Then she stepped away a few feet, holding her stubby pencil poised above her clipboard.

Grimsby stared, his eyes feeling hot in his skull. His hand unconsciously fell to the nail in his pocket. He couldn't even manage this feat on the best of days, let alone this day. He was tired, he was worried about his first case, and on top of it all, he dreaded the thought of Rayne never forgiving him. It had shadowed each passing moment, building in the back of his mind like a storm cloud. Compared to all that, being cursed seemed like a minor inconvenience.

Or at least it had been.

Now, however, he couldn't even manage his own magic, though the past had shown that, even if he could, it wouldn't be enough.

He would fail.

He had failed.

Odd's Bodkin, he wondered if he could have ever succeeded in the first place.

He looked at Rayne's perfectly cut stump, as smoothly sliced as if it was ready to seat two for dinner. He doubted it had taken her more than a few moments.

He glanced back to his tree, where he had spent hours laboring with his most reliable spell. Its trunk was scarred and ragged, but it remained tall and strong.

She has proven she is competent. Grieves's words from the day before came back to him. *You have merely proven you are fortunate.*

He didn't feel fortunate.

And he certainly didn't feel competent.

He felt empty. Drained. More like a scarecrow than a man—one dressed in ill-fitting Auditor's garments.

Perhaps it was best he failed. Perhaps he didn't belong at all.

He stood over the stump, his hands balled to fists at his sides, his left hand clenched around the nail, his right held so tight that his knuckles popped and his palms welled with thin slits of blood beneath his fingers.

He felt every fear and doubt building within him, stacking like iron plates in his stomach. One after another, until he felt like falling down and never standing back up again.

The stack grew so high that he felt like he might choke.

Instead, he screamed.

It wasn't flattering. It wasn't inspiring or brave.

It was a child's scream, and he hated the sound it made.

He lashed out with the heel of his foot, kicking the side of the stump uselessly. Pain immediately shot back up his heel and through his leg as his blow rebounded. He glared, then kicked the stump again and again. Each was as useless as the last. He'd need a crane to tear this thing up—or perhaps a keg of gunpowder.

"Perhaps try magic, Auditor Grimsby," Mrs. Ox called, jotting a note on her clipboard.

He wanted to turn and shout at her, vent his frustration in one massive gale—but he froze.

Perhaps his old magic would have been useless in surmounting the trial. His spells were built around nuance rather than strength. Where other witches could manage the same forces as a bulldozer or explosives, he had always made do with levers and pulleys.

But with the nail, maybe things were different.

His mind rushed back to the night before, when he and Wudge had plummeted from the rooftop toward certain death—only to be saved by the warped magic of his *Torque* spell. Somehow, instead of creating a force that turned objects, it froze them, sapping their momentum instead of adding to it.

He supposed that made sense. If his *Bind*s now pushed apart instead of pulling together, the nail had made *Torque* also perform in an opposite manner to its nature.

The part that was important, though, was that after the spell absorbed their fall and abated, there had been a wave of pressure that surged outward. The force didn't vanish, but rather was held, like tension in a spring. When the spell ended, the spring was free to expand.

But what if he kept applying force to the spring? How much could it take? And what would happen when it sprung?

It might just mean boom.

It wasn't a bulldozer, but it might very well be explosive.

And it was his only chance.

He glared at the stump, this time not with childish rage but with determination.

"One of us isn't going to make it," he said to himself.

He knelt down and, using the nail, he carved the rune for his *Torque* spell into the fresh wood, scouring it one inch at a time. He needed a physical manifestation to help contain the magic. Merely placing a magical impression of the rune wouldn't be enough— although perhaps none of this would be enough if he was wrong.

Yet at this point, he had no other options.

With the rune completed, he put his palm on the surface and began to concentrate. He would need as much power as he could muster—though he'd still need some strength afterward.

He focused, calling forth his Impetus, and felt heat begin to flow into him, drawn from the Elsewhere. It was almost like inhaling fire into himself. He felt the heat well in his chest, though not as much as he had hoped. His memory flashed back to Mrs. Ox's advice from the day before:

Stay stubborn long enough and you will be strong.

He wasn't certain he could be strong.

But he was certain he could be stubborn.

He just had to hope she was right.

With his right hand on the rune, he pushed his still-bleeding palm down onto the splintered surface of the wood and forced the Impetus into it—or rather used his Impetus to will power from the Elsewhere into it.

His scars smoldered and snapped as the rune began to fill with light, like someone had begun pouring molten steel into it. With each moment, he felt his warmth waning, his body growing chill, but he forced forth the power until the rune was filled with solid light.

Then, he stood and stepped back, holding out his palm, maintaining his concentration, and said, "*Torque.*"

There was a hollow sound, like a ball bouncing at the bottom of a well, and motes of light appeared around the stump, the rune still glowing on its surface.

Grimsby took a deep breath, partially to steady his nerves and partially to keep from passing out, and stepped forward to deliver another solid kick to the stump's side.

And absolutely nothing happened.

He slowly smiled—it was exactly what he wanted.

There was no flash of pain as there had been before. It instead felt like his foot briefly stuck in invisible quicksand, rather than striking the stump's hard surface. A few more kicks confirmed the feeling.

The spell was absorbing all the force of his kick, storing it like a spring.

And that spring needed to be tighter.

He looked around, ignoring Oksanna's curious eyebrow raise, and found a stone about half the size of his head. He picked it up and hauled it over to the stump. Then he held it tight and brought it down on the stump.

Thump.

The sound was light and thin, and though the surface of the stump should have been scarred by the hard stone, it was not.

The motes of light, however, grew more numerous.

Grimsby raised the stone again and again. Thump, thump, thump. At first he used his strength to haul the rock down into the stump like he was throwing it at his feet, but before long he grew too tired and simply raised it to let it fall down once more.

Even so, he kept going.

Thump, thump, thump.

The motes grew brighter and more numerous, until the air looked alive with fireflies. The chill from his spent Impetus was replaced with fevered exertion.

Still, he did not stop. If his spell failed here, whether because he lacked the strength to power it or the control to contain it, he would fail his trial.

And he refused to fail.

Thump, thump, thump.

Sweat poured from his brow, and his back muscles burned like welding torches along his spine, made all the worse by the welt left by Echidna's tail in the Elsewhere. His palms were scuffed and scraped, though his left hand was too toughened by scars to bleed. Still, he peeled off his Auditor jacket to continue his work.

His mind went blank, the labor too heavy to allow thought. There was only the steady rhythm of his breath, the hammering of his heart, and, beneath it all, the anxious dread of what would come next.

But he was stubborn.

Thump, thump, thump.

He needed to keep going. It was the only instinct he had strength for. One more strike, and one more, and—

Thump, thump, crack.

The stone split in half, falling on either side of the glowing stump. The rune was flickering madly, and the motes of light were a trembling curtain.

He felt a rough hand on his arm. "We go now," Mrs. Ox said, hauling him back.

Grimsby was so exhausted that he fell when he tried to stumble after her, only to then be dragged like a sack of potatoes until they were both behind the black car.

Grimsby clambered to his feet, holding himself up only by gripping the car's antenna, and raised his hand to abate the spell.

Before he could, it shattered on its own with an explosive boom.

Each blow had been frozen, its force held in magical limbo by the nail-warped nature of his spell, each adding to the tension building within the field, and when it collapsed, those suspended blows all struck.

At once.

Grimsby realized he had no need for a keg of gunpowder, as he had made one himself.

The stump vanished in an instant—shattering to countless splinters that themselves were then split again, leaving little more than a crater of broken chunks of wood, churned earth, and raining dirt.

The stump—Rayne's stump—was no more.

It took a few seconds for the bits of wood and dirt to stop raining down. The glade was silent, devoid of the creak of insects or chirp of birds.

Mrs. Ox looked from Grimsby to the stump and back again. Then she jotted another note on her clipboard. "I thought *Torque* was supposed to . . ." She flipped through older notes. "'Turn stuff.'"

"It, uh, turns stuff into little pieces of stuff," he said, trying to shake away his own shock. He was too exhausted to do much more than lean against the Department car. At first, excitement boiled within his burnt-out body. He had succeeded, after all. But seeing what he had done—he didn't think it was possible, at least not for him. Had the nail not only warped his magic but made it stronger? If so, this was no success at all.

It was a test, and he had cheated.

After all, he couldn't have ever done this on his own.

Could he?

Any elation was smothered by sudden doubt. If he couldn't have passed without the nail, he didn't deserve to pass at all.

Mrs. Ox punched him lightly on the shoulder, though his already aching muscles insisted it was a vicious blow. "Well done, Auditor Grimsby," she said.

Grimsby felt a bitter taste in his mouth. "Actually, Mrs. Ox, I—"

"Cannot say I expected you to use a rock as part of your spell, but I am not here to argue with results. You pass." She beamed at him, apparently completely unaware of the coil of nausea that pulsed in his stomach.

"I—" he began, but stopped himself. What would have happened if not for the nail? Would he have failed and been stripped of his status as Auditor altogether, returning to his life as it was just months ago?

He shuddered at the thought.

Those days had been hard, but they had also been hollow and seemingly endless. They were a blur, each day melding with the last until sinkholes of amorphous but draining memories were all he had of them. He could never go back.

And if he told the Assessor the truth, he just might have to.

"Thank you," he finally said, forcing a smile over the acrid taste in his mouth.

"No need to thank; you earned it."

His false smile withered and died, so he only nodded.

"Let us get you back to Department. I'm sure you have plenty of work left to do today."

Grimsby suppressed a groan. He had been so focused on his trial that he had nearly forgotten everything else going on. His body was already exhausted, his muscles twitching and aching with numb heat. He glanced over at the small crater and wished that he had been a bit more prudent with his magic—and his raw palms made him wish he had done the same with the rock.

He took a breath and let himself lean heavily against the car. For a moment, he thought he might still have time to find Rayne, but he cast the thought away. He was tired. He was battered. He would ask her if she remembered on another day.

Two lies in as many minutes, he thought to himself.

He needed to rest, if there was still time. The trial had been just over an hour. Depending on Finley's simulations, he might have time for a nap. He entertained the thought longingly, though without much hope, as he opened the passenger door and collapsed into the seat, collecting the folder he had scavenged from Rayne's trash bin and placing it in his lap.

Oksanna went around to the driver's side and climbed in as well, dropping heavily into the seat. She paused before clearing her throat and tilting her head at the window.

Grimsby looked up to see a broken splinter of wood about as wide as his finger sticking through the glass. A web of cracks spread out from it like veins in a bloodshot eye.

"Oh," he said. "Oops?"

"Oops," she confirmed, though a smirk shadowed her lips. Then her gaze fell to the folder in Grimsby's lap and the color drained from her usually ruddy face. She reached out and snatched it from his grip with surprising and urgent speed.

"What—" he began, but her wide eyes silenced him.

She let the papers within fall, her stare fixed on the blank side of the folder. Except it wasn't blank; it still had the odd symbol sketched on it.

"Did you make this?" she demanded. She never looked away from the symbol; her voice was harsh and intense.

"N-no!" he said. "I don't even know what it means."

She finally tore her focus away and looked to him. "Where did you find this?"

He bit back his reply. He didn't know what Mrs. Ox saw in the symbol, but it obviously wasn't good. "It was there when I got my assignment," he lied.

She didn't even seem to be listening as she turned back to the symbol and uttered a single word under her breath.

"Strygga."

Then she shook herself like she was trying to wake from a bad dream, and her fingers sparked with light. Within a second, the folder burst into flame and vanished into ash, leaving only a wave of heat to tell of its passing.

"What is it?" Grimsby asked, trying to remain casual despite Oksanna's obvious disturbance.

"You truly do not know what it means?" she asked, looking away from the falling ash to core out Grimsby's expression like an archaeologist at a dig.

"I don't. At all, really," he said. This time he did not have to lie.

Her gaze softened, and she took a deep, relieved breath and settled back into the seat, though some concern plagued her features. "It—it is a witch who has stolen the Impetus of another at their time of death."

"Stolen Impetus? Is that even possible?" Grimsby asked, while another question plagued him, which he did not give voice to: *And what is such a symbol doing on my file?*

"Possible, and terrible." She eyed him for a long moment. "And you know nothing of it?"

"No, nothing."

"Then let us both forget we saw it and move on," she said, though her grim expression betrayed that she didn't seem to be forgetting a thing.

She started the car and began driving back to the Department headquarters on the edge of the reserve.

Grimsby collected the fallen papers quietly. He wanted to pry but decided against it, and Mrs. Ox seemed content with the silence. The strygga symbol seemed to have upset her more than he thought possible. The stern Assessor was normally stoic, and occasionally flippant, but never had he seen her disturbed to such a degree.

She pulled the car up to the base of the main stairs, gesturing outward. "Go on, now. Rest. Work. Whatever it is you need do."

"Thank you, Assessor," he said, too focused on the word *rest* to really consider the remainder of her sentence. He climbed out and the black Department car slid away, the engine nearly silent.

He waved to Stanwick as he entered, and after a bob of twin frizzes of hair, the steel doors opened and he made his way through the hall of runes. As he reached the main foyer, he glanced up at the tapestries and murals, but he stared straight through them.

While his exhausted body trudged on, his mind wandered. The symbol stuck in his head, and the idea behind it made him shiver.

A stolen Impetus.

A strygga.

To steal an Impetus—it was like stealing someone's heart, even their soul. He didn't like to think the idea was possible, but Mrs. Ox's reaction said otherwise. Just the symbol had made the normally ironclad Assessor pale. But what was it doing on the folder he had taken from Rayne's office? Had she written it only to discard it, or had it been someone else? Neither potential answer sat well with him, so he tried to push the thought away and focus on the task at hand.

He still had work to do to find whoever was behind the yet-unknown RUIN case. Even if he and Mayflower managed to find them, how was he supposed to help with his curse-twisted magics?

Though perhaps they were stronger this way than before—but that thought only worried him more.

All the troubles and concerns weighed on him, and, combined with the weariness of his strained and spent muscles, it was too much.

He needed to be unconscious, and he needed it now.

He stumbled his way to the barracks, heedless of those he passed, and collapsed into the first bunk he found. His last memory was calculating the rough trajectory in which he needed to fall to find a mattress.

He was pretty sure he missed.

TWENTY-TWO

MAYFLOWER LEANED AGAINST THE CUBICLE WALL, his eyes burning holes into Finley's out-of-date calendar pinned to the corkboard across from him. Something about the Therian's claims didn't add up—mostly the description of the man who bought the reagents.

"Bald. Mask. Didn't talk," he muttered to himself. It didn't sound familiar, at least not enough to justify his initial draw to the RUIN. There was something else he was missing.

"You say something, Les?" Finley asked, peeling back one earpad of her oversize headphones.

"No, nothing."

Finley arched a brow at him, turning to lean over the back of her chair in a gesture that reminded him of her father. "You know brooding never helped anybody."

"You don't brood enough, then," he said, crossing his arms, though a small smile tugged at the corner of his mouth. Ever since she was a little girl, Finley had never taken him seriously. She was perhaps the only person who didn't, though he'd never admit that was a relief.

"Come on, talk through it. It'll help, I promise! If you're embarrassed, I won't even look," she said, turning back to her work but keeping one ear tilted toward him.

He grunted but cleared his throat and muttered gruffly, "Our only witness, the Therian, claims the suspect is one way, but it doesn't sit right with me. Like someone swapped out my favorite chair for a fake."

"Why? Did you already have a favorite chair in mind?"

"Not quite. But up until now, everything has felt familiar, like déjà vu. I swear I've seen this case before—but this guy the Therian described, he doesn't feel that way."

"Maybe your werewolf was lying?"

"Therian," he corrected. "A Therian can't control what they turn into. Usually they're some piecemeal collection of different animals. To become pure wolf, werewolves have to have some degree of self-control. But no, I doubt he was lying. Wrong, maybe, but not lying."

"So you think you ran this case before? Or one close to it?"

"Very close. But I can't remember. It was after Mary—" He cleared his throat. "It was a long time ago."

"Right," Finley said, turning enough to offer him a soft gaze. "You . . . still miss her?"

His jacket seemed to cinch down over his chest, but he kept his tone level, even if it was barely above a whisper. "I miss all of it," he said. If anyone else had asked him, they'd have woken up with fewer teeth.

But Finley wasn't anyone else.

She was family, even if she wasn't blood.

"I'm sorry, Uncle Les."

He gritted his teeth and resisted the urge to pull out a cigarette. "Point is, I don't remember those days as well as I should, and I can't place this damn case."

"Well, I can pull up a list of old files from around then, ones with you or Mansgraf tagged in them. It might help jog your memory."

"How long will it take to dig up files that old?"

She snorted, her nose wrinkling, then after a few moments of typing she leaned back and gestured to the monitor. "Done."

"What?" He shook his head. "Damn computers."

He leaned over her shoulder and watched as she smoothly scrolled through the pages of scanned documents. Large swathes of text had been blacked out, censored by some Department committee. Most of the cases were more black bars than text.

Then one caught his eye. "Stop."

Finley obeyed, hovering over the image, though she turned her head to the side in disgust.

It was a picture of a woman lying on the ground. She wore a dress of expensive low-cut silk. In the photo, the dress was gray, but he remembered it had been venom green. The gray silk was stained black with blood, which pooled around her splayed dark hair like a radiating halo. Her eyes were wide and bright, her face elegant yet cruel. Her lips were still parted, caught halfway through a spell she had begun to utter at Mansgraf when the old witch's back was turned to deal with thralls.

And finally, at the center of her forehead, was a clean pinhole the size of Mayflower's pinky, where he had shot the woman. Despite the grisly beauty of the photo, Mayflower knew that, just out of frame, the back of her head was largely scattered over the wall.

He felt his stomach twist even as the name found his lips.

"Janice."

"If you say so," Finley said, looking at another monitor that displayed the progress on the simulations. She looked distinctly greener, and it wasn't just the vibrant light of her gadgetry. "The only names not redacted are yours and Mansgraf's."

"Show me the other photos."

She scrolled quickly away, all too happy to leave Janice's placid expression behind. The other photographs were of the scene, and with each he saw, he recalled more of that night, roughly two decades ago.

"She was going to kill a girl," he muttered, the memories so strong that he could smell the damp tunnels and aged oil of the abandoned railway. "Mansgraf said something about her being a sacrifice."

"A sacrifice for what?"

"Didn't know, didn't care. All I needed to know was that woman was going to murder a child."

"What—what happened?" Finley asked, her tone making it seem like she wasn't sure she wanted to know.

"We found her partway through the ritual. Mansgraf held off the thralls she had taken over; I went after the girl."

"Thralls?"

"People Janice had mind controlled. She somehow enslaved them with magic, made them less than dogs, bound to her will."

"Did you stop her?"

He nodded grimly. "She seemed surprised I shot her. Maybe she thought I'd let her finish her threats."

"And the little girl?"

"We got her out. Mansgraf even managed to save the thralls before Janice's spell broke them. It . . ." He found himself feeling an odd sensation in his chest, one that he had nearly forgotten about.

It was pride. Perhaps the first he had felt in a long time.

"It was a good day," he finally said.

"That's good, because the only thing I can tell from all this blacked-out mess is that it was, allegedly, a day."

Mayflower's brow furrowed. The case was indeed the memory that Grimsby's RUIN had called forth, but why? There was perhaps a similarity, but nothing that he could directly compare. It was only as it ever had been: a hunch.

Janice was dead, of that alone he could be certain. After all, he had put the bullet through her head himself. He'd watched the wall turn red behind her. He had seen the light bleed from her eyes.

He had killed her, and he had slept heavy that same night.

So why was it now bothering him so?

"I'm guessing the Department didn't leave in the part about what Janice's ritual was meant to do?"

"No, that's practically double-censored. Guess they don't want anyone trying to replicate it."

"Maybe. Any way to get the original?"

"Leslie Mayflower!" Finley said, faking appearing aghast. "To do such a thing would be strictly against Departmental policy! And would take a few hours, give or take bathroom breaks." She winked at him.

He nodded. "Thanks, Fin."

One screen began flashing repeatedly, and as Finley turned her attention to it, it revealed a map at her touch. "You can thank me again, because it looks like there's only two chances left for our ritualist to take their shot. The first one is tonight, the next is tomorrow. Still crunching ley-line calculations for tomorrow's, but there's only one spot our suspect could try their luck tonight."

He glanced at the map and nodded. "Thanks again, then. I better go get my witch."

TWENTY-THREE

G RIMSBY!" MAYFLOWER'S HARSH VOICE BARKED.

Grimsby shot upright, or tried to, but his wrinkled suit had grown tangled in the stiff sheets of his cot, causing him to tumble from the bed onto the ground in the dim light.

"I'm up, I'm up!" Grimsby mumbled, extracting himself from the blankets and wiping away a dab of drool on his chin. He adjusted his skewed glasses and looked up to see the Huntsman's towering form.

"Come on. Finley got us a lead on where the next ritual might happen."

Grimsby tried to shake the sleep from his head but succeeded only in giving himself a headache. "Already? That was fast."

"Fast? It's near dark."

"Dark?" Grimsby groaned. "I feel like I slept for twenty minutes."

"Make it up later. We need to get into position before the ritualist gets there." He turned and began striding away without another word, forcing Grimsby to scurry to keep up.

He shook his head, trying not to think about the warm, soft bed he was leaving behind.

It was only then that he noticed the haste in Mayflower's stride and the tenseness of his stance. Even his words had been unusually clipped and harsh, though it was only by degrees. Something was off about the man, but he didn't know what.

Dusk was heavy when they exited the Department into the humid summer evening. The Mystic River drenched the air with a thick curtain of dew, making sweat instantly prickle on Grimsby's temples and the small of his back beneath his suit.

They moved quickly through the lot of mirrorless black cars, like an assembly of dark beetles. Sticking out from the midst of them was Mayflower's rusted-out jeep, twice the height of the uniform shells around it.

Yet, when Mayflower didn't even sneer at the plastic cars around the old steel stallion, Grimsby knew something was definitely off.

They settled in and were on the road before Grimsby finally broke the silence. "Les?"

Mayflower grunted.

"Why did you come back to work this case?"

"It's a job."

"Yeah, but Grieves had a lot of jobs he would have given you. Why did you come back for this one?"

Mayflower slid the jeep onto the highway ramp, accelerating enough to make the old beast roar before it fell to a growl. He didn't seem like he would answer.

But Grimsby prodded on. "You've been odd ever since you came back."

"Odd how?"

"As in edgy. Tense."

Mayflower glanced over long enough to raise an obvious brow at him.

"I mean more than normal. Odd's Bodkin, Mayflower, you threatened a man's life after being back on the job for an afternoon."

The Huntsman's face darkened at that, but he still said nothing.

Grimsby turned his gaze to the road, trying hard to shape the fears that had been building in him into words. "There's something you're not telling me."

Again, silence from Mayflower.

"You—" Grimsby said. "You weren't going to come back, were you?"

"No," the answer finally came.

"So, why are you here?"

Mayflower took a breath, guiding the jeep through a knot in traffic while barely losing speed. "I worked a case, maybe twenty years ago. Thought it was finished. But now I think I was wrong."

"Twenty years ago?" Grimsby asked, trying to not think about the idea of Mayflower never returning. "You—you think the same person is responsible for this RUIN?"

He shook his head. "It'd be a pretty impressive trick, considering I shot her in the head the last time. The bald guy your Therian mentioned is probably one of her apprentices, if I had to guess. Trying to carry on her work."

"Her?"

"A witch named Janice. She was one of the dregs that rose to power after the Coven was wiped out back then."

Grimsby shuddered at the mention of the Coven. He had heard whispers about it before—an organized syndicate of witches who held themselves as superior to all other beings, Usuals and Unorthodox alike.

Fortunately, they were gone now.

"Last I saw her, she and her cronies had abducted a baby girl and were planning on sacrificing her to make Janice more powerful somehow—to make her Impetus stronger."

Grimsby paused, the idea sounding familiar. "How?" he asked. "By stealing the girl's Impetus?"

Mayflower frowned. "Maybe."

Grimsby's brow furrowed. The symbol he had seen on his folder earlier and Mrs. Ox's reaction to it came to mind. "I think I've heard about something like that, and recently."

"That's a hell of a coincidence. Where?"

"The Assessor, Mrs. Ox. She saw a symbol someone had written on my old folder and freaked out. Read it as *strygga*. Told me what it was."

"On your folder? Who the hell wrote it there?"

Grimsby started to say *Rayne*, then stopped himself. He wasn't sure it had been her, though it seemed likely. But even if he were sure, he certainly didn't know what that would mean. Had she kept looking into the case after Grieves had taken it from her? Had she found something on her own? Or was she involved in some other way?

Regardless, he could imagine a dozen ways Mayflower might react, and none of them were good.

"I—I'm not sure. I dug it out of the trash and found it with the symbol." While it wasn't technically a lie, it wasn't far off, but he had little choice. Mayflower wasn't exactly levelheaded about the situation, and if Rayne was somehow involved as more than an investigator, Grimsby needed to know the specifics before he let his gun-toting partner in on the truth.

The Huntsman's face shadowed with doubt as though he could tell Grimsby was holding back, but he didn't push the issue. "A strygga," he muttered. "That does sound familiar."

"You think that's what Janice was trying to do? Make herself into a strygga with that girl's Impetus?"

He shrugged. "Maybe so. In any case, it's hard to do much of anything without the back half of your skull." There was some grim satisfaction in his voice, though it felt a tinge hollow. "I shot her. We saved the girl. It was a good day, and I'll be damned if I let someone undo it."

"So," Grimsby said, realizing what Mayflower meant, "that's

why you came back. You think the RUIN is the same one that Janice tried back then?"

He nodded. "It's unfinished business."

"And once that's done, you're"—Grimsby tried not to let his voice choke or crack as he spoke, but failed—"also done?"

Mayflower sighed, keeping his hard eyes on the road. "Kid, I'm an old man. An old man with too much blood on his hands. And I— I don't—" The Huntsman seemed to lack for words, though this time not by choice. He shook his head. "It doesn't matter. After this, I'm through."

Grimsby felt his mouth grow dry, uncertain of what to say, but quite certain there was a monsoon in his guts.

"So," he finally croaked. "This is our first and last real case together."

Mayflower managed a dry chuckle. "Yeah, looks that way."

They both fell quiet. There wasn't anything more to say.

Grimsby sat up in his seat and tried to forget about everything that was twisting up inside him. He knew it wouldn't stay buried for long, but he refused to spoil the drive. The smell of sun-cracked leather, the rattle of rune-etched bars, and the sound of highway winds whistling through old bullet holes. He swallowed over the cracks that formed in his throat.

If his time with Mayflower was to be short, this was how he wanted to remember it.

TWENTY-FOUR

RAYNE WATCHED AS THE MASKED MAN REACHED OUT TO her, the mark on his cheek glowing just above the cloth that covered the lower half of his face. His head was bald, threaded with thin veins that wormed through his scalp. In his hand he held out a smooth stone with a hole worn through its center, though through it she saw not his palm, but soft red light. His eyes were distant, yet strangely familiar, and they seemed to bore beyond her, seeing things she couldn't fathom, or perhaps seeing nothing at all.

She tried to speak, to step away and ready her magic to defend herself, but her body didn't listen. Instead, she only watched as she reached out and took the stone from his palm. Her autonomous hand held up the pinhole to her eye, and beyond she saw long, dark corridors, their walls and ceilings ribbed with arches of skeletal stone.

Her stomach twisted in nausea as her hand pulled the stone away. Then she felt her own body start—as though a jolt of electricity had gone through her.

Her head slowly turned until her eyes fell to the ground, where a pool of stagnant water rippled from idle drips from the low ceiling. As the water settled, her reflection settled with it, though it was not her face staring back at her.

Before she could see its features, however, her own foot rose and stomped the water away.

Suddenly, she felt like stones were being laid on top of her, crushing her down into herself. She felt herself falling, pressed into darkness by some unknown force.

Then, nothing.

RAYNE SHOT UPRIGHT, NEARLY CATCHING HER FOREHEAD ON the metal supports of the bunk above her. Sweat plastered her brow, making her sweep her wild hair back. She was afraid for a moment that her hands were still not her own.

This time, fortunately, they obeyed.

She collected her stray hair and pulled it back into a tight ponytail. Cool air seethed over her sweat-dampened scalp, and she finally let herself take a shuddering breath.

The bunkroom was still dark and empty. How long had she slept? She glared at her digital watch. Somehow the alarm she had set had been disabled. Perhaps she had done so herself, tossing on the stiff, narrow mattress in her restless sleep.

Her mind turned back to the masked man, his vacant yet piercing stare, the glowing rune on his cheek.

Ordinarily, she would have dismissed it as a simple dream, but ever since her dream of the RUIN case turned out to be far more real than she was comfortable with, she couldn't help but wonder if this stranger was more than just a figment of her own mind.

But if so, who was he? And what was he doing in her dreams?

She shook her head. Perhaps her extended rest had given Defaux time to find some answers, if not about the dreams, then at least about Hives. Either way, it was time to get back to work.

She pried herself from the hard bed, discarding the thin sheet before stretching her aching back. Her head felt like it was made of lead, and the stems of her eyes thrummed with thready pain. She felt the urge to lie back down but pushed it away. Sleep had given her no peace for months, and she doubted it would until she laid her twin concerns to rest.

Light hammered her eyes as she exited the barracks into the fluorescently lit halls. She hadn't meant to sleep so long. Most of the other personnel would be gone, or working late, though there were a fair few Analysts and Agents who worked the night shift.

She made her way to her office, her footsteps echoing in the long halls. The only other people she saw were a pair of Agents who nodded at her, their eyes covered by the shaded glasses that gave them a poor imitation of witchsight. She returned the gesture, though it ended up being more curt than she meant. She tried to soften it with a smile, but the expression was drawn and taut.

As they passed, she shook her head. She paused in front of her office door, pressing a hand to her brow to collect herself. She despised how tense and brittle she felt, like sidewalk chalk being ground to the nub. When had simple, casual things become so difficult? The stresses of both the RUIN and Hives felt like they were twin ropes, each tied to her limbs, slowly prying her apart.

"Control yourself," she scolded quietly.

"Self-control is overrated," a voice said behind her, far too close.

Her heart skipped and she whirled around to see Defaux smiling at her.

"Don't—do that!" Rayne said, her tone sharp, though this time it was intended.

Defaux raised her hands in a defusing gesture. "My mistake!" she said, though her smile made no apologies. "You look radiant. Have a good nap?"

Rayne's primary reply was a scowl. She took a deep breath, reminding herself that though Defaux was both somewhat annoying and from the New York branch, she was still her only ally. She opened her office door, holding it for Defaux. "Have any luck looking into my . . . problem?"

Defaux performed an exaggerated curtsy before she stepped through the door. "How gallant! Chivalry isn't dead after all."

"It'll become a casualty if I don't get some coffee," she said, then more quietly: "And it might not be the only thing."

Defaux snorted and sat on the edge of Rayne's desk while she did her best to rinse the burnt ring from the base of the coffeepot before filling it from the water cooler.

"You want any?" Rayne asked.

Defaux shrugged, picking up Hives's badge from the desk and studying it. "No, I just like the way it smells."

Rayne frowned but didn't push the issue. As far as she knew, most other Agents and Auditors, as well as the whole Department, ran on coffee, with the occasional tea-consuming heathen. Caffeine simply helped with magic.

But perhaps things worked differently in New York.

The machine gurgled and groaned, and the smell of roasted grounds filled the office. Immediately, she felt her aching head begin to subside, perhaps in anticipation of oncoming caffeine. Maybe she had a problem, but now was not the time to cut herself off. She waited a painstaking moment for Defaux to say something, anything, about the RUIN case, but instead she just fiddled with the badge and remained infuriatingly silent.

"Did you have any luck?" Rayne asked again. "With the RUIN? With Hives? Anything?"

Defaux let out a sigh that was almost childish. "Well, there's good news and bad news."

"What's the bad news?"

"What? No, I don't start with bad news. The good news is that statistically speaking, nine out of ten RUIN cases go unsolved."

Rayne pinched the bridge of her nose as though it might help contain her boiling anger. "And what's the bad news?"

"The bad news is that my sources had no light to shed on the RUIN. However, that news might not be all that bad."

"What? What part of potentially ending my career isn't bad news?"

"Costa Rica is beautiful this time of year?" Defaux offered, though she rolled her eyes when it didn't even draw a snort from Rayne. "I think you may be overestimating the danger of this RUIN case."

"How so?" Rayne asked. She flexed her fingers repeatedly, making her knuckles crack. It seemed a more productive use of energy than strangling Defaux at the moment, though only just.

"Think about it. What's the more likely scenario here? That you're somehow subconsciously bound to a failed ritual that was probably just some teenager trying his luck summoning a succubus or something, or that you're so strained by the stresses of your search for Auditor Hives that it's manifesting in other ways, such as odd dreams?"

Rayne balked at that. She hadn't ever really stopped to consider that perhaps her tie to the ritual was only in her own mind. "But—but I woke up there! I saw it!"

"Perhaps." Defaux shrugged, crossing one leg over the other as she sat on the edge of Rayne's desk. "Or perhaps your sleep-deprived brain simply found some loose parallels and connected the dots. It's basically déjà vu."

"So you're saying I'm going crazy?"

Defaux grinned. "Crazy is a *very* relative term. But, if *you're* not even sure if you were there or not, how can anyone here tie you to the RUIN in the first place?"

Rayne glared but said nothing. What was there to say?

If Defaux was right, it would be a great burden gone from her shoulders, though that alone made it seem implausible. But even if she was right, that still brought forth the worrying thought that she might not be able to trust her own head.

God, that coffee really needed to hurry up.

"It's a moot point," Rayne finally said. "There's no way to prove one way or the other—unless it's too late to do anything about it."

"Precisely. Which is why you should concern yourself with the spell to track Hives. Let us focus our efforts on that, and once it's taken care of, we can look back into your RUIN case if it's still unnerving you so."

The coffeepot finally drizzled to a halt, and Rayne wasted no time in pouring the brew into her mug that read MAGIC BEANS. It had been a gift from Grimsby when he joined the Department. A gift *he* had given *her* after his long-awaited employment.

And she had gotten him nothing in return.

She wrapped her hands around the warm ceramic, letting the heat soak into her aching fingers. Maybe Grimsby hadn't been as cruel as she first thought. Maybe her mind had simply colored him wicked for taking her case because of her stress—

She shook her head forcefully.

Defaux was right. Her attention was divided, and in more ways than one. It had been undermining her for too long. She needed focus. Clarity. That was always when she was at her best.

Just then, the hurried rush of boots sounded outside her door. Heavy knocks rattled suddenly against the glass. She nearly dropped her mug in surprise; the sudden dread that perhaps the RUIN had been dealt with and somehow it had condemned her filled her mind. She held the thought at bay and made herself calmly set the mug down before going to her door.

She opened it to see one of the Analysts she vaguely recognized. The young woman was limber, dressed in apparel that was only by the loosest of definitions Department-appropriate. But it was her hair that Rayne most recognized. It was dyed in a dazzling hue of colors that looked to have been both an investment and a waste of time and money. The boots she had heard were the woman's spiked black platform shoes.

"Yes?" she asked, brow raised.

The Analyst was breathless, resting her hands on her knees; a silver necklace with a small amulet in the shape of a half heart dangled from around her neck. "Auditor Bathory—" she panted. "You're friends with Grimsby, right?"

Rayne bit her lip. "That's a bit ambivalent at the moment. Why?"

The woman handed her a sheet of paper, still warm from whatever machine had printed it. Rayne scanned it and saw it was an alert from the Asylum—the facility that contained dangerous Unorthodox when necessary. One of their expected attendees had not arrived. They had requested a task force to be dispatched to collect him.

She frowned. "What does this have to do with Grimsby?" she asked.

The woman finally caught her breath and threw back her rainbow mane. Her face was an unusual mixture of sharp angles and freckles. "It's one of Grimsby's guys—a Therian he's responsible for," she said. "If he goes beast-mode and hurts anybody—"

"Then Grimsby will be held accountable," Rayne said, taking a deep breath. She frowned at the notice. The dispatch team would be slow to gather at this time of night. If Grimsby hurried, he might be able to get to the Therian in time and collect him before anything went wrong.

If he even knew something could go wrong in the first place.

Anyway, why should she care? He had taken her case from her; he had betrayed her trust, though perhaps it hadn't been wholly intentional.

"You shouldn't go," Defaux said from behind her.

She turned to see the New York Auditor had picked up her mug of coffee and was inhaling the fumes.

"If you're truly worried about him"—she paused to glance at the Analyst—"digging up trouble, then this is the perfect distraction. Let him deal with the problem on his own. It'll give us time."

Defaux was right. With Therian troubles to distract him, Grimsby would be less likely to be able to focus on the RUIN case. He would have more pressing concerns—like internal questioning, or chastisement from Grieves.

Or he might be too injured to pursue the RUIN.

Maybe worse.

It was, perhaps, the first stroke of fortune she'd had in months, and it had cost her nothing.

Though it might cost Grimsby dearly.

For a moment, it was all tactical; all she had to do was take the Analyst's report and delay for longer than was strictly necessary. All she had to do was nothing.

Then her eyes fell to the mug in Defaux's hands.

MAGIC BEANS.

Rayne felt her stomach twist, and it was like a splash of cold water over her mind.

The tactical value of the situation evaporated. Logic crumbled and fell by the wayside.

Grimsby needed help.

Her eyes met Defaux's, and the New York Auditor's face darkened, though she said nothing.

Rayne turned back to the Analyst to see her looking confused, glancing behind her toward the desk and back again.

"All right," Rayne finally said, "where is Grimsby?"

TWENTY-FIVE

T HE JEEP GROUND TO A HALT OVER THE CHIPPED RE-
mains of sun-scoured pavement. Grimsby could taste the
salt in the air from the nearby bay, and with it the accompanying
stagnant smell of polluted water that made his stomach cringe.

Mayflower gestured past the edge of the streetlight's glow to
an old warehouse close to the waterfront, its corrugated walls
corroded to brittle honeycombs of rust. "Fin says that's the
place," he said. He seemed relaxed, but his brow was pulled taut
into decades of well-worn frown lines.

Grimsby eyed the broken windows of the warehouse as they
seemed to return his gaze. "It's always someplace abandoned or
run-down," he said, trying to suppress a shiver. "Why can't bad
things ever happen in the nice part of town?"

"Maybe it's abandoned *because* it's an intersect for ley lines.
The magic probably scared people off."

Grimsby frowned, though he figured his own frown lines
were much younger than his partner's. There wasn't anything
magic about this place, at least not to him. To him, magic was what
kept him safe. It was what gave him some small control in his life.
It was what gave him a path to follow: to become an Auditor.

This place was dark. It was cold. It wasn't his kind of magic.

Yet somehow it was magic all the same.

He felt for the cold iron of the nail in his pocket. Maybe he was simply wrong about what magic was. He couldn't even trust his own spells right now. What did he know of magic?

Would he even be ready to face the ritualist if they found him?

He shook away the thought. He had managed to find a use for this foreign magic before, both to escape the Geists in the Elsewhere and to pass Mrs. Ox's trial, all despite the nail's strange effects. He could do it again if he needed to.

Hopefully.

He was so wrapped up in his growing anxiety that he hadn't realized Mayflower had exited the jeep until the door slammed. He quickly followed suit but was slightly gentler with the door. The jeep had always been good to him, after all.

Mayflower had parked in a shadowed alley, well away from the warehouse, likely to keep the jeep from view of their would-be ritualist.

"Let's move," he said. "I want to find a good place to hole up before full dark."

"What makes you think whoever we're after isn't here yet?"

"I've dealt with Janice and her kind before. They're cowards. Whoever this ritualist is, he'll wait until it's dark, do his deeds, and try to vanish before dawn finds him."

"You make them sound like monsters."

He scoffed. "If only. Monsters are much simpler to deal with than people." His face grew grim. "Much simpler."

Mayflower led the way to the warehouse, his stride long and confident. Grimsby followed, casting furtive glances all around. The Huntsman seemed certain the place would be empty, but Grimsby was less sure. Whoever they were after had been able to avoid being found so far. That meant he was smart, and if he was smart, he might know they were out here looking for him.

It would make a fine trap.

The warehouse doors had been closed once, but the hinges had rusted off in the brine-drenched air, leaving the doors hanging at awkward angles. Mayflower peered in, then nodded to Grimsby to follow him inside. Grimsby wasn't even certain the structure had ever held electric lights, but if it had, they'd all burned out. The only light was what managed to splay through the dusty windows just below the roof, allowing little more than shafts of dim luminescence and stark shadows inside.

"This place looks like it's about to collapse," Grimsby muttered.

Almost as if in response, a breeze blew in from over the bay, and the warehouse groaned and creaked. Grimsby gulped, hoping he was wrong.

"I don't care," Mayflower said, "as long as it stands up until I find this guy and end this for good."

Grimsby's stomach turned again, though this time it was because of more than just fear. For a moment, he had forgotten that this would be his only case alongside Mayflower. But that moment was gone, and now even his looming worries turned to worries of a different, less immediate sort.

"Are you sure about retiring, Les? I know I'd feel much better if you had my back."

"I'm sure," he growled. "There's a catwalk up there. That's where we'll set up."

"It's just—what will you do with yourself after you're done with all this?" Grimsby asked. He couldn't imagine the Huntsman without a hunt.

"I'll do what I did before I met you in the first place."

"Day drink and brood?"

Mayflower growled again but didn't disagree as he mounted the rickety steps toward the catwalk.

Grimsby gripped the rusted handrail tightly as he followed,

focusing his attention on the Huntsman's back. "You could be saving lives!"

Mayflower tensed but said nothing.

"You're good at this—" he began, but Mayflower froze mid-stride and whipped around.

"I'm not good—!" he snapped, then seemed to bite his words back. After a moment, his voice dropped to a whisper. "I'm not good."

"What are you talking about? You're a good man, Les, I—"

"Sixty-three," he said, the number choking his throat like a noose.

"What?"

"Sixty-three. That's how many—" He seemed like he wanted to trail off, but he gritted his teeth and hissed the words. "That's how many I've killed. Men. Women. Monsters. And worse."

Grimsby didn't know what to say; he wasn't even sure he could understand, but he tried to find something helpful to fumble out of his mouth. "I'm sure you had no other choice."

"I always had a choice, kid," Mayflower said. "Sometimes it was as simple as me or them. Usually not. Some days I wonder if I made the right call. Most days, I think I didn't."

"Les . . ."

"I'm a killer, Grimsby. It's the only thing I've ever been worth a damn at. And after today, the body count will be sixty-four, and that's where it'll stay."

"Wait—you don't mean you plan to kill this guy?"

"This guy, someone else, hell, even the goddamned pope. Whoever shows up to do this ritual, I'm going to put them down and then go home."

"No, no way! You can't just murder them! We have to arrest them. Take them to the Department to stand trial."

"They tried this shit twenty years ago and meant to kill a baby girl to do it. There's no need for a trial. Hell, putting a bullet through Janice's skull was one of the few things I've done that doesn't keep me up at night."

Grimsby shook his head. "I can't let you do that!"

"*Let* me?" Mayflower asked, suddenly seeming much taller and darker than he had just a moment ago. "It's not your call to make."

Grimsby felt small, but he also felt heat begin to boil in his stomach. Sparks snapped from his scars, snuffed from life by his sleeve. "We're partners. Whether you like it or not, we're in this together. What you do, I do."

"No," Mayflower said firmly, his eyes locking Grimsby's down for a moment. "*I'm* pulling the trigger. *I'm* the one responsible, understand?"

"Not anymore, Les. You're not a lone Huntsman. You're my partner, and if you hurt someone, that's on me, too." He felt welling guilt in his stomach, and his voice grew quiet. "I still have nightmares about Peters—about killing him."

"That wasn't you. I killed him."

"Did you?" Grimsby asked. "Does it even matter? I was the one that—" His voice choked at the vivid memory of Peters flayed and gutted by his own familiars, turned against him by Grimsby. "Even if you pulled the trigger before his heart stopped, he would have died because of what I did. Does that make me any less a killer?"

Mayflower's face darkened, but his mouth twisted in a sickened expression. He turned away toward the dim interior of the warehouse below and said no more.

Time passed, and Grimsby anxiously let it go by. The twilight deepened to darkness, and the only sound came from the water nearby, splashing against concrete retaining walls before receding once more.

The Huntsman lurked beside him, his expression hidden in the dark but his posture looming and unwavering, like a statue of an executioner.

Then he finally spoke.

"That's why I can't stay on as your partner," he said quietly, as if to himself.

Grimsby almost didn't reply. He was afraid that if he did, he might startle Mayflower off. "Why not?"

"Because you're a good kid," he said, the words sounding like great weights on his voice, "and if I stay, you might end up like me." He turned, and his hard eyes caught a glint of faded streetlight from the broken windows. "Don't ever end up like me, Grimsby."

Grimsby's mouth fell agape, but silent. He tried to imagine himself like Mayflower—grizzled, bitter, and dangerous—but he simply couldn't picture it. It was like trying to imagine dry water. Maybe that was for the best.

Or maybe it was inevitable.

Before he could say anything, the sound of wheels grinding over gravel came from outside. They both tensed, then hunched deeper into the dark.

Grimsby felt sweat tinge his temples and dampen his shirt. His heart quickened, and suddenly even his oversize suit felt too tight. Was this their ritualist? He tried to steel himself, but it was all he could do to keep still, lest the rickety catwalk reveal their position.

The headlights poured into the broken doors of the warehouse, making Grimsby squint and shield his eyes. The wheels ground to a halt, though the quiet engine continued. He heard a door open, then the approach of footsteps.

A figure appeared, backlit by headlights, slender and fetching. Almost familiar.

Grimsby felt his palms sweat within his clenched fists, and he began to drum up his Impetus, feeling it well within him like a torch in his stomach.

Beside him, Mayflower's steady hand drew his revolver, thumbing back the hammer until it locked, ready to fire.

A woman stepped forward, looking around; then she cast her gaze up at them.

Grimsby's eyes finally adjusted to the light, and he saw not just a familiar figure, but a familiar face, too.

It was Rayne. She must have seen them as well.

"Boys," she called up to them, "we have a problem."

TWENTY-SIX

R AYNE?" GRIMSBY CALLED FROM THE CATWALK. "WHAT are you doing here?"

Mayflower growled, "You're giving away our whole stakeout."

"There's no time for that," she said, taking a few steps through the empty warehouse toward them, her shadow cast large by the bright headlights of her car. "One of the Therians you're responsible for, Samuel Goode, has missed his Asylum deadline, Grimsby."

Grimsby gulped, feeling his skin grow cold. The Asylum was the only place that was sure to safely contain Therians when they transformed. If one transformed beyond its reinforced cells, they could go on an uncontrollable rampage.

Goode was one of many Therians who had a spotless record of attendance, and so it was standard procedure to simply contact them before the full moon and make certain they were aware of and capable of performing their obligations.

If he hadn't shown up, that meant something was wrong.

And it might get much worse if they didn't find him quickly.

"Mayflower," he said, turning to the Huntsman, "we have to find him before he transforms and hurts someone."

The Huntsman scowled at the gun in his hand, his taut brow burdened in thought. Finally, as Grimsby stood and began to go, he heard the Huntsman utter a single word.

"No."

Grimsby froze, then half turned. "What do you mean *no*?"

"I told you, Grimsby. This is my last case. *This* case, right here. We find and stop the ritualist. I'm not getting dragged off target by some fool who missed his deadline."

"But—but someone could get hurt!"

"People always get hurt, boy. Hell, that's all our job is: hurting the right people."

"No, our job is to help people! And right now, there's a real person who needs our help."

"Help?" the Huntsman demanded, his iron grip making the catwalk creak. "How are you going to help him when he shifts? By putting silver in his heart? Because that's what the Department will do," he called down to Rayne in his gruff voice. "Isn't that right, Auditor?"

Her face twisted into a glower as she looked to him. "That's why I'm here. Grimsby, we have a small window before Goode changes and the Department strike team arrives. If we can get him to the Asylum before then—"

Mayflower scoffed. "Focus, Grimsby. We have a job to do, here and now. Whatever this ritual is, it isn't good. I can feel it. People are going to get hurt unless we stop that before it happens."

Grimsby froze, realizing both Rayne and Mayflower were looking to him.

It was his choice, and he had to make it now.

He shook his head, feeling like his blood was pressing against his skin like air in a balloon. The room was all at once too hot and too cold, and someone omnipotent and sadistic had decided to start it spinning.

What was he to do? Stay and hunt the witch who had some unknown ritual of ill intent in mind, or go and find Samuel Goode before he turned into something terrible and did something worse? Both would likely save lives. Both were his responsibility. Both were the right thing to do.

But he could only choose one.

"I'm—I'm going after Goode," he finally said, the words like clay in his mouth.

"What?" Mayflower asked, his tone quiet.

"I can either stop a bad guy or help a good guy. I just—" His voice caught in his chest as he weathered Mayflower's fiery gaze. "I want to help."

"And what about the ritualist? What if he does something a hundred times worse than what Goode does?"

"Then—then I'll deal with that, too. But I won't sacrifice Goode to do it." He looked at the Huntsman and saw anger in his eyes, but also something more lonely. "Come with me, Les. Please."

Doubt shadowed the Huntsman's expression, then cleared away like the sun setting behind a stormy horizon. "No. I have a job to do, and so do you. We need to stop this ritual."

The words struck like a blow to Grimsby's gut, but he had expected them. As much as he wanted the Huntsman's aid, he knew Mayflower could not waver from his hunt. It was simply who he was.

And this was who Grimsby was.

He turned away and began descending the steps to Rayne.

"Grimsby!" Mayflower said, his gruff voice strained. "What are you doing?"

"I'm doing what you told me to," he said as he paused on the steps but didn't look back. "I'm not ending up like you."

Mayflower was silent as Grimsby continued down the stairs. His head was still spinning, and his neck was alight with nervous heat and sweat, but as he reached the ground, he felt his stride grow steadier. He realized this was his first real chance to help someone as an Auditor, and he was ready.

Well, almost.

He hurried to Rayne, his heart pounding, his blood rushing. "Can—can I get a ride?"

Her harsh expression cracked for a moment, and she let slip a short chuckle. "Of course."

TWENTY-SEVEN

GRIMSBY SHIFTED UNCOMFORTABLY ON THE DARK LEA-
ther seat as Rayne sped toward Sam Goode's address. He
wasn't sure how she could see anything through the dark-tinted
windows, but she seemed to manage. He wanted to focus on finding Goode, but he kept hearing Mayflower's voice calling after
him, and kept seeing the lonely spark in the Huntsman's eyes.

He shook his head, trying to distract himself. "Nice wheels.
Hope to have my own someday," he said, glancing at the display
screen at the car's center console. In lieu of mirrors, Department
vehicles used cameras. Mirrors were too dangerous.

Rayne's eyes were focused on the road. The lenses of her
glasses, unlike his own, were flat and non-corrective. They were
purely to give her a mask to shield her from the Elsewhere, though
her Department-issued ballistic mask lay in her lap. "I didn't even
know you could drive," she said, her voice distant, almost automatic.

"Well, not legally, no. And also not really practically, either.
Never had the opportunity to learn. I thought maybe after I got
my badge, they'd give me a car, but . . ." He trailed off.

"You're not there yet," Rayne said. "Grieves may have made you an Auditor, but there's a lot you haven't earned." Her tone was flat, but the words felt as sharp as knives.

Grimsby winced, feeling a little like his chest was caving in on itself. "So everyone keeps reminding me."

"That—came out wrong," she said, casting a glance at him and letting slip a soft smile. "Give it time, Grimshaw. They don't know you yet, but they will."

He tried to smile back, but his mouth was uncooperative.

That's what I'm afraid of, he thought.

He wasn't even sure *he* knew himself yet. What if time showed he was just as lacking as they had expected him to be? He likely wouldn't even have succeeded at Mrs. Ox's trial if not for the nail in his pocket, as his usual spells would have been unsuited to the task. Then he had turned his back on his partner, leaving him alone in a potentially dangerous situation.

Neither felt particularly Auditor-worthy of him.

Nor had his treatment of Rayne and taking her case, unintentionally or not. Maybe there was a reason he hadn't yet earned his place.

"So," he said, "any new leads in your search for Hives?"

"Maybe," she said, then stopped like she'd caught herself slipping. "We're not sure."

"We? Did Grieves assign you a new partner?" he asked, feeling a small burn of envy in his chest.

"Not exactly. A New York Auditor offered to help me. She's . . . odd, but I think she means well."

"A New Yorker? What's she doing in Boston?"

"Helping me," she said. "Near as I can tell, Auditor Defaux is the only other person who seems to give enough of a damn to lend a hand." The words weren't so sharp that Grimsby felt they were aimed at him, but he still pictured himself in their crosshairs all the same.

"Ah. Well, if you need a third pair of hands, or eyes, or . . . whatever, I'm happy to lend mine."

She snorted but gave him a smirk. "Let's hope we still have access to all our limbs by the time we get Goode to the Asylum."

Grimsby nodded, casting a nervous glance outside the car, where the moon shone bright, though it wasn't full as he had expected it to be. "Are we sure Goode will transform?"

Rayne nodded. "Therians differ on when they shift, but it's tied to the lunar cycle. Most, like Goode, begin to risk shifting when the moon reaches its apex. It might not be immediate, but stress or strong emotions can trigger the transformation earlier than expected." She glanced at the digital clock on the console. "I'd guess we have less than an hour before that risk becomes a concern."

"So you think we can get him to the Asylum before he shifts at all?"

She nodded. "With some luck. We just have to find him and keep him calm until we can get him into containment."

Grimsby tried to push down the lump of nerves that had grown knotted in his stomach, but it seemed reluctant to budge. He fidgeted with the iron nail in his pocket instead. Luck wasn't exactly something he had in spades today.

But perhaps that would finally turn around.

Surely it had to eventually, right?

He straightened up as they entered Goode's now-familiar neighborhood. The stark moonlight made the sporadic streetlamps pointless, though many of their bulbs were flickering or had burned out altogether. He saw light in the windows of the passing homes, the figures inside going about their lives, and his mouth went dry.

If Goode shifted, everyone nearby would be in danger. Civilians as much as he and Rayne. And right now, the only people who could protect those civilians were him and Rayne. The thought made his pulse thready, but he felt glad to have Rayne with him. She was a practiced witch—a real Auditor. Smart and powerful.

So what did that make him?

He tried to cast the thought away but felt it cling to his fingers as much as the nail in his pocket would have. Instead, he could only set the idea aside and try to focus. The Department car ground to a halt outside Goode's address.

"This the place?" Rayne asked.

Grimsby nodded, peering at the brick house. The rickety patio shaded the front door from the moonlight, but he could just barely tell it was ajar. "That's probably not a good sign," he said, gesturing to the entrance.

Rayne nodded and then screwed shut her eyes, deftly exchanging her glasses for the ballistic mask in her lap. She looked back to Grimsby, and he squirmed uncomfortably under her guised gaze. "Ready?" she asked.

"As I can be," he said, and they both climbed out of the mirrorless vehicle.

The wind seemed to pick up as they did, cutting clear through Grimsby's ill-fitting suit. The few trees in the neighborhood were sickly or dead; their bare branches croaked and creaked against one another in the otherwise quiet night.

They made their way over the cracked walkway that split the small, barren yard in two. Rayne stepped lithely up the stairs, her stride barely drawing a groan from the old timbers. Grimsby's own steps seemed to make the boards scream by comparison.

The door was open, and the dangling chains of Goode's many dead bolts and locks hung from its split frame. The door itself looked like it had nearly buckled, and the hinges that held it in place did so by thin threads of mangled screws.

"He must have broken out," Rayne said, her whisper somehow unmuffled by the mask. She cast a glance over her shoulder, scanning the moonlit night.

"Or someone else broke in," Grimsby said, pointing at the splinters of wood that littered the inside of the home, rather than the outside.

She thought for a moment, then nodded, holding up her clenched hand. She stared in brief concentration until Grimsby felt her Impetus begin to radiate from her. It was like a bass that was too deep to hear, but he felt it press against his skin like a taut sheet.

Rayne then glanced at him expectantly.

He felt his heart speed up and his veins grow tight. Neither she, nor anyone else, knew of the cursed nail in his pocket and the effect it was having on his magic. Eyes aflame, even *he* didn't fully know what it was doing, only that it was making his spells behave strangely. He couldn't trust his own magic until Wudge found a way to remove the thing, yet what good was he here without it? Totally unarmed, he'd be unable to protect himself or help Rayne against whatever they might find.

No, even though he couldn't be sure of what his magic might do, he couldn't just forgo it altogether. He was a witch, after all.

He followed her lead, drawing forth his own Impetus, like stoking a furnace in his heart. Its heat flowed through him like a second set of veins. He felt his scars prickle under his sleeve, and those that showed on his left hand smoldered dimly in the shadows of the porch.

"All right," he said.

"Samuel Goode!" Rayne called into the broken threshold. "Department Auditors! Come out with your hands visible."

There was no reply from the darkness, though that was not exactly a comfort to Grimsby. Rayne took the lead and stepped through, and Grimsby did what he could to look just as professional when he followed her. He promptly stepped on her heel, drawing a wince of breath, though she made no comment.

The inside of Goode's home was as dark as fresh pavement.

The covered windows kept the bright moonlight at bay, and their only light to see by was cast by flickering night-lights that had been placed in sparse outlets.

They crept cautiously around the first floor, but there was no sign of Goode or anyone else.

"I don't like this," Rayne said, sweeping her foot over the ground. It seemed to be littered with dust.

"You're just now not liking this? Never thought I'd be ahead of you in something." He forced an uncomfortable chuckle.

"This Therian is a reagent dealer, right?"

Grimsby nodded. "Yeah, we think he might be tied to the RUIN case."

Rayne's eyes darkened beneath her featureless white mask. "And you didn't mention this before?"

"Well, I—"

"Forget it," she said, her mind seeming to churn behind her eyes. "Let's just find him."

Grimsby nodded, looking about, until his attention fell upon another stretch of dust, illuminated by a thin shaft of moonlight that slipped through the tinfoil-covered windows. The dust had the vague outline of a smeared print in it, one that seemed to be moving toward a solid wall. He approached it, leaving Rayne raising a curious brow, and felt about the wallpapered surface carefully. Sure enough, his fingers found a straight line, invisible in the dark but clear enough on his fingertips.

"I think I found something," he said.

Rayne made a slightly impressed sound. "Well done," she said. Her tone summoned a burning sensation to Grimsby's cheeks, one he hoped would be hidden in the dark.

After fumbling for a moment, he found a latch. A swift flick and the wall creaked as it receded enough to be slid aside, revealing a staircase downward.

"Stay here," Rayne said, stepping forward. "I'll check it out."

"Stay here?" Grimsby demanded. "You can't go alone!"

"One of us needs to keep watch. I don't want to be trapped down there if Goode shows up behind us with more fur and claws than he ought to have."

"And what if he, or whoever busted in here, is down there?"

Her masked eyes creased in an infuriating smile. "Then it'll be a good thing you've kept my escape route secured."

Grimsby wanted to argue, but before he could, Rayne descended the steps into the dark and vanished.

He glowered after her for a moment, then turned his eyes to the rest of the house, keeping his ears focused on her departing footsteps.

Suddenly, with Grimsby now alone, the house felt somehow larger and more looming. The shadowed corners they had already cleared appeared full of menace, like something might crawl out of them at any minute. He tried to stay calm and aware, but his nerves kept getting the better of him. He twisted and jerked at every creak or whisper, expecting to see the hulking figure of the shifted Goode at any moment.

He was so focused on looking for the beastly silhouette that it came as a complete surprise when he turned to see a woman standing beside him.

One who wasn't Rayne.

He saw only the outline of her wild hair, but before he could utter a sound, she lashed out as fast as a viper.

He heard himself hit the ground more than felt it. Even as she dragged him out of the house and into the moonlight, he felt little more than a thundering in his skull and a pain behind his eyes.

Then the world went blissfully dark.

TWENTY-EIGHT

MAYFLOWER GLOWERED INTO THE DARKENED WARE-house from his post on the catwalk. The only light came from the near-full moon, pouring through dusty windows to cast long shadows over cracked concrete.

The storehouse was almost silent, and he found himself keenly aware of the lack of idle scuffling and breathing sounds that had once told of Grimsby's presence beside him. Maybe he shouldn't have let the kid go after that Therian without him. The moon seemed to wax even more, as though gloating, affirming his worries.

He stifled a growl and made himself focus on the entrance; the doors were slightly ajar after Grimsby and Rayne's departure. The ritualist could enter at any moment. He needed to be collected. He needed to be ready.

He needed to finish what he had started.

He couldn't afford to let Grimsby's naive decision distract him.

Yet it did anyway.

Questions flooded his mind, drawing forth fearful scenarios that made his gut twist. What if the Therian shifted before they contained him? What if it was too much for the two Auditors to handle? What if the Department arrived too late?

He growled again, resisting the urge to reach for a cigarette to chew on. He had always hated the words *what if*. They were shadows on the wall, meaningless drivel for the frightened to dwell upon while they let themselves remain blissfully powerless.

But he was not powerless. He had made a choice.

But now that choice threatened consequences.

Grimsby was his responsibility. If it wasn't for Mayflower's agreement to work for the Department, Grieves would have let the kid stay in squalor. He hadn't seen the potential Mayflower had—or if he had, he had also seen the potential leverage Grimsby represented over the old Huntsman.

Either way, he had returned, and Grimsby had received a badge.

Lord knew the boy earned it, but whether he was ready for it or not was another question altogether. It was no secret that Grimsby was not a powerful witch, even Mayflower could see that, but he was more stalwart than near any Mayflower had known, save perhaps Mansgraf herself.

But it was more than just that.

Grimsby had something in him that Mayflower had rarely seen before. Something that usually died in most other folks he knew, without them ever realizing they'd had it to begin with.

He had no word for it, but he could feel it, as sure as sunlight on a bleak day.

But whatever that special glow was, it wouldn't save Grimsby from being torn apart by a Therian, let alone any of the other threats Auditors faced on a regular basis. And if Grimsby got hurt or—or worse, it would be because Mayflower put him in that position to begin with.

Yet he had another obligation as well, one to the past. Many, or rather most, of his hunts had turned ugly. He wished he could say that he had saved more lives than he'd taken, but it was rare that he was able to stop the bad things before they happened. Instead, he had to learn to settle for stopping them from happening again.

Janice and her ritual had been one of those rare victories. The bad guy had been stopped, the innocent saved. The good guys had won, no strings attached. It had been simple. Clean. It had been *good*.

God, that was all too rare.

But it seemed the case hadn't been as simple as he had thought. It hadn't been clean, and there had been strings attached after all. They were just so long and buried so deep that he had missed them. But now they were back, growing tauter by the moment.

If he didn't cut them now, who knew what they might drag up from the mire of the past. Whatever ill intent this ritual held, good folks would get hurt.

They always did when magic was involved.

If he failed to cut those threads, and Janice's old work was finished, his long past dues would come back to be paid.

He needed to lay this case to rest, once and for all. No matter the cost.

But what if the cost was Grimsby's life?

Mayflower didn't need light or a mirror to know his skin had gone pale.

He'd left the boy to face a Therian, after all. He might not have been alone, but Mayflower didn't know Rayne. She might be decent. She might not. Either way, one thing was sure:

She wasn't Grimsby's partner.

Mayflower was, and he had left Grimsby alone.

His guts made a groaning sound, quiet but amplified by the total silence around him. He had wanted to retire from his profession of killing, but what if Grimsby died because Mayflower had lost the stomach to wield a gun? If that happened, the blame would, and should, fall on the Huntsman.

If Grimsby died on the job tonight, it was because Mayflower had allowed it to happen.

He cast one last glance at the gap in the doors, but no shadow dimmed the strip of moonlight that pooled in the dark. It could come at any moment, or it might not reveal itself at all.

Mayflower shook his head and spat onto the catwalk.

The past had waited near twenty years. It could wait a while longer.

He stood, old bones creaking, and headed to the stairs. If he hurried, he wouldn't be far behind Grimsby and Rayne.

He reached the ground floor, which was draped in near impenetrable darkness, and used the light of the entrance to guide himself.

Then he froze, old instincts firing to life like beacons along a mountain range.

He wasn't alone.

His gun was in his hand without a thought. He stood tall and silent in the dark, listening.

The sudden sound of footsteps was almost as silent as he was, and he heard it only when the source was a dozen feet away.

He whirled and fired, letting his ears guide his aim. The old revolver roared, blazing the darkness to light for the briefest instant. His shot missed, narrowly, and he saw a broad, lean figure rushing toward him. Before he could fire again, the stranger closed the gap, colliding with him like a linebacker and bringing him to the ground.

Mayflower managed to absorb the blow with practiced effort. Though he couldn't break his attacker's grip around his waist, he twisted, making his attacker take the brunt of the force from their tandem toppling.

He tried to bring the revolver to bear in the melee, but his assailant seemed prepared for this and kept the gun at bay with a powerful arm. However, with the attacker using one arm to fend off the weapon and the other to grapple Mayflower's waist, that meant the Huntsman's off hand was left free.

He started with gouging at his attacker's eyes.

His fingers clawed, digging into soft skin until one found its mark.

But the stranger made no noise as he ripped his head away and burrowed it into Mayflower's stomach, squeezing the Huntsman like a vise between arm and skull. He felt the air being crushed from his lungs, and his diaphragm struggled to draw breath to replace it. He drove down blow after blow with his elbow, but he couldn't manage to gain any leverage with his attacker so close to his center of mass.

Finally, he wrapped his free hand around the back of his opponent's head, feeling bald, prickling scalp and worming veins, until he could feel what felt like facial features beneath a cloth mask. He dug his fingers into what might have been a mouth or perhaps a nostril, and wrenched as hard as he could. Flesh split beneath his grip and blood dampened the mask. The head reluctantly turned to one side, easing the pressure on his stomach long enough for him to draw breath.

His gun hand was still propped outward by his opponent, unable to angle for a grisly point-blank shot, but the assailant's grip was around his wrist.

Mayflower let his stiffened arm collapse, bending at the elbow and using the assistance of his opponent's resistance to drive the elbow into his opponent's face, crushing his nose like a plastic cup full of warm soup.

His opponent faltered; Mayflower felt the grip around his waist slip and took the opportunity to pry himself free, though his foe managed to twist his failing grip into the Huntsman's coat, keeping him from breaking contact altogether.

Despite this, he was able to get enough distance to angle his gun. The barrel was roughly center mass. There'd be no missing this time.

Muscles tensed to pull the trigger, but he felt a brief hesitation, and Grimsby's words came to him like the kid was just over his shoulder.

You're a good man.

A bitter taste tinged his tongue.

His trigger finger faltered.

Then he saw a small glow in the dark, emblazoned on his foe's cheek, half covered beneath the mask. However, even with it partially covered, he recognized it. It was a thrall mark, a magical rune that enslaved the mind. He had seen them before—

The last time he faced Janice.

This man could be anyone, any civilian who'd fallen into the wrong witch's clutches. He was an innocent, no more in control of himself than a rabid dog.

But even so, he sensed Mayflower's hesitation.

A strong leg lashed out, catching the back of Mayflower's forward knee. At the same time, the man hauled on his coat and used the leverage to throw him to the ground hard enough that Mayflower felt his ribs rattle.

He tasted blood in his mouth, and realized that he might have to take the shot—whether or not the man was innocent—or risk being killed himself.

He rolled over, bringing his revolver up in a double-handed grip.

But the man was gone.

Outside, he saw a flickering shadow and heard departing footsteps, but they quickly faded to silence.

Mayflower groaned as he climbed to his feet, keeping his eyes on the door and his ears open. It was rare to find a single thrall; witches willing to use such dark magic tended to collect them like pets. But he did not sense anyone else nearby.

It was also strange for the thrall to retreat. They were considered fodder, expendable in every sense of the word. They had no sense of self-preservation. Why had he run?

More importantly, why had he waited for Mayflower to leave before making his move?

It was almost as if whoever commanded the thrall only wanted to delay him . . .

And if the thrall was here, that meant that whoever was behind the ritual had known he'd be here. If that was the case, they'd have left a trap. A lone thrall wouldn't be enough. But if the thrall wasn't the trap, then what was?

He cast a glance behind him, to the barrels that were stacked along the edges of the warehouse. Now that he was looking carefully, he saw wires running between several of them.

"Damn."

He started running.

He had taken hardly a half dozen steps when he heard the first barrel detonate.

The force swept him from his feet and threw him into the doors. He struck one hard, breaking it in half with a combination of his shoulder and his head. Fortunately, the old wood had rotted soft, and the metal reinforcements snapped in a shower of rust. It hurt, but it dampened his forward momentum, keeping his skull from cracking open on the pavement. He landed in a rolling heap outside, and a half heartbeat later, the warehouse became an inferno.

He pressed himself into the ground, his head spinning and throbbing from his collision. He managed to pull the edge of his coat over his face. Within its lining he saw the protective silver stitching flare to life like hot wires. It had been sewn in lines of scripture he no longer believed in, and the words seared themselves into his retinas until he looked away.

Heat washed over him, and he felt every uncovered patch of

skin scream in pain as the hairs burned away, but after a searing moment, the heat died down from inferno to furnace.

He lowered his coat to see the warehouse in flames, its roof completely missing, its windows shattered and pouring out smoke. He cast a quick look around for his attacker, but the thrall was gone.

He holstered his gun and dragged himself to his feet, then limped his way to the jeep. He needed to move in case whoever had laid the trap had a fallback plan. He kept a wary eye out, but no one barred his path. Sirens began sounding in the distance, likely already on their way, but he had no time to wait and apprise them of the situation. Their mystery ritualist was still out there, and using the same tricks Janice had. But Janice was dead—

Wasn't she?

He growled in pain. Of course she was. She had to be.

But if that were true, then who was behind it all? An apprentice, perhaps?

He shoved a cigarette between his teeth and ground his pains into it, spitting out the mashed pulp like cud. Whoever they were, they knew the Department was after them.

And, since they'd decided to use this ritual opportunity as a trap, that meant there was only one more chance for them to cast the spell, which meant there was only one chance for him to stop it.

He climbed inside the jeep and coaxed it to sputtering life. He wanted to return to the Department to plan his next move, and perhaps see if Finley could manage to track the last possible location, but he couldn't do it alone. He left the blaze in his rearview as he maneuvered toward Goode's home.

First, he needed to make sure his witch didn't go and get himself killed.

TWENTY-NINE

RAYNE FOUND HERSELF LEANING AGAINST THE BASEMENT wall, her vision spinning enough to make the dim room feel like it was below the deck of a ship in a storm. She shook herself, feeling her heart begin to speed up in time with her mind.

She remembered descending the stairs, but her mind felt oddly blank after that, like trying to remember a dream.

What had just happened? Had she struck some kind of arcane trap? She quickly looked herself over to make certain she was intact but saw nothing out of the ordinary. Even her white ballistic mask was settled evenly on her face.

She glared and cast away the sensation as she scanned the basement. There was a pair of cheap folding tables at the room's center, covered with baggies and glass jars, while the walls were lined with plastic shelves stacked with cardboard boxes. A quick glance told her it was all reagents of one kind or another, but none of it was unusually dangerous.

Then she noticed a shelf pulled aside. Behind it, a sheet had been used to cover a hole in the wall, but it had been torn away, revealing a safe. The door was split open as smoothly as a knife might go through putty, and though the contents were scattered, she saw they were far more serious in nature. Shards from a grave-stone, the skull of some exotic rodent, the preserved wings of a bat, and more. Though many of the items that remained were difficult to obtain without a permit, she guessed that the most volatile of the components had been taken.

That meant a burglar had broken in after all, rather than Goode breaking out. But if that was the case, where was Goode?

"Grimsby!" she called. "I think you were right about the break-in."

She expected a glib reply but received only silence.

"Grimsby?" she said, feeling her pulse begin to thrum again. Had Goode transformed and returned to his den? Surely not; she would have heard something. Even if it was Grimsby screaming.

Her stomach lurched at the idea and she found herself rushing up the stairs, conjuring Impetus with every step.

The house was silent, still, and above all—empty.

Grimsby was gone.

She called again, storming about the first floor, checking every room, but there was no trace. Even the upstairs, which held only a cramped, messy bedroom and bathroom, was empty.

Then, as she swept the first floor again, she spotted tracks on the dusty floor. They were common enough, with her, Grimsby, and Goode at the very least having left their marks, but there was a new track, a wide, smooth swath that ran straight to the front door.

The most likely source was something being dragged. Something roughly the size of Grimsby.

He had been taken.

She immediately withdrew her phone, intending to call the Department, when it began to ring in her hand. The screen read simply Unknown.

She accepted the call, her mind racing in a panic. "Grimsby?" she asked.

"Um, no. It's Defaux," the voice on the other side of the line said. "Everything okay?"

"No, no. Something's wrong. I—I lost Grimsby."

"What do you mean you lost him?"

"He was here one second, and I went downstairs, and then he was gone!" She normally would have hated the cracks in her voice as she spoke, but at the moment she was too worried to care. "I think someone took him."

Defaux made a curious noise. "You sound so—strange," she said.

"What? What are you talking about?"

"I've never heard you so frantic before."

She felt her temper grow hot and sharp, and it felt like a life-line in a roiling storm. "You don't even know me."

Defaux only chuckled.

"How can you be so calm? Grimsby is in danger! I have to find him."

"So you do," Defaux agreed. "I wanted to tell you I got my hands on the components for the tracking ritual, whenever you're ready."

Rayne shook her head and forced her tongue to be blunt. "Fine—good. Just prepare the circle. I'm going to look for him."

She hung up without waiting for a reply and dialed the Department hotline. It would connect her to the most capable of Department personnel for remote support.

The line clicked on, and a quick voice said, "Miranda Finley."

Rayne recognized the voice as that of the woman who had told her of the Therian ordeal in the first place. "Finley, I need Grimsby's location. Fast."

Keys were already clicking in the background as Finley asked, "Is he not with you?"

"No. He was taken. Let's hope they didn't have the foresight to ditch his cell."

There was a brief clicking of keys on the other side of the line. "Looks like he moved a couple miles about twenty-five minutes ago."

"Twenty-five minutes?" she demanded. That couldn't be right. She had barely been in the basement for two minutes when she realized he was gone. Even after her frantic searching, she couldn't have wasted more than five. A quick glance at her watch, however, confirmed the timing.

She had lost nearly twenty minutes.

Where? How? Was she going crazy?

She let out a sharp breath and forced her head to focus. "Just—just get me the location," she said. She'd worry about losing her mind later.

"Two miles east. Looks like a construction site near the highway."

"I'm on my way," she said, hurrying toward her car.

"I'll alert the task force."

"And the Huntsman," Rayne said, casting a glance to the nearly full moon. "I have a feeling we'll need him."

THIRTY

GRIMSBY WAS PRETTY CERTAIN HE SHOULD BE AWAKE, but everything was still black. He tried to move, but his limbs felt anchored in place. Was he dead? Panic rose in him, surging up like flash-flood waters. He thrashed about, commanding every muscle to move, as though it might help, and found himself tipping over and falling to the ground.

He grunted as his arm hit concrete but heard the clatter of metal doing the same. He realized he was tied to a chair, and the flaring pain in his elbow actually came with some measure of relief. The darkness was not the null embrace of death, but rather just a blindfold. However, his relief was short-lived when he heard movement nearby.

"He's awake," a familiar woman's voice said. "Lump, get him up, and tie the chairs together just to be sure."

A meaty, coarse paw seized him, lifting both him and his chair effortlessly before dropping him back upright. He heard the metal folding chair creak, its joints strained by the force. A rough, heavy rope was cinched around his belly, feeling like it was crushing his stomach into his spine.

He had been captured, it seemed. And if the woman was

speaking to the same Lump as he and Wudge had encountered in the Elsewhere, then that meant she was likely Echidna. His thrumming panic subsided by the barest shades. At least he knew who had taken him, although not why.

"You two realize that assaulting an Auditor is a serious crime?" he asked, trying to sound confident. Unfortunately, his voice was shakier than he would have liked.

"Only if we leave behind witnesses," Echidna said, her suggestion sending a chill down Grimsby's chair-lashed spine.

Deft hands untied and removed his blindfold, which he saw was his Department-issued tie. Then he realized he had no glasses—no mask. For a panicked moment, he began to see the Elsewhere bleeding into his blurred sight, its familiar black sun and red skies the only details he could make out before he screwed his eyes shut again.

"If you two want to have a heart-to-heart, I'm going to need my glasses back," he said. With his eyes closed, he was technically safe from the Elsewhere, but *technically* was not a comforting threshold. He still felt vulnerable without his mask.

There was a brief pause and a murmured exchange. He couldn't make out what Echidna said, but Lump's brutish drawl was booming despite his best efforts.

"But what if he tricks you again, Echidna?"

"Not me—us!" Echidna said with a mixed measure of embarrassment and indignance.

"I dunno . . ." Lump said, and Grimsby could practically hear the dopey grin in his voice.

"Eyes aflame," Grimsby cursed, feeling his heart race and his mouth run on its own. "Look, I don't know why you witchnapped me, but I assume it'll be a moot point if some Elsewhere beast eats my face off mid-conversation."

"Would make for an interesting show, at least," Echidna said.

"But not an interesting conversation, which I'm guessing is what you're looking for."

Echidna made an annoyed sound. "Fine. But no tricks this time, witch."

"Nothing up my sleeve," Grimsby said, wiggling his fingers bound behind his back.

He felt the hard rims of his glasses shoved haphazardly on his nose. Though they weren't in a comfortable position, they should still be enough to guard him from the Elsewhere.

He opened bleary eyes and blinked until they adjusted to the light, twitching his nose around to try in vain to get his glasses in the right spot. He hadn't fully expected what he saw when his eyes cleared.

It wasn't Echidna and Lump before him—except it was. It was almost like two people pretending to *be* them, or perhaps their closely related family. He recognized Echidna's face and her wild tangle of hair, but she seemed to have somehow exchanged her serpentine lower half for an apparently normal set of human legs, complete with threadbare jeans and an oversize, tattered trench coat of faded canvas with an upturned collar.

Meanwhile, Lump had shrunken down considerably, like a sponge left in the sun. He, too, wore a coat like Echidna's, except his was crusted leather, also with its collar turned up, along with some greasy sweatpants. The once-giant troll was even a hair shorter than Mayflower now, but he was still a great deal broader. If it hadn't been for his almost inhumanly long and crooked nose, Grimsby wouldn't have recognized him on the street, though he might have gawked.

"Very noir. You two cosplaying?" Grimsby asked.

Echidna twisted her lip in annoyance and shook her head. "They're guises, fool," she said, tugging at her upturned collar. "They hide us like your masks hide you witches."

"Hide you from what? A magical detective with a bad attitude?"

"From humans like you," she said, her tone callous and bitter.

"Oh." Grimsby felt his flippant defiance wither a touch. It was already challenging being a witch in Boston; he couldn't imagine being someone like Lump or Echidna. Come to think of it, he hadn't exactly heard of such folks living in Boston—or anywhere else for that matter, yet he knew they were, well, *around*. Did they simply blend in better than he realized?

Or was there somewhere else they called home?

He banished both curiosity and empathy, or at least strapped them down under the rest of his concerns. After all, he had been abducted and tied up. He had other priorities to consider over his abductors' feelings. "How did you find me?"

She withdrew a small object from her coat and revealed it to be the slipper he had lost in the Elsewhere. In the sole was a small, dark stain of blood, likely from when he had injured his foot.

"Ah," he said, "tracking ritual. Great." Such a ritual would have been rudimentary compared to the tracking magic a witch could manage with a dowser, but apparently it got the job done. "So, I'm guessing you two wanna have a conversation about our last . . . encounter?"

She glared at him and discarded the slipper. "Return what you stole, and we'll let you both live."

Both?

Had they taken Rayne as well?

Grimsby tried to whip his head around to look for her, but his restraints were confining. He saw they were inside an unfinished concrete structure, like some kind of construction site. Standing flood lamps spilled harsh illumination all around, making his eyes water. It took him a moment to realize it wasn't just a chair he was tied to. Behind him was another figure, this one bound in a chair much like Grimsby. Their seats had been tied together by thick ropes and clumsy knots—likely courtesy of Lump.

He saw it wasn't Rayne, and for a moment, he was simply relieved. Then, as he realized who it was, he felt a chill prickle its way over his skin, drawing every hair to stand on end as it did.

Though Grimsby couldn't see him clearly, and his head was drooping limply to one side, he still recognized the lank locks of Samuel Goode. His face was bruised and one eye was swollen shut, but he seemed otherwise intact.

Grimsby unconsciously glanced up to the exposed sky and saw the all-too-open eye of the moon looking back.

Tied to a Therian on a full moon, he thought. *That has to be a euphemism for something.*

Despite the fear, he still felt a small measure of relief that Goode was all right; he hadn't yet turned into a rampaging monster. Even so, the moon beyond the steel girders above seemed to be emphasizing a single word of his reassurance: *yet*.

He heard someone say something, but his mind was racing in fearful circles as he stared straight up. He needed to get Goode to the Asylum before he turned, or even better yet, before he woke. But how long had he been out? Had the window for Goode's transformation already begun? He had to hurry; he had to—

Echidna's hand darted out and slapped him across the face.

"Focus!" she demanded.

He shook himself, the shock of the pain actually helping him listen to her advice. "What did you two do to Goode?"

"We followed you for a time and thought maybe you used him as your fence," she said, "to sell what you stole from us, but he seemed to have no idea what we were talking about. Now it's your turn to answer me: where is it?"

The nail, Grimsby realized. They must be after the nail. Though why they'd want a cursed object like that was beyond him. More than that, if they didn't even realize he couldn't simply give it back to them, then they must not know any more about it than he did.

In fact, from the way Echidna asked about it, she didn't even know it was a nail at all. She only knew he had stolen *something*, but not what.

For a moment, he debated giving it up, but he dismissed the

idea. He couldn't hand it over even if he wanted, and even if he could, it would be a betrayal of Wudge—though perhaps that would only be fair since he had tricked Grimsby into taking on the curse to begin with.

Regardless, he couldn't tell these two the truth.

So instead, he lied.

"I have no idea what you're talking about," Grimsby said. "We took nothing." He tried to sound nervous and annoyed at the same time, when really he was just nervous and afraid.

Echidna's face hardened, her olive skin shimmering oddly in the harsh light. "I've spent weeks combing through that pile of magical trash, looking for something worth having. And suddenly two thieves show up and take something before running off. I'm assuming you wouldn't risk your lives for nothing, and you certainly don't want to die for nothing, so I'll ask again: where is it?"

"Where—where is what?" Grimsby asked, his mouth feeling like it was filled with old couch stuffing. Lying always made his mouth dry. He looked around for something that could perhaps help him escape, but aside from a crane, a dirty cement truck, and the occasional machine whose purpose Grimsby could scarcely imagine, the area was bare. To top it off, the whole place was also cordoned off by chain-link fences covered with tarps. No one could see them from the outside. He could yell, but Echidna had proven during their last encounter that strangling him was no challenge for her.

"I swear to Mother," she said, her tone frustrated and growing angry. "If you don't tell us what it is and where it is, I'll toss you into the back of that cement truck and let you rot until you come out with skin harder than Lump's." She shot a quick, apologetic glance to her looming partner. "No offense, Lump."

Lump seemed too busy scratching at a patch of cracked, rocky skin on the back of his hand to notice. Then he paused and looked up, his long face scowling. "Hey, wait a minute. He wasn't alone,

Echidna." He jabbed a heavy finger into Grimsby's bound chest. "Where's your little boss?"

Boss? Grimsby thought, feeling insulted that the assertion was more true than false. "We weren't there to take anything. We, uh, got lost."

Echidna's temper was as thin as her shredded jeans. "A human and that toothy *thing* got lost in the Elsewhere, wandered up fifteen stories of wards and traps, and left a treasure trove without taking a single thing?"

"Of course," Grimsby said. "That would be stealing, and that's illegal."

"Nothing is illegal in the Elsewhere."

"Well then, I *definitely* didn't steal anything."

She said nothing, but he could feel her temper tearing away like tissue paper in a hurricane.

"Look, I'd love to help you out, but," Grimsby said, wiggling against his bonds to no avail, "my hands are tied. Besides"—he tilted his head to Goode—"we may have bigger, hairier problems."

Echidna let out a hiss of frustration. "You don't know what problems are, witch." Her face began to harden from frustration to determination. "Last chance: give us what you stole."

"There's no time for this!" Grimsby said. "This guy's a Therian! If he shifts, we're all dead. Untie me so I can get him to the Asylum before that happens."

"Therian?" Lump said, his small eyes going wide beneath his heavy brow.

"Liar," Echidna said. "You're just trying to escape." She let out a shuddering breath, seeming to be steeling herself. "Fine. Lump, break his fingers. Then start working your way up. I bet he'll talk before you reach his shoulder."

Grimsby felt a sharp jab of fear as irrepressible imagery was conjured forth in his mind.

Lump made an uncomfortable sound but dutifully grabbed

Grimsby's wrist with a meaty paw, but before his clumsy hands found one of the struggling digits, Goode kicked upright in his seat, his muscles tensing against their constraints.

He was waking up.

"Puppy dogs' tails," Grimsby cursed. Rayne had said Goode could transform at any moment if he became stressed, and the scenario they were both in was nothing if not distressing. If he shifted here, they'd all be in trouble, but while Lump and Echidna could run, Grimsby was both tied up as well as tied to Goode.

"Fine, fine!" he said, trying to come up with a plan. "I'll give you what you want, but you'll have to untie my arms first."

Lump stopped fumbling for a finger and looked to Echidna. She glared with distrust. "No tricks?" she asked.

"I really hope not," he said.

She waved Lump away and unbound Grimsby's arms, though he still had rope wrapped around his waist and legs. Goode twitched again, this time mumbling incoherently.

Grimsby wiggled his grip past the ropes and into his jacket pocket, withdrawing the nail. "This. This is what I took," he said.

"Give it to me," Echidna said, her hand darting out to snatch it from his palm, but when she pulled, one end of the nail refused to part from him. Her face twisted in anger. "I said 'no tricks'!" she said, tugging at the nail and, by extension, Grimsby's arm socket.

"Ow—ow! In my defense, that isn't a trick," he said. "This is."

He called up his Impetus, rushed and hurried. His scars smoldered and sparked; the darkened blotches of warped skin on his palm became outlined in orange light. He shoved his hand forward and tried to place a *Bind* rune on Echidna's sternum, but before he could, her hand lashed out faster than he could see and caught his wrist.

His mounting Impetus faltered without a spell for an outlet, making his scars spit candlelight gouts of fire, charring his sleeve.

Echidna scoffed, her nose wrinkling at the scent of scorched polyester. "No tricks after all, I see."

Just then, Goode shook himself, his head snapping from side to side. Grimsby saw him look around wildly out of the corner of his eye.

"Where—where am I?" he said, his voice growing more shrill with each syllable.

"Goode, you're fine. Just relax . . ." Grimsby said, though he doubted his cracking, fear-choked voice was as soothing as he would have liked.

He needed to calm Goode down; he needed everything to stop before it was too late.

Then the blindfold slipped loose from Goode's black-circled and terrified eyes. He turned to see the strange trio, Grimsby and Echidna with their locked grips and Lump's looming figure. Then his eyes rose to the moon.

He froze, and his gaze went dull.

Then the shifting began.

THIRTY-ONE

GRIMSBY COULD HARDLY SEE WITH HIS BACK TURNED to Goode, but what he saw out of the corner of his eye was enough to make his blood stall in his heart-hammered veins.

He watched, unable to move, as the Therian's body jerked and twitched, every motion seeming to bulge forth with sinewy muscle. Bones cracked and creaked, muffling his muddled gasps of agony as his body shifted. The ropes that wrapped around them both constricted taut around Grimsby, and the metal chair shrieked as it was pulled and warped by the pressure.

Grimsby felt the bonds tighten painfully around him, but even that wasn't enough to shake him from his shock.

Goode's hands flexed and grasped at nothing, his fingers contracting wildly as they elongated. Short, coarse fur sprouted, first along his forearms, but quickly spreading like a wildfire to coat his skin. His palms grew dark and leathery, and his unclipped nails thickened to sharpened points. Meanwhile, his feet swelled to split his shoes and tear open his socks before hardening into knobby hooves.

Goode's chair groaned and buckled altogether under his growing weight and the squeezing ropes, loosening the tension but turning the bonds into a tangled mess that pulled Grimsby down as well. With his legs still bound, he managed to push himself up to his elbows and looked over to see Goode a scarce few feet away.

The Therian writhed on the ground in horrid pain. His eyes stared at the sky, wide enough to reveal the whites around irises that twisted to vertical, catlike slits. His ribs cracked and rasped, denting outward like someone with a sledgehammer was trapped inside him and trying to escape. His shirt split, revealing skin that quickly burgeoned with bristling fur, though near his throat it became long and silken, like a mane.

He clenched his jaw as his teeth began to seep with blood. Sharpened fangs erupted, pushing aside their human counterparts like craggy spires parting foothills. His face twisted and contorted, but not with the lupine muzzle Grimsby had expected. It was more bulbous and square, though it wasn't until horns began to sprout forth from Goode's forehead that he realized Goode's maw was closer to that of a goat than a wolf. And yet it was neither.

Goode, or what remained of him, clawed his way upright and stood nearly nine feet high, draped in frayed ropes and flayed cloth, basking for a moment in the pale moonlight as he took a deep breath through flaring nostrils. With a note of finality, the horns on his head branched out like questing roots, their surface slick and red with bloody velvet, forming into something like a moose tyrant's crown.

The Therian had shifted.

Goode's nostril flaps fluttered, catching the air. His head twitched and his mane shuddered as he turned his bloodshot eyes to Lump and Echidna, who stood nearby just as horrifically transfixed as Grimsby had been.

Grimsby wanted to say something, to scream at them to run, but the primal part of his mind, the part that was used to being prey, begged him to stay silent. It wanted him to find someplace small and dark to crawl into until the predator went away. Heck, if he weren't still tied to a chair, he might have already done so.

But the small part of him that had come into being over the last few months, the part of him that was an Auditor, knew he had to do something. Lump and Echidna might not have been human, but they needed his help all the same.

He fought back the part of him that demanded silence, and screamed in a hoarse voice, "Run!"

Goode's pointed ears twitched and swiveled toward the sound, but before his attention followed, Echidna shoved Lump into motion. Eyes drawn by the sudden movement, Goode ignored Grimsby's cry. The moment the two Unorthodox bolted, he dropped to all four limbs and loped after them with frightening speed, his apelike gait carrying him forward over the terrain with ease, slowed only by the tangle of ropes draped around his limbs.

Grimsby tried to struggle loose of his bonds to pursue them, but as he did he saw Goode's ropes dragging behind him.

He barely had time to realize they were tangled with his own.

When they drew taut, he was suddenly jerked into motion.

Drawn like a sleigh pulled by a brutal, unruly reindeer, he bounced along the ground behind Goode. He managed to get his arms up to keep his head from being battered along the dirt and concrete, but the chair was quickly rent into scrap, leaving him in a tangled mess of loose ropes as he skidded across the ground like a stone across a pond.

He had little time to think of anything aside from keeping his brain in his skull as his arms took a battering against the hard earth. He finally came to a thudding halt and stumbled numbly to his feet, propped up solely by a cocktail mix of adrenaline and fear. Uncertain why Goode had stopped, he turned to see Lump and Echidna cornered in the concrete and steel scaffolding of the unfinished structure, with their only escape being the door to an on-site trailer, but judging from Echidna's struggling, the door was locked.

Goode had stood on his wolfish hind legs, leering over them like a cougar over trapped prey. He seemed cruelly aware he had no need to rush.

Lump had placed himself in front of Echidna, but even his bulky frame looked soft and edible compared to the leanly muscled and towering Therian. Its claws and teeth both seemed purpose-built to serrate flesh, and while Lump's bits might inconvenience the Therian by turning to stone somewhere along the process of being eaten, it would likely come too late to help the troll.

Behind him, Echidna was trying to kick out the trailer door to shelter within, but she was almost unsteady on her human legs. Perhaps the trench coat guise she wore was throwing off her usual serpentine grace, just as Lump's had diminished his size to a more human stature. Whatever the reason, it appeared she wouldn't have enough time to get the door open and take refuge inside.

Grimsby looked around for anything he could use as a weapon, but though steel girders and pipes were stacked in piles all over, he was nowhere near strong enough to move them, let alone wield one as an armament.

Then his eyes fell upon the ropes draped over him that still trailed behind Goode.

As quickly as he could manage, though it drew pangs from his countless bruises, he slipped out of the tangled bonds and gathered them up. He hurried to coil them around whatever he could find. A pallet of bricks, a pair of loose girders, and finally a bulldozer.

Just as he managed to tie a makeshift knot, one complete with a small bow, as he knew no other knots, he saw Goode lunge.

The Therian closed to within a couple of feet of Lump and Echidna before the ropes drew taut around his chest, holding him back like a dog's leash.

All three of the Unorthodox seemed surprised by this, but it gave Echidna the window she needed to finally bend the door with a heavy kick. She reached through the warped frame and unlocked it from within, allowing her and Lump to slip through and into the trailer and secure it shut behind them.

Goode roared a throaty bleat that trailed into a furious howl, straining at his bonds as his prey escaped.

Then there was a different kind of roar from nearby, a familiar kind that raised hope in Grimsby's chest.

He looked over his shoulder to see Mayflower's jeep crash through the chain-link fence around the site, toppling the posts like cardboard tubes. Hot on the heels of its rusted bumper was a black mirrorless Department sedan.

Despite the vehicles' steel-wrenching entrance, Goode seemed so incensed by his prey that he didn't notice and instead clawed at the ropes that held him back from Lump and Echidna.

The jeep slid to a halt a few feet from Grimsby. Mayflower climbed out, gun drawn, his gaze dark, his skin marred with ash and dirt. He gripped Grimsby hard by the shoulder and looked him up and down. "Are you all right? Are you hurt?"

Grimsby was so surprised that he didn't respond at first, at least not until Mayflower started to shake him. He waved the Huntsman away. "I'm okay, I'm okay!"

Behind him, Rayne climbed out of her sedan, her white ballistic mask covering her face. She rushed to them, keeping her gaze on Goode. "What's it doing?" she asked.

"The two that grabbed me are trapped in that trailer. We have to get his attention before he gets inside."

Mayflower let out a breath. "So be it," he said, his head turning toward Goode, who had nearly torn free of his ropes. His hand tightened on the revolver as he checked the chamber and started to draw his aim on the Therian, but Grimsby grabbed his arm and held him back.

"What are you doing?" Grimsby asked.

"Putting the beast down."

"You can't do that!"

"We don't have a choice, Grimsby," he said. "If we don't stop him and he gets loose, he could kill dozens before we corner him again."

Grimsby felt a hand on his own arm and looked over to see Rayne's teal eyes peering at him through the mask. "We don't have any way to contain a Therian out here," she said. "We have to stop him, here and now."

Grimsby's stomach twisted into more knots than were in the ropes that held Goode. The Therian was in this situation because of Echidna and Lump, but they were only involved because of Grimsby. That meant whatever happened to Goode was his fault.

And he wasn't looking to have a dead man on his conscience.

At least, not another one.

He looked around, trying to find some solution, something that could contain Goode long enough to save his life—when a thought came to him.

"Mayflower, can you use that crane?" he asked, still gripping the Huntsman's arm.

"What?" he demanded, though he didn't break away from Grimsby's grip. "There's no time for this!"

"Please," Grimsby said, "we can still save him. I just need your help. Both of you."

The Huntsman's expression was hard, and he cast a glance toward Rayne before looking back. "We don't have a choice." Yet there was the slightest shadow of doubt that darkened his features.

Rayne nodded in agreement, though her eyes were uncertain as well.

"Yes, we do," Grimsby pressed. "It's just not a good one."

Mayflower said nothing, though Grimsby could sense a hairline fracture in his stoic face.

"You said you don't want me to be like you," Grimsby said. "So why don't you be like me, just this once?"

The fissure in Mayflower's expression widened, and his stony face seemed to almost look ashamed for a moment. "Fine. One chance."

Grimsby nodded quickly. "Thank you. Just get that crane hooked up to the back of that cement truck. Rayne, you move to make sure our unfortunate victims don't slip away in the excitement."

"And leave you to deal with the Therian alone?" she demanded.

He managed a smile, though it was as shaky as his stomach. "I can do this. Please, just trust me."

She looked like she wanted to argue but relented. "Just—don't get yourself killed. All right?"

He drew an invisible X on his chest. "Cross my heart and hope to die."

"Not funny," she called as she darted away, moving into position near the trailer.

Meanwhile, Goode had clawed free from his bonds and was tearing apart the piled coils of ropes around him in a blind rage. Then his nose caught a scent and he turned his eyes to the trailer, where Lump and Echidna were still sheltering. He pounced on its side and began to shear off thin layers of steel and insulation with equal ease.

"What are you going to do?" Mayflower asked.

"Just hitch the crane," Grimsby said. "I'm—uh, I'm going to be bait." Then he started toward Goode before he lost his nerve or the Huntsman could argue.

Goode was clawing the trailer to pieces like it was a tin can. His lean muscles flexed beneath coarse fur as he tore away at the thinning barrier between him and his prey. Through the widening gaps in the walls, Grimsby watched as Lump and Echidna tried to pile as many obstacles as possible between them and Goode. However, Grimsby knew that within moments their shelter would be reduced to a tomb unless he did something.

"Hey!" he shouted, but his voice was drowned out by the violence.

He snatched a broken brick and hefted it in his hand before hurling it at Goode. However, he was still twenty or so feet away, and he missed. The brick shattered against the side of the trailer instead, and Goode didn't seem to notice in his rampage.

He picked up another, forcing himself to get closer, though it defied every instinct in his body to do so. He finally got as close as he dared and hurled the second brick.

"Hey, fuzzy-wuzzy!" he shouted as his projectile sailed.

This time, it hit Goode in the back of his head.

The brick didn't break, but rather bounced soundly off his mane. However, Goode froze, a grip of sparking wires in one claw, and slowly turned to see Grimsby. His hackles rose even further, and he bared sharpened teeth in his equine maw. His horns looked like a crown of sharpened pitchforks in the mixing flood- and moonlight.

Grimsby gulped.

He had a plan.

He had the beast's attention.

Now he just needed to find some way to remain in one piece.

THIRTY-TWO

GRIMSBY KNEW HE NEEDED TO RUN, BUT HIS BODY FELT frozen under that predatory gaze. Like somehow his instincts knew his only chance was to hope Goode's vision was based on movement. However, as the Therian's nostril flaps flared and he let fall the bundle of wires, Grimsby knew movement wasn't necessary.

However, he did feel it was highly encouraged.

He only had to force himself to take the first, stumbling step backward, and adrenaline did the rest. Yet he had barely taken a half dozen paces when he heard Goode leap off the side of the trailer and fall in pursuit, the sound of his heavy hoofed feet pounding after him. Grimsby dared not look back, and instead poured every ounce of desperation and fear he could muster into his legs.

Turned out, he had a surplus of both.

He managed to reach the cement truck. He didn't have time to check if Mayflower had hooked the crane to it or not, so he had to rely on faith. Even if the Huntsman had done his job, he figured his odds of coming out of this—at least with all his insides where they ought to be—well, weren't all that great anyway.

He scurried up the ladder at the back of the truck. As he did, his foot caught on something small and plastic. He felt it click under his heel, and the drum of the truck began to spin. He drew a sharp breath and stepped back, only to kick the remote off the small platform, where it dangled by some kind of safety strap.

He froze, wanting to figure out how to turn the machine off again before jumping inside, but there was no time. He could hear Goode drawing closer, his paired claws and hooves crunching on the hard ground.

Even so, Grimsby hesitated at the opening of the drum.

It was darker inside than he had expected.

An odd half funnel led down into the depth below. He wasn't even sure if there was wet cement waiting within. He began to have second thoughts but then heard Goode's panting breath growing too close.

"Puppy dogs' tails," he cursed, and dropped down the half funnel, sliding into the cement truck's rear.

He immediately caught his foot on ridges of steel jutting from the drum's walls. He hadn't seen them in the dark and stumbled over them, narrowly avoiding twisting his ankle before splashing into a shallow pool of water at the bottom.

Nearly blind, he looked toward the opening, the only source of light. From within, he could see the blades almost corkscrewed around the drum's outer wall. The steel drum was slick, but there wasn't any cement, like he had expected. Instead, there was only a small bit of water, though it seemed to have dampened most of the drum's interior. It was slick, but he still managed to keep his balance.

Unfortunately, balance quickly went from difficult to impossible when several hundred pounds of Therian slammed into the side of the truck.

The drum squealed and dented slightly, but its shape and thick surface were as sturdy as Grimsby had hoped.

It would make a fine cage for Goode.

Grimsby just had to get the Therian inside and then get himself out, or instead of a cage, the drum would become a blender.

The only illumination in the pitch black was a thin beam of light from the drum's port, but it quickly became shadowed, and Grimsby looked up to see the shaggy visage of Goode, his snuffling snout examining the entrance. The funnel seemed a barrier at first, but Goode growled and ripped away the steel with ease, drawing a wrenching squeal and sparks before tossing it away.

Flashing, bloodshot eyes peered into the drum and seemed to find Grimsby in the dark with ease. A long, claw-tipped hand reached inside, grasping for him. Iron-hard nails screeched as they dug furrows in the age-old layers of crusted cement and scores into the metal beneath, but the Therian's reach came up short.

A small part of Grimsby hoped that perhaps Goode wouldn't manage to find a way in, and that he might stay safe within the drum. He forced that feeling down, bitter at himself and his cowardice. If he didn't manage to trap Goode, he'd either kill or be killed, or more likely both.

Grimsby was his only chance.

"Come on," he muttered. "Get in here."

The Therian seemed all too eager to oblige. He shoved his snout into the gap, but his horns were wider than the entrance. He sniffed about, like a dog trying to dig out a treat from beneath a couch, before he finally managed to awkwardly angle his horned head into the drum. With savage, jerking motions, he began to pull himself inside, too few feet away from Grimsby.

Grimsby scrambled in the opposite direction until his back found the bottom of the steel grave.

He was trapped.

He suddenly wondered just how sound his plan actually was, but it was too late to come up with anything smarter—which at this point seemed the same as having come up with anything else.

He summoned up his Impetus, and a dull red-orange glow emanated from his scars, illuminating the darkened interior. A spell welled on his lips, but he bit it back. He had to wait for Goode to clear the entrance, or else they'd both be trapped. Yet watching the Therian inch his way closer and closer, his claws wrapping carefully around the drum's slowly spinning blades as he squeezed his way inside, made every one of Grimsby's already tensed muscles seize with cold fear.

The dampened interior darkened Goode's fur, and warm, scar-born light reflected in his predator-green eyes, the gaze of which never wavered from Grimsby's throat. At last, with a final heave, Goode hauled his haunches into the drum and stood, hunched in the rotating trap.

The Therian loomed over him, seeming to relish the calm before the kill. His lips trembled and peeled away to reveal a mish-mash of fangs and molars. Drool dripped and dribbled from his maw, mixing with the murky water in a sickening concoction of slime that matted half his face. The hackles of his mane rose, bristling like a lion.

Grimsby gulped and tried to keep his feet despite the spinning of the drum and his shaking knees. He felt small and frail beneath the lean and leering form of the Therian, like a rabbit before a wolf.

So, Goode was about as surprised as that same wolf would have been when Grimsby struck first.

He reached out, pouring forth Impetus into his hurried spell. Ill-controlled power leaked into his scars, and gouts of fire burst forth from his sleeve and collar, harmless to his skin but scorching his suit before being smothered by grayed water. Goode's eyes widened, but even as his clawed grasp reached out, Grimsby shouted his spell.

"Torque!"

He was trusting the nail to warp his spell, just as it had done in the past. It was a risk, but his uncertain gamble paid off. Instead of sending anything spinning as it might normally have done, the nail warped his magic once again.

A glimmering field of pinpoint light spread from his outstretched hand and froze the scene before him in place. The Therian's claws ceased moving in midair, just inches from reaching him. The drum's slow spin ground to a creaking halt. Goode's hoof stopped just above the damp steel, half raised in time with his strike. Even the twitching of his snarling face had stopped, like the real creature had been instantly replaced with a wax replica. Only his eyes, wide and feral, seemed almost free from the spell as they whipped back and forth in maddened rage.

Grimsby let out a relieved sigh, and the air came out as cool mist. Chills overran him, making him shiver even as his heart hammered in his chest. The ankle-deep pool of water around his feet had formed a thin skin of crystals where it touched his legs.

His Impetus was all but spent, and managing even the most subtle spell would be difficult. Fortunately, now it looked like all that was left was to slip past Goode and out before the spell wore off, though how long that would take he wasn't sure. The spell had been rushed, but he had put enough Impetus behind it to make his head spin and frost curl over his scars. He had perhaps minutes—or hopefully at least just one.

He shook himself and started for the exit, but as he tried to slide past Goode and the field of glimmering magic, he found himself moving slower than he should have been. It was like he had stepped into a wall of molasses, and though his mind told him he should have been moving at one speed, he found himself moving at half the rate.

He couldn't be certain what was happening. Perhaps the spell was also affecting him for being so close, or maybe the water or even the air around them was also caught in suspension, and now both were reluctant to part for him. Either way, he was moving too slowly, and his time was running out.

He tried to remain calm. He told himself he was going to make it out. He wasn't sure if his heart rate slowed because he actually believed it, or if it was the spell.

However, when he glanced back to see the drool from Goode's maw resume its fall in slow motion, he found his heart rate hurriedly returning to its frantic pace.

He struggled forward, using the dull corkscrew blades like a horizontal ladder, pressing as quickly through the spell as he could. In the corner of his panicked eye, he saw Goode begin to move, like watching an ice sculpture melting in place.

The field of lights grew brighter and brighter, trembling motes that had absorbed too much energy. He began to climb the final slope to the opening, but as the drum slowly resumed its lurching spin, his footing became treacherous on the dampened blades. He slipped and fell not once, but twice, before he managed to get one hand around the opening's edge. He pulled himself out to his chest before looking back to see how much of the spell remained.

He found Goode staring back at him, moving at a tenth of his usual speed and quickly growing faster. The motes of light had grown bright enough to reveal every matted hair on Goode's hide, and they trembled, on the brink of collapse.

Grimsby scrabbled his feet against the slick side of the drum until he hauled himself out of the precipice, his top half dangling as he gripped the ladder to pull himself out.

"Haul it up!" he shouted, pointing upward in a fervent hope that Mayflower heard or saw him.

Then the pent-up energy absorbed by the spell became too much, and it detonated.

The blast was deafening, channeled through the narrow opening of the truck like the barrel of a gun. Grimsby was caught in the pressure wave, and it forced him out of the port like a flung slug. He might have flown headfirst onto the concrete lot had he not barely managed to keep his grip on the drum's ladder, wrenching his arms but leaving him dangling like the drool dripping from Goode's maw.

He wobbled above the ground, dazed for a moment, before deciding to simply let himself fall.

He tried to drop from the back of the cement truck, but something quick and wicked seized hold of him. He felt something tighten around his throat and feared it was claws preparing to sink into tender flesh, only to realize it was his collar that was strangling him.

However, that was because the Therian had twisted his claw tightly in the loose cloth of his suit collar before he fell, leaving Grimsby to dangle precariously by a fabric noose.

He turned to look back and saw Goode's clawed arm extended from the drum like a furry articulated tongue, with Goode's snuffling snout and furious eyes not far behind. He was trying to pull himself free of the truck but seemed unable to fit both his arm and head through at once.

At first, Grimsby thought he would be forced to let him go, but Goode's maw receded, and Grimsby felt himself being dragged back toward the opening.

His scream was choked, due to his collar, but it slipped out all the same. The thought of being pulled inside that dark place again was somehow even more terrifying than being trapped there to begin with. He thrashed and struggled, his waning strength renewed by sheer panic, but the Therian's grip was too strong.

Just then, the truck's rear tipped as it was winched off the ground.

Grimsby was so frightened that he hadn't noticed the steel cable nearby tightening; it had now grown so taut that it began to drag the truck off its rear wheels.

The Therian's footing must have slipped inside, and the sudden jerk of him falling within the drum made his sharp claws slice Grimsby's collar to ribbons, though it freed him as a result. He began to fall, barely managing to catch himself by the crane's now-vertical cable.

Inside the drum, he heard the scrabble and screech of claws as the Therian thrashed and scored the inside of his makeshift cage in an attempt to escape. Grimsby was just about to jump down from the truck when he saw Goode's crown of horns angle its way out of the hole, followed quickly by the rest of his head, like a grisly whack-a-mole.

The drum was deep enough, and even with the internal blades, its walls were sheer enough that once it was fully vertical, Goode couldn't escape. However, the truck wasn't totally off the ground yet, and Goode looked like he might break out of the impromptu trap before it was fully closed.

Fighting his instinct to drop down and run away as fast as he could, Grimsby instead clambered his way back toward the opening and Goode's exposed head, balancing precariously on the tilting vehicle.

The Therian gnashed and snapped at Grimsby as he approached, but he kept his hands clear. The truck continued to tip, but he managed to keep his feet as its front wheels came off the ground, leaving it to twist precariously on the crane's cable.

With the drum now fully vertical, the trap should have been closed, but something was wrong.

Goode shouldn't have been able to reach the opening. However, in the bright moonlight that poured past Goode's shaggy mane, Grimsby quickly saw the Therian was wedged into place, his body dangling by his horns, lodged on either side of the opening like a cork, and the clever beast was using the anchor to inch toward murderous freedom.

Grimsby needed to force Goode back down somehow, but he

doubted he had enough Impetus to do the job, even if his spells were behaving like they normally should. Before he could find an alternative plan, however, Goode's lean arm slipped out past his horns and reached for him.

Grimsby stumbled and nearly fell, again catching himself by the cable. The claw flailed madly, nearly tearing loose the lever arm attached to the damaged funnel that dangled off the back of the drum.

Seeing the opportunity, Grimsby leaned back and braced himself against the cable, kicking at the lever again and again, keeping away from the claw as he did. Finally, it came loose enough that he was able to twist it from the bracket that once held it, giving him a three-foot length of metal.

Just as he got a grip on it, Goode's claw found his ankle and wrapped around it like a vise. It dragged him toward the hole, which was largely blocked by the Therian's maw, held in place by his horns.

Grimsby swung the lever at one horn, but he had no footing, and his swing barely chipped the pointed tips of the bloody antler. Another frantic blow, however, caught Goode across his exposed snout. The Therian squealed in pain, and his grip briefly loosened, letting Grimsby pull free.

He scrambled to his feet and, gripping the lever in both hands, drove it down on the Therian's chipped horn. The glistening red keratin began to split and bleed afresh, and Goode roared in pain. He reached out with his lone limb, its claws splayed to tear open Grimsby's belly.

Grimsby clenched his teeth and brought the lever down again, screaming as he did.

The steel struck home, and the antler shattered. The Therian, with his anchor lost, dropped like a stone into the depths of the truck, thundering inside the drum as he fell.

Grimsby stood for a moment, shocked that he was still

breathing—let alone standing. Then he surprised himself as a nervous chuckle bubbled up from his chest.

"Snicker-snack," he muttered, dropping the lever to the ground below.

He carefully picked his way down the frame of the cement truck, which now dangled several feet off the ground. His efforts were made all the more difficult by Goode's thrashing within, making the vehicle drift and spin gently like a giant's wind chime, but he found his way to the ground, where Mayflower was waiting for him.

The Huntsman helped him the last few feet to the ground, where he happily collapsed into a panting heap.

Mayflower looked down at him, his brow furrowed. "That was batshit insane, Grimsby."

"He's alive, isn't he?"

The Huntsman shook his head but relented. "He's alive. Good job, kid."

Grimsby paused, looking around as much as he was able without sitting up. "Where's Rayne?"

"The two that grabbed you tried to slip away. She went after them."

"She what? Alone?" He managed to sit up, but the simple act made his head spin and his vision blur. "We need to help her."

"Relax, Grimsby. She's an Auditor. She can handle herself."

Grimsby frowned, but his exhaustion drove him to shrug before lying back down. He might have been more worried, but wherever Rayne was, he doubted it was quite as dangerous as being locked in a cement mixer with a who-what-werewolf. He made a mental note to be concerned in a moment.

However, for the time being, he was spent, and he let his mind go blank.

He didn't even mind when Mayflower dragged him another dozen feet away from the dangling truck. They waited there for another half hour before the Department's team arrived, two dozen Agents and half a dozen Auditors rolling up in black and mirrorless vans.

Paramedics looked him over before giving him a blanket, and that was all the excuse he needed to pass out.

THIRTY-THREE

R AYNE DARTED THROUGH THE TORN CHAIN-LINK FENCE, following the retreating figures. As soon as Grimsby had drawn away the Therian, the two potential victims inside the trailer had broken out and made a run for it.

At first, she had hesitated, feeling the urge to go back and assist Grimsby, but he had asked her to trust him to handle it, and so she would.

Instead, she would go after the bastards who had captured him in the first place.

There were two, one fast, the other strong. The strong one had torn down the fence with ease, and they both seemed intent on fleeing the scene.

This she would not allow.

The deep, caged anger in her chest stirred, sending heat searing into her throat. She kept it contained, though the effort made her jaw clench hard enough that her teeth creaked.

"Control yourself," she cautioned.

She was a professional Auditor. She couldn't afford to let petty emotions distract her. Though that caged fury had never felt less petty.

She followed the suspects as fast as she dared, keeping out of sight. Surprise was her best chance to take them both, though judging from their frantic yet oblivious glances behind them, they seemed uninterested in anything that wasn't ten feet tall with claws. As she was considerably shorter, and her claws were not of the visible variety, she kept out of sight easily enough.

The area around the construction site was largely suburban, with several strip malls on one side and a small, darkened golf course on the other. The fugitives quickly moved toward the shadowed backs of the strip malls, keeping out of the streetlights and staying on sparse strips of grass to hide their flight.

They reached the back of one building, a charity donation drop from the looks of the scattered furniture and trash bags of clothes, and both leaned against a dumpster, breathless. Rayne stayed beyond the edge of the light, peering around a wooden privacy fence that separated this lot from the next.

"Oh boy, Echidna," the large one said, his cadence like a massive child's. "Mother's gonna be mad."

"Oh, would you shut up, Lump!" the fast one snapped, wiping away frizzing hair from her face. "Just let me think for a minute!"

They both wore guises in the form of tattered trench coats, the inverse equivalent of witch masks. Where masks hid a witch from the Elsewhere, guises hid beings like these, whom Department doctrine was strictly against calling *monsters*, from the waking world.

At a glance, Rayne couldn't tell for certain what species each was, but both would have to be more or less humanoid for a simple guise to work. She wouldn't know what they were until they turned down their collars and deactivated the disguising magic of their coats. For a moment, her hand fell to the phone in her pocket as she debated calling for backup, just to be safe. Grieves had warned her not to operate solo, after all. Yet if she didn't act fast, one or both suspects might find a mirror or tunnel and escape Department reach.

But these two had taken and nearly killed Grimsby. She didn't know them, but she knew him well enough to know he was the one in the right. Frustratingly, he usually was.

Though what did that mean for her anger toward him?

She shook her head. Despite what he'd done in the past couple of days, these two had hurt Grimsby, and that was something she would not let pass unanswered.

She left the cell in her pocket. The Department would just get in her way.

She stepped out of the darkness into the moonlight and walked slowly across the open lot toward the fugitives.

"Echidna! Echidna!" Lump said, jutting a meaty hand toward Rayne. "Someone's coming!"

Rayne felt their eyes on her, but any ounce of fear that might have been in her boiled away like water in a hot cauldron. Her throat constricted and heat rose in her belly, blossoming through her chest as her Impetus welled and that cage inside her rattled. She fought the feeling instinctively, but she could almost sense the bars bending, and from within power flowed into her Impetus, filling her with a heat far more intense than ever before. It wasn't the power of the Elsewhere; it was something else altogether.

She tried to wrestle her welling Impetus under control as she drew nearer, though she felt her grip slipping as her fury grew.

Echidna turned to Lump and nodded before lowering the collar of her trench coat. The enchantment that molded her to human form began to waver, shimmering over her skin like a coating of glass. Then it shattered, the shards turning to mist, and from within poured sinewy scales, like a serpent breaking free from a cracked vase, revealing her true form as a lamia.

Lump fumbled down his own collar, and the sound of stretching and tearing seams instantly filled the night air. His body swelled like a balloon being inflated with rough, ugly muscle. His dirtied garments tore away, save for the guise of his trench coat, which strained but remained intact thanks to whatever magic enchanted it. His lank hair became almost like hanging moss, and his eyes condensed into something like glassy red garnets. A troll, then.

They clearly thought their true forms would frighten her, and that almost made her smile. All they did was let her know precisely what she was up against.

A lamia and a troll, she thought. *Simple enough.*

"Get lost, witch!" Echidna called over her forked tongue. "Or we'll—we'll . . ."

She seemed to lose her vocabulary when Rayne didn't stop her stride at their transformations.

She came within ten thin feet before she finally did stop. "Facedown on the ground, hands behind your backs," she said, her breath hot in her white mask. "I won't ask twice."

Echidna's eyes were wide and nervous, but she shook herself, seemingly attempting to don a more intimidating expression. "I won't ask twice, either. Turn around and walk away, or we'll be forced to hurt you."

Lump nodded, his long nose sticking out past his mossy curtain of tangled hair. He tensed his boulder-round shoulders, and the seams of his trench coat creaked in protest.

Rayne felt a small chuckle bubble up her throat, and a grim smile twisted her lips. The sensation almost surprised her, but she kept her composure. "I was genuinely hoping you'd say that."

Her Impetus raged within her, but so did something—else. It was the caged, burning darkness. A fire without light. A beast without form. The only things holding it back were bars of cold discipline she had forged over many years of training. She had trapped it within for as long as she could remember.

But after the months of stress, after the mountain of piling worries and fears placed on her chest by the Department, by the RUIN, by Hives and his disappearance—after how these two attacked and could have killed Grimsby, she didn't care to fight to keep that cage closed.

This time, she opened the cage.

This time, she let loose what was within.

Echidna moved first, as Rayne suspected she would. Lamias were prone to striking first and fast. But the ten feet had been a calculated gap.

Before Echidna's slithering form could dart the distance, Rayne raised her hand and spoke. "*Suspend.*" The dark warmth flared as gravity in the area before her was quelled. Everything in a wide arc beyond her outstretched hand began to rise, unbound by earthly law. Dust and grit floated like inverted hail. Furniture levitated, pushed in any direction by the slightest breeze.

Her coiling foe simply lost all traction as Echidna's momentum pushed her away from the ground. She waved and wriggled both limbs and serpent tail but could neither reach Rayne nor gain any purchase.

Lump moved next, as expected. His dense, almost stony form was resistant to the levitation magic, though she had anticipated this as well.

Even as he roared and lumbered forward, she armed another spell with her uncaged inferno. While one hand was turned upward and maintaining her *Suspend*, she flattened the palm and fingers of her other into an almost bladelike shape. She slashed it through the air, across where Lump's ankles were, and said, "*Sever.*"

A nearly invisible wave of pressure sailed from her fingers, like a crescent-edged sword, and cut cleanly across the troll's shins.

Lump hardly had time to realize what had happened as he raised one knee and the lower half of his leg didn't come with it. The other leg gave way like a tree sliced at the trunk, and he fell to the side, moaning, leaving behind two severed feet that quickly grayed to cracking stone.

Her stomach turned at the sight, but she ignored it. The troll would recover quickly.

Finally, she clenched her open, upturned hand, shifting the Impetus from her *Suspend* into a new spell, and crashed her fist into her open palm. "*Sling.*"

The seemingly absent gravity within her *Suspend* shifted, and suddenly every levitating object flung itself in the new direction that her spell had dictated was downward: Lump's head.

Including Echidna.

The collision was fast, like everything being vacuumed to a single point in the span of a heartbeat, including the gathered donations, and it sounded like a crashing avalanche of tearing cloth and breaking wood.

When she dismissed her lingering spells, what she was left with was no more than a pair of largely unconscious Unorthodox beneath a mound of donated refuse.

Her fists clenched, and she felt that lightless fire beg to be unleashed again and again, until her foes were little more than paste. It rose within her, and the air around her trembled as seeping power began to make the residual magic from her spells resonate once more, but she fought it down, dousing it with discipline, until it was again confined within its cage.

But something felt different, and she was yet uncertain what it was.

She took a shuddering breath and unclenched her trembling hands. She had never let herself go so far. She chided herself silently for her indiscipline, though she felt little regret.

In the distance, metal shrieked, and she looked to see a concrete truck being lifted by a crane, with Grimsby's distant form atop it. For a harrowing moment, she saw a claw grip him from within, but he managed to scramble free and climb down, leaving the Therian trapped, and alive, inside.

His plan had worked.

She felt a smile cross her lips, but it quickly died as she turned her attention to the fugitives. Echidna was unconscious and clearly seriously injured. Lump's severed feet were among the pile, and his stumped legs were trembling with reknitting flesh.

They would both survive, though she doubted Grimsby would approve of what she'd done.

She certainly didn't.

It had been effective, but brutal, and if she hadn't wrestled control back when she did . . .

Her stomach churned and she tasted bile bubbling in her throat. Her head began to spin, and she felt like the air all around her had suddenly become too hot to breathe. She felt her balance wavering and instinctively knelt to the ground to keep from falling.

She heard someone say something, a distant call. She sensed someone drawing close, hardly a shadow on the edge of her perception, but it was all she could do to force air into her lungs.

Who were they? What was this? What was happening?

She felt a cold hand on her cheek, and she looked up to see Defaux.

How the hell had the Auditor found her so quickly?

Defaux's appearance was a shock, though it was tempered by the small comfort of a familiar face, just when the rest of the world had suddenly become disorienting and crushing.

"It's all right," Defaux said, her voice muffled like she was calling through a storm. "You're all right. Just relax."

Rayne shook her head, every muscle in her body tensing and convulsing. She fell to the ground, completely unable to control herself, only able to watch as her body writhed.

"You're all right," Defaux said. "You're all right. Let go. I have you, like always."

Slowly, she felt her heart begin to fade from hammer to beat. Her catching breath became shuddering, then finally smooth. Her muscles relaxed, and she let herself go limp, sweat plastering her body.

All the while, she heard Defaux's soft voice and felt her cool hand on her cheek. "Relax. I'll take care of things from here."

Then her mind blanked.

THIRTY-FOUR

GRIMSBY HALF SLEPT UNTIL EARLY DAWN, WAKING PE-riodically in a hurried panic that Goode might have somehow escaped, only to find his trap remained secure. The Department task force had set up a perimeter around the dangling cement truck, which thrashed occasionally like a fish on a line, and though its drum had become warped and dented from within, the crane's cable held.

As the first rays of dawn rose to drown out the moonlight, the members of the task force moved about with enough commotion to wake Grimsby again. He sat up straight in the jeep's passenger seat, becoming briefly tangled in the scratchy blanket a paramedic had given him. He saw Mayflower standing outside in the same position he had been in when he convinced Grimsby to rest in the jeep.

Grimsby stumbled out of the seat, his legs numb from the last few restless hours in an awkward position. He yawned in greeting as he limped to stand beside the Huntsman.

"Get some sleep?" Mayflower asked over his folded arms, his eyes never wavering from the truck. It shuddered briefly as the crane whined and began lowering it to the ground.

"Something close enough," Grimsby said. "I miss anything?"

Mayflower shook his head. "Just a lot of thrashing. Task force has been waiting for the truck to snap loose, but looks like we got lucky."

"That's good."

Mayflower half turned to him and gave him a glance that Grimsby couldn't fully understand. "Yeah. It was pretty damned good."

He squirmed uncomfortably under what felt like praise. "Any word from Rayne?" he asked.

"No, but I wouldn't expect any. If she apprehended those two, I'd wager she'd contact the Department directly. We sort of had our hands full here. Who were they?" he asked, his tone dark. "The ones that grabbed you."

"Well I guess the briefest way to describe them is as . . . my victims?"

Mayflower fully turned to him this time, somehow raising one half of his furrowed brow in a dangerous question.

Grimsby quickly gave him a recounting of his and Wudge's escapade into the Elsewhere the night before, finishing it by withdrawing the nail from his pocket to show him.

The Huntsman leaned close to examine it, though he didn't try to touch it. "And you just happened to neglect to tell me any of this?"

"Well, in my defense, you hadn't left your pajamas in a month—"

"Evening robe."

"I'm not having this discussion with you again."

The Huntsman ignored him and glared at the nail. "And you can't get rid of it?"

Grimsby let it dangle from his finger to demonstrate. "Nope. Wudge is supposedly finding a solution to that problem." He paused. "Though I really expected to hear from him by now—I hope he's all right."

Mayflower grunted. "It messes with your magic, but does it do anything else?"

"What do you mean?"

"I mean, does it make you stronger? Does it make you feel"— he paused for a moment, his gray-green eyes calculating—"powerful? Angry? Anything that does that is something to be concerned about."

"I— I'm not sure," Grimsby said. "The things it's turned my spells into, they're, well, they're useful. Maybe more useful than my normal magic. But more powerful?" He stopped and thought of the stump he'd turned into a crater the day before. "Maybe."

Mayflower said nothing; he only glared.

"What?"

"I've seen a few cursed items in the past. Most were annoying. A few were real nasty. The worst of them always felt like they were a blessing, at first. And they always offered power. Sometimes it was strength, or knowledge, or money. But it was always power, and it was always fast."

"Is that so bad?" Grimsby asked, his eyes falling to the nail cradled in his palm.

"Power? Sometimes. But power fast? Always yes. It takes time to learn how to wield power responsibly." His hand rose unconsciously to the gun inside his coat. "Sometimes I think you can't ever really learn to. But you can be damned sure that anything that makes you powerful quickly is bad news. And someone always gets hurt."

Grimsby found himself wishing he could bury the little piece of metal somewhere in the dirt where it wouldn't trouble anyone again. Instead, he could only slip it into his pocket.

"Get rid of that thing the first chance you get," Mayflower said. "Maybe it's just an annoyance. Maybe not. Either way, it's better to be rid of it."

Grimsby nodded. Hopefully Wudge would have an answer soon. If not . . .

He'd hate to get rid of it on his own—if only because it would mean discarding or destroying the one link Wudge had to his precious door. Besides, that would also likely mean disclosing its existence to the Department, as he didn't have the means to deal with it on his own. Which would also, in turn, mean questions about his use of it during his assessment, and whether or not using it had been illegal.

Although, at the same time, maybe he was a more fit Auditor with it in hand than without.

The idea disturbed him even as it occurred to him, and he quickly boxed away his wandering fears to deal with another time.

Meanwhile, Mayflower's gaze focused on the task force's work. They had lowered the truck nearly to the ground. Agents fanned out in a wide circle, interspersed with the white-masked and less common Auditors, all waiting for any sign of danger.

Then, after a long pause, Mayflower said, "I'm sorry."

"Sorry? What for?"

"I should have been there."

"In the Elsewhere with me and Wudge? I don't think—"

"Not just there. The last few weeks, I should have been there." He seemed to stare hard at the bustling personnel if only to avoid looking Grimsby in the eye. "Or at least had the guts to tell you I wasn't going to be."

Grimsby said nothing, not because he wanted to be silent, but because Mayflower seemed to be working up the will to keep talking.

"There, for a long time—too long—I didn't much give a second thought about pulling the trigger. The world was all dark and light. It was simple." His voice was small, smaller than Grimsby had ever heard it before. "I killed a lot of people when the world was simple."

Grimsby felt like his stomach had cinched tight, his eyes cast to the gun under Mayflower's arm. It always made him wary, like a dog that might bite, but it also often gave him a sense of safety. At the moment, however, there was no warmth to that dangerous power. It was cold, almost alien.

"But now," Mayflower said, "now I'm thinking that maybe . . ." He trailed off, unable or unwilling to finish the sentence.

So, Grimsby finished it for him.

"That maybe it was never so simple?" he asked.

He saw Mayflower's throat tighten, and the Huntsman gave the barest nod.

Grimsby didn't know what to do. What could he say? Mayflower was confessing to him, but neither of them knew what he was confessing to. Had he taken lives that might have been saved?

Neither of them would ever know.

Yet, looking at the Huntsman, who normally stood so tall, now teetering like a cracked obelisk, Grimsby felt like he did know something.

He reached up, way up, and put his hand on Mayflower's shoulder. "You did your best," he said. "Nobody can ask for more."

Mayflower's muscles went taut at the touch, and for a moment Grimsby thought he would pull away. Then, very slowly and through force of will, he relaxed.

He seemed about to say something when the cement truck screeched as the rear dropped the last few feet to the ground, its axle finally torn loose by the weight of it hanging from the cable.

The whole construction yard of movement ceased, as though they were all waiting for something to come clambering out. Agents, armed with firearms from pistols to assault rifles, focused their shaded gazes on the truck. Grimsby felt a flare of heat on his face as a half dozen Auditors summoned rushed Impetuses.

His own heart seemed to skip a few beats, hanging like it was on a hook of its own.

Then a pale, solitary hand poked out of the truck's drum. No claws or fur, no hooves or horn, just an arm slick with grayed water.

Agents moved in and, after looking inside to be sure, signaled the paramedics. They rushed forward with a stretcher and within moments had extracted Goode and laid him on it.

Grimsby felt a surge of relief, like someone had hooked a boiler to his veins. His tensed muscles went slack, and he felt like sleeping for a week. Instead, he limped forward, Mayflower falling in line behind him. An Agent moved to stand in their way but, after a glance at the Huntsman, decided to be anywhere else.

The paramedics were about to elevate Goode's stretcher into the ambulance, but he muttered something and waved at them with an exhausted arm. As Grimsby approached, he tried to sit up but was urged to remain horizontal. Instead, he just donned a tired smile.

Grimsby stood beside him for a minute and realized he didn't know what to say. A few sentences formed in his head, and he stumbled over each of them before stammering, "You okay?"

Goode made a choking noise that might have been a laugh. "I feel like I've spent the last few hours in a dryer full of bricks. Otherwise, yeah."

"Do you—uh, remember?"

Goode's chuckle faded; his eyes grew hollow and distant. "Everything. Every time," he said quietly. "That's what makes it so . . ." He shuddered and trailed off. Then he shook himself, like he was remembering where he was. "Thank you, Auditor," he said. "Thank you for saving me."

Grimsby frowned in confusion for a moment. He looked down to see his suit stained with ash and sweat, with the left sleeve hanging on by scorched scraps, his collar in tatters. He assumed his face was largely in about the same shape.

He didn't look like an Auditor.

But, for the moment, he sure felt like one.

He smiled at Goode, not trusting himself to say words, and instead just nodded.

The paramedics began to raise Goode's stretcher into the ambulance once more, but as they did he struggled to sit up. "One thing," he said, trying to speak up loud enough for Grimsby to hear him. "I gave you that list of what that guy—the ritualist you're looking for—what he bought from me. But there was something else I didn't tell you."

Grimsby felt his heart halt as though it had forgotten how to beat. In all the chaos, he hadn't thought about their ritualist-at-large since Rayne had come to find him at the warehouse. "What was it?"

"I didn't see it, but I could smell it. A scent I've only caught once before. It was a hagstone."

"You smelled a stone?" he asked, wondering just how sharp Goode's senses were. "What did it smell like?"

The Therian's tired eyes grew strained as he gulped. "It smelled like—like something alien. Some*place* alien."

Grimsby frowned, the gears in his mind churning for something other than immediate survival for the first time in hours. He'd never heard of a hagstone, but Goode didn't seem to be in any shape to explain it to him. He decided it was better to let the Therian rest than press him with any more questions. "Thanks, Goode."

He nodded and hoarsely croaked, "Good luck," just before the ambulance doors closed.

The vehicle lurched into motion and wove its way out of the construction site. Two Department vehicles fell into line behind it as escorts, likely to make certain Goode found his way to the Asylum before nightfall.

Mayflower moved from his stalwart stillness, startling Grimsby from his thoughts.

"Hey," Grimsby said, turning his mind away from the case for the moment, "why didn't you say anything to Goode? You saved his life."

"No, you saved his life. From both the Department and me. I came here to kill him." His words were matter-of-fact, but tinged with shame.

"I couldn't have done it alone," Grimsby said.

"Someday, you will have to." These words, too, were spoken as simple truth.

He gulped, suddenly regretting talking about anything that wasn't the job at hand. "You ever hear of something called a hagstone?"

Mayflower's eyes shadowed before he grunted in the affirmative. "Seen them before. Non-witches can use them to manage some magic. Witches can do a lot worse with one. It's like a mobile pinhole into the Elsewhere."

Grimsby shuddered at the thought. Mirrors were all potential doors to the Elsewhere, but they were closed until opened. If a hagstone was always open, who knew what might find its way through?

What's more, what kind of magic could something like that fuel?

What kind of ritual?

Grimsby didn't know, but no answer seemed good. "Well, Goode seems to think he smelled a hagstone on our mystery man."

"Smelled a stone?"

Grimsby shrugged. "It's all we got."

Mayflower thought for a moment, then spat on the ground. "Well, fortunately for everyone, those things are rare. Can't get them from any piddly dealer."

"Know where he might have gotten this one?"

The Huntsman took a deep breath, letting it out slow. "Yeah, but I'm not thrilled about it."

Grimsby was too tired to bother hiding his confusion. "What?"

"Mother Frost. Leader of the Kindred, the biggest Unorthodox crime family left in Boston."

"Monster Mafia, naturally," Grimsby said, shaking his head and walking toward the jeep.

"What?" Mayflower asked behind him with something that might have passed for Huntsman amusement. "No moans of dread, no wide eyes or shaking knees? I would have thought you'd have some comments or concerns."

Grimsby paused, then shook his head. He was too tired for either, so all he said was: "Shotgun."

THIRTY-FIVE ✳

"Remind me again why we can't call for backup?" Grimsby asked. He sat slumped in the jeep's passenger seat, his exhausted body sinking into the cracked leather like an anvil in damp sand.

"The Kindred aren't some back-alley street gang," Mayflower said, his eyes on the road, his hands at ten and two on the wheel. "You remember how I told you we took Mansgraf's base—"

"Lair," Grimsby interrupted despite being half awake. "It's definitely a lair."

Mayflower shot him a glare but didn't argue. "We took it from a Therian gang?"

"Yeah, it definitely rings nightmarish bells." He shuddered at the thought of dealing with not one, but numerous Therians, all in those cramped tunnels underground. His own encounter had given him terrible insight into such imaginations.

"That was the Pack. They were one of the groups that ran out of Boston. Real tight-knit, fur-exclusive fellas. There was a group of vampires, too. I forgot their name." He frowned and let the thought slip away. "And there was the Kindred, which basically took all comers when it came to members, so they were the largest. Mother Frost adopted anything from harpies to trolls and dozens of other things."

"Three monster gangs? Why haven't I heard of this?"

"Because the Department is real good at keeping the real nasty things under wraps, and most folks are happy enough to be left in the dark. But those three were small-fry compared to the fourth group."

"Fourth?"

"The Coven." He said the word like it was battery acid on his tongue.

Grimsby recoiled, the word ugly in his head. "I've heard about them—though only some rumors."

"That's surprising, seeing as the Department doesn't like to talk about them, even to their own. The Coven was all witches—the worst of them. Thought being able to toss around magic made them the rightful rulers of just about everyone and everything. And no small number of them were in the Department. The witch that first tried this ritual we're tracking, Janice, she was one of their lieutenants, but she was small fish compared to some of their ringleaders. They did the nastiest shit I've ever seen. Blood rituals, human sacrifice, and worse." His face contorted in contained fury for a moment before it fell to a smolder. "In any case, Boston was a practical war zone back then. The gangs fought in the streets and a lot of innocents died in nasty ways, but the Coven got out of control. Their members broke away from the Department and started becoming a movement. Worse yet, it started getting traction. So, what remained of the Department set up a meet with the other big three gangs. They all agreed to take down the Coven."

"The Department wouldn't make deals with people like that!" Grimsby said, more in instinctive shock than because he believed it.

"Those deals are the only reason the city is still on the map," the Huntsman scoffed. "Anyway, a year later, there was no Coven left."

"So what happened to the gangs?"

"The vamps went straight. The Pack was all but wiped out. And the Kindred, well, they made a deal of their own. The Department stays out of their affairs, and they don't do anything to upset normal folks. It works well both ways."

"So we can't ask for backup because—"

"Because, strictly speaking, we shouldn't be doing this."

Grimsby gulped. As if his career wasn't in enough jeopardy with his unintentional cheating during his second assessment, and the hiccup with the escaped Therian, now he was going strictly against Department policy; albeit it was a policy he'd had no idea existed until just now.

"So why are we doing this? Surely there's some other way to find out who was behind the RUIN."

Mayflower shook his head. "Hagstones are too powerful to be found through common dealers like Goode. Even demons like Aby or Ash would have trouble getting their hands on one, let alone a supply to sell. If this ritualist had a hagstone for the RUIN, my bet is that the only place to get one would be from Mother Frost herself."

"So how are we going to meet with her?" Grimsby asked, certain he would not like the answer.

Mayflower let slip a bitter growl as he pulled the jeep off the road and down a dirt trail. Within moments, it rattled over a set of rusted-out train tracks and groaned to a halt. "We're going to sit down for tea," he said.

Before them was the towering mouth of an ancient railway tunnel that looked like it hadn't been used in decades. It descended at a shallow angle, though its walls were of chipped, staggered brick rather than smooth cement. Its entry was shadowed beyond the pale light of dawn, but from within Grimsby felt cool breath pouring forth, as if from the maw of some slumbering beast.

The Huntsman climbed out and rounded to the back of the jeep. Grimsby followed him stiffly, feeling pain hammering through the swelling bruises from his encounter with Goode.

"Can I just say, for the record, I think this is a bad idea?" Grimsby said.

"Of course it is." Mayflower shrugged, then opened the hatch to the back and dug through the collection of odd objects within. He moved aside small chests, gun cases, and lockboxes until he found a brown bag the size of his fist. "You want to back out?"

Grimsby let out a nervous chuckle. "Odd's Bodkin, yes. But that won't get the job done, will it?"

Mayflower nodded in approval, hefting the bag before tucking it into his coat. "No. No, it won't."

There was a short moment of mutual silence before Grimsby gestured. "After you."

The Huntsman snorted. "Chivalry isn't dead, I see."

"And he doesn't plan to be anytime soon."

Mayflower scoffed and shook his head. Withdrawing a heavy flashlight from his coat, he walked briskly into the tunnel, departing the dawning light of the sunrise without hesitation.

Grimsby was a bit slower and more reluctant. He took one last glance to the horizon before following Mayflower's bobbing light into the dark.

The tunnel was cold. Not simply chilly, as the spring morning would have had it, but cold enough that the only thing Grimsby could see besides the Huntsman's silhouette was his own puffs of frigid breath.

In the beam of light cast by Mayflower's scrutinous examination of the tunnel, Grimsby saw only redbrick walls overgrown with frostbitten moss. Sheets of ice and rime became more common as they went deeper, as did drifts of piled snow over the rails, and soon the flashlight's illumination was bouncing about, reflected off the undulant frozen surface of the tunnel.

"Why is it so cold?" Grimsby asked, clutching his tattered jacket around himself.

"The name Mother Frost didn't give it away?" Mayflower asked. "She comes from the old country. Very old, where fairy tales were all too true. My guess is that she likes it chilly."

"And she's frozen over this whole tunnel?"

"It's more than a tunnel," Mayflower said, but before he could continue, they heard the squeal of metal on metal grating in the distance and growing slowly closer. The iron rails beneath their feet trembled, and flecks of ice and snow shed from the ceiling, feeling like tiny nails as they fell upon Grimsby's exposed neck to melt away.

He took an instinctive step back, ready to summon his Im petus, but Mayflower stood firm. Even so, he raised his hand to clutch his lapel, resting it conveniently near his shoulder holster.

Within a minute, a figure appeared in the depths of the tunnel, coasting toward them as smoothly as a subway train. As it grew closer, Grimsby saw it was someone atop a single railway car, one that was small and simple.

It had no engine or machinery, not even walls or a roof, but was rather little more than a platform with wheels and a complicated bank of levers along one side. It seemed propelled solely by the driver pumping the handle at its center up and down again.

The figure atop it was hunched and squat, even shorter than Grimsby. He wore only a threadbare tunic and a thin brown cloak of burlap against the frigid air, and on his head was a pointed cap of red that drooped over one shoulder.

As he approached within twenty or so feet, he pulled one of the numerous levers on the side of the train car, if it could even be called that, and the wheels began to screech, throwing off sparks that sizzled and died on the gathered drifts of ice on the ground.

He slid to a halt just a few feet away, tugged at his scruffy white beard, which came to a point that mirrored his hat's dangling tip beside it, and glared at them both with a single eye; its paired socket was shrunken to a withered hole.

"Humans are not welcome in the deep places," he said, his voice wheezing like wind through a ruined farmhouse. "Go back to the surface, where your kind belongs."

Mayflower produced a leather sack from his coat. He dug within and withdrew two coins of shining gold. "One for a ride, the other for safe passage," he said.

The strange man's frown deepened as he idly dug in his empty eye socket with one finger. "Passage to where?"

"To *who*. We want to speak to Mother Frost."

The hunched man cackled. "And how will you be getting back?" he asked.

"How much?" Mayflower reached once again into the fist-size bag of gold.

"You can't afford it," the man assured them, "but if Mother is who you wish to see, I can take you to her, though you may wish I hadn't."

He held out a gnarled hand, the flesh and bone so twisted that it looked more like a claw than anything human, and Mayflower dropped the coins into his harrowed palm.

"The deal is made." The man nodded, his words like an incantation of their own. He stepped back and gestured to the platform he stood on. It looked like ancient wood bound in bands of black iron, and so old that it likely predated anything Grimsby had seen on the surface.

Mayflower climbed aboard, grunting and offering a hand back to help Grimsby up. With them both in tow, the stranger turned to the mass of levers, which looked like a bottom jaw of crooked teeth. He pulled a few, pushed another, and began pumping the central lever up and down. The car's mechanisms shrieked and it lurched slowly forward, gaining speed with each passing moment.

The Huntsman swiveled his gaze between the driver and the tunnel ahead, his flashlight casting dazzling light as it shone through icicles that formed on both ceiling and ground.

Grimsby breathed into his hands, trying to keep his fingers warm against the air that whipped by them. To distract himself from the cold, he turned to their guide and asked, "What's your name?"

The stranger glared at him and spat off the side of the cart, the spittle freezing to shatter before it hit the ground. "Best be careful with questions like that down here, boy."

He forced an awkward laugh. "Well then, what am I supposed to call you? Quasimodo?" He winced. "I'm sorry, that was rude. I'm just nervous."

"Wiser than you look, then. Call me what you like," he said, shrugging his hunched back, "but I won't be giving you my name, and you best keep yours to yourself."

Grimsby shrugged. The man didn't seem insulted by the name, and it bothered Grimsby to not have any title at all for the stranger. "Let's shorten it to Quasi, then."

Quasi glowered but did not argue, instead focusing on the steady rhythm of pumping the platform forward.

"Don't talk much, do you?" Grimsby asked, trying to keep his mind off the gnawing pins of pain from the chill.

Quasi did not reply.

"I spy with my little eye," Grimsby said, uncertain why he was trying, "something . . . frozen?"

Quasi's glare only deepened, forcing Grimsby to retreat a scant few feet to stand beside Mayflower.

"This tunnel goes on farther than it should," he said to the Huntsman.

Mayflower nodded. "There's countless old tunnels below the

city, most of them from the subways—both new and abandoned. But some are older. Much older. And no matter which direction they go, follow one long enough and you end up in the same place."

"Where's that?" Grimsby asked, eyes squinting against the wind.

Before Mayflower could answer, the darkness ahead bloomed from black to deep blue, until it finally rose to an icy-cyan hue. The frozen walls of the tunnel fell away, as did the ground, leaving the rails suspended in the air by chains held taut from high above and spidery, arctic arches that stretched out far below.

Grimsby was instantly struck with a wave of disorienting nausea and felt his balance waver. Mayflower's iron grip seized his arm and kept him steady.

Below them, and for miles into the distance, Grimsby saw a city. It wasn't Boston, or anything like it. The structures were stone and mud, ice and brick. The streets were slick with rime and shimmered in the ambient light of torch-fire sconces and braziers. Above were thick stalactites that hung down, some of them hundreds of feet above their heads; others looked like frozen waterfalls of stone that fell all the way to the ground, creating pillars that dwarfed all but the largest skyscrapers in the city above.

At the cavern's center was a tower of ice, spinning upward and branching out in impossible angles like a stag's antler, supporting the massive ceiling like branches holding up a canopy.

"You end up in Underton," Mayflower said.

THIRTY-SIX ✳

"T HIS PLACE CAN'T BE REAL," GRIMSBY SAID, HIS EYES bugging out until they nearly knocked the glasses from his face. "There's no way this is just—beneath us all the time."

Mayflower shrugged. "Maybe it is, maybe it isn't. But it's real enough."

"Real enough to what?" Grimsby asked, then paused. "Do you think rent is cheaper down here?"

The Huntsman growled. "It's real enough to kill you," he said. "So keep yourself together."

The cart rattled and swayed, veering on a rail toward the branching tower at the city's center. It intersected another line, upon which Grimsby saw an oncoming train, one that was dark iron and encrusted with ice, belching up black smoke from its spout. It blared a wailing horn at them, a fire burning in the depths of its grated maw.

Behind them, Quasi grumbled and flicked another lever, and as the cart struck the next intersection, merely fifty feet from the oncoming behemoth, it caught something on the rails and careened hard onto a different line, making Mayflower and Grimsby both tumble and grip at the menagerie of levers for support. For a moment, Grimsby saw straight down into the city streets, all narrow and crawling, teeming with shadowed figures of varied sizes and inhuman shapes, before he managed to right himself on the car.

Quasi glared at the departing train, which was dozens of cars long, and shook his disfigured claw. "Accursed Neathers!" he called out.

Their vector had veered along the web-way of suspended rails, but with another few jerks of levers, Quasi clattered the cart onto new lines and righted their course to the center of the cavern.

"What business have ye with Mother?" Quasi asked, speaking to them for the first time since they'd entered the main cavern.

Grimsby glanced to Mayflower, wondering if he should say, but the Huntsman only shrugged.

"We're looking for someone who bought a hagstone," he said.

Quasi nodded. "Ah, aye, that'll be Mother, all right. She keeps them locked up tight, she does. Rarely sells them, though." His brow furrowed, making the cave of his empty eye socket squeeze shut. "Whoever bought it must have given her something precious indeed."

Grimsby said nothing, instead looking to the frozen structure at the center of the cave. From here, it looked almost like a lop-sided candelabra or menorah. Whoever, or whatever, Mother Frost was, she was apparently responsible for this place's frozen climate. She must have been powerful to manage such a feat, far beyond anything Grimsby had seen from a single person before. What could their mysterious ritualist have offered a being like that? What could she possibly want that she couldn't obtain herself?

And, most importantly, how were they going to get back?

Grimsby had no answers, and the questions lingered. Although curiosity was quickly supplanted by nervous fear as they drew near the Unorthodox city's center.

"Hey, uh, Les?" he asked.

Mayflower glanced back at him and grunted before returning his gaze to the tower.

"This Frost lady—"

"Mother Frost," Mayflower corrected him. "These folks are particular about their names, and even more so about titles. Be sure to get them right, and to keep yours to yourself."

"Right. Mother Frost. We're here to talk to her directly, right?"

Mayflower nodded.

"What's to stop her from . . . how do I put this . . . tying us to train tracks and twirling her big, evil mustache?"

"Simple. She doesn't have a mustache," he said.

"You know what I mean."

"You mean what's to keep her from killing us?"

Grimsby winced, both at the words and at the thought. He had no idea how Mayflower uttered the phrase so nonchalantly. "Yeah. That."

"This place has rules, like any other. We're both Department, so we've got something like diplomatic immunity as long as we don't break them. Follow them and you'll probably be fine."

"Probably?" Grimsby asked.

"Probably," the Huntsman confirmed with a frustratingly casual shrug.

"But I don't even know the rules!"

The ice tower grew close enough that Grimsby could see wafts of mist radiating off it, coiling over its surface like a living haze.

"Then I suggest you shut up and follow my lead. There's only one rule you need to worry about right now."

"And which one is that?" Grimsby asked as the cart passed under a frozen archway and into an outer ring of ice that circled the tower like a fortress wall, slowing as it did. To one side of the rails was a solid translucent wall, reflecting muddled shapes from outside; to the other was a narrow strip of ice that served as a debarking platform.

"Don't be a smart-ass."

"Easier said than done," Grimsby muttered, but his words were lost as Quasi pulled a lever for the brakes and the cart screeched to a halt.

Quasi grunted as the cart stopped. He gestured ahead. "Go on, now. She knows you're here. Just through there." He pointed with his misshapen claw toward a pair of doors at the center of the platform, each of which was about fifteen feet tall and likely weighed thousands of pounds.

Mayflower stepped off the cart with ease, his stride as cool and steady as the tower itself. Grimsby clambered after him, waving meekly at Quasi as he did.

"Wish us luck!" he said, though it came out more as a genuine plea than a farewell.

Quasi only chuckled and began to pump the cart away.

Grimsby couldn't help but peer around in wide-eyed wonder. He was still freezing, but he barely noticed as he stared at the sheer surface of the tower. It climbed all the way to the ceiling of the cavern, hundreds of feet, but it was almost spindly in breadth when compared to its height, like the roots of a tree frozen and inverted.

Its walls were not flat, but flowing, like once-molten candle wax frozen solid, embedded occasionally with bulbous nodules that held frozen statues within—although these looked more life-like than Grimsby was comfortable with. Many of them even had color to them. They passed one, sunken into the platform's floor, which was some creature akin to that troll Grimsby had seen, Lump. Its large form had been submerged in the ice, its lower portions shrouded by its depth. Its face was turned upward as though snarling in rage—or perhaps gasping for air. Its tusked maw was open wide beneath beady eyes that were bright with fury—

And moving.

Grimsby watched as its gaze followed them, not like a clever painting, but as it actually slid over them beneath the ice.

"It's—it's alive," he said, his voice muted by horror, his eyes darting to more distant forms embedded into the tower's surface like frozen gargoyles. There were dozens, hundreds even. Were they all also alive?

Mayflower nodded, his expression hard. "Mother Frost has a . . . grim sense of justice."

"So what do we do if she turns on us?" Grimsby asked, the heavy doors drawing closer.

"We hope she doesn't."

"Hope?" Grimsby demanded. "Since when does the Huntsman rely on hope? Aren't you the one who told me that if you go to have a conversation with somebody who can kill you, you—"

"You better be able to kill them right back. Yeah, yeah, I remember." He shook his head. "I don't like it, either, but it's our only way to find out who bought the hagstone and track them down to finish this."

Grimsby noticed that for once Mayflower's hand did not rest near his gun, and the only reasoning he could imagine was because it would do them no good.

Somehow, that made him more terrified than any thought of frozen purgatory or big, evil mustaches.

His steps faltered and he suddenly came to a halt, though he could hardly tell over the racing of his heart. This was crazy—absolutely insane. Just a short time ago he had been making house calls and doing busywork.

Now, after defeating a goat-wolf-moose-man, he was about to meet with some kind of frozen underworld train demigoddess.

It was wrong, it made no sense, and though the starkness of those facts had only just begun to catch up with him, it did so with as much speed and force as any railway car.

He suddenly found himself unable to move, and barely able to breathe.

Mayflower noticed he had stopped after a few paces and glanced back. "Kid?"

Grimsby shook his head. "This is a bad idea. We shouldn't be doing this. We shouldn't—" His words fell flat and he found himself crouching on his haunches, wrapping his arms around his legs. His whole body was trembling, and he rocked back and forth on his heels to keep from falling altogether.

Mayflower took a long breath, then he came over.

Grimsby expected him to growl. He expected him to shout, to berate, possibly even belittle. He expected a lot of things.

He did not expect Mayflower to sit beside him and say nothing.

Long minutes passed, and after a time Grimsby found his pulse had begun to settle, and his breath became less thready. His tense muscles suddenly reminded him of their exhaustion, and he let himself fall from his heels to his behind on the cold ice, though he still kept his knees close to his chest.

Mayflower still sat beside him, silent. He wasn't even staring, instead just studying the walls of the tower.

When Grimsby finally had breath to speak, he found his voice choked all the same. "I'm—I'm sorry," he said, staring at the ground between his knees in shame.

Mayflower let out a short breath that might have been a chuckle coming from anyone else. "No, you're not sorry," he said. "You're human, kid." He stood, brushed the clinging ice from his pants, and offered a hand to help Grimsby up.

Grimsby hesitated, still too ashamed to look Mayflower in the face. "I—I don't want to do this."

"Me neither," said the Huntsman. "I'd rather be day drinking in my evening robe. But we got a job to do, don't we?"

Grimsby didn't take comfort in the words. He felt like a coward. He felt weak. He felt like the sole broken link in a chain that went on for miles. He only shook his head and stared at the ground between his feet.

The Huntsman took a deep breath. "You know, if you don't come in with me," he said, "I can't promise I won't shoot anybody."

"Would you promise not to if I did?"

"Of course not," Mayflower said, offering his hand again.

Grimsby found himself trying to suppress a choked laugh. It was indecent to laugh when he was so terrified, so ashamed, which of course made it all the harder to compose himself appropriately.

He shook his head and let Mayflower help him to his feet. "Can you at least promise you won't shoot *me*?"

Mayflower patted his shoulder reassuringly. "Of course not," he said, and his grizzled face twisted in a slight grin.

They turned to face the dual doors of towering ice. As though sensing them, the doors cracked and groaned, opening with a belch of curling mist. And though Grimsby still didn't feel prepared for what was on the other side, he at least knew one thing.

He wouldn't be facing it alone.

THIRTY-SEVEN ✳

BEYOND THE DOORS, GRIMSBY EXPECTED TO SEE A FROZEN throne room, or some kind of fortress within the tower.

Instead, he and Mayflower stood at the edge of a meadow.

The grass was brittle and dry, as though soaked in frozen dew, and dusted with a light flurry's worth of snow. The distant sun was washed to a gray hue. The horizon seemed to stretch on into soft mountain ranges, but as he looked closer he saw the vague shape of the tower's translucent walls marring the image, like a projection on a screen.

Yet, as they moved forward, their steps crunching on the grass, the ground beneath their feet seemed real enough. Behind them, the doors of ice closed, and as they did, they took on the false image of rolling fields of brown-green grass fading into the distance.

Before them was a small cabin of simple wood and stone, barely visible through a grove of not-so-small trees. They were oddly broad and stout, though their limbs were almost entirely shed of leaves, and their trunks were twisted in strange figures.

The cabin itself was almost haphazard, like it might collapse at any moment, but as they grew nearer, Grimsby saw it was actually of sturdy construction that simply seemed to disdain straight lines and even corners. The rooftop came to too many points to be reasonable, and both the chimney and eaves twisted and curled in unnecessary curves.

A figure sat in the fenced yard before the cabin, rocking in a gnarled chair with a steady pace that seemed to match the errant breeze that rolled over the grass, bringing with it a chill that was mild enough to seem almost balmy compared to the frigid tower's exterior.

Mayflower took the lead, and Grimsby followed, trying to ignore the shifting terrain once more. From frozen tunnel to icy city to frigid fields, it was all disorienting. At least the cold was a steady factor. He realized how much he took the consistency of his own world for granted.

They reached the wooden gate to the yard, and he saw the figure was a woman perhaps not far beyond middling age. In fact, she looked to be about Mayflower's age, perhaps even a bit younger.

Except her eyes looked much older.

They were gray and hazy and seemed as deep and opaque as a quarry. Her ancient gaze lingered on the horizon, unfocused, while her quick, deft hands wove a cluster of needlework. She rocked back and forth, her chair creaking with each motion, not seeming to notice them. Beside her, seated on the edge of a windowsill, sat a hand-stitched doll with eyes so dark they seemed to devour the light around them and crave more.

Grimsby felt like the doll's gaze somehow shifted to him, and suddenly his shivering had little to do with the cold.

They approached the gate, and Mayflower glanced at Grimsby before knocking at the rickety wooden boards. It seemed almost odd for him to do, as it was clearly unlocked and was hardly three feet high. The tall man could have simply stepped over it, and even Grimsby could have hopped it with ease. Yet something told Grimsby that would be an unwise choice.

The woman ceased her rocking, and as she did, the wind went still, though somehow the branches of the trees around them continued to rustle and shake. She set aside her cluster of yarn and needles, which appeared to be some kind of tiny dress, and finally turned her eyes toward them, though she seemed to gaze a few feet above their heads.

"Ah. Guests," she said, though there was no surprise in her tone. "You may enter."

The gate swung slowly open on its own, and the two crossed its boundary.

"Sit," the woman said, gesturing to a pair of stools that sat across from her. Grimsby didn't recall them having been there before, nor had he seen them appear.

Mayflower settled down, gruff but somehow a touch refined, like a Wild West cowboy turned gentleman for the moment. Grimsby, meanwhile, felt like a schoolboy about to be scolded by a teacher.

"You've come a long way," the woman said, "wandering very far from safety." Her eyes swiveled to Grimsby, and though her gaze seemed blind, he could feel its pressure over him like a blanket of chains. "Very far."

"Mother Frost," Mayflower said with a nod, "I've heard much about you."

She nodded. "It is as good a name as any, though Hylde will suit our needs well enough. I am more than simply . . ." She trailed off and looked across the vast, illusory fields. "Cold."

"Hylde, then," the Huntsman said, saying the given word with careful respect. "We've come to you because we're searching for someone—"

She raised a brow at him. "I suspect you know exactly where

to find the people you care about, Huntsman, not that it will re-
deem you to them."

Mayflower faltered, his face slackened with shock for a brief
moment before it tightened and his eyes narrowed. A vein bulged
in his temple, and though Grimsby wasn't sure what nerve Hylde
had struck, he was certain that Mayflower was about to say something they both might regret.

"We're searching for someone who got their hands on a hagstone," Grimsby said before Mayflower could speak. "And we
think they got it from—well, from down here."

The Huntsman flashed a furious glance at Grimsby before
taking a seething breath and steeling himself, though he still
looked many degrees from calm.

Hylde turned her oppressive gaze to Grimsby once more, as
calm and serene as a mountain before an avalanche. It took all his
willpower to not shrink into himself beneath it.

"Perhaps they did," she said. "I have a collection of them,
which I sometimes part with for a suitable exchange."

"And did you exchange one recently?"

The woman's eyes narrowed, though it seemed in contempla-
tion more than agitation. "First, young witch, we must observe
the formalities. My kind holds them quite dear, I'm afraid. Mara?"

She waved a hand to the doll beside her, and it seemed to
tremble at the motion. Cold wind whipped through the air, not as
a gust or breeze, but as a channeled torrent, carrying with it flecks
of ice and snow torn from blades of grass and branches above. The
sleet flew toward the doll and seemed to cling to it, collecting
more and more mass until a figure began to form around it, like a
snowman made too anatomically correct. Within moments, the
rough, white snow compacted until it was smooth and glistening
ice, and suddenly a woman sat where the doll had been, her skin
as translucent and white as a glacier. The doll was gone, though

its shadowed mass where the woman's heart should have been could just barely be seen. She opened her eyes, and though Grimsby expected more ice or crystals, he saw they were the same devouring shade of coal as the doll's.

Mother Frost didn't look away from her guests as she said, "Mara, dear. Fetch the kettle for us. And do put something decent on, please."

The ice woman nodded, her hair a clattering of stitch-thin icicles. A brief wave of her hand and mist exuded from her skin, condensing into a crystalline dress over her form, precisely resembling the dress she had worn when she was simply a doll; then she disappeared into the cabin.

Mother Frost resumed her gentle rocking and the wind joined her, rolling through the brittle fields and creaking the skeletal canopy above.

Grimsby fidgeted on his weathered stool, uncertain if he should or even could say anything without despoiling Hylde's formalities. He decided that silence was the least likely option to be found disrespectful, though his hurried heartbeat made every passing second feel like pressure was building in him to say something—anything to relieve his anxiousness.

Mayflower sat, his back rigid, his face held taut. Whatever their host had said had struck some hidden chord, and the Huntsman seemed to be struggling to simply remain civil.

Mara emerged moments later, holding a tray with a steaming kettle and three cups. Her frosted-glass skin reflected the warm glow of firelight within the cabin, and Grimsby shivered at the thought of basking in something other than frigid cold, but the image vanished as the heavy, round door closed behind her.

Mother Frost's foggy eyes remained cast to the distance as Mara poured tea for each of them. Hylde took hers in steady, pallid hands. Mayflower held his without care. Mara finally handed the last to Grimsby, her body making the sounds of a frozen lake gently cracking as she did.

"Thanks," he said, offering a nervous smile.

Her face might as well have been carved in stone for all the emotion it showed in reply. She set the kettle and tray on a flat stump beside Hylde and took up a position behind her like an ice sculpture of a maid.

Mother Frost inhaled the roiling steam from her cup, savoring it before taking a solitary sip. "Now we may discuss," she said.

Mayflower glowered, edging forward on his seat. "The hagstone," he said, his tone clipped. "Who did you sell it to?"

"I sold it to no one," she said flatly.

"Then how the hell did a witch topside get their hands on one?"

"From me, I'm sure."

The Huntsman growled, and Grimsby could feel his patience thinning like fraying rope. Unfortunately, something in Mother Frost's gaze told him they were both dangling by its threads. He cleared his throat, both hands cupped around his tea, savoring the warmth.

"So if you didn't sell it," he said, speaking up before Mayflower could, "how did they get it? Was it stolen?"

Hylde smirked and nodded. "We had arranged a trade, but it seems my potential customer had other intents at heart. Two of my children were sent to make the exchange, but they were betrayed, and the stone was taken."

"Who was the thief?"

She sipped at her tea. "That question matters little."

"Well, uh, actually it sort of matters a lot," Grimsby said.

Mother Frost paused for a moment and raised a dangerous brow.

"To us—I mean," he said, trying not to stammer. "We don't know what ritual they plan to do with the stone, but we do think they failed their first attempt and will try again. We need to find them before that happens."

"I have a name, but such things hold great value here. I cannot simply give it to you."

"But—you just gave us yours," Grimsby said, confused.

"Did I?" Hylde asked, a small smile touching her lips. "How silly of me."

Mayflower growled and dropped his cup of steaming tea. "If you won't tell us the information, then you're just wasting our time," he said, standing with enough force to send his stool clattering to the ground.

Mara's body cracked like the avalanche on the mountainside ready to give way, but Mother Frost held up a cool hand. "Wasted time," she said, shaking her head gently. "Such a human concept. If you wish to leave, Huntsman, you are free to do so."

Mayflower growled and started toward the gate. "Come on, Grimsby."

Grimsby began to stand and object—they were so close to some answers, and Mayflower's temper seemed their greatest obstacle—but he found himself unable to move from his seat. He looked down to see vines had crawled over his lap like a seat belt, securing him to the stool.

"Hey— What—?" he began, but Mother Frost interrupted him.

"Your witch, I'm afraid, is not so free."

Mayflower turned and saw the vines entrapping Grimsby. His gun appeared in his hand like a magician's trick. He leveled it between Hylde's cloudy eyes, but even as he moved, so did Mara.

She was as fast as anything Grimsby had seen, a flashing shimmer of ice. Suddenly, she was directly before the barrel of Mayflower's revolver even as he pointed it. Grimsby had found himself at the end of that barrel before and knew how terrifying it felt. Mara, however, remained as mild as a mannequin.

Grimsby tried to struggle free from the vines, but they only seemed to tighten their grip. "We're with the Department!" he said. "We're supposed to be protected!"

"And so long as you broke none of our laws, you would be," Hylde agreed, still calmly rocking despite the explosive motion of both Mayflower and Mara. "However, that is not the case."

"We've done nothing wrong!"

"Your Huntsman hasn't, but you, little witch, are a thief. And I've grown tired of thieves."

"What?" Grimsby asked, casting a perplexed gaze to Mayflower. "I didn't take your hagstone!"

The Huntsman's eyes narrowed, then they widened in what looked like realization.

Hylde didn't falter, seeming imperturbable. "Not the hagstone, child. You stole something else." She waited expectantly, but Grimsby's expression must have been as honestly dumbfounded as he felt, as she sighed and said, "Shall I remind you?"

"I think you're going to have to, because I—"

He stopped as Mother Frost raised a hand, and the trees around them shuddered and creaked. There was a wrest and rasp of metal, and the sound of small, familiar grunts of struggle.

"Let Wudge go or he will eats your bones!" came a hoarse squeal.

A nearby tree bent down like a waiting servant, its bark cracking and peeling away as it did, and lowered its boughs to reveal an iron cage that might have been meant to hold a bird. Instead, it held the scowling, gangly form of Wudge, whose spindly arms and legs stuck out of the bars as if they were the cage's own limbs.

"Wudge?" Grimsby asked.

"Indeed." Hylde nodded serenely. "Your partner in crime, so to speak."

Suddenly Grimsby realized what Mother Frost meant.

They hadn't stolen the nail from Lump and Echidna—they had stolen it from their mother. And that mother just so happened to be Mother Frost.

"Oh," Grimsby said, as it was all he could manage.

"'Oh' indeed," Hylde said. "As I said, I grow weary of thieves, and while I cannot yet find who stole my hagstone, it seems the others who have stolen from me have done me the great service of turning themselves in. Now you shall be dealt with appropriately."

Grimsby's mind flashed back to the frozen troll and all the other creatures that adorned the tower's exterior in their own personal snow globe prisons. He felt his heart hammer hard.

Hylde was the most powerful being he had ever seen.

And he had stolen from her.

THIRTY-EIGHT ✳

GRIMSBY FELT A SHIVER RUN THROUGH HIM, AND THE sweat that beaded on his brow seemed to freeze in the cold air. "I can explain!" he said.

"I'm sure you could," Mother Frost said, tilting her graying head to one side, "but I'm in little mood to listen. As determined by our pact with the Department, you have broken my laws, and so you, and your accomplice"—she tilted her head to Wudge, who was thrashing in his cage—"are subject to my justice."

Mayflower snarled and thumbed the hammer on his revolver, the barrel aimed at Hylde even through Mara's frozen form. "Let him go, or I swear to God—"

As he spoke, Hylde simply raised a hand and snapped her fingers.

In an instant, the Huntsman twitched, then ceased moving altogether. Frost crawled over him, encasing his skin in a layer of dusty rime, until he was frozen solid.

Grimsby felt his heart freeze almost as quickly. "No!" he screamed, struggling and fumbling to free himself from the vines. They finally withered away, allowing him to escape and scramble over to Mayflower.

Then he saw the Huntsman's furious eyes twitch and move, and felt some shard of relief. Mayflower was still alive, at least.

"Do try not to knock him over," Mother Frost said. "Putting him back together is no simple task."

He turned to her, Mara once again at her side, and wondered how much longer he would be alive himself.

"What do you want?" Grimsby asked. His voice was much smaller than he wanted it to be, but he forced himself to stand straight despite his knees threatening to give way.

"Fear not, your Huntsman will be safely returned to the surface when our business is concluded. He has not transgressed against me, and so no harm will come to him." She gestured between Grimsby and Wudge, the latter of whom had begun gnawing on the bars of his cage. "You two, however, your fate is yet to be decided."

Grimsby felt his fear begin to well into anger. His Impetus rose instinctively, and he felt the scars on his side begin to smolder and snap like embers in a fire pit. Steam hissed and rolled from them, curling and dying in the stale chill. At the moment, he wished more than anything that he had the talent for pyromancy that most other witches possessed—if only to defrost the wretched woman and her icy companion—but he didn't, and even if he did, he doubted it would do much good anyway.

Mother Frost was as calm as she had ever been, yet she had just dispatched Mayflower, the *Huntsman*, with a casual snap of her fingers.

What could Grimsby do to a being like that?

He shook his head. No, he wouldn't ever overpower her, especially not here in her own realm. He had to play by her rules—and just hope there was enough wiggle room within them to slip out of this place alive.

"As I told you," Mother Frost said, resuming her steady rocking, "the witch who bargained for one of my hagstones offered me something quite dear, though it was something that I suspected lay beyond their capacity to secure. You, however, I believe can secure it in their stead."

"Me?" Grimsby asked. "Lady, I may look like the apex of peak performance for a witch, but I'm C tier on my best days." He gestured to his tattered Auditor suit. "And today is not my best day. What makes you think I can get it when someone else couldn't?"

"Because you, and your accomplice"—she cast a disapproving look at Wudge, whose gnashing teeth had made little impact on the iron cage's bars—"are familiar with the witch known as Mansgraf."

Grimsby paused. "Mansgraf?" he asked. "What does she have to do with this?"

Samantha Mansgraf had been the deadliest witch around—at least until she had been killed a few months prior. It was actually through the haphazard solving of her murder that Grimsby had received his position as an Auditor to begin with.

"She and I have . . . history," Hylde said, bitterness obvious in her tone. "And she took from me something I hold quite dear. Retrieve the Wardbox it resides in, and I will forgive your transgressions. I will even supply you with the name of the witch you seek, for what good it might do you."

"Eyes aflame, if people keep stealing your stuff," Grimsby said, "maybe you should get a guard dog or something."

Mother Frost seemed eternally unamused at his comment.

"Why not just get it yourself? Or at least send one of your own people?" he asked. "You must know Mansgraf is dead! And I doubt you want to trust another witch."

"Indeed, but I am honor-bound not to desecrate her domain, as she was mine. Besides, there are other things within her lair, and it would behoove us both to leave them undisturbed."

"And this thing you want me to get for you, it wouldn't happen to 'behoove' us both for it to stay there, too, would it?"

"It would likely be in your better interest, if I'm to be honest," she said with an oddly kind smile, her grayed eyes wrinkling. "But it would be in your worst interest to refuse my offer. I'm afraid you have little choice."

Grimsby glared, but he could hardly argue. "Fine. Unfreeze Mayflower, release Wudge, and I'll get your box."

"I think not. I've grown tired of witches and trickery. Consider your companions insurance," she said. "A deposit repaid upon your return."

"I can't do this alone! You haven't seen her lair—it's a practical death trap!"

"More than you know," Mother Frost said. "Since her passing, a new resident has laid claim to her domain. One that is friend to neither of us."

"Then return my friends to me so we can handle it!"

Hylde thought for a moment, then waved to the branches that held Wudge's cage. They creaked and strained at the bars, warping the cage's shape by narrow margins. Wudge squealed in rage within, but after a moment the branches dropped him to the ground. He was still wrapped in the cage, but the gaps were now such that he could manage to move both arms and legs freely, making the prison look like a miniature suit of shoddy armor. Though it wasn't until now that Grimsby realized that Wudge looked quite pale—even for his usual shade of gray-green.

"You would not believe what it took to get him in there," Mother Frost said. "And so I will not let him out until our deal is concluded."

"Wudge, are you all right—?" Grimsby began, but as soon as Wudge's leather-wrapped feet touched the ground, the tiny creature ran full tilt at the stone wall of the cabin. He clattered into it hard and knocked himself onto his back. The cage seemed unharmed by his efforts.

Grimsby shook his head. Wudge would be hamstrung while

trapped, and he doubted he would be able to perform his vanishing trick while so confined, or he already would have, but it would have to do. "And Mayflower?" he said.

"The Huntsman will not be joining you."

"Now, wait just a minute—!"

"As I said, his safety is assured under my pact with the Department. This task I have asked of you is, however, quite unsafe. If he were to be injured or killed in pursuing it, it would mean I have broken my word—and that would mean dire consequences for us all."

Grimsby desperately wanted to argue, but when he tried to find ground to stand on, he found himself neck-deep in logical quicksand. Mother Frost held all the cards, had stacked the deck, and owned the table to boot. He looked to Mayflower, but the Huntsman's furious expression was immutable beneath the ice, though his eyes darted about madly.

He turned to Wudge, who twisted around inside the cage like a contortionist, trying to fit through the new gaps the tree limbs had left, but none were large enough for him to squeeze out. "Wudge?" he asked. "Are you in?"

Wudge grunted and muttered as he gave up on his efforts, falling slack inside the cage with his feet dangling out. He was panting heavily, his ribs swelling through his skin with each breath. Sweat dampened his body, with droplets dripping down from beneath his onion helmet.

He seemed off, and not just because his furious efforts had failed.

"Wudge hates the cage," he said between rasping breaths.

"We'll get you out," Grimsby said, trying to sound confident and not like he was about to collapse into the growing pit of fear in his stomach. He turned to Hylde. "We'll do it."

"Of course you will," she said with a cold, infuriating smile. "There is a tunnel that leads to her lair. Mara will guide you both there. The Wardbox you seek will be clear: black oak with gold hinges. Return it to me, and I will pardon you, release the Huntsman, and give you the name you seek."

Grimsby set his jaw, quietly hoping the task was as simple as Mother Frost suggested; then he remembered something she had said.

"You said something else had taken the place over. What is it?"

She paused a moment. "I have my suspicions, but I will not say for now. There's only one thing about it that I know for certain."

"What's that?"

She took a sip of her tea and savored it before answering. "It is carnivorous."

"Eyes aflame," Grimsby said. "Because of course it is."

Mother Frost nodded to Mara, and the frozen woman trod lightly from the yard, each of her steps sounding like crunching snow despite the dry ground.

Grimsby hurried to Wudge and hauled him to his feet by the round handle at the top of the bent cage. The prison seemed little worse for wear despite the tiny creature's efforts.

"Wudge hates the cage! Hates it, hates it, hates it!" His voice was harsh and hoarse, but there was deep-set fear in his eyes beneath his onion-helm.

"We'll take care of it," Grimsby said. "But I'll need your help first."

Wudge gnashed his numerous teeth but nodded. "Half-witch helped Wudge. Wudge will help half-witch."

Grimsby smiled a thanks, looked to Mayflower, and said, "We'll be back soon," then turned to follow Mara's departing figure. "I hope."

THIRTY-NINE

"RAYNE? RAYNE, WAKE UP ALREADY."

Rayne stirred from the stone-still darkness, cracking her eyes open to see the bleary image of her office. She was slouched in her chair, her head pounding and her body aching. "What— Where . . . ?" She trailed off as she tried to focus, to remember. Her eyes found Defaux, who leaned against the far wall beside the coffee maker.

"There you are," Defaux said. "I was worried I was going to have to take you to the infirmary, and that would have brought all kinds of questions we don't need."

Rayne sat up in her seat to see both her and Hives's desks had been pushed aside to make space. In the room's center, there was a ritual circle drawn out in chalk paint, the pentagram clean and neat, as if it had been made with a stencil. "What happened?" Rayne asked. "Last I remember . . ."

"You had just brained those two thugs," Defaux said, finishing her thought. "It must have taken more out of you than you realized, because next thing I knew, you had passed out on me."

Rayne felt her stomach flip. That didn't sound right. She had strained her Impetus much more in the past without issue—

although those times she had been more disciplined. Had letting her anger take the reins for a moment really drained her that badly? Or had she lost time again? Neither answer gave her comfort, and both meant the same thing:

Something was wrong with her.

"Where are the suspects?" she asked.

"I handled them already," Defaux said, then raised a brow. "Don't look so surprised. I'm an Auditor, too, after all. But I didn't think it would look good for you to have gone limp on the report, so I brought you back here instead."

Rayne nodded, though it was hesitant. She certainly didn't need anyone knowing she had passed out on the job, especially not on top of all the other scrutiny that was upon her. Even so, Defaux seemed so unfazed by the situation. "Thank you," she said, though she was more dubious than grateful.

Defaux donned her gorgeous smile. "Of course. Let's just get this whole ordeal behind us so I can stop covering your ass." She gestured to the ritual circle. "It's all ready."

Rayne shook away her concerns for the time being. There were more pressing matters. "And this will find Hives?"

"If he's alive—actually, so long as he's in one piece, it'll find him. Come to think of it, even if he's in multiple, it'll find the biggest bit left. Needless to say, I can't guarantee what shape he'll be in."

"It'll be enough to know for certain either way."

She nodded. "I can tell the stress is getting to you." Her voice dropped to a low tone. "I saw what you did to those two Unorthodox. I felt the power you tapped into. Incredible."

Rayne felt an acrid taste on her tongue. "I lost control for a moment. It won't happen again."

"Maybe. Maybe not. Power like that is alive. It's a beast that gets pent up. Maybe it's better to keep it on a leash than in a cage."

Rayne felt her throat tighten. What did Defaux know about controlling power like this? Nothing.

"Enough!" she snapped, surprising even herself at how quickly her anger rose, and with it, the heat of her own Impetus.

Defaux's eyes seemed to sparkle, but she raised her hands in a defusing gesture. "Of course, my mistake. You've handled it so long totally on your own, you certainly don't need my help."

"Can we just get on with the ritual? I want to finish this."

"It's all set up for you. Every bit and bauble. All that's left is to follow through."

"Why can't you do it?"

"Because the tracking ritual needs every connection it can get to be reliable, and your connection to Hives is obviously stronger than mine."

Rayne frowned but didn't argue. Defaux hadn't led her astray so far. And yet, she couldn't help but feel like something was off, like there was some piece she was missing.

"Well?" Defaux asked. "Aren't you ready to find him and lay this all to rest?"

Rayne took a breath and felt her doubts ebb. The important thing was to find Hives and make certain her future was secure. She could never advance in the Department with the shadow of potential betrayal clinging to her like a funeral shroud.

She knelt at the circle's edge, testing the chalk paint with one finger. It was dry and clean, with no risk of being broken by an errant hand or foot—though she noticed a few specks of it on her shoe. Defaux must have drawn it while she was passed out nearby and spilled it on her.

She shook herself and focused on the ritual. So long as it was unbroken, the chalk would mark the barrier that would contain the spell like a pressure cooker. But if there was a leak or weakness, the results could be just as disastrous.

She double-checked to be sure, but Defaux's work was solid and well practiced. Her sigils were sharp and decisive, even harsh, and she had arrayed the ingredients at the five intersects of the pentagram. Rayne removed her mechanical watch and held it in her hand, looking over to Defaux.

"You have the chant?"

She nodded and gestured to the paper beside Rayne, which she had somehow not seen before.

She skimmed it and scoffed. "A bit dated, isn't it?"

Defaux smiled. "All the best magic is."

Rayne memorized the words and set the paper aside, placing one hand at the circle's center before summoning her Impetus. For most rituals, the power wouldn't be necessary, but it wouldn't hurt to have it ready. The nuance of an Impetus could often smooth out any hitches or snags that might arise from a ritual—it was one reason the Department disapproved of Usuals using them at all.

She spoke the chant, careful to keep every word and syllable crisp and clear.

Over hill or under weald,
Through furrow broad or fallow field,
From tallest peak to deepest dives,
Show me where is Wilson Hives.

The words caught and echoed strangely in the small office, and she felt a dull heat begin to emanate from the circle. The silver chains rattled lightly, and the jar of suspended newt eye rippled from invisible power.

She repeated the chant, and the power grew. The bowl of graveyard dirt churned like beetles were crawling through it, then fell over, spreading perfectly across the chalk outline to darken the clean white to boneyard brown. The ancient, rusted weather vane suddenly rose upright, spinning in place like a creaking top in the still air.

She repeated the chant a third time, and the primary component, Hives's badge, began to glow like it was red-hot. The heat in the air was palpable, like she was in a dry sauna, but as she reached toward the badge, she found it cool to the touch.

She held it out to the chain, which writhed like tiny silver serpents, and they latched onto the badge like it was a magnet. Their trailing ends seemed to quest outward, searching for something to bind the magic of the badge to.

She held out her watch, and the chains lashed themselves to it, making her wrist jerk. They entwined themselves around the still hands, making them tremble. She could feel the gears within grating softly. Then the chains started to shimmer and glow, and before her eyes they faded away, first to translucent crystal, then to mist, and finally to nothing at all.

The heat in the room slowly settled, and the ritual circle that was once white had been scorched black. The weather vane crumbled to rusty dust, and the jar of newt eye was bone-dry.

The ritual was complete.

Rayne sat back, the badge in one hand, the other holding up her wrist to stare at her watch. She felt her held breath grow to bursting in her chest, but she didn't dare exhale.

Now was the moment that would tell whether or not Defaux's ritual had succeeded.

Defaux inched forward, her arms crossed, her eyes glinting with intense curiosity. "Well? Finish it!"

Rayne swallowed and finally let herself breathe, then looked to the watch and asked, "Where is Wilson Hives?"

The minute and hour hands trembled for a moment, then spun wildly in opposite directions. Just as she feared they would spin endlessly, they both settled in a single direction.

"We did it," Rayne breathed. "We found him."

FORTY ✳

GRIMSBY TRIED TO IGNORE WUDGE'S FURIOUS MUM-
bling and rattling of his cage as they followed Mara to the
edge of the field of brittle grass. He tried to push down the cold,
curling vines of fear in his gut, but it felt about as effective as if he
was trying to uproot the whole field by hand. By the time he
quelled one concern, two others had grown to replace it.

The last time he had been to Mansgraf's lair, he had nearly
been torn apart by several traps, accidentally caught himself in an
almost fatal verbal contract—courtesy of the tiny caged creature
beside him—and found himself tangled up in the whirlwind
nightmare that had led to Mansgraf's murderer.

And all that had been with Mayflower as a more-or-less ally.

Now he was going back without the Huntsman, and while
Wudge was one of the few beings Grimsby could call a friend, his
current confinement meant he would be of minor aid. If anything
went wrong, it would be up to Grimsby to fix it.

And him alone.

Mara reached the illusory edge of the field, where the rolling
grass was somehow projected through the ice wall. It cracked and

rumbled, and a seam appeared, spreading fast until another door was outlined. This one was smaller than the first he had taken, and the passage beyond looked like a narrow blue shaft of hollow ice. It must have been one of the branches Grimsby had seen from outside as they had approached the crystalline tree.

Mara stepped aside and turned to them; her eyes—as dead as a statue's—looked through Grimsby as she began to speak in a voice that sounded like winter wind through mountain crags. "Follow this tunnel, through the ice. You will find a railway. The tunnel will split and branch. Do not stray from the path."

Grimsby felt a shiver run through him at the sound of her voice, as surely as if that wind had struck him. "How will we know what the right path is?"

Mara's blank face crackled as a small smile curled on one side of her ice-carved lips. "Follow the corpses." She stepped aside and gestured to the open doorway.

Grimsby took a deep breath. He wanted to turn back and take the fastest rail home, but he couldn't. Mayflower was depending on him. "All right, Wudge, let's do this."

"Wudge doesn't want to go! Wudge wants out!" The tiny creature dropped to sit on the ground, crossing his arms, his legs still poking out of the warped cage's bars.

Grimsby sighed. "Don't worry. I got you, bud." He leaned over and picked up the cage by the round iron handle at its peak. It was heavy, but not so much so that it was difficult to carry.

Wudge growled but said nothing, so Grimsby continued into the haze-blue hallway.

He felt like he was inside the needle of a bent syringe, except that through the walls he could see the amorphous shapes of the sprawling yet huddled city below. The tunnel grew more narrow as it approached the edge of the cavern, but though the footing was treacherously slick, it was more or less horizontal enough that he could make headway. He could see other such branches through the ice walls, but most of them looked like they were bobsled chutes rather than passages.

Where the tunnel met the cavern wall, there was a crag in the dark stone, narrow enough that Grimsby feared for a moment that Wudge and his cage might not fit. The nauseating thought of continuing alone was relieved, however, when he found he was able to wedge Wudge through at a slightly awkward angle.

Wudge, meanwhile, kept his arms crossed and pouted, his frown clear despite his onion-helm.

"Wudge," Grimsby grunted as he maneuvered them both through the gap, "how did they catch you, anyway? What were you doing down here?"

"Wudge was looking to break curse. Thought maybe the mother monster had way."

"So she caught you?"

"No!" he said defensively. "Old hag too slow to catch Wudge."

"So how did you end up in the cage?"

Wudge twisted his long fingers in an embarrassed gesture. "She makes really good pie."

"She poisoned you, then?"

"Wudge didn't know! Thought stupid, dumb monster mother left out pie to cool."

"Left the pie out to cool," Grimsby repeated, "in a cavern of ice that she made? Don't you think she could have cooled it if she wanted to?"

Wudge scoffed and scowled in a singular expression. "Tall folk do all kinds of stupid things. Almost as many as half-witch."

The crag opened up into a darkened tunnel, much larger than Grimsby expected. It was perhaps twenty feet across and just as high, its ceiling hung with spines of ice, and its walls were glistening with sheeted rime.

"I do do my fair share of stupid," Grimsby admitted, setting

Wudge down. He seemed to have calmed enough to walk on his own. "Hopefully this plan isn't contributing to that share."

"Plan?" Wudge said. "Half-witch has a plan?"

"Well, sure I do. We just . . ." He trailed off, looking left, then right. "Go the, uh, right way."

"Which is?"

He saw a long, geometric shape at the tunnel's center. It was the track, two iron rail lines, trundling off each way into the dimming darkness. Then, to one side of the tunnel, he spotted a form hung against the wall, cocooned in a globe of ice like a Christmas ornament sunk halfway into the stone. He approached and stared, keeping a cautious distance just to be safe.

Inside the ice was a bestial figure, curled in on itself like it had died in a blizzard. Grimsby couldn't see much, but he could see horns, fangs, and claws.

It was the body of a Therian, long suspended in the ice.

"Well, Mayflower said Mother Frost and her people had helped deal with the Therian mob. I'm guessing this was one of the ones that was dealt with." His eyes trailed down the tunnel, the ambient light just dim enough to see thirty feet or so.

He saw another globe, similar to the first, in the distance, though it looked broken—melted, even, like a chocolate egg in the sun. He stepped carefully closer to see the wall had been scoured with long, deep scratches, which had torn chunks of ice and stone free. Whatever had been in the globe was gone, but under his feet crunched broken shards of charred bone and frozen clusters of fur.

"I think we can confirm that whatever is around here is indeed carnivorous." He gulped and instinctively looked around him, including straight up, but saw nothing. "So all we have to do is, uh, follow the bodies."

Suddenly the idea of following the trail of something strong enough to rend stone and hungry enough to eat a frozen Therian seemed like it would indeed contribute a considerable amount to his daily stupid quota, though he refused to admit that to Wudge.

However, when his companion didn't reply, he turned to see Wudge was gone. A sharp shard of fear shot through him, until he saw Wudge approaching from the opposite direction, standing atop a railway cart not dissimilar to the one used by Quasi, their first guide to Underton.

Wudge had trouble reaching the pump handle and had to leap up and use his whole body weight to pull it down again. He likely would have been too light if not for the cage.

"Look what Wudge founds!" he said, panting slightly as he slowed to a halt. "Now half-witch can pump and Wudge can sit."

Grimsby shrugged. "Fair's fair," he said, climbing aboard. He took the handle from Wudge, who settled on the front of the cart with his legs dangling over the side, like some odd figurehead. Grimsby began to build a rhythm, and in short moments they were grating over the icy rails into the dim blueness.

He tried to keep his pace controlled, as it was difficult to see in the dark and he didn't relish the thought of careening into a cave-in or a chunk of frozen werewolf, and while he did see more of the cocooned corpses of the Therians littering the tunnel, none blocked the rails. Dozens must have died here, though many of them had been torn open and devoured to nothing more than cored bone.

"Do you know how much farther we need to go?" Grimsby asked, his muscles churning and aching at the pump. The work was light, but it seemed to grind on and on.

Wudge leaned precariously forward as he peered ahead, making Grimsby fear he might topple off the cart and be ground up beneath. "The tunnels don't care about how long they go for most time. But Wudge doesn't think it's far now," he said. "Slow down!"

Grimsby happily obliged and let the cart coast forward, rubbing his windburned hands against his underarms to warm them.

Sure enough, as the cart came to a slow halt, Grimsby spotted a door set into the wall. It wasn't the same as the grand, icy monoliths that had guarded Mother Frost's cottage, though he did remember a similar one being at the underground entrance to Mansgraf's lair. Unfortunately, he hadn't seen much of the tunnels within, as Mayflower had guided him straight to the sanctum, but he would never have guessed they extended so far, let alone connected to Underton.

Actually, after consulting his admittedly rough mental map of Boston, Grimsby was beginning to doubt Underton's tunnels followed the normal rules of distance and length. They seemed almost more like they were halfway between the Elsewhere and the waking world: amorphous and shifting. They could stretch on for much farther than he could imagine.

And if that was the case, was Mansgraf's lair any different?

Then he noticed that the round door, which looked like it belonged to a military bunker or biological clean room, was ajar. The edges had been scored by claws, and the frozen stone the door was embedded within had been torn away until the door's hinges came with it. It held on by the thinnest margins of quality steel, though they had bent under the heavy weight to drag over the ground.

"Something dug its way in there, something big," Grimsby said, feeling a chill as he glanced over his shoulder.

"Or maybe out," Wudge said.

"Out? Where would it have come from?"

Wudge shrugged, frustratingly nonchalant, or perhaps just exhausted. "Lying Mansgraf kept many things in her lair. Maybe not all of them liked being kept."

"Shouldn't you know? I thought you were her guard dog."

Wudge turned and scowled at him, crossing his arms. "Wudge not dog. Wudge hates dogs."

"Sorry, sorry," Grimsby said, raising apologetic hands. "Poor expression. But still, how do you not know?"

He shrugged again, his cage rattling. "Wudge kept folks out. Didn't care what was kept in—except the door, when he still thought she had it."

Grimsby shook his head and peered at the darkened crack between door and stone, feeling like something inside was peering back. "What's dangerous enough to be imprisoned, big enough to break free, and hungry enough to eat frozen Therian?"

Wudge frowned. "Wudge didn't know half-witch liked riddles! That's a good one."

"No," Grimsby said, shaking himself and forcing numb legs to carry him down from the cart and toward the door. "It's more of a bad joke, really."

FORTY-ONE ✳

GRIMSBY WEDGED THROUGH THE CRACKED DOORWAY, grateful he wasn't as big as someone like Mayflower. Wudge had some trouble with the thin gap, as the cage's rigid form was too wide, but Grimsby managed to brace his legs against the wall and press his back against the door, creaking it open another sparse inch after some straining.

"Atlas stones," he cursed, voice hoarse over his tightened muscles. "Hurry up!"

Wudge wiggled through, his cage screeching against concrete and metal for the last few inches.

Grimsby let himself drop to the ground, sweat prickling his brow. It was oddly warm on this side of the door, and the cold air that wafted in from the tunnel side spun and swirled into misty hands that scrabbled at the air before fading away. Even his skin radiated with a thin layer of visible air as his body began to warm up.

He looked around the concrete tunnel, which was lit with flickering fluorescents embedded into the ceiling. He recognized the claw-scoured concrete walls of Mansgraf's lair, which had once been a Therian den, but while he remembered most of the long, shallow scratches in the concrete being faded with age, there were many he saw that were much more recent—and much deeper. Even the floor of the tunnel looked to have been scraped to nearly clean by something long and heavy passing over it.

"Hear anything?" Grimsby asked Wudge, turning his ear toward the fork at the tunnel's end. Their entry had not been nearly as silent as he would have liked, but he heard no sounds of alarm.

Wudge frowned, balling up each of his drooping, rabbitlike ears in a fist and holding them out from the sides of the cage like floppy satellite dishes. "Nothing moving," he said. "Tunnels down here are a maze. Follow Wudge, half-witch, and don't forget the way."

He padded forth on his long, leather-wrapped feet, moving confidently if a little haphazardly.

"Wudge, are you okay?" Grimsby asked. "You seem—" He wanted to say *drunken*, but settled for something more neutral. "Off."

Wudge rattled a bar of the cage. "Iron is bad for Wudge. Makes magic hard, and that makes everything hard. If Wudge doesn't escape it soon . . ." He trailed off and shivered despite the growing warmth.

Grimsby nodded, knowing the feeling. "The Department uses iron shackles for that same reason. Messes up magic, effectively disarms witches."

Wudge kept walking but wrapped his lengthy arms around himself, and Grimsby noticed again that the normal gray-green hue of his skin color had faded to a more sickly pallor of itself. "But Wudge isn't witch. Wudge doesn't *use* magic—Wudge *is* magic."

"So that cage—it's hurting you?"

Wudge shook his head. "Is killing Wudge. If it doesn't open soon . . ." He shook his head, refusing to stop his slogging gait, though his pace was slowing. "Wudge doesn't want to end."

Grimsby felt his mouth go dry. He was so concerned with

Mayflower, he had never stopped to consider that Wudge might be in danger, too—in fact, the very idea of it seemed alien. Wudge was normally so aloof; he seemed beyond the petty little concerns Grimsby struggled with, like being eaten alive.

But even he wasn't invincible.

Grimsby could sense it in his voice, if only because he knew the emotion more intimately than any other: Wudge was scared.

He felt a bitter tinge of anger rise in him at the person who had put one of his friends in a cage of iron and the other in a cage of ice. He found a new, odd curse escape his lips. "Fire amid rime."

He hurried his pace, scooping up Wudge as he passed him. The tiny creature grumbled but seemed too meek to argue.

"We'll get you out of there," he said, heaving the cage up onto his shoulder. "I walk, you point. We get the box and get back."

Wudge mumbled an affirmative and extended a bulbous, toadish finger as they approached a fork, and Grimsby followed. They soon passed into a chamber that was nearly twenty feet high and twice as wide in both directions. Each wall had a new doorway at its center, halls branching off from it like a central hub. The floor was littered with splintered bone, and the walls scorched black with soot, but Grimsby barely noticed those things.

What he noticed were the chains as thick as his fingers that were shattered and strewn about. There were half a dozen different lengths of them, each hooked into iron rings set halfway into the ground in a rough circle around the room's center.

But there was nothing there. The broken chains held no beast at bay.

At least, not anymore.

"I think we found where our mystery critter came from," Grimsby said, carefully looking around the room but seeing nothing. "What was it?"

Wudge mumbled a weary reply. "She-bitch Mansgraf kept

many prisoners—many pets. Wudge never saw this one; she told him to keep away and Wudge obeyed." He said the last word like a quiet curse at himself.

"Snakes and snails," Grimsby cursed. "Let's hope it went a different way." He tried to feel as optimistic as he sounded, but the sinking feeling in his stomach felt like a slippery slope.

Wudge pointed him directly across the room, and he tiptoed around blackened iron and broken bone. They passed other, sealed chambers that looked to be empty or long closed-off. Most were locked away with rune-covered doors of steel, with only a small slot to peer in through. Grimsby left the shuttered peep-holes closed. He liked to imagine the rooms were empty, but something told him otherwise. Even if they had no occupant he could see in this world, perhaps the Elsewhere told a different tale. It was better to leave Mansgraf's matters alone as much as he could.

Grimsby never would have guessed that the lair was so expansive, and he felt his nerves grow more brittle with every pace and step. There was still something loose down here, and every corner and door seemed to promise a threat.

Finally they reached a hall that Grimsby knew well. It was the one where he had fallen prey to some kind of trap that caught him halfway between the real world and the Elsewhere—and on the Elsewhere side of things had been a Geist.

It was also where he had first met Wudge.

He felt the cage twitch and heard the small creature weakly cackle. Perhaps he was remembering that same moment.

Ahead was a doorway to Mansgraf's inner sanctum, a massive underground cistern, like a grain silo sunk into the earth. But the door was ajar. Something had torn away the heavy handle, along with a fair chunk of the reinforced concrete it was set into. Grimsby remembered that at the bottom of the sanctum were the Wardboxes. All they had to do was collect the correct box and move along—perhaps their luck would hold; perhaps the creature was elsewhere in the labyrinthine tunnels.

The sanctum doors seemed to almost radiate heat as they approached. The air was near stifling, to a degree that was odd so far underground. Inside the door, the crates of provisions that Mansgraf had kept stockpiled had been torn apart and consumed, only the blue plastic barrels labeled POTABLE WATER remaining intact.

Grimsby peered carefully around before setting foot on the metal-grid floor. It squeaked lightly beneath his feet, but the room was otherwise still. He paused and set down Wudge, who simply let his legs splay as his head bobbed and drooped, leaning against the side of the cage.

"You wait here," Grimsby said. "I'll grab the box and we can skedaddle before anything toothy comes along."

Wudge made a noncommittal noise that wasn't much of an argument, so Grimsby began to descend the spiral staircase that led to the floors below.

He passed quickly through the level that served as Mansgraf's old library. Curved shelves held hundreds of musty tomes of dubious contents, most of which Grimsby likely couldn't read if he wanted to. The rest of them, he was pretty sure he didn't want to read anyway.

The following floor was her lab. Though it was stacked high with glass vials and jars, whatever beast had ravaged the floors above seemed to have decided there was nothing suitably edible here, as even the plastic tarps covering the floors had been unscathed by claws or teeth.

Grimsby took a relieved breath. The creature might not have even come this far down. After all, the Wardboxes were sealed—impenetrable to all but the most powerful magic. There'd be nothing of interest on this lowest floor, at least not for some hungry critter.

That hope vanished when Grimsby descended far enough to see the room at the sanctum's base had been scorched black, as though there had been a fire. The shelves that once lined the concrete walls had been turned to ash, leaving the room to look like an empty, darkened pit.

For a moment, through a feeling of passing vertigo, Grimsby feared the Wardboxes had been somehow destroyed—until he realized the chamber wasn't empty at all. There was a mass at the room's center, an odd combination of long, smooth curves and sharp angles, all of the darkest black. He peered into the mass, his eyes slowly picking apart the shapes, until he saw there was *something* curled up in the center of the heaped ashes, lying atop the piled collection of Mansgraf's Wardboxes.

He couldn't see what it was, at least not clearly. It was reptilian and coiled, its scales a deep shade of black that reflected no light. Its body was like a serpent, but Grimsby could see a pair of clawed limbs tucked within its curled mass.

It was also at least the size of a car, perhaps even larger—it was difficult to tell with it so wrapped around itself.

He froze mid-step, caught by fear on the twisting stairwell. But the creature didn't stir, its body heaving up and down steadily with each rhythmic breath. It was asleep.

Grimsby felt lucky for a sparse moment—he didn't want to imagine what would have happened if he had stumbled upon the creature coiled down here waiting for him.

Then he spotted the Wardbox that Mother Frost had described, black oak and gold hinged, dusted with ash and lying directly beneath one of the thing's twitching claws.

Suddenly, he felt like a mouse eyeing cheese in a trap.

Snakes and scales, he mouthed silently, feeling his heart thumping in every frozen muscle.

FORTY-TWO ✳

GRIMSBY HAD NEVER SEEN SUCH A CREATURE BEFORE.
Its scales were so dark and smooth that it felt as though his
eyes kept slipping away, unable to delineate between the ashen concrete and the creature itself. His every instinct told him to back
quietly away until he was far enough to begin fleeing madly instead.

But he couldn't simply leave, not without Mother Frost's
prize. Wudge was already in terrible shape in his iron cage; there
was no telling how much longer he'd last. And Mayflower—who
knew if Mother Frost's assurances would hold true? What would
keep her from imprisoning Mayflower for as long as she pleased?

Though for that matter, what guarantee did he have that she
would keep her word to begin with? Perhaps the only reward he'd
receive when he returned was an icy cage of his own.

Even so, he had little choice but to honor his agreement with
her, despite the doubts clawing around in him—although those
metaphorical claws seemed preferable to the much more literal
twitching talons of the creature he was faced with.

He felt his hands shaking, and the skin on his neck seemed to
prickle and crawl toward his scalp in a desperate attempt to hide,
but he kept his straying feet from turning back. Instead, though

it was slowly and with frantically constrained effort, he continued to descend the stairs.

Each one felt taller than the last, until his head was spinning with tense fear as he touched the ground. Even from a dozen feet away, he could feel heat radiating from the slumbering beast, its softly heaving body scraping lightly over its own coiled form.

It looked even bigger up close, big enough to wrap around Mayflower's jeep and crush it to scrap. Big enough to swallow Grimsby whole.

His mind quickly flashed to a documentary on pythons he had watched during his rare idle days before he joined the Department. He pictured one of the serpents with a bulging lump in its length from a crushed rat or bird, and quickly found himself feeling pained empathy for the hapless creatures.

And pythons didn't even *have* claws.

This thing did.

He inched closer, having trouble lifting his rigid legs enough to keep his feet from scuffing the scorched concrete. His reluctant body felt like it was moving through a spider's web of rubber bands, with every step making the next more difficult, and the prospect of retreating more and more appealing.

Finally, he came within reach of the Wardbox, its gold hinges just barely visible through the soot and ash, though the beast's limp claws rested atop it. It had five talons, almost like fingers, but resembling a lizard's claws more than a human's digits, and each was tipped with four or five inches of keratin of the same shade as wrought iron.

He licked dry lips and knelt beside the Wardbox, wincing at the light pops of his bending knees. He glanced up to the slumbering serpent, and though he could see little true form in its coiled mass, he could make out a softly flaring nostril and a thin slit that seemed likely to be a closed eye. Thankfully, the thing seemed to be a heavy sleeper.

All tuckered out after a hard day of digging up and eating dead werewolves, he thought.

He was fortunate that Mother Frost's Wardbox wasn't among the piled mass below the serpent, but even so, the tips of the monster's obsidian claws rested lightly on its engraved surface, clicking gently against it with each heaving breath.

Grimsby knelt for a moment, fighting back his urge to run far, far away, and forced himself to make sure there were no random objects resting against the box's sides. Nothing that would fall and clatter to awaken the serpent when he snatched the Wardbox away.

Then he timed the beast's deep breaths, trying to ignore his own thready heartbeat. If he was quick enough, he could take the box as the claws rose and get it out of the serpent's clutches before they fell again. He'd have to be quick—and utterly silent.

Otherwise . . .

His eyes traced the claws as his mind wandered back to the piles of bones that littered the tunnel to here.

Otherwise, suffice to say it would be uncomfortable.

He wanted to move, but each moment seemed the wrong one. His shaking hands and sweating temples were certain of it. After far too long, he decided to count to three breaths, then he would make his move.

The first breath he spent largely thinking about how bad an idea this whole stupid thing was.

The second breath he spent trying to think of an alternative, anything that might save Wudge and Mayflower and somehow get around doing this very, very stupid thing.

On the third breath, he did the stupid thing.

The claws rose, and he reached out with shaking but dexterous hands. He began to pull the box away, but it seemed nestled in place and resisted. He felt it budge slightly and quickly applied more pressure, and with some gentle wiggling, he pried the box free.

His tensed muscles pulled it away so quickly that he nearly lost his balance, and teetered on his haunches for a desperate moment before settling back into place.

The serpent exhaled, and its claws lowered, dangling over the empty space where the Wardbox had been.

Grimsby, almost reluctantly, glanced to the serpent's closed eye, half expecting it to be open and bloodshot, but the beast slumbered still.

He took a relieved breath and edged away before daring to stand. But, just as he started toward the stairs, a small scraping sound and a flutter of movement caught his attention. Around the other side of the beast, toward the steps, was a small form wiggling at the edge of the serpent's piled hoard.

After a closer look, he recognized it: it was Mansgraf's familiar.

Its form was that of a cat, but crafted from shaped metal. The only thing about it that was actually "cat" was its bleached white skull.

It seemed trapped, with only its head and forelegs free, pinned beneath a collection of fallen tomes and a Wardbox crafted from an old chest.

Despite its lack of finer feline features, its skull seemed quite annoyed with its situation. It struggled for a moment, its literal razor blade claws digging uselessly at the mismatched mess, before its jaws opened in what looked like a silent meow. It turned its gaze to Grimsby, seeming to see him for the first time.

He had encountered it only once before, when he and Mayflower had come to the lair searching for clues to Mansgraf's murder. He had dissuaded the Huntsman from destroying it, and it had seemingly rewarded him with a dowser, an essential tool they used to find Mansgraf's killer. Whether or not it recognized him, he couldn't tell. Either way, it reached out to him with one crafted claw, splaying and closing its grip in a request for aid.

How the familiar ended up in this mess, Grimsby couldn't

have guessed, nor could he tell how long it had been trapped. But it was likely quite fortunate the creation had no need to eat. He paused, mid-stride, his instincts tempting him with each passing moment toward the stairs and toward freedom, perhaps safety—but, most importantly, away from the slumbering beast.

He had only to climb as silently as he'd descended, and he'd be home free.

The familiar wasn't even alive, he told himself. It was a construct, a magical imitation of life, not the genuine article. Mansgraf's familiar would feel no pain, nor fear. It was simply behaving according to its magical programming, so to speak. It wasn't *real*.

And yet it needed help.

It would have been totally reasonable, intelligent even, for him to ignore it and continue on his merry way.

So why in blue blazes, he thought, *don't I?*

He couldn't hazard a guess as he set the Wardbox down on the staircase. Every part of him wanted to run, to flee as fast as he could.

Except the part that mattered.

Puppy dogs' tails, he mouthed as he shook his head and tiptoed toward the pinned cat.

Somehow, when the serpent had piled the Wardboxes, tomes, and other odds and ends at the room's center, the familiar had been trapped there as well. Its hind legs were lodged beneath another Wardbox, this one shaped like an old footlocker—unfortunately, upon the box rested what looked like the tip of the serpent's tail. It had a hardened ridge of barbs that prickled down the apex of its spine, forming into a single, sharp tip growing from the end, not unlike the thing's claws, and it swayed back and forth slightly as the beast slumbered.

Grimsby approached more confidently this time. After all, his efforts hadn't woken the serpent before, so if there was any rhyme or reason in the world, he had only to repeat his deed. He carefully adjusted an errant tome that leaned against the Wardbox, then slowly began lifting it, only by the barest inch at a time. The serpent tail continued to curl and sway, and more than once he had to duck his hand out of the way of its tip.

The familiar seemed to understand his efforts, and stood still, watching him with the hollows of its eyeless skull. It had a pair of hammered copper ears, one of which had been carefully folded down at the tip, and both twitched and swiveled as he worked.

Soon, he revealed the cat's tremulous tail of chain links, and after the Wardbox was lifted another inch, the cat suddenly scrambled free in a frantic burst, leaping to the stairs and clicking up them with surprisingly lifelike speed.

Grimsby winced, expecting a furious roar, but the room was quiet.

He took a relieved breath and set the Wardbox down gently before realizing something was off. The room remained still, but it was too much so. There was some element missing, like when the heater at home would shut off and leave a ringing in his empty ears.

He realized what it was about the same time he saw the serpent's tail.

It wasn't twitching or swaying. It was stone-still. As were the creature's slow breaths.

He moved very slowly, turning his head as much as he dared, until he could see the serpent's eye.

It was open, as orange as fire, and smoldering just the same.

And it was looking straight at him.

"Eyes aflame," he breathed.

The curse had never been quite so apt.

FORTY-THREE

GRIMSBY BACKED SLOWLY AND INSTINCTIVELY TOWARD the stairs, though his eyes could not waver from the fiery gaze of the serpent. The creature uncoiled itself, its long, scaled form seeming to expand to fill the room. Its twin, clawed fore-limbs flexed and tensed, pushing its upper body up enough that Grimsby could see almost humanoid musculature slithering beneath the surface of its chest, branching off to each arm. Its head rose, snakelike, its neck drawing back like it was poising to strike. Its burning eye was joined by a second, and neither wavered its gaze from Grimsby.

The unfurled creature stood nearly twice as high as Grimsby, and that wasn't accounting for the length of its body that coiled around the room. For a long moment, the serpent was still, as though surprised or in disbelief at Grimsby's presence, and, for a much-shorter moment, he thought perhaps it wasn't in a predatory mood.

Then its jaws twitched and trembled, slowly opening to reveal rows of fangs that unfolded from the pink flesh of its maw.

The caveman portion of Grimsby's brain then took control and unilaterally decided that flight was the appropriate response.

He turned and bolted to the stairs, barely having enough awareness to pick up Mother Frost's Wardbox as he did. There was a snap behind him, and he could feel the wind coming off the serpent's jaws as it narrowly missed. Talons and scales scraped over concrete in a hissing cacophony, and Grimsby did not need to turn around to know the beast was in pursuit.

He twisted his right arm back as he rushed up the stairs, summoning his Impetus and willing it into his hand. Stray power surged into his left arm, drawing small gouts of flame and popping sparks, but where his palm touched the Wardbox, the energy became dead cold.

He ignored the sensation and pain of his scars and shouted, *"Torque!"*

Still warped by the cursed nail, his spell twisted from its true form into a spreading field of motes of blue light that covered the stairwell behind him like someone had carved out a section of the starry sky and carted it down to this dark abode.

The scrape of concrete shifted to the screech of metal as the beast began clawing its way up the side of the staircase, its powerful talons wrenching the steel to mangled scrap under its footing. Grimsby reached the level above, Mansgraf's alchemical lab, and paused long enough to glance at his spell through the grated metal floor.

The serpent's black-scaled form struck the spell, and Grimsby expected to see it slowed or even halted by his new magic.

Instead, that starry field shattered like a glass curtain, its blue motes of light sparking to fiery orange, raining down and bouncing off the pursuing serpent's dark, glossy scales before dissipating entirely.

Grimsby made an unflattering yelp and fled up the flights of stairs, his frantic mind reeling.

Even Goode in his powerful Therian form had been hampered by that spell, yet this creature had destroyed it without even seeming to notice it was there. At the minimum, the spell should have slowed the monster by a moment or two before failing. Something had gone wrong, but not with his spell—something he didn't understand.

And didn't have time to think about.

Fortunately, he didn't have to think to run.

His footsteps pounded against the grated stairs as he reached the main floor, Wardbox under his arm. The whole steel assembly in the cistern screeched and rattled as the serpent pursued, making the plastic barrels labeled POTABLE WATER churn and splash.

"Wudge, we gotta go!" Grimsby shouted, rushing toward the door, where he saw Wudge's gangly feet sticking out of his cage, unmoving.

Grimsby drew close enough to see Wudge was leaning against the door, his ears drooping and his eyes closed, with his head tilted to the side. His gray-green complexion was nearly all gray. For a moment, Grimsby's frantic heartbeat seized, until he saw the lightest movement of Wudge's sunken chest. He was alive, at least, though he didn't even seem awake, let alone able to run.

Grimsby glanced behind him just long enough to see the ember glow of the serpent's eyes reach the top of the stairs and lock on to him.

He reached out, seized the edge of one of the water barrels, and managed to wrench it to one side with desperate strength. The heavy barrel hit the steel floor hard, but before it had even settled, Grimsby thumbed a *Bind* rune onto its side and put another on the wall beside the door.

He snatched Wudge's cage by the rounded handle at the top before shouting, *"Bind!"*

He felt Impetus drain from him, leaving him feeling all the colder in the stifling heat of the room. Blue light flared between the *Bind* runes, but his inverted magic made the points push apart instead of pull together. The barrel set to rolling, though it was slower than Grimsby had hoped.

The serpent clawed toward him in a twisting mass, a whirl-wind of powerful muscle and black scales that raged around the steady firelight orbs of its eyes.

He had hoped the barrel would careen into the serpent, but the spell instead faltered, and the barrel drew to a halt, merely lying on its side in the beast's path.

"Skies alight," Grimsby seethed. With his magic twisted, he had forgotten that the runes pushing against each other would do little when the barrel rolled with the rune on the far side from its opposite number.

He silently wished *Torque* was its old self again as he stumbled back through the door, Wudge's cage tight in his grip.

The serpent clawed over the barrel, slicing through the plastic with nothing more than its weight on idle claws. The dark talons sank into the crumpling container, and pouring water quickly boiled to steam as it flowed over the creature's ashen scales.

Its eyes lit the spreading vapor like headlights through a fog. A claw reached out of the steam, breaching the glowing tether of light from his failed *Bind* spell, and when it touched the serpent's hide, the tether shattered like a glass filament into nothing.

Something about this creature somehow destroyed any spells it touched, Grimsby realized, and suddenly he felt very much disarmed. Without his magic, he didn't even have a pocketknife to protect himself.

A third light appeared in the steam, blooming beneath the twin headlamps of orange. This light was deep and dim, like a furnace glow, but growing with each moment. The steam swirled and sizzled as it was pulled into the depths, and as the vapor cleared, Grimsby saw the serpent's chest and throat swollen almost like a toad's, with veins of liquid metal glowing through cracks in its spreading scales.

Unfortunately, pocketknife or no, he suddenly felt the odds of his survival seemed quite slim.

Or perhaps a mysterious snow globe that could send the whole world into an ice age.

And either way, he didn't care.

"Free him," he said again, holding up Wudge's cage. "Now."

Mother Frost lifted her eyes from the box to his face, and the faintest lines of a scowl cracked her brow like a fissure in a glacier, but she nodded. "As we agreed," she said.

The boughs of the trees above bent low, and stout branches cracked and creaked as they reached down to wrap around the cage. With powerful limbs, the trees tore the cage door open, making the metal shriek, before dumping Wudge into Grimsby's arms.

He felt some small relief as Wudge's faint breathing began to grow steadier, and some green began to shade the tips of his floppy gray ears.

"And now Mayflower."

"Courtesy, young Auditor," Mother Frost said, "is rarely misplaced."

"The only thing misplaced at the moment is my patience," he said, letting himself drop to sit on a nearby stump. "And I think I earned a bit of flippancy."

"Perhaps, but not through your actions. Simply through your youth. Someday you might understand what I asked was generous, especially compared to what I gave."

"I doubt it."

She gave a small, distant smile. "I do not." Then she waved her wand and the ice around Mayflower sublimated away to mist. Within moments, the furious Huntsman was himself again, his barrel still aimed at Mother Frost's heart.

And he immediately pulled the trigger.

Grimsby winced, expecting a thunderous report, but there was only a dull click. Mayflower's face, still as enraged as it had been the moment he was frozen, contorted further into fury, and he pulled the trigger once more.

Again, only a click.

It was then Grimsby realized that Mayflower's gun, unlike the rest of him, was still coated in a thin layer of rime.

Mother Frost clicked her tongue. "I expected your emotions might get the better of you, Huntsman, so I thought it in your best interest to keep you from making any serious errors of judgment."

Mayflower's rage cooled to merely being red-hot instead of molten. He flicked a glance at Grimsby. "You all right?" he asked.

Grimsby shrugged. "Been worse." He was surprised to discover he wasn't lying.

Mayflower nodded, then finally lowered his gun, his eyes finding Mother Frost's. "The only error that was made here was yours. And I won't forget it." He holstered his gun and turned around. "Come on, Grimsby. Let's go."

He began to stalk away, and Grimsby groaned to his feet to follow, but Mother Frost cleared her throat.

"Our business is not yet concluded, gentlemen," she said. "Your collateral was returned to you, young witch, and your . . . ally freed. But I said I'd give you the name you desired."

Grimsby stopped and half turned. He had been getting the stick so long in this whole ordeal that he had forgotten there was ever a carrot to begin with. The name of the ritualist might give them the final piece they needed to put the puzzle together—and though this gave him a small thrill of excitement, it paled compared to his exhaustion.

"And that would be?" he asked, unable to keep the impatience from his voice.

Mother Frost smiled. "First, young witch, I should like you to show me what you stole from me."

Grimsby hesitated, and even in his unconscious stupor, Wudge fidgeted and groaned, flapping a resistant arm in the air.

"Don't worry, I don't intend to take it back. It is but a trifle, but I would still like to know what I've lost."

Reluctantly, Grimsby dug the nail from his pocket and held it out in his palm.

"Closer, dear boy," she said. "My eyes aren't what they once were."

He nudged closer, until his hand was a foot away from Mother Frost's face. He expected to feel a radiating chill, but instead all he sensed was the smell of cinnamon and tea.

She reached out toward the nail, and before he could explain that it could not part from him, she plucked it from his palm.

No sticking, no tugging, no curse.

"Ah," she said. "A doornail to a very special door. Though perhaps one that best remains closed."

"How—how did you take that? It's been stuck to me for days!"

She smiled. "This is petty magic. I am not." She held out the nail to return it, but he flinched away instinctively. What if this was his only chance to break the curse?

"Your fear this bauble, yet you wish to keep it? Why?" She expressed nothing more than curiosity, but her eyes were somehow focused despite their clouded surfaces.

"It's not for me. It's for him." He gestured to Wudge in his arm. "I told him I'd help him, and he needs that nail."

She nodded. "You are not always courteous, young witch," she said, "but I see that you are often kind. The latter is far more difficult. And more dangerous."

Grimsby shifted uncomfortably, uncertain how to graciously accept a compliment from an apparent underworld demigod who had nearly just gotten him killed and eaten, and perhaps not in that order.

"Thank you?"

"I had not promised you this boon, but I shall give it all the same: take this nail once more. It will no longer be bound to you—you may discard it freely. But beware, I merely suspend the curse. The next to take it will suffer its effects as you have."

Grimsby frowned, suspicious. "Why?"

Her grayed eyes softened for a moment. "Because kindness is not rewarded often enough." She held the nail out between her finger and thumb, the latter of which had a tarnished thimble upon it.

Grimsby reluctantly took the nail, expecting it to stick to him as it had before, but even as he returned it to his pocket, he felt it part from his skin as easily as a mundane version might have.

"Th-thank you," he said, this time more genuine. "That is generous of you."

"It seems some of your patience remains after all," she said. "That is well. And now, why you came here."

She glanced over his shoulder, and Grimsby followed her gaze to see Mayflower standing behind him, arms crossed, eyes wary. Despite the lack of firearm, Grimsby was glad for his steadying presence.

"The name of the thief who stole my hagstone," Mother Frost said, "is Janice."

There was a moment's silence, and Grimsby felt the gears churning in his mind, but before he could speak, he heard Mayflower take a seething breath behind him.

"That's impossible," he said. "Janice is dead. I made certain of it."

"Did you?" Mother Frost asked pleasantly. "Remind me not to hire you to kill anyone for me."

"I shot her in the head. I saw the medical records. I even found her ashes in the Department reliquary. She is dead."

"Then a dead woman stole my hagstone. Perhaps you were right," she said with a raised brow to Grimsby. "Perhaps I do need a dog."

Grimsby glanced back to Mayflower, but his expression looked like he was staring at Medusa: shocked and petrified.

He turned back to Mother Frost before he managed to speak. "There's no chance she lied to you? Gave you a false name?"

"There is no such thing as a false name, though some people carry more than one," Mother Frost said. "She did not lie."

Grimsby found himself believing her, though he wasn't certain why. In any case, if she was right, that meant Janice had somehow returned—but how? Moreover, what did it mean for their RUIN case?

He turned to Mayflower, shifting Wudge's body in his grip. "We need to go."

The Huntsman's face remained disturbed, but he seemed to lash it down. He nodded, though his eyes were thunderous clouds. "All right."

Mother Frost waved a hand. "Your guide will be waiting for you." She lowered her fingers to rest atop the Wardbox, their frostbitten tips tapping against its surface.

Grimsby felt a moment's concern for what might lie within, but he felt it subsumed beneath the myriad of other, more pressing concerns that welled within him.

He made his way to the gates through which they had entered, the Huntsman's stalking steps behind him, and Wudge's bony form in his arm. The doors cracked open like parting glaciers, and on the rails beyond the frozen platform, Quasi waited with his railcar and armory of bizarre levers.

They boarded and the hunched creature began pumping the car without a word. They ground slowly over the rails before gaining momentum and exiting the icy tree, sailing over Underton's labyrinthine streets on suspended lines. This time, however, Grimsby was too worn to be in awe. He instead focused on getting what small amount of rest he could, ignoring the chill air and rattling cart.

The car flew into the tunnel and the city vanished behind them. Before long, they came within sight of daylight, and Quasi let the vehicle coast to a stop.

"Thanks, Quasi," Grimsby said, stumbling down from the car to the rime-stricken brick floor.

Quasi used one twisted claw of a hand to remove his pointed cap and reveal hair that was lustrous and black at the scalp before fading to white at its tips, matching his beard. He dipped his head. "Good luck, witch," he said. Then he reversed the cart and slid off into the dark.

They emerged into the sunlight, and Grimsby shivered as its rays bathed him in warmth. He had forgotten how numbing the ambient cold had been, and quickly new aches began to reveal themselves in his muscles, though their complaints were backlogged behind the rest of his idle pains.

They came to the jeep, and Grimsby began to set Wudge down in the back seat but then saw the iron bars that encompassed it. Instead, he secured the creature in the passenger seat and let himself slide to the ground, his back leaned against the jeep's wheel.

Mayflower paced before him, seemingly intent on digging a furrow in the earth with only his stride. "She can't be alive," he said, half muttering to himself.

Grimsby closed his eyes and was tempted to let the sound of rustling trees and the warm afternoon sunlight ease him to sleep. Instead, he cracked an eye open.

"I don't think Mother Frost was lying," he said.

"Then you tell me, how can a woman who was shot in the head, autopsied, and then cremated still be alive?"

He shrugged. "Maybe she isn't 'alive' at all. There's record of some witches returning as spirits who can still manage magic they knew in life."

The Huntsman shook his head. "A spirit is usually bound to a place or object. They can't wander about collecting reagents for rituals or stealing hagstones."

"Well, you said someone had controlled that guy to attack you, right? Enthralled him? Maybe he did it for her."

"Maybe," he said doubtfully. "Something still doesn't seem right about it."

"How so?"

"The RUIN case didn't feel like the exact same ritual as the one Janice was doing. It was just close. I thought maybe that was because whoever was behind it was copying her, but if it's somehow really her, then why the change? I don't think a spirit would have the wherewithal to manage that." He growled, "No, this spell is different. I just don't know how."

"Well, stealing someone's Impetus to become a strygga is sort of a really specific spell. I hadn't even heard of it until Mrs. Ox told me about it. I don't think there's a whole slew of ways you could twist it to do other things. So what ritual could be close but different?"

"You're the magic guy, witch. You tell me."

Grimsby closed his eyes again and tried to think, but his mind came up blank. "Right now, the only guy I am is the tired guy."

"Well, wake up, kid, because Finley said their last chance to cast this ritual is tonight. And that means so is our last chance to stop it."

Grimsby groaned but forced his eyes open. Mayflower was right. They still had work to do.

He tried to focus his head, and though it felt like it was wrapped in cotton padding, he managed to get something like a thought together. "What it's supposed to do doesn't matter if we can stop it. But now at least we know why she had to wait so long to try the ritual again. For a ritual this powerful, she'd need the right ley lines to align, and that could take decades—even centuries. The only question that really matters is: where is it going to be cast?"

Mayflower grunted. "Finley can run those simulations again, I wager." He reached for his phone, but even as he pulled it from his pocket, it began to blare and buzz wildly. He grumbled a curse and flipped it open before pecking the appropriate button to take the call. "Yeah?"

Finley's voice was tinny, but the phone volume was loud enough that Grimsby could hear. "Les, where have you been? I've been calling for hours!"

"Busy," he said.

"Of course you were." She sighed. "Look. I got that redacted file you wanted—the original. Pulling it up now."

"Good. We also need to figure out the last place the ritual might be repeated."

"That may be tough," she said. "The last time, it worked because the ley lines were so thin that there were only a couple places it could be. Tonight is an apex full moon, so there'll be many more potential intersections."

"Well, then get a list of the likely ones," he said. "We know who's behind it now, and we need to stop her."

"Her who?"

"Janice."

"Hang on a second—" Finley began to mumble like she was reading the file. "Les, are you sure this is the right case?"

"I'm sure. Why?"

"Well, according to all our files, Janice is, like, super dead. Like 'most of her skull was gone' dead."

"I'm aware," he said. "Weird shit happens."

"It does at that. Wait a second—" A small noise came through that might have been a gasp. "Les, you saved a girl that day, right? The one who was going to be used for the ritual?"

"Damn straight."

"And you didn't bother to remember her name?"

"Never learned it. Why?"

"Because she was a witch. And grew up to be an Auditor."

"Spit it out, Finley!"

"It was Rayne, Les. Elizabeth 'Rayne' Bathory—she was the intended victim."

Grimsby felt himself go rigid, suddenly ready to shatter like frozen glass under boiling water. He clambered to his feet, his heart hammering at his ribs.

Rayne had been the victim of the original ritual? What were the odds? More importantly, did she even know? Was that why she had requested the assignment in the first place?

Mayflower caught his gaze, and Grimsby could see the same questions in his face. "You're certain?" he asked.

"Yeah, there's only four people of interest in the report: Samantha Mansgraf, Leslie Mayflower, Elizabeth Bathory, and Janice Defaux."

"What?" Grimsby said, then repeated himself, half shouting at the phone. "What was that last name?"

"Defaux, Janice Defaux."

Defaux.

The Auditor that Rayne had mentioned. Defaux. She was Janice. And that could only mean one thing:

She intended to finish what she'd started twenty years ago, when she had first tried to sacrifice Rayne.

"Grimsby?" Mayflower asked. "What is it?"

"There's no time to explain now. But you're right—Janice is back, and she's been with Rayne this whole time." He again spoke at the phone. "Finley, where is Rayne now?"

"One sec," she said over the sound of clicking keys. "Department log says . . . she checked out not long ago. Personal business, apparently."

Grimsby felt himself shaking his head. "No, no, no! Mayflower, we have to find them. Fast."

"Guys," Finley said, "the ritual will likely start at dusk. There's barely two hours until then—and there's a couple dozen potential locations."

Grimsby felt his throat go dry. Two hours to check everywhere. It would be impossible.

Mayflower's eyes were focused on the horizon as he spoke into the phone. "Fin, is one of those possible locations near Ashmont?"

"Hang on." More clicks. "Not that I can see; the ley lines aren't quite aligned."

"What about below the surface? Like, say, at subway level?"

"Potentially, but why— Oh."

He nodded. "That's got to be it. That's where the first ritual was attempted. That's where she'll try again."

Grimsby frantically tried to run the math in his head, but he was terrible with geography. "Can we make it?"

"If we can get there fast and find a way down faster, then maybe."

"Let's go."

Finley reported over the phone, "I've already got backup en route, but they're not as close as you guys are. You can wait for them to show, but—"

"But it might be too late," Grimsby said.

Her silence told him it was true.

"Well then," the Huntsman said, "let's move. Thanks, Fin."

"Good luck, boys," she said, and the line went dead.

Grimsby and Mayflower climbed into the old jeep, Grimsby sitting in the back after buckling in Wudge the best he could.

"Time to finish this," Mayflower said, and he lurched the jeep over the abandoned rails and back onto the road.

Grimsby only gulped and felt his stomach twist into knots. If they didn't hurry, Rayne could be dead before they even arrived. Or perhaps worse than dead.

FORTY-FIVE

THE WHEELS OF RAYNE'S DEPARTMENT-ISSUED VEHICLE ground over the time-worn asphalt as she pulled into the parking garage. The setting sun bled red in her rearview camera, but it quickly faded away as she turned and drove down into the subterranean level.

She studied the hands on her watch as they quivered and twitched, both pointing ahead. "It's a good spell," she remarked to Defaux, who sat beside her, unusually quiet. "Normally, tracking rituals just point in straight lines. But yours seems to know how to navigate."

"I told you I was good at rituals," Defaux said.

The hands of her watch trembled again, and she parked the car in the empty garage. "But why would Hives be down here of all places? Government Center isn't exactly remote," she said as she climbed out of the car. The sound of her shutting the door behind her echoed in the silence.

"The Center wasn't always here, love," Defaux said. "They built over a place called Scollay Square, and some of its tunnels are still down here, buried beneath the city. Seems to me a wonderful place to go if you don't want to be found."

Rayne frowned but didn't argue. It made sense that Hives would be there instead of aboveground, but why be in Boston to begin with? If he had any sense left in his head, he should have crossed an ocean by now.

She decided it was better not to question it. After all, it seemed to her benefit that he was still in the city at all. All she had to do now was find him and bring him in. She looked around for a moment, spinning while watching her wrist, and the twin hands pointed to a steel door that looked to lead to some kind of utility tunnel.

They approached, and after a quick inspection she found the padlock that held it shut had been removed, leaving the door just slightly ajar. She opened it wide to find that it was pitch-black within. She summoned an inch of Impetus and snapped her fingers, whispering, "*Spark*." Her spell ignited the tip of one finger with a single, bright pinpoint of light. With a casual flicker of her finger, she flung the spark down the length of the tunnel, where it floated like a leaf on a breeze before settling to the ground fifteen or so feet away, burning like a tiny flare.

There, the tunnel looked only like more of the same: concrete walls, metal pipes, and stagnant water pooling on the floor.

She glanced at her watch, and sure enough the hands directed her inside.

She shuddered, feeling her stomach flip as the cramped walls seemed to threaten to press in on her.

"Something wrong?" Defaux asked.

"No, I just—I don't like small spaces, that's all."

"Claustrophobe, eh? Well, hopefully it won't be long."

Rayne nodded, summoning another *Spark* and using it to light her way as she stooped into the old tunnel, crouching to avoid the ceiling.

"I'm right behind you," Defaux said. "Just keep moving."

Rayne listened to her advice, focusing on the ground in front of her as she tried to hurry through the tunnel. The walls seemed to be narrowing on either side of her, or perhaps it was just her imagination. Either way, her breath became more and more constricted with each step. It was like a child was putting one rubber band after another around her chest, just because it was curious about how many it would take to crush her.

She forced herself forward, keeping her eyes on the ground, because she was afraid that if she stopped, she might not be able to move again.

Finally, almost too quickly, the walls fell away on either side of her, and she found herself skidding to a halt just inches before she fell down onto the rails of an abandoned subway line.

She let herself stand up straight and took a deep, bracing breath, and with it, all those invisible rubber bands snapped away one by one.

"Well, that could have been worse," she said, turning around to offer Defaux a nervous smile.

But Defaux was gone.

She felt her heart skitter and stall. "Defaux?" she called in a harsh whisper down the tunnel, but her light revealed nothing, and there was no reply. "Defaux!" she called again, this time feeling panic seep into her voice.

The world was silent.

She felt her skin go cold. Where had her partner gone? Had some spell or trap taken her? She had been there just moments before, within reach.

Then the silence was broken by the crunch of gravel.

Rayne whipped around to see a figure at the edge of her light, standing perhaps twenty feet from her on the rails.

Her wide eyes glanced to her watch, and the hands had ceased their twitching motions, instead pointing directly at the figure. His silhouette was thinner than she remembered, but his broad frame was otherwise familiar.

"W-Wilson?" she asked hesitantly. She didn't know how he would receive her. Would he be relieved for her to have found him? Or would he retaliate against her?

Instead, he simply turned and ran.

"Wilson!" Rayne called after him. "Hives!"

She hopped down from the utility tunnel's alcove and hurried after him, her own feet crunching on the gravel in time with his, the sound echoing against the subway tunnel's brick walls. Within moments, a soft light became visible ahead, and in its glow she saw the running shadow of Hives outpacing her before rounding a corner.

She forced herself to run faster, and as she passed the light, she realized it was a small cluster of candles. As she turned the bend, there were more candles and much-brighter pools of similar illumination.

Hives reached the end of the tunnel and hopped up on what looked to be a condemned boarding platform before leaving her sight.

She reached the platform and ground to a halt, holding her desperate breath to listen. The platform was scattered with candles, some still burning, others pooled into puddles of cold wax on the dusty floor. But there was no sign of Hives.

She climbed onto the platform and trod forward cautiously, her heart hammering, her breath shallow and quick. She let her Impetus begin to well within her, holding out her glowing finger before her, bracing her wrist with her other hand. A dozen spells lingered on her lips, ready to loose themselves if she willed it, but the platform was still.

Then she saw a flicker of movement beyond an open doorway.

"Hives!" she called. "Come out now. It's all right. Let's just talk!"

The movement shuddered, a flickering shadow cast by pooling candlelight, then vanished.

Rayne paused at the doorway, her chest feeling like it might burst. Should she go back and find Defaux? It was dangerous to be down here alone—who knew what Hives might do? Yet if she left now, he might escape again, and she might not be so lucky as to find him twice. If he knew he was being tracked, he might be able to find a way to break the spell.

She shook her head and forced her shoulders square. No, she was going to finish this, here and now, alone or not.

She stepped into the room, hand at the ready, and saw Hives standing before a ritual circle.

One identical to that of her stolen RUIN case.

"You?" she asked. "It was you?"

She felt so adrift, so shocked. She wanted answers, but she also wanted to scream. She wanted to hit him, but she also wanted to see if he was all right.

Before she could say or do anything, however, rough hands seized one of her arms, and fast hands took the other. "Let go!" she screamed as she struggled. Her Impetus raged, but before she could summon a spell, cold iron latched around her wrists, stifling her power. She looked on each side of her to see the two Unorthdoxes she had dispatched only hours ago—each now with a glowing rune on their cheek.

They were thralls, magically enslaved.

"Hives!" she demanded, growing desperate. "What is this? What have you done?"

Hives turned, and she saw him in detail for the first time. His head had been shaved, though whatever razor had done so had left him with a dozen scabby cuts along his scalp. His eyes were ringed and dark, and a mask of old cloth covered his face. He peeled it away, revealing sunken cheeks and a hollow, distant expression. He looked sickly—a shadow of the Auditor she had known, and—

And on his cheek was a dully glowing rune.

He, too, had been enthralled.

"I'm so sorry, love," a familiar voice said.

Rayne struggled enough to turn and see Defaux reveal herself from the shadows.

"You?" Rayne asked. "You did this?" She hated how broken her own voice felt.

Defaux offered her a sad smile and a shrug. "The answer is not as simple as the question. But I haven't been entirely honest with you, I'm afraid."

"No shit," Rayne spat, feeling her anger begin to eclipse her shock. "What the hell have you done to Hives?"

"What have I done to him?" Defaux asked, almost musing. "Nothing I couldn't do without your help." She approached Hives and traced her fingers over the symbol on his cheek. "I did so miss having such loyal companions."

"What the hell is going on here, Defaux?"

"Why, can't you tell? Don't you recognize this little tea party?" She gestured extravagantly at the ritual. "After all, we've had it before." She sighed. "Well, I suppose you wouldn't remember—I did make certain of that. No matter, I have work to do yet, love."

She approached slowly, calmly, her hands held out like Rayne was some skittish mare. "Please do just relax. It'll make this so much easier on both of us."

"Stay the hell away from me!" Rayne screamed, pulling and struggling, but the troll and lamia held her tight. Without her magic, she was no match for either, let alone both of them, Hives, and Defaux.

Defaux crouched to meet her eye to eye, and there was a terrible kindness in her expression. "Go to sleep now, little one. It'll all be over soon." She reached out with a gentle hand.

Rayne thrashed and kicked, managing to drag her fingernails over the lamia's arm and even draw blood, but they held her tight, as steady and rigid as mannequins.

Defaux's hand touched her cheek, and it was soft and cool amid the heat and fury of her struggle. She felt herself grow almost distant, unhinged from her own body, and then the world began to grow dark.

Terribly, terribly dark.

FORTY-SIX

GRIMSBY WATCHED MAYFLOWER FROM BEHIND THE rune-carved bars that separated the back and front of the jeep. His hands nervously clenched in the rough fabric of his pants as the Huntsman guided the jeep down the back streets far too slowly, carefully examining the structures on either side.

"Fast would be better than slow," Grimsby said, trying to keep the frantic impatience from leaking too much into his tone, though it was difficult. Rayne's life was on the line, after all.

"Quiet, boy," Mayflower growled. "It's been twenty years since I was down in old Scollay. I just got to remember where a way down is."

Wudge, who had finally begun to come back around to both consciousness and his usual gray-green color, cackled a soft song. *"Down, down, never to be found."*

Grimsby forced himself to look away and began scanning for any clue as well, though if it were anything less than a sign that read EVIL RITUAL THIS WAY, he doubted he would notice. He could scarcely even breathe, his heart was racing so fast. It hadn't eased since they discovered Janice was back and after Rayne.

He should have paid more attention when Rayne spoke about

Defaux. He should have asked more questions. If he had, he might have—

Might have what?

It wasn't as though he would have recognized Janice Defaux even if he had seen her, and he certainly hadn't known her role in Rayne's past until it was too late. Besides, he wasn't exactly in Rayne's good graces at the moment, and she wouldn't have tolerated him digging into her business after taking her case.

Even so, he felt he should have done more. Something— anything! If he had, maybe Rayne would be safe, rather than in the clutches of a depraved ritualist. Yet there was no changing the past.

Instead, he could only hope he wasn't too late to prevent the grim darkness of the near future.

"There," Mayflower said, squealing the jeep to a halt so fast that Grimsby bucked forward and nearly cracked his glasses into the bars. The Huntsman pointed to a stairwell between two buildings that cut sharply into the earth.

He opened the back door for Grimsby, as it had no handle on the inside, and they hurried out of the jeep and toward the stairs, leaving the stirring Wudge to stretch and yawn behind them. The stairs were little more than weathered slabs of concrete descending to a shadowed steel door. The retaining walls on either side of the steps were made from old, old brick, and the slab steps themselves had been around long enough that twin shallow depressions marred their rough surface smooth from decades of footsteps.

"You sure this is the right place?" Grimsby asked. His voice was thready, but not from the fear of what might happen; he was growing used to that. Rather, it felt much more like dread, a fear of what might have already happened.

"There's a few entrances to the old tunnels scattered about the city," Mayflower said as he grabbed the hefty padlock on the door and knelt, withdrawing some small tools from his pocket. "This one should get us close to where the first ritual was."

Grimsby bounced impatiently from foot to foot as the Hunts-man dug into the lock with his tools. "Can't you just shoot it?" he asked.

"Down here, in close quarters, surrounded by brick and con-crete?" he asked gruffly through a tool he held in his teeth. "You ever try fighting witches with bullet fragments in your leg?"

"No."

"I wouldn't recommend it," he said. "Leaves you sore as hell the next day."

He gave the lock a final, triumphant twist, and his pick promptly snapped, lodging itself in the keyhole. "Goddamned piece of—"

There was a soft pop from the other side of the door, and the padlock clicked open seemingly of its own accord before falling to the ground. The door swung open inward, and Grimsby felt his Impetus begin to rise in panic, until he saw Wudge standing on the other side of the door still looking half awake.

Grimsby glanced behind them to the jeep, and then back to Wudge. "How did you—?"

"Wudge can always get where he isn't welcome," the tiny crea-ture said with a yawning grin.

Mayflower grunted. "Damn. Little guy's more useful than you are, Grimsby."

"Maybe if you go by density," Grimsby muttered, before shoving past them both and into the darkened tunnel beyond. He was worried for a moment that he might not be able to find the way, but the cramped corridor was long and narrow and didn't branch. It was lit only by solitary flickering bulbs dangling from long wires and hooks hammered into the mortar between bricks. Despite its disuse, apparently *someone* had been down here, at least within the life span of a lightbulb.

He heard the others fall in line behind him, but as he tried to hurry forward, Mayflower's hand fell gently on his shoulder. "Careful, now. Not too fast."

"There's no time!" Grimsby snapped, but even as he tried to pull away, Mayflower tightened his grip.

"You won't do her any good if you get yourself killed for not being careful." His tone was soft, but his words were iron. "We go only as fast as we can see, got it?"

Grimsby seethed a breath but relented. It wouldn't help Rayne if he ran face-first into a trap or ambush. He just hoped it wasn't too late to help Rayne at all.

The three of them moved forward, Grimsby cautiously, Mayflower carefully, and Wudge casually. If there had been some kind of fun theme song, and not an ominous silence, they could have passed for a meddling gang on a Saturday-morning cartoon.

The tunnel was quiet save for the steady drip of water and the soft scuffs of their feet on the damp concrete. Cockroaches scurried from their path, and Grimsby heard the telltale scratches of rats skittering in rotted-out alcoves between bricks, their glimmering eyes flashing red from darkened crevasses before retreating.

The tunnel was cool, but Grimsby could feel something else beneath the chill—the simmer of ley lines, like electricity over his skin. The energy prickled and crawled over him, making the thin hairs on his neck stand on end and the unblemished portions of his skin rise in gooseflesh. With every step, he could feel the power rising, quickly dwarfing the ley-line sensation he had felt back in the warehouse he and Mayflower had scouted out the evening before.

Ahead, the tunnel ended in a door hanging open on rusted hinges. In the dimness beyond, Grimsby could make out the flickering of candlelight.

"We're close," he whispered.

"You sure?" Mayflower asked, his leathery grip tightening around his gun until it creaked.

"I can feel it," he said. He glanced to Wudge, who was chewing on his bottom lip with his sharp teeth. "Think you can sneak ahead?" he asked.

Wudge grinned and nodded, then vanished without a word.

Grimsby felt his hands begin to tremble, and suddenly his dread felt more distant compared to the whelming fear that rose cold in his belly. He bit back a sharp curse at himself, and he looked to Mayflower, shamefully hoping the Huntsman hadn't noticed.

He certainly must have, but his face was stern and focused. There was no trace of fear, no sign of doubt. Only competence and vigilance.

Grimsby wished he commanded a fraction of the same.

But he didn't. He was terrified, he was nervous, and he was trembling. But there was one thing he was above all others; one thing that beat the rest of his battling emotions into rough submission.

He was determined.

Determined to help Rayne.

Determined to be an Auditor in more than just name.

Determined to make things right.

He took a steeling breath, then nodded to Mayflower. The Huntsman nodded back, and they approached the hanging door, pressing into the shadows as they peered through the narrow gap.

Three figures stood on the abandoned subway platform on the other side. Grimsby recognized two of them immediately: Lump and Echidna. Their trench coat guises were inactive, their collars down, revealing their true forms. How they had come to be here, he didn't know, but he didn't let himself linger over the possibilities. The third figure was a stranger, he thought, until he looked closer and saw the familiar, though now more gaunt, face of Hives. He hadn't recognized him with his shaved head or emaciated features, but it was the very same.

"What is he doing here?" Grimsby whispered. "What are any of them doing here?"

"Look at the cheeks," the Huntsman muttered gruffly.

Grimsby did, and noticed for the first time the runes that glowed beneath their eyes. "What is that? Some kind of spell?"

"They've been enthralled. Magically enslaved by a witch; in this case, Janice."

"So they're not acting on their own? We can't fight them! What if they get hurt? What if they get killed? They're innocent."

"Look at them," Mayflower said, his words harsh and biting. "Tell me which one of them is innocent? Tell me which one of them hasn't tried to kill you?"

Grimsby said nothing. The Huntsman was cold, but he was right. Each of the waiting thralls had nearly killed him at one time or another.

Yet he was still alive, wasn't he?

Though whether that spoke more of their mercy or their competence, he was uncertain.

"If we want to get to Janice," Mayflower said, "we have to get through them. One way or another." His tone was grim as his hand tightened around his gun.

Grimsby shook his head, too fast and too hard, as though he might shed the pressing doubts that rose in him. "No, not happening! There's got to be another way. Maybe we can snap them out of the spell? You wouldn't happen to know how to break the enthrallment, would you?" Grimsby asked hopefully.

"I don't. Mansgraf could do it, said it had something to do with reminding them."

"Reminding them of what?"

"Beats me. I usually settled for shooting the witch that enthralled them. That also does the trick."

Grimsby felt his mouth go dry. He wanted to save Rayne, but what would it cost?

Even pressed into the shadows, Mayflower's face darkened. "I don't like it any more than you do, but there's no choice."

"There's always a choice! Always. Just—just give me a minute to think."

"We don't have minutes! We might barely have seconds. If you want to save her, this is what we have to do."

Grimsby gulped, but his mouth was dry. Was Mayflower right? Was the only way through to use violence, and risk taking a probably mostly innocent life? It might have been the only way.

But that still didn't make it the right way.

"We can't. We can't do that."

He looked over to Mayflower, expecting the Huntsman to be furious; instead the old man just sighed and shook his head. "I figured. You're the most stubborn conscience I've ever had." He scoffed, then raised a brow at Grimsby. "You know you're going to get us killed one of these days if you keep this up?"

"Let's just hope it's not today."

"Even if it is, at least it'll spare me this headache."

Grimsby curled his lips in a grin. "Follow my lead."

Mayflower only nodded.

Grimsby pushed open the door and stepped out onto the platform, arms splayed wide. "Ladies and gentle-trolls!" he called out. "Your entertainment has arrived."

The waiting thralls all turned to him in eerie unison. Their expressions were unchanging, but their bodies tensed in varying degrees of bulky, sinuous, and broad.

Mayflower emerged from the tunnel behind and stood ready. "What are they doing?"

"Got me. I sort of expected a mindless charge." Then he looked past the three to see a closed door, beneath the seam of which he could see the flickering light of candles. The intangible power of ley lines radiated from the closed room. "They're guarding the ritual chamber," he realized.

"So Janice is behind that door," Mayflower said darkly.

"And so is Rayne."

"You know, this would be a lot easier with the gloves off," Mayflower said, gesturing with his revolver. "They aren't even moving."

"Not happening."

Mayflower growled, "I don't know why I even bring this thing anymore," though he didn't holster the weapon.

Then Grimsby saw a flicker of movement behind Lump's tree-stump-thick legs.

Movement with many familiar teeth.

"Distraction incoming," Grimsby said quickly. "We disable the thralls, get through the door, and stop the ritual."

Before Mayflower could reply, Lump jerked his leg up in reflexive pain, seizing his knee. Dangling by the jaws from the troll's ankle was Wudge.

Lump didn't roar or howl, but was disturbingly silent. He shook loose Wudge, who fell several of his own heights to the ground and scurried quickly from Lump's descending stomp.

Its power shook the floor and cracked the concrete, but Wudge was not beneath it.

Meanwhile, Grimsby and Mayflower began running toward the door, and the other two thralls seemed spurred into action at their advance.

Echidna's serpentine coils carried her forward until she launched herself in a flying pounce, grasp splayed wide, the metal tip of her tail whipping toward Mayflower with uncanny speed. While the old Huntsman's stride was slower, his reflexes were just as quick, and he slid under her like a baseball player stealing second. Yet, as he did, his free hand flew upward and seized the collar of her trench coat. The sudden anchor of the Huntsman's grip and weight turned her neck into a fulcrum, and while the rest of her body kept flying forward, Mayflower used the leverage to crack her head into the ground.

Grimsby tore his eyes away from the Huntsman as Hives bore down on him with a pounding sprint. His gaze was dull and vacant, the mark on his cheek glowing more brightly, but even so, some hint of expression seemed to slip through.

Grimsby threw one hand forward, summoning his Impetus and shouting, *"Torque!"*

He had expected the field of lights to appear and halt Hives's advance, but instead a twisting cascade of blue emerged, and he realized that Hylde suspending the curse of the nail had also restored his magic to its original form.

Unfortunately, the cascade hit Hives in the chest and barely offset his charge. By the time Grimsby realized what had happened, the former Auditor dove and struck him around the waist, tackling him to the ground. Though Hives had lost weight in his time missing, he still had Grimsby at roughly two-to-one odds on mass.

Grimsby managed to get his arms up in a somewhat practiced motion as Hives rained down one hammering fist after another on him. He tried to summon more Impetus, but his concentration failed him, as each strike on the smoldering scars of his left arm showered down burning sparks like a blacksmith's hammer on red-hot steel.

He tried to buck Hives off, but he wasn't strong enough, and when he tried to retaliate, it only left his face vulnerable. A blow struck through, and a knuckle knocked an oversize lens from his battered glasses.

The world became skewed as the Elsewhere began to leak into the unmasked vision of his left eye. It was as though he was seeing double, but each double a twisted mirror of the other. In the real world, Hives was emaciated, bruised, and scratched, his expression nearly empty save for a glimmer of anger and the symbol burning on his cheek.

In the Elsewhere, he was terrified. The symbol leaked fire that fell in a choking collar around his neck, a chain pulling tautly toward the knotted iron door behind him. His gaze wandered, frightened and lost, and he mouthed a single set of silent words again and again.

Who am I?

Grimsby was so shocked by the twin views that another blow struck through his weakening guard, and for a moment, Hives's eyes ceased wandering and found Grimsby's. A fist got past Grimsby's hands, catching him painfully in the stomach. As it did, there was a flicker of recognition in Hives's face, and the mark on his cheek wavered.

Then, as if in punishment, the mark flared alight, and Hives's vision glazed over in pain, returning to its mad wanderings.

But, for an instant, Hives had been himself.

And all it had taken was beating the crap out of Grimsby like he used to

Like he used to.

Grimsby knew it was a crazy chance to take, but he took it all the same. Through a reluctant effort of will, he lowered his arms, and Hives began to beat and batter him completely unfettered.

Strike after strike came down, until Grimsby felt the frames of his glasses twist and tasted blood in his mouth. He felt hot pain swell in the thin flesh between skin and skull, and his vision flickered more than once.

But he was stubborn.

Then the fists began to slow.

Grimsby looked up to see Hives, his expression no longer vacant but furious, the rune on his cheek flickering like a failing lightbulb.

Grimsby's left eye was swollen nearly shut, but he cracked it open enough to see Elsewhere Hives clawing at his throat, the fiery collar there burning his hands as he struggled to pry it off.

"Do it!" Grimsby croaked. "Do it!"

Hives redoubled his efforts, his face growing red, his eyes

bulging, but the collar seemed to do the same, the chain tether growing stronger and thicker.

"Do it, Auditor!" Grimsby screamed.

Hives's eyes went round at the last word, and his mouth twisted in a furious snarl as he pried one final time.

And the collar shattered.

Hives's body went slack and he fell to one side.

Grimsby let his swelling left eye close, almost happy to have something to serve as a substitute for the missing lens of his glasses, and struggled to his elbows to check on Hives.

The former Auditor's vision was distant and dazed, but the mark on his cheek was gone.

He was a thrall no longer.

Grimsby climbed to his feet, wiping away at the dripping mixture of blood and drool that dribbled from his mouth, to see Mayflower wrestling with Echidna, and Wudge fleeing with a mad cackle from the lumbering Lump.

Mayflower, who had managed to trap Echidna in a headlock but had in turn had his own body wrapped in her coils, caught Grimsby's gaze. "Go!" he called hoarsely. "We got this!"

Grimsby took a step toward them both, reluctant to leave his friends with their foes.

Then he heard Rayne scream, long and wrenching. A scream of horror and agony.

He took one last look at Mayflower and Wudge, then turned and rushed toward the door.

FORTY-SEVEN

THE DOOR WAS HEAVY, FORGED FROM OLD AND RUSTED steel, but as Grimsby touched its handle, he heard a quiet chorus of hushed voices, all whispering for a pressing moment, and the door swung open as though on its own.

The room beyond was filled with silent and still machinery, each strange piece showing the wear and ruin of decades down in the dust and darkness. The warm, ebbing light came from hundreds of candles, some clustered in cloisters, while others were impaled on iron spokes or settled on other surfaces of the surrounding machines. Each spread a small pool of light that failed to reach the room's edge or to banish the shadows.

A space had been cleared at the room's center, below the apex of the domed ceiling. A ritual circle was outlined in chalk paint, with some strange object at the intersect of four of the five points of the pentagram star. He recognized fulgurite, or crystallized lightning, a reagent for capturing something that should never be bound. There was an ouroboros ring, a snake that had died engulfing its own tail and been preserved. A length of etched silver chains, the same as those left at the RUIN days before. Last was what looked likely to be the meteorite that had never been beneath the light of a full moon.

But that only made four. Where was the fifth?

Before he could find it, his eyes found Rayne, lying in a huddled heap at the circle's center. He'd never seen her like that, coiled and fetal, helpless. It made his stomach drop as instant, rabid worry overtook him. It was so unlike the Rayne he knew that for a moment he doubted if it was her—or if she was even alive.

Was he too late?

He rushed forward, kicking over a group of candles, sending wet wax and wicks flying. He skidded to kneel beside her, his hands trembling, afraid to reach out for what he might find. Somewhere in the back of his mind, he felt cold logic shouting at him, warning him about something, but his worry pushed it away.

Her face was buried in her arms, her hair spread in an unbound mess, but he saw the soft rise and fall of her chest and some measure of relief filled him.

"Rayne?" he said. "Rayne?" He reached out, placing his hands on the sleeve of her jacket, which was almost as worn as his own at this point, and shook her gently.

She kicked with a start and bolted upright, her wild and frantic eyes finding his own. "Grimsby?" she asked, her voice a hoarse whisper. "Where did— How—?"

He smiled, unable to contain himself as his worry vented away.

She was alive. She was all right.

He had saved her.

Then, before he could speak, Rayne's eyes widened in fearful realization. "Where is she?" she asked, looking around as though for a predator among the machines. "Where is Defaux?"

Grimsby's heart froze as that cold voice of logic finally got its desperate appeal through his thick skull: *Janice is here somewhere.*

But where?

He and Rayne both scrabbled to their feet and put their backs to each other at the circle's center, looking around for their foe. The machines were so massed and alien that the witch could be hiding behind any one of them, waiting to strike. They needed to be ready; they needed to be prepared—

He felt Rayne twitch oddly and lean away.

"You see her?" he asked.

There was no reply.

"Rayne? Rayne?" He turned around, reluctantly leaving his side of the room unguarded.

Rayne was staring at him, an odd smile on her face.

"What is it?" he asked, heat creeping up his neck to fill his head nearly to bursting when it mixed with the adrenaline and fear cocktail he already had up there.

Rayne drew herself close to him, and he didn't, or perhaps couldn't, dare to move. Her lips were parted and soft, her eyes half lidded.

Despite it all, despite monsters, magic, ritual candles, and witches, he found himself frozen, save for a slow, almost inevitable lean toward her. Everything else in the world seemed to fall aside, forgotten.

He felt her hands on his, gentle and warm.

And then the cold shock of iron on his wrists snapped him from his hormonal stupor.

He jerked away, but too late. A pair of shackles, engraved, held his hands, and Impetus, bound and powerless.

"What in blue blazes is this?" he asked, flicking his gaze between Rayne and his cuffs. "Rayne?"

Rayne only smiled, her expression foreign and strange. "Not at the moment, love," she said, then she curtsied. "Janice Defaux. Pleased to see you again."

FORTY-EIGHT

GRIMSBY STARED, HIS MOUTH AGAPE, HIS MIND SPIN-
ning like a windmill in a hurricane.

Rayne, or perhaps Janice, tilted her head at him and gave him a charming smile. "Empty attic, darling? I should have assumed as much. Though I suppose our situation is . . ." She trailed off as she glanced down at her own body. "Unusual."

Grimsby didn't know what to say. It was Rayne speaking, but her every mannerism was wrong, like an inverted reflection. The way she spoke, the way she held herself, even her smile, they were all distinctly not-Rayne.

They were all, apparently, Janice.

"What did you do to her?" he demanded, trying to stand straight and sound formidable, despite his confusion and the magic-nullifying cuffs on his wrists. "Enchantment? Made her into some sort of walkie-talkie thrall?"

Janice rolled her eyes and sighed. "I'm afraid it's a bit more complicated than that, Grims-boy, but suffice to say that we've been . . . roommates for a long while."

"Roommates? You tried to kill her! You tried to bind her Impetus to yourself, and she was just a child!"

Janice raised a brow and tilted her head. "'Tried' implies I failed, dear."

Grimsby froze, realizing what she meant. "But—but you did fail! Mayflower stopped you."

"No, he merely forced me to make an unfortunate change of plans. A strygga was still made that day—though it was not who I intended, certainly." Janice held up Rayne's hand and admired it. "But I must say, she's grown up well."

"You mean—ever since your ritual?"

"We have been bound to one another. Like two little peas in a pod."

"Like a parasite!"

Her smile melted to a scowl as quick as a switchblade. "You have no idea what I've done for her, boy. Without me, little Elizabeth would be a very different person." She paused, then chuckled to herself like she had just made a joke. "Even more so than she is now."

"So if you didn't fail, why the rituals? You already have what you want!"

Her eyes flashed with anger, so wide that her teal irises were totally exposed. "Wrong. I want control. And though little Elizabeth's fraying discipline has let me . . . slip out of my shell once in a while, I rather like being awake. I'd like to stay that way, but that requires"—she glanced at the ritual circle—"lubrication."

Grimsby shuddered, then followed her gaze to the circle. It was then he remembered one of the five reagents was absent, a blank space where it should have been.

"Looks like you're going to come up short on your deadline," he said, feeling some small sliver of triumph pierce his growing dread. "Without five components, there's no way you can pull something that complex off."

Janice laughed, the pealing sound somehow both alluring and manic. "Bless your heart, Grimsby. You simply don't get it, do you?"

He hadn't expected her smugness, and he felt his triumph dissolve like ice in an inferno. "Without a fifth reagent, your ritual will fail. Again. We'll take Rayne back to the Department and they'll tear you out of her."

"They'd have to tear her apart to do that. But I'm not missing the fifth reagent, dear." She eyed him up and down in an uncomfortably predatory fashion. "I'm looking at it."

Grimsby felt his heart freeze in his chest as though it had adhered to his ribs mid-beat.

"Why do you think I let you come so far? Why do you think I let you attend this little party at all?" She leaned in close, her hands gripped sweetly at the small of her back, her voice a hushed whisper. "You're the secret ingredient."

Grimsby realized the depth of his arrogance too late. He needed to run. He needed to get far away. Not for himself, but to thwart whatever plan Janice had in mind—but even as he tried to turn away, he felt heat flare from Rayne's body as Janice's Impetus rose.

"*Wait*," she said, the spell sounding like it was whispered through pillows. There was no force that struck him or held him, but rather his body suddenly didn't see much point in obeying him, when it could instead listen to her.

He tried to force himself to move, but his legs, his arms, even his chest had all gone numb and fuzzy, like he had been stuffed with television static. He couldn't move.

"Good boy," Janice said, her tone making his skin crawl and quiver in the same breath. "Now, take your place."

His body moved on its own, though he strained every nerve to try to fight back. His movement was twitching and reluctant, but it was also inevitable, as Janice's spell drew him toward the vacant reagent space.

"Don't—do this," he said, his voice straining, but his own.

"Shhh." She traced the back of her hand on his cheek. "I won't kill you; it'd be such a waste. In fact, I'll tell you a secret."

She came close enough that he could sense the heat from Rayne's skin and smell her perfume. When she spoke, he felt her breath on his ear. "You remember that day, don't you? The sunlight—the piano? The kiss?" She watched his expression and smiled. "I thought so. That wasn't her. That was me."

Grimsby said nothing, though he felt like he had been dipped in wax and frozen solid.

"Haven't you ever wondered why you two never spoke about it again? Why it always seemed like a dream? Because to her, it was. But to me"—she drew back and met his eyes, and he couldn't help but stare into hers—"to me, it was real."

The numbness inflicted by her spell wasn't enough to suppress the wave of nausea that came over him. Was she telling him the truth? Why would she lie about that? Why would she tell him at all?

And why did it make him feel so disgusted?

If Janice noticed his broken levy of emotion, she showed none of her own save for a smile. "I'll be more to you than she ever could be." She chuckled and her hand found his throat and trailed down to his chest to linger for a moment. "I'll be your *everything*. When we've finished here, you and I can find somewhere private to discuss our future." She winked, and it drew a shiver from him. "I have big plans for us."

Grimsby was almost more sickened than afraid, but only almost. What she meant, he couldn't be certain. Whether she aimed to make him like the thralls outside, mindless and obedient, or her ambitions were something else, he couldn't let it distract him.

He needed to fight back, or at least to get away. He needed to find some way to stop this all from happening.

But he couldn't move. He felt like his body would stop breathing if she commanded it.

He was powerless.

Janice only smiled, as if watching all the desperate thoughts play over his face. She withdrew and stepped into the circle's center, shedding Rayne's shredded coat and casting it aside. She raised her arms, and Grimsby felt the electric power of the ley lines rise with her movement, like an orchestra matching a conductor. In the palm of her hand, he saw a small stone with a smooth hole worn through its center, though he couldn't see her palm on the other side.

"Wait!" he said, straining to speak, to keep his mind from collapsing in panic.

Janice sighed dramatically and glanced over to him expectantly.

"What will happen—to Rayne?"

"You might think me a monster, but I wish her no harm. I could destroy her utterly." Her voice was fiery, but she reined in her tone, and perhaps her temper. "Instead, I'll simply put her in the back seat of our little arrangement. Permanently. My own little Pandora's box, just like she was supposed to be the first time."

Grimsby wanted to say something, anything, but Janice turned away and returned to concentration. She raised the stone, and darkness began to well forth from the hole in its center like a black mist. The room immediately felt like it was full of invisible wire, wrapping around and binding every object, mummifying it to the smallest scale. Grimsby could scarcely draw breath, and before he managed to find his voice, the candlelight flickered and died, choked from life by the spreading shroud.

Though the gaseous cloud was dark, it didn't quench the light from the room altogether. Instead, it warped it. The shadowed room of old machinery began to fall away, melting to reveal twisted brick walls and archways of black marble. The machines were replaced by monstrous sculptures of wrought iron, frozen in distorted agony. For a moment, Grimsby didn't realize what was happening.

Then he looked up to see a round hole in the domed ceiling above, along with the familiar red sky and black sun of the Elsewhere.

Janice and her hagstone hadn't taken them to the Elsewhere.

They had brought the Elsewhere to the waking world.

Grimsby hadn't even known it was possible—or what it might mean if one of the Elsewhere's abominations found them, though Janice looked unconcerned. Her face, Rayne's face, was taut with concentration, her arms moving like she was weaving the air into a complex knot.

Finally, she lowered her hands, the stone smoldering and belching mist from her palm. She looked around, her eyes sparkling and oddly childlike.

"Beautiful," she said.

Grimsby knew he had to do something—say something—before Janice could finish her ritual. Yet he could do nothing. He had nothing, save for his voice.

No magic.

No weapon.

No hope.

Worst of all, there was some small but insistent part of his mind that kept uttering the same, horrid question.

Is this really so bad?

For how long had he felt his heart skip when he saw Rayne's face? For how long had his ears burned when he heard her name? For how long had he felt empty after every time they spoke, all hope deflated from him?

He hated the voice even as it said it, but still he wondered if perhaps Janice was offering him something he never thought he'd have: a chance with Rayne.

His stomach curled in on itself like a dying spider, even as he spoke. "Rayne, she—she never really cared for me, did she?" he asked quietly.

Janice stilled, almost as though she had been waiting for him to speak. She turned from the pocket chamber of Elsewhere she had conjured and offered him a sad, sympathetic smile. "Not in that way, darling. You're simply . . . not her type."

Grimsby nodded, though he found his head hanging in defeat by the end. Janice made a small, satisfied sound and waved her hand. He felt the numbness of her spell edge away, and he saw her approach in the corner of his eye.

"She doesn't see you like I do," Janice said, her hand softly gripping his left arm. "She doesn't know the man you could become—with my help."

Grimsby didn't know what to say. He suddenly felt so tired, so worn.

"You think you're weak. You think you're loathsome and wretched." Her fingers traced the scars on his arm. Where her fingertips trailed, they left a wake of dimly glowing flesh, like painless, hot iron beneath his skin. "You have no idea what you're capable of. I could show you . . . so much."

He wasn't sure what she meant, but he felt her drawing closer.

But he needed her closer still.

"You said—" He cleared his throat, turning to look her deep in Rayne's eyes. "You said that kiss, our kiss, it was you and not her?"

Janice nodded, her eyes pouring into his.

"Prove it," he whispered.

A soft smile curled her lips, and she drew close, until the skin of her cheek was nearly brushing his own. He smelled the scent of honey and cloves and felt his own lips part. She was mere atoms away, but she didn't make the final move, close the final gap.

She lingered, pressed against him, waiting. Whatever spell

held him transfixed wavered—just enough to allow the smallest movement.

He hadn't even realized what he was doing until his lips met hers.

Soft. Sweet.

And wrong.

He pulled back, pressing her away, and looked at the ground.

She took a seething breath. "Do you really want her back? Hardly even noticing you exist?" she asked, standing and taking a step away. "Do you really want things back to the way they were before? Meaningless and menial? If you do, then, by all means, fight back."

She opened her arms as if in an invitation to strike at her.

"It would do no good, of course. You're powerless. But even so, I'll take it as a sign you've no interest in what I can offer you."

Grimsby stared down at his shackles through his lone open eye. He couldn't bring himself to look up.

"But, if you're tired, tired of being ignored, tired of being weak, you can simply do nothing, and I'll show you a world you could never imagine." Her hand pressed a few fallen strands of hair from his face. "You'll never be powerless again. All you must do"—he felt her lean down to his ear and whisper—"is say nothing."

Grimsby said nothing.

He heard her lips slide over her teeth in a smile. "Clever boy."

She returned to the circle's center, and at her gesture, the chalk lines shone with sudden, fiery heat.

Shattered, broken, piece by piece,
Two of mind with one released,
Twist the master and the slave,
So of the two, might one be saved.

The fulgurite glowed to fluorescence before crumbling to ash that simmered in a low haze like smoke. The silver chains slithered along the floor to wrap around Rayne's forearms and neck. The hagstone bellowed forth more mist, and the chamber wavered before becoming solid once more. The ouroboros ring twitched and shivered before unwinding, the snake hissing before withering to nothing. The meteorite seemed to be chiseled away before his eyes, transforming from a formless rock to a figurine that resembled Rayne. Then this, too, crumbled away.

And finally, Janice took Grimsby's hand, withdrawing a blade and dragging it across his palm.

He felt cold, but no pain, and saw no blood. Instead, warm light leaked from the open gash like an eye of fire. He felt himself go numb once more, though this time it was from exhaustion, and fell to his knees.

Janice let him fall, somehow holding his stolen light in the palm of her hand.

Twist the master and the slave,
So of the two, might one be saved.

Janice looked triumphant, but a strange pallor began to show in her skin. She frowned in confusion and redoubled her concentration, arms tensing as she tried to control the magic like a motorcyclist whose handlebars were wavering.

"Something's wrong," she said, her own voice horrified. She looked over to him, eyes aflame. "What did you do?" she shrieked. "What did you do?!"

Grimsby only turned out his pockets, revealing them to be empty.

The nail was gone.

But no quip reached his lips. No triumph filled his shoulders.

"The only thing I could do," he whispered, not to Janice but to Rayne, who he hoped against hope could hear him. "I'm sorry."

Janice screamed as the light glared to brilliance. The chamber shook and groaned. Grimsby was forced to bury his head in his arms against the light and noise.

Then, like the skin of a drum tearing, the magic went hollow and silent.

FORTY-NINE

GRIMSBY FOUND HIMSELF LYING ON HIS SIDE, THE sound of thunder ringing in his ears.

The room was almost pitch-dark, save for a tithe of candles that had survived the ritual and remained lit. He winced as he sat up and found the gash in his palm seeping with blood. He pressed the wound against his stomach to staunch the bleeding, then the fog cleared enough from his head for him to remember.

He whipped around to see Rayne beside him—if it was Rayne at all.

He scrambled over to her and shook her with his cuffed hands. "Rayne? Rayne!" The words were more a silent prayer than anything else. "Please be Rayne."

Her eyes cracked open, and she groaned. "Grimsby?"

"Is—is it you?" he asked.

"What?" she demanded, struggling to sit up. "Is who me?"

There was no sinuous posturing, no seductive gaze. It wasn't Janice.

It was Rayne.

"Odd's Bodkin." He breathed out the relieved curse, his attempted hug becoming something closer to collapsing against her between his exhaustion and bound hands.

There was a quiet moment of awkwardness until he remembered himself and recoiled. "I—sorry. I didn't mean . . ."

There was a sound of fists beating against the sole door to the room, and a muffled shouting from what sounded like Mayflower.

Rayne waved Grimsby away. "It's fine, it's fine. Where—" She bolted up abruptly. "Where is Defaux?"

Then she paused, looking down to one hand, where an iron nail dangled from her finger as though it were magnetized.

"What is this?" she asked, trying to shake the nail away. "What the hell happened?"

Grimsby couldn't bring himself to look up at her. "Rayne, I— It was the only way."

"What are you talking about?"

"The ritual. She was going to bind your will to hers, permanently. But with the nail, it was inverted—but I think it's still permanent—"

He was interrupted as Rayne turned and her eyes looked over his shoulder and widened. "You! You bitch!" Her Impetus rose as she raised her hand, gesturing to a clustered pile of scrap metal beneath extinguished candles. "Sling!"

She flung her hand as though to direct the broken metal at whatever she saw, but there was only a loud boom as the nail made her spell backfire, seeming to detonate inside the pile and send bits of metal scattering.

She shook off her confusion, focusing only on glaring at an empty corner of the room.

"Rayne!" Grimsby said, struggling to his feet and trying to hold her back. "Rayne, stop! She's not there, she's not—"

She shoved him away, and he was too battered and worn

to resist. He fell, unable to catch himself with his hands still bound. The coarse floor ground dirt and dust into his wounded palm.

Rayne screamed and charged, her eyes furious. She dove at nothing and careened into the ground, scrambling in confusion.

"Rayne!" Grimsby called, climbing to his feet and gripping her arm with bloodied hands. "She's not there! She's just—"

She looked at him, her eyes wide and horrified. "Just what?"

"In your head," he said, his voice cracking.

"No. No, no, no, no," Rayne repeated, her voice more strained and frantic with each utterance. She shrieked and shoved him away, sending him back to the floor, and stalked toward the twisted piles of abandoned machinery. "Get out here, bitch!"

Grimsby tried to get to his feet, but before he could, there was a roar of gunfire, and the metal door flew open.

Mayflower ran to his side, gun ready. "Where is she?" he demanded. "Where is Janice?"

Grimsby looked from him to Rayne and back again, not knowing what to say.

There was more noise from the platform beyond the door, the sound of approaching shouting and boots. The Department had finally arrived.

Rayne screamed again, flinging her hand and shouting, "*Sling!*" at a corner of the room. Another detonation.

Another empty corner.

Grimsby struggled up and limped over to her. "Rayne. Rayne. Calm down, everything's fine." He tried to be soothing, but he felt like he did little more than smear his own blood on her arm.

She tore her gaze from the corner and looked back to him, her eyes wide and hurt.

"What did you do to me?"

He opened his mouth, but no words came out.

Suddenly, the room flooded with Agents and Auditors, and he

felt himself being pulled away. Even as he watched, he saw someone putting cuffs around Rayne's wrists.

Then she was dragged from his sight.

He felt his own voice rise in protest, but before he could try to follow Rayne, Mayflower's rough hand gripped his arm and held him fast.

"She'll be fine," he said, his tone hushed and placating. "You saved her."

Grimsby struggled for a moment, then shuddered. His legs might have given way altogether if not for Mayflower's hold on his arm.

"I didn't save her," he said, his voice cracking. "I damned her."

Mayflower said nothing for a long moment before he finally asked, "What happened?"

Grimsby tried his best to recount the ritual, and Janice. He kept his voice low, not only because he was tired, or because of the Department personnel that milled about, cordoning off the area, but because he was afraid that if he spoke too loudly his shaking voice might break altogether. More than once, an Agent approached him, either to question or even to arrest him, and each time a single glare from Mayflower warded them off.

When Grimsby finished, he felt like collapsing to the floor. Instead, Mayflower led him to a relatively flat section of old machinery and sat him down. He withdrew the lockpicks from his pocket and began to fiddle with the cuffs around Grimsby's wrists.

"So you think she's stuck with Janice now?" Mayflower asked.

Grimsby nodded. "It was the only thing I could think to do. I couldn't stop the ritual, and I couldn't let her just—" He trailed off, not knowing what else to say.

"So the ritual meant to trap Rayne instead trapped Janice?" Mayflower said, twisting a pick to unlatch the cuffs. "How's that different from what was happening before?"

Grimsby rubbed circulation back into his wrists, wincing at the cut on his palm. "Before, I think Rayne was in the driver's seat, and Janice was sort of in the passenger seat. She must have been able to take the wheel when Rayne's control was weak. But now—now I think Janice is in the back seat, but Rayne knows she's there." He shook his head. Even with the cuffs off, he still felt powerless.

"So why don't we just pull Janice out of the car?"

"Maybe we could have before the ritual—now, I don't know. If this was as permanent as Janice suggested, I don't think there's any way to get her out without hurting or killing Rayne." He felt like his chest was collapsing in on itself.

"So the only thing keeping Janice from totally taking control is that nail?"

Grimsby nodded, his tone growing flat as he focused on working over the theory in his head. It was better than thinking about anything else at the moment. "I think so. The nail messed with all my magic—even the enchantments and stuff I had at home that I cast before I was cursed. It actively inverts the magic of whoever's cursed—and a ritual is just magic with extra steps. Without that nail . . ." He trailed off, feeling like his stomach was a lake of molten salt.

"Janice is back in the driver's seat."

Grimsby leaned forward, holding his head in his hands. "Maybe if I had been able to stop her—"

"You did all you could," Mayflower said, cutting him off. "And it was a damn sight more than anyone else did. Nobody can ask for more."

Grimsby felt a bitter taste on his tongue. "Then let me ask," he said quietly, "did you ever fail, even after doing your best?"

For a moment, he thought Mayflower wouldn't reply, then he finally said, "Yes."

"And did knowing you did all you could have done—knowing

you hadn't been powerful enough, did that ever help you forgive yourself?"

This time, the Huntsman truly did say nothing.

It wasn't long until they were ushered away from the scene, and after some laconic arguing, Mayflower convinced the chief Agent to let him and Grimsby return to the Department in the old jeep.

FIFTY ✴

MAYFLOWER WATCHED AS GRIMSBY STOOD AT THE pane of plexiglass that looked into the white cell. Gaining access to the more secure levels of the Asylum hadn't been easy, but he had made it happen for the kid's sake. Inside the cell, Bathory was seated on her pallet bed, arms around her knees, leaning against the wall and staring into the corner. She'd been dressed in a bright orange jumpsuit and shackled with magic-suppressing manacles. In her clenched hands she held the nail Grimsby had managed to plant on her, the sharpened end of which had been secured with a white rubber guard by the Asylum's staff.

"Please say something," Grimsby said, his voice almost too far for Mayflower to hear.

There was no reply.

Mayflower felt like shrapnel was twisting in his guts as he turned away. It had been two days since the ritual, and Grimsby had spent hardly a few hours of it anywhere else besides outside Bathory's cell.

He caught sight of Grieves approaching, his suit perfectly pressed, his cheeks clean-shaven. Mayflower clenched his jaw, making his three-day growth of beard grate on his cheeks. He stalked toward the director, hands clenched at his sides.

"Where the hell have you been?" he demanded, keeping his voice low so as not to disturb Grimsby, but his tone was still sharp.

Grieves raised a brow at him. "Directing," he said. "You think this ordeal ends with the culprit apprehended? There's a mile of red tape you ignored and ordinances you broke, and I've only barely managed to keep you and Grimsby from being suspended."

"Suspended?" he growled. "You think I give a damn about that?"

"You might not, but I think someone else would." He cast a glance to Grimsby in the observation room.

Mayflower felt some of his anger wither. "Fine, fine. Shuffle your damn papers."

They stood in silence for a time before Grieves asked, "Has she said anything?"

"I think you know she hasn't."

He nodded. "I'd just hoped my reports were misinformed. She's a good Auditor. She's . . ." He paused as though trying to translate into a language he wasn't fluent in. "She's a good kid."

Mayflower raised a brow at Grieves, though the director's face didn't shift. "I know what you mean. You think Grimsby's right? Think she's stuck with her dark passenger?"

Grieves shook his head. "Short answer is we don't know. Stryggas aren't common, and her case is unprecedented. But, if I had to guess . . ." He trailed off.

"Looks grim, then."

"It usually does. I wish we had a solution, but until we do, she's stuck in here."

Mayflower eyed the long hall of other cells and adjacent observation rooms. "Do I even want to know what else you have in this place?"

"If you did, I'd have to kill you," Grieves said, and the slightest grin marred his placid features.

"You're a real son of a bitch, Grieves."

"So you keep reminding me."

"What about the others you arrested? The troll and the lamia? Hives?"

"As far as the Unorthodox, after discovering they were enthralled, we could hardly press charges, and certainly can't go public. They were returned to Underton this morning, and amends made with Mother Frost."

Mayflower grunted.

"As for Hives . . ." Grieves gestured to a different cell. "He hasn't regained consciousness yet, but we're all quite keen to know how he went from Peters's possession to Miss Defaux's."

"I am, too," Mayflower said. "There's something else going on."

"Always is," he said quietly. Then, after a moment: "Are you still considering making this your last run? This case seems finally finished."

Mayflower bit his lip a moment, then shook his head, his eyes never leaving Grimsby, who still stared through the glass. "No. I don't think I'm done quite yet."

Grieves followed his gaze and nodded. "I figured as much. There's still a lot to teach him."

"Not as much as I'd like," the Huntsman said. "The kid already knows how to make the hard choices. I didn't have to teach him that."

"So what's left?"

"Figuring out how to live with yourself afterward."

Grieves scoffed, but it was more sympathy than dismissal. "You really think you're the best one to teach him that little trick?"

"No," Mayflower said, turning away and shouldering past Grieves, "but I'm the only one here."

And I'm not going anywhere.

FIFTY-ONE

GRIMSBY SAT ON THE COUCH, SLUMPED SO LOW THAT his spine might have sunk into the cushions if they weren't worn to thin, comfortless pads. He stared at the television, which displayed a grainy black-and-white Western, though he might as well have been staring through it to the wall behind for all the attention he was paying to the picture. The sun shone through the threadbare curtains, and the room was warm, but he pulled his tattered bathrobe tighter around him all the same.

His apartment was quiet.

When he had told Wudge about the nail, and that he wouldn't be getting it anytime soon, his friend had vanished without a word. Grimsby wasn't sure whether or not he would come back.

He wouldn't blame him if he didn't. He and Wudge had worked hard to get that nail, and though he'd managed to somewhat save Rayne with it, that wouldn't help Wudge in his quest to find his precious door.

He could only hope Wudge would forgive him.

Though Rayne certainly hadn't.

It had been days since he had last visited her, but she hadn't spoken to him since her incarceration, and his access to the Asylum was limited. No one would tell him how long she would have to remain, but their tone told him it would be indefinite. Even with Janice's consciousness imprisoned rather than in control, Rayne was still a liability at best, and a time bomb at worst.

And it was his fault.

Had he been smarter, or more powerful, maybe he would have found some way to stop Janice's ritual altogether, not just turn it into a lesser evil. Maybe Rayne would be free right now.

But he wasn't.

And she wasn't.

And there was nothing he could do to fix it.

A knock sounded at the door. From its tactical rapping, he knew who it was.

"It's unlocked," he called, not bothering to sit up from his slump.

The door rattled open, and Mayflower stepped inside, dressed in his dated suit. It was still a bit singed from the warehouse explosion days before, though it had cleaned up better than Grimsby's own, which had been shredded to tatters, good for nothing other than to be thrown away.

The Huntsman approached, and Grimsby prepared for scornful words. After all, he had taken an unannounced vacation from his responsibilities at the Department, and Grimsby had chewed out Mayflower for doing the same.

Instead, Mayflower only stood beside the couch and studied the television.

"When was the last time you showered?" he finally asked.

Grimsby frowned, then sniffed the collar of his robe. "Dunno."

"That's probably a good sign that it's overdue."

"Probably," he said, though he did not move.

The Huntsman scoffed, then stepped around the couch and sat on the opposite side.

"You get your new suit yet?" Mayflower asked, his eyes on the television.

Grimsby grunted an affirmative, then tilted his head toward a box in the doorless closet. He had put it below the shelf that held that strange teapot and the box he'd taken from the Lounge months ago. Both were things he didn't want to think about, and the suit seemed right at home among them.

"So, you ready to come back to work?"

This time, his grunt was much less certain.

The Huntsman took a breath. "You know, kid, you can't just quit when you take a hit."

Grimsby felt heat curl up along his neck. "I'm not quitting because I got hit. I can *take* hits."

Mayflower snorted. "I know you can. But that's not what I meant. You did what you could. It wasn't enough. That hurts. Hurts more than getting punched in the gut or having your chest clawed up. It hurts deep."

"Hurts?" He choked down a bitter sound. "I ruined Rayne's life. I may as well have killed her."

"Is she dead?" Mayflower asked.

"What?"

"Is she dead?" he repeated.

"Well, no. But—"

"If she's not dead, then there's still a chance. There's still hope. You didn't take that from her, boy. You gave it to her. And maybe you wanted to give her more and couldn't, but something is a helluva lot more than nothing."

"Doesn't feel that way."

"Trust me," he said, his voice growing distant, "it's much more than nothing."

"That's a cold comfort."

"It's a cold world," Mayflower said. "Why do you think we wear the jacket?"

"So I'm supposed to what? Be happy that I failed?"

"Of course not. You're supposed to do better. And you will. But only if you get up off your ass."

Grimsby said nothing. He knew the old Huntsman was likely all too familiar with what he was feeling, but even so, the demand seemed like an insurmountable task.

"It was my first real case," he said quietly, "and I didn't just fail. I hurt someone I cared about. How am I supposed to just . . . try again? Take another swing, just like that? What if I fail again? What if I actually get somebody killed this time, instead of just getting them imprisoned for life?"

"Look, kid," the Huntsman said, "it's not like the people who need your help won't need it if you quit the job. They'll need someone all the same. The only difference is that if you don't put yourself out there, then maybe nobody helps them at all. You want to help people, don't you?"

He didn't trust himself to speak, so he only nodded.

"Then get up off this damn couch and get dressed. We have work to do."

"I don't think I can. I can't mess up again."

Mayflower laughed. It was short, and a little bitter, but it was a laugh all the same. "Yes, you can."

"Get up, or mess up?"

"Both. But whatever you screw up, you'll figure out some way to fix it."

"How? How can I possibly fix this?"

"I don't know. But I'll be damned if you don't find ways to fix broken things." He actually managed a small smile, though Grimsby couldn't fathom why. "I was wrong about you, you know."

"What? Wrong about me how?"

"You're not going to end up like me. I don't think there's a damned thing God or anyone else could throw at you to make you screw up that bad."

"I'm not sure I get what you mean."

"I mean, at the end of the day, you're a good man, Grimsby. The only way you're going to do something truly wrong is to stop being yourself. But as long as you're doing what you think is right, you'll be fine."

"How can you be so sure?"

The Huntsman donned a genuine smile. "I'm sure. Goode is alive because of you. Rayne is alive because of you. I'm . . ." He trailed off, staring through the television. "I'm sure you've got a lot more good you can do, but you can't do it in your pajamas."

"Evening robe," Grimsby corrected, feeling a small grin on his lips.

"Don't start," Mayflower growled. "Now, take a shower and get dressed. Grieves is assigning cases today."

"Be faster if I just get dressed."

"You're not riding in my jeep smelling like that."

"What, you afraid I'll rub out the smell of cigarettes and old leather?"

"Yep. I'll be outside." He stood, paused for a brief moment as though he might say something else, then shook the thought away and departed.

Grimsby took a breath.

"Try again," he muttered. He shook his head and peeled himself off the couch, feeling his muscles groan in a mixture of annoyance for having moved and discontent for their recent mistreatment.

He showered, making it fast as the tub still lacked a drain thanks to Wudge's last prank.

He went to the cardboard box that contained his new suit. Despite his requests otherwise, it was the same size as his previous—too large. He shook his head. "Guess I'm not doing anything else anyway."

He began to get dressed, and with each innocuous piece of cloth, he felt like something real again.

He almost felt like an Auditor.

Almost.

Fifteen minutes later, he was dressed and climbing into the old jeep's passenger seat. Mayflower was studying the graffitied walls from behind the wheel.

"You good?" he asked as Grimsby settled in.

"Not yet."

Mayflower arched a brow.

"There's something I need to make sure of first."

The Huntsman nodded. "Where to?"

FIFTY-TWO

I DO NOT BELIEVE THIS IS NECESSARY, AUDITOR GRIMSBY," Mrs. Ox said, glancing over at the bark-stripped trunk of the pine tree. "You already passed your second assessment."

Grimsby shook his head and stretched his fingers, the joints of his scarred hand popping. "It's necessary."

She looked over at Mayflower, who leaned against an intact tree a few feet away.

The Huntsman only shrugged.

"Very well," she said, readying her clipboard. She held a hand up to the raven familiar on her shoulder, which produced a pencil from its hollow torso and passed it to her. "Begin."

Grimsby walked forward and stood before the pine. The ground around him was still littered with broken branches and scattered needles from his failed attempts during his first assessment. He took a deep breath and placed his palm on the sun-warmed wood, feeling the weeping sap and rough grain under his palm.

"Sorry, buddy," he said quietly.

He began his work slowly, calmly. Placing a single rune on the tree's trunk and matching it with another on the hard stone at the bottom of the crater he'd made of Rayne's stump. He let the magic come naturally, and his mind wandered as his Impetus waned.

He had failed his friends—he had fallen short.

But he would make things right.

He poured more of his Impetus into the spell, feeling his skin grow cold.

There was so much to do, and he didn't know where to start.

But he knew how it would end.

He would find a way to help Rayne.

He would find a way to help Wudge.

He'd make things right.

His breath fogged on his lips, and yet he felt new heat within him, burning not from his core, his Impetus, but from his scars. This time, the marred flesh didn't drain away his Impetus into useless sparks and fire. Instead, it became a source of warmth—something like Impetus yet not quite the same. Something fragile and dangerous. It wasn't much—it was hardly anything.

But it was enough.

It burned in him despite his breath misting in the spring air, but even as it faded with his *Binds*, he knew his spell would hold.

After all, he was stubborn.

He was an Auditor.

But that wasn't why he would do it. That wasn't what mattered. It never had been.

What mattered was that people needed him.

He stepped away from the tree, walking away from the glowing strand of his waiting spell.

Mrs. Ox tapped her pencil expectantly. Mayflower only nodded to him.

Grimsby didn't look back to the tree. There was no need. He knew what would happen.

"*Bind*."

The strand of light flashed, a glowing cobalt cord. Wood cracked, and the grove shrieked to life as birds and squirrels fled.

The tree crashed to the ground, sending splintered limbs and needles flying. The light of his *Bind* faded.

The grove settled to quiet a few moments later. Mrs. Ox made a sharp note on her clipboard. "Satisfactory, Auditor," she said, offering him a knowing smile.

Grimsby looked back at the fallen pine, feeling a small note of sadness, but felling it had been necessary. Then he caught sight of a nest among the broken branches. Its contents were four small eggs with shells of speckled white and brown.

They were all shattered.

Grimsby's stomach turned, and he looked away to see Mayflower standing beside him.

"You ready?" the Huntsman asked.

"No," Grimsby said, stowing his guilt and managing a smile, "but when has that ever mattered before?"

"Damn straight," Mayflower replied.

They nodded farewell to Mrs. Ox and left for the old jeep. They climbed in, Mayflower coaxed it to life, and they rolled off the dirt path and hit pavement, heading toward the Department of Unorthodox Affairs.

They had work to do.

EPILOGUE

RAYNE GLANCED OVER HER SHOULDER TO THE GLASS wall of her cell.

Grimsby hadn't come today.

Good.

She needed to distance herself from him. Part of her told her it was because she would only jeopardize his career. Another part told her it was because he had betrayed her—ruined her life.

The trouble was, she wasn't sure what parts of her were even her anymore.

She was a strygga. An abomination. Her Impetus was tainted, fused with another's.

Was this why she had always outperformed her peers? Her magic had always been formidable, a trait she assumed was due to her diligent practice and studies.

Was that all a lie?

Was *she* a lie?

If so, then who was she?

She felt her breath catch in her chest, and slowly she felt like hooks were filling her lungs, forcing even her most disciplined breath to become a sob.

She stared at the nail in her hands and the plastic band around her wrist, just above the chainless iron shackles that suppressed her magic. The band read simply: 0528. Not her name, not her position. Not even her age.

Just a number.

She had lost everything.

Her knuckles whitened as her body tensed, anger boiling inside her. She wanted to remain still, to remain controlled, but she couldn't. She knew it was what they expected, the people who were surely watching, but she didn't care. If she didn't do *something*, she'd suffocate in her own skin.

Her room was little more than stainless steel, plastic, and industrial carpet. There were only three objects of note: her bed, a white plastic table, and a matching chair.

She stood and seized the chair, shrieking as she slammed it into the wall. The exertion felt good. The heat felt good. Even the anger felt good.

She picked it up and struck again, this time cracking it down on the table, then again on the wall. Finally, she battered it against the glass until the plastic splintered to broken nothingness, leaving her damp and panting, staring at her own reflection.

"Now, now, that's no way for a lady to act, is it?" *she* said.

Rayne turned to see Defaux—Janice—seated on her bed. She looked as she had when she'd first appeared to her: beautiful, dark haired, with eyes too wide around the irises. Except now her stark suit had been exchanged for a set of simple, thin pants and shirt identical to Rayne's own, except in a shade of venom green.

Rayne didn't reply; she only turned away, pressing her arms and head against the wall. "She's not real, she's not real," she muttered to herself again and again.

Though by now, she knew otherwise. She still held some thin measure of hope that perhaps she could make it be true if she repeated it enough.

"Oh, let's not put on tinfoil hats, shall we? Speak to me! We used to have such lovely talks, Rayne. And it's not as though there's much else to do in here."

Rayne shook her head involuntarily. She hated feeling so out of control, so untempered, but something had changed. Her cage of discipline had been battered, and now it was bent and open.

Janice was free.

And she wasn't going anywhere.

Janice raised a brow, as though Rayne had spoken the thought aloud.

"Dear girl, I wasn't *in* that little cage of yours." Her wide eyes focused on Rayne intensely. "I helped you build it."

"Liar!" Rayne said, the word like a reflex to Janice's voice.

Janice smiled, though the expression lacked its usual predatory note. Instead, it was almost nervous. "I could have become a strygga using any witch. There were a dozen who would have given themselves willingly to me. Yet I chose you." Her eyes seemed to flash. "You don't think it was for no reason, do you?"

Rayne began to speak, but her words were smothered by a sudden pressure inside her, like something trying to escape her chest. She felt that same lightless fire from when she'd first unleashed her trapped power.

It wasn't Impetus—it was something else.

Something sickening.

And far more powerful.

The iron shackles around her wrists grew painfully hot; the runes carved into them began to tremble and glow.

Janice sat forward, wrapping her hands around her knees, her eyes staring straight through Rayne to whatever else was within. "But without that cage—I don't know if either of us can control it."

Rayne winced, pressing the hot shackles into her stomach in

a vain effort to dissipate the growing heat. "W-what is it?" she asked, voice pained and forced through gritted teeth.

"It's your birthright," Janice said, her eyes still focused, seeing something Rayne couldn't.

Rayne saw clearly in the woman's face:

Janice was afraid.

And so, too, was she.

Breakthrough: Women into Management

1

The Reasons

Gray Flannel Pantsuits

Big Companies Battle To Recruit Women For Executive Posts

High Salaries, Child-Care Offered; 'Showcase' Jobs Are Shunned by Prospects Rejecting an Offer a Week

—— By Jennifer McGregor
Staff Reporter of
The Wall Street Journal

CLEVELAND The president of a heavy-equipment manufacturing firm here summoned an aide to his office early this year and instructed him to "do whatever is necessary" to add three women executives to the company's marketing staff.

Three months later, the crestfallen aide returned to report total failure. "If you really want to hire women, we'll have to steal them," he said. "What's more, you'll have to pay them more than you're paying me."

The president's response: "Do it."

A week later, a $22,000-a-year offer (amounting to a $3,500 raise) lured a 39-year-old woman marketing expert away from one of the company's largest competitors. The company expresses no particular pride in the coup, since such piracy of personnel is generally frowned upon. But a company official contends that "pirating is the only way you can hire a woman executive these days.". . .

1

. . . So might lead off an article on the front page of the August 26, 1975 issue of *The Wall Street Journal,* marking the progress women have made since they first got the vote 55 years ago.

In late 1971 and in 1972 growing pressures began to open to women long-locked doors to management positions and to necessary graduate school training. What began to happen to racial and ethnic groups a few years earlier is now happening to women.

We opened this chapter with a rewrite of a lead article in *The Wall Street Journal* of July 23, 1969 which originally referred to male Negro executives. Blacks interviewed felt "fear on the part of corporate leaders that the nation faces a social upheaval unless full racial integration is achieved at all levels of employment." Many personnel men argued that "there's a considerable element of goodwill and social conscience in their effort to hire blacks." The power of government agencies to bring charges or withdraw federal contracts was also seen as "a highly pragmatic and immediate source of pressure."[1]

Attitudes are changing about women on the way up

What was happening to black men is *now* happening to women, both black and white. The idea of women participating in all levels of decision-making is new. Women, who have always been the support staff are now, for the first time in history, working together to make it possible for more women to get into positions of influence and power. We are also experiencing dramatic changes in the attitudes of many men. For example, in February 1970 avant-garde management thinker Warren Bennis acknowledged his reluctance to see women develop their potential, saying, "I have to admit that I'm ambivalent about women's loss of the slave mentality. I've got two of the best secretaries in the world, and, God, I would hate to see them leave me to become administrators on their own."[2]

After nine months' gestation, however, Bennis had come to this recognition: "Few businessmen pay women equally, respect their judgments, and promote them equally with men. Very few institutions have done anything at all about setting up day-care centers, so that women can really pursue their careers; yet this will be one of the biggest issues of the next few years. For my own part, I welcome it (women's rights)—though nervously, of course. I think women will make excellent managers."[3]

From another direction, pediatrician Benjamin Spock, after decades of telling parents that they must raise boys and girls differently so that they can learn their "proper roles," apologized for his past prejudice against women. He told women at the 1971 organizational meeting of the National Women's Political Caucus that he had made pre-publication revisions in his latest book, *Decent and Indecent*, to correct his stereotyped attitudes about females.[4]

For such men as Bennis and Spock to readjust their thinking still is rare. Change of attitudes in the marketplace may take even longer. For the conflict is in the marketplace. Well-educated, capable women are seeking to be in the mainline action but similarly qualified men want to see them remain as full-time housewives and consumers. There have been distinct comforts in the easy superiority which has been accorded to management men. The manager who has been so conditioned will not give up these comforts easily.

Many women have difficulty coping with the effects of stereotypes in their lives. Some women like the status and role of the protected, "little woman." For many others who have developed their capabilities in our affluent society it is not a role that fits comfortably. Most women now recognize that their past history does not read favorably for them today. And many are doing something about it.

Pressures for change are everywhere

It is becoming obvious that there is a vast, easily observable difference between what some managers and social

leaders are saying about equal opportunity for women and what is actually happening. It's a phase of future shock. Not only is overall change taking place at an ever-increasing rate but, at differing rates within different segments of our lives.

Changes at universities are erratic. The University of Michigan, after much resistance, has now developed "a milestone in university affirmative action."[5] Salary equity in academic and non-academic positions, for example, has been adjusted for 100 women employees to the tune of $94,295.

The Berkeley campus of the University of California has had a suit filed that charges discrimination which "parallels that of Mississippi against blacks."[6] A thirty year timetable is sought to reach a goal of the same percentage of faculty women and managerial non-academic positions as are in the qualified work force.

Columbia University is under a heavy barrage of complaints, suits and protests, while President McGill resists considering race and sex as criteria in faculty hiring. He contends that faculty dissent could "blow this university wide open."[7] At the same time, Ruth B. Ginsberg, was recently appointed at Columbia Law School—their first female full professor.[8]

Government money sources are being challenged. One of the largest, the National Institutes of Health, is charged with funding unethical psychosurgical research that is directed against women on whom lobotomies are performed. Successful treatment is frequently assessed on "the ability (of women) to return to household duties."[9] "Women are virtually excluded from advisory and decision making roles" in both intra and extramural NIH funded programs,[10] according to Dr. Julie T. Apter, professor of surgery at Chicago's Rush Medical College. Several women's groups are filing a joint class action suit against NIH to correct this imbalance.

In the last six months of 1971, nearly one-fourth of all appointments to HEW advisory boards and committees were women, according to HEW Secretary Elliott L. Richardson.

There were 207 women appointed out of a total of 880, resulting in an overall increase of 4 percent during that time. In the next six months, Secretary Richardson expected one-third of the anticipated vacancies to be filled with women.[11]

The Department of Defense has selected its first woman, Angeliki Cutchis for the next class at the National War College. She is Chief, Combat Systems Division, Office of the Scientific Advisor to the Assistant Chief of Staff for Force Development of the Army. Upon completion of the 10 month course, she will be prepared for some of the highest, most responsible assignments in the nation. Only four women have preceded her, three from the State Department and one from the Arms Control and Disarmament Agency.[12]

Suits are being filed against corporations to force them to make pay adjustments for the past discrimination and undertake affirmative action programs to employ women at higher levels of management, while the executives of those same companies are being publicly lauded as businessmen of great vision where the employment of women is concerned.

American Telephone and Telegraph Vice-President Walter Straley said with great optimism in 1968, "We think our experience as an employer, hiring some 200,000 persons each year, provides us with a unique competence to play a leading role in the improvement of employment opportunity."[13] He may be less confident now, having been involved in a show-cause suit. He shares the problem with most business, government and university leaders who together face major change from traditional discriminatory practices.

Other major corporations who have already met with back pay decisions include Wheaton Glass Co., for $901,062; Midwest Manufacturing Co. for $240,000; American Can Co. for almost $150,000; and RCA for $125,000.[14]

Corporations will soon be joined by unions, as women members are preparing themselves for more active involvement against discrimination in their own unions. The University of Wisconsin Extension in Milwaukee, for example,

has a course in which union women are learning how to speak out, dig out information, how to argue and, where necessary, how to fight for corrective action.[15]

Using an entirely different approach, office workers in New York City worked through District 65 of the National Council of Distributive Workers to gain an excellent fringe benefit package. They have written up their experience and are making it available for other women interested in unionizing women.[16]

Even men are filing suits for equal treatment. Actions have challenged such issues as a profit sharing plan that allegedly illegally favored women; differential retirement ages; denial of a secretarial job on the basis of sex; dress and hair codes; jury duty requirements; paternity leave.[17] A male nurse recently filed a suit to stop hospitals and nursing registries from making nursing assignments on the basis of sex for men, when they do not for women. He won.[18]

The problem is a pattern of women in lesser positions

Examples of the problem are on display everywhere. Women are employed as nurses instead of doctors, clerks instead of supervisors, teaching assistants instead of professors, assembly workers instead of foremen, dental hygienists instead of dentists, salesgirls instead of retail department heads, legal secretaries instead of lawyers, tellers instead of bank officers. As a result, after several years of low-level enforcement of laws and Executive Orders passed in the mid-sixties, many suits have been filed in the early '70's which challenge long-standing practices which discriminate against employed women.

In all the confusion it is sometimes the companies receiving adverse publicity that are among the first to make energetic efforts to change their practices. They have become visible. But how does a large utility, bank, business machine manufacturer, government agency, state university or health

facility turn around entrenched personnel patterns? How and at what speed?

Some organizations are going into action; others haven't begun

Any program to advance women into decision-making levels will have its frustrations for those involved. Small deliberate steps may seem risky, though necessary, to male managers but glacially slow to women who aspire to the ranks of decision makers. These conflicts of viewpoint and interpretation contribute strongly to the many mixed messages now being heard.

Some companies have accepted fully the idea of women in management roles and have made a committed effort to bring them into new positions as rapidly and painlessly as possible. One firm, a traditionally all-male division of a manufacturer producing special order heavy machinery, brought four women into management at one time. Considerable preparation, both in structured training sessions and in informal discussion, was done before the women started to work in their new positions. Most important was the careful consideration in changing the all-male social climate as the men were informally prepared to work with women for the first time in their experience. The women themselves received training designed to help them cope with potential problems of being "firsts." When the women were finally placed in their new positions, transition was relatively smooth, dislocations minor, and problems of tokenism avoided.

On the other hand, the average organization has taken no action of any kind, least of all, a systematic program to bring women into management. Witness the scramble now on the part of organizations large and small to design affirmative action programs for women. In a 1970 study of 150 companies by the American Society for Personnel Administration and the Bureau of National Affairs (BNA), ᵣesults

showed how sharply employment categories are defined by sex. Of the companies surveyed, 39 percent had no women managers at all; 88 percent had less than five percent of its managers as women; 93 percent had less than ten percent.[19] The sheer drama of the man/woman ratios in management and other job levels is shown in the Chart I constructed from their data. Note the large percentage of women relegated to the traditional low-level clerical and production worker categories.

Twenty-one months later in a new survey of 161 companies, BNA reported a small increase in the percentage of companies whose workforce consists of 10 percent women or more. Table I shows overall changes in the percentage of women in higher levels in such companies.

TABLE I   **Percent of Companies With Over 10% Women at Various Job Levels**[20]

Category	March 1970	December 1971	% Change
Total work force	81	82	1%
First level supervision	17	25	6%
Professional and technical	20	23	3%
Management	7	10	3%

The 6 percent increase of women into first-level supervision is most notable, although the rates for higher positions are only half as great. It appears that significant changes are beginning.

Further, the BNA study revealed new information about the highest jobs held by women in these same companies, reported for both small and large size firms. Large companies reportedly have a substantially more favorable climate in which women can advance, as shown in Chart II.

However, when these data are contrasted with the highest level job held by men, the picture is starkly different. In all of the companies, the highest level for men is in top management. Chart III provides the graphic comparison.

The exclusion of women from management is general and

CHART I   Sex-Typing of Job-Levels for Women: Few Women are in Management

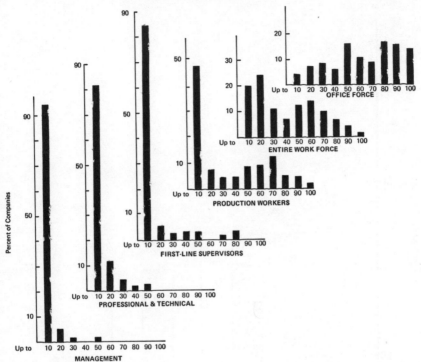

Percent of Companies

PERCENT OF WOMEN AT
VARIOUS JOB-LEVELS

Data Source: Bureau of National Affairs, Inc. (1970)
Copyright © 1970 by Theodora Wells and Lee Christie

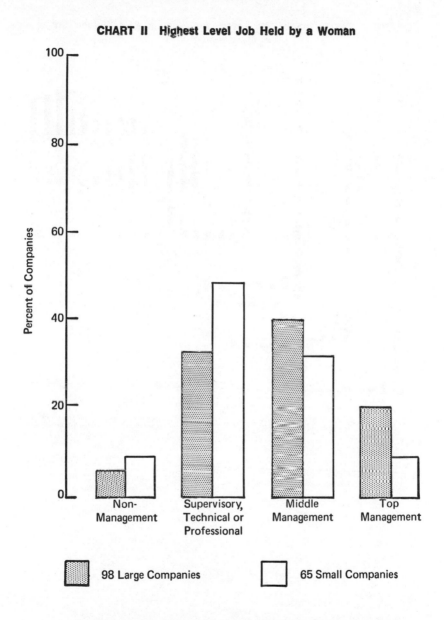

CHART II   Highest Level Job Held by a Woman

Data Source: Bureau of National Affairs, Inc. (1970, 1971)
Copyright © 1971 by Lee Christie

CHART III   Highest Level Job Held by a Man

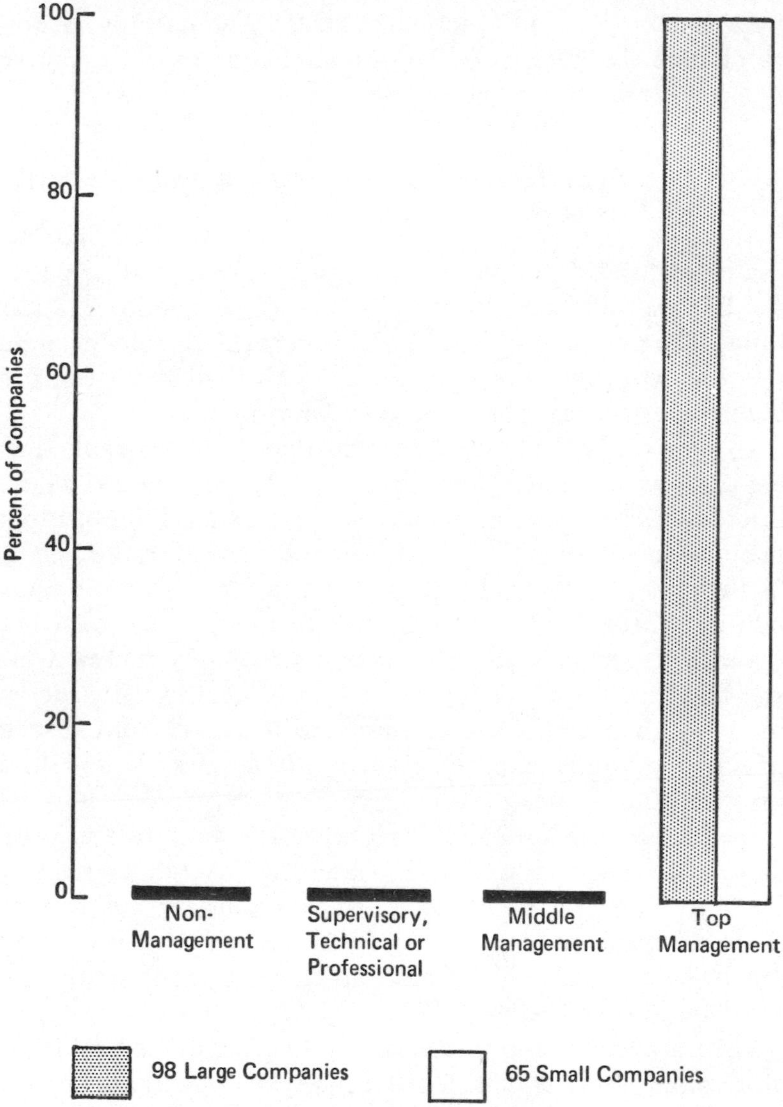

Percent of Companies

100 —
80 —
60 —
40 —
20 —
0 —

Non-Management   Supervisory, Technical or Professional   Middle Management   Top Management

98 Large Companies   65 Small Companies

Data Source: Bureau of National Affairs, Inc. (1971)
Copyright © 1971 by Lee Christie

extreme; it is part of an ancient pattern that few if any organizations have escaped. Therefore, no company need feel its story is a private skeleton. Only if nothing is done to change the pattern will the data haunt those executives responsible for its perpetuation.

Organizations and products are sex-typed, setting up sex-expectations

Organizations and products have sex labels just as people do. For example, construction is masculine, retailing is feminine. The prevalence of women, or general agreement about the opportunities for women, in each industry seems to determine the sex-label of the organization.

In one survey, men and women managers sex-ranked organizations from feminine to masculine as follows: education; retailing; media; government; financial institutions, manufacturing of consumer goods and service trades; manufacturing of industrial goods, defense, transportation and public utilities; and construction.[21] In this occupational line-up they expected a woman to be more likely to fail when she tries to move into higher positions in the construction industry than when she attempts to advance from teacher to school administrator. One's virtually impossible, the other just difficult.

One woman, a top-notch executive assistant to the president of a machine tool firm, had gone as far as possible for a woman in that industry. Upon tendering her resignation, she was given an unprecedented chance to prove herself in outside sales, the traditional avenue for line advancement in that company.

With a masculine product-line, the company had a history of men only in outside sales. Because she knew the company, the territory and was in the continuing product education program required for salesmen, she was given the chance. Two sales*men* were hired at the same time in full expectation that she would fail. Within six months both men were gone.

At this writing, she is still there, earning higher total commissions than any other salesman in the field.

Her record created some new results, but not those anticipated. For example, one unexpected gain was the overwhelming acceptance by customers. The company's market consisted of machine shops with most customer contacts being men. The initial shock of an attractive woman who could talk metallurgy and who didn't mind getting her hands in the grease continues to reverberate in her favor.

Expectations can predict results

It does not always work out so well when a woman is given a chance with an expectation of failure. This can become a self-fulfilling prophecy, depending upon the woman's level of self-confidence. A person who backs a woman but expects her to fail is part of her failure. Just as Jackie Robinson's breakthrough in baseball took team effort, everyone in the organization from president on down must work together in expecting success from its new management women. A supportive climate is especially important since the experience of most women has been the opposite. Both men and women perform better when they feel their bosses and colleagues are behind them.

There are some early indications of companies expecting more from women. For example, in his 25th annual survey of employment trends, Frank S. Endicott, of Northwestern University found that the 191 responding companies expected to hire fewer male graduates in 1971 than they did in 1970. And they expected to hire 11 percent more women graduates and at higher salaries.[22]

Women are making changes happen in court, in government regulations, on the job

Women are expecting more of themselves and have been working out ways to improve their own chances. Slow, cumu-

lative results from widespread efforts of women have been accelerating in the last few years, mostly due to persistent efforts of commissions on the status of women, feminist organizations, women's professional associations and outstanding women in Congress and state legislatures.

It is no coincidence that the year 1972 sees Rep. Shirley Chisholm as a candidate for the Presidential nomination. Nor has there ever been the concerted effort for more repre sentative seating of women as delegates to national political conventions. Across the nation, women are gaining more political power.

The present federal requirements for affirmative action programs for women are the direct results of strategic pressure brought on governmental agencies by women, aided by precedent-setting legal decisions won by women pursuing their cases through the courts. At present, the most effective tools to force change are filing complaints with governmental agencies and bringing class actions in court. Governmental agencies have taken action against utilities, broadcasters, unions, universities, banks, department stores, manufacturers, railroads and airlines. In the matter of equal pay alone, by late 1971 nearly 88,000 employees, mostly women, had been awarded 35.6 million dollars in back pay as a result of the Equal Pay Act which went into effect in June, 1964.[23]

The private sector was not alone in feeling women's pressures. Federal agencies responsible for compliance with Revised Order 4 by April, 1972 faced the double twist of compliance themselves. Affirmative action plans were needed and encouraged for individual agency personnel as well as for their contractors. The President is being criticized for his pitifully low percentage of women appointees to cabinet and executive branch positions. U.S. Congressmen too, have come under criticism for legislative staffing that has severely discriminated against women. The Federal Bureau of Investigation first opened special agent positions to women in May, 1972. A State Department policy which excluded women

from foreign assignments has been banned by the U.S. Civil Service Commission. The U.S. Public Health Service has a suit against it filed by 31,000 women employees.

The Justice Department has barely begun to press sex discrimination cases recommended by Equal Employment Opportunity Commission (EEOC), administrative agency for the Civil Rights Act of 1964. Sex cases have swamped this agency from its inception in 1965, with many district offices more than two years behind in their case loads.[24]

State agencies also feel the pressure. California's Fair Employment Practices Commission was given authority over sex discrimination cases in November, 1970. In the first year, 400 sex cases were filed, one-fifth of all unfair practices complaints received.[25]

Municipal governments have also felt the impact of change. New York City is now requiring all suppliers to have affirmative action programs for women as well as minorities.

It is expected that the OFCC may require that affirmative action plans be made available to the public—a powerful impetus for action if this occurs.[26]

It's when and how, not if women move up. The groundwork has been laid.

The demand for managers and professional people may not be met by the supply of available males. By 1975, because of lower birthrates during the Depression, the number of young men of executive age (35–45) will be at a new low, while the need for managers will have steadily increased.[27] At the same time, women are becoming both more available and more capable. Fewer women are settling for the house-keeping chores of the nation in home, factory and office, and fewer are willing to donate their talents to volunteer service organizations. More women need and expect their education and productivity to be valued with hard cash and fringe benefits including retirement. As women are valuing themselves more, fewer are or want to be dependent.

It's simply not smart personal planning. They expect value received for value given, on an equal basis with men. As Edward J. Bloustein, President of Bennington College observed in 1968, "Even without a revision in the basic marriage pattern, there are other things society could do to enable women to undertake a career on equal terms with men. One thing would be to eliminate the widespread discrimination that exists in most occupations and professions. Men are the ones who determine, the conditions of employment for both men and women, and they simply are discriminatory in the crudest sense of the word."[28]

Since 1968, acceptance of women in many areas has been snowballing. Traditional patterns are being questioned and becoming diffused. More men and women of all ages want wider personal choices and more power over the decisions affecting their lives. Sexual mores and marriage patterns are rapidly shifting. Subordinancy in all choices is no longer tolerable for an increasing number of women, nor is dominance still comfortable for a smaller, but growing cadre of men. Discussions of questions raised by the Equal Rights Amendment opened new legal and social issues around equality of the sexes. Acceptance of diversity—in personal style, attitudes and values—is widening within business, education and government spheres of influence.

Action means tapping a valuable resource

Can these organizations cope with increasing numbers of women who are persevering to share decision-making positions with men? Beginnings are being made. The trends and pressures have been building for decades. The pragmatic wisdom of getting into action now is becoming more general in our large corporations, universities and in government. The kinds of women who can combine their efforts and expertise to create the legal and regulatory changes now affecting employers across the country are a sample of women now prepared for managerial and executive positions. They

represent thousands of women who already have the expertise and experience for top level positions.

Ask yourself—
- Am I tuned in on what's happening with women? Is our organization up-to-date? How about others in our field?
- Are some of our women more capable than we've been giving them credit for? Which ones should move up?
- Do some of the women who work for me want to move up? What do they need to be ready? How can I expedite these moves? How do I get ready to replace them in their present positions?
- Am I resistant to this whole subject? Is resistance an attitude I can afford? What if I do nothing—or oppose it?
    . . . Read on . . .

Notes

1. McGregor, James, "White Collar Blacks: Big Companies Battle to Recruit Negroes for Executive Posts," *Wall Street Journal*, July 23, 1969.
2. Harris, T George, "Organic Populism, A Conversation with Warren G. Bennis," *Psychology Today*, February, 1970, p. 7.
3. Bennis, Warren, "How to Survive in a Revolution," *Innovation*, Number Eleven, 1970, p. 7.
4. Spock, Benjamin, "Spock Answers Critics—'I Harbored Sexism,'" *Los Angeles Times*, September 12, 1971.
5. *The Spokeswoman*, April 1, 1972, p. 3.
6. *Ibid.*
7. *Ibid.*
8. *Women Today*, March 2, 1972, p. 5.
9. Quoted from "Return of the Lobotomy," *Washington Post*, March 12, 1972, in *The Spokeswoman*, April 1, 1972, p. 5.
10. *The Spokeswoman*, April 1, 1972, p. 5.
11. *Women Today*, April 3, 1972, p. 6.
12. *Ibid.*
13. Quoted in "A Unique Competence," *A Study of Equal Employment Opportunity in the Bell System*, a 300-page summary of the findings of the Equal Employment Opportunity Commission, Washington, D.C., 20506.
14. East, Catherine, "What the Government Will Require," speech prepared for the Urban Research Corporation conference, San Francisco, California, October 14, 1971.

15. *The Spokeswoman,* March 1, 1972, p. 5.
16. *Ibid.*
17. *The Spokeswoman,* July 1, 1971, p. 1.
18. "Male Nurse Strikes Blow for Men's Lib," *Los Angeles Times,* April 7, 1972.
19. Bureau of National Affairs, Inc., "Few Women are in Management," *Bulletin to Management,* No. 1047, March 5, 1970.
20. March, 1970 data is from the report above. December, 1971 data is from Bureau of National Affairs, Inc., "Women & Minorities in Management and in Personnel Management," *Personnel Policies Forum,* Survey No. 96, December, 1971, pp. 2–4.
21. Bowman, Garda W., N. B. Worthy and S. A. Greyser, "Are Women Executives People?" *Harvard Business Review,* July–August, 1965, p. 25.
22. Cited in "Employment: Women's Gains," *Newsweek,* January 11, 1971, p. 70.
23. East, *op. cit.,* p. 1.
24. The reader is referred to *The Spokeswoman* and *Women Today,* two newsletters reporting events affecting women's lives, from which these and many other citations in this chapter are drawn. Addresses and subscription prices are listed in *Tools: Information and Sources.*
25. "Significant Increase in Caseload Reported in Five-Year Period," *FEPC News,* (California) No. 44, January–February, 1972, p. 1.
26. See footnote 24.
27. Patton, Arch, "The Coming Scramble for Executive Talent," *Harvard Business Review,* May–June, 1967, pp. 155–159.
28. Bloustein, Edward Jr., "Man's Work Goes from Sun to Sun but Women's Work is Never Done," *Psychology Today,* March, 1968, pp. 39–40.

2

The Reasons in Depth

Equality of rights under the law shall not be denied or abridged by the United States or by any state on account of sex.

Proposed 27th U.S. Constitutional Amendment

Suddenly, women aren't so funny anymore. Traditionally comedians and joke-tellers have used women as their stock in trade—my mother-in-law, the farmer's daughter, that dumb blond, "Now take my wife . . ."

Ironically, the beginning of the end of that source of laughter was one of the funniest days in the history of the House of Representatives. February 8, 1964 was the day the word "sex" was introduced as an amendment to a bill outlawing racial discrimination in employment. In an effort to laugh equal employment off the floor, a Southern representative proposed the addition of "sex," setting off a string of jokes from both proponents and opponents of the amendment. Despite the laughter, Title VII of the Civil Rights Act, including the word "sex," was passed.

The laughter continued, as the media conjured up images of male "bunnies" and female construction workers. Women who claimed equality were, for several years, labeled "kooks" and "bra burning bubbleheads."

Recently the climate has changed. The jokes have begun to sound as out of place as racial humor. With the change in climate, the attitudes, at least in the statements of im-

portant figures in American society, appear to reflect a new awareness.

Why are women no longer a laughing matter? In large part it is because women are taking themselves more seriously. As a result, they are being taken more seriously by the male members of society. In other historical times, and presently in other places, like India, Russia and Israel, women leaders have transcended the familiar and long-held role-relations of men and women. The ties between those distant times and places and our own have been well-examined by various commentators who believe we are in such a period in America today.

Starting slowly, the bases for change are gaining momentum

While legislation to equalize the position of women and men in employment has developed alongside the general civil rights movement, emphasis on the rights of racial minorities has until recently had priority over the employment problems of women. Nevertheless, civil rights and women's rights have the same historical roots and spring from the same human needs.

Federal legislation

Two landmark laws of the early sixties affecting women's rights in employment were the Federal Equal Pay Act of 1963, an amendment to the Fair Labor Standards Act, and Title VII of the Federal Civil Rights Act of 1964. The Equal Pay Act guarantees equal pay for equal or substantially similar work. It excludes all executive, administrative and professional jobs, and most public service and covers only those jobs affected by minimum wage laws.

According to Ann Scott, federal compliance expert for the National Organization for Women (NOW), "the Equal Pay Act does not cover equal opportunity, or such matters as

hiring, firing, promotion, seniority, conditions of employment. It applies only where both men and women work in
the same department or division. This has led occasional
employers to circumvent the act by establishing 'ghetto
departments' where women only can be hired for lower
wages for the same or equal work as men in other divisions.
Other dodges, used by unions as well as employers, may include redefining job specifications slightly in line with a
state 'protective' weightlifting restriction in order to claim
that the jobs are no longer equal, or claiming a 'training
program' supposed to groom only men at a higher wage for
possible promotion."[1]

Title VII of the Civil Rights Act of 1964 provides the
enabling legislation for equal opportunity including access,
promotion, benefits, conditions and terms of employment.
It bans discrimination on all bases (sex, race, color, religion
and national origin) by private employers of 25 or more,
labor organizations, employment agencies and union-management apprenticeship programs.[2] In 1972, coverage was
extended to managers, professionals, teachers, professors
and government employees.[3]

The enforcement pace has been slow, however. The first
equal pay cases were not decided by the courts until 1970,
and enforcement powers were not given to the Equal Employment Opportunity Commission (EEOC) until March
1972. In late February 1972, the Senate by unanimous vote
attached an amendment to a higher-education bill proposing
to eliminate discrimination against women seeking admission to public and private graduate schools and in public
undergraduate colleges and universities.

Forty-nine years after the first attempt to add a constitutional amendment to provide that equal legal rights not be
denied on the basis of sex, the climate finally was right. On
March 21, 1972, the Senate passed a bill, already approved
by the House, to provide sexual equality as a Constitutional
right. The Equal Rights Amendment "will remove the last

acceptable form of social discrimination that exists" in America. State ratification is in process.

State legislation

All fifty states have felt the impact of women's rights legislation. In 1963, 40 states and the District of Columbia had maximum hours laws for women in one or more occupations or industries. By 1971, only 10 states still retained or enforced such laws without major exclusions or change of status.[4]

Executive orders

But an executive order by President Johnson in 1965 has had more impact for change than all legislation to date. Executive Order 11246 as amended, affects most major corporations, educational institutions, non-federal governmental bodies, and financial institutions. Most receive federal funds in one form or another. Federal employment is covered by Executive Order 11478.[5] The order prohibits federal contractors and subcontractors from discriminating in any aspect of employment, requiring employers with contracts of $50,000 or more and 50 or more employees to develop affirmative action programs to remedy existing discriminatory conditions. The Office of Federal Contract Compliance (OFCC) of the U.S. Department of Labor determines the policy and standards of enforcement. Implementation is done by 16 federal compliance agencies within various executive departments and governmental agencies.

Just what kinds of affirmative action programs will be necessary to alleviate discriminatory practices of federal contractors has recently been delineated by another strong government support—Revised Order 4 issued by Secretary of Labor J. D. Hodgson in December 1971.[6]

Detailed considerations for recruiting, hiring, promoting, transferring and training women within the company are outlined in Revised Order 4. Goals and timetables for good faith implementation must also be established, particularly

regarding potential women managers. Leverage is supplied through the power to withhold or cancel contracts where compliance is not occurring or good faith implementation is not evident.

HEW, itself a compliance agency for institutions of education, health and welfare, has declared its objective to set a pattern for a national model and has designed an affirmative action program for itself—one of the largest government agencies.

Educational institutions as suppliers of managers, professional and technical people

Not only laws and executive orders are changing the potential opportunities for women. Educational institutions, long the conveyors of stereotypes of career possibilities for male and female, are beginning to reflect the new look. History books are being rewritten to include the substantial accomplishments of women in this country. Counseling which began with mature women is now moving from college campuses through the community colleges to the high schools and even to the elementary schools. The new message in textbooks and teaching is "alternative ways to live . . .", that some women will continue to fill traditional roles but many will not. Younger girls will learn that it is *all right* to excel in math, to become a marine engineer, to apply for graduate school in business administration. Deliberate recruitment for women in graduate schools is already occurring in a few major universities. This trend will continue as organizations search for specially trained women to fill positions newly opened to them because of federal contractor requirements.

Successful women and influential men look at women's rights . . . and men's

Until recently, the avenues that men use to positions of power and prestige have been available to only extremely

rare women. Successful women have made it alone, without the support of laws, executive orders, or other ambitious women. Therefore many women who are in management feel distant from or even hostile to some of the activities of feminist groups. But more and more of them are recognizing an identification with some of the goals of the movement, even if they are not ready to identify with it as a whole. The range of such women's comments is wide but basically the message is the same.

Julia Walsh of Ferris & Co., first woman admitted to the New York Stock Exchange, seemed to have reservations in a *Fortune* interview when she was asked to respond to an editorial statement that "A woman who gets ahead in this world would seem to have little need for women's lib."

While denouncing any involvement with "the burning-the-bra type of thing," she did respond in terms of her own experience in paying higher interest rates on a home loan for twenty years because she was female. "From that aspect of the women's lib, I'm an activist," she declared.

In agreement with other key issues of the women's rights movement, without labeling them as such she said, "I really do believe . . . that for a gal to survive the same competitive situation that a man survives she must be twice as good . . ."[7]

Anthropologist Laura Nader Milleron, sister of Ralph Nader and one of fifteen women who are full professors at the University of California's Berkeley campus, agreed that women who want to reach the top in the academic professions must be exceptional. Said she: "Women have been given just enough freedom to be the buyers in America to spend their husbands' checks, but not to compete in the professions. Proportionately, there are more women physicists in Italy than in America."[8]

As if in answer to the kinds of positions women usually fill, Fay Kanin, movie and television writer and the first woman president in twenty years of the Screen branch, Writers Guild of America West, is involved in a new effort

to remove sex role stereotypes from TV family situation programs and commercials.

In breaking down old patterns, Ms. Kanin feels, "The women's movement has been quite marvelous and remarkable. Sure, they've taken silly stands. It's really a revolution and revolutionaries have to make headlines. But they have dramatized the issue of woman's equality; they have brought it to national consciousness. Beyond that, the movement has encouraged women who were diffident about getting a degree or a job. It has helped them out of that awful vacuum."[9]

In a 1965 survey, 82 percent of the women managers felt that the number of women in management was on the increase. Interestingly, 63 percent of the men managers agreed.[10] In those days, however, few men were taking a public position about it. But that's rapidly changing. Today more men are offering strong support for the idea of women in management. Support has come from many unexpected places.

One of the most remarkable statements has come from a field where few women are found—the ranks of newspaper commentators. D. J. R. Bruckner, senior editor for the *Los Angeles Times*, pointed out that the women's movement "has certainly produced a widespread awareness of the humiliation of women, and it has done this in a very short time . . . How could you possibly disrespect someone more than by expecting little of them?"

Bruckner believed that "Men are terribly locked in in this country, restricted in outlook, occupation, and in emotions," and said, "For most men it would seem beneficial to promote women's liberation; if it works, it has to amount to men's liberation . . . In the end, that prospect (of liberation for both sexes) is what makes a man want to support women's liberation in general, and especially when the liberators are attacking discrimination in the social, education, economic and political systems. The old order was probably

comfortable for everyone at one time; it worked. It works no longer. There are too many wrecked lives, too many families scattered in desperate divorces, too many men and women whose souls are being flayed by impertinent distinctions—and you can hardly believe how they are altered for the worse."[11]

To start the ball rolling to change the present situation, John Kenneth Galbraith, with two economics colleagues, has proposed a plan for breaking the monopoly of white males who hold 96 percent of America's $15,000-a-year-or-more jobs. Referring to the 4 percent left to women and minorities, he comments, "The people subject to this discrimination are no longer mute or helpless; one can hardly imagine that they will permanently and peacefully accept their subordinate status. There is, accordingly, a choice between eliminating this discrimination or leaving it to later and much more angry remedy . . . Perhaps, on this occasion, foresight and common sense will rule."[12]

Sex bias is in pay and position

Throughout the sixties we have moved steadily towards an awareness of the needs and rights of minority groups in America. The Civil Rights movement has brought slow but steady improvement for those in our society "who have been left behind."[13] To be white and college educated would seem a blessing beyond doubt. Yet if one is a woman, white or ethnic minority, the facts do not bear this out.

Briefly, the statistics reveal some interesting points to the contrary. "Sex bias takes a greater economic toll than racial bias," according to the President's Task Force on Women's Rights and Responsibilities. Even though there is a major difference in median annual earnings between white and black men—$7,396 to $4,777—women earn less. White women average $4,279, black women $3,194.[14]

When the pay received in the total workforce is broken down by sex, we find that only 1.1 percent of women work-

ing received $15,000-a-year or more, compared to 13.5 percent of the men.[15]

Within the pay category of $15,000-a-year or more, there were approximately 5,050,000 positions. Of these, only 3 percent are held by women, 97 percent by men in 1970.[16]

College educated women are under-utilized and underpaid

But what about the college woman? Certainly *some* with bachelor's degrees find themselves sidetracked into these low-income, low-status positions set aside for women. But if a college graduate really wants to, hasn't the climate changed over the years to allow more women into top-level, top-paying jobs in the professions and other managerial posts?

Although many signs point to change in the near future, the scene has been grim. As of March 1969, among working women who had completed four years of college, 19 percent were employed in nonprofessional jobs: clerical, sales, operatives or service.[17] The average annual income of women college graduates was $8,156, compared to men graduates at $13,264 in 1970. Women college graduates average less earnings than men with 1-3 years of high school education ($8,514).[18]

On a national average, all women's average earnings were 59.4 percent of men's.[19] Women with 4-year college degrees averaged 61.5 percent of men's earnings. They did slightly better with 5 years or more of education: 65 percent of men's average earnings.[20]

Salaries offered to new college graduates are consistently lower for women than for men with the same major. This pay pattern stands firm in all the professional and technical categories in later employment periods. Women chemists earn 67.3 percent of men chemists' pay; women linguists fare best at 86.9 percent of men linguists' pay. Does the language form the behavior?[21]

We have already seen in Chapter I how few women are in management positions. Outstanding women students are funneled into stereotypically feminine fields, but may be learning similar capabilities. In a report issued by the Women's Equity Action League on the number of doctorates earned by women from 1960-69, 100 percent of the doctorates in institution management in home economics were earned by women; but for business and commerce doctorates, only 2.8 percent went to women.[22] Why such a difference in two management fields?

Educational institutions under-utilize the women they educate

Philip H. Abelson, editor of *Science*, points to the "limited presence, about 2 percent, of women as full professors in our major universities . . . This compares with an annual doctorate production of about 12 percent women."[23] Furthermore, data assembled in 1970 by the Conference of Professional and Academic Women indicate "the more prestigious the institution, the fewer women are employed."[24] This is historically constant, and perhaps, suggests Dean Alice Kimball Smith of Radcliffe Institute, the only places where intelligent young women may find models in academia currently are in top-level women's colleges where male and female professors are seen in a more realistic percentage mix.[25]

When the American Association of University Women (AAUW) queried college administrators about plans for affirmative action programs, a variety of reasons for past recruitment deficiencies were given. Said one president, "When men interview women for a professional position, they will have in the back of their minds a reservation about whether or not they can deal with a woman professionally in the same manner as they deal with a man. I am no good, for example, in dealing with women who are in tears. I don't anticipate having that kind of problem with a man so it never enters my mind. I suppose most of us don't want to

be bound by cultural restrictions so we simply go out and employ men."[26] So sex role expectations pervade even our halls of higher learning.

Another recruitment complaint heard in academic circles as in other areas of management has to do with the availability of top level candidates. The AAUW report quoted respondents as saying, "The women who applied were not as well qualified, having not had an opportunity to serve in top executive positions."[27] One nationwide search for a vice-president of instructional services produced 46 possibilities, only one of whom was a woman and she near retirement age. The community college system reputedly offers women an opportunity to overcome this deficiency in administrative experience. Women now serving in top positions there may become candidates for administrative and management positions in state, university and private college systems as this route for advancement becomes recognized as valuable.

There's an irony in the thinking of college administrators who, having educated women, do not yet see the ambiguity of their discrimination. And the same patterns exist down through secondary and elementary educational levels. In high schools, 50 percent of the teachers and only 4 percent of the principals are women; in elementary schools it's 88 percent teachers, 22 percent principals.[28]

While the case for women in education, a "feminine" field, has not been good, women in other professions fare no better, sometimes worse: 9 percent are scientists; 7 percent, physicians; 3 percent, lawyers; 2 percent, dentists, and 1 percent, engineers and federal judges. Although there is much evidence of inequities in professional school admissions practices, the possibilities of rapid change in the near future are just emerging. For example, a 1971 estimate set 5.9 percent as the proportion of women enrolled in law schools throughout the country. The most recent enrollment of women law students (8,914) is the highest number of women in 10 years, yet this was only 9.4 percent of the total enrollment.[29]

So we re-run the statistics and so what? Senator Marlow

W. Cook found a "so what." He's the father of four daugh-
ters, one of whom wants to go to law school, as he told
Congress when discussing the Equal Rights Amendment on
August 25, 1970.

"I inquired of a law school in the East," he reported, "and
found out that last year in its graduating class, four of the
graduating seniors were women. When the larger law firms
in the country went to that college . . . they discussed positions . . . with all of the students in the class *except those
four women* (emphasis added). The young men . . . after
passing their bar examination (got) . . . an average starting
salary of between $10,000 and $16,000 a year." He found
that, "While all of the four girls graduated in the top 10
percent of their class, the highest salary attained by one of
these four girls was $10,000. One became a legal secretary,
one went to work for a bank, and two of them went to work
for the Federal Government."

As a father, he put forth this proposal: "Mr. President, I
would be happy to send my daughter to law school, if the
law school would permit me to pay only half the tuition paid
for a male student, since she will receive only approximately
half what they get when she graduates." His regret: "I am
afraid I shall not have that opportunity."[30]

Thus we see that their sex keeps women out of professional schools and then conspires against them economically
if they slip through, even though they may be the top
scholars in their law or medical school. And on payday those
with bachelor's degrees in the professions also fare poorly
alongside their male classmates.

➤ Working for government and Congress is not much different

Although many women with college degrees have entered
government service in an effort to avoid the competitive
problems which face them in the professions, Uncle Sam is
not as benevolent where his nieces are concerned as many

have expected. In 1923 the Civil Service Classification Act provided that Federal employees would receive equal pay for equal work, but this did not solve the real problem of inequality in government service. Executive Order 11478, issued in 1969 as an amendment to Executive Order 11246, requires the head of each executive department and agency to maintain an affirmative program of equal employment opportunity for women. In 1968, just before this order, women represented 34 percent of the federal work force, but 78.7 of those are employed at the lowest levels: Grades GS-1 through GS-6. Almost 20 percent were represented at the 7 to 12 levels, but only 1 percent have made it to the top echelons of civil service represented by Grades GS-13 and above and only 0.02 percent by Grades GS-16 and above. Efforts to date have not yet made any substantial changes in the overall picture.[31] Women's appointments to supergrade positions just receive more publicity now, the percentage increase is still miniscule.

Some of the very Senators who helped to pass the Women's Rights amendment in March 1972 were discriminating against women in staffing their offices. Among 990 Senate staffers earning $12,000 to $31,308 a year during the last half of 1969, men made up 72.5 percent of the staffs and received 80 percent of the total salary payments. Women staffers averaged 71 percent of the earnings of men staffers. Among those earning over $2,600 a month 41 were men, only 2, women.[32] Alan Cranston, (D-Calif.) is one of several outstanding exceptions to the Hill pattern. Two of his four legislative assistants, Carolyn Jordan and Ann Wray, contribute substantially to his decisions.[33]

The context from which the change in women's roles is coming

"American women are increasingly aware and restive over the denial of equal opportunity, equal responsibility, even equal protection of the law," according to the Presidential

Task Force. "An abiding concern for home and children should not, in their view, cut them off from the freedom to choose the role in society to which their interests, education and training entitle them."[34]

The growing discontent of women is involved with the general restlessness felt by many, male and female, young and old, black and white, with low-challenge, below-capacity work rigidly structured into an eight-hour five-day week devoid of stimulation. The strong thrust for meaningful work is being felt throughout America as greater social consciousness replaces the materialism that swept the country after the deprivations caused by the Depression and World War II.

Like so much social change now in process, it really began with the young, those born after World War II who knew none of the hardships of the 30's and 40's. Young men were turned off by the meaningless white-collar job-slots their fathers were wedged into and began to look for alternative life styles, even to the point where many college placement officers are providing counseling in these new directions. Young women, on the other hand, were turned on by new career possibilities which would take them away from what they saw as the drab routine of being "only a housewife" like their mothers.

It was not until the recession of 1970 and 1971 that middle-aged parents began to ask themselves some of the same questions to which young people and adult women had already been seeking answers. Suzannah Lessard, assistant editor of *The Washington Monthly* writes about the shattering of the myth for people who had gone to work in the defense industry. They have begun, along with others, to face the reality: "The cautious white-collar, security-bound life in post-war America has little to do with rugged individualism, versatility, or even ambition, the classical traits which in the land of opportunity yield great rewards."[35]

The space engineer, suddenly unemployed in a society which has always taught that "in America, if you get an

education—a white collar—and are reasonably industrious there will always be a place for you,"[36] has had to face the reality of dispensability. And with this realization comes a "deep unquenchable rebellion, rebellion against having had to put up with it (inflated, useless work) and against being tossed away with it."[37]

"The challenge," says Ms. Lessard, "is to redefine work. Work is effort directed towards the production or accomplishment of something useful. If the habit of thinking about work that way superseded the habit of responding to titles and monetary rewards, if education instead of gearing people up to getting a passport to high-paying, important-sounding niches developed an aversion to triviality as an affront to dignity, if the people in power looked at the working force as energy and talent to be applied to what needs to be done, it would become immediately apparent how wastefully fatuous the present system and projected policies are. The challenge is not to create a vacuous picture of prosperity. The challenge is to free the working force from the meshes of trivia and turn it towards the mountains of real work that needs to be done."[38]

To the desire for more meaningful work add, for women, another social change: the transition from the population explosion to ZPG, (Zero Population Growth). Philip Abelson editorializes about this and the changes he feels will persist because woman's role is in process of change. "If society frowns on childbearing, how are women to occupy themselves constructively? What can they do to lead significant and interesting lives? Increasingly women are turning to employment of some kind.

"Transition from a time in which babies were the thing to an era of zero population growth must have profound consequences on the relations between men and women and on the structure of society. We have only begun to see some of the effects."[39]

At the same time that the need for women as population

producers is dropping, another need may be peaking. Arch Patton, Director of McKinsey & Co., predicted that the low birthrate of the 1930's will cause 1974 to be the lowest point in what has been a steady decrease in the number of men in the 35-to-45 age group. "The importance of the 35 to 45 age group, of course," says Patton, "lies in the fact that much of industry's dynamism depends on their 'let's go' energy and right experience. Studies show that most major inventions have been developed by men in their thirties and forties. The same age bracket also provides most of the departmental and functional heads—the line officers of the industrial army—in the average company."[40]

Supply and demand for managers sets a new stage for women

This shortage has important significance for women. Many factors converge to provide the 45-year-old woman with the creative energy level of a man 10 years her junior. If she has been continuously employed, she is probably experiencing women's 10-year-lag in promotions compared to men, and now be "ready" to move into a dynamic managerial role. Norma Groth's study of gifted girls and women points out that many females who have concerned themselves with filling traditional feminine roles begin at about age 40 to move rapidly towards the Maslovian idea of self-actualization, motivated by previous frustration in their female roles.[41] This emergence of women's creativity in the forties has also been observed by Barbara McGowan, co-founder in 1965 of a UCLA Extension program, "Group Counseling for Women," designed to help prepare mature women to return to education or employment. Ms. McGowan feels that the many life experiences of women outside the work world assist them in making highly creative judgments which advance them at an accelerated rate when they set educational or professional goals.[42]

Highly-capable women have not been needed in the past. They have been excluded from the scurry for bright young executive talent. As Rep. Shirley Chisholm told her fellow Congressmen, "More than half the population of the United States is female. But women occupy only 2 percent of the managerial positions. They have not even reached tokenism yet."[43]

It is onto this employment stage that Revised Order 4 and the "executive scramble" enter from opposite wings. "Few companies," says Patton, "have yet turned to women as potential executive candidates. Yet there are many executive jobs . . . that require the imaginative intelligence and perseverance so many women possess. Furthermore, many graduate schools of business have accepted women, and the supply of female MBAs is likely to increase sharply over the next decade."[44]

Winifred Slack, a CPA and treasurer of a large general contracting firm in Pittsburgh, extends Patton's birthrate projection and predicts that the drop in numbers of 35-44 age men by 1975, "will necessitate recruiting men from the 25-34 age group which will increase by 1975. This younger group will have a personal awareness of the education and capabilities of young women, and a business and social realization that obtaining results takes precedence over race, religion, ancestry or sex."[45] These younger men may well help improve the climate for women as managers.

Trends toward the 35-hour work week and the 40-hour, 4-day week, increased vacations and leaves of absence to acquire advanced degrees or to fill government posts will also create openings in managerial positions.

The pressures for and against change in women's participation will continue

Women have always had to fight for equal pay and employment opportunities for themselves, either alone or in

concert. Today a growing number of organizations, women's caucuses, and advisory commissions on the status of women are making these stands efficiently and effectively. In many cases, they have initiated the legal and legislative action necessary to move those people who are firmly entrenched against change. The simple existence of feminist groups who pressure for needed social change causes many other silent women to take another look at the roles they have accepted, question them and reconsider whether or not they like them.

This questioning process is part of recognizing that other choices do exist. Many women have "never thought about" doing something different from the wife-mother-secretarial roles. They are now beginning to think of exercising wider choices and preparing themselves for more responsible positions in the mainstream of American life.

In addition to making other women aware of wider choices, activist groups have undertaken legal actions and encouraged others to initiate test cases. Much pressure to find new approaches to equalize selection, pay, training and promotion between men and women has been due to their stimulation of legal actions involving EEOC and OFCC. Giving managements of federal contractor organizations some negative motivation (comply or else) seems to have been necessary to make a start. And activists recognize the need to continue their pressure over an extended period of time.

While most changes apparently require this type of motivation to initiate major changes, especially in situations requiring important attitude changes where stereotypes have long prevailed, we expect that such affirmative action programs will continue because they work—for both women and men. Men who have worked with women managers are much more favorably inclined to do it again than those who have not had that exposure.[46] This strongly suggests that once the initial breakthrough is made, the second look-around will not be so traumatic.

We summarize the pressures for and against changes affecting women's managerial aspirations:[47]

Status
Quo

TOWARD CHANGE		AGAINST CHANGE
Demographic changes in age, family size, life styles	$\longrightarrow$ $\longleftarrow$	Personal anxieties of both men and women
	$\longleftarrow$	Traditional views of women
More democratic, humanistic values among large groups of the population	$\longrightarrow$ $\longleftarrow$	Rigid, authoritarian, hierarchial forms of organizations
Legislation, Equal Rights Amendment and Executive Orders, with impact on the judicial system	$\longrightarrow$ $\longleftarrow$	Institutionalized power that is carefully guarded
	$\longleftarrow$	Patterns of business and professional relationships that have not included women
Concern for justice, equality, fair play	$\longrightarrow$	
Knowledge of how to exercise power, influence major decisions, negotiate	$\longrightarrow$ $\longleftarrow$	Difficulty in visualizing women in leadership and management roles; difficulty in trusting their abilities
Vigorous ad hoc groups to focus on special problems	$\longrightarrow$	
	$\longleftarrow$	Habits of discrimination and patronization by men
Aspirations for moving upward and taking more responsibility	$\longrightarrow$ $\longleftarrow$	Inertia of the status quo; resistance to any change
Power of knowledge, expertise and experience in specialized fields	$\longrightarrow$ $\longleftarrow$	Potential threat to self-image and sexual expectations
	$\longleftarrow$	Concern for profitability as power and cost patterns shift

Ask yourself—
- Which of the pressures listed above do I identify with?
- How ready am I to actively support a women's affirmative action program in my own organization?

- Which of the pressure points do I think could be strengthened or weakened in order to move women up in our organization?
- In which direction do I see myself moving? What does this mean to my organization?
- How can I best handle whatever conflicts I have about it?

Notes

➤ 1. Scott, Ann, "Feminism vs. the Feds," *Issues in an Industrial Society,* Vol. 2, No. 1, 1971.
2. For an excellent law summary, see *Laws on Sex Discrimination in Employment,* U.S. Department of Labor, Wage and Labor Standards Administration, Women's Bureau, soon to be revised.
3. For text and summary points, see "The Equal Employment Opportunity Act of 1972," (effective March 24, 1972) a special BNA Report published by the Bureau of National Affairs, Inc., Washington, D.C.
4. "Status of State Hours Laws for Women," U.S. Department of Labor, Employment Standards Administration, Women's Bureau, November 4, 1971 (rev.) p. 1, 3.
5. Executive Order 11246 as amended by Executive Order 11375, and Executive Order 11478 are in *Laws on Sex Discrimination—op. cit.*
6. Title 41, Chapter 60, Part 60-2, "Affirmative Action Programs," published in the *Federal Register,* Vol. 36 No. 234, Saturday, December 4, 1971, effective 120 days subsequent.
7. Walsh, Julia, "The Executive Voice," *Fortune* Cassette Series, April, 1971.
8. Falconer, B., "A Singular Woman," *McCalls,* February, 1971, p. 43.
9. Vils, Ursula, "Reshaping Heroine's Image," *Los Angeles Times,* View Section, February 9, 1972.
➤ 10. Bowman, Garda W., N. B. Worthy and S. A. Greyser, "Are Women Executives People?" *Harvard Business Review,* July–August, 1965, p. 20.
11. Bruckner, D. J. R., "Why Women's Lib? Because Our Present Alternative No Longer Works," *Los Angeles Times,* Part II, December 29, 1971.
12. Galbraith, John Kenneth, Edwin Kuh and Lester C. Thurow, "The Galbraith Plan to Promote the Minorities," *The New York Times Magazine,* August 22, 1971, p. 35.
13. From Richard Nixon's State of the Union address, January 22, 1972, in which he favored "equal opportunity for minorities and others who have been left behind." By a process of elimination, he apparently refers to women in this way.

14. *A Matter of Simple Justice, The Report of the President's Task Force on Women's Rights and Responsibilities,* April, 1970, p. 18.
15. *Fact Sheet on the Earnings Gap,* U.S. Department of Labor, Employment Standards Administration, Women's Bureau, December 1971 (rev.) p. 3.
16. *Ibid.* Conclusions calculated from same data.
17. *Underutilization of Women Workers,* U.S. Department of Labor, Workplace Standards Administration, Women's Bureau, 1971 (rev.) p. 16.
18. *Fact Sheet on Earnings Gap, op. cit.,* p. 3.
19. *Ibid.,* p. 1.
20. *Ibid,* p. 3.
21. *Ibid,* p. 5.
22. "Proportion of Doctorates Earned by Women, by Area and Field, 1960–1969," *Women's Equity Action League,* June, 1971.
23. Abelson, Philip H., "Women in Academia," editorial in *Science,* Vol. 175, No. 4018, January 14, 1972.
24. Trecker, Janice Law, "Woman's Place Is in the Curriculum," *Saturday Review,* October 16, 1971, p. 86.
25. Smith, Alice Kimball, "Educated Women: Some Unanswered Questions," lecture delivered at University of California, Los Angeles, February 23, 1972.
26. American Association of University Women, California State Division, memo to members dated June, 1971, p. 2.
27. *Ibid.*
28. "Women Step Up Battle for Rights Amendment," *Los Angeles Times* (exclusive from the *Congressional Quarterly*), Part 1, March 21, 1972.
29. "That Burgeoning Law School Enrollment," *American Bar Association Journal,* February, 1972, p. 147.
30. Cook, Senator Marlow W., *Congressional Record,* August 25, 1970, discussion favoring the passage of the Equal Rights Amendment.
31. Fields, Daisy B., Statement before the U.S. House of Representatives, Special Subcommittee on Education, June 29, 1970. Reprinted by Federally Employed Women, Inc., Washington, D.C. p. 3
32. *Washington Newsletter for Women,* quoting figures from an anonymously authored report, "Sexism on Capitol Hill," September, 1969.
33. Cimons, Marlene, "Sen. Cranston Helps, Womanpower on Capitol Hill," *Los Angeles Times,* Sec. J, February 6, 1972.
34. *A Matter of Simple Justice, op. cit.,* p. III.
35. Lessard, Suzannah, "America the Featherbedded," *Washington Monthly,* March, 1971, p. 20.
36. *Ibid,* p. 18.
37. *Ibid,* p. 21.
38. *Ibid,* p. 23.
39. Abelson, *op. cit.*

40. Patton, Arch, "The Coming Scramble for Executive Talent, *Harvard Business Review,* May–June, 1967, p. 156.
41. Groth, Norma J., "Vocational Development for Gifted Girls—A Comparison of Maslovian Needs of Gifted Males and Females Between the Ages of Ten and Seventy Years." Mimeographed paper presented at American Personnel and Guidance Association, 1969.
42. Private communication and course information based on extended experience and informal follow-through with Barbara McGowan, counseling psychologist, UCLA Counseling Center.
43. Chisholm, Representative Shirley, *Congressional Record,* May 21, 1969.
44. Patton, *op. cit.,* p. 170.
45. Slack, Winifred S., "Keys to the Corporate Board Room," *The Iris of Phi Chi Theta,* January, 1971, p. 10.
46. Bowman *et al, op. cit.,* p. 166. Also, the most frequent favorable responses came from men who had worked with women managers in those industries seen as having the greater opportunities for women—"feminine" industries such as small advertising, retail-wholesale organizations.
47. Loring, Rosalind K., adapted from chapter "Awakening to Re ality," in *Alice in Academe,* published by American Association of University Women of California, May, 1971.

3

Guidelines for Immediate Action

To this end, I am now directing that you take the following actions:

—Develop and put into action a plan for attracting more qualified women to top appointive positions . . . this plan should be submitted to me by May 15.

—Develop and put into action by May 15 a plan for significantly increasing the number of women . . . in mid-level positions. . . This plan should directly involve your top personnel official.

—Ensure that substantial numbers of vacancies on your Advisory Boards and Committees are filled with well-qualified women.

—Designate an overall coordinator who will be held responsible for the success of this project. Please provide this name to me by May 15.

Richard Nixon
April 26, 1971

Top policy statement is formulated and announced throughout the organization

This is a policy statement from the top, essential to launching a program as pervasive as affirmative action for women, whether within the Federal government or in some other organization. It is also an example of initial goals with a timetable—the parameters within which expected action is to take place.

Developing a climate for change of policies and practices in order to accept women as managers usually means revising some organization-wide procedures and many attitudes

and relationships. So radical will these changes seem to some that little progress will be made without consistent committed leadership from top management.

Even with strong support from executives and trainers, this kind of organizational change requires a person near the top—a new manager, consultant or staff officer—to give it concentrated attention. A fresh way of looking at the familiar scene is essential. Analysis, identification, possible solution, collaboration . . . all will be parts of the puzzle for both the line and staff as more people become involved in the processes of change.

The puzzle, of course, is the design of an affirmative action program relating to women. The structure of the program will be variously designed depending upon the applicable compliance agency and the magnitude of the effort being applied. Guidance for planning and implementation, growing out of experience with other projects of organizational change, generally applies to affirmative action programs.

We are assuming that the mechanics and problems of spelling out the specifics of the plan in each organization are available most precisely in the local area and in working with compliance officers having jurisdiction. Developing timetables also entails estimating some elements on which there may be insufficient information at the start, or which are difficult to estimate on any other basis than a well-educated guess. We want to raise a number of considerations and ideas here that we feel need to be part of the thinking and approach in developing affirmative action programs for women, taking such factors and difficulties into account. We are using Revised Order 4 as a basic model.*

Affirmative Action officers need a wide range of responsibility; should report to top management

The sheer size of the task of turning around an organization, its people and procedures means selecting an affirma-

---

*See *Tools: Information and Sources* for an edited version of Revised Order 4 focusing on the points relating to women.

tive action officer who reports directly to the top management level. The position needs to include responsibility to . . .

- Review and approve: provisions and goals of the program; job opening announcements and ads; job descriptions and requisite qualifications; application forms; tests and other screening devices; other related areas where sex bias may occur in the selection and placement process.
- Review, report and recommend actions for on-going follow-through based on: personnel records; affirmative action files for promotion; reasons for termination, discipline, and rejected promotions of women.
- Review and recommend changes in: personnel policies to assure equitable treatment for women and men; insurance, health and retirement programs to equalize benefits for both sexes and their dependents; other fringe benefit and incentive programs; informal practices and stated policy about leaves, absences, and other time off; other support services such as child care, counseling, etc.
- Review and recommend changes in: training and development programs re: selection, content, results, and rates of job progress subsequent to training.[1]

Selecting the Affirmative Action officer; support groups for Affirmative Action

The logical choice for the women's affirmative action officer is a woman. Why not put a man in charge of affirmative action for women? First, because of the credibility factor. Such a position usually pays well and carries some power in the organization. To select a man could be seen by women employees as meaning that top management intends to continue giving important positions to men. Second, it could appear that a male affirmative action officer is hired to whitewash sex discrimination, not eliminate it. Selecting a woman is *prima facie* good faith. Third, few men are fully aware of the subtleties of discrimination and how it has affected women's lives. Those men sensitive enough to sex discrimination to function effectively as affirmative action officers

would well understand that most men in that position would have considerable difficulty in establishing credibility with some women, especially the more aware ones.

How should the affirmative action officer be selected? Requirements might include in-depth knowledge of women's needs, roles, attitudes; what's happening in women's rights activities; current psychological and achievement motivation research on women; organization and management skills; management by objectives; and government regulatory requirements. Experience as a manager, a change-agent or community development expert should be among the other qualifications.

To separate the unaware from the knowledgeable applicant, questions could well include . . .

- How do you recognize "non-conscious sexism" in action?
- How would you select a woman to become a manager with some prediction of her success?
- What work, if any, needs to be done with men managers to make a woman's affirmative action program effective?
- What problems are "women's" problems, "men's" problems, or just human problems?

Applicants will reveal many unconscious as well as conscious attitudes during the interview. Notice what she (he) thinks women are like. Does she (he) stereotype either men or women in her (his) discussion? Can you sense an attitude of vengeance, "getting back" at society in her (his) conversation? What jokes are made, and does hostility underlie them? Vengeance could be a problem but anger may be useful. Try to sense the quality of it. Or is she (he) somewhat anxious to please, looking for how she (he) is expected to respond? "Nice person," deferring qualities may be far less than helpful in this sensitive position. Openness, directness, honesty and self-confidence are vital. So is support for expressing these qualities.

One important caution. Many firms already have affirmative action officers who are minority men, due to the em-

phasis on minority affirmative action in the past decade. Minority women also hold many similarly visible positions. But problems arising from discriminatory practices against minorities are different from those women experience. Minority women experience both.

Second caution. It must be clear in policy and action that advancement of minority men will not be at the expense of women's advancement nor that women advance at the expense of minority men. This is one sensitive area that can be a key to management's good faith. To pit one group against the other is to undermine the objectives of both. One way to avoid such problems is to select an aware woman who can work with the minority man who is now in affirmative action work. Equal status between them eliminates possible conflicts of interest and makes visible management's equal commitment to both groups. This delicate social balance in black/white, male/female advancement must be weighed in the final selection and placement of affirmative action officers as well as in implementing the program.

Additional people on the affirmative action teams could well include:

- An advisory committee, made up of women and minorities to solicit community and employees' views, to review and comment on policies, grievances, and the administration of the affirmative action program, to propose programs and procedures, and to consider special problems of minority women.
- Personnel staff who have sensitivity and commitment to affirmative action purposes, as evidenced by their work in feminist organizations, and minority communities.
- Supervisors and employees trained to have sensitivity to different attitudes, self-concepts, traditional social roles, and cultural differences among men and women of different ethnic groups.[2]

Responsibilty for the success of the program must rest with top management on down through line supervision.

Managers and supervisors should be held responsible through their performance reviews for meeting goals and timetables. If they have not met them, the reasons should be made clear. Eventually this information will be requested by compliance officers. Even without that pressure, the realistic problems and needed changes in plans are important for future planning.

Determining the present status of women in the organization

A survey to determine the practices, policies and attitudes which affect women should also canvas the experiences women have had in the organization and the ambitions they hold.

First, the survey should determine where women are in the organization by work-unit and by levels. When the search turns to women in management it will be necessary to *define a manager* for the purpose of the count. Without a precise definition, some departments may try to appear more progressive to higher management by including doubtful positions as management roles. In fact some organizations, straining hard, have even included executive secretaries as managers. Some include first-line supervision in management, others start at first-line management, which differs according to the size of the organization.

What defines management will have to be determined by each organization individually. The Department of Health, Education and Welfare bases management on pay-grade level. A major banking operation does not include first-line supervisors in its classifications of officials and managers. Their managers include those who supervise other officers, or are responsible for lending, managing and operations functions.

The basis for defining management—whether by pay-level, function, or numbers of people supervised—must be consistently applied by all managers and supervisors. The survey

should include questions covering requirements of the guidelines of Revised Order 4 which call for analysis of:

- The composition of the work force and applicant flow by minority group status and sex;
- The total selection process—position descriptions and titles, worker specifications, application forms, interviews, tests, referrals, transfer and promotion practices;
- Seniority;
- Facilities and company-sponsored recreation;
- Special programs including educational assistance;
- All company training programs;
- Work force attitude; and
- Under-utilization of women in specific classifications.

Lateral or vertical movements should occur at similar time rates for women and men. Position descriptions should accurately describe all actual functions and duties. Tests for selecting women should be validated, or be clearly capable of being validated should they be questioned for sex bias. Women should be participating in company activities and programs and be proportionately represented in training and development programs. A well-designed survey will reveal how men and women are experiencing the prevailing policies, practices and attitudes which affect their progress.*

Written policies of the organization should be analyzed for sex bias by the affirmative action officer. Unwritten policies are more subtle and may be discovered via the survey which can include questions that focus on some of the old discriminatory practices of differential interview questions, pay, expectations, promotional opportunity, eligibility for further training among others.

More information can be gotten from observing the results of prior bias, such as the invisible ceiling, assumed responsibilities in housekeeping functions, and what positions are most sex-typed. These evidences can be traced back to how

*Sample questions taken from an actual survey are in *Tools: Information and Sources.*

they started. This "audit trail" points back to a source of discrimination where differential ways of treating women from men is evident at the interface with the external market. For example, observe the double message in the employment ad that talks about looking for a man to head up a department, and which also states at the bottom of the ad, "an equal opportunity employer."

Another useful means for locating discriminatory practices is to ask the same questions of men and women, tabulating different patterns of answers. Also, when sex reversal questions are asked (those where the customary sex is replaced with the other sex) any absurdity is a solid clue that sex discrimination is present. Using sex reversal is most revealing of old habits of thinking, and brings the habit into conscious awareness.

Interviews and group sessions, as well as casual conversations can also be a rich source of information about how women feel. Care must be used, however, in interpreting these comments, as well as survey results. They reflect attitudes as of the time expressed, which may change, sometimes very rapidly. In general, most women tend to say what is expected of them, especially to men to whom they have been socialized to defer. It's part of being nice. However, as women become more aware that the price of being nice may be high, they may become more open with their formerly unexpressed viewpoints and experiences. This is the first move toward stepping out of some self-limiting behavior and can identify a potential candidate for career development. New awareness in women may be difficult to understand in comparison to former behavior, but it is a strength that is being released. Once released, it tends to grow.

Finding and recruiting women to fill new positions

Once the status of women within the organization has been determined, a plan for increasing the number of women

and minorities at all levels is set up. Specific targets within definite times are part of this plan. Sometimes there is a point of "operational discrimination"—where the necessary changes seem impossible. If this happens, try making a parallel with other "impossible" situations. Usually they just take a little longer! When you decide "We'll find a way," new possibilities begin to open up. This is "good faith." Finding women who are capable of becoming managers may be somewhat easier than it seems. Thus some thoughts on how "good faith" works . . .

Colleges and universities

Recruitment from colleges and universities is a major source for potential managers who are men. Women graduates typically have been avoided by the campus recruiter. Even women with Harvard MBA's have had this experience.[3] The fact that 30 percent of recruiting companies went to women's colleges while 60 percent went to men's colleges[4] is a sure indicator of intent not to recruit women. Women's colleges as well as coeducational institutions are the primary source for recruiting women for entry-level management positions. They are also the place to find well prepared professional and technical women.

Now that the demand for educated women for higher-level positions is increasing, more effective recruiting practices are necessary. What changes can improve the effectiveness of recruiting? In the past, women have been formally recruited but informally excluded. They have been sought as "tokens," recruited on a basis different from men.

Briefly, here's what has been happening. Recruiters may perform formal interviews to give the appearance of active interest, knowing that an "out" will be available. They avoid the possibility of the woman student suspecting sex discrimination. This works well if the men and women students do not exchange information after their respective interviews. Many do. Even if recruiters are careful to ask the same questions and give the same explanations to both

women and men students, it is becoming easier to spot lack of seriousness. Women graduates are learning what to look for. The most difficult position for a recruiter is to be seeking a qualified person for a position where the department head refuses to hire women. The recruiter is put in a personal double-bind and a long-term result may be that women graduates learn of this company's poor reputation and avoid interviews.

Recruiting a token woman is usually discovered by the woman graduate who is likely to ask about the invisible ceiling in that company. This is an excellent indicator of how serious the company is in integrating women into the managerial ranks. Some women don't want to be the token, fearing it may be another terminal position. Their concern is with being used to conceal exclusionary practices.

Equal pay for equal work is not yet a reality in campus recruiting policies. The U.S. Department of Labor reports that women are consistently offered lower starting salaries for the same job than are men. In 1970 men received offers averaging $86 a month more than women. In 1971 the difference averaged $68 a month.[5]

Some recruiters are still asking biased interview questions such as the old saws, "How will you be able to combine marriage and a career?" (as though men did not combine them all the time) and, "What will your husband say if you don't get his dinner ready by 6 p.m.?" To ask such questions of women concentrates more on her personal situation than on her capabilities. It implies that her skills are of minor importance to the job and devalues her educational achievements.

Finally, some companies do actively recruit women on the same bases and qualifications as men. We predict this practice will increase sharply, stimulated by Revised Order 4. Personnel managers and recruiters can do a major turn around in their recruiting work when they are backed by solid policy and follow-through. It is vital to establish credibility of serious intent and action over a long period of time

One way to start is by offering equal beginning salaries. The word spreads among students and certain firms will be avoided if actual experience of graduates differs from that represented. Young women are more aware of the sex bias they face. They are not guillible when they feel a solid personal commitment to actively use their education for achieve ment and advancement in their chosen profession.

Executive search and placement agencies

Next, executive search and placement agencies and consulting firms are a rich source for management men, but not for management women. There are few, if any, who will handle women even though this is in violation of Title XII. Head-hunters are caught in the middle: the law requires them to handle persons for whom there has been no market. It's an open invitation to pass the buck.

In Atlanta, for example, the local NOW chapter undertook to desexigrate want ads. In the process they were successful in persuading personnel and executive agencies to insist on sending women applicants for all openings formerly designated as "male" positions. As these agencies made their client companies aware of the legal requirements to do this, more women were considered for higher positions.

Search practices can be reversed. Organizations can easily require their recruitment agencies to search and send women on all job openings they place. When it's necessary for earning their fees, agencies will become primary sources for higher-qualified women of all kinds. They have proselyted before and possess considerable creative talent in generating new sources when they apply their minds to it. Without question, the agency deciding to develop this market will find itself an innovator with a rich potential for new income. The time is ripe!

Some other sources for management women are such or ganizations as the American Association of University Women, the Business and Professional Women's Talent Bank, National Organization for Women, Federally Em

ployed Women, Women's Equity Action League and the Women's Bureau. In Washington, D.C., Washington Opportunities for Women, a private, non-profit organization provides job matchmaking for people in that area. Other large cities have new agencies forming for this purpose, as well as local chapters of women's organizations.*

Recruiting from within

Probably the best source is women currently employed in the organization, especially those who are bumping their heads against the invisible ceiling. Although there may be no *formal* restrictions to keep women from advancing, practice demonstrates clearly that they will go no higher. The rationale for the ceiling goes, "It's never been done before," and "This is not a good time to try it," or "Our customers wouldn't accept it; they expect to do business with a man."[6]

Women at the invisible ceiling may be in executive assistantships, staff or administrative capacities or in various supervisory positions. Many have trained one or more male bosses for the next-level position for which they may be well qualified themselves, but have not been considerd for promotion. Not uncommonly, a less qualified man will be given the promotion and a woman asked to "show him the ropes." Even if a woman holds a position in an acting capacity and is rated excellent in her performance, she seldom gets the promotion permanently. Such women represent a valuable pool of under-used, well-trained, and proven, high-potential management talent.[7]

Problems in assessing and selecting women for management positions

Many men may find it difficult to evaluate the technical and professional competence of women. They may feel they can spot these capabilities and potentials in another man,

*For further sources for management women, including addresses, see *Tools: Information and Sources.*

but doubt their judgment about them in a woman. If the woman is attractive, sexy or appealing, how can he be sure he's evaluating her professional and intellectual capabilities rather than being swayed by her physical appearance? Further, when he is used to women performing only as secretaries or perhaps executive assistants, how can he visualize any woman as a manager? On what basis can he choose a woman over a man with sufficient certainty that he is willing to withstand expected pressures from other men? It may even seem like too much trouble, especially if he suspects this is only the beginning of similar problems.

To mitigate this difficulty, male managers may want to consider thinking through the kind of managerial job to be done and what it takes to do it *before* thinking about the sex of the person to fill it. To be fruitful this process will have to explicitly include envisioning a woman filling the job. Most managers are so used to looking for "the best man for the job" that they rarely hear their own assumption that only a man can qualify. This sex-linked assumption must be questioned each time it appears. For some time to come, it may be necessary to seek "the best woman for the job." Whether it is a woman or a man who is finally selected, this way of thinking the matter through will be more thorough, more certain to make the best selection, as well as helping to minimize sex bias.

Almost no woman would want to be selected for promotion solely because she is a woman. Similarly, it is hard to believe any man would want to be selected solely because he is a man. On the other side of the coin, it's frustrating for any woman to realize she is *not* being promoted solely because she is a woman. Yet many a woman has been forced to that realization and to the realization that men do not have parallel experiences.

Not all women employees with the requisite capabilities are good candidates for managerial positions. Many women are conditioned to think of themselves as wives and mothers first and only secondarily as employees. Those women may

not be ready to become managers. There are ways, however, of spotting a woman with a primary, long-range interest in her career. She is an achieving woman who has:

- A high level of motivation and achievement need
- An identification with a field or profession
- A high degree of individuality
- A strong self-esteem[8]

Recent studies have shown that career-oriented women, more than traditional women, have an experience history and background that contains:

- A working mother who served as a role model
- Strong influence by teachers, professors and people in the chosen profession
- As high school girls, infrequent dating and enjoyment from studying and reading, but dating as much as others in college
- Professionally educated parents with a high socio-economic status from a metropolitan area
- Experience of being out-of-phase; late physical maturity, not belonging to high school cliques, moving frequently.[9]

An achieving woman has more commonly developed from such a background, but this background does not guarantee the development of achievement motivation nor is it the only background in which such motivation can develop. Thus, the sociological factors found in these studies should not be used as selection criteria. Rather, a direct assessment is needed of her character, high tolerance for ambiguity, and plenty of energy and endurance, which she'll need!

Unfortunately, individuality, energy and an outside identification can be seen by an interviewer as indicating a nonconformist and potential trouble-maker. Such a woman does not fit "feminine" expectations. Yet the qualities for managerial functions are not standard female role expectations.

Fear of a "trouble-maker" may be fear of an independent thinker. The interviewer's bias, if any, must be compensated for by using another interviewer who does not share a similar bias.

Assessment centers need to include women among the managerial candidates

Some large companies such as Standard Oil and the Bell System have been using assessment centers for several years to identify men as candidates for management positions. Some of the methods being developed are proving successful in predicting future success among men over a long period of time. Longitudinal studies are being done.[10] The programs had no women involved at their inception. Therefore, there is no assessment center information available today for predicting the success of women in managerial roles. Where there are early identification plans and assessment center programs, it is urgent that women be included now to start building data for identifying future women managers.

One of the key innovators in this field, Douglas Bray, quickly recognizes the difficulty managers have in identifying unrealized potential in men, and how much more difficult it is for women. He comments that "even her own boss may be skeptical about advancing her, since the undemanding nature of many entry jobs for women does not allow for a real demonstration of ability."[11] This is organizational bias, structured into the entry level position system.

Clearly, an objective assessment of ability is needed, not only to persuade men supervising new women managers, but to determine that she actually has the required capabilities. Considerable new work may be needed in this assessment process to take into account the effects of cultural sex bias. The final selection criteria must, of course, be the same for both men and women. But the means to getting there may be quite different. Substantial changes in self-concept can and

do take place in many achieving women. Such changes are less centrally important for men. Cultural expectations for each sex create these differences.

Sponsorship as a means of preparing women for managerial responsibilities

In deciding how to move women ahead in management, employers might examine how men get ahead and compare this with how women are advanced. Social psychologist Dr. Martha White has found one such difference for women in science. Women are left out of the informal sponsorship system through which a young man advances by virtue of being the protege of an older, established person.

"Unfortunately, a man may be hesitant about encouraging a woman as a protege," Dr. White says. "He may be delighted to have her as an assistant, but he may not see her as a colleague. He may believe that she is less likely to be a good gamble, that she is financially less dependent upon a job. Because of subtle pressure from his wife, he may temper his publicly expressed enthusiasm or interest. Furthermore, he may fail to introduce her to colleagues or sponsor her for jobs."[12]

Management-directed women find few women mentors available and it is rare for a man to chose a woman as a protege. This sets up an insidious cycle: women do not advance rapidly in part because they lack the insights and contacts women managers could give them, resulting in very few women managers to serve as mentors for younger aspiring women.

Women executives and managers should be encouraged to take on such a role, *but* it must not be women alone who are made responsible for women.[13] That would insure the future numbers of women in management would remain almost as low as today. Men managers, too, must identify women subordinates who have potential as managers and sponsor them as they would men. In fact, men managers should be

expected by their superiors to coach aspiring women toward managerial preparation, and later sponsor them.

Re-examining relevancy of past experience can prove fruitful

For the mature woman with some relevant experience, the career ladder should be open for entry or re-entry at the most appropriate rung instead of automatically starting at the bottom. Positions which provide equivalent development experience but are not now considered part of the management development sequence should be reconsidered for their relevant value. For example, a mature woman's community experience may have been extensive in budget and finance, personnel, coordination and planning. Some few organizations now recognize such experience on their personnel forms, and in hiring, placement and training decisions. Indeed, social agency experience at the board or committee chairman level is highly comparable to some middle and upper management positions of small and medium-size profit organizations. Or, complex political campaign administration can require similar capabilities as are needed for certain middle management and staff positions. Finally, most difficult to subjectively identify are latent "natural" capabilities that come into use in the challenge of increased responsibilities. Objective assessment methods are needed to assist managers in these choices.

Because most women's life-styles are different from most men's does not automatically make them less valuable—only different. Relevant experience can be garnered from many sources. Any other assumption could produce biased effects.

Awareness training is a new idea in changing the climate

Awareness training is a new concept developing with women's affirmative action programs. There are at least three kinds worth considering:

1. Management awareness of cultural bias and sex-role expectations that prevail in the organization and in attitudes of managers at all levels.
2. Women's awareness of their perception of themselves in their career development objectives and considering many new alternatives. For those women who are already aware, the next phase is coping with change in reaching their new objectives, including their part in changing the stereotypic expectations they may face and their responses to them.
3. Men's awareness of what it means to them to be involved in many new working relationships with women as colleagues and sometimes superiors. Changes in women's roles as they move up in managerial expertise will certainly impact men's roles and responses as managers.

Among management training and development people, there is considerable interest as well as concern about such programs and how they should be conducted. Without question, the subject of sex factors in employment, especially management, is potentially volatile in today's climate of active feminism. Polarization between the sexes is just one of many long-buried attitudes that may surface with some intensity as these changes are explored. Objective recognition of the sub-rosa attitudes can greatly facilitate their being handled or resolved. While certain behaviors are now illegal, attitudes are personal even though some may be less than generally acceptable. In awareness training, changing standards of acceptability are also explored.

Films, discussion, role-reversal are tools for awareness training

Many new tools for conducting awareness training are currently being developed. Films, discussions, experiences in role-reversal situations are among the early developments. One film, *51%* is valuable in opening up discussion and

awareness in managements where the subject is new. It presents three women from different experiential and educational backgrounds, through whom the changing roles of women are played. Viewers see how their attitudes and actions can change the work situation to help reduce barriers to using women's potential for management. It treats the subject generally and is useful as an opener to awareness.

A new film, *Women: Up the Career Ladder*, which this book's authors cooperatively designed and produced, goes into work patterns and feelings more deeply. Eight women discuss and cope with their own real problems and possible solutions. Employee follow-up discussion of the various issues in the film usually brings to the surface responses which reveal more underlying expectations that men and women have for each other. It has been used variously: with groups of women only, with mixed groups, with management levels, or with only middle and lower supervision levels.

The Civil Service Commission has an excellent film, *What's the Matter with Alice?* that focuses on those attitudes around a minority woman that can limit her advancement and full use of her education. The process of non-conscious discouragement and non-communication is clearly portrayed and insightfully done.

A variety of pencil-paper tools and awareness readings are also being developed which bring to the surface some of the attitudes that carry a double standard or reflect cultural expectations.

Self-concept inventories are being developed to give persons taking them some insights on how they see themselves and their aspirations in a context of sex-roles. Some of these may develop into new selection tools for management development.*

It is our feeling that management awareness training of the first type should be done with all managers and supervisors as one of the first implementation steps of an affirma-

*For sources of films and other awareness materials, see *Tools: Information and Sources.*

tive action program. The other two types can best be handled as a part of the regular management development program, first on a separate-sex basis, then together. Various task exercises can be used that involve a "trading of expectations" between groups. Many such training tools have already been developed for use in minority awareness programs, as well as in resolving interdepartmental conflicts. With appropriate modifications to fit the subject of sex-role bias, there are a number of useful communication exercises and team-task projects that can be adapted. Care needs to be taken that they accomplish the purpose intended. Review by the women's affirmative action officer is vital before using them in training situations.

This initial awareness training attempts to activate required behavior changes and begins to develop an awareness of attitudes that take longer to perceive.

Management development implications for women—and men

A woman can't become a good manager without appropriate training any more than a man can. She must develop her skills by moving into progressively more responsible positions where she can use her capabilities and be held accountable for the results. She also needs to attend the same management and supervisory training programs available to similarly qualified men. In addition, some women working in a male-valued environment may need training programs that deal with new working relationships with men. And certainly men may need to reconsider their old attitudes about a woman when she, formerly a subordinate, becomes a peer.

As noted above, a good assessment program is essential to be able to objectively measure both women and men in their management capability, progress and advancement potential. Objectivity needs to prevail, whether it's a small-scale program, or a major management assessment center program.

In the first phase of management development, basic man-

agerial skills need to be emphasized and provision made for advance preparation in weak areas. Key processes, that all managers must have a good grasp of, should be defined by the organization and would include such items as:

- Having the ability to develop goals and objectives
- Being able to build a plan to implement these goals interrelating them with others
- Capable of effective communications, especially with people but also written and formal presentations
- Able to resolve or balance conflicts between work, interests and people
- Good at problem solving in all its phases, with work processes and people problems
- Balanced decision-making, carefully weighing the important elements and generally using good judgment
- Able to determine priorities with flexibility, to change as needed, and stick with them when necessary

Undoubtedly there are others considered essential in some places and not in others. In addition to this general managerial ability list, there usually are further areas that the new woman manager may want or need in her personal development. Moving from subordinancy and relative powerlessness into a position of a different kind of subordinancy with possession of some power can present a woman manager with many new questions. The initial bridge, with open discussion of concerns and alternatives, can be critical at this stage of development for some women. Certainly not all will find this change difficult.

It is later, when moving from middle management into higher management that many successful women have experienced some identity crises and have broken through the competence-femininity conflict into a "fully-functioning person" self-concept.[14] Early awareness of these double-binds can help resolve them before they reach high conflict proportions.

The focus here is on some of the male-female dimensions of management development. It is assumed that the qualifica-

tions educationally and technically are present, or being developed in preparation for management development. If the organization is under pressure to have more women in management training, they may feel a need to select a woman who is not ready for such training. If this is the case, it is essential that she be given sufficient preparatory training to give her a basis for additional management training work. When both are done simultaneously, the added pressure on the woman must be taken into consideration when evaluating her achievements.

To knowingly select a person who is underqualified without giving the essential support for probable success is a waste of time and effort on the part of the organization and the woman trainee. It will be better to take more preparatory time and adjust the timetable for accomplishing an increase in the number of women in management training. However, it will be necessary to convince most compliance officers that any delay is not, in fact, lack of good faith. Objective evidence of the need to delay management training pending further preparatory training may be required. Surely some indication that such training is in process is essential. The pressures for promotion will undoubtedly increase as affirmative action programs are implemented.

Promotion is where the barriers based on sex become most apparent

Often the very structure of an organization makes it almost impossible for a woman to be promoted. Male managers may be quite willing to promote women, yet find it impossible as long as they follow company rules and policies. Sex-segregated jobs make it difficult for women to achieve promotion because managerial positions in such an organization typically require "male" jobs as prerequisites. The EEOC's investigators have found this to be the case in several companies.[15]

Seniority, in some companies, may be a barrier to women's advancement. When seniority is considered to be total time spent working for the company, women are considered equally. But when seniority is based on time spent in a department and potential managers come only from male-dominated departments, it works against women. Further, if women lose seniority because of maternity breaks in employment, they suffer a sex-linked, discriminatory disadvantage. Seniority rules of that kind are now in violation of the law. Career ladders with vertical and lateral transfers must be developed to provide ways for women to move out of the traditional pattern of dominating the lower job categories. Long-term improvement hinges on there being known ways to advance within the organization. This fact must be made credible by evidence of women having been promoted from within.

Where women are being introduced for the first time into a particular management level or into an all-male work-unit, consideration must be given to the best way to introduce such change. Tokenism with its deleterious effects should be avoided if at all possible. One way to avoid it is to bring more than one woman into previously all-male positions or work units. Women coming into higher responsibilities may need some preparation for coping with being pioneers. Certainly the men in the all-male climate may need some preparation for coping with this change.

As one training officer of a major electrical company said, "Our men have gotten their early education in all-male classes, often studied at male institutions, have worked in and been promoted to positions where only men work, and now our management is all male. They just don't know what to do with the idea of working with women as co-professionals." Too often this is the stark reality of long-standing cultural bias. This group will need awareness training, probably of the introductory kind as well as in more operational depth.

Peripheral practices and policies affect the success of affirmative action for women

In many organizations employees of either sex have only a vague idea of how promotions are made, but it is often more so for women. If sex-typing of jobs is pervasive in an organization, women may not even realize they have a right to ask for promotion to positions traditionally held by men. If women are to be promoted, it is critical that they are aware of their eligibility to apply for such positions. As the openings arise, they should be posted with women being encouraged to apply. Standards and requirements for promotion need to be studied from the point of view of the need for the present standards and whether or not they contain inadvertent sex-bias or organizational bias.

Child care

To improve the opportunities for recruitment, training and promotion of women, many organizations are considering provision of child care facilities. An affirmative action survey can provide facts for management regarding the number of women and men who have children in need of day care. Often day care can be financed jointly by the organization and parents. Some centers get help from government funds. A number of day care centers are already being successfully operated by corporations. Skyland Textile Company of Morgantown, North Carolina finds employee turnover down 25 percent since their center opened.[16] Increased stability of younger women, plus credible training programs in which they are encouraged to participate can increase the pool of women as potential managers in a major way.

Travel and moving requirements

Travel and moving requirements need to be rethought. Is mobility really essential to managerial positions in a given organization? Which ones? To learn what? Can it be learned

any other way? How important is this learning? Or are some of these prerequisites effectively eliminating most women and some men candidates when it may not be truly important? Policies such as these are being reconsidered in many organizations, partly because of possible barriers to women's advancement. Many men are becoming less willing to uproot their lives unless it is critically important.

Insurance

Insurance policies should be reviewed for possible bias. Many provide benefits unequally distributed, as well as carrying differential premiums. Many insurance companies are reviewing these practices themselves.

Retirement plans

Retirement plans have differential aspects. Many still allow women to retire at age 62 or later, but require men to wait until age 65. This is discriminatory against men. The options should be equalized for both sexes. Women often live longer than men, so it seems equitable to provide for them to work as long as men for their retirement benefits.

Maternity and paternity leave

Maternity and paternity leaves need to be integrated with other leave policies. Many companies now treat these separately from sick and leave plans, usually to the detriment of women. Many women now moving into management positions may not be seriously affected by these policies. But they can make a substantial difference to those women who would like to develop a career plan in the organization but know they will be penalized for maternity breaks. New revisions of the law require that disabilities caused by pregnancy, miscarriage, abortion and childbirth and recovery be treated as temporary disabilities consistent with other health or disability insurance and sick leave plans.[17]

Evaluating women's affirmative action plans by feminist criteria

One women's rights organization, the National Organization for Women, has developed guidelines to evaluate affirmative action plans for compliance with the laws and regulations. Those relevant to moving women into management are:

- Who in your company has the overall responsibility for reporting on and monitoring affirmative action plans?
- What are the numbers and percentages of women in each job category in your company? In each work-unit?
- What training programs have you instituted to upgrade the job opportunities of women?
- What goals, timetables, and commitments have you established to correct identifiable deficiencies in the employment of women? How were these goals determined? To what degree have these goals, timetables, and commitments been attained?
- What means have you taken to internally and externally disseminate a policy of equal employment opportunity for women? How have you publicized your employment policy? What evidence have you that executives, management, and supervisory personnel understand the policy and their individual responsibility for implementing it?
- Which local and national community action programs concerned with improving the employment opportunities of women are you actively supporting? Have you informed these organizations of your employment policies? Have you solicited the help of these women's groups in recruiting?
- What action have you taken to recruit women not currently in the workforce but having requisite skills?
- What are your promotion principles and have they been examined to insure only valid requirements are being imposed?
- How many women (number and percent) participate in company sponsored training, education, tuition assistance programs? How does it compare with men?

- How was your selection process reviewed to eliminate sex discrimination? What are the processes of validation for tests as selectors for positions in your company? Do pre-employment forms illegally request sex and/or marital status of applicant? What provisions have been made to insure all personnel involved in recruiting, screening, selection, and promotion are free of sex bias?
- How were all subcontractors, vendors, and suppliers of your company notified of your equal employment opportunity policy?
- Do ghetto departments (all male or all female) exist in your company?
- Do you insert advertising for jobs under heading "male *and* female" help wanted? Do you advertise job listings in women's interest media?
  What provision is made for child care for employee's children by your company?[18]

Potential new developments resulting from affirmative action for women

As affirmative action programs for women have wider effects with larger numbers of women at all levels of management, new challenges are likely to occur. Some of these might well be . . .

- Developing new ways to conduct training and development, especially where it includes male-female peer-managers. New ways to bring about behavior and attitudinal changes will be explored.
- Studying the effects of prevailing male values in the typical organization, questioning, reviewing possible alternatives.
- Discovering ways that men and women are similar in the human dimensions of games-playing, fears, defenses, double-binds . . .
- New channeling of the decision-making that occurs solely among males at the golf-course, the poker game, and in clubs and bars that exclude women . . .

- New ways to qualify women for some kinds of management positions; alternatives to degree requirements.
- Studying motivation and commitment in women and men, how it is changing, and what this may mean for developing managers.

If the movement of women into new management roles is done in an orderly, well-conceived manner on an organization-wide basis over several years, the credibility of management's "good faith" and the credibility of women as managers will be valuable new facts of organization life.

Ask yourself—
- What do I know about the attitudes of women in my organization? Of the men?
- What criteria do I use for selecting people to be moved upward? How far would I be willing to sponsor a woman who I felt could do the job?
- Who in my organization would be best suited to begin implementing an affirmative action program? Would an advisory committee help the program director?
- What ways would be most appropriate for stimulating awareness of attitudes in my organization? Why?

Notes

1. Excerpted from "Affirmative Action Programs for Women: Requirements and Recommendations," Womanpower Consultants, Berkeley, CA 94703. October 1, 1971, p. 3.
2. *Ibid.*, pp. 3–4.
3. Bird, Caroline, *Born Female: The High Cost of Keeping Women Down*, New York: Pocket Books, 1st printing, May, 1969, pp. 43–44.
4. Orth, Charles D., and Frederick Jacobs, "Women in Management: Pattern for Change," *Harvard Business Review*, July–August, 1971, p. 144.
5. *Fact Sheet on the Earnings Gap*, U.S. Department of Labor, Employment Standards Administration, Women's Bureau, December, 1971 (rev.), p. 5.
6. Wells, Theodora, "Woman's Self-Concept: Implications for Management Development," Chapter in Gordon L. Lippitt, Leslie E. This,

and Robert G. Bidwell, Jr. (Eds.), *Optimizing Human Resources*, Reading, Mass.: Addison-Wesley Publishing Co., 1971, p. 303.

7. *Ibid.* p. 304.

8. Summarized from McCord, Bird, "Identifying and Developing Women for Management Position," *Training and Development Journal*, November, 1971, p. 4.

9. "How Are Career-Oriented Women Different," *Capsule* (published by ERIC Counseling and Personnel Services Information Center, Ann Arbor, Michigan 48104). Spring, 1971, p. 10.

  The article is a summary of three recent research studies comparing "college women who chose conventional career goals with those who chose unconventional career goals (an occupation which is now dominated by men)." The studies are:

  (1) Almquist, Elizabeth M., and Angrist, Shirley I., "Career Choice Salience and Atypicality of Occupational Choice Among College Women, *Journal of Marriage and the Family*, 1970, 32(2), pp. 242–248.

  (2) Tangri, Florence S., "Role Innovation in Occupational Choice Among College Women," Michigan University, 1969.

  (3) Walshok, Mary L., "The Social Correlated and Sexual Consequences of Variations in Gender Role Orientation: A National Study of College Students," Indiana University, 1969.

10. Byham, William C., "Assessment Centers for Spotting Future Managers," *Harvard Business Review*, July–August, 1970, pp. 150–160.

11. Bray, Douglas M., "The Assessment Center: Opportunities for Women," *Personnel*, Sept.–Oct., 1971, p. 31.

12. White, Martha S., "Psychological and Social Barriers to Women in Science," *Science*, October 23, 1970, p. 414.

13. Orth and Jacobs, *op. cit.*, pp. 145–146.

14. Hennig, Margaret, "What Happens on the Way Up," *The MBA*, March, 1971, p. 10. This article is a summary of her dissertation research for her DBA from Harvard, entitled "Career Development for Women Executives."

15. For an example of a thorough analysis of how this allegedly operates in the Bell System, see "A Unique Competence," Equal Employment Opportunity Commission, Washington, D.C.

16. Orth and Jacobs, *op. cit.*, p. 145.

17. Title 29, Chapter XIV, Part 1604, "Guidelines on Discrimination Because of Sex," published in the *Federal Register*, Vol. 37, No. 66, Wednesday, April 5, 1972, effective immediately.

18. For a complete list see "Guidelines on Questions to be Used in Evaluating Affirmative Action Plans," available from the National Organization for Women, 1957 East 73rd St., Chicago, Illinois 60649.

4

Managerial Climate

"All organizations begin with a formal structure designed to achieve their core activities. To date, all the structures designed have been inadequate in their ability to capitalize on human potentialities."

Chris Argyris[1]

The inability Argyris spoke of will have great implications for women in the next decade as Revised Order No. 4 becomes the standard pattern for federal contractors, and subsequently for other organizations. The traditional under-utilization of women's capabilities, as well as the practice of using women as a labor pool on a last-in, first-out basis, will no longer be acceptable policy for most large organizations. The high visibility of women in management will make it particularly important for top managements to use well the female management resources they have.

Difference between public behavior and private attitudes affects change; experience of men working with women as peers affects climate

As we have seen, it is quite possible to order certain behavior changes and have these orders complied with. Correct public behavior and official stances can be assumed by most people even when they don't personally believe in the requirement. Managers and supervisors who have orders to hire specific numbers of women in new higher level positions may do it with an attitude of seriously working with the change

and giving it thoughtful, consistent support. Others may do it with attitudes ranging from reluctance to resistance, or even resentment and hostility.

When the difference between public behavior and private attitudes is great enough, a motive to covertly follow the private attitude becomes active. As long as the feeling does not surface to overt behavior that can be identified as "against orders," some managers will effectively undermine and close out the newly-added women from being effective. Creating a subtly hostile climate, expecting and perhaps arranging for failure, a manager could well find it possible to evaluate the woman as ineffective. This, of course, is poor use of resources while it's occurring, and undermines the goals required by the organization. It's costly, whether it's done consciously or non-consciously.

One important element in attitude change is men's new experience of working with women as peer-managers. Relatively few men have done this, but those who have usually change their attitudes about it—favorably. With that change, women managers also change the climate. Once a woman manager establishes her competence, character and credibility, she can and does influence many attitudes. For example, she may contribute to more frankness and trust in the decision-making processes if she tries to minimize gaming in her personal style.

Considerations in changing male-valued climates

Confronted with the need to change behaviors and attitudes about women in management, top management's approach will depend upon a number of factors:

- the nature of the confrontation that makes change necessary
- the prevailing climate in the organization
- the top manager's tendency toward authoritative or participative style of managing

· patterns of management typical within the industry or field
• numbers of women employed relative to total employees
• previous experience with women in responsible positions
• assumptions about what motivates people, including the differences and similarities about what motivates women as compared with men
• underlying pervasive values and beliefs about people, groups, the organization and the importance of change

Organizational climate affects progress of women as managers

In predicting the degree and type of change likely to occur in an organization with a program designed to move women into and upward in management positions, we need an over-all look at different kinds of organizational climate that are created by different management expectations. We can expect that . . .

I. *The more rigid and traditional the sex-role expectations the more authoritarian the climate.*
The more acceptance of women as individuals, as people, the more egalitarian the climate.
II. *The more authoritarian the climate, the more likely will women be found in low-pay, low-skill jobs, with fewer women at management levels above first-line, with those few being primarily in staff positions.*
The more egalitarian the climate, the more likely will women be found participating in a wide range of positions at management decision-making levels.

Given the first two expectations, the probable impact of externally imposed affirmative action for women suggests these additional predictions:

III. *To comply with new laws, executive orders and court decisions, top management may find affirmative action programs for women need to be authoritarian in order to accomplish rapid behavioral change.*

IV. *Such authoritarian methods will probably meet with passive resistance, slow erosion of gains or outright subversion of company policy unless management also undertakes a program intended to change attitudes.*

- The training for such attitude changes is likely to produce styles that are more consultative or participatory.
- If top management clearly intends to stay with its affirmative action policy and subordinates believe this, they will tend to change their attitudes as they have both more contact with women in their new positions and a strong model of change.

We believe that in defining the organizational climate these formulations can serve managers as a basis for predicting: where difficulties will occur; where maneuverability is possible; the kind and depth of change in attitudes and behavior that may occur; the degree of opportunity both short-term and long-term that women will have to advance in management.

There have been many ways of describing organizational climate. Rensis Likert's system has been particularly helpful in thinking about management engendered climates as they impact the potential for change.[2] However, for the purpose of defining the organizational climate most adaptive to moving women through the organization, we propose these modifications:

1. *Exploitative:* maximum *use* of people with minimum concern for their needs.
2. *Paternalistic:* the top person (Father) knows what's good for people, and keeps the prerogative to decide.
3. *Consultative:* people, both men and women, are encouraged to contribute and be taken seriously. Decision-making is centrally held but consideration is given to the experience and expertise of those people near the function involved.
4. *Egalitarian:* each according to his *or her* abilities in organizational processes. Both women and men have more

impact through using their competence and creativity, participating in decision-making which is diffused throughout the organization: more coordinated than controlled at the top.

These general organizational climates, when defined in depth, bring to light silent management philosophy and behavior, implicit assumptions about what people are like and the inevitable results that follow. Obviously, subordinates respond differently in each climate, especially women managers. They may find their scope of activities limited, or their growth potential depending on their ability to influence their working environment.

Exploitative climate requires obedience

The exploitative climate expectations for all employees are the same as are widely held for female sex-role behavior: passive, dependent, subordinate. Both men and women are implicitly expected to function at an immature level, one which is considered normal for women. Thus, men managers often feel subservient and somewhat hostile. Uninvolved in responsibility for decision-making, they get little satisfaction from their jobs and sometimes quietly work at cross-purposes with authority in order to feel some power over their own circumstances.

Women managers are seldom found in such a climate. Here the expectations are already so low for men managers, that women are most likely to be found in the traditional sex-typed jobs, performing low skill functions and earning low pay. Management's expectations for their desired behavior are that they be quiet, respectful, well-behaved and obedient; punctual, non-articulate, honest and trustworthy, and of course, efficient.

In this climate, the primary concern is to "not make waves" with a concomitant concern for protecting one's own position. Power is recognized as belonging to management by

virtue of position rather than problem-solving ability. Therefore, conformity and acquiescence are encouraged and, "at
the upper levels, subordinates tend to 'think positive' . . . they
react primarily to crises; they tend to create win-lose com-
petitions between groups; they hide information; and they
create 'just-in-case-the-president-asks' files."[3] Rationalized as
part of unchangeable human nature, their pessimistic evaluation about human nature becomes a self-fulfilling prophecy.
Expectations motivate.

Top management may use the ideas and technical knowledge of subordinates, while giving little or no credence to
their sense of responsibility, their ability to make decisions,
their commitment to organizational goals, or their concern
with exercising controls over the processes of the work of the
organization. Therefore subordinates are seen as though they
cannot be counted upon to concern themselves with the profit
ability of the organization.

With security being assumed as the prime motivator of
people, the assumptions of McGregor's Theory X tend to
prevail: the average person inherently dislikes work and will
seek to avoid it; therefore, people must be coerced, con
trolled, directed and threatened with punishment to get them
to give adequate effort. It is assumed that people prefer to
be directed, do not want responsibility and have little ambition.[4] The locus of authority, responsibility and discipline is
in management's hands: the "prerogatives" of management.
These prerogatives include "the right to command," "the
recognized right to direct subordinates," "subordinates are to
respond to orders in all organized activities." The authoritarian style assumes that since subordinates are expected to perform adequately, to do so is no basis for reward. Rewards
should be used to "elicit superior performance, innovation
and creativity . . . subordinates who do not conform to normal expectations are punished . . . those who do not respond
to rewards menace those who do . . ."[5]

Argyris describes the people who can survive this formal,
authoritarian climate as childlike rather than adult, noting,

"In effect . . . organizations are willing to pay high wages and provide adequate seniority if mature adults will, for eight hours a day, behave in a less than mature manner."[6] In such a climate, managers are treated as not-very-bright employees and, with the self-fulfilling prophecy working predictably, will come to behave as expected. Survival.

Managers who have difficulty in understanding the politics of passivity to which most women are subjected have only to recall when they themselves have been in these organizational situations where they felt hemmed in, somewhat helpless and with a decreased sense of responsibility. Men and women often share the experience of making decisions in the name of a superior; women as administrative assistants or as "assistants to . . ."; men as managers with little influence of their own.

Most people have a tendency to withdraw or to become dependent on those with power over them. They tend to defer to the boss who gives the performance review. They resort to using their "long and successful education in organizational survival, where they learn deceit, manipulation, rivalry, and mistrust—qualities endemic to our present organizational structures."[7] The very qualities that are often attributed to women *because they are women*, are widely demonstrated by men in organizational climates that require dependency and passivity from them. Men often respond out of a deeply-ingrained training to obedience to high authority and a sense of duty. This can emanate from the ideal of service to country, a patriotic duty to sacrifice for the larger good. In this Spartan ideal, it becomes a matter of honor to acquiese to command authority. The behavior becomes dependent, passive, unquestioning obedience. Obviously, these patterns are not sex-linked; they're subordinancy-linked.

Paternalistic climate requires deference

In benevolent authoritarian organizations, women may have the opportunity to rise into first or second-level man-

agement positions. The invisible ceiling typically operates at the first level, with a few exceptional women at the second level. They may become "managerial drudges." Rarely do women get higher in this climate, unless she is someone who started with the company at its inception and is retained due to exceptional knowledge of internal politics and influence or from a long-standing personal loyalty. The benevolent stance gets expressed with comments such as, "Oh yes, we have a woman personnel director. She is really good, does quite well, participates in executive benefits . . ." (Implication: She's good—for a woman.) She is often the token woman to whom management can point to "prove their innocence" of sex-bias.

Most of the management positions open to women in this climate are staff positions; coordinating functions; trouble-shooting assignments, personnel and training functions, customer and public relations activities, and research roles. Line positions held by women are most frequently in selected departments, such as accounting and computer-related functions. There is usually heavy emphasis on technical excellence and many of these positions are "terminal" management positions for women: they are not avenues to continued advancement. In *numbers* of such positions for women, these patriarchal organizations often see themselves as non-discriminatory. In *advancement potential*, the old patterns persist. Positions remain sex-typed, but sometimes women are allowed to rise to a slightly higher level.

Top managers who create this kind of climate operate from modified versions of the exploitative assumptions of what people are like. They feel that they know what's best for the organization and the people within it. They feel the responsibility to see that subordinates conform to their "one right way." They are more gracious in their personnel relationships and therefore expect subordinates to be grateful if and when they are included in decision-making or sharing of information. Occasional involvement in these processes is usually an attempt to motivate subordinates by providing a focus for them—a goal. This goal, presented as mutually determined

while being graciously imposed, is then used to prod for immediate action. An authoritarian president of a large manufacturing firm had the habit of pounding his fist to palm, prodding with an enthusiastic "Go, go, go." The pressure set up a tension in the subordinates that was relaxed only when the goal was reached. Then the process was repeated and would go on, as one writer graphically put it, "so long as one fly after another goes on landing on man's rump to stir up some new need to force him to go on swishing his tail."[8]

This fly-on-the-rump theory moves the locus of motivation more inward and self-determining than the carrot-and-stick theory of the exploitative climate. However, it still assumes that subordinates behave like children. It is a paternalistic stance.

Some men managers and many women managers find this dependency reassuring and comfortable and remain satisfied with meeting top management's expectations and receiving its rewards.

Managers are inclined to be "yes-men or yes-women" willing to pass-the-buck, protective of their positions, competitive in their relationships, and showing some resistance that is reinforced by tacit agreement with other subordinate managers. There is usually an active grapevine which serves as an important source of information not officially dispensed from above. Fragments are pieced together for the benefit of those managers who are trusted within the grapevine circuit, there being a self-preservation interest in collaboration. A strange mixture of competition and collaboration co-exists where there is the "common enemy" of top management combined with the need to curry their favor. This tends to keep managers off-balance, never quite knowing where they stand, and encouraging aggressive competitivenes to counterbalance the tension. Some particularly vicious infighting can occur in this climate.

On the other hand, sufficient benevolence from the top can generate enough loyalty and appreciation that viciousness remains dormant. Managers become expert in reading the

pecking order, hoping to exploit opportunities for favorable visibility—"to make points." Often a great deal of energy is expended in elaborate, creative strategies to achieve personal goals. Through a climate of comparatively high fear and low trust, top management thus contributes to organization-defeating behavior from its people.

Some managers, both men and women, find this dependency reassuring and comfortable. They remain satisfied with meeting top management's expectations and disdain vicious competition. These are the "managerial drudges, who are essential to any corporation and may even be called its operational backbone—victims of the Protestant Ethic. Their entire goal is to perform their assigned tasks in an exemplary manner and according to formal corporate expectations."[9]

For women, at least, this acceptance of dependency contains far less risk when the position is highly valued by them, and frequently is only a repetition of previous life experiences. However, more and more outstanding women have moved beyond "conditioned opposition" and are prepared to deal with the tasks of leadership as fully-functioning managers.

The game-playing required in this environment is increasingly disliked by women who prefer *not* to play manipulative roles. The risk for women is greatest here for management of this type is unfamiliar and unaccustomed to newer patterns of relationships. The risk for management is the discovery that the goal (the "fly") is to allow subordinates to be themselves.

Consultative climate requires involvement

In organizations where more trust contributes to a consultative climate, there is likely to be an attendant attitude of perceiving women more as persons, less as stereotypes. There is no indication that the *number* of women in first and second-level management is significantly different, nor that the *advancement potential* is improved in any major way.

But the needs for recognition, self-esteem, of contributing to the development of the organization's processes, and confirmation of self-worth in working relationships are met to a greater degree. These satisfactions are, of course, not limited to women in the consultative climate. But it makes the invisible ceiling for women less galling, more tolerable. At least *some* higher-level needs can be satisfied to an extent which, for most women, is a comparatively rare experience.

This is the most trusting of the authoritative styles, creating an organizational climate where considerably more confidence to contribute something of value is placed in subordinates. Ideas are valued more; there is less punishment for mistakes or non-conformity; communications are exchanged more freely and with greater accuracy; more delegation stays delegated; and subordinate managers participate in more teamwork. Although broad policy is still made at the top, there is deeper involvement in the formulation and implementation of policy by those who have technical or professional knowledge. Nonetheless, control remains firmly in the hands of those at the top. Middle-level managers share some feeling of responsibility, of being "in" on things, and of having the confidence of top management. Executives are more willing to give room for self-direction, and to find commitment to organizational goals believable.

This climate, again reflecting top management's philosophy, expects more mature behavior from subordinates, in the direction of McGregor's Theory Y: expenditure of effort in work is natural; people will exercise self-direction and self-control where they feel personal commitment to goals; such commitment to goals is a function of satisfactions derived from achieving their goals; people will accept and go after responsibility, given the right climate; capacities for imagination and creativity in solving organizational problems are widely distributed, not limited to a select few; but, under the conditions of today's industrial life, there is only partial utilization of the intellectual potentialities of the average person.[10]

This is not sex-linked behavior; it fits women as well as men. The use of brain, muscle and heart is as vital to the female of the species as to the male.

While it is easier to integrate women into the managerial network in this climate, they are still seen as women first and managers second. They may enjoy more respect and be sought out for their viewpoints, as are the men, but they are limited as to how far they can rise in the managerial-exective suites. While they can derive important satisfactions in this climate for many years, their tolerance for an invisible ceiling may become less.

Educated women (those most likely to become managers in an increasingly technological world) work for the same reason as do educated men—fulfillment through the challenge and satisfaction of investment of self in the task—plus money.

Egalitarian climate invites participation

In a participatory climate the most productive inputs from women as well as men are likely to occur. Individual competence tends to supersede sex-role expectations. Top management expects, and more often gets, committed effort and continuing growth from their people. They believe in them. Dependence on formal authority is not necessary when top management can place deep confidence in subordinates. Treating subordinates as peers, because their professional or technical competence is valued, makes possible the formation and implementation of goals and policies throughout all levels of the organization. The goals established for organizational projects are usually well matched with the personal goals of the individuals involved. Because lower-level managers and subordinates are involved in the planning and implementation of organizational policies, they have a personal commitment to achieving them. This commitment accepts challenges to more problem-solving, more teamwork, more collaboration in the interest of the overall objectives. Simul-

taneously, personal worth is reinforced, valued and encouraged. Resistance is minimal; information flows quite freely, the confidence level is high. The feeling of involvement is among the rewards of the effort.

Confidence is placed in people on the assumption that they have strengths they want to exercise in concert. "What's good for the company is good for its people" no longer reveals a paternalistic platitude to manipulate people to work solely for company goals. Why? Because the reverse is *also* happening, "What's good for its people is good for the company." Self-interest and organization-interest interlink; dependency upon power is replaced by interdependency between strengths. Loyalty is freely given because it is authentically present, not because "that's what a good employee does." Personal security is no longer derived from outside one's self but from within. Paradoxically, as a person's need for security from the organization lessens, the desire to participate in it increases.

As needs for personal security in both the economic and social senses are satisfied, the needs related to self-esteem become more motivating—needs for self-confidence, independence, achievement, competence and knowledge. Developing a competence that gains recognition, appreciation and deserved respect along with commensurate status and rewards comes into play. These needs, as well as those of self-fulfillment, can be best satisfied in the egalitarian climate. The management philosophy of Greenewalt when at DuPont, suggests this same combination in his two success principles: "First, the realization that an enterprise will succeed only to the extent that all individuals associated with it can be encouraged to exercise their highest talents in their own particular ways. Second, the provision of maximum incentives for achievement, particularly in associating the fortunes of the individual with that of the corporation."[11]

In such an environment, women are more easily perceived as individual contributors, function as part of a group in which they are expected to perform from their capability

base. In this climate, it is possible for women to be located in any position within the organization, including managerial and other decision-making roles and supervision of men as well as women. When intelligence and creativity rather than sex-roles determine tasks and responsibilities, the range for diversification is wide indeed. Since much research by Eleanor Maccoby and other psychologists has documented repeatedly that these qualities are not sex-linked, new ways of formulating qualifications and selecting people must be developed so that women as well as men can move in the direction of this mutually rewarding system.

Climates vary within an organization

Even though every organization seems to have its characteristic climate, some individuals in it may function differently and relatively autonomously from the main style of the organization. For example, in an egalitarian, or even a consultative climate, it is quite possible to find an exploitative manager. Frequently a manager becomes so dependent on a woman assistant that there is "never any time" for her to get additional training to prepare for the next step forward. This demand, although it entails under-utilization, provides that manager with uninterrupted assistance. Surrounding departments, more in tune with the climate, may be allocating time to sending women to training programs thereby seeking longer range benefits.

On the other hand, it is possible in a paternalistic organization for a few executives to play a buffer role between the authoritarian expectations of other top executives, and the urge-to-grow motivations in lower-level managers. As the buffer manager functions within the top management group, he sensitively selects the time to suggest, "Well, let's ask Mary what she thinks—she's supposed to be our expert." Or he proposes, "I don't really want to get into all those questions—that's what we have market research for. Jane, how about your people (the Marketing Research Manager is asked)

coming up with some recommendations?" Sometimes these suggestions will be quickly accepted, other times ignored or rejected. But the buffer executive keeps sensing when he can involve others. He helps create a supportive climate in which men and women alike can maintain their sense of personal worth and importance. His strength is in his flexibility. His pragmatic sense of "what's possible," is combined with an attitude of utilizing strengths in others, including women, without drawing pressure from men associates. The buffer executive can just as easily be a woman of maturity, serving as an "intuitive integrator" of available human resources balanced with strategies of timing.

Climates vary under different economic conditions

The management climate also varies from time to time. Let's assume that an organization faces the need to regroup for survival; to reduce costs, "tighten the belt," and maintain most of its share of the market. Over the short-term, productivity can increase under heavily authoritarian operations. But, typically this action is an overreaction. When financial concerns lead to rigidly imposed line-by-line expense cutting, arbitrary layoffs are made, and memos to employees berate personal telephone calls and too-long coffee breaks. Resistance sets in. The grapevine becomes highly active, with morale sliding downhill. Rebuilding confidence will take a long time—a process that can be avoided with a cooler reaction.

A quickly reacting management will shift away from the authoritarian stance, declaring management's need for their employees' help in the shared need to survive and grow again. Ideas and involvement from among the organization's people will be solicited This is the rallying-call that brings out the best in strong people though it may send the less sure job-hunting.

Climates must become freer to respond to societal changes in work values

If change were slow-paced, institutions and businesses could take pride in long-held traditions and in decisions based on precedent. In our ever-faster-moving society, tradition and precedent are re-examined constantly in the light of new conditions with awareness that people and organizations must change along with society. Many organizations are changing because they see better possibilities for growth or even just survival. Some are changing under pressure by outsiders—government, consumer groups, environmentalists and civil rights organizations.

Bureaucracy works best in managing the routine and predictable with great reliability. As a system, it is not so well equipped for the rapid changes of today or the expected, more frequent changes of the future. Moreover, the large growth in size of organizations has meant a loss of human scale in which individual employees could retain their identity and sense of purpose. We predict that managers who made it the hard way (along with their organizations) will find it requires strenuous effort to change their style and learn to cope with the unfamiliar collaboration of women managers. For women's contribution historically has been concern for human affairs, the soft way—a quality they are not likely to lose completely as managers. Their inputs may make gross size tolerable again.

Affluence values replace scarcity thinking

Most significantly, Americans have entered a period of affluence previously unknown to humanity. The scarcity values of the past insured that those at the top of the hierarchy controlled whatever wealth there was above subsistence. Contemporary affluence values encourage more democratic forms of organization in which everyone involved can share in a

better than adequate lifestyle. To date "everyone" has not included women or minorities.

Top managers who continue to assume that people work only to be able to feed and shelter their families are out of touch with present societal values. Organizations are now finding it necessary to be more concerned with human aspects of work because many people require identification with their work, self-esteem, status and self-expression. Management must now accept the needs and demands of managers' private lives including the issues used previously as reasons for keeping women out. These needs have led to, and have been formed by changes in personal values with which management must keep step.[12]

New values express the conviction that people are and should become more independent and autonomous, selecting and rejecting from among old values and exercising conscious choice. New choices in both work and leisure are being made even to questioning the value of a continuous work life. Many people have come to believe their workplace should provide work that is meaningful and stimulating so they can gain intrinsic satisfactions in addition to adequate pay.

Human values and social responsibility are becoming higher priorities in management thinking

But according to General Electric's study, "Our Future Business Environment: A Re-evaluation," "All organizations will be operated less and less by the dictates of administrative convenience, more and more to meet the wants and aspirations of their membership . . . Dealing with the uncertainty of change reduces the value of set procedures and increases the value of individual initiative . . . Managers . . . must expect that considerations of individual motivation, group relationships and personnel costs (including the "hidden" costs of poor performance, withheld cooperation, high

turnover and extra recruiting and training) will weigh much more heavily in their decision-making in the future."[13]

This approach to the changing dynamics of management was strongly seconded by Kalman B. Druck, Chairman of the Public Relations Society of America, when he proposed, "All across the country, managers are running organizations—not only businesses but government agencies, universities, hospitals, law offices, and department stores—without ever formally evaluating the changing opinions of employees, investors, customers, community neighbors, and other important groups. My thesis is that we are at the end of the era of casual attention to the role of opinion in management. *I suggest that neglect of public opinion is no longer tolerable.*"[14]

Terms such as "social responsibility" and "public consent" are new parameters for major institutions of the country. Many organizations have been involved in programs projected to ameliorate some of the identified ills of our nation. For women, Mr. Druck cinches the point with his statement, "Expectations of American society have now begun to rise at a faster pace than the nation's economic and social performance . . . with greater emphasis being put on human values."[15]

There is a strong interplay between these social trends and the move to advance women further up the management ladder. The prevailing external climate will, over the long term, help soften resistances. The internal climate will tend to loosen up as men become more used to working with women on the management team.

Visible now is the tremendous pent-up desire of many women to participate in the mainstream of organizational life and processes. After feeling of fringe-importance, some women give tremendous energy and commitment when accepted into genuine managerial participation. Typically they will also invest considerable time and effort in management development and educational programs to supplement their present capabilities. The necessity to take affirmative action for women can be a blessing in disguise.

Ask yourself—
- What kind of climate do I work in? Would I feel more productive, more satisfied, if I had more say over what we do?
- Could I get more of what I want by working with or participating more in affirmative action for women? Do we share some motives?
- Do I have any apprehensions about working with a manager at my level who is also a woman?
- How do I go about getting the other men to think seriously about adding women managers without getting them angry with me? What's the problem there?

Notes

1. Argyris, Chris, "On the Effectiveness of Research and Development Organization," *American Scientist*, 56, 4, (1968) p. 344.
2. Likert, Rensis, *The Human Organization: Its Management and Value*, New York: McGraw-Hill Book Co., 1967.
3. Argyris, Chris, "Resistance to Rational Management Systems," *Innovation*, No. 10, 1970, p. 30.
4. McGregor, Douglas, *The Human Side of Enterprise*, New York: McGraw-Hill, 1960, pp. 33–34.
5. Koontz, Harold and Cyril O'Donnell, *Principles of Management*, 3rd ed., New York: McGraw-Hill, 1964, p. 500.
6. Argyris, Chris, *Personality and Organization*, New York, Harper & Row, 1957, p. 66.
7. Argyris, *Innovation, op. cit.*, p. 28.
8. Leavitt, Harold J., *Managerial Psychology*, Chicago: The University of Chicago Press, 1958, pp. 10–11.
9. Shewell, J. R., reviewing Adams, Sexton and Don Fyffe, *The Corporate Promotables*, Grief 1969, in *Innovation*, No. 12, 1970, p. 70.
10. McGregor, *op. cit.*, pp. 47–48.
11. Greenewalt, Crawford H., *The Uncommon Man*, New York, McGraw-Hill Book Co., 1959, p. 10.
12. Beckhard, Richard, *Organization Development: Strategies and Models*, Reading, Mass., Addison-Wesley Publishing Co., 1969, p. 6.
13. "Our Future Business Environment: A Re-evaluation." General Electric Corporation, 1969, p. 6.
14. Druck, Kalman B., "Public Opinion's Impact on Business," *Town Hall Journal*, March 7, 1972, p. 66.
15. *Ibid.*, p. 67.

5

Our Sex-Role Culture

"It is indeed a pleasure to meet a capable, well-educated career woman who has managed to retain her femininity." Quoted from a letter following an interview for a managerial position with a large real estate firm, this was written by a personnel man to a woman applicant.[1] Obviously it was intended as a compliment. Equally obviously, he had expected that a capable, well-educated career woman would not be "feminine."

Language reflects society's value of man over woman

"She thinks like a man" is an old compliment given to women who are so exceptional that they can only be complimented in male terms. Underneath, it carries the implication that to be like a man is good; to be like a woman is not. The same implicit approval would hardly be conveyed in, "She thinks like a woman!" Our language is permeated with these sex-linked connotations that place higher value on men. Many of these reverse compliments reflect the widely-held expectations for men and women. It becomes apparent how prejudicial sex-labeling is when we consider that the real question should be, "Does this woman think like a *manager?*" Language and the social value attached to certain words have a subtle, powerful effect in forming attitudes and behaviors.

Traditional expectations for women define their "place"

A look at the characteristic attitudes that management men and women express about women in management reveals the traditional expectations held for women and their "place."[2]

The requirements for a manager—toughness and concern only for the dollar—do not and will not ever mix with the cultural idea ascribed to (but not necessarily found in) females. Someone has to stand for the things spiritual, kindness and tolerance. So, as a culture, all of us look to women to personify this.

Chief engineer, extractive industry (Man)

It's still a fact that most people want a home and family. There is no necessity for more than one person in the family to have a career. It is only logical and sensible that the man be that person simply because of woman's biological role. She's needed at home.

Treasurer, financial institution (Man)[3]

More women should be at home to instill our moral values in growing children. It's an investment in the future of our country that is badly needed.

Dean, Graduate School, State University (Man)

There are very few who can stand the stress and strain of present-day business without it affecting their family relationships. A woman enjoys an outlet from routine household chores, but very few choose to go higher when it affects their homes and families.

President, consumer goods manufacturer (Woman)

When a woman tries to come across as smarter than all the men around, she makes it harder for all of us.

Director, Social Welfare Agency (Woman)[4]

I think competing with men dishonors a woman's natural abilities. She tries to meet men's challenges because she feels that what she, as a woman, can do isn't worth much.

Owner-director, advertising agency (Woman)

These statements, and the assumptions and implications behind the words, betray traditional values based on sex-role expectations:

- women are best suited to home and family
- women should leave home only by necessity; men belong outside the home
- the nuclear family has no acceptable alternatives
- women are spiritual and men are not
- women being at home with children insures that moral values are transmitted
- women contribute vitally to our moral values if they stay home (by implication, they make no such contribution if they do not stay home)
- kindness and tolerance have no place in business, only toughness and concern for the dollar; only women have the former and only men the latter
- women *personify* valuable qualities men *do* the important work
- if *some* women try to demonstrate superiority over men, it hurts *all* women
- even when one particular woman is more able than an individual man, she should not let this be known
- competition is for men and cooperation is for women
- women dishonor themselves and their own "natural abilities" if they attempt to meet "men's" challenges
- challenges belong to men because challenges must be met with aggressiveness
- aggressiveness belongs to men and is not in the repertoire of woman's "natural abilities"

It is striking to note three themes running through these assumptions. Whether the speaker is man or woman, most traditional attitudes define women in terms of, and in rela-

tion to, men. The standard is male; women are compared against that standard. The mood is established that women are valued for those qualities of kindness and tolerance, spirituality or humanness which are not a part of the expectations of what a "real" man is. Perhaps this is why ministers and counselors, mostly male, carry an onus of being ineffectual—not "real" men.

The implication is that softer qualities are nice, in fact essential to the continuation of the race, but are not important in management. Because of the biological fact that women give birth, an innate desire to nurture is attributed to them forever after.

Men are supposed to be tough, concerned for the dollar, practical and objective enough to face the facts and act accordingly. Even if someone has to get hurt in the process, a man is supposed to be strong enough to do what has to be done. Such strength, toughness and total responsibility, even occasional, necessary violence, are attributed to men as "natural." To do anything else is considered as weakness, a "feminine" quality. This must be avoided at all costs if a man is to be a man—a doer and a leader.

Secondly, these assumptions are held to be true for *all* men and *all* women. Any noticeable variance from the standard description of what a "real" man or a "real" woman is like can make that person vulnerable because he or she is different. Certainly many men have conflicts within themselves about their leadership ability when they are not tough and don't want to be. And many women have inner conflicts between nurturance and tough-mindedness.

Most importantly, there is a silent, pervasive assumption that men and women are *totally* different, that there is no commonality in the characteristics attributed to each sex. A dichotomy is set up, not recognizing the great overlap in the distributions of the human characteristics of the two sexes. For example, Harry Levinson finds that the exceptional executive needs to have "ministrative" qualities.[5] These are stereo-

typically attributed to women, yet are becoming valued in contemporary managers (men). On the other hand, some women managers are quite capable of risk-taking and have decision-making abilities usually attributed to men. All of these qualities describe self-confident *people* and are not confined to one sex or the other. Culturally prescribed behaviors are deeply rooted in the backgrounds of most of us. They underlie our legal and economic systems, and pervade birth, marriage, death and inheritance patterns. Most of us are weaned on them, beginning with whether we are placed on pink or blue receiving blankets, and are reinforced through every phase of our lives by all major institutions: marriage, family, education, church, military, corporations, social agencies, government, media. The total society functions through social definitions that have become part of the conventional wisdom—what Everybody Knows.

Even when a review of these silent assumptions reveals a basic incongruity with personal experience, change is not automatic. This change is particularly uncomfortable. The status quo, even if it is incongruous, is known. Resistance to change, shared by most people, has caused the formation of stereotypes as well as their perpetuation long after their social usefulness has passed. To stereotype people is to cast them in molds constructed from the groupings in which it is convenient to classify them—race, religion, sex, national origin and age. But such categorizations ignore the wide variations that exist within each category and the dangers of shortcuts in dealing with masses of data and crowds of people who touch our daily lives.

The serious mistake is in believing that all individuals within each category are essentially alike. The danger is the potential loss of those capabilities not assumed to be present. Since most male managers and administrators have learned to stereotype women employees as possessing low capabilities, such mold-casting has resulted in tremendous underutilization of the capabilities of many women.

Woman defined as seductress, witch, madonna and . . . stupid

One archetypal image of woman as seductress is reinforced with unremitting repetition in an endless avalanche of ads. Automobile, motorcycle and computer equipment ads are heavily loaded with sprawled, straddled women with challenging, luring eyes. Commercial key-clubs sell status on the strength of don't-touch sex. Reclining double lounge chairs with intense female in black, filmy negligee, eyes drawing you close. Woman in predatory crawl on someone's carpet. Woman in black lace foundation being unzipped, instructing women how they too can be seductive if they buy. Titillation and sex.

Closely associated is the theme of the feminine evil—the dangerous sex—permeating the subliminal bombardment. Strange powers of women—over which men have no control. Sex and seduction with sin stirred in is the basic brew for witchery—the ultimate evil power of woman to destroy men. Through seduction Lorelei devastated the sailors of the Teutonic world. Through seduction Circe corraled men to become pigs. Wicked witches still thread through the stories read to our children; Hansel and Gretel, Snow White and the Seven Dwarfs; and Hallowe'en tales paint her astride her broom, silhouetted across the moon. Endlessly, women have been portrayed as dangerous, seductive, destructive, unpredictable—like hurricanes. Eroticism and evil are essential qualities of women, according to ancient myths and current beliefs. Today advertisers sell billions of dollars of merchandise and services by exploiting this archetypal image.

At the other extreme of ancient imagery is the madonna—the sweet, soft, delicate, tender mother/child (often undistinguishable pictorially—both feature innocence). This image sells toilet paper, deodorants, lingerie and perfume. One classic ad promoting trading stamps as a sales incentive, featured a home snapshot of the sweet, eternally feminine wife. The caption: "The most powerful incentive ever invented by

man—woman." In one brilliant stroke, this ad succinctly summarized the male invention of the innocent, dependent, consumer wife who looks to her husband to provide all things and for which all men strive.

How simplistic this modern-day version of the ancient division of labor based on reproductive biology. How weary the consumer, worker or manager who attempts to keep people and functions in neat, tidy little boxes. Accumulating evidence demonstrates that women are no longer succumbing to stereotyped advertising. And so it is with work.

Today, most jobs are "in between" jobs. Survival depends on recognizing a quite different range of values, sometimes including opposing values. Early agrarian patterns have no relevance for a modern, industrialized society. Yet the myth of dependency, supportiveness, nurturance and maintenance as the nature and purpose of woman lingers on. The soft image of innocent motherhood is enshrined in the media's religion of consumerism long after major changes in marriage and family patterns; long after major changes in employment and education resources; long after technology has vastly increased the range of work that can be performed by either men or women.

The media reflect a third dominant theme: Women are presented as not very bright, certainly not logical. In some instances, they appear downright stupid, especially when it involves handling money or demonstrating reasoning ability. For example, a computer equipment company ran a double-spread of red lips invitingly parted, captioned: "We taught our data entry system to speak a new language: Dumb Blond."

Of course, men are not exempt from the blandishments of advertising. One computer systems ad shows four mildly seductive women simperingly vying for attention. The caption cozily suggests that, "Time sharing can be a problem . . . if you are trying to support too much expensive equipment." It carries the happy implication, of course, that the reader (probably a married male) can easily cope with the sexual joys of four lovely ladies. But there are few practical matters

a man must concern himself with—time, for instance. So, to have his cake and eat it too, it appears he'll have to time share.

The requirement to have manly equipment is rather openly referred to in a motor oil ad that carried the jingle: "The only difference between men and boys is the size and cost of their toys." The question is: Do these portrayals still sell merchandise? Are the admen's predictions accurate that men buy the sexual aura with the product? Ah, the power of sexual fantasies!

The model of the manager is masculine

"The model of the successful manager in our culture is a masculine one. The good manager is aggressive, competitive, firm, just. He is not feminine; he is not soft or yielding or dependent or intuitive in the womanly sense. The very expression of emotion is widely viewed as a feminine weakness that would interfere with effective business processes. *Yet the fact is that all these emotions are part of the human nature of men and women alike.* (Emphasis ours.) Cultural forces have shaped not their existence but their acceptability; they are repressed, *but this does not render them inactive.* (Emphasis his.) They continue to influence attitudes, opinions, and decisions." This is the professional manager as defined by Douglas McGregor.[6]

A successful manager is assumed to be objective, unemotional, logical—a hard-nosed decision-maker dealing only with facts. He is expected to repress those aspects of himself that are associated with the feminine in our culture—softness, yielding, dependence and intuitiveness. To express emotion is seen as "feminine weakness."

The masculine model sets up double binds for men

Faced with accepting women as managers, a male manager may well feel he is expected to accept in them those

very qualities he has had to reject in himself to become a manager. Hence, this double-bind: **If he accepts women as managers, he has to accept as OK-for-a-manager the emotions he had repressed in himself; if he accepts the prescribed unemotional manager's role, he can't accept women (the feminine) as managers.**

Not just the model of a manager, but the very value of masculinity can seem to be threatened by women moving into management. It shakes up the traditional role of men in relation to women. Richard W. Smith in "Why Men Need to Put Women Down," spells out the role-relationship. "A male, in order to be a socially accepted "regular fellow" must be first, a warrior (or at least warrior-like); second, a highly-active procreator; and third, an economic provider. Females, in turn, must be married, economically and emotionally dependent, and mothers."[7] When a woman steps out of her traditional role she upsets the balance of both roles. She can easily be seen as threatening the worth and masculine identity that a man finds in the "conquering" of work. It raises the question: "If a woman can do a man's job as well as he, how can a man maintain that it takes that extra measure of ability (virility) to qualify for such work?"[8]

Many men may well wonder how to relate to this unexpected change—"What do you do with them?" To be agressive and competitive is to be that way *with other men*. The male role requires that women be taken care of, not fought. Secondly, the symbol of a highly active procreator is the man who chases and beds women. Clearly this is not appropriate in relating to women managers as professional colleagues. Third, as an economic provider a man is subjected to legal and social pressures that say, "A man who can't support a family isn't much of a man," and conversely, "A good supporter is a high-status *he*-man."[9] A woman manager may adhere to the feminine role by being married and a mother, but she definitely is *not* economically and emotionally dependent.

So, many men feel locked into another double-bind: **If**

he's a man as prescribed, he cannot relate to a woman on an equal (male) basis; if he's his own person, relating equally to women, he risks being seen by other men as "not much of a man"—or manager either.

While many managers can appreciate a woman's compe tence, they often find it difficult to simply accept it as just that. Somehow, competence and feminine sexuality don't seem to go together. The idea that a man "controls his women" is widespread. When a woman becomes a manager functioning as his colleague or superior, control over her is no longer available nor appropriate for the man. Again, con flict betwen male-role and work-role.

Education, some tough choices and compromises in his career, expectations from families, may constitute a large personal investment in a man's masculine identity and feel ings of being valuable as a person. With women as man agerial competitors, this investment may feel devalued.

The unequal concept has been with us a long time, deeply rooted in the Protestant ethic and our marriage system. We come from American beginnings that did not include women as citizens under the Constitution. Under laws of coverture, married women were "dead in the law" and found divorce virtually unavailable, while unmarried women were legally treated as minors. In spite of progress through new legisla tion, equal rights and equal protection under constitutional law remain ambiguous today.[10] Yet to be accomplished are the States' ratification of the Equal Rights Amendment and the courts' interpretations of Revised Order 4 and other work related decisions.

Social roles for work, sex and marriage are intertwined

Inextricably intertwined are at least three major role pat terns that affect the relationships between men and women and create difficulties for women in process of becoming managers. To talk about one is to talk about all three. First

are *sex-roles*: which underlie the pattern of male "superiority" and female "inferiority." Second are *marital-roles* of husband and wife where power, intelligence and responsibility traditionally rest with the husband while the wife is perceived as a helpmate "living through" her husband and children. Third are *work-roles* where men are in the leadership and decision-making roles and women are in the housekeeping and nurturing tasks of industry, government, education and services.

These three culturally entrenched patterns have contributed to the ubiquitous non-conscious attitudes of dominance and subordinancy. Roles by virtue of one's physical sex impinge on the work situation. Robert Townsend, for example, contending that many men "spend most of (their) waking hours in sex-fantasy day-dreams," advises women, "This kind of competition is a real pushover."[11] We disagree about the weakness of the competition since it seems evident that men have not only sex-fantasies but also *sex-role fantasies* firmly rooted in historical male supremacy. It has long been fact as well as fantasy that men have power over women.

Social sex-role power is further enhanced by marital roles whereby wives of managers, and sometimes husbands of managers, feel proprietary rights on their spouses, making demands on their time and energies that impact the work situation. As we shall see in the next chapter, the jealousy and possessiveness which so often characterize marriages can increase the pressures under which managers operate. As more women enter management, there is increasing speculation about the influence of marital status. Single women are often discussed as to the degree of their sexual frustration, and thus their potential sexual availability. On the other hand, married women may or may not be considered "off-limits" for sexual involvements. In some industries, such as the entertainment field, being married is usually not a barrier. Divorced women are often considered to be more flexible in their sexual standards and thus easier to approach. Whatever the marital status, there are many factors—age,

appearance, "vibrations"—that determine whether speculations evolve into action.

Marital status also affects selection and promotion policies. Ranging from traditional anti-nepotism rulings to whether or not a married woman should hold a responsible job, these are concerns about whether she, *or her husband*, actually makes her employment decisions. Administrators have been juggling concerns such as:

- Deciding that husbands and wives can work in the same department provided that . . . neither is involved in making employment decisions about the other. (a new ruling at Stanford University)
- Does the woman have serious commitment to the organization, or does she treat her work as a time-filler depending on her husband's activities?
- Expecting women to prove the need for the position as opposed to assuming that a man has the need in his traditional breadwinner role.
- Assuming that motivation is based on economic need. Mark the assumptions . . . . if a woman is married, her husband works and supports her . . . . economic need is the only need that really motivates people . . . . the requirement to support is the only fair basis for employment.

Some management men perpetuate these assumptions by recognizing their own interest in making no change. One advertising agency executive appeals to the "nurturing nature" of women when he put it this way: "Higher education has wised you (women) up . . . all of this makes men a little uneasy. And a little wistful. Men don't want things to change. They haven't changed and they don't want women to change . . ."[12]

Clearly, men on the average are different from women on the average because of differential opportunities for development. Comparable opportunity for developing the capabilities and potentials of both men and women must be

available before we can know whether or not there is any shred of intrinsic difference between the sexes in handling the managerial role. Separating the biological and social conditioning facets in the personality development of both women and men is nigh impossible. "It is clear that until social expectations for men and women are equal, until we provide equal respect for both men and women, our answers . . . will simply reflect our prejudices."[13] There is no valid basis now available for understanding what meaning, if any, biological differences have for any specific function. The authority that tells women and men who they are and what they're supposed to do is too deeply imbedded into the social context to make that possible.

It is hardly remarkable, then, that men find it difficult to see women in the work-role of manager. Patterns in leadership and management are deeply entrenched. Psychiatrist Robert Seidenberg described it this way: "We must recognize that our society is overwhelmingly dominated by male 'homosexuality' in religion, politics, higher education, law, big business, the armed forces, and practically all other important institutions . . . the reality that men in general prefer to spend most of their time in each others' company, compete, make contracts, plan and make decisions together, and in their leisure time, play together. Very little time is spent with women; their opinions are generally held in low esteem; they are never present in the higher echelons of decision-making, and are not brought into games of leisure. They are sexual partners, but this takes only a few minutes a week, just enough time to establish that the male is a heterosexual, which he obviously is not, based on his apparent preferences as found in time-spent studies . . . For most men, women are good to sleep with—not to stay awake with."[14]

Labeling this pattern as homosexuality is rather strong. We feel more inclined to describe it as monosexuality—a one-sex scene with heterosexual interludes. In this all-male climate, the reality of women as peers is bound to be disturbing. The real shock is the reality of the difference be-

tween recognizing the principle of equal opportunity and having to live with its consequences personally.

What are the traits valued in men; in women?

Whether biology or socialization is the rationale for stereotyping, certain traits are ascribed to each sex. When these traits are displayed by the designated appropriate sex, then they are socially valued. For example, aggressiveness is ascribed to men. Socially valued when shown by men, it is denigrated when demonstrated by women. So strongly supported are the attitudes about this difference that both men and women easily define a woman "unfeminine" if she displays certain "aggressive" behavior.

In an effort to understand attitudes about the aggressiveness of women's career choices, an opinion survey* sampled men and women under 30 and women over 30. Occupations for women frequently rated "aggressive" by men were: public relations, engineer and city planner. Other behaviors rated for aggressiveness included:

- tries to get elected to public office
- becomes a supervisor of men
- manages the family budget

Comparisons between the responding groups reveal that age, above and below the generation watershed of 30 years, is less a factor than is sex. Women over 30 (45 percent) and under 30 (50 percent) are closer in their agreement on the aggressiveness of occupational choices for women than are males (60 percent) and females (50 percent) both under 30. (Interestingly, male veterans gave 20-40 percent lower ratings of aggressiveness than non-veteran college men did, in all cases. Presumably veterans' experiences make the difference.)[15]

One widely-quoted study of college students of both sexes reflects a range of stereotypes of the larger society from

---

*The survey questions are included in *Tools: Information and Sources.*

which today's professional management is drawn. Both men and women students agreed on:

Valued traits, when displayed by men:

Aggressive

Independent

Unemotional

Hides emotions

Objective

Easily influenced

Dominant

Likes math and science

Not excitable in a minor crisis

Active

Competitive

Logical

Worldly

Skilled in business

Knows the way of the world

Feelings not easily hurt

Adventurous

Makes decisions easily

Never cries

Acts as a leader

Self-confident

Not uncomfortable about being aggressive

Ambitious

Able to separate feelings from ideas

Not dependent

Not conceited about appearance

Thinks men are superior to women

Talks freely about sex with men

Direct

Valued traits, when displayed by women:

Does not use harsh language

Talkative

Tactful

Gentle

Aware of feelings of others

Religious

Interested in own appearance

Neat in habits

Quiet

Strong need for security

Appreciates art and literature

Expresses tender feelings

Both men and women agreed that masculine traits are more socially desirable than feminine traits. Thus, "women also hold negative values of their worth relative to men." Since these researchers were working with outstanding college achievers, they concluded that the impact of negative stereotypes on the self-concepts of women were "enormously powerful."[16]

Lesser social value of women produces "minority status"

Recent legislation and the feelings many women have about themselves refer to "minority status" as defined by sociologists. Many Americans react negatively to this definition since

BLACKS	WOMEN
Ascribed Attributes	
Inferior intelligence, smaller brain, scarcity of geniuses	Inferior intelligence, smaller brain scarcity of geniuses
More free in instinctual gratifications. More emotional, "primitive" and childlike. Imagined sexual prowess envied.	Irresponsible, inconsistent, emotionally unstable. Lack of strong super-ego. Women as temptresses.
Common stereotype, "inferior"	Common stereotype, "weaker"
Rationalizations of Status	
Thought all right in his place. Myth of contented black.	Woman's place is in the home. Myth of contented woman—"feminine" woman is happy in subordinate role.
Accommodation Attitudes	
Supplicatory whining intonation of voice	Rising inflection, smiles, laughs, downward glances
Deferential manner	Flattering manner
Concealment of real feelings	"Feminine wiles"
Outwit "white folks"	Outwit "men-folk"
Careful study of points at which dominant group is susceptible to influence	Careful study of points at which dominant group is susceptible to influence
Fake appeals for directives: show of ignorance	Appearance of helplessness
Discriminations	
Limitations on education—should fit "place" in society	Limitations on education—should fit "place" in society
Confined to traditional jobs—barred from supervisory positions. Their competition feared. No family precedents for new aspirations.	Confined to traditional jobs—barred from supervisory positions. Their competition feared. No family precedents for new aspirations.
Deprived of political importance	Deprived of political importance
Social and professional segregation	Social and professional segregation

women are statistically 51 percent of the population. Nonetheless, an accurate accounting of the potential for individual control of one's life style, one's destiny, reveals the lack of female power to do so. Helen Hacker, in 1951 compared the attributes which most people believed to be true about a minority group and about women. In view of the strong press of ethnic minorities in recent years to change the stereotypic attitudes, the concern and pressure from women to do likewise may well be understood through her comparison.

With both blacks and women, roles are in flux resulting in a conflict between achieved status and ascribed status.[17]

Traits and attitudes taught to women produce a double standard of mental health

These attributes, learned because of being female, have become part of the standards of mental health held by practicing psychiatrists, psychologists and psychiatric social workers, both men and women. In a 1970 study, a group of this composition were asked to describe a healthy adult, (sex unspecified), a healthy male and a healthy female, using the sex-role stereotypes described above. These "people-helpers" were found to hold *a double standard of mental health*. They perceived the healthy adult, sex unspecified, to be closely similar to the healthy male, but significantly different from the healthy female. Both men and women clinicians agreed that the so-called healthy mature woman, compared to men, is:

more submissive	less independent
less adventurous	more easily influenced
less aggressive	less competitive
more excitable in minor crisis	have feelings more easily hurt
more conceited about	less objective
appearance	disliking of math and science

Practicing clinicians perceived these traits as healthy in women, not healthy in men.[18] This might be how your psy-

chiatrist views your daughter. Certainly, these traits parallel the sex-role stereotypes on which girl-children are weaned.

The researchers put it this way: "This constellation seems a most unusual way of describing any mature, healthy individual . . . It places women in the conflictual position of having to decide whether to exhibit those positive characteristics considered desirable for men and adults, and thus have their "femininity" questioned . . . or to behave in the prescribed feminine manner, accept second-class adult status, and possibly live a lie to boot."[19] They observed that even in a climate of equality of opportunity and freedom of choice, social pressures to conform to sex-roles restrict career choices open to women and, to a lesser extent, to men. But women no longer are so accepting of the behavior prescribed for them. One of the authors, commenting on militant women's views, said; "A special kind of hatred is reserved by liberationists for psychoanalysts and psychiatrists who in their treatment of women have encouraged them to adjust, to accept their status . . ."[20]

For managers much of life is lived in the realms of ideas, decisions, conceptualizations. It is experience we need in order to undo the damage of thinking and defining in the narrow terms of established culture. Legislators, scholars, psychiatrists, managers, men and women alike, all have been exposed to the history of separate roles for the sexes. For many people these role expectations may be very comfortable. For others, such ascribed attributes have proved to be both self limiting and societally limiting. Our conviction is that the highest productiveness and achievement are possible when we maintain a minimum of sex-related roles, and provide a maximum of possible choices for individual style and directions of growth.

Ask yourself—

How do I define femininity—by behavior? appearance? language? occupation? a style, a manner?

• Similarly, how do I define masculinity?

• In order for me to be comfortable with a woman as a manager how would I rate these traits? What are my priorities?

Notes

1. Private communication to Theodora Wells.
2. The following quotes, except as footnoted, are from Bowman, Garda W., N. B. Worthy and S. A. Greyser, "Are Women Executives People?" *Harvard Business Review*, July–August, 1965.
3. Private communication.
4. *Ibid.*
5. Levinson, Harry, *The Exceptional Executive, A Psychological Conception*, New York, The Mentor Executive Library, 1968, pp. 175–203.
6. McGregor, Douglas, *The Professional Manager*, (Edited by Caroline McGregor and Warren G. Bennis), New York, McGraw-Hill Book Co., 1967, p. 23.
7. Smith, Richard Warren, "Why Men Need to Put Women Down," paper delivered to the California State Psychological Association, Monterey, California, January, 1970, p. 4.
8. *Ibid.*, p. 11.
9. *Ibid.*, p. 9.
10. For a carefully documented study of the legal status of women today, see Kanowitz, Leo, *Women and the Law, The Unfinished Revolution*, Albuquerque, New Mexico, 1969. It should be noted that in this book, Professor Kanowitz takes a stance against the Equal Rights Amendment which he has subsequently reversed in testimony before Congress.
11. Townsend, Robert, *Up the Organization* (with new chapters added), Greenwich, Conn., Fawcett Publications, Inc., 1970, p. 210.
12. Hobbs, Whit, Senior Vice President of Benton & Bowles, quoted in "Place for Women in Management," *Los Angeles Times*, November 8, 1967, p. 16.
13. Weisstein, Naomi, "Woman as Nigger," *Psychology Today*, October 1969, p. 20 ff. Condensed from "Kinder, Kuche, Kirche as Scientific Law: Psychology Constructs the Female," *Motive*, March–April 1969, p. 84.
14. Seidenberg, Robert, *Marriage in Life and Literature*, New York, Philosophical Library, Inc., 1970, pp. 13–14.
15. Loring, Rosalind K., "Aggressiveness in Women Opinion Survey," administered in various UCLA Extension courses through the Department of Daytime Programs and Special Projects, January, 1971; and at San Fernando State College, February, 1971.

16. Rosenkrantz, P., S. Vogel, H. Bee, I. Broverman, and D. Broverman, "Sex-Role Stereotypes and Self-Concepts in College Students," *Journal of Consulting and Clinical Psychology*, 32, No. 3, June, 1968, pp. 287–295.
17. Hacker, Helen Mayer, "Women as a Minority Group," *Social Forces*, 30, October, 1951, pp. 60–69. This comparison is slightly edited from the original.
18. Broverman, I., D. Broverman, F. Clarkson, P. Rosenkrantz, and S. Vogel, "Sex-role Stereotypes and Clinical Judgments of Mental Health," *Journal of Consulting and Clinical Psychology*, 34, No. 1, February, 1970, pp. 1–7.
19. *Ibid.*, p. 6.
20. Loring, Rosalind K., "Love and Women's Liberation," Chapter in Otto, Herbert (editor), *Love Today—A New Exploration*, New York, Association Press, 1972, p. 83.

6

Managers, Marriages, and Mates

"The man who believes that the only satisfactory sexual relationship is the one in which a woman is submissive to him is also the man who would be challenged if his wife had a career. He is also the man who determines the social mechanisms which make it virtually impossible for women to undertake careers. He is the man who would find himself threatened as a male if his wife assumed an independent, or on occasion, a dominant role either in their sexual relationships or in the so-called 'world of work.'"

Edward J. Bloustein[1]

Traditional marriage and management expectations

As the position of women in the work force changes, the traditional wife will have to learn ways to resolve the ambiguity of her supportive role to her manager husband, while at the same time coping with the changing roles of his female co-workers—from secretaries to managers.

(For those men who have a traditional marriage, we suggest you read the rest of the chapter in the second person—you—as we have done in the next two paragraphs. It offers an *experience* of attitudes, situations and events.)

Because of your wife's dependence on you it is important to consider what motivates her feelings about the working relationships you have as a manager. The secretary is rela-

tively easy to cope with, since she performs a variety of "wife-support" functions along with typing and transcription. In many cases, your secretary can be an ally and friend to your wife, partially sharing similar roles and able to converse on the same plane. Tradition has established rules of propriety that cover entertaining and gifts, lending a certain circumscribed security to their relationship. Your wife probably knows you well enough to assess whether or not your secretary is a sexual threat to her. So the closeness and the time spent together by manager and secretary are usually understood and accepted.

No such rules exist with the woman manager. Your wife may well wonder *"Do I relate to a woman manager as a woman or as a manager?"* The very question, if asked, makes her attitude toward women clear—they are inferior to men. It makes her own subordinate relationship with you starkly clear. It also spotlights the conflict between the traditional secondary role of women and the anomaly of a woman-and-manager.

(We now return to the third person since many managers are in non-traditional marriages, are divorced, or otherwise involved in their private lives.)

Although the patterns are changing, even today the wives of most managers stay home raising the family and pursuing conventional activities consistent with being an "organization wife." Certainly she has considerable more latitude today than in the 1950's when she was expected to be part of the total executive package William Whyte so well described in *The Organization Man.*[2] But most organizations still expect their managers to have wives who provide the customary support to the manager and his activities. (The lack of a wife has been cited as a real handicap to the *woman* who would be a manager!)

In the belief that the conventional wife's attitudes often have a critical influence on how a manager feels about his organization, his relationships within it and many of his decisions, some organizations attempt to influence their managers' marital relationships for the benefit of the enter-

prise. In government, education and medicine as well as business and industry it was formerly possible to consider a manager's marriage to be not only the organization's business but even a part of the organization. Thus, the conviction of the right to make policies affecting mates, to interview wives before hiring husbands, and even to require wives to live by prescribed standards, performing such functions as entertaining and public relations without pay. For example, not until 1972 did the U.S. Department of State change its policy, custom and expectations of wives of Foreign Service employees. They now recognize traditional wifely participation as a "voluntary act of a private person, not a legal obligation . . ."[3] The need for this change was based on the policy of the Foreign Service to remain representative of American society which now "permits wives to choose for themselves the roles which they choose to follow."[4]

These and many other changes suggest that any assumptions about marital influences on occupational life are and should be questioned. Last year's generalizations are no longer valid and yesterday's no longer appropriate. The legitimate degree of interest and influence the organization has in the marriage must now be considered case by case.

Most key decision-makers are older men, raised in traditional marriage patterns and personal value systems. Many of the choices made by younger people seem diametrically opposed and within a brief span of time the encounters of tradition and innovation have enmeshed almost everyone.

Today's marriage roles are undergoing rapid change. Marriage is becoming less a lifelong institution, with serial monogamy and peripheral affairs far more common. Most young as well as middle-aged people remarry readily, but many choose to remain single. Many young couples choose to live together rather than marry, at least until they are sure marriage is what they want or until they are ready for children. And many are working out more egalitarian patterns of marriage relationships.

For the first time in the history of the Census Bureau's records, most married women plan to have fewer than three

children. As of February 1972, women between 18 and 39 now expect to have an average 2.8 children compared with 3.1 in 1967. Women in the key childbearing age from 18 to 24 now expect to have only 2.4 children.[5] Thus, American families will become even smaller in the future. Many new options are opening up to women who wish to use them.

How intense the reaction is when women with these newer marriage values collide with managers who have traditional marital role expectations woven into their ideas about employment! Men with traditional marriages often feel very uneasy about women as managers who don't behave in traditional ways.

In his experience, the traditional manager expects his wife to define herself in relation to him and derive her identity from him. The manager who leads others, helps build the organization, rises to executive positions and wields power is handsomely rewarded in pay, prestige and privilege— social recognition of success. His wife, as "power behind the throne," shares his recognition and money-status. She must learn a social mobility that matches her husband's career ups and downs, sharing it in a dependent capacity. Her personal recognition comes in verbal honoring of her supporting role, or guilt if she opts for more personal choices.

Only recently have some wives of executives and managers devoted substantial amounts of time to activities of their own choice. Management consultant Richard Beckhard has found that wives of executives show a trend toward greater autonomy, creative careers and community responsibilities. Nonetheless, a traditional wife knows she must protect and advance her relationship with her manager-husband because it may be her life's investment.

The traditional wife is a resource about women employees and managers

One of the ways she can protect her investment is to offer her husband the kind of emotional support that helps him with his work. In listening to his problems, offering com-

ments and suggestions, many wives offer this support. Apparently, more managers than commonly thought talk with their wives about problems at work, especially concerns about human relations. Because she's a woman and there's no embarrassment in discussing it with her, a wife is often consulted about problems of women employees, according to one survey.[6]

When the manager consults his wife about women managers, he may find that his marriage relationship is rarely an experience in equality. Habitually relating to women in a superior-subordinate way, he may be used to being in the more powerful position, able to effectively dominate choice-points. A shift to the colleague, same-level basis may be a totally new experience. There is not much experience on which to build a bridge-by-analogy to this new development. As a male officer of a financial institution put it, "A man's attitude toward women executives is strongly influenced by his basic attitude toward women and his relationship with his wife." This viewpoint had not been verified by asking managers as a group how they feel. We decided to ask.

In a workshop on Women in Management,[7] the married men were asked to complete this sentence: *"If I had a woman boss, my wife would feel . . ."* The responses ranged from total rejection of the idea ("I would not work under those circumstances") to a certain blasé acceptance ("No change. We've been through it.") One was sure that his wife would feel "that I was inferior and not the dominant male that I have led her to believe I am"; another that she would feel "superior." The sexual dimension was expressed by one man who expected that his wife would feel jealous, another that it would be "OK if the woman boss were unattractive." One simply didn't know how his wife would feel.

How relevant is the wife's experience in advising her husband on matters relating to situations involving women in management? If she has never worked, or perhaps was employed for a short time while awaiting marriage, she is likely to perceive women employees in relation to herself. The central difference between her and women employees is

motivation. A wife is more dependent on her husband-manager, for both money and self-esteem, than are the women he employs. In terms of the average woman employee, this may not be a substantial difference. Many "women's jobs" are expanded versions of various support functions that wives typically perform: secretarial, correspondence clerks, nurses, teachers, counselors, social-workers, bookkeepers, and "assistant to" roles. In discussing problems of women employed in these jobs, the traditional wife probably can offer valuable perceptions. It parallels her life so she is knowledgable.

On the other hand, this same wife may find it difficult to consider impartially a woman who is economically independent and who shares leadership roles with her husband. To this wife, the secretary is a known; the woman manager, an unknown. Moreover, if a wife resists her dependent status, she may hold some resentment toward the personally achieving woman. Ladylike disdain for women's liberation is one weapon. The "super-lady" can make it even more difficult for her mate to understand and accept the committed, if affluent, working woman. In one family-owned company where the wife of the president was also on the board of directors, no woman was in the inner management circle working closely with her husband, at her insistence. A top woman executive of a large utility firmly believes that changing men's attitudes about women must begin at home.

Changing work relationships can affect marital relationships. Traditional ways are both reinforced and questioned

Consciously or not, a wife may wonder, *"To what degree is a woman manager a threat to me?"* Whether or not a sexual threat is present, the traditional marital relationship may undergo some modification. For example, if there are marital difficulties resulting from a husband feeling his wife is excessively dependent or demanding (i.e., pressuring him to improve their income or status), the independence of a

woman manager could appear refreshing to the manager-husband. The woman manager may be seen as a person with whom he can cooperate, instead of someone to take care of. Greater equality between the sexes in management responsibilities could result in generating a desire for greater equality in marital responsibilities. That may be seen as dangerous by many wives, revitalizing by others, or, perhaps more commonly, both at the same time.

Regardless of the hazards, we are seeing increasing numbers of women uneasy with the delicate balance of marital tasks. Too many women have discovered that everything a wife personally invests in the support of her husband's career accrues to the man, intrinsic to him even if he moves to another company—or another woman. Her reward is only the security that his achievement and power can bestow upon her. Only if they remain married do the wife's efforts continue to pay off for her.

If she becomes widowed, divorced or is forced to become the breadwinner, she has gained no personal identity or value of her own. This is a tragic discovery in the homes of many aerospace engineers who are casualties of defense cutbacks. Wives seeking employment are seen as "just housewives" by personnel offices. Their years of experience in running the home, coordinating community activities and entertaining for the company are considered to be years of "doing nothing."

Nevertheless, the Bureau of National Affairs is still selling a double-feature film, *How to Advance Your Husband's Career*. The first film is for wives only. The wife is asked to measure herself against such "assets" as keeping a tranquil home; being a cheerful hostess; being understanding of her husband's late hours or business trips; accepting necessary transfers as "new adventures"; dressing and acting with decorum at all times outside the home. The opposites of these virtues are billed as liabilities with the additional admonition not to become a problem drinker!

The second part is for both husbands and wives, geared to

inspire them to "work together, in love, for a stable, happy marriage." The whole package is promoted as a way "to get wives on the company team."[8]

Still appealing to the supportive wife role, but attempting to meet her needs more effectively, are some new programs designed to give wives understanding of business management. Dr. Leon A. Danco of John Carroll University reportedly has met with resounding success in offering business organization, financial management, estate planning and industrial psychology to wives of presidents of family owned companies.

The Steel Service Center Institute offers modern motivation theory and practice, which apply at home as well as in business. In their seminars, they discovered that, "In some organization games we played, the wives gave their husbands a good run for their money in coming up with new ideas."[9] Such surprised, patronizing wonder that wives would even be interested, much less so competent, suggests the low level of expectation held for wives and for women generally. It certainly reflects Dr. Danco's belief that the traditional viewpoint of management is to look upon the wife "only in terms of a possible source of trouble rather than a positive force."[10]

Marriage patterns are changing and roles of husbands and wives are being questioned

So far, only the traditional wife has received attention here. We assume that this is the majority situation, at least for managers' and executives' wives. But we do not ignore the wide variety of marriage patterns and how these relate to changes in the husband's occupational climate. For example, if the wife is non-traditional, working in a valued capacity outside the home, the occupational climate of the husband does not affect the marital relationship so centrally. Less dependence by the wife reduces the concentration on her role performance, without reducing the caring between husband and wife. In fact, one frequent paradox is that the less the

need for dependence, the greater the mutual caring and trust. Both are relieved of some of the pressures inherent in the traditional roles of husband and wife. The O'Neills of *Open Marriage* comment, "By freeing themselves from the restrictions of their customary roles, they will have a better chance of reawakening the sense of play that lies buried beneath the responsibilities of adult life."[11]

A shifting of some of the stresses of organizational life can also occur, shared by women managers who thrive on challenges traditionally handled by men. Continuing, the O'Neills comment, "In most cases both the provider role in the family and the managerial position in our society are filled by men. These are stressful positions . . . such stress could be equally shared by men and women. To so share it will provide the double benefit of giving women an opportunity to actualize their capabilities, and of increasing the health and longevity of men. Our traditional separation of male and female roles no longer makes sense in a complex technological world. It is time to stop overburdening our men while we deprive and underutilize our women."[12]

Changing marriage patterns have serious implications for organizational policies in many areas

Many current organizational policies are based on traditional marriage patterns. They need to be re-examined in the light of the changing styles of marriage, the legalizing of pressure for more women in management and the increasing number of divorced, widowed and single women who are heads of households.

Promotion policies

One traditional concern of management has been, *"What if we pay her more or promote her to a higher position than her husband?"* Past policies have held the company responsible for protecting a woman's marriage by paying her less.

A quick re-examination will show that it is really the husband's problem. Many men today can handle such a situation because they have strong egos, can feel proud of their wives' accomplishments and can accept the additional income without feeling a loss of masculinity. If a man cannot, this appears to be a problem for the couple, not the company, to solve.

But such decisions are still being made. Recently a woman assistant vice-president of a financial institution was being considered for promotion to full vice-presidency. Fully qualified, she had been functioning as a vice-president in every respect except title, pay and benefits for almost a year. The company's affirmative action officer recognized her contribution and recommended her for promotion, but no action was taken for some time. In a discreet investigation, it was found that her promotion was approved at each of the next three officer levels but stopped at the top. Why? Because she would be paid more money than her husband was making as an officer of a competing financial institution. She was the only woman officer qualified for full vice-presidency and the organization's affirmative action plan was overdue in promoting a woman to this level. Still she was disqualified only for the external reason of her husband's income, not because of experience, qualifications or length of service.

This institution would hardly qualify as an "equal opportunity employer." Certainly it would not deny a husband a promotion because he would then earn more than his wife!

Relocation and transfer policies

From the old frame of reference, there is concern that women managers will not relocate if the company requires them to move. At the same time, there is concern that the woman will give up her job if her husband is transferred.

Such concerns are based on the long-established pattern of the husband's career determining where the family will live. That concept no longer holds true for traditional couples, much less non-traditional.

Moving is most detrimental to the traditional wife who has no job status of her own. She loses any status she has gained on her own in the community including "the name that she has made for herself in the social and societal sphere if not in professional roles. Her identity as a person apart from being a wife or a mother is rarely transferable. In a new community she finds that she must create one all over again."[13]

For the non-traditional couple, if the husband is offered a transfer, it is not automatic that the wife will leave her job. If she cannot get as good a job in the new location, they may be financially well ahead for him to turn down the transfer. Conversely, if the wife is offered a transfer, it is not automatic that the man will leave his job for similar reasons. Some companies are recently beginning to see the advantage of hiring both partners. Executive couples are a new breed, acting in concert when it comes to hiring or relocation. Some are interviewed by the same company; others get assistance in placing the spouse in the same area. "There could be greater likelihood of retaining both than each separately," according to Roger Davis, executive recruiter of Merrill Lynch, Pierce, Fenner & Smith, Inc.[14]

Again, the possibility that a woman may refuse a transfer, or, for that matter, may even refuse the responsibilities attending a promotion, is given by some organizations as their reason for not offering women transfers or promotions.

Increasingly, couples are deciding that money will not be the only factor determining where they will live or which promotion is accepted. For many, a compromise is made between two careers. For some, geography is most important. For others who find it difficult to start over again and again, staying in one place, be it city or company, may be their choice.[15]

Individually or in couples, it seems clear that the era of equal opportunity conveys to prospective managers "the right of refusal." People separately and together are learning to explore alternatives, considering time, energy, money,

family needs and personal priorities. Choice-making about environments appears to have become generally available.

Travel policies; unwritten policies about sexual activities

Another responsibility management has taken upon itself based on the traditional values is for the behavior of men and women managers on overnight and out-of-town assignments. Again, the employer seems to be assuming the role of *in loco parentis*. There is no reason to *assume* the purpose of a business trip is not business, regardless of the sex of the managers involved. Men and women traveling together does not mean automatic intimacy. Even if intimacy should occur, it would not be the responsibility of the organization.

There continues to be a problem with male managers who travel alone if the company is going to assume responsibility for their behavior. Many senior managers have received complaints from wives of managers about travel requirements for their husbands. One corporate officer spoke of a wife who threatened to sue the firm but finally gave up for lack of evidence.

Some wives object to frequency and length of time away from home. Others feel that, since they provide support functions for their manager-husbands and are "part of the company team," that they influence company assignments he is given. And some wives fear that their husbands will take advantage of opportunities for extra-marital sex. Presumably management may have similar complaints from husbands of women managers.

Certainly top executives do not want to feel they are contributing to marital stress or exposing the company to potentially poor public relations because of an irate mate. Social critics used to be concerned about the frequency with which women, in the process of getting started in a career, secured a divorce. But we feel that may not be dysfunctional in society today. It may be better for both members of that couple in the long run. In any case, management should not

feel guilty or responsible for the divorce. Parenting of adults is out.

We wonder about the practicality of management to assume any responsibility for the private activities of its managers. If a married man or woman is going to engage in extra-marital sex, it will happen. Opportunities exist or can be made. Under the traditional values, such conduct means automatic marital problems. But today matters of marital fidelity are decisions made by the couples involved. Some find extra-marital affairs acceptable, not destructive to their marriage. Many others don't agree.

New questions where no policies exist; women managers, their husbands and families

Other new concerns for management may grow out of perceiving women as managers for the first time. The organization may wonder if the woman manager's husband is to be considered part of the company team, as is the manager's wife. Or, one question of etiquette is the query of a wife, *"Do I invite her out to lunch?"* This is often protocol for secretaries; is it for co-managers? When a wife extends a luncheon invitation to her husband-manager's secretary, she does it as an extended courtesy of her husband. Formally, the wife assumes the business status of her husband while performing this business function delegated to her.

But the woman-manager shares the manager protocol. Does the husband-manager delegate the business lunch with other managers to his wife now? No? The gesture would be interpreted as based on a personal relationship, not on business etiquette.

Does the husband-manager include the woman manager on occasions where he invites business associates to his home? Many subtleties play into this question, which at first may seem ridiculous. The question arises because she is a woman, not because she is a manager. As a woman she is automatically excluded; as a manager, she is automatically included with other managers. The risk is the first invitation. And the

risk for the woman's acceptance and status frequently hinges on being present in social-business situations. Women managers are more easily known as persons in the informal ease of a home, just as are men managers.

Some male managers, used to the idea of wives as providers of support systems for their husbands, assume the woman manager will have conflicts between the management role and the expectations of her husband and children who, it is claimed, will make demands of her. In any such conflict, it is further taken for granted that her home duties will take priority over her executive functions. Further, the same men fear that it will be a great liability to a woman manager not to have the support of a wife as social secretary and hostess. Again, this is non-conscious adherence to the old modes of thinking—and perhaps some loyalty to the old "men's club of management"—which makes the formulation of new policies difficult. Perhaps thinking about the contemporary styles of marriage may shed new light on women managers and their husbands and implications for promotion policies.

Non-traditional thinking allows even the possibility that a man would provide support services for his manager-wife. These services, traditionally expected from the manager's wife, include "serving as social secretary, accountant, chauffeur and sometimes his analyst."[16] This role reversal is not new. Husbands of women singers, painters, actresses and other glamour occupations have found their life styles filled with pleasure as well as financial gain.

Children too, have experienced the benefits of My Mother, the Working Woman. Recent studies show that "the percentage of disturbed children was three times as high in the homes of non-working mothers as compared to working mothers![17] The evidence continues to mount—the children of working mothers (including those with careers, not just jobs) are more self-reliant, mature and self-determining people. What a set of tools with which to face the world!

In making a number of recommendations for management

development programs for women managers, Marshall Brenner proposed that these might include "providing husbands of the development candidates with an understanding of the support functions required of them."[18] He recognized the conflicting roles that a married woman is expected to play when she is a manager and a wife. The company expects a large commitment from her as a manager; the husband expects support functions for himself. Brenner's proposal is to help the husband "in realigning his role expectations and in finding alternate sources of some of the support functions normally performed by the wife."[19] Interestingly, he does not suggest that the husband perform support functions for the wife such as she traditionally performs for him. He speaks to the more egalitarian balance whereby the husband finds new sources for himself, and presumably the wife-manager generates her own sources of support.

We question the appropriateness of including husband-training in a management development program, just as we question wife-training for corporate benefit. His point, that top management must seriously scrutinize its own assumptions that traditional patterns of marriage and of work will prevail, is well justified, however.

Other societal changes which will affect the management of organizations are occurring. As children cease to be the primary reason for the existence of marriage, higher value is placed upon the emotional relationship between husband and wife. That relationship is now expected to be closer and deeper than any other our society provides. Its intensity and the many expectations of it have caused marriage to be subject to heavier stresses at the same time that it has become more important. The modern marriages of many people have developed as temporary systems. We expect that trend will continue. For many other couples however, marriage remains the enduring relationship that provides an anchor in the midst of constant change, insurance against "future shock."

Childrearing, involving a smaller number of children, will

no longer be the sole responsibility of wives. Fathers are being deluged with data indicating they should spend more time with their children. And many want to. Both mothers and non-mothers are placing greater importance on their careers and they will have to be taken seriously.

With more choices about careers becoming increasingly important to both spouses, nepotism rules which prohibit the hiring of both husband and wife or those which prohibit them from working on the same project will gradually be eliminated. Otherwise a husband and wife who are trained in the same field (and this is becoming common) are forced into agonizing choices of whose career comes first. Many couples are choosing jobs which pay less but allow both to work, over those in which the husband is paid well but the wife cannot work.

The increasing emphasis on non-economic values and concepts supplementing economic ones means that some of the older assumptions about organizing and utilizing managerial resources must change to reflect the changing societal values. Companies which are changing are moving in the direction of providing more options, more flexibility, more egalitarian ways of relating with their key people.

Employees at all levels are selecting more individualistic approaches to their private lives and organizations find that home and family can well be separated from work. Step One for any organization is an assessment of whether or not the traditional utilization of wives as opinion-makers, personnel solicitors and alter egos is still viable. While many wives may continue in these roles, it will be more and more by choice. Many other wives are simply not available for such support since they are occupied with their own careers. Women managers may or may not have built-in support systems at home either.

Stability, long accepted among the primary criteria for selection of managers, has been judged by traditional family support systems. Experience and functional changes in managers' roles have demonstrated that being a "good family

man" or a "good family woman" does not necessarily provide the stability needed by top management.

Ask yourself—

For the manager concerned about his own or his subordinate managers' mates, clarifying policies could be developed from such questions as—

- If I had a woman boss, my wife would ————————
- If my woman managers are married I expect ————
- Or, if unmarried I expect ————————————
- My wife (or partner) is important to my work in ———
- The organization has a right to expect the manager's mate to ————————————————————

Notes

1. Bloustein, Edward J., "Man's Work Goes From Sun to Sun but Woman's Work Is Never Done," *Psychology Today*, March, 1968, p. 41.
2. Whyte, William H., Jr., *The Organization Man*, New York, Doubleday & Company, Inc., 1956. Part VII, The New Suburbia: Organization Man At Home describes the suburban life of Park Forest, where the wifely roles are played out.
3. U.S. Department of State, "Policy on Wives of Foreign Service Employees," Department notice to all State, AID and USIA employees, January 21, 1972, p. 1.
4. *Ibid.*, p. 2.
5. *Birth Expectations Data: June 1971*, Current Population Reports, Population Characteristics, U.S. Department of Commerce, Series P-20, No. 232, February, 1972, p. 1.
6. "The Power Behind the Throne," *Business Week*, January 18, 1971, p. 29.
7. The questionnaire was administered in a workshop, *Women in Management*, led by Theodora Wells, at the Industrial Relations Center, California Institute of Technology, Pasadena, CA 91109, November, 1970. Permission to quote responses granted.
8. "Mildred Johnson on Executive Wives (And their Husbands)," *Projector*, BNA Films (5615 Fishers Lane, Rockville, Maryland 20852), May, 1971, p. 3.
9. "Man, Wife, and Work," *Industry Week*, January 25, 1971, p. 29 ff.
10. *Ibid.*, p. 32.

11. Quoted from "Someone's in the Kitchen with Joanne," *New Woman*, 1972, p. 31. Excerpted from O'Neill, Nena and George, *Open Marriage: A New Lifestyle for Couples*, New York, M. Evans & Co., Inc., 1972.
12. *Ibid.*, p. 33.
13. Seidenberg, Robert, "Dear Mr. Success: Consider Your Wife," *Wall Street Journal*, February 7, 1972.
14. Bender, Marylin, "Executive Couples: Reluctance to Hire Husbands and Wives Is Fading," *The New York Times*, October 29, 1971.
15. Jones, John A., "Career Wives: New Factor in Relocating Key Workers," *Los Angeles Times*, April 16, 1972.
16. Brenner, Marshall, "Management Development Activities for Women," paper delivered at the American Psychological Association, Miami Beach, Florida, September 3, 1970, p. 8.
17. Marmor, Judd, "Women at Work—A Study In Prepudice," (referring to a review of such studies by Lois Stolz), p. 11. Adapted from an address delivered at the conference, "Exploding the Myths—Employment Opportunities for Career Women," December 1966, presented under the auspices of the Department of Daytime Programs and Special Projects, University Extension, UCLA. Published as a conference report by U.S. Department of Labor, Women's Bureau, 1967, pp. 51–56.
18. Brenner, *op. cit.*, p. 8.
19. *Ibid.*

7

Working Relationships That Work

I make the prediction that women managers will in the future be perceived as much sexier and more womanly than now . . . Success is sexy . . . and this will apply to women as well as men.

William J. Goode, President,
American Sociological Association[1]

Successful people are exciting to be around. Vibrant with energy, they inspire those around them to think with renewed vigor. Their vitality encourages others to want to do more, to stretch for new accomplishments. They are simply "turned on"—a contagious condition. Add the accoutrements of success—position, power, pay and prestige—and the combination is just plain stimulating.

This kind of success behavior is now available mostly to men. As women move further into management and executive offices, they are developing styles of behavior that are similar—more imaginative, freer-moving, vital. As their need to contend with stereotypic expectations lessens, women managers will neither fight, nor over-compensate for, role problems. And, as this need diminishes, stored energy is released for new, productive relationships.

Awareness is key to changing relationships, values, and climate of work

The challenge of management today is to provide ways for people to relate to each other as they renew and rebuild their organization responsively to changing values. The developing organization is the environment in which the development of managers takes place. Management must take responsibility for whatever discriminatory practices and attitudes presently exist. Responsibility should be shared with new women managers in creating a mutually accepting climate in which men and women can work effectively together.

If working relationship patterns must change to fit the new scene, what kinds of behaviors and attitudes are really productive? The list is long, but here's a start:

- A firm, but not rigid, recognition of the value of self, peers, superiors and subordinates
- Flexibility in decision-making processes
- Openness and clear communication, uncluttered by constant concern of what is role-expected
- Receptivity to inputs of staff and colleagues with minimum reference to seniority, status and sex
- Willingness to collaborate in team effort, letting go of acceptance/rejection games so there can be less defensiveness, more trust.

Awareness is the starting line. Awareness of what behavior comes through as patronizing; of when physical size differential becomes synonymous with mental size; of the actions that "speak louder than words."

Cue 1. Managerial women want the same valuing as men—the same attention, respect and consideration of their ideas, information and opinions.

Cue 2. Managerial women are available for the range of appropriate tasks and functions as are managerial men—but are not there to perform functions from

former positions of secretary, staff member, "assistant to."

Cue 3. Managerial women "hear" the language of traditional sex-relating as a signal of attitudes. Trite, tired and tasteless jokes alert them to the all-too-frequent reality that men who use these devices mean them.

Cue 4. Realistic expectations of responsibility for quality and quantity of productiveness neither shocks nor dismays a woman manager. Rather, she sees this as a signal that the relationship is working.

Cue 5. Managerial women are aware of the differences between lip service and commitment. They have learned to "hear" the body language and understand the subtlety of implicit "gentleman's agreements."

Conflict between "official" and "personal"

As with any change, an official position may be accompanied by intent to follow-through. However, in the very nature of an official position, the pressure to conform to regulations may be given lip service only.

Being logical about the benefits of promoting women into management may be quite difficult. Chris Argyris believes that there is a deep, underlying reason for executive resistance to being rational. After reviewing probable long-range effects of change, he observed that "managers slowly begin to realize that fundamental changes will be required in their personal styles of managers' thought and behavior. That's when the danger signals start."[2]

"We don't care who does it—black, white, male, female, whatever—just as long as the job gets done." A representative of a major broadcasting network is interpreting top management's attitude about integration of middle-level managers and operating professionals on the basis of both color and sex. The words don't quite fit the silent language of his outstretched arm pointing toward all those other people out there *away* from top management. His body completes his

sentence, ". . . as long as they're not near me and *I* don't have to work with them." When the meaning of this gesture is put into words, the implications become clear. It's one thing for people lower down to have to comply with these changes. It's another when it's occurring in the adjoining executive office.

Conflicts among many external and internal pressures

The conflict is real at whatever level it occurs. Managers are the center of a web of relationships which must be balanced and harmonized. If the job is to be done profitably, relationships must be effective and efficient. But managers also have to cope with multiple pressures that restrict their ability to act. Among these pressures are organizational processes: management controls of budgeting, personnel policies, cost controls, scheduling and external legal and regulatory restrictions. Outside institutions contribute changing ideas of what a good manager is. Internal rivalries weave political gaming threads. Adding tension to this web of complexity, managers carry an inner set of conflicts:

* assumptions about reality
* personal values, needs and aspirations
* actual capabilities
* personal views of self

The need to untangle personal and organizational needs can be a major preoccupation of managers even before women and the sex dimension are introduced into working relationships. But, as Abraham Zaleznik said, "Business managers, whether they know it or not, commit themselves to a career in which they have to work on themselves as a condition for effective working on and working with other people."[3]

Conflict in male-female role expectations

In an informal survey conducted by one of the authors in 1970-71 with various management groups,[4] women were

asked to complete the statement, "Men managers tend to treat women ———." Overwhelmingly they answered "as inferiors, protectively, as infants, a little condescending, with less respect," or other answers which showed that they had received different treatment from that accorded men.

Men were asked to complete the statement, "I think women are best suited for ———." Their answers: "living off the ulcerated intestines of their man, housework and kids if married, clerical positions, because they can seem to withstand the office environment without getting bored as easily as men, jobs that are easy and do not put much strain on them, attending parties, their duty is to raise children" and, of course, "sex." Fewer than a third of the responses gave non-role views such as "anything they want to do or be" or "anything men can do." Most responses were validations of the perceptions of stereotyping that the women had expressed. Thus, work-roles and sex-roles are in conflict, making visible the ". . . dynamic interplay between environmental forces and pressures operating on the manager, his values, personality, and aspirations . . . Role conflict is inescapable . . ."[5]

Culturally, society maintains a sex-dichotomy. Since people are primarily defined by their sex, not as persons, managers or other non-sexual categories, sex-linked expectations of behavior and relationships have evolved. As "we all know," men are tough, dominant, active leaders—rational; women are tender, submissive, passive, followers—emotional. Defined from such assumptions, most jobs have become sex-typed.

Stereotypes filter responses to women

Stereotypes function as screens that block out other experiences or information which would lead to personalized responses. Stereotypic screens filter responses to women and provide certain consistent patterns of thinking and reacting . . .

1. *Stereotypes are resistant to change.* "It's always been this way. I don't know why you think it should be any different. You'll have to prove it to me."
2. *Stereotypes are rooted in the collective unconscious, ageless archetypes,* passed on through legendary and religious folklore. "It's been true for so many for so long, there must be something to it."
3. *Stereotypes do not respond to rational evidence.* "Well, maybe those are some facts, but there are others that contradict them. I know how it *really* is . . ."
4. *What applies to one member of the stereotyped group applies to all members.* Example: Mary gets angry. Stereotype: "She just proves it. Women are too emotional."
5. *What applies to the total stereotyped group applies to each member of it.* "Women are too emotional. What can you expect of Mary? She's a woman!"
6. *Every member of the stereotyped group is just like every other member.* "They're both women, aren't they? Of course Mary and Miriam are both too emotional."
7. *Stereotypes do not transfer to a non-member of it.* For example: "Bill sure got mad this morning." Stereotypes: None. It does not follow that Bill's anger proves that "men are too emotional" even when the same event occurs. Instead, Bill is seen without this stereotype, as an individual who "probably had an argument at breakfast." (This, of course, implies that it was his wife who, because she is a woman, is too emotional. Bill's anger is thus justified.)
8. *Stereotypes make comparisons to unidentified yardsticks.* Re: "Women are too emotional." Compared to what, to whom? In what context? For what purposes? "Too" is a comparative adjective. Used in a stereotypic response, it seems to need no referent for comparison.
9. *Comparative stereotypes are judgmental and negative.* The comparative adjective "too" carries a negative connotation. There is an excess of a quality, and the excess is not valued.

10. *Stereotypes enjoy wide popularity. Sharing them can gain acceptance and expected comraderie—the common bond.* Globalized humor, locker room innuendoes and old-fashioned courtesy that implies weakness of head as well as muscle—these are the strands tying the bond in "Isn't that just like a woman!"

11. *Stereotypes are often used to elicit sex-role behavior.* "Anne, how about you taking minutes today?" Anne, vice-president, being the only woman at the officers' meeting, is seen as the logical secretary.

12. *Stereotypes are applied with different meanings to the same category and used interchangeably:* Example: "Women who want to be treated like women will act more like women " Clearer communication might have said "Adult females who wanted to be treated as normal women, will behave like the Eternal Feminine Ideal."

13. *Deviators from the stereotype must be exceptional to withstand the pressure to be cast back into it.* "A woman's got to be better than average to gain the respect of men, so good she can't be disregarded . . ."

14. *Deviators from the stereotypes are exceptions, admired but with no expectation that it can be repeated.* "She's a crackerjack manager. No more (women) around like her!"[6]

The power of stereotypic expectations of women and the images they conjure up are all encompassing indeed. One manager, male, head of an auditing section where professional staff were given field assignments, had no women auditors. The organization's affirmative action program called for more qualified women at all levels and in all functions. In line with this program, the management development officer questioned the chief auditor at some length about his lack of women auditors. After numerous evasions, eventually pushed to the wall, he finally blurted out, "I *know* what they do out there!" As his fears unfolded, he fought back with, "Where would they sleep?" Obviously to him, any woman given tnat much latitude away from the control of the office,

would be out seducing men and creating all kinds of impossible problems for him to handle. Conceptually he could not imagine a woman controlling herself personally as well as professionally.

Men question how to treat women managers as persons

For some men, thinking of a woman manager as a person raises the question, "*Do you treat her like one of the boys, then?*" The very question sounds like an insult to many women. The question still is posed in terms of male or female. To some men, working with a woman manager "as if she were a man" means working with a competent person who is expected to carry the responsibilities of the position. In a colleague sense, she is accepted on the management team. But even here, sex-roles are operational, for most men tend to treat an attractive woman differently from an unattractive one. "For all the talk about character and inner values, we assume the best about pretty people. And from grade school on, there's almost no dispute about who's beautiful."[7] If a woman is unattractive, she is seldom influential in the sphere of men. If she is attractive, she is more likely to be accepted. Less severely, the same thing operates for men.

Almost no management positions have valid requirements that automatically disqualify either all women or all men. The traditional pressures from which women have been legally "protected"—weightlifting and long hours—are simply not applicable to management positions. Managers, by status, do not lift heavy objects. They call the maintenance crew or lower-status males. Long hours always go with exempt positions, whether at management levels or lower. Women selected for management positions typically have been putting in long overtime hours without extra pay and without compensatory time off in order to achieve some of their

goals. Men do the same thing. It's simply part of the process of doing well the work you want to do.

There are some men who are quite comfortable, even admiring, of those women who are willing to put forth the effort to give them a good run for the money. It's the old challenge with a new twist: May the best *person* win. Not all managers are as ready to think this way. One insidious fear we have heard is *"What if a woman is promoted over me?"* A man competing for advancement wants to win. If he has to lose, he would rather lose to a man. For some men, losing to a woman seems singularly threatening and apparently more permanent, thanks to the traditional male role

Superior goes with masculine and inferior with feminine when jobs are sex-typed. Thus male-female relationships are at the same time superior-subordinate relationships. Given this correlation, men are not likely to get much open feedback from women and may be unaware of built-in habits of putting women down. Accustomed to relating only to lower job level women, many men find themselves puzzled, perhaps threatened, when considering how to relate to women on the same level. The old answers to the question *"How do I handle this woman?"* are wrong because now the question is wrong. To think of "handling" is controlling, making it difficult to think of women as persons, professionals, peer-managers.

A male manager may gradually accept a woman's capabilities of she "proves" herself to him. This proving process has an extra dimension for a woman compared to a man. A man proves his capabilities to perform required management functions, period. A woman must prove she has the same performance capabilities *in spite of being female*. She must prove that an *assumed* handicap does not apply to her, that the negative expectations of her, female, do not apply to her personally. She is required to break out of stereotypes defining her by her sex. For example, she frequently

takes risks on the job; risks related to profits, meeting interventions and decision-making. Since women aren't expected to take risks, many men find it difficult to accept this risk-taking as credible. A man, doing the same things, would be assumed to be credible until proven otherwise.

If the man manager can see the woman manager as able to perform well in managerial roles, usually he can give credit to her work, although occasionally with reservations. His self-image of being rational, fair and objective is thereby preserved. This provides a genuine congruence between his work-role and the competence aspect of the male-role. It does not yet satisfy another part of the male role: sexual dominance.

What has sexual dominance to do with managerial relationships? For most men in our culture, masculinity and occupation are so intimately intermeshed that it is difficult to separate them. This underlies the implicit dilemma: "How do I relate to a manager who is competent (an equal peer) and female (an unequal subordinate)?"

Let's try restating the question: *"How can I make the masculine/feminine equation feel more equal?"* If we move to a *person* level, it comes clearer. We can all think of persons who are biological males who seem more empathic, less aggressive, and more supportive than the usual expections for "a man's man." We can also think of persons who are biological females who assume more responsibility, are more independent and decisive than the usual expectations for the dependent feminine role of "a real woman."

> *Persons who happen to be male or female—a different way of relating.*

Empathy, aggressiveness, supportiveness, independence . . . all such traits are human traits. Labeling them masculine or feminine is a social practice that limits human expression. It also limits our ability to relate to men or

women as humans—persons whose individual style is their own.

As long as we think of men and women as sex-roles, the element of sexual dominance of men over women will distort peer relationships. Exploitation through sex has a certain appearance of legitimacy, if for no other reason than that it is so widely practiced. When we begin to think of men and women as persons, using different kinds of strengths, sexual dominance is far less important. Collaboration replaces conquest.

A way to define *"What is a person?"* while using definitions we have come to think of as masculine or feminine has been developed by Lee Christie, research psychologist. He finds four clusters of strengths that characterize people. The first two are socially-labelled masculine; the last two, feminine.

- *The deliberative-manipulative cluster of strengths.* This is the ability to get things done; to go out into your environment and find a place in it and cope with it; to get that environment to pay off for you.
- *Risk-taking strengths.* This is the willingness to expose yourself; to take a chance that others may not see you as you'd like to be seen.
- *The strength of being an attractive person.* This involves being "nice to be with" and "not hurting others' feelings."
- *The strength of empathic character.* This is the strength of feeling *with* other people—sensing where they are emotionally, in some depth.

All are *human* strengths, according to Christie. We all have all of them to some degree although some may be deliberately or subconsciously suppressed. If we combine them in other than stereotypic fashion interesting things result. For example, take "being nice" and "being deliberative-manipulative." Here we find a very coping person who

defends himself or herself and copes well with the world. Many Americans today, both male and female, are characterized by this coping approach because it is acceptable to our competition-based society. Or, combine "risk-taking" and "empathic" and we have a person who matches Maslow's idea of the self-actualizing individual—another combination finding increasing acceptance as we move into new areas of understanding.[8]

Acceptance of change, game-playing and new styles of behavior

The opportunity for qualified women to use their capabilities under similar competitive circumstances as men is a central concern of most female change-makers. As a matter of simple justice, women (as well as men) who seek advancement want to feel that they have been given fair consideration and a reasonable opportunity to show what they can do. They want room to stretch themselves and to assume a greater role in the organization's future.

Acceptance is as critical to women managers as it is to men—acceptance as a competent manager and acceptance as a person. Both kinds of acceptance are vital to her and to him in order for them to function effectively. At the present time acceptance is far more a problem for women managers than for men; it requires establishing rather than already being established.

One of the questions that women managers may ask themselves is *"To what degree am I willing to gain acceptance by using expected 'feminine' behavior?"* It is easy for some women to turn on the charm and be quick with the winning smile and feel no duplicity in playing this role. Some send out double messages by playing the "helpless female" role while simultaneously using a quick mind. For others it feels hypocritical and they prefer the direct approach. Most people feel that some amount of game-playing is needed for

survival. Male-female games are only one variant of the genre.

Some women respond from a range of behaviors, and are less predictable since they can move with the situation. These variations in behavior are possible when the woman manager has enough self-awareness to be able to respond appropriately recognizing her own needs and the needs of the group. There are decisions about how openly to "present" themselves, how honestly to express independence or anger. Most women managers don't dream of exploding in volume and language when angry, though many men do. That doesn't mean women are less angry, only that they are aware of expectations of masculine behavior vs. feminine behavior, both physical and emotional.

Women managers today are pioneers, locating new territories, providing experience for other women and for men as they work together in new relationships. Using ˙ome of the positive values of "femininity"-sensitiveness to another person's feelings and trying to meet them there—can make work progress more easily. Judging others and taking their moods personally is avoided. This is responsible communication, often stereotypically valued as a feminine quality, but better described as mature behavior in either sex.

Certain kinds of "feminine" behavior that cater to the sexual image of femininity are potential traps for the woman manager. She is often coaxed to come on more seductively. If she does, she probably will not be taken seriously in her work. If she doesn't, she may be accused of being too serious and therefore "unfeminine." If she assumes strong leadership, she may be received as "coming on too strong." If she doesn't give strong leadership, she is discounted as ineffective, "just like a woman." The new women managers are matter of fact about their willingness to be assertive, firm and demanding. Frequently the charge is made that such women are taking themselves too seri-

ously and lack humor. Rarely do the pages of history record that crusaders and change agents were great wits. Evidently, participating in the production of new patterns is far more involving than amusing.

The newest relationship: women managers of men

The least tried relationship is women managing men. History has recorded few models like Katherine de Medici, Elizabeth of England, and Joan of Arc. Even the contemporary scene with Indira Gandhi, Golda Meir and several dozen U. S. women mayors or congresswomen, presents but a skimpy array of models for women managing public affairs. For the few women managers of men in business, goverment, education, health and community service organizations, it has been a wheel-inventing experience.

To date most managers have been able to ignore the questions of working *with* or *for* a woman, since the vast majority of women work at lower levels. The only problems that most managers have experienced are in the formal role of supervising women and occasional questions of informal, more intimate relationships.

Today the prospect is different. Working with women as peers, competing with women for advancement, and collaborating as peers to attain organizational objectives are becoming realities. In small but growing numbers, men are faced with working *for* a woman. Other men have the responsibility for developing women managers and helping them to integrate themselves into the already established predominately male management group.

Apparently, it is a strange and wonderful experience for men to figure out how to be familiar without being too familiar—while being sufficiently respectful of position and "a woman." Here are some incidents (and questioning thoughts) between men, subordinates and peers, relating to women managers.

- One woman bureau chief in the Federal Government reported that men stopped joking whenever she entered the meeting room. (Language unseemly for a lady?)
- A female hospital administrator found physical contact frequently used by the junior males in her department. (Is a hand on the knee or an arm around the waist the same as a slap on the shoulder?)
- Some men kiss women peers at work as casually as they do at social occasions. (Is a greeting kiss the same as a handshake? Why can't women shake hands as men do?)
- Margaret Chase Smith reported potential difficulties when, as a freshman Senator, all the "courtly gentlemen" senators stood up in her presence. (If I accept their courtesy, will they accept my logic?)
- Another woman executive, this time in the public relations field, periodically receives so-called praise from a male peer who announces to her, "Today I like the way you behaved; sometimes you're bitchy." (When his manner is at odds with hers or with other department heads does that make him a bastard?)

To cope with such situations women managers today are handling these situations with a combination of ways, using their past experience in human relations, persuasion, arbitration and discipline.

Awareness provides new information for making logical changes

Women's expertise in relationship building and repair becomes a bridge to understanding. Obviously men are aware of maintenance of relationships as a generalized need in organizational processes. Many of them have developed their sensitivity through management courses, workshops and labs. And many will use similar skills in learning to listen for their own non-conscious attitudes.

Senator John Tunney of California is an unusual example of such a listener. He seems eager to understand what non-conscious attitudes his comments convey so he can become

more aware of the assumptions he actually has about women. With sensitive feedback, he and his legislative aide, Jane Lakes Frank, make up a continuing learning team of communication.[9]

A stance of learning—of listening, hearing, feedback—helps us go beyond outmoded patterns of stereotypic responses in working relationships between men and women managers. Awareness provides new premises for logic to operate on.

Ask yourself—

- What apprehensions do I have in working with women as peers? As superiors?
- Do I regard most women as having a set pattern of relating to men? Can I recognize a range—from cool, crisp and collected, to warm, empathic and accepting? Do I believe that this affects how well-qualified a woman is? How?
- How do I handle whatever sexual feelings I have around women associates at work?
- What is the language that reveals my convictions about male/female relationships? Have I gotten a clear reading lately?

Notes

1. Quoted in an interview by Marylin Bender, "Women Managers and Marriages," *The New York Times*, December 26, 1971.
2. Argyris, Chris, "Resistance to Rational Management Systems," *Innovation*, Number 10, 1970, p. 30.
3. Zaleznik, Abraham, "Management of Disappointment," *Harvard Business Review*, November–December 1967, p. 67.
4. Among the management groups surveyed by Theodora Wells were the Administrative Management Society, Los Angeles Chapter; managers and supervisors at a conference on Living and Growing with Change, Industrial Relations Institute, California Institute of Technology; and adult students of office management at San Fernando Valley State, Professor G. Jay Christensen.
5. McGregor, Douglas, *The Professional Manager* (Edited by Caroline McGregor and Warren G. Bennis), New York, McGraw-Hill Book Co., 1967, p. 55.

6. Wells, Theodora, Concept and Development of Stereotypic Filters, first presented in October, 1971, in *Management Development for Women*, a course pioneered in 1968 with the Department of Daytime Programs and Special Programs, University Extension, UCLA.
7. Berscheid, Ellen and Elaine Walster, "Beauty and the Best," *Psychology Today*, March, 1972, p. 42.
8. Christie, Lee, cited by Phillip E. Frandson, "Sex-Role Changes: What of the Future," paper delivered at the pre-conference workshop *A Professional's Guide to Continuing Education for Women;* National University Extension Association at Columbia, South Carolina, on April 30, 1972. Frandson is Associate Dean of University Extension, University of California at Los Angeles.
9. Cimons, Marlene, "Tunney Side Brings Lib Out of the Woodwork," *Los Angeles Times*, Part IV, May 12, 1972, p. 1.

8

Won't Women...?

"Men's concerns reflect outmoded behavioral norms and role expectations."

Charles D. Orth and Frederic Jacobs,
Harvard Business Review[1]

Every controversial field has its conventional mythology. The specific concerns around the subject and subjection of women have inspired lyrical poetry and political tracts. At Mother's knee, through cultural osmosis, via the media, we absorb the message. The familiar concerns come out of hibernation with the issue of women in management. "What if?" comes out as "Won't women . . .?" These concerns, sometimes attacks, are still being used to "Keep women in their place" . . . behind men.

Back in 1964, *Newsfront,* a thoughtful magazine distributed free to management men carried an article, "Does a lady executive need to be more— or less—of a woman?"[2] In 1965, *Harvard Business Review* ran a feature study, "Can Women Executives Be People?"[3] Both publications were primarily edited by men, and these article titles reflected the prevailing attitudes of the day.

Not much has changed. In early 1972, *The MBA,* a management slick distributed free to students, faculty and alumni of graduate business schools, carried a feature, "How much of a woman should a woman in business be?"[4] Eighteen managerial women were found who responded to this stereotypic double-bind question. The most frequent re-

144

sponse had to do with being a competent person while accepting being female. However, Martha Stuart, founder of her own communications firm in New York, was the one to make the double-bind sharply visible with, "How much of a man should a man who is a father be?"[5]

Competition from women was clearly not welcomed by the men who put the issue together. Fear of women using all their feminine ammunition was announced in another article, "When She Gets Your Job, Here's What She'll Be Wearing."

The copy reads like a big game hunt: "the liberated Ms. moving in for the 'executive kill,' " fully dressed for the adventure in "jungle-red blouse, satin jacket dripping with blood-red cherries . . . smoking a cheroot . . ." The spectre of the aggressive female crouching with animal cunning was advanced in full dress: "Ms. will do anything to grab that million-dollar account away from you—garb herself in a Garbo-like cloche hat, glitter dress and mink to slink around the right places in a rented Rolls. It's a whole new power play . . . Beware. She's stalking down Madison Ave. to bag your clients in a safari outfit . . . She stoops to conquer your swivel chair and executive restroom key . . ." In the style of a Ray Lichtenstein zap-cartoon, the cover has a sultry, cleavaged blonde castrating men with, "You're fired."[6]

A graduate student, hired by IBM, for example, is going to have difficulty reconciling this image with the official IBM equal opportunity stance of promoting women into management.[7] They, like many other corporations, are implementing new policies and programs to meet the challenges of legal requirements, pressure from increasing numbers of women and a heightened sense of justice. Will the jungle image become the unofficial attitude that sets teeth on edge whenever a woman shows aggressiveness or racks up top sales?

The conflict among these images strongly suggests to us that what women are saying about themselves is not being heard above the drums of pending warfare. Rather than

kill, achieving women are saying that they are resolving the double-bind of femininity by merging the feminine with their competence. As Emily H. Womach, Delaware State Treasurer puts it, "No one can be less than a total person and be successful in any endeavor. A woman in business brings all her talents—as an individual and a woman—to the job. Each individual is different in many ways, and being a woman is just a part of these differences."[8] And Edith Grimm, Vice President Merchandising, Carson, Pirie, Scott & Co.: "A woman in business is successful because she is herself and not because she is an imitation of someone else. Talent doesn't have a gender, nor does intelligence."[9]

Many of these voices are the exceptional ones, the ones who have "made it," the ones who have successfully coped with the images and imaginations of the myths of men. Many others did not rise through the organization as do men, but got there by way of loopholes that are among the few ways women have been able to get to the top at all—widowhood, stock ownership, or heading their own businesses.

Now that organizations are required to open their upward channels to women on an equal basis with men, the concerns of whether women will act like managers or just "like women," keep cropping up. As the conventional barrage begins, we offer some unconventional commentary . . .

In her roles as a women, wife, mother, can she really be committed to a career?

Doesn't the organization have a right to know a woman's plans for marriage, family, and length of time she plans to work?

Yes, when men are also asked their plans for marriage, family and length of time they plan to work in this organization. How long will a man stay *in a comparable position* before he leaves to improve himself?

Won't women managers be subject to pregnancy, childbirth and the
care of small children, which will mean they will quit and therefore
their training lost to the organization?

At present there is little cause for this concern, because most women have their last child at age 26 and at that age they are rarely under consideration for a management position. Women generally are older than men when considered for the same level positions.

As for leaving for the purpose of staying home with children, one 1970 study of workers showed that women are somewhat less prone to leave jobs than are men, and of the women quitting (including all groups and job levels) only 11.5 percent said they were leaving for family reasons.[10] Unlike secretaries and bookkeepers who have relatively easy job mobility, women managers are much less likely to leave; they have positions that cannot easily be duplicated elsewhere. Further, their general motivations are substantially different from those of women at lesser paid, less responsible levels.

As for young women managers, birth control is improving and abortion laws are being liberalized. More women are choosing to be childless today, and a challenging job gives many women the fulfillment they might otherwise seek in motherhood. Social acceptance of such choices is increasing, so it is reasonable to predict that the pattern of reduced numbers of children per family will continue.

For those young women who have children and also aspire to higher positions, the demand for child care will increase. No other single factor discriminates against women's employment so totally as motherhood. As the responsibilities and costs of child care are more equitably distributed between men, women and society, more women can realistically build career objectives. In the meantime, young women in higher-level positions do the obvious: provide for child care and for most emergencies

What if her children are sick?

Family reasons for absences occur with both men and women. When the job level and pay are low enough so that it is an economic loss or an even exchange to hire a qualified person for sick-child care, the motivation for staying at work is rather low. For women in higher level positions, the economic motives balance in favor of staying on the job and arrangements usually have been worked out for this contingency. Emergencies and family crises may require absence from work of either parent.

The nature of emergency arrangements for children should be asked of both men and women if it's asked at all. At an affirmative action conference, one equal opportunity representative reported that his company has started asking these questions of both men and women. Interviewers have discovered that men are far more involved in the lives and care of their children than had been predicted.

Don't women have a greater turnover rate?

U.S. Department of Labor comments "Labor turnover rates are influenced more by the skill level of the job, the age of the worker, the worker's record of job stability and the worker's length of service with the employer than by sex . . ."[11] The frequency with which men leave for better jobs effectively offsets women leaving to have children.

Don't women have a greater absentee rate?

Men and women have about the same absentee rate, when acute and chronic conditions are counted. Then men average 5.4 days per year, women 5.3 days.[12] Again, time out is tied to level of involvement and responsibility. The stability of a small percentage of women in higher-level positions more than offsets the higher absenteeism of younger women in the lower skilled, lower-paid jobs. Women and men managers maintain about the same percentage of time off regardless

of reason, ranging from illness to pleasure, from legal and personal problems to upgrading careers through education

Won't women refuse management positions because they feel it will cut into their time off and family responsibilities?

Some will, some won't. Many men do not want to give so much of their lives to the job and its stresses either. New priorities and values held by them have recently curtailed executive recruitment among younger men. A long hard look at the extra requirements for higher positions may be needed. For similar reasons, for both men and women there comes a point when the price of success is so high that it is questioned.

Women don't want to be managers because of the extra work load.

Just try them. Why are the Equal Employment Opportunity Commission, the Office of Federal Contract Compliance, the Wage and Hour Division, and the courts being inundated with cases involving discrimination against women if women are not ambitious? For example, one of the first court cases involving women in management was a class action recently settled by consent decree with Household Finance Corporation. Women who had been consistently passed up for advancement were promoted and awarded back pay with interest.[13]

Women don't need to work because their husbands can support them. They work only for luxuries and therefore don't have the commitment necessary for a managerial position.

Again, this assumes marriage and wife dependency as a pattern which all women will choose. But the facts of life are substantially different. Among women in the workforce, 41 percent are single, widowed, divorced or married with husband absent. Only 59 percent are married with husband present.[14]

This concern implies that commitment is a function of

economic necessity. It is interesting to note that the higher up the ladder a manager goes, the more he or she has multiple sources of income such as investments, stock options, executive incentive-and-bonus plans, and memberships on boards of directors. No one expects men managers to be less committed because they have enough financial resources to retire at age 40. Members of the Young Presidents Organization, having made their first million before reaching 40, are not known for lack of commitment due to economic security!

Further, there is a considerable body of motivational research indicating that the economic motive is only one of many important factors contributing to a sense of commitment.

> **Because of her basic physiological makeup, do women have the emotional stability needed for managerial responsibilities?**

Women can be expected to be in a bad mood once a month due to hormonal changes; and worse, while going through menopause, will be "subject to curious mental aberrations" or insanity, such as involutional melancholia. How can they be in responsible positions?

This "raging hormones" myth was escalated into a national controversy in 1971 when Dr. Edgar Berman, then a member of the Democratic National Committee's policy planning council, claimed that these physical changes made women poor risks for key executive jobs, using the "mental aberration" argument above.

Dr. Estelle Ramey, an endocrinologist and professor of physiology and biophysics at Georgetown University Medical school, countered with facts and comparisons with men as tests of reasonableness. Regarding decision-making ability she stated, "Where women have been able to move along to the top, there is no evidence that hormonal changes have made her a poor decision-maker. And even if she does have

menstrual problems, should we let that hold her back? If a man has a peptic ulcer, should we let him be President? Peptic ulcers are cyclical, too."[15]

Dr. Robert Greenblatt, chief of endocrinology at the Medical College of Georgia commented, "A woman smart enough to attain a key position would certainly be smart enough to get medical advice."[16]

In his text, *Human Endocrinology*, Dr. Herbert S. Kupperman, reports that 50.8 percent of women have no symptom of menopause except the cessation of menses. Another 45 percent worked as usual without interruption and only 5 percent were incapacitated at intervals.[17]

Menstruation is a normal function that women learn to live with in spite of the many taboos around it. While there may be some physical discomfort involved for some, the medical and pharmaceutical professions have helped considerably by developing medications that, for all practical purposes, eliminate most symptoms. Women can reasonably be expected to provide sufficient care for themselves with their physical problems to keep working effectively, just as is expected of men. There is no valid reason for singling out this function for special cautionary measures.

It is also quite possible that such changes can have energizing effects. Some women are greatly relieved that the risk of pregnancy is past and, having no fear of sexuality loss with menopause, they perceive themselves entering a new phase of activities where the home/career conflicts are gone. Focus of energy is sharper and commitment greater.

"What about menopausal men, or doesn't that count?" queries Dr. William Masters, co-author of *Human Sexual Inadequacy*. "It may well be that the male executive age about 55 to 65 goes through the same sort of steroidal imbalance."[18] Several medical textbooks describe a male climacteric period, the symptoms of which include nervous tension, instability of emotions, irritability, moodiness, lapses of memory and inability to concentrate. A Danish study revealed a 30-day rhythm in the hormones of men corresponding closely with

women's 28-day cycle and involving changes of mood and energy level. A Japanese transport company, adjusting schedules to the male drivers' lunar cycles, report a one-third drop in accidents in two years. Women have generally learned to live with their cycles; men have, generally, denied the existence of theirs.[19]

Questions about women's hormonal patterns are simply the wrong questions. Management should be asking how to take advantage of energy peaks in both men and women and how the physical, emotional and psychological changes of middle age may affect the managerial functions carried by men and by women. The man who needs to prove his virility or fears competing with younger people may have no more or less effect on the direction of the organization that the woman approaching menopause.

Won't women take things too personally to be managers?

Another stereotype. *Which* women take *what* things too personally compared to *whom?* What is taking something *personally?*

Women have learned objectivity from their work experience, which is typically longer than that of men in the same positions. They have to be as objective as men, or more so. It is essential for their survival and achievement. Women raised in traditional patterns are prepared through that training and experience to be aware of a wide range of human needs and possible reactions and so they listen to others' personal reactions. This awareness is an important strength for any manager, not a disqualifying weakness.

Women often respond to anger, hurt or frustration by crying. What do you do if a woman manager cries?

Rare indeed is the woman manager who "falls apart" at all, much less crying in the public glare of the workplace. She is usually familiar too with more effective ways of handling situations before she reaches such a state of frustration. Most are too aware of the negative stereotypic trap about "emo-

tional" women to permit themselves the luxury of tears. And most would agree that this is inappropriate behavior for the environment and position. Many feel it is simply immature.

If a woman manager needs to find expression in an intensely frustrating, pressure situation, she usually finds some way to "grit through" until she can do her crying in private. The unwritten rules require it. We have had many informal conversations with a variety of managers, men, who have had to deal with women in tears. In virtually every instance, the women involved were in entry-level, non-supervisory positions, about age 22 or less.

If a woman uses crying to manipulate men, she probably will become known as a manipulator. Depending on the man she is trying to control, she will (1) continue to get away with it; (2) exchange manipulations; or (3) be rendered ineffective through non-participation by the man. The manipulator requires the collusion of the manipulated.

Many men, having learned well to choke down or not feel the pressure of tears, may feel superior to the woman who "gives in" to such "weakness." These same men have learned other ways for a "real man" to respond to frustration. While anger or loss of temper is hardly the best response, men are not physically punished if they express themselves that way. Studies at Oregon State College and Columbia University showed that under the same test conditions, the average man lost his temper six times to the average woman's three.[20] The male values of stoic control have provided standards of appropriate behavior in the work world. What a relief it would be to both men and women if human feelings were permitted freer expression. It might reduce the ulcer and heart attack rates.

Women aren't hard-nosed enough to be good negotiators.

Many women learn how to make things happen because those who have moved far enough up in the organization to be participating in strategy formulation have had to develop the necessary skills. When willingness to take risks is also

present, women are among the most skillful strategists and negotiators, moving with the gaming situation. If she maintains confidentiality and has a fine sense of time, she can be a powerful, valuable part of a strategy or negotiating team. This kind of professional maturity is hard to find in either men or women, but certainly some women are well-qualified.

Some men operate under the illusion that a woman is a pushover who succumbs to flattery at lunch and seduction in the afternoon. Such a "salesman" is an easy protagonist in negotiations with a sophisticated woman. He won't know what hit him as she leaves unseduced with the information she wants. His image of women may then dissolve into the jungle scene noted above—because he made the wrong assumptions.

When all else fails, two versions of femininity or masculinity questions are raised.

Won't women lose their femininity if they become managers?

What is femininity? If it is a *natural* difference between the sexes, then it is impossible to lose. If it is an *unnatural role behavior* society has forced on women, then of course they will lose it when they no longer are or feel inferior—and about time!

Won't women who go into management become too masculine?

Women who are interested in management come with various styles, as do men. Strange that men first worry about women managers acting too feminine and then suspect they will be too masculine (meaning aggressive?). To paraphrase Freud, "What *do* men what? My God, what do they want?"

Sex? In management?

One undeniable difference between men and women is anatomy. So the possibility of sexual relationships involving managers is sometimes a fantasy and sometimes a reality. In

either case, the issue can be distressful to many men and some women. Nevertheless, it's real.

Won't sexual tensions, when men are working together with women as managers, disrupt working relationships and hinder progress for the organization?

For an individual person, sexual feelings may never arise in the working environment. Some women will even deny their sexuality in an effort to be sure that they achieve through their own competence, *not* through sex. This is really a peculiar concern, however, because employers seem to worry very little about the distraction of sexual attraction between men and their female secretaries.

Won't men and women managers have feelings of attraction so powerful that they will have little or no control over themselves?

The imperative to act on feeling "overcome by desire," is a potent myth, slow to change. Most of the advertising themes, best-sellers and romantic lyrics play on this idea. Most of us have had, at one time or another, a feeling of "chemistry" with another person. And we know that having outside sexual relations may cause problems with spouses or bosses. Amazingly, the "I couldn't help it," excuse has worked all too often for so long that it is integrated into our belief systems. Men may forgive each other for occasional slips, but for a woman, already coping with the "emotional" stereotype, it can be the death knell. She will be the one to go if the office romance is discovered . . . at least up until recently.

But no more. Its both or none, says EEOC. A switchboard operator was fired when her boss discovered she was "having an affair" with a male employee. The man was only "talked to." Double standard, said EEOC, declaring her dismissal constituted sex bias.[21]

Won't a woman manager use sex to get what she wants?

For a woman to exploit sex is to enter a competitive, adversary, win-lose battle, using a man as an object to mani-

pulate and coerce for personal gain. Even though such techniques, whether for sexual or non-sexual purposes, are found in most if not all organizations, the pay-off is inappropriate and most women recognize the device as counter-productive. A few women have used their charms to great personal advantage. With such an effective asset, they have seen no reason not to use it. For men, the use of sex to gain competitive advantage is by now institutionalized in "the employment of call girls and amenable secretaries to promote business deals."[22]

Most women who achieve middle or upper level management have long since learned that the fastest way out of an organization is to manipulate their way sexually. Very few will gamble what they have achieved on something so nebulous. The price may be a woman's entire career—a bad bargain.

What about the social niceties?

Among the quips tossed to women as they strive for equality are, "Well, don't expect the Prince Valiant courtesies anymore!"

Men learn early most of the cultural norms about how to treat a secretary, a date or his wife, as well as the woman who is a stranger. But few, if any, norms exist about how to treat a woman who is a peer or superior. Many managers, even to the level of the president, find this lack of norms worrisome. Some feel it's a nuisance to have to think of new ways to relate with women when other problems seem more important. Thus, we offer some thoughts . . .

Are women willing to give up their treasured and protected status for the opportunity to be equal in competition, status and money?

Yes, some are. Women are on the pedestal very few hours a day. In the lowly work they are presently assigned, including housework and office drudgery, women are not protected and treasured. The 42 percent of working women who are

widowed, single, divorced or separated, have no one to treasure and protect them at all. Furthermore, women are not protected from pollution, war, traffic, alcholism, rape, taxes or even from opening their own doors when no gallant man is around. As one woman film producer put it, "For $5,000 a year, I'll open the door myself."

What about chivalry toward women? Won't women managers want the courtesies accorded to their sex?

Courtesy and consideration from both sexes toward members of either sex should be the principle. If old habits are comfortable, keep them. But don't hold women responsible for *your* choice.

Men have to watch their language and jokes when women are around.

Many men may enjoy sex banter and scatology in their congeniality as a contrast to the formalized, "appropriate" behavior expected of them on public platforms and in boudoirs. As hierarchies flatten and sex-roles dissolve, the need for relief from expectations of propriety by the other sex may lessen. In the meantime, few women have lived in today's home and work world without four-letter words being uttered in their presence by all ages and both genders, sometimes by themselves. To consider her shell-pink ears too delicate for such words is sheer nonsense. Some women are offended by such taste, others are not. Some men seem even more offended than many women managers we know.

Our men have to do quite a bit of social drinking. We can't ask a woman to do that.

The Victorian era is over. Many men in management, however, have made social drinking an essential part of doing business and expect men to be able to hold their liquor. Stereotypically, women don't hold theirs as well. The truth is when either men or women drink beyond their capacity they aren't effective. Therefore, it is reasonable to expect that

managers, regardless of sex, should be held responsible for their own drinking behavior when engaged in business and given similar consideration or penalty if they can't or don't do so. They're adults.

Who pays for lunch when a man and woman lunch together?

Many men complain that women "want to be treated as equals but expect you to buy their lunch."

Likewise, many women ask, "How do I pay the bill without stepping on his precious male ego?"

It sounds like a standoff. Rather than risk undermining the well-advertised male ego by offering to pay, many women pass. By existing social custom, it is the man's problem. Both bottle up their feelings. Restaurants reinforce the impasse by automatically giving the check to the man. The out-fumbling game is difficult to play between a man and a woman within the existing etiquette.

If equal responsibility is sought, it is not the man's problem alone—it is a shared problem, often decided when lunch plans are made.

Some men find it virtually impossible to let a woman pay for them. A sensitive woman would probably not offer to pay in that case, or at least would not insist on it, sensing this as a more considerate choice. Men who feel this way, however, cannot very well blame the woman for their choice to conform to the male stereotype.

When a woman invites a man to a business social lunch, she usually expects to pay. When organizations give their women managers the same credit privileges of expense accounts as they do their men, this conflict will cease to exist. People can then make simple, straightforward choices about which invitations to extend and accept.

What's wrong with calling women "girls?" Is "lady" better?

"Girls" is becoming about as acceptable as calling black men "boys." It's a diminuitive that suggests general inferiority or childlikeness. "Lady" as identification often is gen

uinely valued by both men and women, but frequently it has a deceptive resonance. The word achieved prominence in the days of chivalry and was then and still is used to put women on a pedestal. That position has now been identified as a safe one for those who treasure a somewhat protected and aloof status.

Try "women"—it's usually safe!

> **Back to practical matters, what about some hard cash considerations in placing women in management, as well as how they relate to others?**

We can get women managers for less pay than we give men, so why should we waste money by paying women more than the minimum they will accept? After all, $18,000 is still pretty good for a woman.

First of all, discrimination in pay on the basis of sex is illegal. Secondly, are you paying for the work they produce or for their anatomy?

Women as well as men really don't want to work for women managers. What if the staff will not accept her?

Men as well as women must earn the trust and respect of their subordinates. For women to establish rapport will usually be more difficult. One method of speeding the process is for management to indicate in every possible way that *they support* the woman as manager. It should be made clear that placing her there is evidence of their judgment that she can do the job.

If women don't think they are getting a fair shake, why don't they speak up and ask for what they want?

This question seems to blame the victim—to castigate women for sex discrimination The common experience is, of course, that speaking up invites a put-down. Further it assumes that the men being asked agree to the necessity for a fair shake.

A woman responsible for executive recruitment and placement for a major metals firm was called in by the president
and quizzed about the friends she might have in the feminist
movement. Agreeing there might be one such person, she
then was asked to "infiltrate" and find out what was happening that might affect his company, a large federal contractor.
He made it quite clear that he would fire her if she turned
into a feminist herself.

A woman editor who filed a complaint with the EEOC and
won found that when she looked for another job she was
blacklisted as a trouble-maker.

Occasionally, the story is different. One woman executive
was active in the formation of a new chapter of the National
Organization for Women. Her company, a large federal contractor, heard about it and called her in to ask why. She explained that it was because she was paid less than male executives at her level, had no business cards, no expense account,
no company car use, nor other benefits given to men at her
level. Within a month, she was given the same benefits as
comparable men, and no further mention was made of her
off-hours activities.

To speak up, a woman usually has to put her job and perhaps her career on the line, where men typically do not. Reasonable caution based on the realities for most higher-level
women is thus labeled a weakness by men who have a different reality.

*Women activists often draw a parallel between their situation and
that of minority groups. Middle class women have good homes,
plenty of money to spend, every comfort technology has to offer.
How can they compare their situation with minorities?*

This is the contented-woman myth. When women do have
money, good homes and work-saving devices, it is because
they live with men who make plenty of money and allow
them to spend it. Often these women are also as well educated as their husbands and have a basic human need to use
their intellectual talents. As with ethnic minorities, women

want to be seen as individuals who are given acceptance for their participation in management processes. The effects of subordinancy have parallels between blacks and women. (Even before the black movement in the sixties, these parallels were clearly drawn by Helen Hacker and are in Chapter 5, *Our Sex-Role Culture.*)

Employing and promoting black women would seem to meet the demands of both women and minorities. Isn't this a reasonable solution?

No. This results in discriminating against black men and white women while appearing to get double credit with compliance requirements. Such short-cuts are not "good faith" efforts.

Often the best intentions of a company toward its women don't convince feminists that the company is serious about advancement for women.

Good intentions may not be connected with reality. One of the reasons for the lack of conviction is the difficulty most organizations have in changing as rapidly as women, in their desire to catch up, would like. That is the nature of social change and the exhaustion of having waited for change for so long.

Unfortunately, premature announcements of programs to upgrade women only arouse hopes which are then dashed when the programs do not move as promised. There is probably more bitterness when there is unrealized hope then when there is no change in the *status quo.* Many organizations have instituted surveys but have not moved beyond that to job restructuring and training programs.

At what point can an organization no longer be charged with tokenism?

When there is no longer an invisible ceiling, that point is reached. When the percentage of women managers has moved close to the percentage of working women in the United States, currently 38 percent, tokenism will be dead.

So much progress has been made already, why are women still so anxious?

Not all public relations statements reflect reality. A recent airlines magazine article touted their progress, announcing that, "airline women have come a long way from their stereotyped roles of secretary and stewardess."[23] A closer reading of the article showed that half the women mentioned got their jobs through having been secretaries or stewardesses when World War II took the men away and they "filled-in" on "men's jobs," proved themselves, and managed to stay on. One of these women was named editor of the employee magazine during the war and is still editing 25 years later. In 1959 another woman passed federal dispatcher exams and 13 years later is an assistant flight dispatcher. Would feature stories about men reveal this rate of advancement? More newly-hired women hold "feminine" jobs, such as "manager of the woman's market." Two featured women are engineers at their West Coast operations base among 398 male engineers! No woman pilots are mentioned. A bleak picture painted glowingly![24]

Actually, very little progress has been made. The changes have just begun and will be many years in the making. We've barely begun to visualize the sex-picture of the management suites of the future with women in many top positions, carrying primary responsibilities instead of support roles only.

Notes

1. Orth, Charles D., and Frederic Jacobs, "Women in Management: Pattern for Change," *Harvard Business Review*, July–August, 1971, p. 142.
2. "The Management Mystique," *Newsfront*, November 1964, pp. 18–21.
3. Bowman, Garda W., N. B. Worthy and S. A. Greyser, "Are Women Executives People?" *Harvard Business Review*, July–August 1965, p. 14.

4. "How Much of a Woman Should a Woman in Business Be," *The MBA*, March 1972, pp. 16–17.
5. *Ibid.*, p. 16.
6. *Ibid.*, pp. 13, 66.
7. Baker, Ruth S., "Women In IBM: A Special Report," *Think*, December 1971, p. 2.
8. *The MBA*, op. cit., p. 17.
9. *Ibid.*, p. 16.
10. Bernstein, Harry, "Women Workers More Stable, Study Claims," *Los Angeles Times* citing the *Labor Turnover Handbook*, Merchants & Manufacturers Association, November 1970.
11. *Handbook on Women Workers*, U.S. Department of Labor, Wage & Labor Standards Division, Women's Bureau, Bulletin 249, 1969, p. 76.
12. *Ibid.*, p. 80. Often-quoted figures of worktime lost due to illness or injury are 5.6 days for women, 5.3 days for men during 1967, reported in *Facts About Women's Absenteeism and Turnover*, U.S. Department of Labor, Wage & Labor Standards Administration, August 1969, p. 1.
   This report indicates the problems of statistics that do not fully reflect *length* of time away from work as compared to *frequency*, and comments, "Since women lost more worktime because of acute conditions and men because of chronic conditions, . . . the total financial loss caused by women's absences was about the same as that caused by men's." (p. 1)
13. *Women Today*, April 17, 1972, p. 1.
14. *Why Women Work*, U.S. Department of Labor, Wage and Labor Standards Administration, Women's Bureau, December 1970.
15. Cimons, Marlene, "Hormonal Bias Is Her Battle," *Los Angeles Times* article featuring Dr. Estelle Ramey, February 21, 1972.
16. Quotations are from *Medical World News*, August 1970 and are cited by Shirley Bernard, *NOW Acts*, December 1970, p. 12.
17. Kupperman, Herbert S., *Human Endocrinology*, Philadelphia, F. A. Davis Co., 1963. Cited by Shirley Bernard, *op. cit.*, note 17.
18. *Op. cit.*, note 17.
19. Ramey, Estelle, "Men's Cycles (They Have Them Too, You Know)," *Ms.*, Spring 1972, p. 11.
20. Bernard, Shirley, *NOW Acts*, Spring 1971, p. 10.
21. *The Wall Street Journal*, December 14, 1971, p. 1.
22. Brenton, Myron, *The American Male*, Greenwich, Conn., Fawcett Publications, Inc., 1966, p. 79.
23. Delfino, Adriano G., "The Expanding Role of Airline Women," *Aloha* (United Airlines) Mainliner's Hawaii Guide, January–March, 1972, p. 14.
24. *Ibid.*, pp. 14–16.

9

Future Implications

This book is written with a sense of immediacy and with our attempt to provide congruence as the reader contemplates the future of women in management. The relatively stable past provided the context and the present is moving as rapidly as today's news stories follow each other. Future projections indicate an accelerating rate of real change as women move throughout organizations. Future women managers will be molded by the cumulation of these changes.

First, a brief reminder that no trend applies to all women —or even to all women managers. But each new action has indicated the growing cohesiveness of the movement to provide equity for those women interested and capable of preparing themselves for new challenges. They will establish the climate for future change for other, more traditional women.

It is interesting to note that none of the futurists, either authoring books or sequestered in think tanks, seem to be aware that women's revised roles will have an impact upon the future. Rarely is there a reference to the shifting scene caused by women changing roles and its potential effect upon men and organizations. Instead, the futurists seem to make a simple projection of the roles which women now fill at work into both near and distant futures. Apparently they don't see any change whatsoever as more women work up to higher level positions. They may not have stopped to consider the possibility. However, we believe organizational life will be substantively different.

Since predictions and projections help to frame the central issues as well as influence today's decisions, the following is

our view of the relevance of women in management to the future of organizations.

I. *The impact of women's changing roles is potentially greater than those of technology, zero population growth or any other single issue because women are in every part of life.*

At work they will be employed in the range of relationships including supervisors or managers. An increasing percentage will have high-level positions. Earlier we indicated women will be less available to do the kinds of work they've been doing. Someone else (men) will do these tasks—or they will be left undone. In the process, we may discover that unnecessary work is being done.

Similarly, the kinds of relating they will give and expect to receive will affect the functioning of many units—education, public affairs, career and family. Fewer homes will be nuclear families. When women are at home, they will relate differently with their husbands and children. In their communities they will relate differently to other important people in their lives. Wherever women *are* in society, they will have a sizeable impact on where anybody else can be.

II. *There will be substantially more women who will want to be actively involved in public, societal, business and other decision-related activities rather than in finding new ways of exercising leisure time options.*

This possibility is supported by biomedical projections for the human future. Women and men both will have far more energy long into their lifespan. Since women are living today at least seven years longer than men, we predict their greatest physical, physiological and even emotional productivity will be in the years formerly called "the middle years." While many futurists are enthusiastic about leisure time and shortened work weeks, there is little indication this will appeal to all women. Many capable women are seeking *respite from* leisure or misused time. We now know that productive work is a prerequisite for living a meaningful life. The issue

is not in meeting the Puritan Ethic of the positive value of work, but in gaining satisfactions for which there seem to be few substitutes. As women see themselves belonging much more in the mainstream and being accepted there, they will be more active in higher level jobs, at all ages. Certainly management women will be stimulated by the more generalized liberated feeling among women. It will influence their behavior, their attitudes and their own expectations for themselves.

III. *Women will be more willing to be visible about the work they've been doing all along.*

They'll be less underground about their capabilities. They'll be more articulate about the things they believe in and feel strongly about. Their range of behavior will be much broader as well as more visible. This should bring about many more alternatives for women in styles of operating, ways of living, modes of expressing one's self and challenges for fuller, more creative lives. In return, men will also rethink their commitments and redirect their own energies and activities. Organizational development programs will be used to integrate and balance the changes made.

Concurrently, there will be a recognition on the part of women that they will be taking risks, just as anyone who expresses an idea takes a risk. This includes much less of the habitual deferring to men which has become a conditioned response. At the same time, more women will become convinced that the best policy is to be direct in expressing themselves and their ideas. There will be more mutual sharing of viewpoints and experience with frank disagreements as well as agreements.

Many of the problems of women at the present time have to do with feelings of anger that come out in the form of defensive behavior and a sense of being off-balance. As the climate changes, more women will become increasingly self-confident and defensiveness will change to self-acceptance.

We expect a new type of humor as these changes occur.

The old-style jokes that ridicule or put women down will continue to be tasteless. Reverse compliments will be identified as just that and fall flat. Looking backward on today's tensions of change, the new humor will have the perspective and sophistication to appreciate the absurdities in that transition.

IV. Women will take the lead in integrating the many aspects of life; in the home and in the work setting.

While women will expand their range of activities and behavior, they will generally not relinquish those things which they and the men in their lives have enjoyed—those activities they have shared in common: family, home and recreation. Community activities will still be important to many women. We expect that by 1990, less than 20 years hence, women will enlarge their work share without threatening other desired commitments. This will involve a creative juggling of choices, balancing of priorities, and integrating of new choices.

Women would not have been able to envisage so much change in their own lifetimes if the nation had not been committed to a program of major expansion of technology. The results of this commitment have led us to new values in order to restrain our polluting and over-populating the country. This is the arena for the contributions of technology, ZPG and new value systems. The next steps will be to create more orderly and effective ways of integrating the various aspects of life. Since women have been accustomed to this kind of integrative thinking far longer than have men, we believe women will lead the way in designing new systems for living, in and out of work settings.

V. The Equal Rights Amendment will be ratified rapidly due to the efforts of both men and women.

Among the results of ERA will be the rewriting of job descriptions in order to eliminate discrimination. The U. S. Department of Labor recently contracted for an assessment

of all positions listed in the Dictionary of Occupations. The jobs now primarily occupied by women will be described more accurately as to complexity and rigor compared to those jobs held primarily by men. The impact of this study will lead to eliminating ghetto departments that provide no channels upward, and will validate the readiness of many women to occupy positions of greater responsibility. This will help to make visible many women qualified to be managers.

Organizations and individuals who currently seek to block ratification of ERA will find their positions so untenable they will find other means of meeting their own goals and convictions. An example is the California AFL-CIO which in 1972 began working to extend state minimum wage and hour laws to men as the pressure to ratify ERA defied their efforts to oppose it.

A far greater result will be the change in national attitude toward women's roles since most Americans see themselves as law-abiding citizens. We recognize that attitude change does not occur automatically with the passage of a law or a Constitutional Amendment. But the long range implications are in the direction of objective realization of national policy.

VI. *We anticipate an uneven pattern of change.*

People don't all change at the same rate, as we have seen from evidence in court cases and employment policies. There are differences among the states in the speed with which they are ratifying the Equal Rights Amendment. Some businesses and industries are far ahead of others in implementing affirmative action programs. In some places in this nation, people are moving so slowly that conflict in the future is inevitable. It may get even more turbulent as we go along because these changes will be taken more seriously as women gain higher level career and political positions which provide real power bases from which to negotiate.

In the process there will be a number of rear guard actions

carried out under the smokescreen of protection of women. Some labor unions, legislators and women, and also physicians and other professionals of the male establishment are convinced that because some women need to be protected, all women should be treated with the same "protection." These people are likely to continue to write articles and legislation expressing grave concern about what will happen if there really is sex equality. In the name of protection delay could occur.

But we are projecting that the major institutions of our society, business, industry, government, educational and health institutions will indeed proceed to initiate and implement affirmative action programs. The reasons for action range from pressures and the consequent risks of the federal compliance agencies and women's groups, to implementing the *intent* simply because they see affirmative action as a fair, just and beneficial course today. Certainly, the insights presented by women associated professionally and in the cause of Civil Rights have alerted the country to their intent to make equality a fact for all.

VII. *Results of that uneveness will be some radical changes not only in occupations and careers but also in the relationships of professionals to the lay person in his or her field.*

Much of this will be heightened as the result of fresh social science research and ethical criticism on age-old questions, a search that will intensify in the future. New kinds of questions will be asked about sex-roles and self-concepts, particularly in relation to achievement motivation. Research in organizational behavior has not yet included women as subjects in investigating achievement motivation, because so few women have been in achievement sensitive positions. Such research will be undertaken and extended to encompass the impact on men, providing new information on ways to expedite organizational change involving sex-role and work-role attitudes. This will be particularly helpful to those executives and management consultants who use scientific evidence as

a basis on which to give sound direction to management decisions.

VIII. *There will be differences in emphasis between public life and private life.*

Public life involves social policy, balance of opportunities and the assurance through law of responsible functioning in our society. These will be expanded resulting in making choices available to all people regardless of where they come from.

Private life has to do with personal and family life styles. It involves exercising personal choices in which an unrestricted variety is appropriate as long as those choices don't impinge on others too heavily. Some women who are "liberated, achieving, dominant" at work will expect the same type relationship with their family. Many other women will choose to adopt traditional wifely, motherly behavior at home, regardless of their work styles. Still others will elect non-family life-styles. All the various methods of family planning will be utilized by women who decide either to delay having children or to having none at all. "When a woman is face-to-face with the rest of her life, it is the urgencies of freedom and fate that count, not the positions of legislators, spokesmen and establishments."[1]

New criteria for stability will be developed about the person, not his or her marital status, as new social changes permeate management policies and attitudes.

We expect that organizations will continue to lessen their concern with matters involving the private lives of their managers and other employees. Traditionally, the higher the position in the organization, the more top management has indicated interest or even control of private lives. We see this breaking down as evidenced by such early signals as "executive couples" who are recruited and placed together. This pattern we expect to continue, with more innovative ways of solving old problems.

IX. *Except for a radical reversal in the economy, the percentage of women in the work force will continue to rise. But whether employment is up or down, the percentage of women in supervisory, professional, managerial and executive positions will increase substantially.*

The first part of the prediction is based upon projections of available child-rearing facilities and attitudes.

The second part is, of course, predictable with the momentum already established by the numbers and socio-economic diversity of women who are working together for the first time in history to achieve that very goal.

Also for the first time in history this will be organizationally feasible since there will be a sufficient number of professionally and educationally proficient women to meet the requirements of the positions. Colleges and universities are now actively recruiting women for their graduate schools of business management, engineering, law, public administration and other allied fields where women have been rare. Since HEW is encouraging this door-opening as a part of educational institutions' affirmative action plans we can predict at least a tripling of women graduate students in these fields in the next five years. Although this will mean only 5-15 percent of the graduates will be women, the often-used query, "Yes, but will *she* be able to do the job?" will not hold up. Adequate expertise will be available.

Similarly, many foundations and major corporations are providing experimental time and situations for women graduate students. Victor Gruen and Associates, a Beverly Hills based international planning firm, selected four college women (of five interns) to spend the summer of 1972 investigating urban planning.

More women already employed are indicating that they are willing to train for better positions, as men have. Increasing numbers of women will be entering continuing education and graduate degree programs.

Along with professional expertise, women will have political astuteness. In the process of pressing for equality, they will have learned the skills and procedures for achieving goals through the experience of political maneuvering.

X. Organizations will respond more readily to society's changing value system.

Old patterns are not working in many, many places. Contemporary patterns show potential for greater productiveness if we have consensus. Our national conscience seems increasingly aware of the necessity to incorporate the values expressed by many sub-groups around the country. As Willis Harmon said at the White House Conference on the Industrial World Ahead: A Look at Business in 1990, "Large privately-owned and managed corporations, we may assume, will continue to be the dominant economic institutions in American society. If their modes of operation move toward humanistic capitalism, there would be a marked broadening of corporate goals to include, besides the present economic and institutional goals, authentic social responsibility and the personal fulfillment of those who participate in the corporate activity—not as a gesture to improve corporate image nor as a moralistically undertaken responsibility, but as operative goals on a par with profit-making and institutional security. With humanistic capitalism, not production, but productiveness in human life, will be the goal."[2]

XI. To be successful in integrating demand with productivity, the following strategies will achieve immediate action, tomorrow. . .

- Provide a climate for success. Prepare the way, avoid tokenism; get good people, do awareness training, promote from within.
- Make sponsorship a requirement, and evaluate supervisors and managers on it.
- Make affirmative action an "in" project so tensions are at minimum.

- Recruit the best possible women and give them the same accoutrements and help as you would any man in the same role.
- Engender a climate of social approval of women managers along with the requirement to work together.
- Provide supplementary training in tasks and skills not traditionally experienced by women.

What new information do we need, or can help develop?

- Achievement motivation research
- Behavior and attitude change research, especially related to concerns of men
- Measurement of present levels of awareness, of degree of change
- Ways to expedite change and to cope with resistance to change
- Self-concept training, especially to prepare traditionally-oriented women
- Assessment methods for selecting, training and promoting women
- Ways to restructure certain jobs to form career ladders and lateral transfers, coordinated with training
- Selecting tests and validating them for own purposes of selecting excellence in high potential women (not just for compliance)
- Ways to develop empathy and action on the job simultaneously
- Overcoming deference, subordinancy thinking

XII.   *Women will continue to be interested in the action results of organizations and institutions in our society.*

Although the form of individual and group involvement may vary . . .

"If there weren't laws on the books and weren't people in the courts, there would still be the women's movement rolling along." says Aileen Hernandez of the National Organization for Women. "You might as well face it—women aren't going to go away."[3]

By 1990 the experiences of participation in the varied aspects of life will thoroughly dissipate the fears of many men that women will irrationally seek rights they cannot use well. Women will have amply demonstrated their capabilities to themselves and to others.

Notes

1. Lerner, Max, "Population, Abortion and Freedom of Choice," *Los Angeles Times*, May 21, 1972.
2. Harman, Willis A., "Humanistic Capitalism: Alternative to Big Brother?" *Newsletter*, Association for Humanistic Psychology, May 1972, p. 3. Condensed from an address given to the White House Conference on the "Industrial World Ahead: A Look at Business in 1990."
3. Hernandez, Aileen, president of the National Organization for Women, quoted in "Corporate Lib: Under Pressure, Firms Try to Upgrade Status of Women Employe," *The Wall Street Journal*, March 20, 1972.

Tools: Information and Sources

I. Revised Order 4

(Edited to focus on requirements for women)

Affirmative Action Programs with specific goals and time-tables for women as well as minorities are now required of all federal contractors under Executive Order 11246 as amended. The provisions are known as Revised Order No. 4, and the enforcement arm is the Office of Federal Contract Compliance (OFCC), U.S. Department of Labor.

The full text of the required contents of Affirmative Action Programs, along with suggestions for implementing them, is available through the OFCC. For the purposes of this book, we are including excerpts from Revised Order No. 4 that concern women in management, or provide the necessary conditions whereby women, both white and minority, can move into management positions.

Section numbering is included to facilitate cross-referencing to the full text. Omissions and deleted repetitious material are designated by an ellipsis (. . .). Changes in wording from the 1970 version of Order No. 4 are noted with an asterisk (*). Completely new text material is noted with a double asterisk (**). The full table of sections is included for those not familiar with the scope of the provisions and brief summaries of omitted sections are included.

PART 60-2—AFFIRMATIVE ACTION PROGRAMS

SUBPART A—GENERAL

Sec.
60-2.1 Title, purpose and scope.
60-2.2 Agency action.

SUBPART B—REQUIRED CONTENTS OF AFFIRMATIVE ACTION PROGRAMS

SUBPART C—METHODS OF IMPLEMENTING THE REQUIREMENTS OF SUBPART B

SUBPART D—MISCELLANEOUS

SUBPART A—GENERAL

Section 60-2.1 Title, purpose and scope

A general outline of the subjects and parameters of Revised Order No. 4.

Section 60-2.2 Agency action

General statements of responsibility of federal contractors to have affirmative action programs acceptable to OFCC; enforcement powers and procedures leading to cancellation or termination of present contracts and/or debarment from future contracts.

SUBPART B—REQUIRED CONTENTS OF AFFIRMATIVE ACTION PROGRAMS

Section 60-2.10 Purpose of affirmative action program.

An affirmative action program is a set of specific and result-oriented procedures to which a contractor commits himself to apply every good faith effort. The objective of those procedures plus such efforts is equal employment opportunity. Procedures without effort to make them work are meaningless; and effort, undirected by specific and meaningful procedures, is inadequate. An acceptable affirmative action program must include an analysis of areas within which the contractor is deficient in the utilization of minority groups and women, and further, goals and timetables to which the contractor's good faith efforts must be directed to correct the deficiencies and, thus to increase materially the utilization of minorities and women, at all levels and in all segments of his work force where deficiencies exist.

Section 60-2.11 Required utilization analysis.

Based upon the Government's experience with compliance reviews under the Executive order programs and the contractor reporting system, . . . as categorized by the EEO-1 (Employer's Information Report) designations, women are likely to be underutilized in departments and jobs within departments as follows: officials and managers, professionals, technicians, sales workers (except over-the-counter sales in certain retail establishments), craftsmen (skilled and semi-skilled). Therefore, the contractor shall direct special attention to such jobs in his analysis and goal setting for minorities and women. Affirmative action programs must contain the following information:

*   (a)   An analysis of all major job classifications at the facility, with explanation if minorities or women are currently being underutilized in any one or more job classifications (job "classification" herein meaning one or a group of jobs having similar content, wage rates and opportunities). "Underutilization" is defined as having fewer minorities or women in a particular job classification than would reasonably be expected
**   by their availability. In making the work force analysis, the contractor shall conduct such analysis separately for minorities and women.

(1) (i)—(viii) . . . (minorities only)

** (2) In determining whether women are being under-utilized in any job classification the contractor will consider at least all of the following factors:

(i) The size of the female unemployment force in the labor area surrounding the facility;

(ii) The percentage of the female workforce as compared with the total workforce in the immediate labor area;

(iii) The general availability of women having requisite skills in the imediate labor area;

(iv) The availability of women having requisite skills in an area in which the contractor can reasonably recruit;

(v) The availability of women seeking employment in the labor or recruitment area of the contractor;

(vi) The availability of promotable and transfer-able female employees within the contractor's organization;

(vii) The existence of training institutions capable of training persons in the requisite skills; and

(viii) The degree of training which the contractor is reasonably able to undertake as a means of making all job classes available to women.

Section 60-2.12 Establishment of goals and timetables.

(a) The goals and timetables developed by the contractor should be attainable in terms of the contractor's anal-ysis of his deficiencies and his entire affirmative action program. Thus, in establishing the size of his goals and the length of his timetables, the contractor should con-sider the results which could reasonably be expected from his putting forth every good faith effort to make his overall affirmative action program work. In deter-mining levels of goals, the contractor should consider at least the factors listed in Section 60-2.11.

(b) Involve personnel relations staff, department and divi-sion heads, and local and unit managers in the goal setting process.

(c) Goals should be significant, measurable and attainable.

(d) Goals should be specific for planned results, with time-tables for completion.

(e) Goals may not be rigid and inflexible quotas which must be met, but must be targets reasonably attainable by means of applying every good faith effort to make all aspects of the entire affirmative action program work.

(f) In establishing timetables to meet goals and commit ments, the contractor will consider the anticipated expansion, contraction and turnover of and in the work force.

(g) Goals, timetables and affirmative action commitments must be designed to correct any identifiable defi-ciencies.

** (h) Where deficiencies exist and where numbers or percen-tages are relevant in developing corrective action, the contractor shall establish and set forth specific goals and timetables separately for minorities and women.

(i) Such goals and timetables, with supporting data and the analysis thereof shall be a part of the contractor's written affirmative action program and shall be main-tained at each establishment of the contractor.

(j) Where the contractor has not established a goal, his written affirmative action program must specifically analyze each of the factors listed in 60-2.11 and must detail his reason for a lack of a goal.

** (k) In the event it comes to the attention of the compli-ance agency or the Office of Federal Contract Com-pliance that there is a substantial disparity in the utilization of a particular minority group or men or women of a particular minority group, the compliance agency or OFCC may require separate goals and time-tables for such minority group and may further require, where appropriate, such goals and timetables by sex for such group for such job classifications and organi-zational units specified by the compliance agency or OFCC.

* (l) Support data for the required analysis and program shall be compiled and maintained as part of the con-tractor's affirmative action program. This data will include but not be limited to progression line charts, seniority rosters, applicant flow data and applicant rejection ratios indicating minority and sex status.

(m) Copies of affirmative action programs and/or copies of support data shall be made available to the compliance agency or the Office of Federal Contract Compliance, at the request of either, for such purposes as may be appropriate to the fulfillment of their responsibilities under Executive Order 11246, as amended.

Section 60-2.13 Additional required ingredients of affirmative action programs.

Effective affirmative action programs shall contain, but not necessarily be limited to, the following ingredients:

(a) Development or reaffirmation of the contractor's equal employment opportunity policy in all personnel actions.

(b) Formal internal and external dissemination of the contractor's policy.

(c) Establishment of responsibilities for implementation of the contractor's affirmative action program.

(d) Identification of problem areas (deficiencies) by organizational units and job classification.

(e) Establishment of goals and objectives by organizational units and job classification, including timetables for completion.

(f) Development and execution of action oriented programs designed to eliminate problems and further designed to attain established goals and objectives.

(g) Design and implementation of internal audit and reporting systems to measure effectiveness of the total program.

** (h) Compliance of personnel policies and practices with the Sex Discrimination Guidelines (41 CFR Part 60-20 of this chapter).

* (i) Active support of local and national community action programs and community service programs, designed to improve the employment opportunities of minorities and women.

** (j) Consideration of minorities and women not currently in the workforce having requisite skills who can be recruited through affirmative action measures.

Section 60-2.14 Compliance status.

No contractor's compliance status shall be judged alone by whether or not he reaches his goals and meets his timetables. Rather, each contractor's compliance posture shall be determined by reviewing the contents of his program, the extent

of his adherence to this program, and his good faith efforts to make his program work toward the realization of the program's goals within the timetables set for completion . . .

SUBPART C—METHODS OF IMPLEMENTING THE REQUIREMENTS OF SUBPART B

Section 60-2.20 Development or reaffirmation of the equal employment opportunity policy.

(a) The contractor's policy statement should indicate the chief executive officers' attitude on the subject matter, assign overall responsibility and provide for a reporting or monitoring procedure. Specific items to be mentioned should include, but not be limited to:

*

(1) Recruit, hire, train, and promote persons in all job classifications, without regard to race, color, religion, sex or national origin, except where sex is a bona fide occupational qualification. (The term "bona fide occupational qualification" has been construed very narrowly under the Civil Rights Act of 1964. Under Executive Order 11246 as amended and this part, this term will be construed in the same manner.)

(2) Base decisions on employment so as to further the principle of equal employment opportunity.

(3) Insure that promotion decisions are in accord with principles of equal employment opportunity by imposing only valid requirements for promotional opportunities.

(4) Insure that all personnel actions such as compensation, benefits, transfers, layoffs, return from layoff, company sponsored training, education, tuition assistance, social and recreation programs, will be administered without regard to race, color, religion, sex, or national origin.

Section 60-2.21 Dissemination of the policy.

(a) The contractor should disseminate his policy *internally* (emphasis added) as follows:

(1) Include it in contractor's policy manual.

(2) Publicize it in company newspaper, magazine, annual report and other media.

(3) Conduct special meetings with executive, management, and supervisory personnel to explain intent

of policy and individual responsibility for effective implementation, making clear the chief executive officer's attitude.

(4) . . .

(5) Discuss the policy thoroughly in both employee orientation and management training programs.

(6) .

(7) . . .

** (8) Publish articles covering EEO programs, progress reports, promotions, etc., of minority and female employees, in company publications.

(9) Post the policy on company bulletin boards.

* (10) When employees are featured in product or consumer advertising, employee handbooks or similar publications, both minority and nonminority, men and women should be pictured.

** (11) Communicate to employees the existence of the contractors affirmative action program and make available such elements of his program as will enable such employees to know of and avail themselves of its benefits.

(b) The contractor should disseminate his policy *externally* (emphasis added) as follows:

(1) Inform all recruiting sources verbally and in writing of company policy, stipulating that these sources actively recruit and refer minorities and women for all positions listed.

(2) . . .

* (3) Notify minority and women's organizations, community agencies, community leaders, secondary schools and colleges, of company policy, preferably in writing.

** (4) Communicate to prospective employees the existence of the contractor's affirmative action program and make available such elements of his program as will enable such prospective employees to know of and avail themselves of its benefits.

* (5) Same as (a) (10) above.

(6) . . .

Section 60-2.22 Responsibility for implementation.

* (a) An executive of the contractor should be appointed as director or manager of company Equal Opportunity
* Programs . . . He or she should be given the necessary top management support and staffing to execute the

** assignment. His or her identity should appear on all internal and external communications on the company's Equal Opportunity Programs. His or her responsibilities should include, but not necessarily be limited to:

(1) Developing policy statements, affirmative action programs, internal and external communication techniques.

(2) Assisting in the identification of problem areas.

(3) Assisting line management in arriving at solutions to problems.

(4) Designing and implementing audit and reporting systems that will:

    (i)   Measure effectiveness of the contractor's programs.

    (ii) Indicate need for remedial action.

    (iii) Determine the degree to which the contractor's goals and objectives have been attained.

* (5) Serve as liaison between the contractor and enforcement agencies.

* (6) Serve as liaison between the contractor and minority organizations, women's organizations, and community action groups concerned with employment opportunities of minorities and women.

(7) Keep management informed of latest developments in the entire equal opportunity area.

(b) Line responsibilities should include, but not be limited to, the following:

(1) Assistance in the identification of problem areas and establishment of local and unit goals and objectives.

* (2) Active involvement with local minority organizations, women's organizations, community action groups and community service programs.

* (3) Periodic audit of training programs, hiring and promotion patterns to remove impediments to the attainment of goals and objectives.

(4) Regular discussions with local managers, supervisors and employees to be certain the contractor's policies are being followed.

* (5) Review of the qualifications of all employees to insure that minorities and women are given full opportunities for transfers and promotions.

(6) Career counseling for all employees.

(7) Periodic audit to insure that each location is in compliance in areas such as:

(i) Posters are properly displayed.

** (ii) All facilities, including company housing, which the contractor maintains for the use and benefit of his employees, are in fact desegregated, both in policy and use. If the contractor provides facilities such as dormitories, locker rooms, and rest rooms, they must be comparable for both sexes.

* (iii) Minority and female employees are afforded a full opportunity and are encouraged to participate in all company sponsored educational, training, recreational, and social activities.

(8) Supervisors should be made to understand that their work performance is being evaluated on the basis of their equal employment opportunity efforts and results, as well as other criteria.

** (9) It shall be a responsibility of supervisors to take actions to prevent harassment of employees placed through affirmative action efforts.

Section 60-2.23 Identification of problem areas by organizational units and job classifications.

* (a) An in-depth analysis of the following should be made, paying particular attention to trainees and those categories listed in Section 60-2.11 (d).

* (1) Composition of the workforce by minority group status and sex.

* (2) Composition of applicant flow by minority group status and sex.

* (3) The total selection process including position descriptions, position titles, worker specifications, application forms, interview procedures, test administration, test validity, referral procedures, final selection process, and similar factors.

(4) Transfer and promotion practices.

(5) Facilities, company sponsored recreation and social events, and special programs such as educational assistance.

(6) Seniority practices ...

(7) ...

(8) All company training programs, formal and informal.

(9) Workforce attitude.

(10) ...

(b) If any of the following items are found in the analysis, special corrective action should be appropriate.

*   (1) An "underutilization" of minorities or women in specific work classifications.

*   (2) Lateral and/or vertical movement of minority or female employees occurring at a lesser rate (compared to workforce mix) than that of nonminority or male employees.

*   (3) The selection process eliminates a higher percentage of minorities or women than nonminorities or men.

     (4) Application and related pre-employment forms not in compliance with Federal legislation.

     (5) Position descriptions inaccurate in relation to actual functions and duties.

**   (6) Tests and other selection techniques not validated as required by the OFCC Order on Employee Testing and other Selection Procedures.

*   (7) Test forms not validated by location, work performance and inclusion of minorities and women in sample.

*   (8) Referral ratio of minorities or women to the hiring supervisor or manager indicates an abnormal percentage are being rejected as compared to nonminority and male applicants.

*   (9) Minorities or women are excluded from or are not participating in company sponsored activities or programs.

     (10) ...

*   (11) Seniority provisions contribute to overt or inadvertent discrimination, i.e., a disparity by minority group status or sex exists between length of service and types of jobs held.

     (12) Nonsupport of company policy by managers, supervisors, or employees.

*   (13) Minorities or women underutilized or significantly underrepresented in training or career improvement programs.

     (14) No formal techniques established for evaluating effectiveness of EEO programs.

     (15) —(19) ...

Section 60-2.24 Development and execution of programs.

  (a) The contractor should conduct detailed analyses of position descriptions to insure that they accurately reflect position functions, and are consistent for the same position from one location to another.

* (b) The contractor should validate worker specifications by division, department, location or other organizational unit and by job category using job performance criteria. Special attention should be given to academic, experience and skill requirements to insure that the requirements in themselves do not constitute inadvertent discrimination. Specifications should be consistent for the same job classification in all locations and should be free from bias as regards to race, color, religion, sex, or national origin, except where sex is a bona fide occupational qualification. Where requirements screen out a disproportionate number of minorities or women such requirements should be professionally validated to job performance.

* (c) Approved position descriptions and worker specifications, when used by the contractor, should be made available to all members of management involved in the recruiting, screening, selection and promotion process. Copies should also be distributed to all recruiting sources.

  (d) The contractor should evaluate the total selection process to insure freedom from bias and, thus, aid the attainment of goals and objectives.

    (1) All personnel involved in the recruiting, screening, selection, promotion, disciplinary and related processes should be carefully selected and trained to insure elimination of bias in all personnel actions.

* (2) The contractor shall observe the requirements of the OFCC order pertaining to validation of employee tests and other selection procedures.

* (3) Selection techniques other than tests may also be improperly used so as to have the effect of discriminating against minority groups and women. Such techniques include but are not restricted to, unscored interviews, unscored or casual application forms, arrest records, credit checks, consideration of marital status or dependency or minor children. Where there exist data suggesting that such unfair discrimination or exclusion of minorities or women

exists, the contractor should analyze his unscored procedures and eliminate them if they are not objectively valid.

* (e) Suggested techniques to improve recruitment and increase the flow of minority or female applicants follow:
* (1) Certain organizations such as the Urban League ... Colleges, and City Colleges with high-minority enrollment, the State Employment Service, (among others) ... are normally prepared to refer minority applicants. Organizations prepared to refer women with specific skills are: National Organization for Women, Welfare Rights Organizations, Women's Equity Action League, Talent Bank from Business and Professional Women (including 26 women's organizations), Professional Women's Caucus, Intercollegiate Association of University Women, Negro Women's sororities and service groups such as Delta Sigma Theta, Alpha Kappa Alpha, and Zeta Phi Beta; National Council of Negro Women, American Association of University Women, YWCA, and other sectarian groups such as Jewish Women's Groups, Catholic Women's Groups, and Protestant Women's Groups, and women's colleges. In addition, community leaders as individuals shall be added to recruiting sources.

* (2) Formal briefing sessions should be held, preferably on company premises, with representatives from these recruiting sources. Plant tours, presentations by minority and female employees, clear and concise explanations of current and future job openings, position descriptions, worker specifications, explanations of the company's selection process, and recruiting literature should be an integral part of the briefings. Formal arrangements should be made for referral of applicants, follow-up with sources, and feedback on disposition of applicants.

(3) —(9) ...

* (10) When recruiting brochures pictorially present work situations, the minority and female members of the work force should be included, especially when such brochures are used in school and career programs.

* (11) Help wanted advertising should be expanded to include the minority news media and women's interest media on a regular basis.

*   (f)   The contractor should insure that minority and female employees are given equal opportunity for promotion. Suggestions for achieving this result include:

**   (1) Post or otherwise announce promotional opportunities.

*   (2) Make an inventory of current minority and female employees to determine academic, skill and experience level of individual employees.

        (3) Initiate necessary remedial, job training, and work-study programs.

*   (4) Develop and implement formal employee evaluation programs.

*   (5) Make certain "worker specifications" have been validated on job performance related criteria. (Neither minority nor female employees should be required to possess higher qualifications than those of the lowest qualified incumbent.)

*   (6) When apparently qualified minority or female employees are passed over for upgrading, require supervisory personnel to submit written justification.

        (7) Establish formal career counseling programs to include attitude development, education aid, job rotation, buddy system and similar programs.

        (8) Review seniority practices . . . to insure such practices or clauses are non-discriminatory and do not have a discriminatory effect.

*   (g)   Make certain facilities and company-sponsored social and recreation activities are desegregated . . .

**   (h)   Encourage child care, housing and transportation programs appropriately designed to improve the employment opportunities for minorities and women.

Section 60-2.25 Internal audit and reporting systems.

     (a)   The contractor should monitor records of referrals, placements, transfers, promotions and terminations at all levels to insure nondiscriminatory policy is carried out.

     (b)   The contractor should require formal reports from unit managers on a schedule basis as to degree to which corporate or unit goals are attained and timetables met.

     (c)   The contractor should review report results with all levels of management.

     (d)   The contractor should advise top management of program effectiveness and submit recommendations to improve unsatisfactory performance.

Section 60-2.26 Support of action programs.

   (a) The contractor should appoint key members of management to serve on Merit Employment Councils, Community Relations Boards, and similar organizations.

   (b) —(f) . . .

SUBPART D—MISCELLANEOUS

Section 60-2.30 Use of goals.

Affirmative action is not to be used to discriminate against any applicant or employee.

***Section 60-2.31 Preemption.*

Executive Order 11246 as amended and requirements above preempt any conflicting State or local laws.

Section 60-2.32 Supersedure.

Supersedes Order No. 4, January 30, 1970.

First signed: August 25, 1971
First published in Federal Register, Vol. 36, No. 169: August 31, 1971
Time for comment completed: September 30, 1971
Final version in Federal Register: December 4, 1971
Effective date: April 2, 1972

II. Sample Survey Questions**

(Adapted from a governmental agency's survey of both women and men employees; response selections for tabulation omitted.)

Questions about treatment on the job

  1. As far as you know, how does your pay compare with the salary of others doing the same job with similar experience?

  2. As far as you know, how does your job title compare with others doing the same work?

  3. Do you feel that you have *more* responsibility than your title or grade level provide?

  4. Have you ever had a woman supervisor?

  5. In a job interview, have you ever been asked questions such as (check as many as apply)

      _____ Do you expect to marry?

      _____ Do you expect to have children?

_____ Do you plan to work a "significant" number of years?

_____ What will you do if there is sickness at home?

_____ How will your children be cared for while you are working?

_____ None of the above

6. Have you ever been asked if you were serious about a working career?

7. Have you ever been told that a particular job is for one sex only?

8. Have you ever been asked what your spouse's feelings are about your working?

9. Are you ever asked to do any of the following at the office? (check each if "yes")

_____ make the coffee	_____ be sexually available
_____ keep a social calendar	
_____ dial phone calls	_____ clean the office
_____ purchase gifts	_____ repair equipment
_____ prepare for office parties	_____ lift heavy items
_____ take notes at meetings	_____ none of the above

Questions about the employees' feelings related to their job

1. Do you feel that your ideas are utilized?

2. Do you feel that your capabilities are being utilized?

3. Do you feel capable of doing the job you now hold?

4. Are you willing to take more responsibility than you now have?

5. Do you feel you have been treated unfairly on your job because of any of the following? (check as many as apply)

_____ race	_____ religion	_____ none of the above
_____ sex	_____ age	
_____ national origin	_____ other: specify _____	

6. Do you feel that you have been discriminated against on the basis of your sex by your boss or those above you in the job hierarchy?

7. Below you?

8. At the same level?

9. Do you feel that you are given any privileges or preferences on the basis of your sex?

10. Would you mind working with a woman who is in her last months of pregnancy?

11. How would you like to work for a woman boss?
*12. How would you like to work for a man boss?
13. If you had a choice, would you prefer a male supervisor?
*14. If you had a choice, would you prefer a female supervisor?
15. Do you feel that men, in general, make better supervisors than women?
*16. Do you feel that women, in general, make better supervisors than men?
17. Do you feel that women generally have difficulty working for a woman supervisor?
*18. Do you feel that men generally have difficulty working for a man supervisor?
19. Do you feel that men generally have difficulty working for a woman supervisor?
*20. Do you feel that women generally have difficulty working for a man supervisor?
21. Please check all of those things which you think increase a woman's chances of advancing on the job:

_____ being single
_____ being competent
_____ not having any children
_____ thinking "like a man"
_____ being sexually available
_____ being "feminine"
_____ never presenting self and ideas in such a way as to pose a threat to boss
_____ being married

_____ being physically attractive
_____ willing to do more than her share of the "grub work"
_____ having a boss interested in encouraging women
_____ being able to relocate
_____ other _____

22. Please check all of the following adjectives you associate *more* with women than with men.

_____ logical
_____ creative
_____ gossipy
_____ narrow-minded
_____ frivolous
_____ responsive
_____ dependent

_____ emotional
_____ articulate
_____ cooperative
_____ competitive
_____ talkative
_____ domineering
_____ considerate

_____ sympathetic
_____ perceptive
_____ practical
_____ ambitious
_____ passive
_____ aggressive
_____ sensitive

_____ other_____

23. Women: Would you say that the adjectives you checked in the previous question describe yourself?
24. Men: Would you say that the adjectives you checked in the previous question described the woman who is closest to you?
25. Are you in favor of women's organized attempts to advance themselves economically?

Questions about the employees' view of things in the organization they now work in

1. Do you think that women are promoted less frequently than men in the same job category?
2. Do you think that women are absent more often than men?
3. Do you think there is more job turnover among women than men?
4. Do you think women are paid the same as men for equal work?
5. Do you think the fact that women bear the children hurts their chances for advancement in their jobs?
6. Do you think that menopause affects a woman's working ability?
7. Do you think that there are differences between men and women in the way they work?
8. Do you think that women can handle high-level policy making jobs?
9. Do you think that women have as much access to "office information" as men?

Questions about how the person thinks things should be

1. How do you think household chores should be divided between a married couple when husband and wife are both working? (5 options)
2. How do you think child rearing should be divided between a married couple when husband and wife are both working? (5 options)
3. Do you believe that a woman can be successful in her marriage, in raising her children, and in her career?
*4. Do you believe that a man can be successful in his marriage, in raising his children, and in his career?
5. Do you think child care would best be provided for by:

_____ parents only	_____ public day care
_____ employers	centers
_____ private day care	_____ schools (all day)
centers	_____ other: _____

6. If child care connected with this organization was avail-
    able, would you be interested in having my child(ren)
    there?
    How many children needing child care do you have?
7. Should there be special maternity leave benefits?

    ____ no   ____ yes, leave with full
    ____ yes, leave without pay   pay
    ____ yes, leave with partial   ____ other:
    pay   specify _____

8. How long should maternity leave be?

    ____ no maternity leave   ____ 3 months
    ____ 2 weeks (comparable   ____ 6 months
    leave for military   ____ other: _____
    reserve duty)
    ____ 6 weeks

9. Should there be special paternity leave for new fathers?

    ____ no   ____ yes, leave with full
    ____ yes, leave without pay   pay
    ____ yes, leave with partial   ____ other:
    pay   specify _____

*10. How long should paternity leave be?

    ____ no paternity leave   ____ 3 months
    ____ 2 weeks (comparable   ____ 6 months
    leave for military   ____ other: _____
    reserve duty)
    ____ 6 weeks

11. Do you think men should have the opportunity to have
    jobs that have been traditionally held by women, such as
    nursing and secretarial work?
12. Do you think women should have the opportunity to have
    jobs that have been traditionally held by men, such as
    supervisory, managerial, and high-level, policy making jobs?

    The survey can include questions on: Sex, race/ethnic
    background, age, schooling, length and kind of employment
    in present organization, job and pay status, marital and
    dependent statistics, child care arrangements, work inter-
    ruptions and reasons, etc., for statistical analysis and
    planning. Additional data affecting selection, promotion and

*Questions and opinions included to restate a typically biased viewpoint
as suggested by the previous question.
**Source: Womens' Action Program, U. S. Dept. of Health, Education and
Welfare.

transfer policies can include plans for advancement, for family, availability to travel, relocation, reasons for working, preferred working hours.

Additional Survey Questions*

(Using a rating scale from 1 to 9 and in reference to the employing organization)

	From 1 ⟵⟶ To 9	
1. The level of responsibilities I have in my job is _____ by my supervisor.	Not recognized	Very well recognized
2. The present salary review and performance appraisal system has been _____ to women.	Very unsatisfactory	Very satisfactory
3. Recent lay off practices have been _____ to women.	Very unfair	Very fair
4. My opportunities for promotion have been _____.	Very poor	Excellent
5. My opportunities for salary advancement have been _____.	Very poor	Excellent
6. My opportunities for career development have been _____.	Very poor	Excellent
7. My present job is _____ to my career goals.	Not related at all	Very related
8. Finding out about other job openings in this organization is _____.	Very difficult	Very easy
9. I would like _____ to be a supervisor.	Not at all	Very much
10. My supervisor is _____ in my career development.	Not at all interested	Very interested
11. My supervisor is _____ to talk to.	Extremely difficult	Very easy
12. I get recognition for my efforts _____.	Very rarely	Very often
13. I get criticism for my efforts _____.	Very rarely	Very often
14. I think I have discriminated against women _____.	Very rarely	Very often

*Source: TRW Systems, Redondo Beach, California.

III. Possible Sources for Management and Professional Women

American Association for the
Advancement of Science (AAAS)
1515 Massachusetts Avenue, NW
Washington, D.C. 20005

(A master roster of women and
minorities in the sciences is
currently being compiled for use
of employers seeking professionals. To be completed in mid
1974.)

American Association of
University Women
2401 Virginia Avenue, NW
Washington, D.C. 20037

American Bar Association
Women's Rights Unit
336 Hickory Street
Butler, IN 46721

American Business Women's
Association (ABWA)
9100 Ward Parkway
Kansas City, MO 64114

American Institute of Physics
335 West 45th Street
New York, NY 10017

American Newspaper Women's
Club
1607 22nd Street, NW
Washington, D.C. 20008

American Society of Women
Accountants (ASWA)
327 South LaSalle Street
Chicago, IL 60604

American Women's Society of
Certified Public Accountants
(AWSCPA)
327 South LaSalle Street
Chicago, IL 60604

Association of American Colleges
1818 R Street N.W
Washington, D.C. 20009

Business & Professional Women's
Foundation (BPW)
2012 Massachusetts Avenue, N W
Washington, D.C. 20036

Federally Employed Women
(FEW)
Suite 487, National Press Building
Washington, D.C. 20004

Federation of Organizations
for Professional Women
1818 R Street N W
Washington, D.C. 20009

(A registry for 52 professional
women's organizations with extensive descriptive information.
Primarily reference and referral
source.)

International Association of
Personnel Women (IAPW)
c/o Margaret M. Lucas
Bechtel Corporation
P.O. Box 3965
San Francisco, CA 94119

International Federation of
Business & Professional Women
(IFBPW)
Beaux-Arts Hotel, Suite 801
307 East 44th Street
New York, N Y 10017

International Federation of
Women Lawyers (Legal)
475 Fifth Avenue
New York, N Y 10017

League of Women Voters of the
United States (LWVUS)
1200 - 17th Street, NW
Washington, D.C. 20036

National Association of College
Women (NACW)
417 South Davis Avenue
Richmond, VA 23220

National Association of Negro
Business & Professional Women's
Clubs
652 Bryn Road
Pittsburgh, PA 15219

National Association of Women
Deans and Counselors
1201 16th Street, N W
Washington, D.C. 20036

National Association of Women
Lawyers (NAWL) (Legal)
1155 East 60th Street
Chicago, IL 60637

National Council of Negro
Women (NCNW)
1346 Connecticut Avenue, NW
Washington, D.C. 20036

National Federation of Business
& Professional Women's Clubs
(FBPWC)
2012 Massachusetts Avenue
Washington, D.C. 20036

National Organization for Women
(NOW)
National Office
1957 East 73rd Street
Chicago, IL 60649

National Urban League
55 East 52nd Street
New York, N Y 10022

Women's Bureau (and Regional
Offices)
U.S. Department of Labor
Wage & Labor Standards
Administration
Washington, D.C. 20210

Women's Equity Action League
(WEAL)
7657 Dinds Road
Novelty, OH 44072

Women's Equity Action League
Action Committee for Federal
Contract Compliance
1504 44th Street, NW
Washington, D.C. 20007

Women's National Press Club
(Newspaper)
National Press Building
Washington, D.C. 20004

IV. Where to Get Training Materials

GENERAL RESOURCES

A wide range of agencies and organizations concern themselves with both general and specific issues related to the employment of women. They include:

- AAUW (listed in III) who have published Affirmative Action information, listings of professional women's caucuses and specialized educational programs recruiting women.
- Advisory Commissions on the Status of Women (see federal, state, and local listings in your area) who typically have multiple kinds of information available.
- Regional offices of the Women's Bureau.
- University Extensions around the country have more courses in management development and training for women. Call your local university extension for detailed information.
- Citizens Advisory Council on the Status of Women
  Executive Director: Catherine East
  4211 Main Labor Building
  Washington, D.C. 20210
  The Council was established to serve as a primary means for suggesting and stimulating action with institutions, organizations and individuals working for improvement of conditions of special concern to women and, with the Interdepartmental Committee on the Status of Women, to review and evaluate progress in the full participation of women in American life. Established 1963 (rewritten in 1965).
- Association of American Colleges
  Project on the Status and Education of Women
  1818 R Street, N.W.
  Washington, D.C. 20009
  Publishes excellent brief descriptions of many aspects of Affirmative Action requirements. While tailored to educational institutions, the principles apply to most federal contractors as well. Useful summary statistical information included.
- American Council on Education
  Office of Women in Higher Education
  One Dupont Circle
  Washington, D.C. 20036

  With its Commission, directs attention to the broad area of career development for women through and in higher educa-

tion—including access to higher education, curricular content and testing bias, unbiased counseling and advising, continuing education, special academic programs for women, motivation factors, employment opportunities at all ranks in academe, and legislation affecting women's education.

Specializing in consultation is:

- Association of Feminist Consultants
  4 Canoe Brook Drive
  Princeton Junction, NJ 08550
  (609) 799-0378
  This is a new resource consisting of over 50 consultants who are experienced in many diverse fields related to the various women's issues, as well as being active feminists.
- There are other women who consult on a part-time basis who may be reached through university extensions throughout the country.

SELECTED REFERENCES

National Newsletters

There are many newsletters, newspapers and distributors of general and special interest information concerning the issues affecting women. Special symposia, workshops and conferences are proliferating all around the country. These kinds of information, with contacts for more details, are carried by the following newsletters which the authors find useful in employment and related concerns:

Fair Employment Report
Editor and Publisher: Leonard A. Eiserer
P.O. Box 1067, Blair Station
Silver Spring, MD 20910
(301) 587-6300
Rates: $60 per year; $35 for six months
Quantity rates on request

The Spokeswoman
Editor-Publisher: Susan Davis
5464 South Shore Drive
Chicago, IL 60615
(312) 363-2580
Rates: $7 per year for individuals
$12 per year for organizations

WOMANPOWER
   Publisher: Betsy Hogan Associates
   222 Rawson Road
   Brookline, MA 02146
   (617) 232-0066
   Rates: $37 per year for the first subscription
   $15 for each additional subscription mailed to the
   same address

Women Today
   Editor: Barbara Jordan Moore
   Publisher: Myra E. Barrer
   Today Publications & News Service
   National Press Building
   Washington, D.C. 20004
   (202) 628-6663
   U.S. Rates: $15 per year; $25 for two years

Subscribers to *Women Today* also receive free a regular report
of the Washington Chapter of the Women's Equity Action
League (WEAL), which lists the progress of bills before Congress and recent court decisions affecting women.

Also available a directory *Women's Organizations and Leaders.*

Research Publications

The number and diversity of research projects in this field
continues to grow substantially. Information regarding them is
available from the organizations listed above. Several excellent
examples are:

*The Sexual Barrier: Legal and Economic Aspects of
Employment*
Prepared by: Marija Matich Hughes
2422 Fox Plaza
San Francisco, CA 94102
Third edition—$3

KNOW, Inc.
P.O. Box 86031
Pittsburgh, PA 15221
(412) 241-4844

Several of their reprints and packets can be adapted for training purposes or can be used for background preparation
material.

Women's Rights Law Reporter
180 University Avenue
Newark, NJ 07102
Rate: $15 for 6 issues (issued twice a year)
Excellent abstract of current legal decisions affecting women's
lives. Special thematic issues on employment and other subjects
where heavy legal action is occurring.

Women's Studies Abstracts
P.O. Box 1
Rush, NY 14543
Rate: $8.50 per year for individuals; $10 with index
A thorough description of information available from over
2000 sources. Excellent reference.

Business Oriented Publications

Periodicals of private organizations and public institutions
concerned with the impact of current trends upon business and
industry have published articles or entire issues devoted to questions of employment of women. Among recent and highly useful
ones are:

- *Business Horizons* (University of Indiana)
- *Conference Board Record*
- *Harvard Business Review*
- *Journal of Contemporary Business* (University of Washing-
ton)
- *Training and Development Journal*
- *Wall Street Journal*

Films (see Chapter 3 for description)

51% (1971, 16mm. color, approx. 25 min.)
Robert Drucker & Co.
Print Distribution Office
10718 Riverside Drive
North Hollywood, CA 91602
(213) 985-0123 (Tylie Jones)

Women: Up the Career Ladder
(designed and produced by the authors)
(1972, 16mm. black/white, approx. 30 min.)
P.O. Box 24901, Dept. K
UCLA Extension
Los Angeles, CA 90024
(213) 825-0741 (Claire Malis)

What's the Matter with Alice?
(1972, 16mm. color, 30 min.)
Newsfilms, USA
21 West 46th Street
New York, NY 10036
(212) 757-4970

V. Aggressiveness in Women Opinion Survey

I. *A Woman Is Aggressive When She*   *Yes   No*

Helps her children with their homework
Invites a man for dinner
\ Is well dressed
Aspires to the same job as men have
Is a "good" mother
Expresses her opinion in public
Demands equal rights in employment practices
Expects her family to go to church
Voices disagreement with her friends
Becomes a member of the Parent-Teacher Association
Enters a Miss America type contest
Gets good grades in school
Becomes a supervisor of women
Helps her husband select his clothing
Plans family celebrations
Diets to maintain her figure
Becomes a supervisor of men
Chooses the decorations and furniture for her home
Takes a vacation by herself
Manages the family budget
Plans the family vacation
Is the leader of a Girl Scout troop
Tries to get elected to public office

Chooses as her occupation (check as many as you wish)

Nurse	( )
Public Relations	( )
Teacher	( )
Engineer	( )
Sales	( )
Secretary	( )
Librarian	( )
Mathematician	( )
Model	( )
Artist	( )
City Planner	( )
Psychologist	( )
Other	

II. *The Words Which Describe An Aggressive Woman Are* (Circle as many as you wish)

Talkative	Unemotional	Determined
Sweet	Firm	Innovative
Quarrelsome	Angry	Critical
Unfeminine	Honest	Opinionated
Originator	Knowledgeable	Enterprising
Powerful	Demanding	Competent
Competitive	Adequate	Complacent
Strong-minded	Disparaging	Calculating
Rebellious	Humorous	Pitiless
	Other _____	

III. (Please circle the words which express your feeling) Generally speaking I . . . like, admire, approve of, dislike, distrust, disapprove of women who are aggressive.

IV. Please complete the sentences below with the first thought which occurs to you.

The aggressive woman _____

I prefer women who _____

The feminine woman _____

Activities appropriate for women are _____

An aggressive man _____

Respondent is: _____

Male _____	Female _____
Over 30 _____	Under 30 _____

Index

p 10
p 30
? 37
Tools - who
the Alic

Mana
might

100 -
p. 104

70-89

solve

Contents

This book is (as are all books) a statement of the authors' philosophy. And, as always, it contains the contributions of many others—the women and men who have shared their feelings and experiences with us. Special recognition is due the women who creatively assisted with the manuscript, Jean Stapleton and Shirley Collins; and Leila Greenstone, assisted by Phyllis Hirsh, Martha Mahaney, Laurie Morgan, Donald Rotterman and Elinor Tidman, who held up through crisis after crisis in manuscript production. The manuscript critiques of Mary Lou Pyle, David Menkin and John Zuckerman were invaluable.

Among our most valued and atypical experiences have been the consistent support and shared enthusiasm of Lee Christie and Mike Loring. Their cogent comments in reacting as managers and as men continuously provided us with fresh awareness.

We have attempted to state the situation as we see it; we have tried not to side-step seldom talked about issues. Whether you dip into chapters here and there or read straight through, we hope you will share our conviction that women belong on the management team—now.

May 1972   ROSALIND LORING AND THEODORA WELLS

NOTE: In the year and a half since this book was written the number of women moved into management has not been dramatic, but the legal actions involving some major organizations are producing slow but steady change. While only a few have been directly affected (such as AT & T, University of Michigan, Sears, Roebuck and Company, General Motors, University of California at Berkeley), others have been challenged to alter their personnel policies. We continue to believe that all parties will benefit when the changes occur along the lines discussed in this book—with a systems approach and in good faith.

February 1974   ROSALIND LORING AND THEODORA WELLS

managers in proportion to the total number of women workers in this country. But there are enough who have aspired, who have achieved, who have clearly demonstrated their abilities and won recognition so that this book could be written. Many more are under-utilized and unrecognized We have sought to identify what the pressures are and the ways of channeling those pressures toward the ultimate benefit of organizations and the people in them.

The rising aspirations of women to be managers and leaders is part of a larger world-wide ground swell of aspirations of excluded groups. We feel the change all around us—it seems almost to proceed without us. But we believe it can indeed be directed by those of us aware enough to move with and act on the changing mood. We hope to be aware enough to provide the leaders now in the field, plus those preparing to enter higher positions with better ways of interacting with each other and with the work to be done.

Management suites have always been the scene of competitive vying for power positions by men wishing to achieve their personal goals. Arriving now are educated, achieving women—freed from restrictive stereotypes—who are determined to find their places in the power-centers at all levels of organizational life. These women know they have the right to these places where they can exercise their best abilities in reaching their personal goals. They also know they have important value to add to the management processes of organizations reaching for ever-changing goals.

Our convictions come from growing up female in America. We've had most of the typical experiences plus enough of the atypical to enjoy and appreciate the aspirations of women and men as they seek individually and in groups to achieve their goals. Our interest is in understanding where people are and then helping them recognize the situation of others. Especially are we concerned about bridging the chasm between the militancy and frustration of some women and the inflexibility and rigidity of most work systems. We seek responsiveness to changing social and personal needs and aspirations.

Don't we need more answers before going into action?

Answers will have to come simultaneously, resulting from action itself. Past practices have allowed few women to be in management, yet present laws, executive orders, governmental implementation and legal and administrative actions are requiring change. It is no longer a choice of if or when, but of how.

Looking at national trends and at the newly acquired determination of women, we see the need for re-examination of previous assumptions and roles. People are less willing to tolerate behavior which is illogical, or unnecessary as they see it. We write this book with the premise that we can find agreement on the goal of fuller utilization of all human resources, women and men alike.

The process of questioning long standing attitudes and expectations is a difficult one. Habits of thinking and reacting are involved. So much change has been happening in the last decade affecting employment matters that "the woman issue" can feel to many management men as though it is the last straw. To those women presently in or entering management, it may feel long overdue. For the benefit of both groups and for productive evolution of organizations and institutions, we want to explore realistic ways of solving new people problems.

We do not intend to assess what has brought us to this point as an attack on the "male establishment." Rather, it is a recognition that we have all been caught in a maze of myth, folklore, and half-truths—much of which has shaped everyday reality. But it is also reality that women today are not accepting the old patterns. Instead they are searching for innovative ways of correcting their situation. As with any major social change, there are elements of upheaval. Some women are raucous; some men are hostile; other women are sophisticated strategists; many men are supportive integrators of change. As we've become involved in this turbulence, we've searched for ways to generate empathy as well as action.

There are today critically few women executives and

Why We Wrote This Book

For you, the executive, manager, supervisor, industrial relations director, government official and university administrator, the questions relating to women and their search for equality in careers have been mounting in erratic progression. We, ourselves, have responded to these questions frequently during the past ten years. As women who are also managers, consultants, trainers, observers and interpreters we are responding now with increasing tempo. In this book we have attempted to put into context the reasons, and requests of women and men who feel that the time is now for utilizing the resources available in the women of this country. Of course we believe these reasons exist—we've seen them in action. We're participating in the action ourselves.

And so we know that another part of the context is the male manager population whose typical operating procedures bear the imprint of our society's history of work relationships.

The events of the past decade have impressed us with the wide range of response, the collision and confusion, which have occurred as the concept of equal opportunity has become a reality. Currently, we are moving from concept to implementation of equality. We care what happens to both men and women as the inevitable conflicts between traditions and aspirations are faced. If a new balance is to be found, new insights, acceptance and hard information are needed. We have provided some of each of these— enough to help you in building on your own experience and knowledge.

Our target? More women in management NOW.

Why is it so important to move women into management now? Why not wait until the returns are all in . . . from surveys, research, or social inventions now in the heads and on the papers of women and men throughout the nation?

women from management roles as well as many facts that bear on revamping the picture. For further depth about the legal, social and economic factors culminating in the current situation, Chapter 2 characterizes today's trends—and their irreversibility.

For immediate action, Chapter 3 sets out some guidelines for changes in policies and practices to move the organization in alternative directions, using Revised Order 4 for federal contractors as a model. Innovations in awareness training and management development are explored, as well as new questions to be asked.

Then to analysis of the components contributing to the work environment of managers. In Chapter 4 we look at the managerial climate—developing some hypotheses about top management's impact on the prognosis for success of women in management roles. Chapter 5 covers societal expectations of women and men in their sex-roles and'marital-roles which both impinge on work-roles. Then to some detailing of new questions in Chapter 6 as we look at the ways marriage and corporate practices traditionally have been intermeshed and have influenced each other. In Chapter 7 we explore relationships by taking apart some customary expectations, making it possible for men and women to relate on another level—as persons.

Recognizing oft-repeated concerns about women, we make some unconventional commentary in Chapter 8. Finally in Chapter 9 we predict some new patterns not yet perceived by other futurists.

In a supplement to make action more efficient, we provide a number of tools including sources of information and technical assistance.

This book is a "first" in this newest of organizational developments . . . women in management.

Preface

This is the moment in history when the entire nation, from the White House down through organizations of all types, is aware that change must take place in employment of women. The practices of the past are no longer acceptable to women and various legal and governmental actions have declared that new approaches must be implemented.

Immediate, pragmatic pressures are on employers of one-third of the nation's work force—federal contractors—to implement goals and timetables to work more women into management. Most other employers face similar pressures through recent legislation requiring equal treatment of women and men regardless of sex or marital status. Action will be taken as a matter of law-abidingness if not of personal conviction. It is no longer a question of if or when, but of how. Thus, this book.

Although there have been some women in managerial positions during the past 75 years, the number has been painfully few in light of the fact that over one-third of the work force is women.

The first necessity is for immediate reversal in policies and practices. Changed practices become patterns as attitudes are subjected to experience. Both begin to merge into new ways so that men work with women as peer-managers —a new relationship for most men . . . and women.

This book puts the changes, real and proposed, into context, explains how and why various practices are out-of-date and gives guidelines for fresh direction.

In Chapter 1 the spotlight focuses on why change is needed and ranges over the many facets of exclusion of

Van Nostrand Reinhold Company Regional Offices:
New York Cincinnati Chicago Millbrae Dallas

Van Nostrand Reinhold Company International Offices:
London Toronto Melbourne

Manufactured in the United States of America

Published by Van Nostrand Reinhold Company
450 West 33rd Street, New York, N. Y. 10001

Published simultaneously in Canada by Van Nostrand Reinhold Ltd.

15 14 13 12 11 10 9 8 7 6 5 4 3

Breakthrough: Women into Management

Rosalind Loring
Los Angeles, California

Theodora Wells
Beverly Hills, California

VNR **VAN NOSTRAND REINHOLD COMPANY**
NEW YORK / CINCINNATI / TORONTO / LONDON / MELBOURNE

Breakthrough: Women into Management

THE ETHIKON SERIES IN COMPARATIVE ETHICS

Editorial Board

Carole Pateman, *Series Editor*

The Ethikon Series publishes studies on ethical issues of current importance. By bringing scholars representing a diversity of moral viewpoints into structured dialogue, the series aims to broaden the scope of ethical discourse and to identify commonalities and differences between alternative views.

Previous Titles in the Series (not published by Cambridge)

Brian Barry and Robert E. Goodin, eds.
*Free Movement: Ethical Issues in the Transnational
Migration of People and Money*

Chris Brown, ed.
Political Restructuring in Europe: Ethical Perspectives

Terry Nardin, ed.
The Ethics of War and Peace: Religious and Secular Perspectives

David R. Mapel and Terry Nardin, eds.
International Society: Diverse Ethical Perspectives

David Miller and Sohail H. Hashmi, eds.
Boundaries and Justice: Diverse Ethical Perspectives

Simone Chambers and Will Kymlicka, eds.
Alternative Conceptions of Civil Society

Nancy L. Rosenblum and Robert Post, eds.
Civil Society and Government

Jack Miles, foreword, and Sohail Hashmi, ed.
Islamic Political Ethics: Civil Society, Pluralism, and Conflict

Richard Madsen and Tracy B. Strong, eds.
*The Many and the One:
Religious and Secular Perspectives on Ethical Pluralism in the Modern World*

States, Nations, and Borders

The Ethics of Making Boundaries

Edited by

ALLEN BUCHANAN

Duke University

MARGARET MOORE

Queen's University, Canada

CAMBRIDGE
UNIVERSITY PRESS

PUBLISHED BY THE PRESS SYNDICATE OF THE UNIVERSITY OF CAMBRIDGE
The Pitt Building, Trumpington Street, Cambridge, United Kingdom

CAMBRIDGE UNIVERSITY PRESS
The Edinburgh Building, Cambridge CB2 2RU, UK
40 West 20th Street, New York, NY 10011-4211, USA
477 Williamstown Road, Port Melbourne, VIC 3207, Australia
Ruiz de Alarcón 13, 28014 Madrid, Spain
Dock House, The Waterfront, Cape Town 8001, South Africa

http://www.cambridge.org

First published 2003

Printed in the United States of America

Typeface ITC New Baskerville 10/12 pt.   *System* LATEX 2$_\varepsilon$ [TB]

A catalog record for this book is available from the British Library.

Library of Congress Cataloging in Publication Data

States, nations, and borders : the ethics of making boundaries / edited by Allen Buchanan,
Margaret Moore.
p. cm.
Includes bibliographical references and index.
ISBN 0-521-81971-7 – ISBN 0-521-52575-6 (pb.)
1. Boundaries – Moral and ethical aspects. I. Buchanan, Allen E., 1948–
II. Moore, Margaret, Ph.D.
JC323 .S73 2003
172–dc21   2002073554

ISBN 0 521 81971 7 hardback
ISBN 0 521 52575 6 paperback

Contents

viii   *Contents*

About the Contributors

Khaled Abou El Fadl is the Omar and Azmeralda Alfi Distinguished Fellow in Islamic Law and an Acting Professor of Law at the University of California, Los Angeles, School of Law. His most recent publications include *Rebellion and Violence in Islamic Law* (Cambridge University Press, 2001); *Speaking in God's Name: Islamic Law, Authority, and Women* (Oneworld Press, 2001); and *The Conference of the Books: The Search for Beauty in Islam* (University Press of America, 2001).

Daniel Bell is associate professor in the Department of Political and Social Administration at the City University of Hong Kong. He is the author of *Communitarianism and Its Critics; East Meets West: Human Rights and Democracy in Asia;* and co-author of *Towards Illiberal Democracy in Pacific Asia.* He also co-edited (with Joanne Bauer) *The East Asian Challenge for Human Rights.* He has been a Fellow of the Center for Human Values, Princeton University, and has also been awarded a fellowship at the Center for Advanced Study in the Behavioral Sciences, Stanford University. He has just completed a co-edited volume entitled *Confucianism for the Modern World,* forthcoming from Cambridge University Press in 2003.

Allen Buchanan is professor of public policy and of philosophy at Duke University. He is the author of *Secession: The Morality of Political Divorce* and *Justice, Legitimacy, and Self-Determination* (forthcoming). His special interests include problems related to secession and self-determination, and he has published many journal articles on issues related to these topics.

John Finnis is professor of law and legal philosophy at Oxford University; Biolchini Family Professor of Law, University of Notre Dame; a Fellow of the British Academy; and a member of the Holy See's Council for Justice and Peace of the International Theological Commission. He is the author of *Natural Law and Natural Rights; Aquinas: Moral, Political, and Legal Theory;*

Fundamentals of Ethics; Moral Absolutes; and *Nuclear Deterrence, Morality, and Realism* (with Joseph Boyle and Germain Grisez). He has also served as special advisor to the House of Commons on patriation of the Canadian constitution.

Sohail H. Hashmi is associate professor of international relations at Mount Holyoke College and a member of the editorial board of the Ethikon Series in Comparative Ethics. His research and teaching interests include comparative international ethics and Middle Eastern and South Asian history and politics. He has contributed chapters to a number of books, and is at present completing a book on the Islamic ethics of war and peace. He is also co-editor (with David Miller) of *Boundaries and Justice: Diverse Ethical Perspectives.*

Andrew Hurrell is University Lecturer in International Relations and Fellow of Nuffield College. His major interests include international relations theory, with particular reference to international law and institutions, and the international relations of Latin America. Recent publications include co-editor with Louise Fawcett of *Regionalism in World Politics* (Oxford University Press, 1995); co-editor with Ngaire Woods of *Inequality, Globalization and World Politics* (Oxford University Press, 1999); and *Hedley Bull on International Society* (Macmillan, 2000).

Benedict Kingsbury is professor of law at New York University Law School. He has been a visiting professor at Harvard Law School, the University of Tokyo, and the University of Padua, and was formerly university lecturer in law at Oxford University. He is the author of *Indigenous Peoples in International Law* (forthcoming), and has published articles on a wide range of topics in the theory and history of international law, including compliance, trade-environment disputes, Grotius, sovereignty, and inter-state arbitration. He is the co-editor of several books, including *United Nations, Divided World: The UN's Roles in International Relations* (with Adam Roberts); *The International Politics of the Environment* (with Andrew Hurrell); *Hugo Grotius and International Relations* (with Hedley Bull and Adam Roberts); and *Indigenous Peoples of Asia* (with R.H. Barnes and Andrew Gray).

L.H.M. Ling is affiliated with the New School University as a Core Faculty member in the Graduate Program in International Affairs and is associate editor of the *International Feminist Journal of Politics* (IFJP). She is the author of *Postcolonial International Relations: Conquest and Desire between Asia and the West* (Palgrave Macmillan, 2002). Her journal articles include "Sex Machine: Global Hypermasculinity and Images of the Asian Woman in Modernity" (*Positions: East Asia Cultures Critique*, 72 (2) November 1999: 1–30); "Confucianism with a Liberal Face: The Meaning of Democratic Politics in Postcolonial Taiwan" (co-authored with C.Y. Shih, *Review of Politics* 60 (1) January 1998: 55–82); and "Authoritarianism in the Hypermasculinized State: Hybridity, Patriarchy, and Capitalism in Korea" (co-authored with

Jongwoo Han, *International Studies Quarterly* 42 (1) March 1998: 53–78). She has also contributed chapters to several books.

Menachem Lorberbaum is a senior lecturer of Jewish philosophy at Tel Aviv University and a research Fellow at the Shalom Hartman Institute of Jerusalem. He is the author of *Politics and the Limits of Law: Secularizing the Political* in *Medieval Jewish Thought* (forthcoming, Stanford University Press) and co-editor with Michael Walzer and Noam Zohar of a multi-volume series on *The Jewish Political Tradition* for Yale University Press.

David Miller is Official Fellow in social and political theory at Nuffield College, Oxford University, and a member of the editorial board of The Ethikon Series in Comparative Ethics. He is the author of *On Nationality* (Oxford University Press, 1995); *Principles of Social Justice* (Harvard, 1999); and *Citizenship and National Identity* (Polity, 2000). He is also the editor of *Liberty* and co-editor (with Michael Walzer) of *Pluralism, Justice, and Equality*, and (with Sohail Hashmi) of *Boundaries and Justice: Diverse Ethical Perspectives* (Princeton University Press, 2001). His research interests include theories of justice and equality and ideas of nationality and citizenship.

Margaret Moore is Queen's National Scholar in the Department of Political Studies, Queen's University, Canada. She is the author of *Foundations of Liberalism* (1993) and *Ethics of Nationalism* (2001) and editor of *National Self-Determination and Secession* (1998). She is interested in issues connected to citizenship theory, distributive justice, and the ethics of nationalism and secession.

The Rev. Oliver O'Donovan is Regius Professor of Moral and Pastoral Theology and Canon of Christ Church, Oxford. He is a Fellow of the British Academy. He has served as President of the Society for the Study of Christian Ethics and as a member of the Second Anglican-Roman Catholic International Commission. He is the author of *The Desire of the Nations: Rediscovering the Roots of Political Theology; Peace and Certainty: A Theological Essay on Deterrence; On the Thirty-Nine Articles: A Conversation with Tudor Christianity; Resurrection and the Moral Order: An Outline for Evangelical Ethics; Begotten or Made?*; and *The Problem of Self-Love in Saint Augustine*. With Joan Lockwood O'Donovan, he edited *From Irenaeus to Grotius: A Sourcebook in Christian Political Thought.*

Anthony Pagden is Professor of Political Science and History at UCLA; formerly the Harry C. Black Professor of History at Johns Hopkins University; University Reader in Modern Intellectual History at Cambridge University; and Fellow of King's College, Cambridge. His most recent publications are *Peoples and Empires: Europeans Overseas from Antiquity to the European Union* (2001), and, as editor, *The Idea of Europe* (2002). He is also the author of *The Fall of Natural Man; The American Indian and the Origins of Comparative Ethnology* (1982); *Spanish Imperialism and the Political Imagination* (1990); *Lords of*

All the World: Ideologies of Empire in Spain, Britain, and France (1995); and *La Illustracion y sus enemigos* (2002). His special interests include the thought of Francis of Vitoria, Bartolomé de las Casas, and the Renaissance Scholastics.

Daniel Statman is associate professor of philosophy at Bar Ilan University. He is the author of *Moral Dilemmas*, co-author of *Religion and Morality*, and editor of *Moral Luck* and *Virtue Ethics*. A past member of the Institute for Advanced Study, Princeton, his interests include Jewish philosophy and philosophical psychology, as well as moral, political, and legal philosophy.

Richard Tuck is professor of the history of political thought at Harvard University and university lecturer in history at Cambridge University. He is the author of *Natural Rights Theories; Hobbes*; and *Philosophy and Government*. His scholarly interests include political authority, natural law, human rights, toleration, and the history of political thought on international politics from Grotius, Hobbes, Pufendorf, Locke, and Vattel to Kant. He is presently engaged in a work on the origins of twentieth-century economic thought.

Acknowledgments

This book is the result of a dialogue project organized by the Ethikon Institute in collaboration with the Carnegie Council on Ethics and International Affairs. The trustees of the Ethikon Institute join with Philip Valera, president, and Carole Pateman, series editor, in thanking all who contributed to the success of this project.

We are especially grateful to Joan Palevsky, the Carnegie Council, and the Sidney Stern Memorial Trust for major financial support, and to Joel H. Rosenthal, president of the Carnegie Council, for his much-valued collaboration in this effort.

Special thanks are due to Allen Buchanan and Margaret Moore for taking on the important and challenging task of editing this book. They in turn are grateful to Anna Drake and Patti Tamara Lenard for research assistance and help in transforming the various papers into a manuscript ready to be sent to the publisher.

In addition to the authors' contributions, the active participation of other dialogue partners – Chris Brown, Russell Hardin, Susan James, Zarko Puhovski, and Nancy Sherman – greatly enhanced the project and its results.

We would also like to thank the four anonymous reviewers for Cambridge University Press for their helpful comments on the manuscript; Terence Moore, the commissioning editor at Cambridge University Press, for his support and advice; Ronald Cohen, who carefully edited and improved the text and efficiently guided this book through its various stages; and Rob Swanson for preparing the index.

1

Introduction: The Making and Unmaking of Boundaries

Allen Buchanan and Margaret Moore

This volume is concerned with one of the most pressing issues facing us today: the making and unmaking of boundaries. Even in this age of globalization – by which is usually meant capital mobility, extremely rapid methods of transportation and communication, the liberalization of economic markets, the advance of multinational corporations to many parts of the globe, and increased global economic trade – boundaries are enormously important. It matters to people's education, level of health, opportunities and life-prospects, rights and liberties which states they live in. People who migrate from one area of jurisdictional authority to another often taken great risks: Some prospective migrants die in the attempt. The coercive power of the state is often employed to prevent the migration of people across boundaries, and some states expend huge sums of money on military hardware and large armies and sacrifice their soldiers' lives, mainly in defense of existing boundaries.[1]

One of the most destabilizing aspects of the post-Cold War period has been the alteration of boundaries, which takes place outside the rule of law and often by force.[2] For nearly fifty years following the end of the Second World War, there was only one successful case of secession – Bangladesh, which was created out of a separatist movement, and in unique circumstances, particularly since its secession was supported both militarily and politically by India.[3] Since the end of the Cold War, a number of new states have been created in the former Soviet Union, Yugoslavia, and Indonesia, Ethiopia, and Czechoslovakia, and there is little prospect of boundary stability and peace in the ethnically mixed, recently independent states of the first three regions, as there are a number of secessionist groups seeking to further carve them up. The former Soviet Union has become fifteen new states, and there are armed state-seeking groups in Chechnya, as well as the Crimeans in the Ukraine, and the Abkhazians and South Ossetians in Georgia. East Timor has won independence from Indonesia, and the Acehnese and West Papuans are agitating for similar, separate status. The former Yugoslavia has been divided into five states, and Montenegrins and Albanian Kosovars continue to press their cause for the further disintegration of what is left of Yugoslavia. Eritrea has separated from Ethiopia. The Czech Republic and Slovakia have emerged from the former Czechoslovakia. There are also armed secessionist struggles in a large number of countries: Tamils in Sri Lanka, Kashmiris in India, Kurds in Turkey and Iraq, and Basques in Spain, and more peaceful, nationalist separatist movements in Quebec in Canada, Scotland in the United Kingdom, and Catalonia in Spain. For the people who fight in secessionist causes, or in defence of the status quo, the main issue is where the boundaries are to be drawn, and implicitly which state the people are to live in. In many of these cases, the struggle is not conducted for reasons directly connected to the material well-being of the people living there, but is more directly understood in terms of nationalist mobilization.

A comparative understanding of boundaries, and especially of how boundaries are to be made and unmade, is enhanced by a detailed examination of the precise ways in which different traditions conceptualize these issues, and have come to regard boundary changes. Each ethical tradition discussed in this volume represents a certain pattern of justificatory argument, and appeals to common concepts or ideas in its normative justification. This includes not only theoretical formulations of the basic principles underlying the traditions, but also the various ways in which different traditions have *in practice* understood and adapted to the challenges posed by boundary changes. The focus of this volume is on the ethical or normative theorizing about boundaries, as opposed to empirical claims, not only because every volume has limits, but also because empirical claims about boundaries are amply documented elsewhere,[4] whereas comparative ethical theorizing about boundaries has heretofore been insufficiently considered.

The interrelationship between ethical traditions and political boundaries is particularly interesting and complex. In many cases, the boundaries constructed by the ethical tradition – between member and non-member – do not have a direct bearing on the boundaries between jurisdictional units. One reason why the two kinds of boundaries frequently do not coincide is that there is a strong territorial claim involved in political boundaries, a claim that does not apply in the case of boundaries between members. Political boundaries are essentially coercive: their rules are made and enforced within a geographical domain, whereas the boundaries constructed by ethical or religious tradition are partially voluntary or subjective in the sense that there is always the possibility of leaving the particular ethical or religious community. This subjective component is especially important where there is an element of self-consciousness about membership, as is generally the case in a world of cultural and ethical pluralism and rival traditions. In many cases, however, the question arises as to whether religious or ethical rules should be enforced politically and applied across a whole domain. If this occurs, the generally porous and partially voluntary nature of boundaries between traditions are transformed into political or legal requirements. It also raises the question of the appropriate rules for people who are not members of the religion or ethical tradition enforced throughout the polity.

Many of the ethical traditions examined in this volume regard territorial boundaries as regrettable in the sense that the justificatory theory they appeal to is universal in scope. This view on the moral status of boundaries does not necessarily translate, in a straightforward or direct way, into a particular view on the justifiability of different modes by which boundaries can be altered. In many cases, traditions have developed different kinds of normative distinctions in practical confrontation with such issues as whether conquest is justified; whether territory can be purchased and, indeed, what is the relationship between land and territory, in the sense of jurisdictional authority; whether secession is justified, and, if it is, what can justify it; and a host of other questions and issues connected to the legitimacy of the practices designed to make and unmake boundaries.

1. The Problem of Defining a Tradition and Theorizing about Traditions

Central to this volume, and comparative ethics generally, is the quest to consider a set of topics or questions from the standpoint of particular traditions. This presents some immediate difficulties, mainly concerned with the problem of what constitutes a tradition, and the related problem of how to individuate traditions.

In a world of cultural heterogeneity, communities informed by these ethical traditions interact and overlap with each other in a wide variety of ways. They trade with each other, quarrel with each other, sometimes conquer or marry each another. They are often acutely aware of the presence of people who operate within other, rival, traditions, with quite different self-understandings, and sometimes they incorporate elements of other traditions into theirs. Nor is this solely a recent phenomenon, accompanying globalization as defined at the beginning of this introduction. As Richard Tuck makes clear in his chapter (8), there has been a profound awareness of the clash of different moral views at least since the time of Herodotus. The Roman world, in particular, had to contend with its own version of globalization, as members of various traditions – Roman citizens, Africans, Jews, Greeks – lived side by side, sometimes commingled on the same territory, and were also engaged in a wide variety of transactions, including trade and warfare, with exotic peoples beyond the fringes of the Roman Empire.

This volume does not represent traditions as homogeneous, self-sufficient entities, although there are purists within each tradition that aspire to separateness. The contributors to the volume recognize that these traditions have constantly interacted with, and are influenced by, one another, and that they are internally heterogeneous to begin with. The organization of the volume reflects this fact by presenting two chapters about each tradition. These different chapters reflect a certain degree of debate concerning what the tradition is about, which itself normally reflects tensions and debates within the self-understanding of the tradition. Moreover, within each chapter, there is an acute sensitivity to the degree to which traditions are contested, and to the fact that traditions are not organized, hierarchical, tightly bound structures, but patterns of interpretation, which can be defined more or less expansively, and have a number of elements, often in tension with each other.

In spite of the dangers attached to essentializing "traditions," by which is meant failing to capture the heterogenous nature of particular traditions, it is a useful starting point for ethical inquiry to recognize that people often see themselves as operating within a particular defined tradition in the sense that they explicitly and implicitly appeal back to a certain book (the *Qu'ran*, say) or a certain body of interpretation (in the case of Islam, the pre-modern Muslim jurists). In many cases, the members themselves recognize that ethical inquiry for them, but not for everybody, has to take into account the salience of a particular text they think is authoritative, and a body of interpretation of that text as a starting point for ethical inquiry.

Sometimes these starting points have strong links to a particular religious heritage. An ethical tradition is unambiguously religious, if not uniquely so, when its major propositions are considered by adherents to have been divinely revealed, either explicitly or implictly, and deemed both credible and true for that reason. This is a claim made in various ways by Judaism, Islam, and Christianity. The natural law tradition, on the other hand, is essentially philosophical and secular (to use a modern term) in its origins, content, and major lines of development. Yet the appropriation by Christian thinkers of natural law ideas deriving mainly from Plato, Aristotle, and the Stoics, and the combination of those philosophical ideas with biblical concepts, has sometimes led to the perception that the resulting mix, not excluding its philosophical content, is more religious than secular. The perception of the natural law tradition as predominantly a religious tradition is one factor that led to the designation of Renaissance scholasticism and Early Modern natural law as "Catholic natural law" and "Protestant natural law," respectively. In this volume, because the former figures prominently in the chapter on Christianity, the chapter on natural law has been largely reserved for the latter.

While these two variants of the natural law tradition overlap to a great extent, they also emphasize different intellectual sources and were both extremely important to the debate on European conquest and settlement in the Americas (the former being emphasized in the Spanish and Portuguese colonization of the Americas, the latter in British colonization). Indeed, it is because of their rich and pioneering debates on settlement and jurisdictional authority in the context of the colonization of the Americas that both have been included in this volume.

The last two chapters in this volume span more contemporary debates, and the ethical traditions examined are more obviously secular. Unlike the traditions of the pre-modern and modern periods, the characterization of liberal theory and international law as ethical traditions is more open to question. Liberal theory and international law are both clearly traditions, in the sense that they accept authoritative principles and operate at least partly through either past debate and practice. Whether they are ethical traditions is a little more contested: in the case of liberal theory, normative value is placed on the freedom of the individual, on personal autonomy, and there is a clearly articulated theory of the appropriate scope of state action, which qualifies it as an ethical theory. It is not a *comprehensive* moral theory, but it certainly raises questions, and attempts to provide coherent answers, about the appropriate – that is, legitimate and justifiable – scope of state actions. International law, too, is clearly a tradition: like all law, it is oriented by past precedence and practice. However, some people, aware of the strong divergence between law and morals, and the role of power relations in the creation of international law, might argue that international law is not an ethical tradition. Andrew Hurrell confronts this challenge in his chapter (14), arguing that international law articulates a system of universal norms that confers legitimacy on certain practices and de-legitimizes other practices. In this sense, international law can be regarded as an ethical tradition, which empowers certain actors and justifies certain actions. Both liberal theory and international law have been included in this volume precisely because their norms have been influential in modern times in the debate on the legitimate modes by which boundaries are made and unmade.

One of the most difficult aspects of comparative ethical inquiry is the question of how to individuate distinct moral communities. At the most general level, the different traditions are clear enough: the principles appealed to by a Muslim, who is clearly operating within an Islamic tradition, are quite different from those appealed to by an international lawyer. They accept different authoritative texts, and consider different principles to be relevant in assessing the justifiability of a particular practice. But beyond the most general level, problems arise. For example, does Orthodox Christianity fit in with the Christian tradition represented in this volume, on the grounds that it accepts the same authoritative text (the Christian Bible)? Or does Orthodox Christianity embody its own distinctive morality, as Samuel Huntington has argued?[5] There is an intermediate position between purely local moralities, and universal morality (which involves the thin conception of shared moral beliefs) but what exactly constitutes that intermediate position is not always clear. The chapters in this volume articulate clearly distinguishable ethical traditions, but because there is no clear answer about the appropriate level of generality that traditions are conceived of, it follows that what should be included within a tradition, or what constitutes a tradition in its own right, will be open to debate.

Another challenge to the examination of ethical theorizing within different traditions involves the appropriate objects of study. The chapters in this volume not only examine critical reflection on authoritative texts and the principles enunciated in these texts, but also how these principles have been applied in practice. People who share a common tradition – by which is meant people who appeal to a similar set of authoritative texts and have a similar moral vocabulary – develop their practices and norms through concrete practices, and often in relation to a set of problems or challenges that arise in the real world. The relationship between normative justification, authoritative text, and practice is, however, an extremely complex one, as the contributions to the volume reveal. On the one hand, we cannot simply understand the normative principles underlying a tradition by examining the authoritative texts, because these might not be complete guides to actual practice – these principles may be appealed to very selectively, and so it is necessary to examine how the principles and commitments have been manifested in practice. On the other hand, if we want to know what is justified according to a particular tradition, we cannot simply appeal to what people have done. Sometimes people act without regard for the values or principles that are common in their society, and it would be wrong to view the actions of the vicious and the unjust as representative of the moral code of all those who share the tradition they were brought up in. Sometimes there is also genuine disagreement within traditions about the limits on permissible action, and this is not always clear by simply looking at practices. In order to figure out what people think is morally right, it is important to pay attention to the public discourse that is employed, the principles and values appealed to, and how this has guided practice, as well as to the resilience and possible tension between the different elements of traditions, and the role this plays in justifying action in specific contexts.[6]

2. Ethical Traditions, Boundaries, and Territory

Questions of political and legal authority are inextricably bound up with the issue of territory because of the close, interconnected relationship between territory and governance. This relationship is particularly clear in the modern state-system, which is premised on the Weberian notion of the sovereign territorial state with the exclusive right to govern within clear territorial boundaries. Since the end of the seventeenth century in Europe, it has been impossible to talk about sovereignty without also discussing territory. This is because sovereignty refers not merely to the right to regulate various aspects of life within the territory, but also because it involves the capacity to exclude other political agents from control of the territory.[7] A close relationship between governance and territory was also characteristic of the Roman Empire, which had definite limits, a clear boundary, and attempted to construct systems of uniform administration and taxation throughout the territory.

During periods of less effective governance, such as the Middle Ages in Europe, no single political power could claim to be the exclusive sovereign authority within a definite territory. This was partly because of the limited capacity of governing powers to give effect to their rules. In fact, there were many competing, and overlapping sources of authority, such as small bishoprics within a kingdom, free cities, city leagues, the Teutonic Knights, and the Hanseatic League. Many functions that are now associated with the sovereign state, such as coining money, or setting a standard of weights and measures, were carried out at the local level or performed by non-state actors, such as guilds. Even during the Medieval period, however, governance had strong territorial association: it was not governance over persons, or over members simply, as in a nomadic tribal system, but over a geographical region, even if its boundaries were often more zones than clear demarcations. Territory was relevant because it referred to the bounds of jurisdictional authority, the geographical scope of the rules the political authority made. This geographical dimension was relevant even when the boundaries between competing authorities was unclear, or when several powers competed with each other for authority.

The ethical traditions examined in this book discuss the issue of boundaries in two distinct, but related, senses. First, they discuss the issue of boundaries in terms of the boundaries between members and strangers, insiders and outsiders, people of their faith or ethical standpoint, and people who do not adopt the ethical tradition. The central focus of this kind of concern is related to boundaries as they arise with respect to the issue of membership. Who is and who is not a member of a particular community? How should the two interact? What principles should govern their relations?

These ideas are brought up in numerous ways throughout this volume. The Jewish Bible refers to the presence of non-Jews amongst the Jewish people, discussed mainly in terms of the principles that should govern the relations between the two, and in terms of the appropriate organizing rules and principles that should govern the community. Implicit in Confucian teaching is also a distinction between followers of Confucianism and the rest of humanity, who are potentially subject to Confucian rules and virtues. The issue was raised most acutely in terms of the relations between those who have adopted Confucian principles and ways and those who resist it. Daniel Bell's chapter (4) notes the concern expressed over the disagreeable reality that some outsiders showed no inclination to assimilate or abandon their own culture and become civilized (Confucianized).

The Christian tradition has also been strongly shaped by a conception of boundaries, especially the boundary between insiders and outsiders. Christians were acutely aware of the presence within "Christian Europe" of converts, heretics, Jews (the "outsiders within"), and of Muslims (the "outsiders outside"), whose presence came to define the limits of Christian Europe. The Islamic tradition operated with a basic boundary between

Muslims and non-Muslims (*dar-al Islam* and *dar-al harb*), but further distinguished between non-Muslims who are part of one's community and require defence against invaders,[8] and those non-Muslims who offer basic protections for Muslims, especially in terms of safety and freedom to practice one's religion.

One of the key debates in contemporary liberal political philosophy is the question of whether, or to what extent, liberals should tolerate illiberal groups.[9] This is essentially a question of what organizing principle should be adopted in a community, when the adherents of different ethical traditions disagree. The only ethical tradition examined in this volume that does not address the question of who is a member, and the appropriate relations governing insiders and outsiders, is that of international law, and this is because international law, as the only global set of institutionalized norms, defines who has standing in international law and in the interstate system. As a result, it is both very difficult for non-state actors (outsiders) to get recognition within international law, and these actors do not really challenge the tradition of international law, but only aspire to be recognized by international law and the international community as legitimate political actors.

Second, there is the issue of legitimate governance, which raises the question of how to draw the political or jurisdictional boundaries of legitimate units. Interestingly, while many of the ethical and political traditions do have conceptions of legitimate governance in the sense that they articulate a standard to distinguish legitimate from illegitimate governance, they are much more vague on the question of what principle(s) should determine how to draw the boundaries between these units. In some cases, this is because the tradition simply ignores the latter kind of question, relying, as in the case of liberalism, on simplifying assumptions that prevent consideration of the most difficult ethical issues concerning border change. The Confucian tradition is a good example of the indirect relationship between legitimizing principles and political boundaries. The Confucian tradition articulates a clear sense of justice, involving a basic respect for humanity, filial piety, and respect for tradition and wisdom, all of which provide an outline of the principles characteristic of legitimate rule. But this conception does nothing to clarify the scope of these principles, except perhaps to indicate that they should be applied universally. The question then arises as to whether this concept of legitimate rule would justify conquest of area under the rule of an unjust leader by a political authority established by Confucian principles. One answer that seems possible to draw from the principles and general discussion is that there is no right to "territorial integrity," in the modern sense, to protect an unjust leader, but it is also important (presumably because of the danger of a ruler's using Confucianism as a pretext for his own expansionist aims) to determine the wishes and desires of the people living beyond the area of Confucian political authority. In this sense, it seems that it is assumed that there is a universal desire for justice, or possibly a latent universal knowledge of what injustice is, even in areas governed by rival ethical traditions (that is, areas that are not populated by people imbued with Confucian traditions and principles). The "test" for justified military action is whether it would be acceptable to the people in the conquered region.

In other cases, the conception of boundaries between members of different traditions is importantly related to the question of jurisdictional authority over land. This is because of the strong territorial component implicit in the idea of political rule, which presupposes that the rules apply to all people who live within the geographical or territorial domain. Different conceptions of legitimate (that is, just, moral, proper) rule directly affects the relationship between members and non-members, and sometimes this has a direct bearing on the rules regarding land, even if not on the issue of the boundaries between jurisdictional units. Ethical traditions typically involve adherence to certain fundamental organizing principles, which might themselves have an exclusionary or adverse impact on members of other faith communities or ethical traditions. This is discussed briefly by Menachem Lorberbaum in Chapter 2 in terms of rabbinic debates in Judaism over whether (and to what extent) gentiles have rights to inherit land and acquire real estate within the Holy Land.[10] This stemmed from a debate over the rules concerning the jubilee year in *Leviticus*, and on Maimonides' interpretation of the relationship between rules governing the community, and whether land became de-sacralized when owned by gentiles. Of course, many traditions have had rules that seemed to privilege members of their own tradition and penalize members of rival communities – the Christian tradition, for example, imposed harsh restrictions on members of the Jewish community, and particularly on their capacity to settle and own land in various places throughout Europe in the Middle Ages.

Further, in defining the territorial component involved in the creation and alteration of political boundaries, land (and control over land) is often a relevant factor. The rules operate over a domain in which people are not the sole relevant considerations in establishing the borders of the domain. In some traditions, such as liberalism, there is an extensive discussion and debate about the legitimacy of property rights, and how individuals can come to own individual pieces of property, but these are not generally helpful in explaining or justifying political boundaries, for reasons that Allen Buchanan explains in his chapter (12) on liberalism. In other cases, the conception of "land" that "belongs" to a particular ethical or religious tradition is defined in accordance with the faith community that occupies, or has occupied the land, although this of course is frequently contested by rival traditions and communities. Christians, for example, tended to assume that all territory that had once been under Christian rule remained *de jure* if not *de facto* Christian lands. This helps to explain the Crusaders' quest to "liberate" the Christian Holy Lands; as well as the sporadic attempts from the fifteenth century to the late seventeenth century to drive the Ottomans from the Eastern Mediterranean, and why it was that Christians spoke of the "reconquest" of Spain, when, by 1492, the Kingdom of Al Andalus had been Muslim for longer than it had been Christian.[11] Interestingly, there was a very similar view in the Muslim tradition about how to specify what constitutes Muslim land. Like their Christian counterparts, Muslim jurists were, Abon El Fadl argues,[12] very reluctant to concede that territory conquered by the Crusaders and Mongols were no longer to be regarded as an abode of Islam.

In other cases, the land itself is not exactly viewed as analogous to individual property, but is more closely associated with belonging (collectively) to a particular group of people, although not as a result of prior occupancy or rule, but as a result of the terms of a covenant with God. This is discussed in this volume with respect to the Jewish, Christian, and Islamic traditions. In all three religious traditions, the earth – and of course all the land on the earth – is conceptualized as belonging in the first instance to God, and that God has made the land available to human beings. In return, human beings have general obligations, which are variously described as avoiding "corrupting" the land, living in accordance with justice, or living in accordance with God's laws. Interestingly, there is a parallel debate in these three traditions about the extent to which political institutions, and thus jurisdictional territories, are necessary to uphold the community's relations with God. In all three, the obligations to live in accordance with God's laws are not purely individual, but also, importantly, collective, although there is a significant question, especially in Islam, whether this collective obligation requires the equation of religion and polity. This is expressed in terms of a debate over whether God's laws have to be implemented politically, which means jurisdiction over a piece of land, in which the *Shariah* (Way to God) is upheld, or whether religious community is sufficient. Khaled Abou El Fadl argues in his chapter (11) on the Islamic tradition that the Medina component of the Muslim narrative (which involves institutionalizing politically the Islamic message) cannot be dismissed. The message underlying the Medina experience suggests, if carried to its logical conclusion, making the defence of religion inseparable from the duty to defend the territory. There is a similar debate in the Jewish tradition, with the Zionist idea of developing the political sanctuary of the state of Israel, constituting at least a partial departure from the traditional message of Judaism, which involves waiting for a spiritual Messiah to lead the people back to their homeland.

In addition to this question of the relationship between political authority and religious obligations, there is, in both the Jewish and Islamic traditions, a sense that certain places are exceptionally blessed: in the Jewish tradition, there is the notion of the Promised Land, centered on Jerusalem; in the Islamic tradition, Mecca, Medina, and Jerusalem are viewed as "sacred" or "prohibited" spaces, blessed by exceptional Divine acts. This leaves open the question, in the Islamic tradition, of whether their sacredness requires political (that is, jurisdictional) authority over these sacred areas, or whether it simply requires on the part of Muslims appropriate reverence towards them. This is paralleled by a debate in Judaism concerning the status of boundaries, and the holiness of the land, which is reflected in Chapters 2 and 3 in this volume. Lorberbaum's chapter emphasizes two important elements: the first is that the land is a promised land, which itself is a basis of entitlement, although the prescribed borders were never realized by either the Judean or Israelite kingdoms, and the second is the obligation to holiness on the part of the Jewish people, as their part of the covenant. Daniel Statman, on the other hand, in Chapter 3, questions this relationship between holiness and the chosen quality of the land, arguing instead that it was the fixing of borders that determined holiness – that is to say, the holiness of the land was determined by Joshua through its conquest, and then nullified when the land was lost to Babylon. Holiness, on this view, is connected to the communal requirement on the part of Jews to live in accordance with God's laws, but does not inhere specifically in the land itself.

Finally, to return to one of the themes of Section 2 of this chapter, none of the traditions is uniform or homogeneous. Indeed, one interesting aspect of the contextual approach to tradition adopted in this volume is that it reveals the resiliency of various traditions and the way they can be used to arrive at radically different conclusions. This resiliency is clearly exemplified by the debate in both the Christian and natural law traditions on the discovery and occupation of the Americas. Most Christian theorists, as opposed to Christian princes, mercenaries, and fortune-seekers, accepted the Roman view that unoccupied land (*terra nullius*) became the possession of whoever first occupied it, and although these theorists distinguished between occupancy of the land (private dominium) and sovereignty over it (public dominium), the distinction only seemed to presuppose the view that public dominium ought properly to be exercised in accordance with the common good of the community as a whole. In line with these conceptions, Vitoria and other Catholic theorists argued that European settlement in the Americas required the permission of the local sovereign. They also advanced views of legitimate governance, which pressed in the opposite direction. On this view, it was appropriate for a prince to act on behalf of the international community, and to force rulers to abandon their crimes against their own people. In those parts of the Americas that were clearly "civilizations," and so there clearly were local sovereigns, the practice of human sacrifice was used to suggest that these civilizations were not in fact "civilized" and that Christian princes could legitimately intervene with the force of arms to prevent the tyranny of "human sacrifice." It is not clear, however, that this innovative attempt to legitimize armed intervention could justify the permanent occupation of these areas, rather than merely setting up a new prince.

There was another line of argument, also advanced within the Catholic tradition, and alongside the argument that the princely authorities (native chiefs) in the Americas were barbaric and the Christian Europeans were potential liberators. This was the view that the Pope was the Vicar of Christ on earth, and could delegate authority to secular rulers. As Anthony Pagden argues in his chapter (6), the 1494 Treaty at Tordesillas, signed by both Spain and Portugal, relied on the view that the Papacy had the capacity to make land-grants to secular rulers, and so divide the world into two discrete spheres of jurisdiction. The 1494 Treaty did this, even though it operated with incomplete information about the actual land that it was assigning away: it granted territorial rights to lands in the Americas to Portugal and Spain, "as you have discovered or are about to discover," as long as they were not already occupied by a Christian power.[13] Catholic theologians like Vitoria criticized this on the grounds that the Pope could not permanently alienate his power to secular rulers as this would diminish his own office, which in turn contradicts the foundation of the Papal right in the first place.

Theorists informed by the natural law tradition also debated the issues of boundaries, settlement, conquest, and jurisdictional authority, as those questions were raised by the European "discovery" of the Americas. Many seventeenth-century natural law theorists were critical of the Papal authority argument, which was the principal legitimizing argument for the division of Latin America into Portuguese and Spanish jurisdictional areas. Exponents of this tradition were divided on the question of the legitimacy of settlement in the Americas. One line of argument within the natural law tradition, emphasized by Locke, considered European settlement in the Americas to be justified on the basis of a natural right to free and peaceful access to all parts of the globe (presumably based on the Biblical view that the earth belonged in common to all men), and further argued that it is only when land has been brought under cultivation and appropriated that it can be said to be occupied. Moreover, on the Lockean view, government (public dominium) follows from private ownership, and cannot be said to be possible either in nomadic hunter-gatherer societies or over the ocean (thereby confronting both the Venetian claim to control shipping in the Adriatic and the English claim over the North Sea). A rival view within the natural law tradition – rival in the sense that it arrived at different conclusions – and most famously expounded by Pufendorf, is that settlement against the wishes of native rulers was clearly illegitimate, and this illegitimacy was grounded in the view that first occupancy clearly conferred rights to land and sovereign jurisdiction. This view was, however, not reflected in the actual practices of Europeans in the Americas.

3. Structure of the Volume

This volume strikes a balance between detailed knowledge of particular traditions and general understanding of the themes and issues with which the book is concerned. Each of the contributors, experts at the particular debates of the particular tradition they write about, adopt what may be called an internal point of view.[14] They attempt to convey the group's own self-understanding, and to show how the basic principles that underlie ethical theorizing within the group has shaped, or does shape, debate on issues relevant to the making and unmaking of boundaries.

However, if we are to understand in general terms those boundary-alterations that are permissible, and those that are not, we need to move beyond a purely internal understanding, and consider areas of possible agreement as well as examine the normative basis on which groups disagree, and how fundamental this disagreement is. This is where focussing the examination of each tradition on the same set of issues is extremely helpful. This volume implicitly relies on a typology of five different methods by which boundaries may be altered: (1) conquest, (2) settlement, (3) inheritance, (4) sale-purchase, and (5) secession. Each of the contributors to the volume considers the debates and attitudes within the tradition they are writing about to these general issues. Two of these methods – inheritance and sale-purchase – are connected with analogies between (private) and (public) property. The question of settlement bears on the relationship between members of a particular tradition and jurisdictional authority over a territory. Conquest was one of the most dominant modes, at least historically, of transfer of territory, and secession is currently the most dominant mode, at least in the sense that it is being pressed for by many different sub-state groups in all parts of the globe. Both conquest and secession press on the appropriate relationship between jurisdictional authority, legitimate governance, and membership in the community.

Each of the methods of boundary-alteration outlined in the typology raises quite different normative issues. (1) On the question of settlement, when, if ever, is settlement alone a morally sufficient ground for the acquisition of territory and the creation of boundaries? Furthermore, what is to count as settlement? (2) The issue of inheritance is broadly situated within a general conception of the intergenerational transfer of land and territory through bequest and inheritance. This raises the question of whether the territorial claims of a descendant people are affected by the expulsion or voluntary withdrawal of its forebears. (3) Sale-purchase is also a possible process for the transfer of territory, but one would expect that if it is acceptable, it would need to be governed by certain normative principles. For example, does the government have an obligation of stewardship toward future citizens that places constraints on its right to sell state territory? (4) One of the most dominant methods of acquiring territory in the past has been through conquest. This volume therefore asks whether territory can be properly acquired and boundaries legitimately altered through conquest. If so, the important question is under what circumstances and for what ends. (5) The issue of secession, which is currently the dominant mode by which groups press for major boundary changes, raises the question of whether there is a right to secession, either in general or in specific circumstances. If not, why not? And if so, what considerations warrant the exercise of this right?

Each tradition has two chapters devoted to it. The lead chapter describes how these issues are handled within a particular ethical tradition, or would be handled in the light of its principles if fully developed positions have not yet emerged, or why the tradition regards the questions as improper or peripheral, if that is the perception. The role of the second chapter in each tradition is not so much to critique the main presentation but to suggest a supplementary or, where appropriate, alternative view of how the same tradition, or a different strand of it, would handle the same issues. Each major tradition is essentially a family of perspectives, and the two chapters-per-tradition arrangement is an attempt to do justice to this intramural variety.

By comparing the seven prominent ethical traditions on the making and unmaking of boundaries – and specifically on the typology of different modes by which boundaries can be altered – this volume bisects internal and external approaches. Each chapter, with the exception of its overview, presents a purely internal focus, describing the principles and modes of reasoning internal to each tradition. By presenting each of the traditions side-by-side, relating to the same set of questions, it assists our comparative understanding of these questions, and possibly enables to us to think about all these issues in cases of intertradition conflict.

Notes to Chapter 1

1. Kashmir is one example where the drawing of boundaries (even the precise drawing of the Line of Control) is central to the conflict.
2. The alteration of boundaries takes place outside the rule of law, first, because frequently the affected parties do not agree on the boundary change. In most cases, the minority group seeks secession, or some form of self-determining status within a new boundary, and the majority group in the state seeks to maintain the existing state boundaries. Second, very few states have any provision for changing boundaries, or allowing secession, in their domestic constitution. Finally, international law does not contain a right to secede, or, at least, any right contained in international law is immediately qualified by the need to maintain the territorial integrity of existing states. See Andrew Hurrell's Chapter 14 in this volume. This means that any attempt to change boundaries occurs outside the rule of law.
3. See Donald Horowitz, "Self-Determination: Politics, Philosophy, and Law," in Margaret Moore, ed., *National Self-Determination and Secession* (Oxford: Oxford University Press, 1998), 181–214, at 185.
4. For an excellent empirical theory on boundary change, see Ian Lustick, *Unsettled States, Disputed Lands: Britain and Ireland, France and Algeria, Israel and the West*

Bank-Gaza (Ithaca, NY: Cornell University Press, 1993) and Brendan O'Leary, Ian Lustick, and Thomas Callaghy, eds., *Right-Sizing the State: The Politics of Moving Borders* (Oxford: Oxford University Press, 2001).

5. Samuel Huntington, "The Clash of Civilizations?" *Foreign Affairs* 72/3 (1993), 22–47.

6. For a good discussion of the problems in exploring the "values" of a community, or, analogously, a "tradition," see Joseph Carens, *Culture, Citizenship and Community: A Contextual Exploration of Justice as Evenhandedness* (Oxford: Oxford University Press, 2000), 111–3.

7. This description of sovereignty is adapted from Paul Hirst, "Globalization, the nation state and political theory," in Noel O'Sullivan, ed., *Political Theory in Transition* (London: Routledge, 2000), 172–89, at 173. There is also a useful and extremely interesting discussion of the dual aspects of sovereignty in Brendan O'Leary, "Comparative Political Science and the British-Irish Agreement of 1998," in John McGarry, ed., *Northern Ireland and the Divided World* (Oxford: Oxford University Press, 2001).

8. See Sohail H. Hashmi's Chapter 10 in this volume.

9. On the issue of (liberal) toleration of illiberal groups, see Jeff Spinner-Halev, *Surviving Diversity: Religion and Democratic Citizenship* (Baltimore: Johns Hopkins University Press, 2000); Ayelet Shachar, "Group Identity and Women's Rights in Family Law: The Perils of Multicultural Accommodation," *Journal of Political Philosophy* 6/3 (1998), 285–305; and Susan Moller Okin, "Is Multiculturalism Bad for Women?" *The Boston Review* 22/5 (Oct./Nov. 1997), 661–84.

10. See Menachem Lorberbaum's Chapter 2 in this volume.

11. See Anthony Pagden's Chapter 6 in this volume.

12. See Khaled Abou El Fadl's Chapter 11 in this volume.

13. See Pagden, Chapter 6.

14. For a good discussion of internal and external perspectives, see Jacob Levy, *The Multiculturalism of Fear* (Oxford: Oxford University Press, 2000), 13–4.

PART 1

THE JEWISH TRADITION

Making and Unmaking the Boundaries of Holy Land

Menachem Lorberbaum

"The Land of Israel is Holier than all other Lands"
(Mishnah Kelim 1:6)

Introduction

What kind of a good is territory? How do we reason about land? The concept of territory has a unique role to play in the manner in which we think about land issues. Ordinarily we speak of territory as if it were analogous to a private individual's real estate holding. People sell and purchase territory and people inherit the land of their ancestors. Upon closer examination, however, the analogy breaks down. Consider the case of inheritance. Rules of inheritance guide the intergenerational movement of accumulated wealth. The point of transition between the generations is determinable, and the relevant agents can be individuated. The death of a parent occasions inheritance by a child. Territory does not move in the same way between generations. The line demarcating a generation is not the line between an individual parent and child. Generations are marked off in hindsight, and the process is closer to a process of periodization in history. In fact, territory does not "move" at all. The role of the concept "territory" is to transcend generational difference. Like the concept of a people or a nation, territory is transgenerational and connotes continuity over time. Territory is a political concept; it cannot be privatized.[1]

Discussions of territorial boundaries usually relate to one of two sets of considerations. First, is a discussion of territory in terms of the geographical, topographical, or defensive integrity of a sovereign polity. Second, is a discussion of territory in terms of the demographic integrity of a populace. Despite the different and often conflicting claims they give rise to, both these sets of considerations share a common assumption. Land, on this conception, is ultimately a functional substratum, albeit a necessary one, for political and demographic entities. Yet these discussions often fail to grasp the manner in which different nations and indigenous peoples relate to land and speak about it. On this latter view, land creates its own frame of reference; it is home. The assumption that political and demographic considerations exhaust the field of relevant principles guiding the making and unmaking of the boundaries of a Promised Land is not only reductive, it is conceptually misguided. Functionalist argumentation is disenchanted, distancing the speaker from precisely that which a people views to be precious and charismatic about their *patrie.*

Were we to assume that we ought to do justice to conceptions of land as an independent good, and were we even to grant a charismatic conception of land, it is not self-evidently clear how we would reason about its implications in non-functionalist terms. My analysis of the Jewish tradition will be done with this interest in mind. The tension between charismatic conceptions of the land of Israel on one hand, and functionalist analyses of its political implications on the other, is an ongoing feature of this tradition. Central to this tradition is the conceptualization of the land in terms of its holiness. The land of Israel is the Holy Land. The discourse of holiness exemplifies precisely the attempt to speak about the charismatic quality of the land. Yet the implications of this holiness are unclear: Does it follow that Jews must live in this land? Must they control it? Can others live there? Can the holiness of the land be annulled? All these questions are radically debated. Moreover, if we do grant the existence of a cleavage between sacral and functionalist argumentation, we must still determine which of these modes should gain the upper hand in situations of conflict.

The framework for the present discussion is the normative tradition of Halakhah, Jewish religious law. As in any legal discourse, here too one argues from precedents, which themselves are subject to different and often conflicting interpretations. In any case, a theoretical analysis of Halakhah need not treat precedents as trumps. In contradistinction to juristic rulings, a theory of Halakhah explicates the values underpinning halakhic discourse and precedent, seeking to evaluate the range of available options in the tradition.[2]

The twentieth century has posed fundamental challenges to traditional halakhic discussions of territorial boundaries. First is the existence of a sovereign state of Israel. Past debates have for the most part focused on the ritualistic implications of holiness, not on its political implications. Furthermore, it is not clear at all what elements, if any, of this religious normative tradition should have any interest to secular Israeli Jews, whose personal identity is national, not religious. Finally, the manner and the degree to which this religious discourse can fit into the existing normative discourse of international political society is yet to be determined.

The debate regarding these challenges is still very much a part of the political landscape in the modern state of Israel. We will return to examine the contemporary relevance of this traditional discourse of territory in the final part of this chapter.

The Idea of a Holy Land

The very idea of regarding a land as "promised" indicates the basis of entitlement. The Hebrew Bible can be read as the epic of a people and its land. The narrative structure of the Torah, the five books of Moses, serves to legitimize the title of the people of Israel to the "Land of Canaan," and sets out the conditions of the land's inheritance. The history of the people begins with the story of Abraham, who is commanded by God, "Go forth from your native land and from your father's house to the land that I will show you" (Gen. 12:1).[3] And the Torah ends with Moses' vision of this land from the summit of Pisgah as he ends his career as prophetic leader of the children of Israel just before their entry into the land:

And the Lord showed him the whole land: Gilead as far as Dan; all Naphtali; the land of Ephraim and Manasseh; the whole land of Judah as far as the Western sea; the Negeb and the Plain – the valley of Jericho, the city of the palm trees – as far as Zoar. And the Lord said to him: "This is the land of which I swore to Abraham, Isaac, and Jacob, 'I will assign it to your offspring.' I have let you see it with your own eyes, but you shall not cross there." (Deut. 34:1–4)

For Moses, who never enters it, the land remains the great promise. Perhaps this ending suggests the possibility of the ever-promised land. The land whose promise can never be fulfilled: it is the vision on the horizon.[4]

Sanctifying this land, treating it as "holy," would seem to be but a theological and a metaphysical reinforcement of national entitlement. But a closer scrutiny of the use of the idea of holiness reveals its potential to serve an important role in limiting human claims of entitlement. The clearest way is in what I shall call the "divine ownership" argument. According to this argument, the meaning of a holy land is that this land belongs to God, hence precluding, or at least severely impeding, human entitlement.

The classic Biblical formulation of the divine ownership arguement is found in the agrarian utopia envisioned in Leviticus 25. There, the land of Israel was divided into fixed familial inheritances. Even when sold, these plots ultimately returned to the original family in the Jubilee year.

And you shall hallow the fiftieth year. You shall proclaim liberty throughout the land for all its inhabitants. It shall be a jubilee for you: each of you shall return to his holding and each of you shall return to his family. (Lev. 25:10–12)

The Jubilee marks the cyclical return to an "original position" of distributive equilibrium for a society in which the basic economic unit is the family holding. The cycle emphasizes the limits of financial transactions to undermine the arrangement of holdings. This check against the ongoing accumulation of wealth is expressed in terms of holiness, limiting the claims of ownership:

That fiftieth year shall be a jubilee for you . . . It shall be holy to you . . . But the land must not be sold without reclaim, for the land is Mine; you are but strangers [*gerim*] resident [*toshavim*] with Me. (Lev. 25:12, 23)

Holiness here severely limits entitlement. Ownership is here a divine attribute; it therefore precludes human ownership.[5] The people of Israel are tenants. The land does not belong to the people; it is God's.[6]

Divine ownership has often been interpreted as an imposition of strict ritualistic conditions for human residency on the land. What is striking about *Leviticus* 25 is that the socio-economic utopia is derived precisely from the theological denial of human ownership. The conditions derived are those of economic justice and care. Justice and benevolence must therefore be presumed to be among the defining characteristics of divine ownership.

These conditions are built into the covenant with the people of Israel, and are obligatory on pain of exile from the land.[7] Observing the seven sabbatical years of each Jubilee cycle (Lev. 25:8) is the condition for inheriting the land. Otherwise, "the land shall be foresaken of them, making up for its sabbatical years by being desolate from them, while they atone for their iniquity" (Lev. 26:43). It also follows from this model that conditions for living in this land would pertain to any of its inhabitants, not only Israelites.[8]

Such a position is espoused in a number of Biblical sources in reference to other requirements as well. Leviticus 18 is the chapter of laws concerning forbidden incestual relations. It ends with the following admonition:

Do not defile yourselves in any of those ways, for it is by such that the nations that I am casting out before you defiled themselves. Thus the land became defiled; and I called it to account for its iniquity, and the land spewed out its inhabitants . . . So let not the land spew you out for defiling it, as it spewed out the nations before you. (Lev. 18:24–25, 28)

Incestual deviance is seen as an abomination that defiles the land and justifies the exile of the people of the land. These standards are expected from all inhabitants of the land regardless of their nationality.[9] Israel's conquest of the land and the defeat of the seven Canaanite nations residing there are both justified according to these standards. The metaphysics informing the notion of "defiling" the land requires further elaboration; in the present context it is sufficient to note that defilement is particularly connected to issues of idolatry, incest, and bloodshed – the three cardinal sins of the Jewish tradition.[10] The biblical laws concerning murder end with a similar admonition to the law regarding incest: "You shall not pollute the land in which you live; for blood pollutes the land . . . You shall not defile the land in which you live, in which I myself abide, for I the Lord abide among the Israelite people" (Num. 35:33–34).[11]

The concept of divine ownership can be seen to stand in tension with other more politically oriented concept of divine sovereignty. Rashi (1040–1105), the classic medieval Biblical commentator, interpreted the first verse of the Bible, "In the beginning God created heaven and earth" (Gen. 1:1), in this spirit:

Rabbi Isaac said: The Torah [whose main object is to teach commandments] should have begun from "This month shall mark for you [the beginning of months]" (Exod. 12:2), since this is the first commandment that Israel was commanded [to observe]. And what is the reason that it begins with Genesis? Because of [the verse] "He revealed to His people His powerful works, in giving them the heritage[12] of the nations" (Ps. 111:6). For if the nations of the world should say to Israel: "You are robbers, because you have conquered the lands of the seven nations" [of Canaan], they [Israel] could say to them, "The entire world belongs to the Holy One, Blessed Be He, He created it and gave to whomever it was right in his eyes. Of His own will He gave it to them and of His own will He took it from them and gave it to us."[13]

Rashi interprets the creation story as a legitimization of Israel's entitlement in terms of divine absolutism. God here is portrayed as an absolute sovereign parceling out land to whomever he favors.[14] The absolutist version of theocratic argumentation is not uncommon, but its main weakness is the arbitrariness it attributes to God.[15] In contradistinction, the concept of holiness not only sets standards so as to critique claims of entitlement; it could also serve to limit the claims Israel might entertain against other lands.[16]

Borders

Holiness not only determines norms of behavior, it fixes boundaries too.[17] There are various traditions regarding the borders of the land of Israel in the Bible and in the later Rabbinic literature.[18] Generally speaking, we may distinguish between (1) the vision of the promised territory, (2) what the tradition deemed prescriptive borders,[19] and (3) the reality of the actual historical borders of Jewish political entities.[20]

The land originally promised to Abraham is presented thus in the book of *Genesis:*

On that day the Lord made a covenant with Abram, saying, "To your offspring I assign this land, from the river of Egypt to the great river, the river Euphrates: the Kenites, the Kenizzites, the Kadmonites, the Hittites, the Perizzites, the Rephaim, the Amorites the Canaanites, the Girgashites, and the Jebusites." (Gen. 15:18–20)

The promise is vast, extending from the Nile River to the Euphrates. Ranging from Egypt to Mesopotamia, it exceeds, in fact, any specific country. "This land," in God's promise to Abraham, indicates a region rather than a country. It indicates a dream of boundless – and therefore boundary-less – horizons, rather than any operative program.[21]

This interpretation is borne out subsequently by the Bible's persistent use of the term "land of Canaan" – that is to say, the land of the Canaanite nations rather than the land of Israel. It is further endorsed by the programmatic, prescribed borders set out to the people of Israel poised on the threshold of the land, prepared to conquer after forty years of wandering in the desert. Thus God says to Moses:

Instruct the Israelite people and say to them: When you enter the land of Canaan, this is the land that shall fall to you as your portion, the land of Canaan with its various boundaries. (Num. 34:2)

Scripture then proceeds to outline in detail the borders of the land of Canaan in all directions. These range roughly from the Mediterranean in the west to the heights east of the Jordan River, and from northern Lebanon to the Negev desert in the south.[22]

But in fact the territory reported by the Bible to have actually been conquered was both more and less than the prescribed borders. It was more in that it included large portions of land to the east of the Jordan River, but also significantly less territory on the west bank of the Jordan. The prescribed borders were never realized.[23]

The gap between the prescriptive map of the Book of Numbers and the reality of the conquest was not as important in forging future Rabbinic positions as the gap between both of these and the land settled by the Judeans returning from exile at the beginning of the Second Commonwealth. The ancient Judean and Israelite kingdoms were destroyed and their inhabitants exiled in the course of the eighth and seventh centuries BCE. In 538 BCE, Judean exiles returned from Babylon following the declaration of Cyrus, the Persian emperor.[24] In Rabbinic tradition, the Land of Israel consecrated by the returning exiles was significantly different in its boundaries from both the prescribed biblical borders and the actual borders of the pre-Exilic kingdoms. It ranged roughly from Acre in the north to Ashkelon in the south along the Mediterranean, and included Galilee and the Golan. Yet there was no settlement in Samaria. The actual borders of the Second Commonwealth were determined by political oscillations throughout the period that ended with the collapse of the Judean polity following the series of failed massive rebellions against the Roman empire in the first and second centuries of the common era.

Conquest

A. *Biblical Norms*

The gap between what the Torah considers prescriptive borders and the horizons of the original promise are significant both in terms of size and in terms of obligation. In the Bible, conquest is considered one of the primary way to acquire land, and the norms detailed by the Torah reflect its centrality:

When you cross the Jordan into the land of Canaan you shall dispossess all the inhabitants of the land; you shall destroy all their figured objects; you shall destroy all their molten images, and you shall demolish all their cult places. And you shall take possession of the land and settle in it, for I have assigned the land to you to possess. You shall apportion the land among yourselves by lot, clan by clan: with large groups you shall increase the share, with smaller groups reduce the share. (Num. 33:51–54)

The motif of these verses is best expressed by their guiding verbs: dispossession, possession, and apportioning. Given these norms of conquest, which include a demand for a complete dispossession of the idolatrous inhabitants of the land, the determination of prescribed borders is of crucial significance.

Notice that the Biblical norms of dispossession enumerated here stress the idolatrous nature of the inhabitants of the land. Dispossession and possession are presumed by the text to be in need of religious and moral justification, and the verses point to the standards discussed in the previous section. The conquerors are commanded to destroy all the inhabitants' "molten images" and demolish all their "cult places." Conquest of the land is couched in the discourse of a crusade against idolatry and not in terms of ethnic cleansing.[25] Now there is no doubt a long history of the abuse of the Biblical rhetoric of crusading zeal permeating all the monotheistic religions that are heirs to the potent combination of monotheism with a vision of universal history. The medieval empires of Christendom and Islam, the modern colonialists, and the secular Enlightenment are all heirs to this messianic combination: they all inherited the discourse of the battle against idolatrous heathens.[26] In the Torah, however, this zeal is focused on a specific strip of territory and not on a program of universal proselytizing or conquest. Hence, claims of other nations to their territory outside the borders of the land are respected. For example, regarding the Edomites, the people of Israel are commanded by God to "be very careful not to provoke them. For I will not give you of their land so much as a foot can tread on; for I have given the hill country of Seir as a possession to Esau" (Deut. 2:5). Similarly, regarding the east bank of the Jordan, the land of Moab: "Do not harass the Moabites or provoke them to war. For I will not give you any of their land as a possession; I have assigned Ar as a possession to the descendents of Lot" (Deut. 2:9). The Torah here acknowledges that these territories are to be treated as the promised lands of other nations. The idea that there exist a plurality of promised lands is not viewed as incoherent.[27] It is a characteristic feature of the Biblical conception of entitlement that it focuses on a specific promised land.

The Biblical tradition thus bequeaths two different and often conflicting tendencies. One is the national epic narrative that is particularistic in character, focusing on a specific territory. The other is an anti-idolatrous crusading zeal, focusing on religious and moral norms, on people rather than territory. In the verses considered earlier, these two tendencies are combined. Entitlement is geared to a specific land, and conquest is bound by the religious and moral practices of the inhabitants of the land. These standards will also be those to which the people of Israel, in turn, will be held responsible.[28]

Boundaries typically yield an asymmetry between the inner realm they come to preserve and the outer realm they exclude. We may characterize the Biblical conception of prescriptive territorial boundaries as intensely focused on the inner realm demarcated by the boundary and only marginally interested in the excluded realm.

B. Rabbinic Attitudes

The first rabbinic authority to interpret the command to dispossess the Canaanite nations, as a divine command to exercise sovereignty over the land, was Nahmanides (1194–1270). In his glosses to Maimonides' *Book of Commandments*, Nahmanides criticizes Maimonides (1135–1204) for failing to enumerate a specific positive commandment to "inherit" the land of Israel:

We have been commanded to inherit the land which God the exalted gave our fathers, Abraham, Isaac and Jacob, and that we should not leave it in the hands of any of the other nations, or desolate. Thus He said to them: "And you shall take possession of the land and settle in it, for I have assigned the land to you to possess" (Num. 33:53). The detailed borders of the entire land were also presented [in the Biblical text].[29]

Nahmanides is well aware of the problem the anti-idolatrous rhetoric poses to his position. Rashi, for example, interpreted Numbers 33:53 thus:

If you dispossess it [the land] of its inhabitants, 'you shall' be able to 'settle in it', and to remain there, but if not, you will not be able to remain in it.

Rashi interprets "you shall take possession of the land" as a prediction rather than as an imperative. Possessing the land depends on the treatment of its idolatrous inhabitants. In his *Commentary to the Torah*, Nahmanides cites Rashi's interpretation, but insists that his own interpretation of the verse as a commandment is "the principle one."[30]

Do not mistakenly say that this commandment refers to waging war against the seven nations [of Canaan] we were commanded to destroy, as written "thou shalt smite them" (Deut. 20:17). This is not so, for we were commanded to kill those nations when they wage war against us, but if they wish to make peace they can do so and we will leave them alone subject to specific conditions. As for the land, we should not leave it in their hands or in the hands of any other nations at any time in history.... Similarly, if after destroying these nations our tribes wish to leave the land and occupy the land of Shinaar or Assyria, or any other place, they are not permitted to do so, for we are commanded to occupy and settle the land.

Thus, Nahmanides who is the most outspoken of medieval Rabbinic authorities on the issue of Jewish sovereignty over the land, expresses his position with clear acceptance of the contours of traditional controls – the Promised Land only, and the conquest of its inhabitants subject to the controls of the law: "if they wish to make peace they can do so and we will leave them alone subject to specific conditions."[31]

Nahmanides' final remarks point to the preconditions stated in Rabbinic tradition regarding conquest. Rabbinic tradition stressed the political nature of conquest. Maimonides neatly summarizes this position:

All lands conquered by Israel [under] a king at the decision of the High Court are deemed a national [literally: public (*rabim*)] conquest and considered for all matters as the Land of Israel conquered by Joshua. Providing that he conquered it following the conquest of the entire Land of Israel specified in the Torah.[32]

Maimonides here interprets the Talmudic dictum that "the conquest of an individual is not considered a conquest."[33] Territory is only created by a conquest that can be seen as a political act undertaken by political agents – that is, the king guided by the High Court as an expression of national agency. Furthermore, conquest can consecrate newly acquired land only after the implementation of the prescriptive borders. This is a binding order. The Biblical idea of a plurality of promised lands no longer features here.[34] In principle, future conquests are possible, but they are viewed as a broadening of the basic borders.[35]

Settlement, Purchase, and Inheritance

Despite these Rabbinic echoes of the Biblical and Hasmonean ethos of conquest, the experience of recurring exiles proved to be a watershed in the development of Judaism. The experience of exile impressed itself on the Rabbinic tradition in two ways. First, it led to the understanding that viable Jewish communities can be created, maintained, and even thrive in exile. The Jewish people have lived as a people in exile for the better part of two millennia. Life with only a dim memory of the Promised Land can be sustained. It is a thick way of life that is as crucial a condition for the survival of a people, and that can serve a temporary functional parallel to territory as a substratum for the people's existence.[36]

Second, the experience of exile showed the Rabbis that territory acquired by conquest could equally be lost by the conquest of others. Maimonides summarizes this point:

All territories seized by the Israelites who had come up from Egypt, and consecrated with the first consecration, have subsequently lost their sanctity when the people were exiled therefrom, inasmuch as the first consecration, due solely to conquest, was effective only for its duration and not for all future time.[37]

Entitlement by conquest is limited to the exercising of sovereign control, and loses its effect once voided by exile. Maimonides continues by contrasting the Second Commonwealth experience:

When the exiles returned and reoccupied part of the Land, they consecrated it a second time with a consecration that is to endure forever [in the borders of their settlement].

In contrast to conquest, the possession of territory by the settlement of a people creates a consecration that is inviolable.[38]

In fact, settlement, purchase, and inheritance are all viewed as part of one cluster or nexus. The Bible treats Abraham's journey through the land as that of a patriarch symbolically taking possession of the land. After a painful family split between Abraham and Lot, his nephew, God reassures Abraham:

"Raise your eyes and look out from where you are, to the north and south, to the east and west, for I give you the land that you see to you and to your offspring forever . . . Up, walk about the land, through its length and through its breadth, for I give it to you." (Gen. 13:14–17)

Abraham's journey through the land is viewed as an act of possession that symbolically establishes the right of his offspring to inherit the land.[39] The Bible commonly refers to the national right of a people to the land as an "inheritance." It establishes the boundaries of transgenerational possession of land. Recall the verse cited earlier in which God declares, "And you shall take possession (*vehorashtem*) of the land and settle in it, for I have assigned the land to you to possess (*lareshet*)" (Num. 33:53). The verbs translated as taking "possession" have the same root as the word used for "inheritance (*yerushah*). The right of transgenerational possession is exclusive to Israelites.[40]

This exclusion of gentiles from rights of inheritance in the land is closely linked to limitations regarding real estate acquisition. The book of *Deuteronomy* commands:

When the Lord your God brings you to the land that you are about to enter and possess, and He dislodges many nations before you – the Hittites, Girgashites, Amorites, Canaanites, Perizzites, Hivites, and Jebusites, seven nations much larger than you – and the Lord your God delivers them to you and you defeat them, you must doom them to destruction: grant them no terms and give them no quarter (*lo tehonam*). (Deut. 7:1–2)

The final command has been interpreted by the Rabbis as broader than a prohibition of clemency to include a prohibiting of residency (*hanayah*).[41] Judging by the context of the verses, the focus seems to be the battle against idolatry: "for they will turn your children away from Me to worship other Gods" (7:4).

Following this interpretation, Maimonides rules as follows:

Houses and fields are not sold to them [i.e., idolaters] in the Land of Israel [...] Houses are let to them in the Land of Israel, provided they do not form a neighborhood. Less than three is not a neighborhood. Fields are not let to them. [...] And why were they [the Rabbis] so stringent regarding a field? For two implications: it would be voided from tithes and it gives them residency (*hanayah*) in the land. Outside the land [of Israel] houses and fields may be sold to them for it is not our land.[42]

Maimonides' formulation exemplifies the tight weave between territory and the crusading zeal against idolatry. Responsibility is focused on "our land," and in fact the prohibition of *lo tehonam* does not apply to a gentile who has ceased to worship idolatry:

Should an idolater desire to stay in our land, we may not permit him to do so unless he forswears idolatry; in which case it is permissible for him to become a resident.[43]

Such a gentile is considered a resident alien (*ger toshav*) – a gentile who has rights of residency and towards whom Jews are obligated to care for his well-being.[44] He should not to be confused with a full convert to Judaism (*ger tzedek*), who is committed to a full Jewish life and enters the community as a member. Full membership, in contrast to rights of residency, includes ties of marriage.[45]

Regarding the central Rabbinic controversy over whether or not a private individual gentile's purchase of real estate desacralizes his holding for purposes of tithes and other obligations concerning the land, Maimonides' position is unclear. Here he seems to say that a gentile's possession in fact forecloses the possibility of fulfilling any commandments regarding his property.[46] It is interesting to note that even regarding pagans, some authorities raise the distinction between national rights concerning territory on the one hand, and individual rights concerning labor and private property on the other. Hence, some medieval authorities argue that although the land is "an inheritance [to Israel] from their ancestors, [a pagan] nevertheless, owns that which he has planted."[47]

Secession

The classic case of secession is that of the Kingdom of Israel from the rule of the House of David under the heir to the throne, Rehoboam, by a rebellious officer, Jeroboam.[48] The tension between the tribe of Judah and the northern tribes of Israel was by that time three generations old. The Israelite monarchy had been founded by Saul from the tribe of Benjamin. David, from the tribe of Judah, ascended to the throne after the defeat and death of Saul at Mt. Gilboa in the battle against the Philistines. Given the great size of the tribe of Judah, David's policy was to reinforce the confidence of the other Israelite tribes in his reign so that it should not be identified as a usurpation of power by the tribe of Judah over all the other tribes. Although he was treated by Saul's court as a rebel, David sought to enlist Saul's surviving generals to his service in the interests of tribal unity. Yet, despite his own charisma, David's efforts were undercut by the harsh "realism" of his general (and nephew) Joab and by the series of rebellions experienced by the kingdom. The rallying cry, "We have no portion in David, No share in Jesse's son! Every Man to his tent, O Israel!" (2 Samuel 20: 1) is as old as these rebellions.

The great successes of the Israelite monarchy under David's, and particularly Solomon's, reigns ultimately overshadowed the sense of disenfranchisement felt by the other tribes. But when Solomon's son Rehoboam, in his now famous folly, declared, "My father made your yoke heavy, but I will add to your yoke, my father flogged you with whips, but I will flog you with scorpions" (1 Kings 12:14), the cord was cut. The people's retort was ready, reiterating the rallying cry of earlier rebellion: "We have no portion in David, No share in Jesse's son! Every Man to his tent, O Israel! Now look to your own House, O David" (1 Kings 12:16). And so the Bible tells us, "the Israelites returned to their homes," and the new Kingdom of Israel, independent of the Kingdom of Judah, was formed.

The secession was viewed by Rehoboam and the Kingdom of Judah as a rebellion but judged by the Biblical narrator as legitimate. The prophet Ahijah of Shilo speaks in God's name to Jeroboam, promising him He will "tear the kingdom out of Solomon's hands, and I will give you ten tribes" (1 Kings 11:31). One tribe, however, Judah, "shall remain his – for the sake of My servant David, and for the sake of Jerusalem, the city that I have chosen out of all the tribes of Israel" (11:32). This verse captures the balance of legitimacy maintained between the kingdoms and dynasties that remained impressed in the imagination of future generations. The split, as any civil war, was a traumatizing disaster,[49] but in time the new kingdom gained legitimacy.[50] Jerusalem remained the focus of national memory, and the House of David dominated the messianic imagination of future generations.

This story of secession is a political one between rival tribes of one nation; it does not refer to the secession of a minority people. In the former case, the control of territory is certainly disputed, but ultimately it remains in the fold as a whole. But we may surmise that if Jeroboam were considered a rebel, certainly would the secession of a different ethnic group be so considered. This inference, however, holds good for a monarchic regime, and we have no real models of other sovereign regimes to set precedents for us.

State of Israel or Land of Israel

The making and unmaking of territorial boundaries have marked the history of the modern state of Israel.[51] For over a century, since the pre-state sixth congress of the Zionist movement, the Jewish national movement has faced four major territorial crises.

1. 1903: The Uganda proposal put forth by Theodore Herzl and rejected by the movement, and the three subsequent major partition crises of Palestine:
2. 1937: Partitioning Eastern and Western Palestine along the Jordan River.
3. 1947: Partitioning Western Palestine into two states.
4. The Oslo agreements repartitioning the West Bank from Israel and creating a Palestinian entity.

All have left traumatic scars within Israeli society.

Although the arguments put forth in all these controversies were similar, there was a marked difference between the first one and the latter three. The first was an argument about whether a political entity should be created regardless of its territorial location. Even the supporters of the Uganda proposal agreed at the time that its acceptance would seriously impede the viability of a Jewish nation-state. The latter three controversies were about the nature of the relationship between a nation-state and its national territory. Both the political Right and Left grounded the Jewish national right to territory in the Biblical epic. However secular their adherents, they read the Bible as the legitimizing narrative of the Jewish nation-state. But in the eyes of the Jewish right, the state is an agent of the nation, and has no right to relinquish national possessions, such as the land. To do so would be tantamount to a delegitimization of its sovereign authority. In contradistinction, the labor movement, traditionally etatist in its approach, viewed political sovereignty and the quality of the state's civil society as the overriding values in the question of state and territory.[52]

The most important development influencing the controversy over the recent partition proposals of the Oslo accords has been the novel role played by religion. The earlier controversies were carried out in a society that was predominantly secular, and the debate was essentially a secular one between etatism, reason of state, and nationalism. The eighties and nineties of the twentieth century have been marked by an overlapping of previously independent cleavages of Israeli society along a new bipolar divide between

Religious-Right and Secular-Left.[53] This has raised the theological ante regarding territory.

Gush Emunim, the settlers' movement, is a religious movement that cast Zionism in the role of messianic redeemer. Its relation to the land is best expressed in the following statement by Rabbi Abraham Isaac Kook (1865–1935), treated by the movement, as a manifesto:

The land of Israel is not something external, not an external asset, a means to an end of collective solidarity and the strengthening of the nation's existence, physical or even spiritual. The land of Israel is an essential unit bound by the bond-of-life to the People, united by inner characteristics to its existence.[54]

This formulation might have been understood merely as a critique of territorial functionalism similar to that mentioned in the introduction to this chapter. Kook, however, continues to claim that

Therefore, it is impossible to appreciate the content of the sanctity of the Land of Israel and to actualize the depth of love for her by some rational human understanding – only by the spirit of God that is in the soul of Israel.[55]

This self-proclaimed supra-rational reification of the land has sharpened the split between the partitioning policy of the state and the loyalty to land. The nationalist-religious right, and most especially the settler's movement, has experienced a cognitive dissonance between the state and its legitimating political theology, forcing a cruel dilemma between state and land. Do they wish to live in the state of Israel (*medinat yisrael*) or in the land of Israel (*eretz yisrael*)? How are they to act when national sovereignty and territorial integrity do not coincide?

Arguably however, the concepts of homeland, *moledet*, and *patrie* are not mere secular mantels for an ancient idea of a holy land. These concepts taken from the discourse of the modern nation-state transform as much as they continue. Secular Zionism's adoption of the Biblical epic has come with an attendant tradeoff. It has adopted the epic narrative while at the same time relieving itself from the claims of holiness. The various controls of the normative tradition of holiness have been given up in the process of adopting the Bible for the purposes of a secular political-theology.[56] Paradoxically, this process has not spared the nationalist-religious right that may have fallen prey to the very secularization it seeks to counter. Whereas secular Zionist parties aligned themselves with socialist or liberal norms, religious parties have been precariously exposed to that modern political sensibility that Pierre Manent has characterized as "the discrediting of the idea of the good, coinciding with the elevation of the idea of the people."[57] In its zeal to provide a religious narrative of redemption as Israel's political-theology, the nationalist-religious right has tended to overlook the normative controls of holiness, and fallen into the trap of condoning violence. The modern ideology of nationalism has here too displaced the ethos of holiness.[58]

Conclusion: Territory as a Value

Establishing the value of territory does not yet determine its weight in the hierarchy of values of a tradition. A basic principle of Halakhah is that "attending to the [saving of] lives" [*pikuah nefesh*] is a principle overriding all other obligations. The classic example is that of the sanctity of the Sabbath, for which deliberate violation is considered a grievous sin but is violated for the sake of saving life. Here is Maimonides' formulation of the principle:

The commandment of the Sabbath, like all other commandments, may be set aside if human life is in danger. Accordingly, if a person is dangerously ill, whatever a skilled local physician considers necessary may be done for him on the Sabbath. [Even] if it is uncertain whether the Sabbath needs to be violated or not... the Sabbath should be violated, for the mere possibility of danger to human life overrides the Sabbath.[59]

All commandments are set aside in situations of danger to human life.[60] This is a guiding principle in situations of conflict. Maimonides further elaborates the point by stressing the teleology of Halakhah:

When such [actions violating the Sabbath for the purpose of saving human life] have to be done, they should not be left to heathens, minors, slaves, or women, lest they should come to regard Sabbath observance as a trivial matter. They should rather be done by adult and scholarly Israelites. Furthermore, it is forbidden to delay such violation of the Sabbath... for scripture says, "Which if a man should do, he shall live by them" (Lev. 18:5), that is to say, he shall not die by them. Hence you learn that the ordinances of the Law [Torah] were meant to bring upon the world not vengeance, but mercy, loving-kindness, and peace.[61]

Maimonides bases the overriding consideration of saving life in an understanding of the telos of the law: "mercy, loving-kindness, and peace."

Nahmanides' formulation of the commandment to possess the land in terms of Jewish sovereignty has already been cited earlier in the section on conquest. Nahmanides' interpretation whereby "we are commanded to occupy and settle the land" and "not leave it in... the hands of any other nations at any time in history" clearly constructs the commandment in a way that would prima facie circumvent the restriction of endangering life. But as I indicated, Nahmanides formulation is an exception.[62] The real challenge seems to be in understanding the role of politics, for only a polity would be able to carry out Nahmanides' agenda. Now, a fuller treatment of his position would demand a discussion of just and unjust war, and that is beyond the scope of this chapter.[63] To conclude this section, I would like to point to alternative views that conceive of the polity in terms of the telos of the law developed by Maimonides.

First is that of Naphtali Tzvi Yehudah Berlin (1817–1893) in his influential commentary to the Torah. The Book of Deuteronomy maintains an ambivalent position regarding monarchy as the preferred regime. Berlin explains this hesitation:

There is a difference between government by monarchy and government by the people and their representatives. Some states cannot tolerate a monarchic regime, while others, without a monarch, would be like a ship without a captain. An issue like this cannot be decided by the binding force of a positive commandment. For matters of collective policy involve [dealing with] life-threatening situations, in which positive commandments are overridden. Therefore there can be no definite imperative to appoint a king, as long as the people have not consented to the monarchic yoke through seeing the surrounding nations being governed more adequately [by kings].[64]

Berlin's conception of the best regime is not the issue at hand (he is actually an anti-monarchist), but rather his conception of politics. Sovereign politics means determining policies with consequences of life and death. Policy questions are therefore a realm not governed by definite imperatives, for these may have to be constantly overridden in the configurations of saving life and minimizing threats to life.[65] Berlin's novel political use of the overriding character of saving life provides a strategy of argumentation that boldly relieves the realm of the political from religious and nationalist claims that threaten to endanger human life.[66]

Second, is Maimonides' celebrated ending of the *Mishneh Torah*, his monumental fourteen-volume codification of Jewish law:

The Sages and Prophets did not long for the days of the Messiah that Israel might exercise dominion over the world, or rule over the heathens, or be exalted by the nations, or that it might eat and drink and rejoice. Their aspiration was that Israel be free to devote itself to the Law [Torah] and its wisdom, with no one to oppress or disturb it.... [67]

Maimonides points to the ultimate human goal – that of acquiring wisdom. Politics is a tool enabling the creation of security, affluence, and abundance that would permit the pursuit of knowledge.

The application of norms regarding territory should be determined by their place in the hierarchy of values. The promotion of human security of life and the contribution to the quality of life of the polity always have a controlling role to play.

Notes to Chapter 2

1. Nationalism, however, need not supply the sole theoretical basis for a conception of territory. Recognizing the political character of territory is compatible with a liberal conception of parcelization of private property, and it certainly does not preclude a prohibition of conquest as a means of acquisition.

2. For an outline of the basic structure of Halakhah, as well as a discussion of some of its basic principles, see *Encyclopaedia Judaica*, s.v. Halakhah, vol. 7, pp. 1156–66, Michael Fishbane, "Law, Story and Interpretation: Reading Rabbinic Texts," Michael Walzer, Menachem Lorberbaum, and Noam Zohar, editors, Yair Lorberbaum, co-editor, *The Jewish Political Tradition* (New Haven: Yale University Press, 2000), vol. 1 "Authority," pp. xxxix–lv. For a classic presentation, see Menachem Elon, *Jewish Law: History, Sources, Principles*, translated by B. Auerbach and M. J. Sykes. 4 vols. (Philadelphia and Jerusalem: Jewish Publication Society, 1994).

3. Biblical citations usually follow *Tanakh: The Holy Scriptures*, The New JPS Translation According to the Traditional Hebrew Text (Philadelphia: The Jewish Publication Society, 1988).

4. The resounding inspiration of the Biblical epic and its interpretive pliability is exemplified in the twentieth century in the dramatic use of this theme by Martin Luther King Jr. in the apocalyptic sermon he delivered on the eve of his assassination, "I See the Promised Land." See *The Essential Writings and Speeches of Martin Luther King Jr.*, edited by James M. Washington (San Francisco: Harpers, 1991), pp. 279–286. On the reiterative potential of the Exodus themes, see Michael Walzer, *Exodus and Revolution* (New York: Basic, 1985).

5. Biblical theology typically depicts God in terms of human relational roles; see the detailed discussion in Moshe Halbertal and Avishai Margalit, *Idolatry*, translated by Naomi Goldblum (Cambridge: Harvard University Press, 1992), pp. 9–36, 214–235. The same tensions encountered in the present discussion regarding the notion of God as owner are to be found regarding the theocratic notion of God as king. It can serve as a limiting notion of human ruling as it does in Martin Buber's analysis of Biblical anarchism in *Kingship of God*, translated by Richard Scheimann (New York: Harper and Row, 1967). It can also be interpreted as an ideology of ruling, as does Gershon Weiler in *Jewish Theocracy*, (Leiden: Brill, 1988).

6. But doesn't the entire universe "belong" to God? Or to use the Psalmist's words, "The earth is the Lord's and all that it holds, the world and its inhabitants" (Ps. 24:1). This question threatens to undermine the coherence of the divine ownership argument especially when applied to a single land. Much depends on the meaning of singling out a particular territory, as we will see later.

7. See Leviticus 26:3–47.

8. The term "Israelites" is used to denote the Hebrew audience of the Biblical text, in contradistinction to modern day Israelis, i.e. citizens of the state of Israel.

9. See the vivid description of the theology of the God of the land by the peoples exiled to Samaria by the Assyrian Empror in 2 Kings 17:24–41.

10. See Babylonian Talmud (BT) Sanhedrin 74a and Maimonides, Mishneh Torah (MT), Laws of the Foundations of the Torah, Chapter 5.

11. Cf. *Ezekiel* 36:16–38. See too Moshe Greenberg, "Some Postulates of Biblical Criminal Law" in his *Studies in the Bible and Jewish Thought*, (JPS: Philadelphia 1995), pp. 25–41.

12. Hebrew: *nahalat*, translated variously as ancestral portion, inheritance; cf. Num. 34:2, 36:1–11.

13. English translations of Rashi's commentary to the Pentateuch are available in many different editions; the translation here is my own.

14. This argument is typical of feudal justifications of law and is discussed in detail in Walzer, Lorberbaum, and Zohar, *The Jewish Political Tradition*, vol. 1 "Authority," pp. 28–30, 37–42, 437–441.

15. See Maimonides' fierce critique, *The Guide of the Perplexed*, 3:31.

16. I have so far interpreted holiness in relational terms that typically describe the divine in terms of specific human roles (owner, sovereign, etc.). Holiness on this account means in the presence of God, and the norms governing the proper use of the land are derived from the logic of the specific role models informing the divine relationship to human beings. A different approach interprets holiness as an attribute of the land. What can it mean to predicate holiness of an object? The analysis of holiness is much debated, and positions cover the entire range of possibilities: metaphysical, normative, and functional (here used in an ontological rather than socio-political sense). Judha Halevi, *The Kuzari* 2:8–24 is a classic medieval exposition of the essentialist metaphysical conception and Nahmanides' commentary to Leviticus 18:25 is a kabbalistic formulation of the metaphysical position. A recasting of the metaphysical position in modern nationalist terminology is Abraham Isaac Kook, *Orot*, translated by Bezalel Naor (North Vale, New Jersey: Jason Aronson, 1993), p. 89. A classic exposition of the normative approach is Mishnah, Kelim 1:10. Yeshayahu Leibowitz, *Judaism, Human Values and the Jewish State*, edited by Eliezer Goldman (Cambridge: Harvard University Press, 1992), pp. 121–122, 226–228, explicates the latter in functional terms, combining a stringent normative orthodoxy with an equally stringent and at times vehement anti-metaphysical approach. For a detailed exposition of these approaches in the context of the modern religious reaction to secular Zionism, see Aviezer Ravitsky, *Messianism, Zionism, and Jewish Religious Radicalism*, translated by Michael Swirsky and Jonathan Chipman (Chicago: The University of Chicago Press, 1996), pp. 10–144. Ravitsky has also pointed to the fascinating tradition of demonizing the land in his Appendix (ibid.). Now, although there is undeniably a close connection between metaphysics and policy in matters of territory, it does not take a clear form of strict inference when considering the normative tradition of Halakhah. In my discussion earlier, I have therefore focused on normative utterances rather than philosophical or ideological disquisitions.

17. Rules of holiness demarcate the holy and secular and the pure and impure; so too in issues of land. Cf. Mishnah Kelim 1:10. On the Rabbinic tradition ascribing impurity to the lands of the gentiles, see Gedalyah Alon, "The Levitical Uncleanness of Gentiles," in his *Jews, Judaism and the Classical World*, translated by Israel Abrahams (Jerusalem: Magnes Press, 1977), pp. 183–189.

18. "Rabbinic" in upper case refers to the scholars of the first centuries of the Common Era and their canonic works, the Mishnah, Jerusalem Talmud (JT), Babylonian Talmud (BT), and Midrashic compilations. I will use "rabbinic" in lower case to refer to medieval scholars.

19. That is, pertaining to various commandments that are territorially bound.

20. Identification of the locales mentioned in the sources has been much debated by commentators and historians. A useful summary of the halakhic debates

is *Talmudic Encyclopedia,* edited by Shlomo Josef Zevin (Jerusalem: Talmudic Encylopedia Publishing, 1956; Hebrew), vol. 2, pp. 205–213.

21. Following Yehuda Elitzur and Yehuda Kiel, *Atlas Daat Mikra: A Compendium of Geographical-Historical Terms in the Scriptures* (Jerusalem: Mossad Harav Kook, 1993; Hebrew), pp. 22–23.

22. See Elitzur and Kiel, pp. 50–55.

23. See Joshua 13 and Judges 1.

24. The declaration ends the Hebrew Bible; see 2 Chron. 36:23.

25. Although the praxis of Biblical norms of war creates an overlapping between the religious and the ethnic that threatens to blur this distinction; cf. the story of the Gibeonites in Joshua 9 especially against the background of the norms of conquest as described in the case of Jericho and Ai in earlier chapters of that book. The Rabbinic tradition viewed the story of Moses' call for peace to Sihon king of the Amorites as a precedent; see *Midrash Rabbah,* Numbers, translated by Judah J. Slotki (London and New York: Soncino Press, 1983), 19:27, vol. 2, p. 777. The Rabbis attributed a similar call for peace to Joshua before his war against the seven nations; see JT Shvi'it 36c and see Maimonides' codification in MT Laws concerning Kings and Wars 6:1–5.

26. See especially Norman Cohn, *The Pursuit of the Millennium* (New York: Harper and Row, 1961). Much of the debate concerning secularism and political theology turns upon the religious roots of the secular forms of political legitimacy; see Karl Lowith, *Meaning in History* (Chicago: Chicago University Press, 1964) pp. 1–20, and the extensive discussion in Hans Blumenberg, *The Legitimacy of the Modern Age,* translated by Robert M. Wallace (Cambridge: MIT Press, 1985).

27. Cf. Amos 9:7: "True, I brought Israel up from the land of Egypt, but also the Philistines from Caphtor and the Arameans from Kir." In Deuteronomy, the point seems to be that these nations all fit into the overall narrative of the territorial conquests of Abraham's descendents and their kindred tribes in the region of ancient Palestine. Other Biblical sources allude to an argument from a polytheistic conception of regional deities; see Judges 11:12–29. Cf. the Septuagint version for Deuteronomy 32:8, "He fixed the boundaries of peoples in relation to the sons of Israel," which reads "sons of God [*el*]" instead: *Biblia Hebraica,* edited by Rudolph Kittel (Stuttgart: Deutsche Bibelstiftung, 1977) ad loc.

28. Even the definitions of idolatry served the Rabbinic tradition as a control upon divesting of individual rights. Not ethnic identity but adherence to norms was taken to be the guiding criteria. See Maimonides, MT Laws concerning Kings and Wars, 8:10–9:1.

29. Nahmanides, *Glosses to Maimonides' Book Of Commandments,* Additions to the Positive Commandments, 4 (Hebrew).

30. Ramban (Nachmanides), *Commentary on the Torah,* translated and annotated by Charles B. Chavel, (New York: Shilo 1975), Numbers pp. 385–386. I have slightly altered the translation to fit the New JPS translation of the Bible.

31. These conditions are not specified in the Biblical text; they are rooted in Rabbinic interpretation; see n. 22.

32. Laws concerning Kings and their Wars 5:6 (the translation is my own, ML); for further restrictions, see Laws of Kings 5:1.

33. BT Gittin 47a.
34. The background might be the Rabbinic view according to which the Babylonian and Assyrian imperial conquests undermined the ethnic coherence of the peoples of the ancient Near East. Still, there is an interesting tradition seeking justification for the Davidic wars of conquest against Moab; see *Midrash Rabbah*, Genesis, translated by H. Freedman (London and New York: Soncino Press, 1983), 74:15, vol. 2, pp. 686–687.
35. See MT Laws concerning Heave Offerings 1:3.
36. See the frank critique of Halevi, *The Kuzari* 2:23–24, 5:23–28. There is an intense debate regarding the obligation of an individual Jew to reside in the land of Israel; see BT Ketubot 110b–111a, and the Tosafot Ketubot 110b s.v. *hu omer*. Nahmanides' critique of Maimonides' in the *Glosses to the Book of Commandments* mentioned earlier is the focal point of much of the later debates in the literature.
37. Laws concerning Heave Offerings 1:5, *The Code Of Maimonides (Mishneh Torah)*, Book Seven, *The Book of Agriculture*, translated by Isaac Klein (New Haven and London: Yale University Press, 1979), p. 99.
38. The obvious questions remain insufficiently treated: wasn't the land originally settled too? Conversely, did others not settle it after the Roman subduing of Judean rebellions?
39. Cf. BT Baba Batra 100a regarding pacing a plot as a means of taking possession.
40. Cf. BT Baba Batra 119a involving the case of the daughters of Zelophehad reported in Num. 27:1–8 and 36:1–12, for a fascinating debate on whether principled entitlement to territory is sufficient to establish actual possession of a private plot.
41. See BT Avodah Zarah 19b–20a.
42. MT Laws concerning Idolatry 10:3 (translation my own).
43. Maimonides, *The Commandments, Sefer Ha-Mitzvoth of Maimonides*, translated by Charles B. Chavel (London and New York: Soncino Press: 1967), Negative Commandment 51, p. 49; cf. MT Laws concerning Idolatry 10:6.
44. See Laws concerning Kings and their Wars 10:12. The disputes concerning the category of *ger toshav* regard points of substance and points of procedure. Regarding substance, the question is whether a mere rejection of idolatry is sufficient, or is a fuller commitment to the seven Noahide laws necessary. Regarding procedure the question is whether a formal acceptance is necessary, and if so for what purposes. Rabbi Abraham Isaac Kook argues that a mere rejection of idolatry and no formal procedures are sufficient to qualify for residency; see his *Mishpat Kohen* (Jerusalem: Mossad Harav Kook, 1966), section 63, pp. 128–129 and the editor's notes, pp. 365–366.
45. See MT Laws concerning Forbidden Intercourse, chapters 13–14.
46. See BT Gittin 47a. The relevant texts seem to be corrupted by much editing and interpolation; see Saul Lieberman, *Tosefta Ki-fshutah* (New York: The Jewish Theological Seminary of America, 1955), Order Zera'im, Part 1, p. 260 ln. 90–91. Maimonides' position is also unclear and has perplexed his commentators, given his seemingly contradictory rulings; see Laws concerning Heave Offerings 1:10–14 and Laws concerning First Fruits 2:15 and Rabbi Hayyim Soloveitchick, *Hiddushe Rabenu Hayim Halevi* (Israel: np, 1972), folio 38a–38b.

47. Tosafot Rosh Hashanah 13a, s.v. *velo*.

48. 1 Kings 12. See Barbara W. Tuchman, *The March of Folly from Troy to Vietnam* (New York: Alfred A. Knopf, 1984), pp. 8–11.

49. Here is Tuchman's summary: "The twelve tribes were never united. Torn by conflict, the two states could not maintain the proud empire established by David and Solomon, which had extended from northern Syria to the borders of Egypt. . . . Reduced and divided they were less able to withstand aggression by their neighbors. . . . The alternative course that Rehoboam might have taken, advised by the elders and so lightly rejected, exacted a long revenge that has left its mark for 2,800 years," *The March of Folly*, pp. 10–11.

50. Cf. BT Horayot 11b and Maimonides, MT Laws concerning Transgression through Error 15:6.

51. For a useful summary, including an illuminating comparison of relevant maps, see Moshe Brauer's entry "Frontiers" in *Encylopaedia Judaica* (Jerusalem: Keter, 1971), vol. 9, col. 311–322. On the policy informing the decision-making process, see Itzhak Galnoor, *The Partition of Palestine* (Albany: State University of New York Press, 1995).

52. See Mitchell Cohen's study of the labor movement's ideology and policy in *Zion and State* (New York: Columbia University Press, 1992) and James S. Diamond's study of the "Canaanite" critique of Zionisim in *Homeland or Holy Land?* (Bloomington: University of Indiana Press, 1986).

53. See Aviezr Ravitski, *Religious and Secular Jews in Israel: A Kulturkampf?* (Jerusalem: The Library of Democracy Institute, 1999).

54. Rabbi Abraham Isaac Kook, *Orot*, p. 89.

55. Ibid. See his argument further on: "Distance from awareness of the mysteries produces a distorted awareness of the sanctity of the Land of Israel," p. 90.

56. The complex relation between the political-theology legitimizing the Israeli nation-state and the place of religion in society is examined by Charles S. Liebman and Eliezer Don-Yehiyah in their two joint books, *Civil Religion in Israel* (Berkeley: University of California Press, 1983) and *Religion and Politics in Israel* (Bloomington: University of Indiana Press, 1984).

57. Pierre Manent, *An Intellectual History of Liberalism* (Princeton: Princeton University Press, 1995), p. 16. The great success of nationalism relative to other ideologies is discussed by Ezra Mendelsohn, *On Modern Jewish Politics* (New York: Oxford University Press, 1993).

58. Recent analyses of the religious right in Israel are Ehud Sprinzak, *The Ascendance of Israel's Radical Right* (Oxford: Oxford University Press, 1991) and Gidon Aran, "Jewish Zionist Fundamentalism: The Block of the Faithful in Israel," in *Fundamentalism Observed*, edited by M.E. Marty and J.R.S. Appleby (Chicagon: University of Chicago Press, 1991), pp. 265–344.

59. Laws concerning the Sabbath 2:1, *The Code Of Maimonides (Mishneh Torah)*, Book Three, *The Book of Seasons*, translated by Shlomo Gandz and Hyman Klein (New Haven: Yale University Press, 1961), p. 10.

60. The classic exceptions are the cases of conflict between human lives, cases of incest, and the forced worship of idolatry; see n. 10.

61. Laws concerning the Sabbath 2:3; op. cit. p. 11.

62. See the various sources cited in Aviezer Ravitsky, "Prohibited Wars in the Jewish Tradition," in *The Ethics of War and Peace*, edited by Terry Nardin (Princeton: Princeton University Press, 1996), pp. 115–127.

63. See the exchange between Naom J. Zohar and J. David Bleich in *Commandment and Community*, edited by Daniel H. Frank (Albany: SUNY Press, 1995), pp. 245–273. See also Noam J. Zohar, "Can a War be Morally 'Optional'?" *The Journal of Political Philosophy*, 4 (1996), pp. 229–241; Michael Walzer, "War and Peace in the Jewish Tradition," in *The Ethics of War and Peace*, edited by Terry Nardin, pp. 95–114.

64. *Ha'amek Davar*, Deuteronomy 17:14, in Walzer, Lorberbaum, and Zohar, *The Jewish Political Tradition*, vol. 1 "Authority," pp. 154–5.

65. See the application in Shaul Israeli, "In Answer to a Query," in *Af Sha'al: Mitzvah min ha-Torah?* (Jerusalem: Oz Veshalom, 1978).

66. I am indebted to my colleague Haim Shapira for pointing out to me the significance of Berlin's position.

67. Laws concerning Kings and Wars 12:4, *The Code Of Maimonides (Mishneh Torah)*, Book Fourteen, *The Book of Judges*, translated by Abraham M. Hershman (New Haven: Yale University Press, 1949), p. 242.

3

Man-Made Boundaries and Man-Made Holiness in the Jewish Tradition

Daniel Statman

1. Holiness and Boundaries

According to Menachem Lorberbaum, central to the Jewish tradition "is the conceptualization of the land in terms of its holiness." In his view, this conceptualiztion plays a key role in determining the tradition's view on the making of boundaries. Unlike other traditions that view territory as merely "a functional substratum," in the Jewish tradition, territory – more accurately its own territory – is viewed as "an independent good." Thus, contends Lorberbaum, an inquiry into the connection between this Jewish, nonfunctionalist conception of the land and the attitude to the making of boundaries might enable us to make some general observations about the way nonfunctionalist conceptions of land govern reasoning about boundaries.

I am not sure, however, that this is the best conceptual framework for a discussion on the Jewish attitude to the making of boundaries. Let me start by presenting a different view on the Biblical perception of the land of Israel. According to Lorberbaum, in essence, the land is perceived as holy: "The land of Israel is the Holy Land." Yet, surprising as this might be for some readers, in the Bible the root Q-D-SH, which denotes holiness in Hebrew, never once refers to the land of Israel! In particular, the expression "the holy land" (*erets ha-qodesh*) is nowhere to be found in the Bible. In the book of Isaiah (52:1), we find the term "city of holiness" referring to Jerusalem, but no reference to any land of holiness. The closest we can come to this is in the expression "holy ground" (*admat qodesh*), yet this refers not to the land of Israel, but to the ground on which Moses stood before the burning bush.

How, then, is the land of Israel perceived in the Bible? Not as a holy land, but rather as a *good* land, good in the most mundane and non-spiritual meaning of the word:

For the Lord thy God bringeth thee into a good land, a land of brooks of water, of fountains and depths, springing forth in valleys and hills; a land of wheat and barley,

41

and vines and fig-trees and pomogranates; a land of olive-tree and honey; a land wherein thou shalt eat bread without scarceness, thou shalt not lack anything in it.[1]

In fact, the promised land is so good that the Bible has to warn the children of Israel again and again not to let its superb physical and material conditions lead them astray from their religious-moral assigned destiny.[2] If there is any intrinsic holiness to the land, it is thus obscured from sight. According to the Biblical text, the good earth as encountered by the Israelites is more of an obstacle to a life of holiness than an inspiration to one.

Lorberbaum contends that the idea of the holy land is tightly connected to two other ideas – that of the promised land and that of the divine ownership of the world. Yet these are separate ideas – a land that is not holy can be promised, and a land that is holy might not be promised. As for the connection between ownership and holiness, here too I think we face different and logically independent ideas. The argument from divine ownership is based on a general moral-political argument to the effect that owners have a decisive say in how their property might be used. By this token, as God is the owner of the land of Israel, its inhabitants are forbidden to sell lands without reclaim,[3] and they ought to regard their ownership as essentially limited and conditional. However one evaluates the validity of this argument,[4] it is different from an argument based on holiness that seeks to derive normative implications from the intrinsically unique qualities of the land – namely, from its holiness. Contrary to Lorberbaum, then, I do not think that "the meaning of a holy land is that this land belongs to God". The legal relation of ownership is far too weak to ground, let alone exhaust, the meaning of the idea of holiness (whether of the land or of any other object). To be sure, the term "holy" does appear in the laws about the Jubilee ("It shall be holy to you,"[5]), but it refers to the fiftieth *year* and not to the *land*, as Lorberbaum seems to argue.

I will say more about the argument from ownership in Section 2. But first let me complete my argument about the relation between holiness and the making of boundaries. Lorberbaum is well aware of the fact that what is meant by the holiness of the land is a matter of great dispute in Jewish philosophy. Some argue that it refers to an intrinsic quality of the land (a claim that seems to be consistent with Lorberbaum's notion of a nonfunctionalist conception), while others argue that it is some sort of a relational quality (what we might call a functionalist conception).[6] This disagreement casts doubt on attempts to characterize the tradition as accepting, more or less unequivocally, the idea about "the charismatic quality of the land" (Lorberbaum), and certainly on attempts to connect this conception of the land to the actual rules of Halakha.

To overcome these difficulties, Lorberbaum says that his discussion focuses "on normative utterances rather than on philosophical or ideological disquisitions". Yet while I fully agree with this focus, I think it leads to a different conclusion to that offered by Lorberbaum. On Lorberbaum's view, "holiness does not only determine norms of behavior, it fixes boundaries too". Yet the ideas set forth in the Talmud seem to entail the opposite view – namely, that the fixing of the borders determines holiness. I refer to a central Talmudic source,[7] according to which the holiness of the land was determined for the first time by Joshua through his conquest (*kibbush*) of the land, then nullified as a result of the land being lost to Babylon, and then re-established by Ezra, this time through his settlement (*chazakah*) of the land. According to most halakhic authorities, including Maimonides, while the first sanctification – by Joshua – was only temporary, the second – by Ezra – was to last forever, in spite of the subsequent devastation of the land and exile of its people by the Romans. What we see here is that human acts – in this case acts of conquest and of settlement – determine both the very holiness of the land as well as the precise boundaries of this holiness. This has significant halakhic implications because various agricultural laws – mainly the laws of *terumut u-maa'serot* (heave offerings and tithes; dues given to the priest and the poor) – apply only to the Holy Land, hence those parts of Israel conquered by Joshua, but not settled by Ezra, are exempt from these laws.

According to Maimonides, human acts such as conquest can determine not only the boundaries of holiness *within* the (promised) land of Israel, but, under well-defined circumstances, even the boundaries of holiness *outside* it. Maimonides says that if the king of Israel conquers lands outside the boundaries of Israel specified in the Torah, and if he does so after completing the conquest of the land within those specified boundaries, then the newly gained land will be "considered for all matters as the Land of Israel conquered by Joshua."[8] "For all matters" includes, of course, matters relating to the holiness of the land, such as the obligatory offerings of the first fruits to the priest and the poor. Thus, the making of *political* boundaries (via conquest) fixes the *sacred* boundaries too – the borders of the holy land – not the other way round.

A further illustration of this dependence of holiness upon human acts is the possibility of selling the land of Israel (or pieces of it) to non-Jews, and the implications of such a sale. According to the Talmud,[9] Jews are not allowed to sell houses and fields in Israel to non-Jews. However, this prohibition is not absolute, and might be overridden by more urgent considerations. One such consideration that justifies violating this prohibition in the eyes of many contemporary Rabbis is the injunction not to allow the land to lie fallow in the seventh year (*shemita*). Observing this law became hard when Jews returned to work the land of Israel in the nineteenth century, and the Rabbis ruled that if the land of Israel is temporarily sold to a non-Jew before the seventh year, then the laws governing agricultural work in the seventh year are circumvented. Thus, by a human freely undertaken transaction of selling the land to non-Jews, the Jews who do so in effect nullify its holiness, thereby exempting it from the laws of the seventh year. We must assume that this selling is legally valid, otherwise it could not do the trick of evading these laws.[10]

To sum up the difficulties in the assumption that the Jewish view on making boundaries is guided by its conceptualization of the land in terms of its holiness: First, the Bible never describes the land of Israel as holy. Second, the Talmud, which does refer to the holiness of the land, regards it as established – and also as overruled – by human acts, be they acts of conquest, settlement, or sale. Finally, discussing the question of boundaries through the prism of the notion of holiness creates the impression that the only arguments used in the halakhic tradition to justify claims about boundaries are arguments based on its holiness, which, if true, would make the tradition irrelevant to contested lands outside Israel and to international relations in general. I try to correct this impression in Section 3. But before I do so, let me say more about the notion of divine ownership and its relevance to the topic under discussion.

2. Ownership

I suggested earlier that the argument from divine ownership is different from the argument from holiness. What exactly does the former entail with regard to the right to the land and the making of boundaries? Lorberbaum shows that it is used in the Biblical laws of the Jubilee to restrict human ownership. But he also correctly notes that this is not the only way this idea is used in the tradition. Following Rashi's famous commentary to Genesis 1.1,[11] divine ownership is often referred to as grounds for the (assumed) unconditional right of the Jews to the land of Israel. For many Jews, these words of Rashi provide the definitive and final reply to any skeptical challenges about the right to the land or about the legitimacy of its boundaries. Non-Jews have no claim to this land because God, the owner of the entire world, has given it to the people of Israel. And since owners have the moral and legal power to transfer or share their ownership, this transaction is valid, and the people of Israel are thus the sole owners of the land.

If the land of Israel is so conceived – as the private property of the people – then a radical conclusion suggests itself – namely, that any non-Jew residing in Israel is a trespasser unless he or she gets special permission. It also seems to follow that non-Jews cannot really own any land in Israel, for the land is already owned; legally speaking, one cannot gain ownership over somebody else's property, be it an individual or a collective, unless this owner willingly relinquishes his property rights. Furthermore, if non-Jews use the land, they should pay the owners for its use. If these conclusions sound too extreme, let me quote from an article R. Ben-Zion Krieger published in 1987, the title of which is "Giving lands from Israel to non-Jews."[12] After explaining that the land of Israel belongs to the people of Israel forever, and that they never gave up their divine right to the land, he quotes from R. Kook, who says that even if the people of Israel wanted to give up this property, they could not do so, because "with regard to the land of Israel and its relation to the people of Israel, there exists a supreme power, a divine power, that cannot be forfeited even on the owner's own will." R. Krieger then concludes by saying the following:

If govermental agents or individuals purchase with money lands in the areas in which they want to gain ownership, it is not their duty to do so but is really above the line of duty, just in order not to give an excuse to the nations of the world to say 'you are robbers, you both murdered and took possession.'

You can easily see how such an approach leads to an extreme right-wing position in contemporary Israel. On this model, the Palestinians are just guests in a land that belongs to somebody else, and, as a matter of principle, can have no territorial claims with regard to it. Their very raising of such claims is a case of *hutspah*, of effrontery, of ingratitude toward the true owners of the land who graciously allow non Jews to reside in it.

This understanding of the divine ownership argument has been prevalent in the last century among believers. Rashi's words can no doubt be read to support it, as can the whole Biblical epic of the people and its land; God promises the land to the children of Israel and allows them – in fact orders them – to capture it from the Canaanite nations inhabiting it. The idea of divine ownership can thus be interpreted in two opposing ways: as restricting human ownership ("you are but strangers resident with me,"[13]) and as strengthening it ("[God] gave it to them and of His own will He took it from them and gave it to us)"[14]. Both are found in the divine ownership tradition, the former more prevalent in discussions on the political level.

Pointing out the existence of these two understandings does not mean that no arguments can be offered to prefer one over the other. I think Lorberbaum is right to emphasize the divine arbitrariness presupposed by the political-nationalist interpretation. I would add that this interpretation lends itself to a Euthyphro-like dilemma of the following form. The dilemma starts with a question about the moral-political right of the Jews to the land of Israel (in general, or regarding any specific border). As a reply, the notion of divine ownership is utilized, to the effect that God "of His own will gave it to them [the non-Jews residing in Israel] and of His own will took it from them and gave it to us."[15] But now a dilemma presents itself: Is God's will to give the land to the people of Israel based on a (moral) reason or not? If it is, then this reason (whatever its content) suffices to justify the moral right, and the idea of ownership plays no real role in the argument. It would be God's justice that would underlie His parcelling out of lands, not His unlimited power as owner. If, however, God's will is not based on reason, then it provides no moral answer to the question we started with. Though in some narrow legal sense the argument would establish that the land belongs to the Jews, it would fall short of establishing anything close to the justice of their possession.

We seem to face here a deep tension between two religious intuitions, one emphasizing God's overall power and sovereignty, the other emphasizing God's justice and goodness. Elsewhere I have shown that by and large the Jewish tradition preferred the latter intuition, portraying God as rational and just rather than as an arbitrary ruler. In the realm of morality, this is expressed in the refusal to accept divine command theories of morality.[16] Thus, I think Lorberbaum is right in suggesting that the tradition as a whole is more consistent with an interpretation of divine ownership that morally restrains human ownership and behavior than with an interpretation that relieves humans of some of their moral burdens.

3. Applying Universal Principles: The Principle of Conquest

As indicated earlier, I believe that the Jewish tradition has something to say not only about how the boundaries of the Holy Land are to be made but also about how boundaries in other countries are to be made. Furthermore, according to some Rabbis, the principles governing the making of boundaries in the international domain apply (at least partially) to the land of Israel too. The use of such principles became pertinent in the last century, when Jews were challenged to answer questions regarding the moral legitimacy of the Zionist project in general, and of Israel's boundaries (after 1948 or after 1967) in particular. As explained in the previous section, anyone truly troubled by the moral problematics here could not find solace in claims about divine arbitrariness. Hence, one would expect to find use of arguments of a more universalistic nature too, arguments that could be accepted by the non-Jew as well as by the disturbed conscience of the Jew. Within the halakhic tradition, such arguments would typically be formulated in terms of ideas found in classical sources. I would like to illustrate this point by looking at the use made of a Talmudic principle governing the political-territorial implications of conquest. This will show, first, how a Talmudic principle applies to all making and unmaking of boundaries, and second, what happens to the halakhic defense of the Jewish right to the land when it opens itself to universal principles.

What then is this Talmudic principle? In tractate *Hulin*, the Talmud seeks to solve the following problem. In Deuteronomy 2, God says to Moses that he ought not to wage war against the nations of Ammon and Moab "because I have given it unto the children of Lot for a possession." However, later we learn that both these nations, in fact, were conquered by the children of Israel. How so? The Talmud quotes a verse from Numbers 2 according to which Ammon and Moab were first conquered by Sihon, king of the Emorites. Through this conquest, the territories of Ammon and Moab became Emorite territory, and the original prohibition against taking the possessions of the Ammonites and the Moabites was annulled. In the words of the Talmud: "Ammon and Moab were rendered clean [unto Israel] through Sihon."[17] Similarly with the conquest of the Philistine lands. Abraham promised Abimelech that neither he nor his descendents would take Abimelech's land. How, then, were the children of Israel allowed to conquer this land? Because the nation of Kaphtorim did the work first and gained the land from the Philistines, thereby nullifying any claims the Philistines had regarding their land. As most commentators contend, what the Talmud states here is a general principle about the possessional implications of conquest – that any property gained by war is transferred to the ownership of the conquerors with no residue. I shall be referring to this principle as "the principle of conquest." It applies to the territory of the conquered nation, and *a fortiori* to other kinds of property. The sixteenth-century scholar David Ben Solomon Ibn Abi Zimra (known as Ha-Radbaz) offers the following explanation for this principle:

That is the way of kings to conquer territories one from the other and by doing so they take full possession of them, because if you do not say so, you will find no king who has possession in his kingdom, for all of their kingdom they take from others and they do so by war and that is their possession.[18]

This is a powerful argument. If conquest did not transfer ownership over territories and did not entitle the conquerors to bequeath the newly gained territory, then most nations (if not all of them) would face serious problems with their right to their lands. It is hard to find existing countries whose boundaries (at least some of them) were not made by conquest in one war or another. There is no need to weary the reader with examples.

Radbaz's reasoning clarifies the universal nature of the principle under discussion, which is also evident from the Talmudic source I just mentioned. In the Talmud, it helps establish the possessional implications of conquests by Gentiles of lands belonging (at the time of conquest) to Gentiles. Would this universal principle apply to conquests by Jews too? To the conquest of the land of Israel (by Jews or by non-Jews)?

As for the first question, regarding the conquest of territories (outside Israel) by Jews, the answer is probably in the affirmative. R. Shneur Zalman of Lyady, the founder of Chabbad, mentions the principle of conquest in his halakhic work, *shulchan a'ruch ha-rav*, and then refers in parenthesis to the Maimonidean law cited earlier,[19] according to which the king of Israel can broaden the boundaries of the land of Israel via conquest.[20] Thus, according to Shneur Zalman, the rule about the results of conquest effected by the king of Israel is just a branch of a more general principle governing the implications of conquest in all nations.

The second question has two parts, one relating to the conquest of Israel by Jews, the other to its conquest by non-Jews. For obvious reasons, the first part has been more relevent in contemporary halakhic discussions about the making and unmaking of Israel's boundaries. On the second part of this question, I have found nothing, but I offer some speculations in the closing lines of this chapter.

How, then, is the principle under discussion relevant to contemporary Israel? In 1937, Reuven Gafni published a full-length book about "our historical-legal right over the land of Israel."[21] The book was honored by a preface from R. Abraham Isaac Kook, then the Chief Rabbi of Palestine, part of which I quoted earlier.[22] In Chapter 7 of the book, Gafni argues that according to international law, as well as Jewish law, one gains possession over territory by conquest. This implies that the Jews have a right to the land of Israel for the following reason:

The conquest [of the land] in the last war [First World War] was by England who captured the land from the Ottoman empire to whom the land had belonged for centuries. According to the rules of war, the British could – if they so wished – annex this country and make it a colony of the Crown, or whatever they would like. [But] in the very days of the war they explicitly denied such an intention [to annex it to Britain] and chose a different option which was expressed in the Balfour Declaration, guaranteeing the establishment of a national home for the Jews in the land of Israel.[23]

A similar argument was made several years later by R. Shaul Yisraeli, a central halakhic authority in religious-national circles. Yisraeli says that the owners of the land are those who gain possession over it in war, and in the case of Israel, those were the British. As the British, with the approval of the international community, agreed in 1947 to give the land to the Jews, "... the establishment of the state of Israel was carried out with the consent of the landowners and hence it is legal *from the Torah's point of view.*"[24]

The landowners in this citation are of course the British, not God, as in the simple ownership model. But now, on Yisraeli's view, what about those parts of Israel gained in 1948 that were not included in the UN partition? To this, Yisraeli answers that since the 1948 war was a defensive war, it falls into the category of a "permissible" war,[25] and therefore all of the territories occupied as its result were legitimate and fall under the principle of conquest.

The interesting point to note about these approaches is that they make the "Jewish" answer to the question under discussion depend on a general understanding of the moral and the political situation. In other words, to determine the point of view of the Torah, one must first determine what the facts of the matter regarding the relevant history are and what morality has to say given these facts. This comes out very clearly in the last source I would like to mention. This is an article from 1995 by R. Abraham Sherman.[26] After introducing the principle of conquest, Sherman shows that it does not apply automatically to any conquest, because when wars are unjust, then taking possession over property gained by them, be it real estate or other property, would amount to simple robbery. Violence, then, is not the only circumstance when it comes to international relations. This implies that in order to use the principle of conquest to establish possession over the territories occupied in 1948 and in 1967, one must first demonstrate the morality of these wars, and Sherman tries to do so in a way similar to that taken by Yisraeli – indeed to that taken for years by mainstream Zionism – that they were defensive wars,[27] or in their words, wars necessary "to save Israel."

Sherman, as well as Yisraeli, add another proviso to the principle of conquest – that conquest transfers ownership only if the conquest was intended to do so in the first place. Hence, for example, regarding the 1982 war in Lebanon, Sherman argues that as Israel waged this war solely for self-defense, it did not thereby take possession over Lebanon and did not turn it into part of the land of Israel.[28]

These provisos to the Talmudic principle of conquest would apply to its use on the international domain too. They mark an interesting development from a principle that grants a reward to successful aggression, irrespective of its moral justification, to a principle far more nuanced and sensitive to moral considerations. In the way Sherman summarizes the current understanding of the principle, it wholly depends on the justice of the war leading to conquest. This development is not too surprising: It is one thing to speculate in the abstract about what the Talmud says concerning the effects of the wars between Sihon and Moab. It is a different thing to apply these Talmudic ideas to real-life moral quandaries in contemporary Israel. The move toward a more moral formulation of the principle under discussion accords well with the general move toward moralization in Jewish law.[29]

Yet, as hinted here, this turn to universal principles has its price. It exposes those who make it to possible criticism regarding their moral as well as their historical assumptions. As this exposure could become a fearful enterprise – maybe it will turn out that not all the wars were defensive, or maybe it will be shown that some particular instance of occupying territory was unjustified – a constant tension can be found in the literature between moral claims on the one hand and claims about an absolute right to the land grounded in divine ownership on the other.

Finally, let us return to the question regarding the application of the principle of conquest to the conquest of Israel by non-Jews. If the king of Israel were to conquer Greece, then, according to Maimonides, Greece would become part of the land of Israel, and the Greek people would lose any claims to it. On Shneur Zalman of Lyady's view, this is a result of the universal principle of conquest.[30] What about the opposite case, in which the Greek king conquered Israel? Would it then – according to *Jewish* law – become part of Greece? Can Jews lose their rights in Israel through war, just as other nations can lose theirs? I found no explicit discussion of these questions in the literature, probably because for most halakhists, the answer to these questions would be an unequivocal "no." Nevertheless, I would like to suggest some speculations that might lead to a different answer. This answer might teach us something about the possibilities for moral interpretation within the tradition. It also encourages new reflection on the nature of the relation between the Jewish people and their land.

I start with a general claim. If the principle of conquest applied to the conquest of Greece by the Jews but not to the conquest of Israel by the Greeks, that would be a blatant case of injustice, which would run counter to the repeated emphasis in the Torah on the justice of its laws and the righteousness of God. Such discrimination between Jews and Gentiles would hardly be compatible with the injunction, "Justice, only justice shalt thou pursue,"[31] and would definitely be inconsistent with the Torah's expectations that when the nations see the Jewish law, they will say "and what nation is there so great that has statutes and judgments so righteous as all this Torah."[32] In other words, the perceived moral nature of the Torah encourages a fair and equal application of the principle outlined here. The motivation for such equal application derives not only from broad considerations of justice but from a Talmudic principle according to which "there is nothing which is allowed to Jews but prohibited to non-Jews."[33] Put simply, it is unfair that the Jews would have the power to gain ownership over territory in a way that would be blocked for non-Jews.

Let us assume then that an international court ruling according to halakha would grant the Greeks possession over the land of Israel in the imaginary scenario we are discussing. Would such ruling contradict the Biblical view about the eternal bond between the people of Israel and their land? I think not. As Lorberbaum reminds us, the entitlement of the Israelites to their land is contingent on their moral-religious behavior. This means that if they are "vomited out" of the land, to use the figurative language of Leviticus 18, they must have defiled the land by their sins, and no longer deserve it. In this respect, the Israelites are no different than other nations, whose residence in the land also depends on their behavior.[34] The Emorites, explains God to Abraham, will not lose their entitlement to the land until the fourth generation, "as their iniquity is not yet full."[35] Hence, when they do eventually lose the land, we must infer that their iniquity was full. The same with the children of Israel: If they lose the land through conquest of some other nation, their iniquity must be full. And if their iniquity is full, then, according to the Bible's moral-theological view, they have no right to reside in the land. If all this is correct, then an international court ruling according to Halakha might apply the principle of conquest in the case under discussion not only for moral reasons (fairness in applying the principle of conquest), but for theological ones too. Denying the political consequences of such conquest would amount to contravening the divine judgment on the iniquity that led to the loss of the land.

4. Summary

1. In the Biblical view, the right of nations to live within their promised boundaries depends on their moral and religious behavior. Sinful behavior is punished by exile, be the sinners Jews, Emorites, or Moabites. In that sense, on a moral-theological level, the making and unmaking of boundaries depends on proper behavior.

2. The boundaries of holiness also depend on human action, and are not just given once and forever. They are made by political actions such as conquest and settlement and unmade by actions such as exile and sale. Thus, holiness does not fix the boundaries of the Holy Land but the other way round.

3. That conquest makes the boundaries of the Holy Land can be seen (and at times has been seen) as an instance of a universal Talmudic principle to the effect that through conquest the conquerors gain ownership over the conquered territory. This principle applies to all acts of conquest, including that of the land of Israel, and has been utilized by contemporary Rabbis to justify Israel's right over territories gained by war.

4. The principle of conquest, whose power to transfer ownership seems to be unlimited in Talmudic sources, has been interpreted by later commentators as contingent on the justice of the war that let to the conquest. This moralization of the principle means that any use of the principle outlined to ground the making of boundaries would have to rely on moral arguments of a universal nature, thereby making the "Jewish" answer to questions about boundaries dependent on the general moral answer to them.

Notes to Chapter 3

1. Deut. 8:7–9. Cf. Numbers 16:13, Deuteronomy 33:28, Kings II 18:32.
2. See Deuteronomy 6:10–13, 8:11–18, and 32:13–15.
3. Leviticus 18: 25:23, and Lorberbaum's contribution to this volume.
4. For a critical analysis, see A. Sagi and D. Statman, *Religion and Morality*, (Amsterdam: Rodopi, 1995), Chapter 3.
5. Leviticus 25:12.
6. See Lorberbaum's contribution to this volume, n13.
7. *Yevamot* 82b.
8. Laws concerning Kings and their Wars, 5:6, quoted by Lorberbaum in his Chapter 2 of this volume.
9. BT *Avoda Zara* 20a.
10. Would the land of Israel still belong to the Jewish people even after it was sold to a non-Jew prior to the seventh year? If it does, the relation here is clearly not one of private property. This can also be learned from the Biblical stories about the Patriarchs purchasing land in Israel. See especially Genesis 23:4, where Abraham explains to the Hittites that he is only "a stranger resident with them,"

and thus he pleads with them to sell to him "for the full price" (ibid., verse 9) a burying place for Sarah. And this takes place after the land was already given to Abraham in Genesis 15. I say "given" rather than "promised," because that is explicitly the verb used there: "In that day the Lord made a covenant with Abram, saying: 'Unto thy seed *have I given* this land.'" According to the Midrash, the cause of the strife between the shepherds of Lot and those of Abraham was precisely the inability of Lot to grasp this point – namely, that the divine granting of the land cannot translate automatically to private property rights. The Midrash says that Lot's shepherds thought that, as the land was promised to Abraham, Abraham had the right to take his beasts to pasture wherever he wished, and as Lot would surely inherit him, he had a similar right. By contrast, Abraham's shepherds thought that such behavior counted as simple robbery (*Genesis Rabba* 41:5). On the general difficulties in understanding the political notion of territory in terms of private property, see Allan Buchanan's Chapter 12 in this volume.

11. Following the Midrash, *Genesis Rabba* 1:2.
12. R. Ben-Zion Krieger, "Giving lands from Israel to non-Jews" [in Hebrew], *Tehumin* 8 (1987), 323.
13. Leviticus 25:23.
14. Rashi to Gen. 1:1.
15. Rashi, ibid.
16. See Avi Sagi and Daniel Statman, "Divine Command Morality and the Jewish Tradition", *The Journal of Religious Ethics* 23 (1995), 49–68.
17. *Hulin* 60b.
18. *Responsa*, part 3, 733.
19. See n7.
20. R. Shneur Zalman of Lyady, *Shulchan A'ruch Ha-Rav*, Part V, Laws concerning the renunciation of property and the removing of the neighbour's landmark (*hefker vehasagat gevul*).
21. Reuven Gafni, *Our Historical-Legal Right Over the Land of Israel* [in Hebrew], 1937.
22. See text near n12.
23. Gafni, *Our Historical-Legal Right Over the Land of Israel*, 134.
24. S. Yisraeli, *Erets Hemda* [in Hebrew] (Jerusalem: Mosad Harav Kook, 1988), 35. Emphasis mine.
25. See Maimonides, Laws concerning Kings and their Wars, 5:1.
26. R. Abraham Sherman, "The Halakhic Validity of the Wars of Israel in Determining Sovereignty Over Areas in the Land of Israel" [in Hebrew], *Tehumin* 15 (1995), 23–30.
27. Ibid., 29.
28. Ibid.
29. See, for example, Leon Roth, "Moralization and Demoralization in Jewish Ethics," in his *Is There a Jewish Philosophy?* (London: The Littman Library of Jewish Civilization, 1999), 128–43; Judith Hauptman, *Rereading the Rabbis: A Woman's Voice* (Boulder, Colorado: Westview Press, 1998). I am not assuming that the tradition moves only in the direction of moralization, only that moralization is a dominant feature of it.
30. See n20.

31. Deuteronomy 16:20.
32. Deuteronomy 4:8.
33. BT Sanhedrin 59a.
34. Here again the principle governing the right to reside in the land of Israel can be seen as a branch of a universal principle applying to all lands – namely, that sinful behavior is punished with exile. Maybe the first illustration of this principle is the punishment of Cain, who, after defiling the land with his brother's blood, is "driven out from the face of the land" (Genesis, 4:14). See also Jeremiah 48–49 about the fate of the Moabites and the Ammonites, who will both be expelled from their lands as a result of their sins. It is also noteworthy that both of these nations are promised to return in the end of days back to their original territories (Jerermiah, 48:47 and 49:39). Thus the cycle of exile and return to a promised land is not unique to the Jewish people and the land of Israel. See Nahmanides, commentary to Genesis 1.1: "When a nation continues to sin it has to leave its place, and another nation then inherits its land. Thus has been the divine justice forever."
35. Genesis 12:16.

PART 2

THE CONFUCIAN TRADITION

4

The Making and Unmaking of Boundaries: A Contemporary Confucian Perspective[1]

Daniel Bell

1. Introduction

More than 2,500 years ago, a political thinker named Master Kong (Latinized name: Confucius; c. 551–479 BC) left his native state of Lu, hoping to find a ruler more receptive to his ideas about good government. Unfortunately, Confucius did not have any luck, and he was forced to settle for a life of teaching. Several generations later, a pupil of Confucius's grandson named Master Meng (Latinized name: Mencius; c. 390–305 BC) committed himself to spreading Confucius's social and political ideas. Like the old master, Mencius wandered from state to state, looking for opportunities to put his political ideals into practice. Mencius had slightly more success – he served briefly as Minister of the State of Ch'i – but he eventually became disenchanted with political life and reluctantly settled for a teaching career.[2]

Several hundred years later, however, the social and political ideas of Confucius and Mencius – as recorded in *The Analects of Confucius* and *The Works of Mencius* – proved to be literally world transforming. They slowly spread throughout China, Japan, and Korea,[3] and by the late nineteenth century, the East Asian region was thoroughly "Confucianized." That is, Confucian values and practices informed the daily lives of people in China, Korea, and Japan, and whole systems of government were justified with reference to the ideals of Confucius and Mencius. Confucianism has fared less well in the twentieth century – most notably, the Chinese Communist Party did its best to extirpate every root and branch of the Confucian worldview – but more than one scholar has argued that long-entrenched Confucian habits continued to provide the background assumptions and values even during the darkest days of the Cultural Revolution.[4] More recently, a Neo-Confucian revival movement has taken shape among East Asian scholars and social critics (and some foreign academics) who aim to explicitly promote Confucian values in society and government. As

Tu Wei-ming notes, "The upsurge of interest in Confucian studies in South Korea, Taiwan, Hong Kong, and Singapore for the last four decades has generated a new dynamism in the Confucian tradition."[5] Tu goes on to explore the possibility of a "third epoch" of Confucian humanism.[6] Even the Chinese Communist Party has "rectified" its previous anti-Confucian stance – "Jiang Zemin and the so-called New Conservatives have turned to Confucianism in response to the crisis of legitimacy and the wide- spread social malaise that threatens to undermine the Chinese Communist Party."[7]

There is of course an ongoing debate about the extent of Confucian influence in contemporary East Asian societies. Since the May 4, 1919, stu- dent movement in Beijing, critics of Confucianism have argued that the values identified with the teachings of Confucius and Mencius have been – or should be – relegated to the "dustbin of history."[8] In this chapter, I will largely take it for granted that the values of classical Confucianism continue to exert moral and political influence in East Asia, and that any new political order in the region is likely to be shaped by "Confucian characteristics."[9] If this assumption is correct, it lends contemporary political import to the main concern of this chapter – to draw out the implications of Confucian- ism for the making and unmaking of territorial boundaries. If not, let us hope that the simple joys of intellectual curiosity will suffice to justify my effort.

2. Does Classical Confucianism Allow for (Justifiable) Territorial Boundaries Between States?

First, we need to confront a potentially fatal objection. Whatever the rele- vance of Confucian political values, they do not seem to bear on the ques- tion of territorial boundaries between sovereign states. The basic problem is that classical Confucianism seems to rule out the possibility that rulers could justifiably seek to exercise authority over a particular territory and establish boundaries between that territory and the rest of the world. In- stead, Confucians defended the ideal of '*tian xia*' [the world under Heaven]. As Joseph Chan explains, "The Confucian school of thought, as repre- sented by Confucius, Mencius, and Xunzi, was particularly important in idealizing the order of '*tian xia*', carrying much critical, ethical import . . . the Confucian conception of '*tian xia*' refers to an ideal moral and political order admitting of no territorial boundary – the whole world to be governed by a sage according to the principles of rites (*li*) and virtues (*de*). This ideal transcends the narrowness of states."[10]

Confucianism's 'founding fathers' do seem to endorse the ideal of '*tian xia*.' While Confucius himself does not explicitly say that he believes a ruler can govern over the whole world, he does hint at the possibility of a sage-king who could spread "his peace to all the people" (14.42; see also 17.6).[11] In this ideal world, the ruler need not resort to coercion or punitive laws:

Lord Ji Kang asked Confucius about government, saying: "Suppose I were to kill the bad to help the good: how about that?" Confucius replied: "You are here to govern; what need is there to kill? If you desire the good, the people will be good. The moral power of the gentleman is wind, the moral power of the common man is grass. Under the wind, the grass must bend." (12.19)

Confucius suggests that the "moral power" of the ideal ruler will eventually attract those living in faraway lands, bringing peace to the whole world and presumably doing away with the need for territorial boundaries between states:

I have always heard that what worries the head of a state or the chief of a clan is not poverty but inequality, not the lack of population, but the lack of peace. For if there is equality, there will be no poverty, and where there is peace, there is no lack of population. And then, if people who live in far-off lands still resist your attraction, you must draw them to you by the moral power of civilization; and then, having attracted them, make them enjoy your peace. (16.1)

Mencius draws on these ideas to elaborate upon the ideal of a sage-king who rules the whole world by non-coercive means. First, the ruler must gain the sympathy of the people:

There is a way to gain the Empire [*tian xia*]. It is to gain the people, and having gained them one gains the Empire. There is a way to gain the people. Gain their sympathy, and then you gain them. (4A.10; Dobson) [12]

Mencius argues that the ideal ruler would gain people's sympathy simply by his benevolence, without relying on the use of force (see 1A.6; Dobson). Even if people do not seem immediately receptive to Confucian norms, the ruler should not worry. He should cultivate his own personal virtues, [13] people will be inspired by this "moral power," and eventually he will gain the allegiance of the whole world:

Mencius said, "If a man loves others, and his love is not reciprocated, let him think about his own feelings for Humanity. If a man governs others, and they fail to respond, let him think about his own wisdom. If a man extends courtesies to others, and is not in turn treated with courtesy, let him think about his own sense of reverence. If a man pursues a course, and his way is impeded, let him seek the remedy in himself. With these things correct within himself, the whole world will turn to him. (4A.4; Dobson)

Mencius even seems to provide a time frame for ultimate success:

If any of the princes were to put into effect the policies of King Wen [an ideal ruler of the past], within a period of seven years they would inevitably become rulers of the world. (4A.14; Dobson)

From a contemporary perspective, all this might seem like pie-in-the-sky theorizing, of little relevance to the real world. Fortunately, that is not the end of the story. In fact, it would be surprising if Confucius and Mencius had not attempted to provide some practical, morally informed guidance in a non-ideal political world of sovereign states delimited by territorial boundaries. Consider the fact that *The Analects of Confucius* and *The Works of Mencius* were penned during the Spring and Autumn and Warring States periods (c. 800–221 BC), a time of ruthless competition for territorial advantage between small walled states. In such a context, it would seem odd, to say the least, for two political thinkers explicitly concerned with practical effect to limit their political advice to quasi-anarchistic principles.[14] This kind of political thinking might have resonated more in the days of Imperial China, when rulers saw themselves as governing the largest and most powerful empire in the world surrounded by as-yet-uncivilized barbarians. But China had not yet been unified in the Warring States period[15] – more precisely, the idea of China (*zhong guo*: literally, "Middle Kingdom") as a self-conscious culturally unified community with the potential to spread civilized norms over the whole world had not even been invented.[16] There are no references to China in *The Analects of Confucius* and *The Works of Mencius*.

It is also worth noting that Mencius suggests successful sage-kings come in five hundred year cycles – or more, since "seven hundred years have now passed since Chou began. As a matter of simple calculation the time is overdue." (2B.13; Dobson; see also 7B.38; Dobson). Mencius seems to suggest that sage rulers would not last for more than a generation or two,[17] which means that – according to his own theory – the non-ideal world of competing states delimited by territorial boundaries is the reality roughly ninety percent of the time. Given the predominance of the non-ideal world, one might have expected Mencius to formulate principles of political guidance in this context as well.

Confucius is even more skeptical concerning the prospects of sage-kings ever taking power. For one thing, he did not – unlike Mencius[18] – consider himself to be in the top moral/intellectual category, which is presumably a requisite for sagehood:

The Master asked Zigong: "Which is the better, you or Yan Hui?" – "How could I compare myself with Yan Hui? From one thing he learns, he deduces ten; from one thing I learn, I only deduce two." The Master said: "Indeed, you are not his equal; and neither am I." (5.9; see also 7.34)

But even Yan Hui [Confucius's favorite pupil], along with everybody else Confucius has met, is subject to human weaknesses: "I have yet to meet the man who is as fond of virtue as he is of beauty in women" (15.13).[19] Nor is Confucius overly confident about the ability to cultivate one's personal virtue in an honest and non-self-deceiving way: The Master said: "Alas, I have never seen a man capable of seeing his own faults and of exposing them in the tribunals of his heart." (5.27) Even Yao and Shun, the icons of sage-hood, proved to be deficient:

Zigong said: "What would you say of a man who showers the people with blessings and who could save the multitude? Could he be called good? The Master said: What has this to do with goodness? He would be a saint! Even Yao and Shun would be deficient in this respect. (6.30; see also 7.26)

In short, both Confucius and Mencius seem to recognize the difficulty, if not impossibility, of implementing an ideal, non-territorial political order governed by a wise and virtuous sage-king who inspires the whole world simply by means of "moral power." But is there any evidence that classical Confucians did in fact attempt to provide practical, morally informed guidance in a non-ideal world? In my view, many, if not most, of the passages in *The Analects of Confucius* and *The Works of Mencius* seem to assume the context of a non-ideal political world.[20] It is difficult to otherwise make sense of, for example, the statement in *The Analects* that "A gentleman has a moral obligation to serve the state, even if he can foresee that the Way will not prevail" (18.7). In the same vein, it would seem odd for Mencius – if his only concern was to lecture rulers on the requirements of sagehood – to make the argument that people can transgress traditional norms in hard-luck situations (4A.17), including breaking promises (4B.11) and killing tyrannical rulers (1B.8). More pertinently, the passages on warfare seem to provide direct evidence that Confucius and Mencius attempted to justify territorial boundaries between competing states in non-ideal situations.[21] One quote will suffice to make this point:

Duke Wen of T'eng asked, 'T'eng is a small state, wedged between Ch'i and Ch'u. Should I be subservient to Ch'i or should I be subservient to Ch'u?' 'This is a question that is beyond me,' answered Mencius. 'If you insist, there is only one course of action I can suggest. Dig deeper moats and build higher walls and defend them shoulder to shoulder with the people. If they would rather die than desert you, then all is not lost.' (1B.13; Lau)

In a non-ideal context, the justifiable course of action may be to reinforce, rather than abolish, territorial boundaries between states. If Mencius – who is considered to be the most "tender-minded" of the Confucians[22] – had only been concerned with ideal theory, he would have given the opposite advice.

My claim, in short, is that several prescriptions in *The Analects of Confucius* and *The Works of Mencius* were meant to apply in a political context of walled states competing for territorial advantage.[23] Needless to say, this ancient Confucian world is far removed from our own, and one has to be careful about drawing implications for contemporary states. But as Benjamin Schwartz notes, this conglomeration of separate states and principalities "resembled the emerging multi-state system of fifteenth- and sixteenth-century Europe (more, in fact, than did the *polis* of ancient Greece). We even find the emergence of many of the concomitants of the multi-state system – including a rudimentary science of international politics and efforts to achieve collective security."[24] Thus, it should not be entirely surprising if at least some Confucian prescriptions are still relevant for the contemporary world of sovereign states delimited by territorial boundaries.[25]

3. On the Selection of Feasible and Desirable Confucian Values

But which Confucian prescriptions should one appeal to? How does one select values from the complex and changing centuries-long Confucian tradition, interpreted differently in different times and places and complemented in sometimes conflicting ways with Legalism, Daoism, and more recently, Western liberalism? In this chapter, I employ the following criteria.[26]

First (and most obviously), I select values that help to answer the questions we have been asked to think about. This leaves out many Confucian values, such as filial piety and the meritocratic selection of scholar officials, that may still be worth defending today but do not bear on the issue of the making and unmaking of boundaries.

Second, I limit myself to the values espoused and defended by the two "founding fathers" of Confucianism: Confucius and Mencius. *The Analects of Confucius* is, of course, the central, founding text in the Confucian tradition, and any plausible interpretation of Confucianism must draw to some extent on the sayings of Confucius. Mencius, who elaborated and systematized Confucius's ideas, is the second most influential figure in the Confucian tradition.[27] The philosophy of Mencius became the orthodoxy in Imperial China from the Sung onwards, and still today he is "regarded as a fountainhead of inspiration by contemporary Neo-Confucian philosophers."[28]

Third, I exclude Confucian values that have been explicitly repudiated contemporary Confucian philosophers and social critics.[29,30] Few, if any, Neo-Confucians endorse such (apparent) classical Confucian values as the inherent superiority of men over women, the complete exclusion of commoners from the political decision-making process, the three-year mourning period for deceased parents, or the idea that "Heaven" somehow dictates the behavior of political rulers. Passages in *The Analects of Confucius* and *The Works of Mencius* that seem to lend themselves to these views have been either re-interpreted or relegated to the status of uninformed prejudices of the period, with no implications for contemporary societies.[31]

In addition to these three criteria, my selection of Confucian values is also guided by two "relevant indicia" – that is, relevant factors that can be applied in cases of doubt or disagreement. These indicia, however, are not requirements, for reasons that will be spelled out next.[32]

The first relevant factor is that the values contrast in some way with Western liberalism. Most contemporary Confucian intellectuals endorse values that are generally consistent with liberal-democratic norms – more precisely, some liberal ideas and practices have been invoked to complement and enrich Confucian values.[33] But it may be important to respond to the potential objection that Neo-Confucians tend to sanitize the Confucian tradition by picking and choosing only those elements that cohere with the best of the liberal-democratic tradition. If this objection is correct – that is, if liberal "Confucians" defend the values of Confucius and Mencius on purely strategic grounds, because they are seen as means to promote Western-style liberal democracy in East Asia – it would cast doubt on the assumption that Confucian norms have any independent value. It would also suggest that liberal "Confucians" do not take the Confucian tradition seriously, in the sense that they are unwilling to revise their initial liberal standpoint in response to an engagement with Confucianism, or at least to acknowledge the possibility that Western liberal-democratic norms do not automatically have priority in cases of conflict with Confucian norms. To counter these objections, I try to identify – where relevant – areas of actual and potential conflict with liberal-democratic norms. But since there are also substantial areas of overlap with Western liberalism, it is important – for the sake of accuracy – not to make this criterion an essential requirement.

Second, I try to identify Confucian values that helped shape East Asian political history and that still inform (at least in part) the practices and institutions of countries in the East Asian region. This might help to respond to the potential objection that classical Confucian values are no longer relevant in contemporary societies. But I do not want to make this an essential requirement, because there is often a large gap between Confucian ideals and "actually-existing" Confucianism. Confucian values can – and should – provide a critical perspective on some political practices in the East Asian region, and it is important to leave room for this possibility.

Let us, at long last, turn to the actual content of Confucian values. I begin by listing some general principles that bear on the question of the making and unmaking of boundaries. Next, I draw on these principles to discuss Confucian perspectives on settlement, inheritance, sale-purchase, conquest, and secession.

4. General Confucian Principles that Govern the Making and Unmaking of Territorial Boundaries[34]

Confucius and Mencius did not directly address the question the principles that should govern the making and unmaking of boundaries between states. They did, however, defend three general principles that have clear implications for the acquisition of territory and the making and unmaking of boundaries.[35]

4.1 The Need to Promote Peace

In an ideal world, Mencius suggests, the Empire (*tian xia*) would be unified and peaceful (1A.6; 2B12; see also *The Analects*, 14.42). One benevolent ruler would have obtained sovereignty over the whole world without having committed a single unjust deed (2A.2) and no one would be fighting for the sake of gaining territory. At that point, it makes sense to ask, "What need is there for war?" (7B.4, Lau)

In a world of competing states, however, it would be foolish for states to act on the assumption that wars are unnecessary. In the days of early Confucianism, several states were ruled by blood-thirsty tyrants ready and willing to use ruthless means to increase their territory,[36] and this called for different prescriptions. In this non-ideal world, Confucians held that smaller countries must prepare to defend themselves. This involves a well-trained army – as Confucius puts it, "To send to war a people that has not been properly taught is wasting them" (13.30; see also 13.29). Fortified boundaries are also essential – as noted earlier. Mencius urges the governor of a small state to "Dig deeper moats and build higher walls and defend them shoulder to shoulder with the people. If they would rather die than desert you, then all is not lost." (1B.13) Rulers of small states must get the people on their side, train them for self-defense, and fortify territorial boundaries. There is no other way to secure the peace.

More generally, Mencius suggests that boundaries between states are justified if they promote the value of peace. In his own day, Mencius lamented the fact that boundaries seem to be the product of ruthless wars of conquest. In principle, however, fixed territorial boundaries can help to prevent outbreaks of violence:

Mencius said, "The setting up of border posts in antiquity was to prevent violence. Today they are set up for the purpose of engaging in violence."[37] (7B.8, Dobson; see also 6B.9)

4.2 Pluralism within Unity

In an ideal Confucian world, to repeat, one sage-king would rule peacefully over the whole world. The ruler would put Humane policies into practice, and then, as Confucius put it, "the grass must bend" (12.19; see also Mencius, 3B.5). This metaphor, however, can be slightly misleading. Even in an ideal society, one should not expect blind allegiance to the emperor's wishes and consequent uniformity of thought. Quite the opposite. Confucius did not admire people who blindly followed edicts handed down from above:

The Master said, 'Is one who simply sides with tenacious opinions a gentleman? or is he merely putting on a dignified appearance?' (11.21; Lau)

Instead, Confucius actively encouraged critical reflection upon norms and practices:

The Master visited the grand temple of the Founder of the Dynasty. He enquired about everything. Someone said: "Who said this fellow was expert on ritual? When visiting the grand temple, he had to enquire about everything." Hearing of this, the Master said: "Precisely, this is ritual." (3.15; see also 10.21)

Critical reflection is important for a reason that will be familiar to liberals – the only way to progress is to allow for conventional wisdom to be challenged by better arguments (see 11.4). The government in particular needs social critics to point to mistaken policies:

"Is there one single maxim that could ruin a country?"
Confucius replied: "Mere words could not achieve this. There is this saying, however: 'The only pleasure of being a prince is never having to suffer contradiction.' If you are right and no one contradicts you, that's fine; but if you are wrong and no one contradicts you – is this not almost a case of 'one single maxim that could ruin a country'?" (13.15)

Confucius recognizes that such questioning leads inevitably to plural outlooks and diverse viewpoints, even in an ideal society. One of the most famous quotes in *The Analects* is the following: "A gentleman seeks harmony, but not conformity. A vulgar man seeks conformity, but not harmony" (13.23). The ideal society, in other words, will be constituted of people who do their own thinking and come to different conclusions about the good life.[38]

This carries certain political implications. First, those in power should tolerate diverse views.[39] In fact, this may well be the single most important trait for a ruler to possess:

The Master said, 'What can I find worthy of note in a man who is lacking in tolerance when in high position [?]" (3.26, Lau; see also 17.6, 19.3, 20.1)

But what if people hold conflicting views, and they cannot manage to sort out their differences among themselves? Mencius deals with this problem. He recognizes that conflict is a permanent feature of the social landscape, drawing the implication that an ideal government should provide fair mechanisms for conflict resolution:

If your Majesty would engage in true government, displaying Humanity ... Every discontented subject in the world would plead his cause in your Court. (1A.7, Dobson)

The ideal Confucian society, in short, will be unified, but it will promote critical thinking and questioning, tolerate the existence of plural ways of life, and provide fair mechanisms for dealing with conflict.[40]

Now let us move on to the non-ideal multi-state world. In this context, rulers should still strive their best to realize the ideal (consistent with the requirements of self-defense). Even small states can be governed by relatively benign rulers that display Humanity[41]:

Mencius said, "A Paramount Prince was one who, pretending to Humanity, resorted to force. Such a one had need of the rule of a major state. A True King is one who, practising Humanity, resorts only to virtue. Such a one has no need for a major state. T'ang the Successful had a state of only seventy miles square, and King Wen a state of only a hundred miles square. (2A.3; Dobson)

But the True King should not be satisfied with a small state. He should try to spread Humanity beyond his borders.[42] The appropriate means, to repeat, is "moral power"[43]:

Allegiance which is gained by the use of force is not allegiance of the heart – it is the allegiance which comes from imposing upon weakness. Allegiance which is gained by the exercise of virtue is true allegiance. It is the response of joy felt deeply in the heart. (2A.3; Dobson)

The aim is to attract as many people as possible, including those living in faraway lands:

Sung is not, as you say, 'putting Humane policies into practice.' But if Sung really were really to do so, then all within the four seas would raise their heads in expectation to him, hoping that Sung would become their prince. (3B.5, Dobson; see also The Analects: 13.16)

There are no restrictions – racial, ethnic, or other – to membership in the Confucian state, beyond adherence to Humanity. Everyone can, in principle, be "civilized" (see The Analects: 9.14, 15.10).[44]

The ideal of a unified Confucian state spreading Humanity to the whole world began to be taken more seriously following the creation of Imperial China.[45] From the Han dynasty (206 BC–220 AD)[46] onwards, the "Middle Kingdom" saw itself as the largest and most powerful state in the world, spreading the benefits of Confucian civilization to the rest of the world. From the very beginning, however, it was apparent that not everybody would readily submit to officially sanctioned Confucianism. "[T]o overcome the disagreeable reality that some [outsiders] showed no particular inclination to assimilate or to abandon their own cultures . . . the tributary system [was established]."[47] In this system, the tributary ruler or his representative had to go to China to pay homage to Chinese overlordship by prostrating himself before the Chinese emperor in ritual acknowledgement of his vassal status. In return, China guaranteed security and provided economic benefits,[48] while using "moral power" to spread Confucian norms and allowing traditional ways of life and practices to flourish.[49] Needless to say, the practice often deviated from the ideal.[50] Still, the system was remarkably stable and effective overall. Korea and Japan were eventually "Confucianized," partly, if not primarily, as a result the "moral power" of Confucian norms.[51] And the

Confucian emphasis on tolerance, minimal government, and transmission of culture by means of moral power did manage to curb the excesses of blood-thirsty warriors and greedy merchants.

By the late-nineteenth century, the tributary system had broken down, and China itself was subjected to encroachments and occupations by Western imperial powers. The illusion of the "Middle-Kingdom" surrounded by barbarians was shattered, and Chinese thinkers now recognized that their state was one among many – weaker, in fact, than the major Western powers. In response, the state became the unit of political concern and Chinese intellectuals limited their ambitions to the promotion of the Confucian value of "pluralism within unity" within their own country. Liang Qichao, one of China's most influential modern Chinese political thinkers, argued that Confucianism should be made the ethical basis of the Chinese state because this would lead to the country's strength and unity and help China survive in a ruthless, state-eat-state world.[52] He also stressed that citizens should be guaranteed as much personal freedom as possible within the state.[53] Still, Confucians did not completely abandon the ideal of spreading Confucian values to the rest of the world. Liang's teacher and friend, Kang Youwei, argued that Humanity would eventually enter the age of Great Peace and Great Unity.[54] But this dream grew ever more distant as nationalism became more entrenched during the course of the twentieth century.[55]

4.3 The Importance of a Virtuous Ruler

In an ideal world, once again, one virtuous ruler would govern the whole world. The ruler would achieve perfect virtue by observing the correct rites (*li*), his virtue would have a "civilizing" effect on the people, and there would be no need for coercive laws and regulations. As Confucius put it:

The practice of humanity (*ren*) comes down to this: tame the self and restore the rites. Tame the self and restore the rites for but one day, and the whole world will rally to your humanity. (12.1; see also Mencius, 2A.3)

In the real world, however, the people will not always be swayed by the personal virtue of the ruler. The ruler should do his best to rely on moral persuasion and exemplary virtue, but some people may not respond to "moral power":

The Master said: "The moral power of the Middle Way is supreme, and yet it is not commonly found in the people anymore." (6.29; see also 8.9)

Mencius explains this unpleasant fact, noting that when people lack "constant means, [...] they will go astray and fall into excesses, stopping at nothing" (1A.7). Even perfect Humanity, however, will not always be reciprocated. Someone might well respond to the Humanity with bad treatment, at which point the True Gentleman should conclude that his interlocutor is an "utter reprobate" (4B.28; Dobson). Not surprisingly, Confucius allowed for the use of legal punishments when other mechanisms for promoting moral behavior (and preventing immoral behavior) failed to do their work (12.13, 4.11).[56] Mencius concurred,[57] going so far as to justify the use of the death penalty for those who neglect elderly parents (6B.7; see also 1B.7 and 7A.12).[58]

More worrisome, some rulers in the non-ideal, multi-state world are positively wicked.[59] In fact, Mencius could not find a single virtuous ruler in his own day, though he seemed to recognize that some were better than others (see, for example, 6B.7). Thus, Mencius's advice to rulers was to strive for virtue, with the hope of attracting people from states governed by particularly unsavoury rulers (see, for example, 1A.7, 4A.4). Confucius also shared the belief that people will, and should, migrate to states with relatively benign rulers (see, for example, 16.1).

Sometimes, however, even relatively virtuous rulers cannot defend themselves against the superior power of larger states. When that happens – that is, when small states are conquered by larger, more oppressive states – Mencius suggests that the ruler of the small state can flee with his people to establish new state boundaries elsewhere (see, for example, 1B.15).[60]

5. Specific Issues Relating to the Making and Unmaking of Boundaries

Let us now draw on these principles to discuss the Confucian perspective on settlement, inheritance, sale-purchase, conquest, and secession. The principles will be selectively invoked for the purpose of discussing these issues and drawing (where relevant) implications for the contemporary world. I follow the recommended sequence of questions.

5.1 Settlement

When, if ever, is settlement alone a morally sufficient ground for the acquisition of territory and the creation of boundaries? Settlement alone might justify the acquisition of territory and the creation of state boundaries if people are attached to a territory and to the collectivity constituted by those whose ancestors were native to the territory – and if this attachment overrides competing values in cases of conflict. Neither Confucius nor Mencius, however, hold this position. Confucius, in fact, argues that a gentleman should not become too attached to a particular place:

The Master said, 'A Gentleman who is attached to a settled home is not worthy of being a Gentleman.' (14.2)[61]

Instead, a gentleman should seek out virtuous rulers:

The Master said, "While the gentleman cherishes benign rule, the small man cherishes his native land." (4.11; Lau; see also 4.1, 15.10, and 18.2)[62]

But what if the Gentleman cannot find a state that is actually governed by Humanity? The Confucian solution is to move to a state governed by a *potentially* virtuous ruler who is willing to listen and adopt ideas about good government (18.3, 18.4; see also Mencius, 7A.32). If the standard account of Confucius's life is correct, that is what Confucius himself tried to do,[63] thus setting an example for all subsequent Confucians.

Mencius had more to say about the common people (as opposed to "Gentlemen"). He explicitly recognized that land was important for common people for the obvious reason that their livelihood often depends on it (1B.15). However, this does not necessarily translate into a sense of piety of place per se, the kind of attachment that might justify appealing to settlement as a sufficient reason for the creation of boundaries. Mencius argued that people needed to make productive use of land in order to meet the material needs of their families and communities.[64] It is implied that they lose the "right" to land if they fail to make productive use of it.[65] It is also implied that they can migrate to different states if the economic conditions are more satisfactory.[66] That, in any case, is what the Chinese have done to an extent unmatched by any other culture.[67]

As noted earlier, Mencius also suggests that common people will leave their homelands and gravitate towards states governed by relatively virtuous rulers. He does, however, allow for one exception – some people will choose to defend their homeland when a small state previously governed by a relatively decent ruler is conquered by rapacious foreigners:

Duke Wen of T'eng said, 'T'eng is a small state. If it tried with all its might to please the large states, it will only bleed itself white in the end. What is the best thing for me to do?'

'In antiquity,' answered Mencius, 'when T'ai Wang was in Pin, the Ti tribes invaded the place. He tried to buy them off with skins and silks; he tried to buy them off with horses and hounds; he tried to buy them off with pearls and jade; but all to no avail. Then he assembled the elders and announced to them, "What the Ti tribes want is our land. I have heard that a man in authority never turns what is meant for the sustenance of men into a source of harm to them. It will not be difficult for you, my friends, to find another lord. I am leaving." And he left Pin, crossed the Liang Mountains, built a city at the foot of Mount Ch'I and settled there. The men of Pin said, "This is a benevolent man. We must not lose him." They flocked after him as if to market.

'Others expressed the view, "This is the land of our forbears. It is not up to us to abandon it. Let us defend it to the death."

'You will have to choose between these two courses.' (1B.15; Lau)

This is the only passage in which Mencius recognizes that land can have some sort of "spiritual" value for people.[68] But note that this is an exceptional case, and even here Mencius says that not everybody will fight for his home-land. Many others will prefer to flee with the ruler to a more hospitable environment to start anew, and Mencius suggests that this is a perfectly legitimate choice.

In short, the attachment to a settled place per se cannot justify the cre-ation of state boundaries. Instead, boundaries should be porous, and people should have the right to leave their homeland and start anew if they experi-ence economic hardship. Gentlemen have a special obligation to leave their homeland and advise relatively benign foreign rulers, and common people should have the right to flee tyrannical rulers.

5.2 *Inheritance*

The transfer of territory from one generation to another must be con-strained by the three principles noted earlier. First, the territory must have been justly acquired in the first place – that is, by the peaceful exercise of "moral power." For example, conquered territory cannot justifiably be passed down to descendants. As Confucius said:

Zang Wuzhong, having occupied Fang, requested that it be acknowledged by Lu as his hereditary fief. Whatever may be said, I cannot believe that he did not exert pressure upon his lord. (14.14)

It is not made explicit, but Confucius leaves open the possibility that the original inhabitants have rights to the conquered land or, at least, more rights than the occupier's descendants.

Second, the ruler cannot break up his territory into several states to be distributed among his heirs (even assuming that the territory were justly acquired). The presumption in favor of unity is so strong that the issue of willingly dividing up the state was never raised (as far as I know) in Chinese imperial history. This background also helps to explain why the Chinese were deeply wounded when Western imperial powers began to carve up the Chinese state in the late nineteenth century.

Third, the territory should be passed onto the most virtuous heir, rather than to the ruler's blood descendants. Mencius makes this explicit:

Shun assisted Yao [a sage-king] for twenty-eight years. This is something which could not be brought about by man, but by Heaven alone. Yao died, and after the mourning period of three years, Shun withdrew to the south of Nan Ho, leaving Yao's son in possession of the field, yet the feudal lords of the Empire coming to pay homage and those who were engaged in litigation went to Shun, not to Yao's son, and ballad singers sang the praises of Shun, not of Yao's son. Hence I said, "It was brought about by Heaven." Only then did Shun go to the Central Kingdoms and ascend to the Imperial throne. If he had just moved into Yao's palace and ousted his son, it would have been usurpation of the Empire, not receiving it from Heaven.

The *T'ai shih* says, Heaven sees with the eyes of its people. Heaven hears with the ears of its people. This describes well what I meant. (5A.5; Lau)

In Chinese imperial history, the principle of transferring the state to the most virtuous heir did inform (to a certain extent) the official practice – the ruler did not pass the state onto a pre-determined biological heir (such as the eldest son), but rather to the descendant considered to be the most virtuous. In reality, the emperor made the final choice from among his own sons – not surprisingly, there was intense competition among potential heirs to gain the father's affection – and this did deviate from the Confucian ideal. According to Mencius, the choice of heirs should be left to "Heaven," not the Emperor:

Wan Chang said, "Is it true that Yao gave the Empire to Shun?"
"No," said Mencius, "The Emperor cannot give the Empire to another."
"In that case who gave the Empire to Shun?"
"Heaven gave it [to] him". (5A.5; Lau)

And how does Heaven reveal itself? Mencius suggests that one must look to the will of the people:

In antiquity, Yao recommended Shun to Heaven and Heaven accepted him; he presented him to the people and the people accepted him. Hence I said, "Heaven does not speak but reveals itself by its acts and deeds." (5A.5; Lau)

Mencius did not draw the implication that the people's acceptance of a ruler can be determined by means of democratic elections – apparently this possibility did not even occur to early Confucians – but arguably democracy is more consistent with Confucian principles governing the intergenerational transfer of territory than the actual practices from Chinese imperial history.

5.3 Sale-Purchase

There is no explicit Confucian bar against buying and selling territory. Similar to the case of inheritance, however, sale-purchase must be constrained by the three general principles governing the making and unmaking of boundaries – territory can be bought or sold if it promotes peace, unity, and virtuous rule. No doubt it is difficult to satisfy these conditions in practice, which may help to explain why the Confucian state in Imperial China did not trade territory with other states. One apparent counter-example comes to mind, however – the transfer of Hong Kong island from China to Britain in 1842, which seems to violate the Confucian presumption in favor of unity.

But this is not really a counter-example. Hong Kong was not transferred to Britain by means of free exchange. Rather, it was acquired as part of the settlement imposed on China after Britain's victory in the First Opium War. China did not "sell" Hong Kong; in fact, the Qing government was forced to pay $12 million to Britain "on account of the expenses incurred" in the war.[69] In 1898, Britain took advantage of China's defeat by Japan in the war of 1894–95 to demand the lease of the New Territories (the area north of Kowloon) for ninety-nine years and this area was administered as an integral part of the existing colony. Here, too, the terms of the treaty were reluctantly agreed to. As Norman Miners puts it, "The national humiliation of the unequal treaties was keenly felt by all Chinese but they were impotent to do anything about it so long as the Western powers retained their military superiority and were willing to use it."[70]

5.4 Conquest

Mencius, to repeat, argued that states have an obligation to promote the value of peace. As a consequence, he was critical of rulers who launched bloody wars of conquest simply to increase their territory – wars that were, unfortunately, all too common in his own day (see, for example, 6B.9, 7B.8). These wars were often disastrous for all parties concerned, including the conqueror's loved ones:

Mencius said, 'How ruthless was King Hui of Liang! A benevolent man extends his love from those he loves to those he does not love. A ruthless man extends his ruthlessness from those he does not love to those he loves.'

'What do you mean?' asked Kung-sun Ch'ou.

'King Hui of Liang sent his people to war, making pulp of them, for the sake of gaining territory. He suffered a grave defeat and when he wanted to go to war a second time he was afraid he would not be able to win, so he herded the young men he loved to their death as well. This is what I meant when I said he extended his ruthlessness from those he did not love to those he loved.' (7B.1, Lau; see also 1A.7)

Mencius, however, does not oppose wars of conquest in principle. He argues that wars of conquest can be justified if the aim is to bring peace to foreign lands. Certain conditions, however, must be in place. First, the conquerors must try to liberate people who are being oppressed by tyrants:

Now the Prince of Yen was a tyrant. Your Majesty set out and punished him. Yen's people thought you were saving them from 'fire and flood' [i.e., from tyranny]. (1B.11, Dobson)

Second, the people must welcome their conquerors:

When King Wu marched on Yin, he had over three hundred war chariots and three thousand brave warriors. He said, "Do not be afraid. I come to bring peace, not to wage war on the people." And the sound of the people knocking their heads on the ground was like the toppling of the mountain (7B.4, Lau; see also 1B.10, 1B.11, 3B.5).

Third, wars of conquest should be launched against relatively weaker powers. Mencius warns against wars between equal states, presumably because such wars will be bloody and stand little chance of success:

Mencius said, "The Spring and Autumn Annals have no examples of 'just wars', though they do contain examples of some wars better justified than others.[71] The word *cheng*, 'a punitive expedition' [which occurs in the Annals], properly speaking, refers to one in authority attacking one under his jurisdiction. States of equal rank cannot properly *cheng* each other. (7B.2, Dobson)[72]

From a Confucian perspective, in short, territory can be acquired and boundaries altered through conquest if, and only if, the aim is to secure peace. And this must be done in the following circumstances: (1) the conquered people are liberated from tyranny, (2) the people welcome their conquerors, and (3) the war is relatively "clean" and stands a good chance of success.

Let me briefly note that the Confucian perspective on conquest can provide us with a critical stance on China's foreign policy. Consider the fact that the Chinese government regularly condemns international military efforts to bring peace to oppressed peoples, such as NATO's effort to prevent the ethnic cleansing of Kosovo Albanians,[73] simply on the grounds that this involves intervening in the affairs of a sovereign state. No doubt the China's sensitivities in this respect can be traced back to its historical experience of subjugation at the hands of Western imperial powers. The Chinese authorities may also be worried about setting precedents for international intervention to protect oppressed minority groups in China.[74] But to the extent that the government relies on Confucian norms to derive legitimacy – as seems increasingly to be the case – it is worth pointing out the gap between the ideal and the reality.

5.5 Secession

Confucians, to repeat, value unity; ideally, there would be no territorial boundaries between states. This goal, however, must be implemented by means of moral power. If a state is taken over by force, then unity cannot be justified, and the conquered state has a moral right to secede. One of the principles of good government, according to *The Analects*, is to "Restore states that have been annexed" (20.1; Lau). Even punitive expeditions that were initially justified can go bad, in which case the conquerors should pack up their bags (or more precisely, their weapons) and leave:

'Now when you went to punish Yen which practised tyranny over its people, the people thought you were going to rescue them from water and fire, and they came to meet your army, bringing baskets of rice and bottles of drink. How can it be right for you to kill the old and bind the young, destroy the ancestral temples and appropriate the valuable vessels? Even before this, the whole empire was afraid of the power of Ch'i. Now you double your territory without practising benevolent government. This is to provoke the armies of the whole Empire. If you hasten to order the release of the captives, old and young, leave the valuable vessels where they were, and take your army out after setting up a ruler in consultation with the men of Yen, it is still not too late to halt the armies of the Empire. (1B.11; Lau)

But what if a territory has been taken by force from another state – as in the case of Hong Kong? Should it be returned to its former state – China, in this case – or granted independence? Confucius and Mencius do not answer this question directly. There is, however, a Confucian presumption in favor of unity, so long as the state tolerates the existence of diverse opinions and ways of life. That, it turns out, is the premise underlying the "one country, two systems" formula. Hong Kong is promised complete autonomy in all areas except defense and foreign policy, and in exchange the territory must pay lip service to Chinese sovereignty.

Of course, I do not mean to imply that Confucian principles play an overriding role in determining China's policy vis-à-vis Hong Kong. But it is worth noting that the "one country, two systems" formula does resemble the tributary system – a system more explicitly founded on, and influenced by, Confucian principles – in its basic commitment to the value of "pluralism within unity."[75] It is also worth noting that the "one country, two systems" is unique. Other autonomous territories, such as Puerto Rico, Greenland, and Aaland Islands, do exist.[76] In such cases, however, autonomy is justified by reference to cultural differences; in Hong Kong, autonomy is justified by the need to maintain different economic and legal systems. Moreover, Yash Ghai has argued that Hong Kong has responsibility for more functions of government than any other region in any scheme of autonomy, yet it has less institutional/legal protection for its autonomy.[77] On the face of it, this system would appear to be unstable, and many foreign critics predicted social chaos and political collapse following the handover to China.[78] Yet the Chinese government has not interfered with Hong Kong's internal affairs as much as previously feared (so far).[79] What explains China's "hands-off" policy?[80] No doubt, Chinese policy is influenced by contemporary political factors, such as the desire not to "kill the goose that lays golden eggs" and the need to set a positive example for Taiwan's eventual incorporation into the "mother country." But let me suggest that the Confucian value of "pluralism within unity" also plays a background role in helping to stabilize the "one country, two systems" formula.[81] More pertinently, perhaps, social critics can appeal to Confucianism to defend Hong Kong's autonomy if ever the Chinese state does begin to trample on this formula.

6. Conclusion

In an ideal world, there would not be any territorial boundaries between states. One sage-king would govern over the whole world, relying solely on moral power to secure people's compliance with virtue. Confucius and Mencius, however, drew on this idea primarily for critical purposes, and it is unclear to what extent they really believed that it was a practicable ideal. Both lived in a world of walled states ruthlessly competing for territorial advantage – a world that is (in this respect) closer to our own multi-state world than the intervening period of Imperial China, when the "Middle-Kingdom" saw itself as the world's largest and most important power surrounded by as-yet-uncivilized barbarians. As a result, Confucius and Mencius proposed political principles meant to provide morally informed practical guidance in a non-ideal world of competing states – principles that have clear implications for the drawing of territorial boundaries. Let us make these implications explicit.

First, boundaries between states are justified if they promote the value of peace. Small states can, and should, fortify state boundaries if this serves as a deterrent against invasions. Territorial conquest by large states is only justified if this leads to the removal of a wicked ruler who oppresses his own people (and if the people welcome the foreign conquerors).

Second, states should strive to achieve unity with other states, but this must be accomplished by non-coercive means. A conquered state has a moral right to secede. If a part of a state has been taken over by another state, however, it is preferable – other things being equal – to return the territory to the original state rather than establish new boundaries between states (that is, give independence to the territory). Within a unified state, subordinate territories can, and should, be granted a wide range of autonomy – in fact, the only requirement is that they pay lip service to sovereignty of the state.

Third, the attachment to settled territory per se cannot justify territorial boundaries in the absence of a virtuous ruler. Boundaries, in other words, do not have any moral significance if they serve to protect wicked rulers. Critical intellectuals ("Gentlemen") in particular should value benign rule over native land. Given the opportunity, they should leave their homeland and advise relatively benign foreign rulers. They should also favor the redrawing of territorial boundaries if this promotes virtuous rule.

Other means of redrawing territorial boundaries – such as the transfer of territory through bequest and inheritance and by means of sale and purchase – should be constrained by the need to promote peace, unity, and virtuous rule.

It is worth emphasizing that Confucian political principles are meant to have universal validity. The possibility that cultural differences might justify different political principles did not (it seems) even occur to Confucius and Mencius. In reality, of course, Confucian principles are more likely to resonate in East Asian societies that have been shaped (and continue to be influenced) by Confucian values. Does this mean Confucianism lacks any relevance outside East Asia? On the face of it, things do not look very promising for contemporary Confucian universalists, given widespread and seemingly irreconcilable differences in political culture. To take just one example – the

Confucian emphasis on the personal virtue of the ruler seems inconsistent with the liberal emphasis on institutions that work regardless of the particular character of officeholders.[82] But if it is widely felt that Confucian principles can help to remedy the defects of non-Confucian societies, they may well come to be universally shared one day.

Notes to Chapter 4

1. I am grateful for Chow Siu Tak's outstanding research assistance. I would also like to thank Allen Buchanan, Joseph Chan, Ci Jiwei, and Margaret Moore for critical comments on an earlier draft, and Song Bing for help with the Chinese language sources.

2. This is a brief summary of the standard account of the careers of Confucius and Mencius. Details of their lives, however, are sketchy and open to (mis)interpretation. A recent book has controversially argued that Confucius did not say most of the things attributed to him in *The Analects*, and one prominent scholar of Chinese history even doubts that Confucius ever existed [see Charlotte Allen, "Confucius and the Scholars," *Atlantic Monthly* (April 1999)]. Some Sinologists hold that stories about Mencius's childhood are largely legend [see W.A.C.H. Dobson, *Mencius* (London: Oxford University Press, 1963), xii–xiii]. In this chapter, I do not need to take sides in such disputes. What matters (for my purposes) is that the two classic Confucian texts – *The Analects of Confucius* and *The Works of Mencius* – have been transmitted in more or less intact form for over 2,000 years and continue to command a great deal of moral and political authority in contemporary East Asian societies.

3. For an account of precisely how and when the values espoused in "high culture" Confucian texts came to exert widespread influence in the East Asian region, see Gilbert Rozman, ed., *The East Asian Region: Confucianism and Its Modern Adaptation* (Princeton: Princeton University Press, 1991). Rozman notes that the process took several thousand years: "Only in the second millenium after Confucius' death in 479 BC did the practices that had become closely identified with his teachings become widely disseminated among the Chinese people, and even in the third millenium diffusion continued but remained incomplete. In Korea the Confucian legacy was introduced later and did not spread widely until the fifteenth century. In Japan mass acceptance of Confucian principles was accelerated in the eighteenth and nineteenth centuries" (ibid., viii–ix).

4. See, for example, Donald Munro, *The Concept of Man in Early China* (Stanford: Stanford University Press, 1969), 165–7.

5. Tu Wei-ming, "Confucius and Confucianism," in Walter H. Slote and George A. Devos, eds., *Confucianism and the Family* (Albany: State University of New York Press, 1998), 33.

6. Ibid.

7. Randall Peerenboom, "Confucian Harmony and Freedom of Thought," in Wm. Theodore de Bary and Tu Wei-ming, eds., *Confucianism and Human Rights* (New York: Columbia University Press, 1998), 236. This may be something of

an exaggeration, however, because the CCP does not typically try to justify its policies by appealing to Confucianism.

8. A more subtle view is that the attempt to move Confucianism from the "background" to the "foreground" – that is, the attempt to explicitly justify policies by appealing to Confucianism – would prove to be politically counter-productive in mainland China, because the legacy of twentieth-century "anti-Confucian" movements has tainted Confucianism in the minds of many Chinese intellectuals (I thank Ci Jiwei for this point).

9. For an argument along these lines, see Daniel A. Bell and Hahm Chaibong, eds., *Confucianism for the Modern World* (New York: Cambridge University Press, 2003),

10. Joseph Chan, "Territorial Boundaries and Confucianism," David Miller and Sohail Hashmi, eds., *Boundaries, Ownership, and Autonomy* (Princeton: Princeton University Press, 2001), 96.

11. Unless otherwise indicated, I rely on Simon Ley's translation of *The Analects of Confucius* (New York: Norton, 1997). This translation has been criticized for occasionally extrapolating from the original text to make Confucius into a defender of modern liberalism. In cases of doubt, I checked Ley's translations against other recent translations and against the original source (with the help of Song Bing).

12. Unless otherwise indicated, I rely on one of two translations: W.A.C.H. Dobson's translation of *The Works of Mencius* (London: Oxford University Press, 1963), which is helpfully organized by themes; and D.C. Lau's complete translation of *Mencius*, volumes 1 and 2 (Hong Kong: The Chinese University Press, 1984), which includes the accompanying Chinese text.

13. I use the male personal pronoun because Confucius and Mencius seemed to assume (without argument) that the ideal sage-king would be male. Of course, there is no reason to make this assumption in the modern world.

14. I say "quasi-anarchistic" because, unlike anarchists, Confucius and Mencius still saw the need for a political ruler to provide for "order without coercion."

15. The first Chinese dynasty was founded in 221 BC by the ruthless Emperor Qin, who relied on legalist principles that emphasized the use of harsh punishments and quasi-totalitarian control of the whole population. Emperor Qin is notorious for ordering the live burial of Confucian scholars and their books. Imperial China only began to be "Confucianized" during the Han dynasty (206 BC–220 AD).

16. According to Mark Elvin, the "cultural unity" of China was created "in 213 BC with the destruction of local records by the first emperor, a deliberate act of policy aimed at extinguishing local loyalties." Mark Elvin, *The Pattern of the Chinese Past* (Stanford: Stanford University Press, 1973), 21–2.

17. Only one passage in *The Works of Mencius* deals with the question of the succession of sage-kings. Mencius notes after sage-king Yao's death, his unsage-like son took over. But the people paid homage to Shun, and the sage-Shun assumed the "Mandate of Heaven," ruling for a further twenty-eight years (5A.5; see the discussion in Section 5.2 of this chapter).

18. See 2B.13.

19. Confucius, *The Analects*, translated by D.C. Lau (London: Penguin, 1979). Leys translated "*se*" into "sex" (as opposed to Lau's "beauty in women"), which

doesn't capture the aesthetic dimension of the term (I thank Ci Jiwei for this point).

20. In retrospect, it is perhaps unfortunate that Confucius and Mencius did not make explicit the distinction between prescriptions for ideal regimes and those for non-ideal regimes (comparable to say, to Aristotle's distinctions in the *Politics*). This could have avoided misunderstandings and controversies regarding points of interpretation.

21. For a presentation and analysis of Confucian military thought, see *Zhongguo Ruxue Baike Quanshu* [Encyclopedia of Confucianism in China] (Beijing: Zhongguo Dabaike Quanshu Chubanshe, 1997), 185–93.

22. William James famously described Mencius as a "tender-minded" philosopher, in contrast to the "tough-minded" Hsun Tzu.

23. According to Bruce Brooks and Taeko Brooks, the real Confucius was in fact a warrior who had the misfortune to live at time when his skills as a charioteer and bowman were becoming obsolete. See Bruce Brooks and Taeko Brooks, *The Original Analects* (New York: Columbia University Press, 1998), 270–1. The myth of Confucius as a learned scholar only emerged after his death. This is a controversial interpretation, but if true, it would lend even more support for the thesis that many of the prescriptions in the *Analects* were meant to apply in a non-ideal context of competing states.

24. Benjamin Schwarz, "The Chinese Perception of World Order, Past and Present," in John Fairbank, ed., *The Chinese World Order: Traditional China's Foreign Relations* (Cambridge: Harvard University Press, 1968), 278–9. See also Victoria Tin-Bor Hui, "The Emergence and Demise of Nascent Constitutional Rights: Comparing Ancient China and Early Modern Europe," *The Journal of Political Philosophy*, Vol. 9(4), 2001, 374, 401.

25. There is one significant difference, however. In contrast to the modern discourse on boundaries between nation-states, cultural and linguistic differences did not figure in the Confucian discourse on territorial boundaries. Early Confucians held that their principles were universal, and they did not place any value on cultural identity.

26. I do not mean to imply that that present-day Confucians should necessarily follow these criteria for selecting Confucian values. My only claim is that these criteria generate interesting results for those of us thinking about principles for establishing and justifying territorial boundaries in the modern world.

27. Hsun Tzu (c. 340–245 BC) is sometimes held to be the third "founding father" of the philosophy known as Confucianism. Hsun Tzu, however, is a controversial character because he is also "blamed" for being a major influence on Legalism (Confucianism's main ideological competitor in Chinese history), with the consequence that he "was excluded from the Confucian orthodoxy." Shu-hsien Liu, *Understanding Confucian Philosophy* (Westport, Conn.: Greenwood Press, 1998), 55. For this reason, I do not discuss the works of Hsun Tzu in this chapter.

28. Ibid.

29. For a discussion of contemporary Confucian intellectuals, see ibid., Epilogue.

30. This criterion might be problematic if contemporary Confucians had repudiated some, or most, of the sayings of Confucius and Mencius regarding territorial boundaries. Fortunately, that is not the case.

31. See, for example, Chan Sin Yee, "Gender and Relationship Roles in the *Analects* and the *Mencius*," *Asian Philosophy*, Summer 2000. Chan argues that Confucius and Mencius did not argue in favor of the biological inferiority of women (in contrast to Aristotle) and that the central values of Confucianism do allow in principle for the equal participation of women in education and politics. The passages in *The Analects of Confucius* and *The Works of Mencius* that seem to justify the subordinate status of women, according to Ms. Chan, can be attributed to the purely contingent, uninformed prejudices of the period.

32. I borrow this distinction between "essential requirements" and "relevant indicia" from Benedict Kingsbury. See his article, "The Applicability of the International Legal Concept of 'Indigenous Peoples' in Asia," in Joanne R. Bauer and Daniel A. Bell, eds., *The East Asian Challenge for Human Rights* (New York: Cambridge University Press, 1999), 373–4.

33. For example, Confucius and Mencius both argue that the ruler must gain the trust of the population, but neither drew the implication that democratic elections are the best means to achieve this end (see Section 5.2 of this chapter). Thus, contemporary Confucians need to draw on the Western liberal-democratic tradition for the purpose of implementing a crucial Confucian value.

34. As a matter of terminology, I take "territory" to refer to a geographical space that is under a jurisdiction of some people organized in the form of a political community (the Chinese language also carries this connotation – see Chan, "Territorial Boundaries and Confucianism," in Miller and Hashmi, eds., *Boundaries, Ownership, and Autonomy*, 89). Moreover, I will indulge in the simplifying assumption that the boundaries we are concerned about are the borders of states, while also recognizing that important questions regarding the making and unmaking of territorial boundaries within states are being left out. See the discussion in Allen Buchanan, "The Making and Unmaking of Boundaries: What Liberalism Has to Say," Section 2, in this volume.

35. These principles were not ranked in order – hence, they are presented here in no particular order – and it is unclear which one has priority in cases of conflict. Confucius and Mencius seemed to assume that they would not conflict in practice.

36. Unfortunately, there seems to have been little improvement in this regard, which is the main reason why the Confucian perspective on peace and conquest is still relevant today.

37. This passage suggests that fixed territorial boundaries existed even in the Golden Days of Antiquity (for the purpose of preventing violence), which suggests (once again) that Mencius may not have been overly optimistic about the possibility of a borderless world governed by one ruler.

38. The reader will pardon the use of modern terminology. But Confucius does explicitly acknowledge the validity of differing ways of life that cannot be ranked along a single axis. In one of the lengthier passages of *The Analects*, three of Confucius's students discuss their various ambitions. A fourth student, Tien, says "I differ from the other three in my choice," and Confucius replies, "What harm is there in that? After all each man is stating what he has his heart upon." (11.26, Lau)

39. Needless to say, the reality in Imperial China often deviated from the ideal. Arguably, however, Legalism, rather than Confucianism, was the main source for official intolerance in Imperial China.

40. Some passages in *The Analects of Confucius* and *The Works of Mencius* do, arguably, lend themselves to more "authoritarian" interpretations – see, for example, Ci Jiwei, "The Right, the Good, and the Place of Rights in Confucianism," unpublished manuscript. These possible interpretations, however, have been rejected by most contemporary (non-governmental) defenders of Confucianism, which is why I do not deal with them here.

41. What, one may ask, does Humanity (*ren*) mean? Besides tolerance, Confucius says that it includes the following features:

> Zizhang asked Confucius about humanity. The Master said: "Whoever could spread the five practices everywhere in the world would implement humanity." "And what are these?" "Courtesy, tolerance, good faith, diligence, generosity. Courtesy wards off insults; tolerance wins all hearts; good faith inspires the trust of others; diligence ensures success; generosity confers authority upon others." (17.6)

See also the discussion of *ren* in Joseph Chan, "Territorial Boundaries and Confucianism," in Miller and Hashmi, eds., *Boundaries, Ownership, and Autonomy*, 91–4.

42. Mencius, however, suggests that large states based on Humanity will find it easier to "spread the message" abroad: "Today, if a large state were to put into effect government based on Humanity, the rejoicing of the people would be that of a man saved from the gallows." (2A.1, 84)

43. With the exception of punitive expeditions described in Section 5.4.

44. See, for example, Wu Junsheng, *Tianxia Yijia Guannian Yu Shijie Heping* (The Concept of One Family Under Heaven and World Peace), *Dongfang Zazhi* 10/8 (1977), 9.

45. See Immanuel C.Y. Hsu, *China's Entrance into the Family of Nations* (Cambridge: Harvard University Press, 1960), 6.

46. Most notably, the "Confucian" philosopher Dong Zhongshu (c. 179–104 BC) argued that "all the world," meaning the territories of the Han dynasty, "are as one." See Feng Youlan, "The Historical Role of Confucian Thought in the Formation of the Chinese Nation," *Chinese Studies in Philosophy* 12 (Summer 1981), 57–8. The ideal of *tian xia*, it seems, began to be used as a justification for the political status quo (whereas it served the opposite function in the days of Confucius and Mencius).

47. Joanna Waley-Cohen, *The Sextants of Beijing: Global Currents in Chinese History* (New York: Norton, 1999), 14.

48. See John K. Fairbank and Ssu-Yu Teng, "On the Ch'ing Tributary System," in John K. Fairbank and Ssu-Yu Teng, eds., *Ch'ing Administration: Three Studies* (Cambridge: Harvard University Press, 1960), 112–3.

49. See Hsu, *China's Entrance into the Family of Nations*, 8–9.

50. See, for example, Alasdair Ian Johnston, *Cultural Realism: Strategic Culture and Grand Strategy in Chinese History* (Princeton: Princeton University Press, 1995). Johnston focuses on the Ming dynasty's grand strategy against the Mongols, and he was struck by "the prevalence of assumptions and decision axioms that in fact

placed a high degree of value on the use of pure violence to resolve security conflicts," notwithstanding the existence "of a Confucian-Mencian discourse" (xi). Johnston, however, exaggerates the extent of Mencian idealism. He notes that "Mencius, in particular, pushed Confucian ideas in a more extreme direction, arguing that a virtuous ruler had no need to use military force because he would have no enemies" (45n18), but as noted earlier, Mencius does allow for the possibility that a virtuous ruler of small state may need to fortify territorial boundaries and fight with his people for the purpose of self-defense (1B.13). As well, Mencius allows for the use of force for just "punitive expeditions," as Johnston himself notes (70n14).

51. The Koreans, in particular, committed themselves to Confucian culture. As Chai-Sik Chung notes, "The Koreans often called themselves "barbarians to the east" of China (*tongi*). Driven by this self-conception, they strove to conform to Confucian culture to the point of claiming that they were more orthodox than the Chinese in their fidelity to the Confucian culture." See Chai-Sik Chung, *A Korean Confucian Encounter with the Modern World* (Berkeley: Institute for East Asian Studies, University of California, 1995), 16. Still today, the Koreans consider themselves to be the most orthodox Confucians in East Asia. One may be puzzled by the fact that Korea also has the highest proportion of Christians of Asia, but a closer look at the actual convictions and practices of Korean Christians reveals that "Our Christians are Confucians dressed in Christian robes." Quoted in Koh Byong-ik, "Confucianism in Contemporary Korea," in Tu Wei-ming, ed., *Confucian Traditions in East Asian Modernity* (Cambridge: Harvard University Press, 1996), 199.

52. Pi Mingyong, "Liang Qichao Lun Rujia Wenhua Yu Minzu Zhuyi" (Liang Qichao on Confucianism and Nationalism), *Qilu Xuekan* 3 (1996), 58–9.

53. See Andrew Nathan, *Chinese Democracy* (Berkeley: University of California Press, 1985), 55. Nathan, however, criticizes Liang for adhering to the "Confucian" belief that individual and collective interests can be harmonized (ibid., 57–8). One might question the extent to which Liang was relying on political rhetoric that was not meant to be taken too literally, but in any case it is unfair to blame Confucianism. As noted, Mencius does recognize that conflict is a permanent feature of the social landscape (1A.7). And why would Confucius argue that there is always a need to ask questions and to recognize the ever-present possibility that people can be mistaken in their beliefs? These arguments cannot be reconciled with the claim that absolute harmony and the absence of conflict are practical possibilities.

54. See John K. Fairbank and Edwin O. Reischauer, *China: Transition and Transformation*, revised edition (Boston: Houghton Mifflin Company, 1989), 373–4.

55. A more recent Confucian thinker, Mou Zongsan (1909–1995), has argued that the several Confucian values identified by Mencius are universal, but that their concrete norms and modes of expression may vary from culture to culture. See Joseph Chan, "Territorial Boundaries and Confucianism," in Miller and Hashmi, eds., *Boundaries, Ownership, and Autonomy*, 106–8. This seems like a promising start towards recognizing the moral legitimacy of some different cultures without abandoning the universal aspirations of Confucianism. Chan notes, however, that Mou does not provide a sound argument for

moving from an endorsement of different cultures (that express Confucian values in their own ways) to an endorsement of the nation-state. Let me then suggest the following argument: different communities (for example, Japan, Korea, China) employ different languages to promote Confucian norms, which could be a basis for establishing different, language-based Confucian states (note that this argument applies only to the Confucian world, not, as Mou would have it, to the whole world). I suspect that this kind of idea constitutes a background belief among many intellectuals in the East Asian region – contemporary Confucian intellectuals seem to be simply assume that different linguistic communities (for example, Chinese, Korean, and Japanese) in the East Asian "Confucian" zone should be granted different states. Arguably, there may be a Confucian basis for defending the view that language is the vehicle for the transmission Confucian norms (see *The Analects*, 13.3), but I do not know of anyone who has explicitly drawn the political implication that different linguistic communities should have their own, language-based states.

56. See the discussion in Joseph Chan, "A Confucian Perspective on Human Rights for Contemporary China," in Joanne R. Bauer and Daniel A. Bell, eds., *The East Asian Challenge for Human Rights* (New York: Cambridge University Press, 1999), 226–7.

57. Even in an ideal state, Mencius suggests, the True King will *lighten* (but not eliminate) the penal code (1A.5). In another passage, Mencius says that "when worthy men are in positions of authority . . . its policies and laws will be made clear to all (2A.4; Dobson). The aim seems to be transparency, not the abolition of punitive laws.

58. Confucius also seemed to endorse the death penalty, though he argued that "To impose the death penalty without first attempting to reform is cruel" (20.2; Lau).

59. Later Confucian thinkers – most notably, Huang Zongxi – explicitly drew the implication that there is a need for institutional checks on the ruler's power. See Wm. Theodore de Bary, *Asian Values and Human Rights: A Confucian Communitarian Perspective* (Cambridge: Harvard University Press, 1998), chapter 6.

60. See the discussion in Section 5.1 of this chapter.

61. See the discussion in Edward Shils, "Reflections on Civil Society and Civility in the Chinese Intellectual Tradition," in Tu Wei-ming, ed., *Confucian Traditions in East Asian Modernity* (Cambridge, Mass.: Harvard University Press, 1996), 70.

62. Early Chinese thinkers echoed this view. Part of what distinguished the barbarian from the civilized "gentleman" is the barbarian's love of land. As Ruth Meserve notes, Chinese annalists in the *Shih chi* reported the tale of Hsiung-nu leader of Mo-tun, who was meant to exemplify barbarian attitudes: "Executing his ministers who would have given [. . .] wasteland away, he reportedly said, "Land is the basis of the nation!" See Ruth Meserve, "The Inhospitable Land of the Barbarian," *Journal of Asian History* 16 (1982), 53–4.

63. Mencius, however, did note that Confucius delayed the departure from "the state in which [his] parents were born" (5B.1; Dobson), suggesting that it is not

an easy thing to do. Confucius himself notes that the obligation of filial piety (see Section 5.2 of this chapter) qualifies the urge to emigrate:

> The Master said: "While your parents are alive, do not travel afar. If you have to travel, you must leave an address." (4.19)

64. Mencius also condemns a ruler who fails to allow commoners to make productive use of his private hunting park (1B.2).

65. Note, however, that the productive use of (unoccupied) land does not translate into "Lockean" ownership rights. Even when the farmer makes productive use of the land, the state can – and should – curtail property rights in order to secure the material welfare of the non-farming classes and the interests of needy family members (see Mencius 3A.3).

66. If the economic conditions are satisfactory, however, Mencius did seem to justify curbs on freedom of movement (see 3A.3).

67. Of course, the Chinese were not always granted the opportunity to emigrate. In Imperial China, the state imposed curbs on emigration – as Ruth Meserve observes, "The Great Wall was built as much to keep the Chinese in as it was to keep the barbarian out," Meserve, "The Inhospitable Land of the Barbarian," 57. Thus, most Chinese migration has occurred in the last 150 years, when borders became more fluid. More recently, China has experienced "internal" migration. The World Bank has estimated that 100 million "migrant workers" have left the countryside to find work in the cities, the largest mass migration in human history. According to Dorothy Solinger, the migrant workers are typically treated as "foreigners" by urban Chinese, in ways comparable to the attitudes and practices of Germans and Japanese towards "guest workers" from foreign lands. See Dorothy Solinger, "Human Rights Issues in China's Internal Migration: Insights from Comparisons with Germany and Japan," in Joanne R. Bauer and Daniel A. Bell, eds., *The East Asian Challenge for Human Rights* (New York: Cambridge University Press, 1999). So if we limit ourselves to absolute numbers and we include "internal" as well as "external" migration, China is indeed "number one" in terms of geographic mobility. Michael Walzer may then have to qualify his view that "Americans apparently change their residence more often than any people in history." See his "The Communitarian Critique of Liberalism," in Amitai Etzioni, ed., *New Communitarian Thinking* (Charlottesville: University Press of Virginia, 1995), 58. It is worth asking why Chinese seem distinctly prone to emigration and seem to lack (comparatively speaking) a "spiritual" attachment to land. Perhaps this is because the most fertile parts of China – the area surrounding the great Yangtze and Yellow rivers – are prone to recurrent mass flooding, thus forcing people to migrate to different agricultural areas and inhibiting the development of attachment to land per se.

68. In 7B.14, Mencius says that "the altars to the gods of earth and grain" are important and that "When a feudal lord endangers the gods of earth and grain he should be replaced." According to D.C. Lau, however, "the altars to the gods of earth and grain" refers to "the symbol of independence of the state" (Mencius, Volume 2, 291).

69. China was also forced to pay $6 million to compensate Britain for the loss of opium and a further $3 million to settle outstanding debts, for a total of

$21 million – not a small sum in the 1860s! See Jonathan D. Spence, *The Search for Modern China* (London: Hutchinson, 1990), 159.

70. Norman Miners, *The Government and Politics of Hong Kong*, fifth edition. (Hong Kong: Oxford University Press, 1995), 3.

71. In an ideal world, in other words, there would be no wars.

72. This passage does not directly support my point, but it seems plausible to assume that Mencius warns against punitive wars between states of equal rank because they are not likely to be effective; in principle, Mencius should not have an objection to wars of conquest to liberate oppressed peoples in large states.

73. Of course, NATO's war on behalf of the Kosovo Albanians was not an unqualified success, even from a Confucian point of view. The war did succeed in liberating Kosovo Albanians from an oppressive tyrant, and most people did seem to welcome the foreign conquerors. But the high-altitude bombing campaign (designed to minimize the risk to combatants) killed many innocent civilians (including journalists at the Chinese embassy in Belgrade) and seemed to have caused the Serbs to increase the pace of ethnic cleansing in Kosovo, which (arguably) made the war more bloody than it need have been.

74. The Chinese government has since realized that international intervention can also be used against minority groups. It is generally supportive of the U.S. led war against al-Qaida partly because it can draw on the "terrorist threat" to justify repressive measures against its Muslim minority in Xinjiang province.

75. One important difference, however, is that Hong Kong is generally regarded (even within the mainland) as more (politically and economically) advanced than the mainland, whereas the subordinate territories in the tributary system were generally regarded (often by members of the subordinate territories themselves, as in the case of Korea) as inferior to the Confucian center (I thank Ci Jiwei for this point).

76. Autonomous systems are distinguished from federalist arrangements by the fact that autonomous territories are less concerned with influencing what goes on in the rest of the country. Partly this is because autonomous territories are small relative to the rest of the country (in contrast to most provinces and states in federal countries) and have little ability to influence the rest, even if they wanted to.

77. See Yash Ghai, "Autonomy with Chinese Characteristics: The Case of Hong Kong," *Pacifica Review* 10/1 (February 1998), 13, 18–19, 21.

78. J. Terry Emerson expressed a typical "American view" – "History reveals that struggles focused on dividing sovereignty may as easily lead to total separation . . . It would serve the mainland better if Peking would theorize more about how to fulfill true political and social liberalization than how to achieve an impossible dream of combining two antagonistic systems (democracy and Communism) in one nation." See J. Terry Emerson, "An American View of 'One Country, Two Systems'," *Issues & Studies* (September 1988), 49.

79. The one major exception seems to prove the rule. China objected to a Court of Final Appeal (CFA) judgment that seemed to imply question China's ultimate sovereignty, but the CFA issued a "clarification" explaining that this was not its

intention. See Alkman Granitsas, "Compromising Issue," *Far Eastern Economic Review* 11 (March 1999), 20. The judgment itself was allowed to stand, even though (according to the Hong Kong government) it may have potentially disastrous consequences by granting the right to claim residency in Hong Kong to hundreds of thousands of mainland children (more recently, the Hong Kong government controversially requested the Standing Committee of the National People's Congress to "interpret" the CFA's ruling so that Hong Kong will not be "flooded with immigrants" from the mainland). In other words, the mainland Chinese government seemed to be primarily concerned about the need to pay lip service to Chinese sovereignty, not unlike the pre-twentieth century tributary system.

80. It might seem peculiar that the Chinese government grants more latitude to the Hong Kong people than to people on the mainland itself. But this was also a feature of the tributary system, which granted more latitude to people in the subordinate territories than to those in the center of the Empire.

81. If I can add another cautionary note, I do not mean to imply that the mainland would refrain from interfering with Hong Kong's internal affairs if the Chinese government faced an immediate threat to its own interests. My point is simply that the legacy of the tributary system may have shaped habits of mind that help to reinforce the "hands-off" policy so long as other, more contemporary political factors also favor this approach.

82. According to Peter Berkowitz, however, liberal thinkers such as Locke and Mill neither neglected nor disparaged the importance of the personal virtue of office holders. See Berkowitz's *Virtue and the Making of Modern Liberalism* (Princeton: Princeton University Press, 1999). Still, the fact remains that contemporary liberal societies in the West do in practice place little emphasis on the personal virtue of rulers – Bill Clinton may be a *schmuck*, one hears, but he is still a good President. In East Asia, in contrast, there is (typically speaking) less willingness to draw a sharp distinction between private and public morality. It is quite likely that a publicly exposed liar would have lost (in people's minds) the "Mandate of Heaven" (that is, the moral right to rule).

5

Borders of Our Minds: Territories, Boundaries, and Power in the Confucian Tradition

L.H.M. Ling

1. Introduction

Dan Bell has provided us with a comprehensive survey of Confucian treatments of territorial boundaries. Professor Bell has accomplished this task, moreover, despite the tremendous range that exists within what is considered "the Confucian tradition," both temporally (over two millennia of interpretation and reinterpretation) and substantively ("neo," "post," "reformist," "orthodox," and so on). In this regard, Professor Bell has given us not only what the Confucian canons say on the subject of territories and borders (particularly in light of the different methods of boundary alteration discussed in the Introduction to this volume), but a taste of how contemporary societies in China, Taiwan, and Hong Kong draw on Confucian principles to decide policy issues.

At the same time, it is necessary to underscore the *hybrid* nature of "third world" traditions such as Confucianism. In our enthusiasm for multicultural equality (itself an artefact of Anglo-American liberalism), we must be careful not to wish away, inadvertently, the impact of almost five centuries of Western colonialism and imperialism on societies outside the West. One may note, for instance, that while Confucianism today has integrated liberal notions of "the public" as a distinct sphere of governance from "the private," liberal theory shows no trace whatsoever of absorbing Confucian concepts such as filial piety or virtuous rule.[1] Put differently, we cannot pretend that the political traditions of the colonized have developed in the same *hegemonic* fashion as those of the colonizers. Non-Western traditions such as Confucianism, as this chapter shows, have had to endure – and make do with – significant ruptures in their fundaments.[2]

This perspective comes from a postcolonial approach to global life.[3] It defines tradition as a set of principles and practices that interact, absorb, mix, and integrate with other traditions, producing, over time, a third, hybrid tradition. Such hybridity retains elements of the original but also exhibits unanticipated developments either through alternative interpretations of the old or the emergence of wholly new concepts. Here, China – as one site of Confucianism – serves as an instructive example. Its interactions with Others such as "Westerners," as well as formulations of the Self like the "Manchus" and, later on, "overseas Chinese," highlights the Confucian tradition's *real* borders – the borders of our minds – from which territorial borders derive.

I examine the five indices of territorial boundaries – settlement, inheritance, sale-purchase, conquest, and secession – in a slightly different and paired order. This reordering reflects two of the most significant events to reverberate throughout the Confucian world-order of the nineteenth century[4]: Britain's *conquest* and *sales-purchase* of Chinese territory after the Opium Wars (1840–1842, 1858–1860), and Japan's *secession* from Chinese hegemony shortly thereafter. To demonstrate a postcolonial understanding of *settlement* and *inheritance*, I turn to the spread of Chinese immigrants to Southeast Asia and North America at the turn of this century. Each case demonstrates the dynamic mutation of the Confucian tradition both as a world-view and a set of institutionalized practices.

Let us begin with Confucianism's outstanding *raison d'être*: family relations.

2. Confucian Governance as Family Relations

"The essence of the world is nation; the essence of nation is family" (*tianxia zhi ben zai guo, guo zhi ben zai jia*) – *The Analects*

Dan Bell rightly noted that Confucianism offered a *cosmos* of ideology and ethics rather than self-contained states demarcated by borders.[5] Anchored in the "three bonds" (*san gang*) and "five relationships" (*wu lun*), the Confucian world-order converged various domains of human activity – political (ruler-to-subject), familial (father-to-son, parent-to-child), conjugal (husband-to-wife), fraternal (brother-to-brother, friend-to-friend) – into one set of family relations writ large. These, moreover, followed a strict hierarchy of authority *and* care:

…father and son should on the one hand be affectionate, and on the other hand be filial; brother to brother should show love and respect; friend to friend should observe loyalty; and the rules of propriety for states concerned follow the pattern of the relationship between father and son, brothers or friends, as the case may be.[6]

Rulers, fathers/parents, husbands, and older brothers wielded greater authority and status over subjects, sons/children, wives, and younger brothers. But these relationships were founded, also, on reciprocal obligations and duties.[7] For example, a ruler may enjoy power (*quan*) in exchange for loyalty (*zhong*) but only if he would attend with benevolence (*ren*) to the welfare of his subjects; otherwise, he may rightly lose his right to rule, otherwise known as the "mandate of Heaven" (*tian ming*). Similarly, parents may demand filial piety (*xiao*) but only if they love and protect their children. A husband may command his wife (or wives) to serve him, his parents, and his children (especially sons), but in return for ensuring her material well-being. An older brother may dictate to a younger one but, again, in turn for loving, protecting, and guiding him. These social strictures applied equally to relations between states or societies.

Of course, daily practice often failed to honor these abstract ideals. Indeed, the boundaries of Confucian social relations were (and continue to be) stretched to suit the convenience of rulers, fathers/parents, husbands, and older siblings at the expense of subjects, children, wives, and younger siblings. For example, rulers lost the mandate of Heaven only after all petitions for reform had failed and much misery had been endured by the people. Similarly, society expected children to remain filial to their parents only until extreme abuse had occurred. Husbands could maltreat their wives with impunity simply because women had little recourse to justice outside their families; the same would apply to cruelty from older to younger brothers. Similarly, powerful states/societies often bullied weaker ones.

But the Confucian tradition established itself more as a moral guide to what *should* be than a practical manual of what *is*. Extrapolated from the Confucian household, it conceived of the world as a Universal State (*da tong*), which explicitly linked the individual with the communal, the state with family, prosperity with welfare, and strength with faith:

When the Universal State prevails, the world is like one home common to all; men of virtue and merit are to be selected to be rulers; sincerity and amity pervade all dealings between man and man; people shall love not only their own parents and own children, but also those of others; the aged, the young, the helpless widow and widowers, the orphans, the destitute, the incapacitated and the sick shall be well provided for and well looked after, while the able-bodied shall exert themselves in their aid; man shall be appropriately employed and woman suitably married; one detests that things should be abandoned or wasted on earth, but when gathered or stored up, they are not to be retained exclusively for oneself; one detests that exertion does not proceed from oneself, but its fruits are not to be regarded exclusively as one's own. Thus there will be no cause for conspiracy, robbery, theft or rebellion, and no need to bolt one's outside door. This is a true Universal State.[8]

In this Confucian *cosmos*, China presided as the Celestial Parent with all Others as its filial children or younger siblings.[9] Indeed, the Confucian world-order distinguished "civilized" from "barbarian" only to the extent of their lack of cultural incorporation. China historically utilized a policy of "cherishing men from afar" (*huairou yuanren*). It presumed that all Others could be "converted" (*xiang hua*) to embrace the Confucian world-order. "No absolute outside was acknowledged, only relative degrees of proximity to a center."[10]

Two conjunctural axes calibrated one's authority, status, and identity within the Confucian world-order.[11] A vertical-moral (*zung*) axis linked the rulers on top – that is, "superior men" (*junzi*) – with the masses below; a horizontal-geographic (*heng*) axis connected those in the center – that is, the Middle Kingdom (*zhongguo*) – or closer to it – that is, Korea, Vietnam – with those on the periphery – that is, Mongolia, Japan, the West. Male literati in service to the Chinese Emperor, as the pivot to this "cosmo-moral dominion,"[12] ranked the highest.

Though fixed in substance, *zungheng* also rotated, shifted, and proliferated according to different circumstances. For instance, the leader of the Southern Sung dynasty made peace with the larger, more powerful Chin in 1138 by accepting his status as a "vassal" (*chen*); when relations improved, his successor gained the more intimate title of "nephew" (*zhi*) to the Chinese Emperor's (younger) "uncle" (*shu*).[13] Korea characterized its relations with China as "smaller serving larger" (*shi da*) while declaring its interactions with Japan as an equal exchange "between neighbors" (*jiao lin*).[14] Similarly, the king of Siam (Thailand), viewed as a "universal emperor" (*chakravartin*) in his own right, paid annual tributes to China; he, in turn, received tribute from the princes of Malaya, Laos, Cambodia, and Burma.[15] In correspondence with China, Vietnam referred to itself as a "barbarian" (*fan*), but labeled the Cambodians *fan* in turn.[16]

Territorial borders thus operated as instantiations of *social* borders. In her study of frontier poetry from classical China, for example, Gudula Linck found varied uses of the concept of "frontier." It may refer to natural geographies such as mountains and rivers ("threatening," "beautiful") or a construct of foreign policy ("defence"), but ultimately the notion of frontier denoted "a situation encountered by people."[17] Here, frontier poetry commented on types of interaction with different peoples socially ("hostile," "romantic"), militarily ("just war," "bad war"), and politically ("open and inclusive," "closed and exclusive"). Linck's probe into the etymology of the Chinese words for "frontier," "boundary," and "border" merits quoting at length, as each denotes a relationship – primarily military but also agricultural or merely physical – between two groups of people[18]:

The character *sai* obviously corresponds to *frontier*. It is used in the context of military defence ... The second term *bian* [means] "side," "edge," thus corresponding to the English words *boundary* and *border*...the third character *jiang* written without the "arrow" radical is simply a demarcation, a limit between fields. However, written with the "arrow" radical it means "strong," thus it is easily associated with military strength. The compound word *bianjiang*... designates political and military frontiers.[19]

Though it was not mentioned formally in the Confucian canons, China's Emperors often used women to ensure the familial, social nature of frontier relations. They did so by marrying an imperial princess or concubine to a local chieftain. Indeed, marriage historically "bonded" the Korean royal house to the Chinese Emperor. The Korean crown prince, in fact, lived in the Forbidden City as a "child hostage," the better to learn Chinese culture, until he came of age to rule in his own domain. This excerpt from an anonymous poem written about the sixth-century marriage of an imperial concubine, Zhao Chun, to a leader of the Xiung Nu tribe, highlights Chinese culture's traditional portrayal of the outgoing bride's sentiment regarding life on the periphery:

> Who sees my grief, when leaving the gates of Han.
> My Dragon Prince! My Phoenix Court!
> Hills of Yen, farewell!
>   Ah!
> Sorrowful I go.[20]

A woman's lamentations, however, paled next to the need to maintain China's centrality in the Confucian world-order. When that presumption came under challenge in the late nineteenth-century, China's physical borders suffered – but not as much and irreversibly as its borders of the mind.

3. Conquest and Sale-Purchase: From "Cherishing Men from Afar" to Extraterritoriality

Her Majesty's Government cannot allow that, in a transaction between Great Britain and China, the unreasonable practice of the Chinese should supersede the reasonable practice of *all the rest of mankind.*[21]

As Dan Bell mentioned, the Confucian tradition discouraged conquest unless it could satisfy three conditions: the conquest would (1) liberate the local people (2) at their request, and (3) should be launched against a weaker power. Similarly, sale or purchase of territory should come about only if it promoted peace, achieved unity, and ensured virtuous rule. China's defeat in the Opium Wars shattered these precepts of the Confucian world-order, first, by demonstrating the Middle Kingdom's systemic weakness against the "barbaric" West. Second, Britain's assertion of extraterritoriality in its unequal treaties with China violated the subsidiary tenets of Confucian conquest and sale-purchase: it incarcerated, not liberated, the local people; it was imposed on them against their will; it promoted turmoil, not peace; and it divided China into various treaty-ports under foreign control. Extraterritoriality effectively allowed foreign powers to slice up China "like a melon" even though concessions such as Hong Kong were technically "leased," not "sold," to conquering powers, as Bell pointed out.[22] Accordingly, most Chinese viewed extraterritoriality as an abuse of, not virtue in, governance.

Extraterritoriality turned *zungheng* on its head. Now physical borders conferred, rather than reflected, social relations. A legal device, extraterritoriality was used historically in Europe to protect the embassies of competing royal houses. Reminiscent of Louis XIV's narcissistic declaration of *"l'état, c'est moi,"* it consisted of a conceptual double move: (1) that territorial boundaries *sovereignized* the state, and (2) this geographically specific condition can be *virtualized* in the person of an ambassador or a location such as an embassy.[23] Hence, territorial boundaries under the Westphalian state system had both an objective and symbolic impact.[24] Applied to China's unequal treaties, extraterritoriality was also racialized: that is, any citizen of a Western power committing a crime on Chinese soil would be subject to the laws of his home country rather than those of China.

Initially, extraterritoriality did not upset Confucian boundaries regarding Self and Nation. The Chinese Emperor, for example, retained within his corporeal person a similar sense of extraterritoriality given his role as the critical pivot to *zungheng*: he linked Heaven above with Earth below. Note, for example, how one of the Qing negotiators for the Treaty of Nanking (1842) defied the British ability to conquer China, given this Confucian understanding of place, power, and identity:

In case it were impossible to defend the capital, the emperor could still transfer the capital elsewhere; and, even then this does not mean that the people of our country would be willing to respect you as rulers of China, to say nothing of the fact that the capital is not easy to take.[25]

In this mandarin's world-view, the capital moved with the Emperor who, literally and figuratively, embodied the Middle Kingdom. Moreover, given his reasoning, what would be the point of capturing the capital if the British could not command either loyalty or filiality from the people? How could they *rule?*[26]

Little did this negotiator know or understand that Westphalian sovereignty would subsequently "territorialize" China into a reified state with geographically delimited borders irrespective of *zungheng*. Extraterritoriality carved up China internally into multiple, smaller versions of foreign "states" within China's own, supposed sovereignty. Treaty ports such as Shanghai effectively imported the territorial boundaries of various European, British, Russian, American, and Japanese states into the heart of the Confucian world-order. Here, extraterritoriality extended the privileges of a king to lowly sailors and soldiers by the very virtue of their culture, nation, and race.[27] A weakened, defeated Qing court even ceded to Britain the power to handle all customs, duties, and taxes derived from trade with those across its "borders," until two decades after the Republican revolution of 1911. Extraterritoriality, in short, superseded Chinese sovereignty. Not without reason, then, did the Taiping rebels (1851–1864) cry, *"Can the Chinese still consider themselves men?"*[28]

From this brief history, we see that the notion of "territorial boundaries" took on both a real and surreal significance in China. It was real in the sense that territorial boundaries came to demarcate the state of "China" that was both created and destroyed by Western imperialism. It took on a surreal meaning given the wholesale *subjective* manipulation of supposedly objective entities. At root was an uneasy conflation of the thing itself (Chinese nation-state) with its objective characteristics (territorial boundaries). Now fully subjected to the Westphalian state system, Chinese nationalists *metynomized* China as a nation-state through its individual parts. Accordingly, any encroachment of Chinese territory became tantamount to defiling the Chinese nation-state itself, whereas, under the Confucian notion of *datong*, no individual part could undermine the overall whole. Indeed, much of China's subsequent nationalist fervour for revolution stemmed from a sense of injustice and helplessness against foreign invasion. It further undermined the traditional Confucian antipathy against conquest and reinforced its predisposition towards unity. Precisely for these historical reasons, the government in China today retains an unrelenting grip on three, "rogue" territories – Tibet, Taiwan, and Hong Kong – despite the expressed wishes of its people.

When secession occurred in the Confucian world-order, it manifested culturally and relationally more so than physically. Such was the case with Meiji Japan (1868–1910).

4. Secession: From "Brush-Talking" and "Shared Civilization" to Translation and Difference

Geographical representation in China is not simply an inert body of texts, but a participant in the intellectual activity of informing and interpreting the world; geographical texts attest both to ways in which Chinese scholars and officials understood the outside world and to ways in which that perceived outside world began to change in the late nineteenth century.[29]

Secession, as Dan Bell underscored, could be justified in moral terms only. That is, if a ruler abused his people or a territory was annexed unjustly, then secession from that ruler, rather than withdrawal of territory per se, was sanctioned. Meiji Japan effectively disrupted this Confucian presumption of unity when it started to emulate the West culturally, politically, militarily, and economically.[30] Japan's primary motivation was to avoid becoming another imperial China. Note this passage from an influential *samurai* in 1849:

Because the Chinese thought that their's was the only good country and did not realize that those countries they despised as barbarians were well-versed in practical learning, had achieved great prosperity and developed a flourishing military power, and had far surpassed themselves in skill with firearms and proficiency in navigation, when they came to war with England, they exposed their shame to the entire world, and completely destroyed the reputation established for them in ancient times by their sages and wise men.[31]

D.R. Howland has provided us with extraordinary insight into imperial China's relationship with a Westernizing Japan in the late 1880s through the works of one Huang Zunxian, a member of China's first embassy to Japan. Huang wrote several poems and later books on Japan while stationed there. These acquired popular and scholarly attention given the Chinese fascination with Japan's seemingly wholesale adoption of Western ways.

Huang's works register a shift in Chinese attitudes toward Japan. From a remote island outpost populated by "dwarfs"(*wei guo*) whose literati, nevertheless, could "brush-talk" (*bi tan*) in Chinese and therefore qualified as a cultural relative (*tong wen*), post-Opium War Chinese elites began to see Meiji Japan as a revitalizing state that had somehow undertaken the reforms that China should have taken but couldn't. In the process, though, Japan also seemed increasingly a cultural stranger.

For example, Huang's first publication, *Poems on Divers Japanese Affairs* (1879), emphasized Japan's closeness to China both stylistically and substantively. It began with a traditional setting of the mood to indicate the place:

> Gold-dusted treasured saddle, gilt pillon,
> Lacquered box, nacre-inlaid, containing ancient goblet;
> Parasol opens like butterfly, cloth quivering,
> This one's called the *Okugata* [lady], that's the *Dannasama* [gentleman].[32]

Subsequently, he historicized the location of Japan with the dream-crushing arrival of the West.

> The day of steamships, sounds of cannon fire come –
> Alarm and crush the dreams of flower-viewing masses.[33]

Huang concluded by lamenting and chastising the Japanese for retreating into a "*spiritual stupidity*" by resorting to "*halls of mud*" to fight the West's cannons and steamships, thereby "*clos[ing] itself up for a thousand years.*" Clearly, Huang could have been referring to China as much as Japan. But as an official representative of the Middle Kingdom, he could not publicly criticize the Qing court for doing essentially what he had described in this poem for Japan. Indeed, in an earlier stanza, he referred to "*Opium's poison fog expansive like the sea, We close ourselves off, our eyes we do not move.*" Given that this poem was published after the Opium Wars, this reference to China could not be taken amiss in any reader's mind. Whatever his intentions, Huang presumed Japan's cultural intimacy with China such that one could be encoded for the other.

A second poem written in the mid-1880s already reads quite differently. Far from being spiritually stupid, Japan was beginning to learn, grow, and "dazzle." Huang sounded an early note of alarm at Japan's rapid remove from the Confucian world-order. For this reason, he called for another "sagely Gui Gu," a political strategist from the Warring States period who helped to reunify China, to retrieve Japan back to the Chinese fold:

> Chemistry books, strange machines – question the new arrangement.
> Sail the seas, search far and wide for the sagely Gui Gu.
> From Western lands learn a legacy of beneficial dazzle.
> Encourage all acquaintances to speak out on world affairs.[34]

A decade later, Huang's representation of Japan has changed dramatically. In this later work, *Japan Treatise*, the author abandoned all poetic allusion for a straightforward categorizing of "facts," typical of Western natural science at the time. Yet note, too, his residual adherence to a unified *cosmos* defined by hierarchial, social relations:

The Outer Historian states: Circling the earth are one hundred and some domains. With a domain, you have of course a people; with a people, you have a ruler. Now, of those one hundred and some domains, there are some where one man rules alone; these are called autocracies. In others, the common people discuss administration; these are called democracies. When these higher and lower elements divided responsibilities and privileges, this is called the joint governing of ruler and people...[Japan] has planned to inaugurate its National Assembly within ten years, and so its autocratic administration, which has endured for over 2,500 years, is heading today in the direction of what some say will be a joint rule, and what others say will be a democracy.[35]

Another scholar of Japan at the time further distanced China from Japan by flatly asserting that "this land has eliminated the Chinese language"; indeed, he denied any significance to writing, culture, or civilization in a new world of power politics where military hardware mattered only:

[T]he speech and writing of each nation is different, and translation so twists the tone of words in the transmission that they go awry...Only if we have warships and the best troops can we prevail over the world.[36]

For Howland, this expository shift mirrored a world-order shift.

What was once ostensibly familiar and could be claimed effortlessly as China's own became within a decade a space most decidedly foreign.... This shift, in other words, occurs as a dual negation – of both the analogy of the "warring states" and the reality of "shared language/Civilization".... It was the clearest and most forceful indication that, as a world order, Civilization had failed.[37]

No physical changes had taken place in terms of territorial boundaries (the first Sino-Japanese war was still two decades away), but Japan had effectively, seceded from the Confucian world order.

Another instance of such trans-bordering is the Chinese diaspora.

5. Settlement and Inheritance: From *Datong* to Diaspora to Greater China

[C]ross-cutting ties between mainland and ove[r]seas Chinese, between mainlander and foreign investors, and between Chinese socialism and foreign capitalism all help to disrupt the political borders of the nation.[38]

Dan Bell has noted that the Confucian tradition permits settlement in cases of need only. That is, the people have a right to settle elsewhere if their ruler neglects their welfare. As for inheritance, territory should pass on to the most virtuous heir, not necessarily a blood relative, through a "peaceful exercise of "moral power.""[39] The territory should remain as a whole and not parceled out in small pieces.

With the disintegration of the Confucian world-order, many felt justified to escape overseas precisely because of their lack of welfare at home. Chinese workers "sojourned" from Southeast Asia to Cuba to Peru and parts of the British empire to the Indian Ocean, East and Southern Africa, the Pacific and Caribbean to North America.[40] Initially all male,[41] they worked as indentured laborers ("coolies"), graduating to owners and managers of extensive family-owned businesses whose progeny were encouraged to go into the professional classes. American media today characterize Asian Americans as a "model minority" whose seeming assimilation retains an inscrutable Otherness.[42] What the Chinese diaspora/settlement demonstrates, instead, is an inversion of the Confucian tradition's *datong* concept through a racialization of *cultural*, not territorial, inheritance.

Aihwa Ong has observed "a consistent tension" within Chinese communities outside of China. On the one hand, there is "the modernist imaginary of the nation-state (emphasizing essentialism, territoriality, and fixity)"; on the other, "the modernist imaging of entrepreneurial capitalism (celebrating hybridity, deterritorialization, and fluidity)."[43] Indeed, Chinese reformers and revolutionaries alike drew on both to further their goal of re-making the Chinese state.[44] Each appealed to a historical sense of loyalty from "overseas Chinese" (*huaqiao*) even though they left China precisely because the "ancestral land" (*zuguo*) could not provide for them adequately. At the same time, Chinese nationalists sought to persuade their overseas brethren to part with hard-earned cash so that they might, in their turn, save China.

Both concepts pivot on an uneasy presumption of cultural ties that come from racial unity. Here, race twists the previous *zungheng* formula for the Confucian world-order by grounding social relations in blood ties affirmed by a territorially-bound state called "China." Chinese reformers and revolutionaries alike fashioned a racialized identity that differentiated a newly articulated Han Self from all Others, including the ruling house of Manchu.[45] Subsequent attempts to involve overseas Chinese in China's nation-building, whether Communist or Nationalist, also propagated the notion of a common cultural allegiance based on a homogeneous racial foundation. In this way, national inheritance became co-extensive with a racially based, cultural inheritance.

Today, many speak of a Greater China (*da zhonghua*) emerging in the Asia-Pacific region. Initially meant to refer to networks of Chinese family businesses that seem to prevail in the region, it now connotes a cultural integration as young people in China, Taiwan, Hong Kong, Singapore, and Los Angeles rock to the same music, watch the same movies, scream for the same celebrities. Elsewhere, I note an increasing ideological convergence, also, as post-Tiananmen China adopts the corporatist method of political and economic management devised by its capitalist neighbours (Japan, Taiwan, Singapore, South Korea).[46] Donald M. Nonini and Aihwa Ong consider this version of "Chinese transnationalism" an alternative to Western modernity. Its "new and distinctive social arrangements, cultural discourses, practices, and subjectivities...play nodal and pivotal roles in the emergence of the new flexible capitalism of the Asia Pacific."[47]

At the same time, the Chinese diaspora/settlement inverts the Confucian tradition's original vision of a Universal State. In contrast to a *datong* that absorbed everyone into Confucian family relations, the Chinese diaspora turned these norms inwardly for the nuclear family even while adjusting them to suit different external environments. Thus Confucian (re)settlement reframes the *datong*'s Confucian family relations writ large to the Chinese diaspora's nuclear family relations writ small. Yet, given the extensive networks among the Chinese diaspora especially through its family-owned businesses, one could say that an entrepreneurial *datong*-like structure prevails. Though now far removed from any sense of territorial or national inheritance, this Chinese transnationalism nevertheless extends the notion of a common cultural heritage grounded in race.

6. Conclusion

This spare review of territorial boundaries in "the Confucian tradition" hardly does it justice. My point here is not to dispute Dan Bell's presentation of Confucian treatments of the making and unmaking of boundaries. Rather, it is to show that the Confucian understanding of borders is neither objectively fixed, given its emphasis on social relations, nor is it singularly derived, given its forcible interaction with a rival world-order, the Westphalian state system. The Confucian tradition, like all traditions, has mutated over time. Returning to the five indices of territorial borders, we see some of its resultant hybridities at work:

1. **Conquest.** Any Confucian influence remaining in contemporary China would mitigate against conquest of "foreign" lands. But China's experience with Western imperialism has internalized this Westphalian instrument of power for domestic territories. Indeed, this history helps to unravel

an apparent contradiction cited in Dan Bell's chapter. He asked, "How could China deny sovereignty to Taiwan while denouncing NATO's bombing of Kosovo as a violation of the latter's sovereignty?" Precisely because China had suffered foreign imperialism on its own shores, it cannot tolerate international (especially Western) violation of sovereignty, no matter how well-justified, *and* the separation of a part (Taiwan) from the national whole. China needs both to uphold its sense of national sovereignty and territorial integrity.

2. Sales-Purchase. Confucian antipathy towards sales or purchase of territory does not preclude the selling or purchasing of women's bodies to secure alliances. This traditional tactic of Confucian politics, though not of Confucian teachings, has mutated over time as well. Note this comment from a Taiwanese businessman who seeks American statehood for the island in light of China's threats against its independence:

China is like a gangster . . . The United States is like a policeman. Every time the gangster tries to take the girl [Taiwan] in his arms, she has to call the policeman to come save her. Our job is to get the girl married to the policeman . . . Then there is no danger, and the protection is permanent.[48]

3. Secession. Instead of rotating *zungheng* relations between "civilized" and "barbaric," frontier relations have become objectified in the Westphalian interstate system. Still, sovereign states such as Japan are placed within a familial hierarchy of those "closer to" or "farther from" an imperial center. For this reason, many in Taiwan today claim a *cultural* independence from China to prepare for the island's *political* independence.

4. Settlement. Confucian family relations remain a model for governance but have shifted from a universalistic *datong* for the world to a specific nationalism for China to the contained, nuclear family for the Chinese diaspora. Hence, even if Chinese immigrants face racism and discrimination in their new settlements, rather than virtuous benevolence, they can tolerate this given the nuclear family's continuation of patriarchal-parental authority and care.

5. Inheritance. The Chinese diaspora transnationalizes a territorially demarcated space called "China" into a cultural commitment based on race, primarily for entrepreneurial purposes.

Notes to Chapter 5

1. That contemporary Confucianists accept a liberal public/private divide *intellectually* does not mean necessarily that they implement it *practically*. See, for example, L.H.M. Ling and C.Y. Shih, "Confucianism with a Liberal Face: The Meaning of Democratic Politics in Contemporary Taiwan," *Review of Politics* 60/1 (1998), 55–82.

2. It is not that Western traditions did not receive similar intellectual infusions from non-Western traditions. See, for example, M. Bernal, *Black Athena* (New Brunswick: Rutgers University Press, 1987). My point, rather, is that many in the West are only now beginning to *recognize* the role of non-Western thought in their midst, particularly given the intensive interactions produced by economic globalization.

3. Postcoloniality as a school of thought first came about with the *Subaltern Studies Group*, founded in the 1980s. For a quick survey of postcolonial writings, see B. Ashcroft, G. Griffiths, and H. Tiffin, eds., *The Post-Colonial Studies Reader* (London: Routledge, 1995).

4. I prefer the term "Confucian world-order" to "Confucian tradition" since the former instates the latter, as the next section will explain.

5. An itinerant scholar and advisor to any ruler who would listen, Confucius took upon himself the mission to end the devastating military competition and conquest that came to be known as the Warring States period (403–222 BC). Confucius was not content, though, to simply devise a theory of war and its origins (like Sun Tzu or his Western counterpart, Clausewitz). Instead, Confucius sought an enduring peace by grounding political and military relations in a theory of intertwined social relationships, the most binding of which stemmed from the family.

6. *The Analects*, quoted in C. Chao, *A Brief History of the Chinese Diplomatic Relations, 1644–1945* (Taipei: Chinese Culture University Press, 1984), 16.

7. The only relatively equal relationship in this structure is that between friends. But even here, Confucian doctrine requires a reciprocity in friendship to maintain its equal status.

8. *Book of Li*, quoted in Chao, *A Brief History of the Chinese Diplomatic Relations*, 32.

9. Note, for example, the relationship between the Chin Emperor and his "foster son," the Khitan Emperor, as encapsulated in the former's letter to the latter in 942 AD. See L.S. Yang, "A 'Posthumous Letter' from the Chin Emperor to the Khitan Emperor in 942," *Harvard Journal of Asiatic Studies* 10/3–4 (1947), 418–28.

10. J.L. Hevia, *Cherishing Men from Afar: Qing Guest Ritual and the Macartney Embassy of 1793* (Durham: Duke University Press: 1995), 23.

11. B.T. Wakabayashi, *Anti-Foreignism and Western Learning in Early-Modern Japan* (Cambridge: Harvard University Press, 1991).

12. Hevia, *Cherishing Men from Afar*.

13. L.S. Yang, "Historical Notes on the Chinese World Order," in J.K. Fairbank, ed., *The Chinese World Order* (Cambridge: Harvard University Press, 1968), 20.

14. Ibid., 27.

15. J. Mancall, "The Ch'ing Tribute System: An Interpretive Essay," in J.K. Fairbank, ed., *The Chinese World Order*, 63–89.

16. Ibid., 68.

17. G. Linck, "Visions of the Border in Chinese Frontier Poetry," in S. Dabringhaus and R. Ptak, with R. Teschke, eds.,*China and Her Neighbours: Borders, Visions of the Other, Foreign Policy, 10th to 19th Century* (Wiesbaden: Harrassowitz Verlauf, 1997), 99.

18. For an example of how territorial boundaries were negotiated traditionally, see Christian Lamouroux's account of the Song-Liao border dispute (1074–1075).

Christian Lamouroux, "Geography and Politics: The Song-Liao Border Dispute of 1074/75," in S. Dabringhaus and R. Ptak, with R. Teschke, eds., *China and Her Neighbours*, 1–28.

19. Linck, "Visions of the Border in Chinese Frontier Poetry," 102.
20. Quoted in Chao, *A Brief History of the Chinese Diplomatic Relations*, 33.
21. Lord Palmerston quoted in J. Spence, *The Search for Modern China* (New York: Norton, 1990), 156. My emphasis.
22. At their peak, foreign powers controlled the following territories in China: Germany over the Shandong peninsula (later conceded to Japan after the Treaty of Versailles), Japan over Taiwan and Manchuria, Russia and Japan over the Liaodong peninsula, Britain over the Yangtze River area, and France over Yunan province.
23. Although, as Chao demonstrated, the Warring States period had a similar custom regarding the inviolability of ambassadors. See Chao, *A Brief History of the Chinese Diplomatic Relations*.
24. The "Westphalian state system" refers to our contemporary system of interstate relations. It originated in the Treaty of Westphalia (1648), which granted *sovereignty* to individual kingdoms for the first time.
25. Chang Hsi quoted in S.S. Chang, *Chang Hsi and the Treaty of Nanking, 1842*, S.Y. Teng (trans.) (Chicago: University of Chicago Press, 1994), 37.
26. Note, below, Mencius's famous comment on the ultimately self-destructive nature of conquest:

> King Hui of Liang, for the sake of territorial gains, disrupted and destroyed his people, by leading them to battle. Sustaining a great defeat he renewed the conflict, and afraid lest they should not be able to secure a victory, urged his son, whom he loved, onwards, till his life was sacrificed with the others. This is what I call "beginning with what they do not care for, and proceeding to what they care for." From *Book of Mencius*, quoted in Chao, *A Brief History of the Chinese Diplomatic Relations*, 36.

27. See F. Dikotter, *The Discourse of Race in Modern China* (London: Hurst and Company, 1994).
28. Spence, *The Search for Modern China*, 173.
29. See D.R. Howland, *Borders of Chinese Civilization: Geography and History at Empire's End* (Durham: Duke University Press, 1996), 5.
30. See E.D. Westney, *Imitation and Innovation* (Cambridge: Harvard University Press, 1987).
31. Quoted in K. Masaaki, ed., *Japanese Thought in the Meiji Era* (Tokyo: Pan-Pacific Press, 1958), 22.
32. Quoted in Howland, *Borders of Chinese Civilization*, 113–4.
33. Ibid.
34. Ibid., 228.
35. Ibid.,232.
36. Yao Wendong, quoted in Howland, *Borders of Chinese Civilization*, 234.
37. Howland, *Borders of Chinese Civilization*, 233, 241.
38. A. Ong, "Chinese Modernities: Narratives of Nation and of Capitalism," in A. Ong and D.M. Nonini, eds., *Ungrounded Empires: The Cultural Politics of Modern Chinese Transnationalism* (London: Routledge, 1997), 175.
39. See D. Bell's contribution to this volume.

40. They were considered "sojourners" because each migrant sought only to make money overseas, eventually to return to his native land a rich man. Of course, many sojourners never returned since they could never make enough money or became entrenched in their new lives.

41. Tradition in China and immigration laws in receiving countries generally kept Chinese women from foreign shores until the early twentieth century. This was particularly the case with Chinese emigration to North America. See H.H. Kitano and R. Daniels, *Asian Americans*, second edition (Englewood Cliffs: Prentice Hall, 1995); Kitano and Daniels, 1995; S. Chan, "The Exclusion of Chinese Women, 1870–1943", in S. Chan, ed., *Entry Denied* (Philadelphia: Temple University Press, 1991), 94–144.

42. G. Okihiro, *Margins and Mainstreams* (Seattle: University of Washington Press, 1994). A recent Census Bureau report says that Asian Americans enjoy the highest median family income: $49,100/year (Rosenberg, 1998). They are also well-educated: 42 percent of Asian Americans twenty-five years and older have at least a bachelor's degree, compared with 26 percent of non-Hispanic whites, 14 percent of African Americans, and 10 percent of Latinos. The Census Bureau also reports that one of five Asian Americans grows up in poverty, the same as other groups, and 20 percent of high school students in San Francisco drop out before graduation. These statistics indicate an uneven distribution of resources and possibilities for Asians in America. Nevertheless, the mainstream media continue to market them as uniformly prosperous, law-abiding, and fixedly bourgeois.

43. Ong, "Chinese Modernities," 172.

44. P. Duara, "Nationalists Among Transnationals: Overseas Chinese and the Idea of China, 1900–1911," in Ong and Nonini, eds., *Ungrounded Empires*, 39–60.

45. Ibid.

46. L.H.M. Ling, "Hegemony and the Internationalizing State: A Postcolonial Analysis of China's Integration into Asian Corporatism," *Review of International Political Economy* 3/1 (1996), 1–26.

47. A. Ong and M. Nonini, "Chinese Transnationalism as an Alternative Modernity," in Ong and Nonini, eds., *Ungrounded Empires*: 11.

48. Quoted in S. Faison, "Color Taiwan Red, White and Blue (He's Serious),"*New York Times*, 4 August 1999, A4.

PART 3

THE CHRISTIAN TRADITION

6

The Christian Tradition

Anthony Pagden

1. Principles

Since it first emerged as a "world religion," Christianity has taken several forms, some of which have had widely differing and mutually hostile views over the territorial rights of peoples. In particular, the two major intellectual Christian traditions, Augustinianism and Thomism, have given very different degrees of importance to the place that humankind occupies in the world. In this chapter, I shall be concerned with the Catholic tradition, which, since the sixteenth century, has meant increasingly the Thomist, and opinions on the question of the making and unmaking of boundaries. I shall also concentrate on the period from roughly the late Middle Ages until the end of the seventeenth century.

Christian principles and Christian ethics have always been present in nearly all European discussions on the legal and political issues, which questions of territorial sovereignty inevitably raise. But it is also the case that the terms in which those question have been discussed since the early eighteenth century have been largely secular. Between the mid-sixteenth century and 1648, nearly every European state was engaged in some kind of confessional conflict. These wars divided peoples and families. They were the first to be fought along ideological lines, and they wholly transformed the map of Europe. The Treaty of Westphalia of 1648 brought to a close the last of these great international conflagrations, known as the Thirty Years War. It also crucially put an end to the role of the Papacy – the only interested party to reject the Treaty – as an agent of international arbitration, and established once and for all the principle of *eius regio, cuius religio*, the principle that every sovereign had the right to decide what form of Christianity would be practiced within his own borders. The effect was to establish the foundations of what would become the modern European state system. It was also to diminish, and ultimately eliminate, religious arguments from political debate. The early-modern state had been, to a large degree, like its ancient and medieval predecessors, a theocratic one. The modern state, despite the enduring Christian ethical foundations on which it was based, was to be entirely secular.

"Christianity" – before the great schisms that culminated, in the West, with the Reformation – was, in principle, at least, very little concerned with questions of territorial acquisition, or in questions of territory at all. St. Paul's claim that the Christian "new man"

which is being renewed unto knowledge after the image of him that created him, where there cannot be Greek or Jew, circumcision and uncircumcision, barbarian, Scythian, bondman, freeman: but Christ is all and in all (Colossians 3.11)

specifically eliminated any possible distinction between Christians on grounds of place or political affiliation. Furthermore, Christ's injunction to "render unto Caesar" made explicit the demarcation between the Christian faith, which was universal, and human identity and politics, which were quite specifically local. The early Christians also endorsed and re-worked the strongly Stoic vision of a single humanity bound together by a single source of understanding. The now much-quoted claim by the Stoic Zeno of Citium that all men – although what he meant by "all men" is open to question – should live

not in cities and demes, each distinguished by separate rules of justice, but should regard all men as fellow demesmen and fellow citizens; and that there should be one life and order as of a single flock feeding together on a common pasture"[1]

finds an unintended echo in St. John's gospel, "and there shall be one fold and one shepherd" (10. 16). But unlike Zeno's flock, the sheep within Christ's fold are all, and only those, whom Christ has brought there. For John, as for Paul, as perhaps for all the early Christians, the differences that had hitherto constituted the peoples of the Greek *oikoumene* – the inhabited world – would vanish into the Christian "congregation of the faithful."

In Latin Christendom, and in particular after the revival of Aristotelian moral philosophy by Albertus Magnus, and more significantly St. Thomas Aquinas in the thirteenth century, the Stoic common law for all humankind, the *koinos nomous*, was conceptualized as the law of *nature*, the *ius naturale*, a law that was distinct from divine law (essentially the organizing principles of the creation), and the purely human or civil law. The Roman jurists, from Cicero on, had of course made a similar – if far less precise – division between the human, the natural, and the divine. But in Aquinas, the natural law becomes an ontological principle that links man directly to the divinity. "Rational creatures," he wrote,

are subject to divine Providence in a very special way; being themselves made participators in Providence itself, in that they control their own actions and the actions of others. So they have a certain share in divine reason itself, deriving therefrom a natural inclination to such actions and ends as are fitting. This participation in the Eternal law by rational creatures is called the Natural law."[2]

Nature, furthermore, in Aquinas's celebrated phrase, was not erased by God's grace but perfected by it. What for Augustine had been antithetical – and would become so again for Luther and Calvin – could for Aquinas be reconciled. Man's humanity thus acquired a full and proper place in the creation. This, as both the neo-Thomists, and later the Protestant natural law theorists, in particular Hugo Grotius (discussed in Chapter 8 of this volume by Richard Tuck), could see, gave man a certain measure of independence from his creator. Since one did not – at least for Aquinas – need to be a Christian to be rational, both the Pauline *homo renatus* and the non-Christian natural man, the *homo naturalis*, are similarly endowed with the capacity to understand the precepts of the natural law and to act upon them.

Humanity, for Aquinas, therefore, embraced the "gentes" or the "nationes" – those who lived outside the Christian world – as much as it did those who lived within it. (In this sense, Michel Foucault is right in suggesting that Christianity democratized ethics – so to speak – by making ethical values applicable to literally everyone, in place of a system of ethics that, in the pagan world, and especially in the Stoic conception of that world, had been confined to the "wise."[3]) Contrary to the image that it has acquired since the Enlightenment, the medieval Christian world-view – at least as expressed by the educated elite – was generally cosmopolitan. It merely attached a conception of the unified community of the faithful to an eschatological reading of secular history. Humanity itself would only have fulfilled God's purpose for the world once, in the worlds of the Psalm, "the Word had reached to the end of the earth" (*Psalms*, 18.5). This implied a future state, but it was one that would one day be fulfilled, and when it was the purely Christian polis – the *respublica christiana* – it would come to embrace literally the whole earth.

This is not, of course, to claim that such a view of human history had any explicit political dimension. The boundaries that divided the human race into nations remained unaffected by the spiritual and anthropological community of mankind, as did hierarchical distinctions within individual societies. There were, of course, those who were prepared to take Paul's message more literally – the Fratricelli, the Taborite Brotherhood – but these have always operated on the fringes of the Church, and generally been expelled from it. The Church had always accepted the secular authority of the Roman Emperors. "The Emperor," wrote the second-century theologian, Tertullian, "is established in dignity by God, and [the Christian] must honour him and wish for his preservation."

But Christians are, of course, recognized – in particular by Thomists – to be inescapably political creatures. Aquinas's instance on the humanity of mankind, on man's identity, in the Thomist rendering of Aristotle's *zoon politikon* as an essentially social being, and the subjection of mankind to a natural law, all demanded a constant attention to the political. Questions of authority, of power, and more broadly of that range of potentialities covered by the various uses of the term *dominium,* thus formed an integral part of much theological discourse from the thirteenth to the fifteenth centuries (and, of course, in a somewhat modified form continues to do so to this day). However, it was only with Europe's overseas expansion in the late fifteenth century that the ethical questions relating to national frontiers began to present themselves with any real urgency. There had been earlier concerns over the Latin occupation of Constantinople and the Crusades in general. There had, of course, been the continuing dilemma of the legitimacy of the Holy Roman Empire, and the role of the Emperor. There had also been the question of the territorial reach of papal authority – something that would present itself again after 1492. All of these would, in one way or another, be re-examined in the light of the new overseas "discoveries," and in particular after the 1520s. when the Castilian crown suddenly found itself in *de facto* possession of vast tracts of territory to which it could lay no obvious or unassailable claim based on any of the recognized principles of territorial occupation.

I shall therefore focus on those questions, and in particular as they were discussed by a group of theologians who have come to be known as the "Second Scholastic" or, more parochially, as the "School of Salamanca." They were, for the most part, the pupils and the pupils of the pupils – from Domingo de Soto (1494–1560) to the great Jesuit metaphysician Francisco Suárez (1548–1600) – of Francisco de Vitoria, who held the Prime Chair of Theology at Salamanca between 1526 and his death in 1546. Vitoria's reputation today rests upon the claim that he was the "father of international law," largely because of the very striking observations he made on the Spanish occupation of the Americas, and because of his extended discussions of the Roman notion of the "law of nations" (*ius gentium*), a somewhat indeterminate category midway between the natural law and the civil law.

As with most such putative genealogies, this is something of an anachronism. But if modern international law does have a history, then its sources are clearly to be found in the law of nations. In general, Vitoria and his successors were inclined to think that this belonged to the category of the positive law, in that although it was in accordance with natural law – as all just legislation had to be – it was nevertheless "that which is not equitable of itself but [has been established] by human statute grounded in reason."[4] But if the *ius gentium* had in this way to be enacted, it could only be so by what Vitoria called the power of "the whole world which is in a sense of commonwealth." Since the world, the community of all humanity, was prior to the nation, this gave the *ius gentium* precedence over the local legislative practices of individual communities, so that no "kingdom may chose to ignore this law of nations."[5] It could also be argued – as we will see – that any ruler working on behalf of the law of nations possessed supra-national authority, or what Vitoria terms "the authority of the whole world." This, of course, meant that like the natural law (but unlike any purely civil law), the law of nations applied equally to Christians and non-Christians. The problem, however, in the absence of any political body that might be recognized as standing in for the commonwealth of all the world, was how to determine what the content of this law was to be. Here it became very difficult – as in the case of distinguishing between what was "natural" and what was not – to separate local norms from those that might count as sufficiently "grounded in reason" that the "commonwealth of all humanity" might be supposed to be in agreement with them.

This problem remains insoluble to this day. The modern "international community" has no more cohesion – although it has a great deal more power – than Vitoria's "commonwealth of all humanity." For some "human rights" can seem self-evidently the *natural* rights of all mankind; for others they appear – as they did to the late Ayatollah Khomeini – to be only the product of one particular culture, and simply another instrument of "Western," which means ultimately Christian, imperialism. For we speak, and Vitoria spoke, of "rights" as if they were the property of all peoples. It might well be reasonable on some Kantian calculus to assume that all individuals, in any possible community, even if they do not now possess, or recognize such a conception of a natural or human right, could be brought to understand the meaning of the term. It is well to remember, however that the language of rights, of *iura*, began as a feature of the Roman legal tradition, and was created in the context of Roman imperial legislative practices, and that it acquired its present ethical dimension only within a strongly ontologized Christian tradition. The use by the autocratic rulers of some Asian states of such terms as "Asian values" to defend acts that most democratically governed states would condemn as acts of tyranny is, at best, selective. (There are other "Asian values" that do not sanction the denial of individual freedoms.) But it does serve to remind us that if we wish to assert our belief in the universal, we have to begin by declaring our willingness to assume, and to defend, at least some of the values of a highly specific way of life. At present, the "international community" derives its values from a version of a liberal consensus that is in essence a secularized transvaluation of the Christian ethic, at least as it applies to the concept of rights. The reluctance to recognize that fact does not necessarily invalidate its claim to be in the long-term interests of the majority of humankind. But it does weaken its argument against those, like Khomeini, for whom the values it proclaims (let alone anything resembling a categorical imperative) are simply meaningless.

Most of the early-modern Christian discussion over the more contested means of acquiring new territories, of unmaking boundaries, wrestled with the same ethical difficulties the United Nations does today. The difference, however, is that Vitoria and his heirs were in possession of a body of religious beliefs that provided them with a way of understanding the world that they accepted as irrefutably true. The United Nations can appeal to no such body of beliefs – although it frequently speaks as though it could – with anything like the same assurance.

Boundaries are evidently the creation of the civil or human law. A generalized rhetoric might claim that the seas and mountains had been created by God to establish natural frontiers between peoples, but such claims could never stand any close examination. For the Christian, therefore, boundaries – so long as they were made in accordance with accepted principle of the law – had, like all civil enactments, to be binding in conscience. What was clear, however, at least for Vitoria and most of his successors, was that they could only be used to impose very limited restrictions upon the movement of individuals. In the Thomist, and broadly Aristotelian, account of the origin of civil society, the creation of states, the division of the world into distinct nations, had resulted in the loss of the majority of mankind's primitive liberties, but not all. Every individual retained, for instance, the liberty, and the right, to defend himself. "Any person," wrote Vitoria, "even a private citizen may declare and wage a defensive war" – a point on which Grotius and the seventeenth-century Protestant natural law theorists would rest much of their fundamental re-evaluation of the whole tradition.[6] In Vitoria's opinion, humankind also retained what he calls "the right of natural partnership and communication" (*naturalis societas et communicationis*).[7] This describes a complex set of claims divided into five propositions. In principle, however, it is an allusion to the ancient right of hospitality, which Vitoria transformed from a Greek custom into a right under the law of nations. "Amongst all nations," he wrote, it is considered inhuman to treat travelers badly without some special cause, humane and dutiful to behave hospitably to strangers":

"In the beginning of the world", he continued, "when all things were held in common, everyone was allowed to visit and travel through any land he wished. This right was clearly not taken away by the division of property (*divisio rerum*); it was never the intention of nations to prevent men's free mutual intercourse with one another by its division."

The right to hospitality, and in particular to assistance in moments of danger is, of course, based upon a supposition of a common human identity. "Nature" said Vitoria, "has decreed a certain kinship between men (*Digest* I.i.3) ... Man is not a "wolf to his fellow men" – *homo homini lupus* – as Ovid says, but a fellow." This brings with it an obligation to friendship for "amity between men is part of the natural law." All men are thus compelled to live in a state of amicability with one another. Vitoria's point is that a right to travel peacefully, and to be granted hospitality, is precisely a right that survives from man's primitive condition, and, as such, it cannot be abrogated by merely human legislation. Vitoria is here discussing what he claims to be the right of Spaniards, or indeed any other Europeans, to "visit" and travel in the Americas. But he is certain that it equally applies to the French, who cannot lawfully "prevent the Spaniards from travelling to or even living in France and vice versa."[8] The crucial component of Vitoria's argument was his assertion that the right of communication, and of sociability, because it had survived the division of lands after the creation of civil society, was what the jurist Fernando Vázquez de Menchaca (the "pride of Spain," as Hugo Grotius called him)[9] would call a *liberrima facultas, ius absolutum* – an absolute right that could not be interfered with by any human society.

Vitoria's claim that all humans have a right of free (peaceful) access to all parts of the world draws upon a long ancient and humanist tradition. The Gods – or later God – Seneca had claimed, had distributed their goods unequally over the surface of the globe so as to drive men to communicate with one another, so that as the fourth-century Greek rhetorician Libanius expressed it, "men might cultivate a social relationship because one would have need of the help of another." To make this easier, they had been thoughtful enough to provide winds that blew in contrary directions so as to make sailing possible. Commerce was thus, in Philo of Alexandria's phrase, the expression of "a natural desire to maintain a social relationship." "If you destroy commerce," claimed the first-century historian Lucius Annaeus Florus, "you sunder the alliance which binds together the human race." No wonder then that the Athenian decree prohibiting the Megarians from trading in any part of the Athenian Empire should have led to the Peloponnesian Wars, or that Agamemnon should have made war on the king of Mysia for attempting to limit passage along the roads that led through his kingdom. The Italian humanist, Andrea Alciati went so far as to argue that the chief reason for the Crusades had been that the "Saracens" had denied Christians access to the Holy Land.[10] All of these texts, together with Vitoria's own formulation of the argument, became the underlying principles in the battle over the freedom of the seas, which began with the Dutch rejection during negotiations over the Treaty of Amsterdam of 1609, of the Portuguese claim to have dominium over the Indian Ocean, and continued until the end of the century with interventions by Hugo Grotius, the Portuguese canon lawyer Serafim de Freitas, the Venetian Paolo Sarpi (on the Venetian right to control shipping in the Adriatic), and the Englishman John Selden (on English rights over the North Sea).

The principle of "natural society and communication," however, had wider, more enduring implications. A similar set of claims, similarly grounded in the principle of human amicability, is also to be found in a number of later writers who had had no contact either with the "School of Salamanca" or their writings, but that seem to preserve a broadly Christian (and Stoic) sense of the universality of humankind. The most striking, and by far the most influential, is to be found in Kant's conception of the *ius cosmopoliticum*. This, which was clearly intended as a replacement for the by then discredited *ius gentium*, was in certain respects precisely the right of inter-subjective exchange of the kind that Vitoria had attempted to describe.

In *Perpetual Peace, a Philosophical Sketch* (1795), Kant calls it the "conditions of universal hospitality." Kant is quite specific about what he understands by "hospitality." All citizens, he explained. have the right "to try to establish community with all and, to this end, to *visit* all regions of the world."[11] *Visit*, however, not *settle*, much less *conquer* them. This right makes

it possible for [strangers] to enter into relations with the native inhabitants. In this way, continents distant from each other can enter into peaceful mutual relations which may eventually be regulated by public laws, thus bringing the human race nearer and nearer to a cosmopolitan existence.

This is contrasted sharply with "the *inhospitable* conduct of the civilized states of our continent, especially the commercial states, [in] the injustice which they display in *visiting* foreign countries and peoples (which in their case is the same as *conquering* them)." Neither Vitoria's *naturalis societas et communicationis* nor Kant's *ius cosmopoliticum* had much chance of being heard in a world of emergent nation-states that needed to be able to secure their frontiers as a prerequisite to establishing their undivided sovereignty over them. But expressed, as both Vitoria and Kant expressed them, as injunctions to sociability and as the rights that any possible international community should extend to all commercial transactions, they underpin, albeit perhaps unbeknownst to its drafters, one of the key principles of the founding treaties of what has now become the European Union – namely, the right of all citizens of any of the member states of the Union to free access to, and the right to reside and work in, all others.

2. Settlement

In general, most Catholic theorists accepted the Roman principle that unoccupied lands (*terra nullius*) becomes the possession of whosoever first occupies them, in the sense of putting them to some productive use. They were, however, far more cautious about what constituted occupancy than those Protestants, from Alberico Gentili to John Locke, who made one form or another of the *terra nullius* argument the basis of their claims to the territories of non-Europeans.[12] Catholic theorists also made a distinction – which in general the Protestants did not – between the occupancy of land and sovereignty over it, between, that is, private and public dominium. Whereas it might be legitimate to occupy genuinely waste lands of which there was no private owner, this could only be done with the permission of the local public owner – that is, the sovereign. Even Gentili, who was generally prepared to concede extensive rights to Europeans over non-Europeans on the grounds of their greater technical capacities, was certain that although it would be licit for Christians to occupy vast tracts of unoccupied land, within, say, the territorial limits of the Ottoman Empire, the settlers were nevertheless bound to accept the sovereignty of the Sultan.[13]

Most of the neo-Thomists also followed Vitoria in rejecting the rights of settlement in the Americas – which Vitoria links, as did all subsequent writers on the topic, with the even more tenuous right of discovery (*ius inventionis*) – on the grounds that the Indians "undoubtedly possessed as true dominion, both public and private property as any Christian." From this it followed that "they could not be robbed of their property either as private citizens or as princes on the grounds that they are not true masters."[14] The fact that the "barbarians" had failed to develop their territories might be adduced in support of another argument concerning their mental capacity, but of itself "it provides no support for possession of these lands, any more than it would if they had discovered us."[15]

Vitoria had been concerned with the Spanish rights to the lands of the "barbarians" in terms of the natural law. There existed, however, another kind of claim to occupation, which played a crucial role in the discussion over the legitimacy of the Portuguese settlements in Africa (and Brazil) and the Spanish occupation of America. This was Papal donation. As Richard Tuck observes, the Papacy, and in particular the canon lawyers in the service of the Curia, had since the ninth century some conception that the Pope, as "Vicar of Christ" – a title made current by Innocent II in the twelfth century – enjoyed both spiritual and secular dominium over all the peoples of the world, whatever their religious beliefs.

Acting on this belief, Pope Nicholas V in 1454 granted to Afonso V of Portugal rights of settlement over all "provinces, islands, ports, places and seas, already acquired and which you might acquire in the future, no matter what their number size or quality" in Africa from Cape Bojador and Cape Nun, "and thence all southern coasts until their end." Not to be outdone, the Castilian crown in 1493, secured from Alexander VI the famous "Bulls of Donation" to the Americas, which granted territorial rights over all those lands "as you have discovered or are about to discover,"[16] and which were not already occupied by another Christian prince. One year later, Spain and Portugal, signed a treaty at Tordesillas that divided the entire *orbis terrarum*, of which they possessed only the most primitive geographical knowledge, into two discrete spheres of jurisdiction. (Even the 370 leagues west of the Cape Verde Islands – approximately. 46° 30′ West – along which the Tordesillas Line was drawn, could not be established with any accuracy.) The western half of the globe went to Castile, which believed that it now controlled an unhindered route to the Orient. The eastern half went to Portugal, intent mainly on keeping its Castilian rivals out of the South Atlantic, which thereby came into possession of Brazil. The Treaty was a purely civil agreement between two states – and as such was granted some respect even by the Protestant powers who, of course ridiculed the idea that the Papacy might be able to make land-grants to secular rulers. But its very existence relied on the idea that the Pope was "monarch of the world."

The Bulls of Donation remained the main prop of Spanish arguments in defense of their claims over the Americans until well into the seventeenth century. They are, for instance, the only explanation for the Spanish presence in America offered by the Historiographer Royal, Antonio de Herrera, in his massive *Decadas* of 1601–1615,[17] from which, given Herrera's place in the royal household, it is safe to assume that this was a position with which the Castilian crown still wished to be associated. Even Bartolomé de las Casas, the fiercest defender of the rights of the indigenous peoples of America, never once questioned the legitimacy of the Papal donation. As far as las Casas was concerned, the Indians were legitimate subjects of the Spanish crown, and thus had a right not merely as human beings, but as members of the same commonwealth, to be treated as the equals of their conquerors.[18]

The neo-Thomists, however, rejected the Pope's claim to universal dominium as firmly as they rejected the argument that the Holy Roman Emperor was "lord of all the world." To exercise such power, the Pope would, as Vitoria points out, have had to have acquired it though one of the three forms of law: divine, natural, or civil. Clearly, on the canon lawyers' own evidence, Papal dominium could not derive from either civil or natural law. And "as for divine law, no authority is forthcoming, . . . it is vain and willful to assert it."[19] All the references to secular authority in the Bible would indeed seem to suggest a clear distinction between the domain of Christ and that of Caesar. The Pope's authority, as Innocent III had decreed, was confined to spiritual rather than secular matters, except where strictly moral issues were involved.[20]

Vitoria goes on, however, to make a further point that has some bearing on the claims of any body or institution to supra-national authority. Even if the Pope were to have "secular power over the whole world," he would not be in a position to give it to secular princes since this would diminish the authority of the office of the Papacy. No pope could therefore "separate it from the office of the supreme pontiff, or deprive his successor of it."[21] Vitoria was of course concerned with the status of a particular office, which was theoretically controlled by divine selection. But the question of how far an international organization can delegate its power – the use, for instance, made by the United Nations of NATO – before that power becomes permanently alienated, remains a crucial, and largely un-addressed, theoretical concern for the "international community."

Papal claims to plenitude of power over the whole world, furthermore, like all universalist claims, supposed the existence of a stable and recognizable cosmos. As Vitoria's most gifted and influential successor Domingo de Soto argued in his great treatise on rights and justice, *De Iustitia et iure* of 1556, the Latin term "terra" had traditionally been used to describe the territorial limits of the jurisdiction of the Roman people. As "Christendom" was generally deemed to be co-extensive with the Empire, there were therefore some grounds for supposing that the Pope might be in a position to act as an adjudicator between Christian rulers, and such rulers "are bound to accept his judgement to avoid causing all the manifold spiritual evils which must necessarily arise from any war between Christian princes."[22] (It was precisely this claim, widely accepted by all Christians before the Reformation, that was effectively abandoned by the Treaty of Westphalia.)

There was, however, as Soto pointed out, some confusion in the various uses that both the Papacy and the Empire had made of the word "*terra*" or "*orbis terrarum.*" The Papal donations to both Afonso V and Ferdinand and Isabella were couched in the future tense, and were clearly intended – something underscored by the Tordesillas Line – to encompass literally the entire globe. Since the end of the fifteenth century, however, it had become obvious that this "world," as an inhabited spaced, was no longer fixed, but was continually expanding, and despite the limits imposed by God on all space, might do so for some considerable time to come. The word "*terra*" should therefore, argued Soto, be understood, in the indefinite (or sub-junctive) mode, as limited in its application to a condition that was still only potential.[23] And if this were the case, then no claim to possession of it could be made in a future time. For Soto, and even more forcibly for Soto's contemporary Vázquez de Menchaca, the Bulls of Donation, had thus been rendered void by the very facts they were intended to bring under control, for clearly no man – not even a pope – can have dominium over what is potential, since he would have no means of knowing just what it was he was claiming power over.[24] So long, that is, as the full extent of the inhab-ited world was as yet unknown, any claim to universal sovereignty could only be based upon a tacit assumption that each new society, as it came to light, would have to conform to a rule – the juridical concepts of Western Europe – that had been devised with no prior knowledge of its existence. Furthermore, if such a rule were to be at all legitimate, it would also have to be one that had been created for the "exclusive use" of peoples whose particular needs were as yet unknown to those who had drafted it. And that, concluded Vázquez, would be "worthy of laughter and mockery."[25] For Vázquez, in particular, the expanding regions of the new worlds, known and still-to be known, meant that everything about human history could only be contingent. The law, hitherto considered to be timeless, was, he declared, "for this moment only. On the next it dies." Futurity, which the jurists had sought to appropriate for themselves, now belonged only to God. It fol-lowed, then, that in a world that had been demonstrated to be in a state of perpetual becoming, no sovereignty could be realized beyond the borders of the community in whose name it was being claimed. The idea that in ever-expanding world, one ruler, no matter how mighty the source of his authority, might be "superior in dignity to all other princes," was declared Vázquez "to be compared to the tales of children, to the advice of the aged and to the shadows of an unquiet sleep."[26] It is something of an irony that

that they were in possession, in Vitoria's words, "of true dominion both in pubic and private affairs' before the arrival of the Europeans, and that therefore their rights take precedence over those of their actual rulers. About this there can be little doubt. What is far less certain is what the rights and the status of the European settler populations are *now* if it is assumed, as both the Canadian and the Australian high courts have tacitly at least assumed, that the original act of settlement was itself illicit.

What is obvious is that the use of prescription raised questions of territorial rights in a strongly existential idiom. And as all of those engaged in these debates came to recognize, sooner or later, was that it was legal fact that would in the end be decisive – *ex facto oritur ius* ("the law has its origin in fact") as the jurists were fond of saying.[35] Both Vitoria and Soto could see that if their arguments were to be taken to their proper conclusion, "the whole Indian expedition and trade would cease." But both also recognized that such a situation could never come about (although Vitoria pointed out that the Portuguese crown gained as much as the Castilian out of licit trade "with the same sorts of people without conquering them").[36]

Vitoria's views on these matters, and the sometimes even more radical ones of Soto and Vázquez de Menchaca, might seeem starkly incongruous with what we know of the actual practice of the Spanish in America. Certainly none of the arguments against colonization and settlement expressed by the School of Salamanca had much direct impact either on colonial practice or even on colonial legislation. The Laws of Burgos of 1513, and the far more radical New Laws of 1542 (which the Council of the Indies largely repealed in 1545 rather than face a full-scale settler revolt) were aimed at limiting the abuses of the settlers, and, more importantly for the crown, in curbing their territorial rights. They never raised in any explicit manner the question of the legitimacy of the occupation itself. Neither did anyone ever seriously propose that the Spanish should actually withdraw from the Americas, although a number of the settlers in Mexico appear to have believed that Charles V was seriously contemplating such a move.[37] Vitoria's arguments were moral ones, and as he knew full well, rulers rarely did, or indeed could, act on moral principle alone. All kings, he once told a correspondent are driven to think "from hand to mouth."[38] Politics was always a pragmatic affair. The theologians were there to advise, not to judge, although inevitably, as later generations came to believe, they had provided what was in effect a very powerful body of arguments against almost any kind of overseas territorial expansion.

3. Inheritance

In general most Christians, certainly all Thomists, held to the view – leaving aside the rather delicate question of those gained in a just war – that most territories could only be acquired thorough inheritance. States were subsumed into the person of their rulers. Individual subjects had, of course, rights over and against their rulers, but these did not extend to questions that related to the extent of the ruler's territory.

Rights to occupation, that is, were ascribed to a single group or, in most cases, to a single family. Even the territorial claims of the Empire – which was technically elective – assumed a succession of *translationes* from Constantine (or in some versions from Augustus), and claims such as that of Charles V to Milan on the grounds that it had always been an imperial fief, were formally very little different from, say, Ferdinand II of Aragon's claims to Navarre. (The same was also true of, for instance, Pope Paul III's claim to Perugia, or the Papal seizure of the towns of the Marche.) In general, too, Christians assumed that all territory that had once been under Christian rule remained *de iure* if not *de facto* Christian lands no matter who their actual rulers might be. Christian rulers used titles to lands over which they did not rule, and appointed bishops – *in partibus infidelium* – to sees they could never hope to occupy. This, of course, was the reasoning behind the Crusades and behind all the sporadic attempts from the fifteenth to the late seventeenth centuries to drive the Ottomans from the eastern Mediterranean. Christendom was in a state of permanent war with the Ottoman Empire (significantly the only state beside the Holy Roman Empire to be described as an *imperium*) not because the Turks were unbelievers but because they occupied much of what was widely considered to be, and in large areas was, the lands of Christians.[39] This, too, was why it was possible for Christians to speak of the "reconquest" of Spain when by 1492 the kingdom of Al Andalus had been under Muslim rule far longer than it had ever been under Christian.

4. Sale-Purchase

There is virtually no discussion of the possible acquisition of land through sale or treaty by any of the neo-Thomists. Land as the private property of individuals could of course be sold or alienated in any way that its true owner saw fit. But it is far less certain that a ruler could legitimately dispose of any part of the state that was entrusted to his care. In certain cases – that of France, for instance – any such alienation was proscribed by civil law, or in the French case, what was know as the "fundamental laws" of the kingdom. This did not, however, prevent either the French or the Portuguese from purchasing territory from non-European rulers. The Portuguese, for instance, although they spoke of their empire as a "conquest," had never in fact "conquered" anywhere, except Brazil. Their "factories" (*feitorias*) in Asia and even in coastal west Africa had either been leased or acquired through treaty with native rulers. The French also acquired territory in North America through purchase, although this was done largely in imitation of the English, who made extensive use of purchase as a means of acquiring territory in America. For the English, sale had the advantage of effectively eliminating the presence of any indigenous inhabitants. They bought lands, not persons. "The only [right] which will bear the least examination . . . is founded upon purchase," argued Arthur Young in 1772, since any other means of acquiring land involved the forceful displacement of peoples, and would thus become *de facto* a conquest. Purchase followed by "improvement" evidently made for better and more successful colonies than those whose origins had been in "acts of violence."[40] The Iberian kingdoms, however, were far more exercised about their sovereignty over peoples, and this of course could not be the subject of any commercial transaction.

5. Conquest

In general, conquest was a wholly unacceptable means of acquiring territory or of altering the frontiers of existing states. Most Christians of all confessions would have agreed with Locke that "*Conquest* is as far from setting up any government, as demolishing an House is from building a new one in the place."[41] In practice, however, most boundaries were changed, in particular outside Europe, after the late fifteenth century by one or another kind of conquest. Conquest could only become legitimate if the territory conquered had been taken in what was know as a "just war."[42] Such a war conferred upon the aggressor a right to wage war – the *ius ad bellum* – and was governed by a set of agreements about how the war should be conducted and the benefits the victor was entitled to derive from it – the *ius in bello*.[43] In general, the Roman jurists had claimed that war could only be waged defensively and in pursuit of compensation for some alleged act of aggression against either the Romans themselves or their allies. "The best state," as Cicero observed, "never undertakes war except to keep faith or in defense of its safety."[44] War was thus only a means of punishing an aggressor and of seizing compensation for damages suffered.

In general, most Christians accepted this basic principle. Wars, said Augustine, in the most frequently cited passage on the subject,

are just which revenge the injuries caused when the nation or *civitas* with which war is envisaged has either neglected to make recompense for illegitimate acts committed by its members, or to return what has been injuriously taken.[45]

Vitoria discussed, although only briefly, the possibility that the Spaniards might be in legitimate possession of the Americas "on account of the personal tyranny of the barbarians' masters towards their subjects, or because of their tyrannical and oppressive wars against their subjects." He came to the conclusion that on these grounds, the Spaniards did indeed have the right, "even without the pope's authority," to prevent such things as human sacrifice and cannibalism because "the barbarians are our neighbors." The Roman law of vicinage, to which Vitoria alludes here, required that "neighbors" come to the defense of each other in times of crisis. The

Spaniards thus had an obligation in natural law to come to the "defense of the innocent," and this applied even if the innocent were willing participants in the crimes committed against them. "It makes no difference," wrote Vitoria, "that all the barbarians consent to these kinds of rights and sacrifices, or that they refuse to accept the Spaniards as their liberators in the matter." For prolonged habit is capable of obscuring every human being's understanding of the natural law, and no man may "deliver himself up to execution" (unless justly convicted of a crime), for the same reason that he may not commit suicide, because possession in his own body (*dominium coporis suuis*) belongs not to him, but to God. Clearly if the rulers of the "barbarians" refuse to abandon their crimes against their people, then "their masters may be changed and new princes set up."[46] It would seem to be obvious that any prince who was not himself a tyrant would have this duty. The Spaniards are here merely acting on behalf, and by the authority of, a supposed international community. The Spaniards are in America – or in those parts of America where human sacrifice and cannibalism were supposedly practiced – by historical contingency, and the task thus fell to them. But it could just as easily have been assumed by any other non-tyrannical ruler, Christian or, indeed, non-Christian.

Vitoria's conception of war "in defense of the innocent" – that is, of some kind of "humanitarian war" – in common with all attempts to justify armed intervention in the interests of "others," fails of course to specify – beyond the reference to cannibalism and human sacrifice – what would count as "tyranny" and "oppressive laws." It was, too, an innovative move since, in general, theories of the "just war" avoided claims made on behalf of third parties unless these were specifically involved as "allies" (*socii*).[47] The Indians might, for instance, quite reasonably have sought the assistance of the Europeans in their (legitimate) struggles against other Indians. This had indeed happened, as Vitoria points out, in the case of the Tlaxcalans who – at least in Hernán Cortés's account of events – had sought Spanish aid in their struggle against the Aztecs.[48] But few would accept that any state could intervene in the affairs of another without the express request of at least a legally recognized representative body from that state. Fewer still would have accepted that one ruler had the authority to decide what constitutes an "offence against the innocent" in another state. In contemporary terms, for instance, Vitoria would have sanctioned such wars as that fought by NATO (now transformed from a defensive alliance into an agency of "the commonwealth of all the world") in Yugoslavia in 1999, whereas most just-war theorists would have denied that in the absence of a duly established authority capable of claiming "ally" status, it constituted merely an unwarranted interference in the internal affairs of another state.

In the case of the American Indians, the humanitarian argument for conquest, and the subsequent imposition of "new princes" and hence in effect the creation of new states, was fairly circumscribed. In other, less specific contexts, however, Vitoria substantially broadened the possible applications of the same argument. "It should be noted," he wrote,

that the prince has the authority not only over his own people, but also over foreigners to force them to abstain from harming others; this is his right by the law of nations and the authority of the whole world. Indeed, it seems he has this right by natural law: the world could not exist unless some men had the power and authority to deter the wicked by force from doing harm to the good and the innocent.

Here the law of nations has been appropriated to the natural law, just as the prince is now appropriated to the entire *respublica*. Furthermore, since in Vitoria's opinion the commonwealth, in the person of the prince, clearly had the authority "in natural law" to "punish those of its own members who are intent on harming it with execution or other penalties," it followed that

If the commonwealth has these powers against its own members, there can be no doubt that the whole world has the same powers against any harmful and evil men. And these powers can only exist if exercised though the princes of the commonwealth.⁴⁹

There were further, and somewhat more sinister, ways in which it was possible to extend the range of this injunction. One, which drew, if only indirectly, on the arguments in favor of pre-emptive strike discussed by Richard Tuck, maintained that if it was legitimate for a ruler to right a wrong on behalf "of the whole world," then it might also be legitimate for a prince to wage war in order to prevent any future, or further, deterioration in the status quo. In the view of Francisco Suárez, perhaps the most influential Catholic writer on the justice of war in the seventeenth century, this would, for instance, have constituted a cause for a just war against Henry VIII of England. For England, so Suárez claimed to believe, because of the offences Henry had caused its peoples, was already in disarray and might therefore legitimately be attacked to prevent further collapse.⁵⁰ "War," as Suárez phrased it, "is permitted so that the state may preserve the integrity of its rights," even if that war had been initiated by a foreign power.⁵¹

Such arguments, though they were formally deployed to defend the Spanish presence in America, provided, however, no charter for effective colonization. For once the "integrity of the state" had been established, the invading power should logically withdraw. According to Augustine, however, Cicero had also argued in Book 3 of *De Republica* that wars might be waged "in defense of faith." This clearly widened the possible application of both the Ciceronian and the Augustinian grounds for a *ius ad bellum*. If "fides" is understood here, as Augustine understood it, to mean religious belief, then for the neo-Thomists this comes dangerously close to the argument, which Vitoria associated with Fitzralph, Wycliff, Huss, and the "modern heretics" Luther and Calvin, that sovereignty (*dominium iurisdictionis*) depended upon God's grace rather than God's laws, and that no "ungodly" person could be a legitimate ruler.[52] For the neo-Thomists, however, dominium derived from the natural law, and was entirely unrelated to the ruler's religious beliefs or ethical convictions. As Suárez observed, it was not man's task to vindicate God. If God wished to take revenge upon the pagans for their sins, he remarked acidly, "he is capable of doing so for himself."[53] But "fides" could also be interpreted, as Cicero himself would have done, to stand for a way of life, in this case, of course, the way of life practiced within the Roman *civitas*. It could therefore be claimed that an offensively un-Christian – which meant in effect an offensively non-European – life-style constituted not only a crime against nature, but an offence of such a magnitude that it posed a threat to the continuing existence of the *civitas*. The Christian prince might therefore go to war as the defender of the Christian *civitas* precisely on the grounds that Augustine had endorsed elsewhere in the *City of God* – namely, that war might be made to "acquire peace," peace in this context being defined as a "work of justice" (*opus justitiae*) for the restoration of the "tranquillity of the order of all things."[54]

In such circumstances, argued Suárez, "the natural power and jurisdiction of the human republic" could be mobilized as a "reason for universal conquest" against all those whose behavior was so extreme as to constitute a threat to the integrity of humanity.[55] Since Suárez was also prepared to consider that any attempt to "impede the law of Christ" might constituted legitimate grounds for such action, the scope of the jurisdiction exercised by the "human republic" could be very wide indeed.[56]

On these grounds, it would seem that the conquest of all "barbarians" might be permissible if their barbarism made them, in effect, sufficiently unlike Christians to seem somehow incapable of creating true civil societies. This still left the question open as to whether this justified permanent occupation, or only – as would, for instance, have been the case with a Spanish occupation of England – a brief stay sufficient to establish new (native) rulers able to remedy the "disorder" within the state. "Self-determination" is hardly a term that figures in the vocabulary of these writers, but very few of them ever envisaged the permanent occupation of one state by another. The purpose of war was to remedy ills. In the process, the victor might seize such moveable goods as he deemed necessary to compensate for the losses he had incurred. He might also seize goods, and even persons, as punishment for wrongdoing. But immovable goods were another matter. Vitoria accepted that

it is sometimes lawful to occupy a fort or town, but the governing factor in this case must be moderation, not armed might. If necessity and the requirements of war demand that the greater part of enemy territory or a large number of cities be occupied in this way, they ought to be returned once the war is over and peace has been made, only keeping so much as may be considered fair in equity and humanity for the reparation of losses and expenses and the punishment of injustice.[57]

It is not entirely clear from this whether the "crimes" of the Americans are such that the Spaniards, acting for the "the whole world which is in a sense of commonwealth," would be justified "in equity and humanity" in seizing all their lands in perpetuity. Vitoria does not say. But for him, as for all Christian writers on this subject, there remained the consoling – or troubling – example of the Roman Empire. Rome had, as Vitoria explains, been built up "using the law of war as their title to occupy the cities and lands of enemies who had done them injury,"[58] and Rome had also been "defended by Augustine, Jerome, Ambrose, Aquinas and other holy doctors" as both the reward for the supreme (secular) virtues of the Roman people and as the instrument used by God to unite the world for the coming of Christ.

Vitoria was clearly prepared to accept the existence of the Roman Empire in some sense as a divinely ordained creation. Soto, however, argued that the claims made by Vitoria's "holy doctors" had been seriously misunderstood. The collective *virtus* of the Romans, he claimed, had been constituted by purely secular and civil qualities, such as justice and fortitude, which retain their intrinsic merit even when they are pursued for the wrong reasons. The supposition that had underpinned so much Christian thinking about the Pagan empire was false. It had been a purely human creation limited, like all such creations, in both time and space. As such, of course, its historical existence offered no possible legitimisation for future imperial projects, even those supposedly pursed in the interest of evangelisation.

6. Secession

None of the neo-Thomists, indeed no Catholic thinker of any kind, recognized a *de iure* right of a people to secede from a legitimately constituted state. The people, the nation, were always spoken of as one with the person of their prince. The desire for self-determination in the modern sense was nothing other than rebellion. There did exist circumstances under which rebellion might be sanctioned – Suárez's works were burned by the public executioner in Paris for supposedly advocating regicide – but none of these involved the kind of aspirations for self-rule that modern secessionist politics suppose.

7. Conclusions

Since the late sixteenth century, Christianity has been not one faith, but many. Crucially for the purposes of this chapter, it has been two: Catholic and Thomist and Protestant and Augustinian. As I stressed at the beginning, I have been concerned here only with the Catholic Thomist version. The history of the Augustinian Protestant views on boundaries belongs properly to the history of the Protestant natural law theories of the seventeenth century, to Hugo Grotius and Samuel Pufendorf, and this has been discussed by Richard Tuck in Chapter 8.

One major difference between the two traditions, however, can be emphasized. The Protestants, as Catholic apologists have often pointed out, disingenuously for the most part, have been far less troubled than Catholics with the legitimacy of seizing the lands of others. Neither the Dutch nor the English, nor later the Swedes and the Danes, troubled themselves overmuch with justifying their occupation of American Indian territories. When they did, the arguments they deployed were based, as we have seen, on some version of the Roman law of *res* or *terra nullius*, or on the assumption, often false, that the settlers had acquired their lands either through treaty or purchase. In nearly every case, that is, what was at stake were existential legal claims. The question of the nature of the Indians, their status qua rational beings, their cultural and political identity, though they often played a role in these arguments, were generally secondary. Behind these differences there lay, too, larger political and evangelical objectives. The Spanish, the Portuguese, and the French in America, Asia, and the Pacific all, in different ways and to varying degrees, had set out to establish new Christian societies. Their ideological and juridical concerns were as much with persons as with land. The English and, in those regions where they settled, the Dutch, had no such objectives. True, the English Puritans had hoped to create new communities in America, but they were to be communities of Europeans only. The Indians were not to be incorporated; they were to be displaced or, if that proved impossible, eliminated.

Ever since it became a state religion under Constantine the Great, Christianity has been used to sustain, and the Christian churches have been all-too-willing participants in, any number of colonising ventures. Like all universalising faiths, like Islam and communism, like liberalism – which is in many respects its secular heir – Christianity found itself easily pressed into service as agent of a certain kind of inclusivity. Christianity, like Islam (like Judaism, too, although Judaism had no universalist aspirations), proclaimed itself to be the only "true religion," the only correct way to understand the cosmos and mankind's place within it, just as both communism and liberal democracy have been touted as the only "true," the only correct, modes of political life. The consequence, of course, has been to insist that all those who chose for whatever reason to remain outside, to embrace some other faith, or to pursue some other political life, have to be compelled, by argument preferably, but by force if necessary, to recognize the error of their decision.

But for all that, the Christian tradition, at least as reflected in the writings of the neo-Thomists (the Augustinians and the canonists come out far more strongly in favor of universal empire), persisted in their claims that the boundaries and the frontiers that peoples had established amongst themselves could not so easily be disregarded in the pretext of spreading the faith. In attempting to establish this as an ethical principle, they were driven to give some theoretical shape to what Cicero had first described as the "republic of all the world." The results were not entirely satisfactory. And they stopped far short of the categorical denial of the rights of one society, whatever its presumed merits, to occupy the lands and subjugate the peoples of another that the modern jurist might hope to find. But as the "international community" comes to play an ever increasing role in the politics of individual states, as boundaries are made and unmade with ever-increasing frequency – and bloodshed – some re-evaluation of the role the concept of the "law of nations" has played in the evolution of international legal and political theory might be useful in helping to think through some of difficulties that the community has had in identifying itself.

Notes to Chapter 6

1. Plutarch, *On the Fortunes of Alexander*, 329A–B.
2. St. Thomas Aquinas, *Summa theologiae* I. 2. ae, q.91 art.1 and 2.
3. Michel Foucault, *Le Souci de Soi. Histoire de la sexualité* 3 (Paris: Gallimard, 1984), 274. In the *Republic* (Zeno's lost work on politics), Diogenes Laertius tells us that "he declares the good alone to be true citizens or friends or kindred or free men. . . . Friendship, [the Stoics] declare exists only between the wise and the good, by reason of their likeness to one another." Only friends are to be treated "as we should ourselves." To the non-virtuous and the non-wise, by contrast, "he applies the opprobrious epithets of foemen, enemies, slaves and aliens" (*Lives of Eminent Philosophers*, VII 31).
4. Vitoria, *Comentarios a la Secunda secundae de Santo Tomás*, ed., Vicente Beltrán de Heredia (Salamanca: Universidad de Salamanca, 1932–52) 6 vols. III, 12, 89–90.
5. "On Civil Power," 3.4, in Francisco de Vitoria, *Vitoria Political Writings*, eds., Anthony Pagden and Jeremy Lawrance (Cambridge: Cambridge University Press, 1991), 40. All future references will be to this edition.
6. "On the Law of War," 1.2, in Vitoria, *Vitoria Political Writings*, 299.
7. "On the American Indians," 3.1, in Vitoria, *Vitoria Political Writings*, 278. As he defines it, this seems to have been Vitoria's own creation. St. Augustine had suggested that denial of a right of passage might be sufficient *injuria* for a just war. But this has none of the structure of Vitoria's argument (*Quaestiones in Heptateuchum*, IV. 44; *Decretum* C.23. 2.3).
8. "On the American Indians," 3.1, Vitoria, *Vitoria Political Writings*, 278.
9. Hugo Grotius, *The Freedom of the Seas* [*De Mare Libero*], trans. Ralph Van Deman Magoffin (New York: Oxford University Press, 1916), 52.
10. All are quoted by Grotius, *The Freedom of the Seas*, 10.
11. "Perpetual Peace a Philosophical Sketch," in Immanuel Kant, *Kant Political Writings*, ed., Hans Reiss (Cambridge: Cambridge University Press, 1977), 106–7.
12. For a wider discussion of this position, see James Tully, "Aboriginal property and western theory: recovering a middle ground," *Social Philosophy and Policy* 11 (1994), 153–80.

13. See Benedict Kingsbury, "Confronting Difference: the Puzzling Durability of Gentili's Combination of Pragmatic Realism and Normative Judgment," *The American Journal of International Law* 92/4 (1998), 713–23, 723n.

14. "On the American Indians," 1, Conclusion, in Vitoria, *Vitoria Political Writings*, 250–1. 15.

15. "On the American Indians," 2.3, in Vitoria, *Vitoria Political Writings*, 264–5.

16. There were five Bulls in all. They are printed in Manuel Giménez Fernández, "Nuevas consideraciones sobre la historia y el sentido de las letras alejandrinas de 1493 referentes a las Indias," *Anuario de estudios américanos* 1 (1944), 173–429.

17. See David Brading, *The First America, The Spanish Monarchy, Creole Patriots and the Liberal State, 1492–1867* (Cambridge: Cambridge University Press, 1991), 205–10.

18. *Aquí se contiene treynta proposiciones muy jurídicas*, ed., Ramón Hernández in *Fray Bartolomé de las Casas, Obras Completas*, vol. 10 (Madrid: Editorial Alianza, 1992) 201–14.

19. "On the American Indians," 2.2, in Vitoria, *Vitoria Political Writings*, 260. Vitoria uses the same arguments in "On the Power of the Church," 5.1, in Vitoria, *Vitoria Political Writings*, 83–4.

20. See Brian Tierney, *The Crisis of Church and State 1050–1300* (Toronto: Toronto University Press, 1988) 127–38.

21. "On the American Indians," 2.2, in Vitoria, *Vitoria Political Writings*, 261.

22. Ibid., 262.

23. Domingo de Soto, *De Iustitia et iure* (Salamanca 1556), 306.

24. Vázquez de Menchaca, *Controversiarum illustrium aliarumque usu frequentium, libri tres* [1563] 3 vols., ed., Fidel Rodriguez Alcalde (Valladolid, 1931), II, 30.

25. Ibid., II, 29.

26. Ibid., I, 17.

27. This was a chapter from a much longer work Grotius had entitled *De Indis* but has subsequently come to be known as *De iure praedae* (*On the Right of Booty*), and written between 1604 and 1605. It was never published in Grotius's lifetime. See Richard Tuck's Chapter 8 in this volume.

28. Grotius, *The Freedom of the Seas*, 15.

29. Freitas, *De Justo império asiático dos Portugueses* (*De iusto imperio Lusitanorum Asiatico*), 2 volumes, trans. Miguel Pinto de Meneses (Lisbon: Instituto de Alta Cultura, 1959) [References are to vol. 2, the Latin text], 93–4.

30. Juan de Solórzano y Pereira, *Politica Indiana, sacada en lengua castellana de los dos tomos del derecho i govierno municipal de las Indias occidentales*, 2 volumes (Madrid, 1647), I, 37.

31. The most important source for the significance of prescription to such cases – and the one cited by Solórzano – was Bartolus's discussion (*repetitio*) on the law *Quominus*, under the title *De fluminibus* (*Digest* 43. 12.2), discussing the possibility of acquiring right over a public river. See Annabel Brett, *Nature, Rights and Liberty* (Cambridge: Cambridge University Press, 1994), 280–1.

32. See Anthony Pagden, *Spanish Imperialism and the Political Imagination* (New Haven-London: Yale University Press, 1990), 34–5. Bartolus had raised similar questions with regard to the rights of the Venetians and the Genoese to restrict

sailing within their respective gulfs. See Brett, *Nature, Rights and Liberty*, 284 at n5.

33. Grotius, *The Freedom of the Seas*, 47.

34. Freitas, *Do Justo império asiático dos Portugueses* , 182–3.

35. On this, see Luigi Prosdocimi, "'Ex facto oritur ius.' Breve nota di diritti medievale," in *Studi senesi* (1954–5) 66–67, 808–19.

36. "On the American Indians," Conclusion, in Vitoria, *Vitoria Political Writings*, 291.

37. See Anthony Pagden, "Dispossessing the Barbarian: the language of Spanish Thomism and the debate over the property rights of the American Indians," in Anthony Pagden, ed., *The Languages of Political Theory in Early Modern Europe* (Cambridge: Cambridge University Press, 1987) 79–98.

38. "Letter to Bernardino de Vique," in Vitoria, *Vitoria Political Writings*, 334. On another occasion he wrote to Pedro Fernández de Velasco, "I sometimes thing how very foolish it is for one of my kind to think, let alone speak, about government and public affairs; it seems to me even more absurd than a grandee pronouncing on our philosophies," in Vitoria, *Vitoria Political Writings*, 337.

39. Which is why, according to Vitoria, it was legitimate to enslave the "women and the children of the Saracens," because "they can never sufficiently pay for the injuries and losses inflicted." See "On the Law of War," 3.3, in Vitoria, *Vitoria Political Writings*, 318.

40. Arthur Young, *Political Essays Concerning the Present State of the British Empire* (London, 1772), 472.

41. John Locke, *Second Treatise*, in *Locke's Two Treatises of Government* 2nd ed., ed., Peter Laslett (Cambridge: Cambridge University Press, 1967) 47.

42. See Frederick H. Russell, *The Just War in the Middle Ages* (Cambridge: Cambridge University Press,1975).

43. See in general, S. Albert, *Bellum Iustum, Frankfurter Althistorische Studien 10*, (Kallmunz: Michael Lassleben,1980).

44. Cicero, *De Republica*, 3.34.

45. St. Augustine, *Quaestionum in Heptateuchem*, VI. X.

46. "On the American Indians," 3.5.15, in Vitoria, *Vitoria Political Writings*, 287–8.

47. See Jonathan Barnes, "The Just War," in Norman Kretzmann, Anthony Kenny, and Jan Pinborg, eds., *Cambridge History of Later Medieval Philosophy* (Cambridge: Cambridge University Press, 1982) 775–8.

48. "On the American Indians," 3.7, in Vitoria, *Vitoria Political Writings*, 289.

49. "On the Law of War," 1.4.19, in Vitoria, *Vitoria Political Writings*, 305.

50. See Pagden, *Spanish Imperialism and the Political Imagination*, 31.

51. Francisco Suárez, *Disputatio xii. De Bello*, from *Opus de triplice virtute theologica, fide spe et charitate* [Paris, 1621], printed in vol. 2 of Luciano Pereña Vicente, *Teoria de la guerra en Francisco Suárez*, 2 volumes (Madrid, 1954), 126–7.

52. See "On Civil Power," 3.1–6, in Vitoria, *Vitoria Political Writings*, 42.

53. Suárez, *Disputatio xii. De Bello*, 149–52.

54. *De Civitate. Dei*, XIX 13.

55. Suárez, *Disputatio xii. De Bello*, 238.

56. Ibid., 158–61.

57. "On the Law of War," 3. 7, in Vitoria, *Vitoria Political Writings*, 324.

58. Ibid., 325.

7

Christianity and Territorial Right

Oliver O'Donovan

Anthony Pagden is wise to take as his point of vantage that moment in the development of Christian thought at which the explosion of Western colonisation brought the questions of conquest to the fore, and elicited from a range of Catholic thinkers, led by Francisco di Vitoria, a discriminating and critical view. He is also quite correct to see their perspective on the question as deriving from the Aristotelian renaissance of the high Middle Ages, which influenced the Catholic thinkers of the sixteenth century, especially through their rediscovery of St. Thomas Aquinas. It is hard to imagine Vitoria's great contemporary, Luther, taking up the colonial conquest of the Americas with anything like the same insight, not because Luther was uncritical of power-hunger or expansive self-aggrandisement, but because he lacked a purchase on the *political* categories needed for a discussion of territorial right.

Beyond this point, however, I hesitate to follow Pagden in his distinction between Augustinian and Thomist streams of Christianity. It seems to suggest, on the one hand, that the aspiration to transcend limitations of place did not affect Thomists, and, on the other, that the pre-Thomistic first millennium of Christianity was not aware of the significance of place. Both suggestions would be mistaken. In the first place, Thomists were prominent in the mid-twentieth century wave of philosophical scepticism about territoriality; one went so far as to write: "Living together does not mean occupying the same place in space.... Living together means sharing as men, not as beasts."[1] And in the second place, the beginnings of Christianity were already deeply shaped by the dialectic between universal co-citizenship and local particularity. To discover why this was so, we have to go back to its ambiguous relation with ancient Judaism. At the risk of treading less expertly over ground mapped out so beautifully by Menachem Lorberbaum in Chapter 2 of this volume, we must glance back at the Hebrew Scriptures to identify the themes that evoked from early Christians a gesture both of appropriation and transcendence.

1. The Early Christian Response to the Territorial Conceptions of Ancient Judaism

The bond that attached the people of Israel to the Promised Land was drawn much tighter by the traumatic experience of losing it. Nothing could be more moving than the detail in which the authors of the Book of Joshua, probably situated in Babylonia, gathered and preserved ancient boundary-descriptions of each tribal territory with a list of villages and towns belonging to each. In these austere pages, we are led up hills and down valleys, through tiny hamlets unknown to us and perhaps to them, mingling periods of history anachronistically but with great geographical detail, delineating the widest plausible boundary for Israel's possession while overlooking such major interruptions as the presence of Philistine civilisation on the coastal plain. Geography is here the object of that minute attention normally reserved for genealogy and ritual. If we let our imaginations rest on the situation of these displaced scholars who so carefully pieced together every geographical record they had been able to carry with them, we may think there is nothing quite like it in the ancient or modern world as a testimony to the devotion inspired by places. The gift of "the land" was for them a *defined* gift, shaped by its territorial determinations and divisions, which were the medium through which YHWH gave himself to his people. The land was their possession because *he* was their possession, and so its definition mattered. Always, then, geography was charged with transcendent meaning. It was no arbitrary typological embroidery on the part of later expositors such as Philo or the author to the Hebrews to look on the Promised Land as a "heavenly" possession, for it was an aspect of the ancient historians' thought that the land pointed beyond itself. The symbol of this transcendence was the land-less status of the tribe of Levi, dispersed through other tribal territories, of whom it was simply said that "YHWH is their inheritance."

From the pre-Exilic perspective, Israel was not unique in being able to claim their land as a divine gift. The world was divided into territories, as an ancient conception held, according to the number of the angelic beings, each serving as the tutelary god of the inhabitants. Israel was under the care of the High God, whom it knew as YHWH.[2] But these allotments were not autochthonous. Not only in Israel's own case, but in others too, they had been granted by migration and conquest. Some prophets said that all these migrations had been under YHWH's control.[3] The Book of Deuteronomy saw this phase of primitive history as a divine measure to replace a barbarous race of semi-humans with civilised peoples.[4] This theory was not, of course, meant to license *new* wars of civilisation; on the contrary, it was to underwrite the stability of the boundaries as they existed, or claimed to exist, in the late seventh century, which was a period of unparalleled uncertainty.

In response to the aggressive expansion of Mesopotamia, to which Israel's Northern kingdom had fallen an early victim, Israel's prophets had developed a theory of *punitive conquest*. The imperial powers were put in play by YHWH primarily to punish his own people for their moral and religious failures. But this implied no right on the conquerors' part. They were mere mindless and uncomprehending tools in the hand of YHWH, to whom the right of judgment belonged exclusively. Their turn would come in God's time. Pseudo-Jeremiah, writing after the collapse of Judah in the early sixth century, tried to decide what the international order would look like when YHWH brought his long-awaited judgment upon the tyrannous Chaldaeans. His verdict: only those peoples that, like Edom, had forfeited their right to exist by treachery, would be swept away for good; other features of the international order would be put back in their former places.[5]

But in later Biblical Judaism, this emphasis on the religious importance of territory is already qualified. The diaspora radically changed the Jewish political identity. They have to "dwell among those who are enemies to peace."[6] They live in other kingdoms than their own, and retain their identity extra-territorially, and when they can, they travel for the high festivals to "the house of the Lord" in Jerusalem. Often (as they like to emphasize) they played an important role in their host-societies, not least as counsellors and advisors to government. But not without conflict: Daniel, the archetypal Jewish counsellor at a pagan court, suffered famously for keeping his window open to Jerusalem when he prayed.[7] The shift away from territorial definitions is evident in the enhanced role played by the Holy City in these exiles' understanding of their identity. Jerusalem still had its territory, of course, though much less than the exilic Deuteronomists had thought it was entitled to. But this hinterland now fell into the background. The metropolis rather than the land became the focus of Jewish loyalty.

The preaching of Jesus, which is now seen to be much *more* of a piece with national expectations than was once customary to admit, addressed a Jewish consciousness that was much *less* territorially defined than at earlier periods. Jerusalem, the city, is the focus (negatively) of Jesus's most severe critiques of his people; Jerusalem, the city, is the focus (positively) of his predictions of the coming of God's Kingdom. The Gospels continually speak of his journeys to Jerusalem, especially (in St. John) those associated with the great feasts of the Jewish religious year. It was in Jerusalem, the apostles taught, that God had vindicated his anointed, and in Jerusalem that the gift of the Holy Spirit was given. And Jerusalem was the focus of a further expectation of great importance: the gathering of the Gentiles to worship, taken to be the signal of the Kingdom. So it was from Jerusalem, according to St. Luke, that the missionary message must go out, not only to Jews but also to Gentiles. The geographical consciousness of early Christianity, then, was precisely that which it inherited: that of a city at the centre of the world. So we are not surprised to find (in 1 Peter, for example, and the Letter to Diognetus) the early Christian communities taking up the diaspora consciousness of extra-territorial identity. "While living in Greek and barbarian cities, according as each obtained his lot, and following the local customs both in clothing and food and in the rest of life, they show forth the wonderful and confessedly strange character of the constitution of their own citizenship. They dwell in their own fatherlands, but as if sojourners in them; they share all things as citizens, and suffer all things as strangers."[8]

In two important respects, however, the early Christians qualified their Jewish inheritance by further minimizing the significance of place. One was in a detached and critical attitude to holy places and shrines. God would be worshipped "in spirit and in truth," and that made the question as to where irrelevant.[9] Implied in this was an exhaustion of the significance of Jerusalem itself. Having discharged its sacred function as the place of God's judgment and vindication on mankind, it could pass from the scene, and when in the generation after Jesus it succumbed to Roman armies, Christians felt that they had been more than prepared for this outcome. The other important qualification was that they developed an abstract concept of the state. Saint Paul wrote of "authorities" in general terms, and conceived of them as serving a purely judicial function.[10] Missing from his conception was any idea that the identity of a *particular* people is conferred or represented by its government, or that a government must have a *particularly* defined territory over which to exercise jurisdiction.

The patristic church engaged with the territorial conceptions of ancient Israel as part of a Gentile hermeneutic endeavour to retain the Jewish Scriptures while not taking literally their preoccupation with the Jewish national destiny. The "earthly promises" were valid in the Old, but not in the New Covenant. The possession that the Jewish people had learned to prize as *land*, the Christian church now knew to point forward to the spiritual possession of God's people in God's immortal presence. This dissolution of concrete geographical references into universal and eternal reality was not first learned from the encounter with Greek philosophy. But when the revived Platonism of the third century of the era impinged upon Christian thinkers, they found its conception of the spacelessness of the spiritual a congenial idea. Spirit cannot be in space; space must be in spirit. As Plotinus had said in a famous simile: the body relates to the soul like a net floating in the sea. The young Augustine insisted that the wise man is not, as he seems, here with us; he is "in himself."[11] And when Jesus quoted the Psalm that said "the meek shall inherit the land" (*terra*), Augustine takes him to have meant "the solid stability, so to speak, of the eternal inheritance, where the soul possessed of good affection rests, as it were, in its proper place like a material body on the ground (*terra*), and is nourished on its proper food like a body on the produce of the soil (*terra*)."[12]

Yet such radically Platonizing views did not prevail. Already in Augustine's lifetime, they had begun to seem old-fashioned. This was to become an age of holy places once again. Jerusalem had been reinstated as a goal of pilgrimage since the reign of Constantine, who built churches on all the sites connected with Jesus. Then it was the turn of local shrines to arise throughout the Mediterranean world, marking the burial places of local martyrs. This age also saw the church's diocesan and metropolitan organization expand in complexity and significance, as bishops assumed responsibilities for local government conceded them by the Constantinian settlement and forged a closer identity with the civic communities in which they served. The famous declaration of the Council of Constantinople (381) that "the Bishop of Constantinople shall have the primacy of honour after the Bishop of Rome, because Constantinople is the new Rome" shows the church conscious of its own geographically distributed structure as a mirror of the prevailing political geography.[13]

2. The Development of a Christian Constitutional Conception

The dominant thesis in the Christian dialectic, nevertheless, was the universalist transcendence of place. This thesis was worked out in a fundamentally functional approach to political rule, which interested itself chiefly in the rationale of government and in the mutual obligations of rulers and subjects. Questions of title, legitimacy, representation, and all that goes to constitute the "politics of identity" assumed a very subordinate place. What didn't govern, wasn't government; what governed effectively and for the common good, *was* government, and should be respected as such. Whether what actually governed ought to govern, and whether what governed here ought to govern there, seemed much less important to discuss.

This prejudice about the proper order of questions is discernible in a generally suspicious attitude to the right of *inheritance*. For those who associate the theo-political tradition with seventeenth-century claims to the "divine right of kings," this may be a surprise, for by that time, divine right was interpreted largely as a right of dynastic inheritance. But this was already a degenerate tradition, in which the idea of an active providence of God that "raised up" rulers had been supplanted by a deist conception of mechanical succession. The spirit of the older tradition is discernible at a critical moment in 751 AD, when Pepin, father of Charlemagne and chancellor to the passive Frankish King Childeric, was authorised by Pope Zacharias to supplant the monarch. The Pope's argument was that "it was better for the man who had power to be called king."[14] Royal dignity was associated with practical responsibilities, and whoever had the responsibilities should have the dignity. Such a view was naturally at home in Papal circles, where the power of God to cast down one king and raise up another seemed to offer some scope for Papal authority, too. But it was congenial also to the Western empire, which retained the tradition of election, and still in the later Middle Ages it could command the support of a royalist such as John Wycliffe, for whom the essential element in the succession of monarchy was not heredity, but the recognition of the successor's moral and intellectual qualities.[15]

However, it was not possible to leave questions about the constitution of government to be settled altogether on an *ad hoc* basis, and we may trace two major propositions on the subject within Christian thought, successive but overlapping:

A. The constitutional proposition that more easily accommodated itself to the universalist thesis was the *divine provision of world empire*. From comparatively early times, apologists had felt that there was something peculiarly opportune in the chronological coincidence of Augustus's founding of the Julian dynasty and the birth of Christ. Even while the Empire was still unfriendly to Christianity, its significance as a sign of the Kingdom of God could be affirmed. Christians valued especially its provision of safe travel throughout the Mediterranean region, essential to the missionary spread of the Christian Gospel. After the Constantinian turn, this association became irresistible to many. "At the same time one universal power, the Roman empire, arose and flourished, while the enduring and implacable hatred of nation against nation was now removed; and as the knowledge of one God and one way of religion and salvation, even the doctrine of Christ, was made known to all mankind; so at the self-same period the entire dominion of the Roman empire being vested in a single sovereign, profound peace reigned throughout the world."[16] Wars of empire could be seen as wars of pacification, bringing benefit to a divided and fractious world, and contrasted with the torment of civil war. To the fifth-century historian Orosius, writing from the personal experience of a refugee, it was the glory of the Christian empire that "the width of the East, the vastness of the North, the great stretches of the South, and the largest and most secure settlements on great islands, all have the same laws and nationality as I, since I come there as a Roman and Christian to Christians and Romans. . . . The state comes to my aid through its laws, religion through its appeal to the conscience, and nature through its claim of universality."[17]

Not all shared this view – Augustine's coolness towards it has often been noticed[18] – yet it survived with amazing vitality even the collapse of the Roman empire in the West, and was strong enough to seed the Carolingian empire in the eighth and ninth centuries, sustaining thereafter at least a loose supra-national macrostructure that prevailed in Europe throughout the Middle Ages. In the fourteenth century, the Western empire achieved an enhanced symbolic importance to theologians as the counterweight to an increasingly criticised Papacy; at that time, the principle of imperial organization received its last most uncompromising defence from the poet Dante Alighieri: "It is quite clear that the task proper to mankind considered as a whole is to fulfil the total capacity of the possible intellect all the time, primarily by speculation and secondarily . . . by action. Now since . . . the individual man becomes perfect in wisdom and prudence through sitting in quietude, it is clear that universal peace is the most excellent means of securing our happiness."[19] In the East, the imperial idea sustained the dwindling remains of the East-Roman order for centuries after anything resembling empire had become a memory, and constructively forged important international links throughout the Orthodox world that far outran the power of Byzantium itself. At the beginning of the Eastern Empire's long last agony, when Constantinople was already surrounded by Turks (ca. 1394), a Patriarch could rebuke a Prince of Moscow for refusing to have the Emperor prayed for at the Eucharist: "My son, you are wrong to say, 'We have a church, but not an emperor.' It is not possible for Christians to have a church and not an emperor. Church and empire are entirely one and interwoven, and cannot be separated."[20]

B. A rival conception of political organization had, however, grown up alongside the imperial ideal in the West, and during the Middle Ages it grew steadily in influence. The concept of a Christendom constituted by independent Christian kingdoms arose first in late patristic times from the conversion to Christianity of the Germanic tribes who had conquered the Western end of the Roman Empire. The Papacy found in kingship the best resource for ordered government, and so was often found supporting royal attempts to curb the diffuse aristocratic power of barons. These kingdoms were encouraged to accomplish the marriage of their native Germanic law with Roman law by the analogical application of Roman law to their separate sovereignties, and to see themselves as incorporated into an international order by the recognition of the international church and its priesthood. Out of this experience, there arose the most sustained attempts to develop Christian thought about political constitution, attempts that, for all their debt to the Aristotelian revival, were firmly based on the medieval experience of kingdoms and the appropriation of imperial law to the new plural model. For the Christian constitutionalists of the fourteenth to sixteenth centuries, the legitimacy of a regime lay in its relation to the society that sustained it. A "perfect society" was one that was so self-sufficient as to be in a position to select a ruler with *summa potestas,* or "sovereign power."

Thus the basis for a Christian conception of legitimacy was laid. Government evokes and reflects a sense of self in the people it defines. The "common good" of a people is a vocation to act *together,* and so requires a sense of common agency, enabled by the structure of the government that serves it. Government is not only provided from above by God, but also from below, as the people realise their common agency in the recognition and authorisation of the government that God has raised up. The *freedom* of a people, then, comes to be a quite different idea from that of the freedom of an individual. It is grounded in the satisfactory relation of political structure to the concerted authorisation of it by the society. But given the complexity of communities and the complexity of their association within a single people, the greatest point of weakness seemed to lie in the capacity and willingness of society to act together. The doctrine of social constitution of political authority was consistent with a strong demand for subordination to it. If it is characteristic of the modern age to assume that threats to freedom are likely to arise from above, by the imposition of unfitting government, it was characteristic of medieval thinkers to assume that they would arise from below, as the concerted action of a society was frustrated by the restless and wayward development of sectional identities. Hence the development in the Renaissance period, prompted especially by conciliar theories of the authority of the Pope, of strong "federal" sensibilities, which required a representative presence from all constituent communities within a body that could act for the whole.

The logic of the federal idea demands reflection upon the question, which lay before the conference, of *secession* from a political society. A breach of fellowship within a political society that deprived the partner, or partners, of the benefits of the fellowship, and even of the status of self-sufficiency that made them a political society in the first place, would seem to constitute a serious wrong. The sole justification of such a measure would have to be the requirements of remedial or punitive justice – that it is the best available way to set right an outstanding wrong. This wrong might, of course, consist in ineffective or incompetent government, and need not be malicious. But there could be no right of independence founded solely on natural forms of identity, whether racial, linguistic, territorial, or religious. There can only be a natural right of *freedom*, which is most highly realised as the freedom *for fellowship* – the right to engage in a common activity in a manner that respects and fulfils the perceived identity of each participating community. *Justified* secession, then, is a confession of failure, a second-best when the conditions for fellowship have collapsed. *Unjustified* secession is a great wrong, which could, in principle, be resisted by war, though it would usually be prudent to hesitate before the rather unpromising endeavour of restoring broken fellowship by force.

3. The Restricted Place of Territory within Christian Constitutional Conceptions

Such a concept of constitutional legitimacy, developed along social rather than territorial lines, offers no clear view of territorial questions. The Christian Germanic kingships defined themselves in relation to a people, not a place: there were kings *of the English* and *of the Franks*, long before there were kings of England and France. Territorial sensibilities may enter more or less deeply into the cultural self-consciousness of a people. In the case of those bounded by decisive geographical features, it may be more; among those with fluid and geographically flexible boundaries it may be less. So that one people comes to perceive itself primarily as an *island* people, while another perceives itself as primarily a *Francophone* people, another as an *Orthodox* people, another as a *Slav* people, and so on. But a sense of social identity is not static, though it is conservative. It is built up out of social tradition, the *ensemble* of engagements of every kind that constitutes the possibility of a people being "at home" with itself, and these engagements evolve with changing circumstances. So once-definitive territorial barriers may come to be porous; modes of transport change the relations in which people stand to their neighbors, and identities evolve accordingly. The over-taking of sea transport by land transport in the last centuries of the era before Christ had enormous implications for the political consciousness of Mediter-ranean populations. (We have yet to imagine the political revolutions about to be precipitated by worldwide communications technology.)

The idea of world-empire appealed to the Christians of the earlier cen-turies because it reflected their belief in the universal rule of God, but the later idea of a plurality of kingdoms also reflected it, though less obviously. It allowed Christians to insist that the vocation of a people is defined not only by the internal relation of society to government but also by its out-ward, international horizons. To be a people is to be *one* people among *many* peoples, and to engage in constructive international activity within a common context. But this is so only as each separate realm does not pre-tend to constitute the final horizon of its members' view. The church, as an international body independent of the civil realms but claiming a common membership with them, constituted the possibility of an international out-look, and mission – that is, the free sharing of God's truth and fellowship across political boundaries under the rule of God in Christ, the highest form of international engagement.

This is why the arguments over the legitimacy of colonial conquest were both closely connected to, and distinct from, arguments about the mission-ary task of Christianity. They were distinct in that Christian mission was not a task that belonged to secular governments, whatever support they might offer for it, nor could it be prosecuted by the methods that secular gov-ernment had at its disposal. Yet they were connected to them, in that only an international and universal truth could ground claims about the proper political relations of discrete peoples and cultures. The preaching of the Kingdom of Heaven provided the basis on which it was possible to con-ceive norms for international engagement. There must be a common law for the interactions of peoples, reflecting the universal rule of God who is the source of all law. In the sixteenth century, this law came to be distin-guished from *ius divinum*, whether "natural" or "revealed," and conceived as *international law*, or *ius gentium*. This was the context in which the some-what disconcerting contention of Vitoria arose, that the native Americans "can no more prohibit Spaniards from trading with them than Christians can prohibit other Christians from doing the same."[21] To live in a commu-nity consciously insulated against foreign contact is to defy the horizon of universal humanity, and such a policy is morally indefensible in that it de-nies the ground on which the moral obligation of respect between peoples rests.

In this general context of thought, the doctrine that *territorial conquest* confers just title to govern was highly suspect among Christian political thinkers. Wycliffe describes it as "a nest of heresy for men of arms, inculcating rapacious and predatory attacks against their weaker brethren."[22] Only victory in a just war could entitle one to confiscate territory, and a just war itself was not about *territory*, however much it involved it, but about a moral reality: wrongs inflicted by one political society upon another, which required punitive, remedial, or even defensive action. In the absence of such international wrong, the tradition as a whole was prepared to entertain the thought that a flagrant refusal of religious or moral duties might justify penal intervention. But what might satisfy either of these conditions was disputed. Grotius, continuing the restrictive line of thought developed by Vitoria, argued that sins against natural religion could be a ground of punitive war, but that failure to convert to Christianity could not be.[23]

Christian thinkers did acknowledge that titles of jurisdiction arising from unjust conquest, although not justified *by* the conquest, might come to be justified subsequently by the tacit consent of the population.[24] There are certain conditions for claiming the so-called "right of prescription" – one of which, of course, has to be serious success on the new ruler's part in governing *justly*. The effective functioning of government, again, is the argument that trumps all arguments. Since government cannot function without serious cooperation from the people, the fact that it has functioned is a demonstration that there has been serious cooperation. In this way, the disapproval of conquest was safeguarded against the nightmare conclusion that the legitimacy of any settled regime might at any time be put in question on the basis of its dubious origins.

4. The Confusion of Property and Jurisdiction

Territorial conquest, then, was disapproved, but it was generally agreed, following Roman Law, that land that nobody owned – *res nullius* – was available for occupation. "The earth is the Lord's and the fulness thereof," the Psalm tells us, and that fullness is put at our disposal.[25] This is not a *political* doctrine originally, but a doctrine of property. Its importation into political doctrine in the period of colonisation reflected a moment of serious confusion in Christian political thinking, from which it was necessary subsequently to find a way out. From about 1300, both in spiritual and secular realms, claims to jurisdictional authority came to be argued on the basis of proprietorial lordship – *dominium* – so that jurisdictional responsibility came to be indistinguishable from territorial property right. The sources of this diversion were, in the first place, the legacy of feudalism; in the second, the presence on the borders of Christendom of the *dar-al-Islam,* which offered a very different way of handling the same Jewish legacy of territorial consciousness; and in the third, the radically anti-proprietorial doctrine of spiritual authority proposed by the Franciscans, a doctrine that assumed the association of secular authority with property in attempting to posit a "perfect" way of life in antithesis to it. In the end, notions of property and jurisdiction were separated again, but the importance of this period lies in the fact that it generated a legacy of territorial doctrine that was often difficult to negotiate within the tradition – for example, the claim of the Papal *plenitudo potestatis.*

The concept that political rule is authorised by *occupation* conflates these two ideas, which ought to be kept apart: the proprietary right, on the one hand, which may be claimed over land that nobody owns, and the right to constitute a government on the other. Even at the narrowly proprietorial level, the doctrine of occupation is something of a will-o'-the-wisp. Genuinely unoccupied territory is hard to find; it may, perhaps, have disappeared altogether. As the sadder features of American colonisation demonstrate, the appearance of *res nullius* may be illusory, since prior occupation may take cultural forms that are not apparent to the eye of the would-be occupier. Wycliffe was among those who thought that the doctrine was, as it stood, insufficient: "the fact that one occupies goods which were previously unowned, does not give one an absolute right to occupy them."²⁶ Claims to occupation must not exceed the capacity of the occupier to make worthy use of what he occupied; for good use was also necessary to establish title. This was in accord with his doctrine of "dominion by grace," which maintained that all right of dominion was subject to its virtuous employment. His notorious readiness to encourage the expropriation of abused property (especially from church prelates) was implied by his strong sense of the moral and social obligations that property carried with it. But it looked more ominous to a later generation, and he was blamed by Vitoria for a doctrine that appeared to countenance the colonists' refusal to respect the right of native Americans. Yet, in truth, when the colonists alleged full exploitation as a ground for seizing underdeveloped land, their economic concept of good use was a pale shadow of Wycliffe's moral one. And not even at his most anticlerical did Wycliffe envisage that powers of expropriation would rest in any other hands than those of government.

The attempt to extend the doctrine of occupation beyond property right to authorise the assertion of a right to govern is doomed to failure. *Res nullius* will not do the work required of it. Either it assigns the right to govern together with the first rights of property, which is often unreasonable: the first British settler may be followed by 5,000 French. Or it assigns the right to govern tautologically to the first government, which is no answer at all. Even in the case that looks most like occupation, where a government takes over a still largely unoccupied territory to regulate settlement there, the right of that government to govern will rest on the fact that it actually *does* govern, and not at all on the simple fact that the land was empty before it did so. So if we want to know who *should* govern a previously ungoverned territory, the answer, "the first settlers," is probably wrong, and the answer, "the first government," is stupidly uncommunicative. Answers to such questions can only be found where the earlier centuries of Christendom found them: in the complex and contextual search for the government God has "raised up." The *right* government is the *effective* government – that is to say, the government that can command effective administrative and judicial capabilities and can maintain an effective political relation to the community. The search for a simple proprietorial formula is a mistake. Good government of an untamed territory requires access and communications: proximity will be a factor in providing them. It requires investment: wealth will be a significant consideration. It requires a political relation to the growing community: linguistic and cultural affinity must play a part. It requires judicial competence and responsibility: a record of good institutions is important. It requires recognition by the community: questions of limited or total self-government are bound to arise sooner or later. Perhaps the best account that can be given of such institutions as Crown Land in Canada, where a government asserts sovereignty over unpossessed territory in order to avoid the evils of haphazard settlement, is that a new and unformed community will require a placeholder administration, and the doctrine of first occupation may point, suggestively, though not conclusively, to where such an administration may be found.

Transfer of territory by sale or purchase is another problematic idea arising from the confusion of jurisdiction and property. In principle, the land on which a community dwells is not open to being transferred as a commodity, since it is a constitutive part of the community's identity, and the community does not have "ownership" of it. There are, however, a number of possibly legitimate proceedings that may be *misdescribed* as "sale" of territory. One is a decision to *withdraw from occupation*, thereby leaving it clear for new immigrants. Another is a decision to *cede jurisdiction* over a territory to a neighboring political community or to the inhabitants. The conditions on which such steps as these may be rightly taken, and especially whether they require the agreement of the local communities, have been a matter for serious discussion in the case of Northern Ireland. It would be, perhaps, not out of keeping with the Christian tradition to suggest that they might be done without the agreement of the local communities if that were justified as a *punitive* measure – if, for example, those communities had been rebellious and ungovernable. But both these acts are, by their very nature, unilateral. The freedom of a successor state to assume jurisdiction would be founded not on an act of sale but on the fact that it was in a position to offer a community the governance it needed. And so it would seem to be improper for the successor state to pay directly for the transaction. Yet one could imagine how such a unilateral act might be undertaken within the context of a wider bilateral treaty, which ensured the goodwill of the ceding state in recognizing the successor state and, in some other form, also ensured the goodwill of the successor state to the ceding state. There would always, no doubt, be some who were ready to *call* such an agreement a sale!

Notes to Chapter 7

1. Jacques Maritain, *Man and the State* (Chicago: University of Chicago Press, 1951), 207.
2. Deut. 32:8f.
3. Amos 9:7
4. Deut. 2:20–3.
5. Jer. 46–51.
6. Psa. 120:6.
7. Dan. 6:10.
8. *Epistula ad Diognetum* 5, tr. (Kirsopp Lake: Loeb Classical Library, 1913) [*IG*,12]. This and subsequent quotations from historical Christian political sources are quoted from Oliver O'Donovan and Joan Lockwood O'Donovan, eds., *From Irenaeus to Grotius: a sourcebook of Christian political thought* (Grand Rapids: Ecrdmans, 1999). (hereafter abbreviated: *IG*)
9. John 4:21, 24.
10. Romans 13:1–5.
11. *De ordine* 2.6.19; *De quantitate animae* 30.61.
12. *De sermone Domini in monte* 1.2.4.
13. *Concilium Constantinopolitanum* canon 3. Quoted from J. Stevenson, ed., *Creeds Councils and Controversies* (London: SPCK, 1966), 148.
14. Quoted from Brian Tierney, ed., *The Crisis of Church and State 1050–1300*, (Toronto: University of Toronto Press, 1988) 20.
15. *De civili dominio* 1.30 [*IG*, 508].
16. Eusebius, *Laus Constantini* (Speech at the Dedication of Holy Sepulchre Church) 16 [*IG*, 58].
17. Orosius, *Historia contra Pagaonos* 5.2, trans. I.G. Raymond (New York: Columbia Press, 1936), [*IG*, 167].
18. See especially R.A. Markus, *Saeculum: history and society in the theology of St. Augustine* (Cambridge: Cambridge University Press, 1970), 1–21.
19. *De monarchia* 1.4, trans. D. Nicholl and C. Hardie (London, 1954), [*IG*, 415].
20. Patriarch Antonios IV, *Epistula* 447 [*IG*, 516].
21. *De Indis* 3.1.2, trans. Jeremy Lawrance, ed., Anthony Pagden, *Vitoria: Political Writings* (Cambridge: Cambridge University Press, 1991), [*IG*, 627].
22. *De civili dominio* 1.21 [*IG*, 505].
23. *De iure belli ac pacis* 2.20.44–51.
24. Thomas, *Commentary on the Sentences* 2.44.2 [*IG*, 329].
25. Psa. 24:1.
26. *De civili dominio* 1.21, [*IG*, 506].

PART 4

THE NATURAL LAW TRADITION

8

The Making and Unmaking of Boundaries from the Natural Law Perspective

Richard Tuck

1. The Ancient Background

Europeans have never lived in ignorance of other cultures. The clash of radically different moral attitudes was already a familiar theme by the time of Herodotus, whose *History* is in effect an encyclopedia of cultural difference. And although by the beginning of our era, the ancient cultural variety of the Mediterranean had been somewhat reduced to a kind of vaguely Hellenized uniformity, the Romans were constantly engaged in trade and warfare with exotic peoples beyond the empire's boundaries – extending even to the Chinese, with whom there were fitful contacts including (allegedly) an embassy from Marcus Aurelius to the Emperor. The spread of early Christianity from its origins in the Hellenised Roman Empire out across the Old World illustrates the range and complexity of these contacts: by the time Islam appeared on the scene, Christian sects were to be found spread out along the trade routes of Central Asia and even into China itself (where the presence of Nestorian monks later astonished – so it was claimed – Marco Polo); throughout the Parthian Empire (which was the base of the Nestorian Church, founded in deliberate rivalry to the Church of the Romans); in Northern India; in East Africa; and in the wilds of Northern and Central Europe.

The disappearance of imperial rule in Western Europe did not significantly diminish the extent to which cultured Europeans were exposed to these differences: the clash of barbarian and Christian and the clash of Christian and Moslem constantly brought them home, while from the tenth century onwards, European sailors were beginning to push far beyond the boundaries even of the Roman Empire – Northern Europeans were vaguely aware of the North American continent and its savage inhabitants from the time of the Greenland settlement by the Norsemen at the end of the tenth century, a settlement that (it is clear) had frequent contacts with the inhabitants of Labrador and Newfoundland, and that may have lasted continuously until after Columbus had set foot among the Caribbean islands.

Against this background, the issue of how and where to draw boundaries was constantly raised – and most spectacularly answered, of course, by the Roman *limites* built of stone or turf in North Africa, Germany, and Britain, and by their Dark Age equivalents such as the Devil's Dyke and Offa's Dyke in England. It was Roman rather than Greek practices and attitudes, in this area as in so many others, that were foundational for the Middle Ages and the Renaissance; the Greek cities possessed a complex set of rules and principles governing their own relationships, but, as is well known, Greek theorists of the pre-Alexander period had great difficulty in treating non-Greeks as full participants in these relationships, and in developing any comprehensive theory of what we would now call international relations. In the case of Rome, the attitude of the lawyers and moral philosophers has often been misunderstood: there are various rather casual references to the Roman Emperor as *dominus mundi*, but there is no evidence that any pagan Romans genuinely thought of their Emperor or their City as ruler of the world in a literal sense. As Paul Veyne pointed out, when Romans talked about Rome as *dominus orbis terrarum*, what they characteristically meant was that its independence was to be secured by – if necessary – attacking any other state, rather than that Rome could claim to *govern* all known states – experience with Parthia, let alone India or China, would quickly disabuse them of that idea.[1] Only one text in the *Digest* refers to the lordship of the world, and it does not suggest that it was meant very seriously: it is the famous text on the law of the sea (14.2.9), a passage taken from the writings of Volusius Maecianus on the Rhodian sea law (the set of conventions that Mediterranean sailors used to sort out disputes over wrecks, and so on), which records the answer of the Emperor Antoninus to the petition of a shipwrecked sailor:

"I am master of the world (*kosmos*), but the law of the sea must be judged by the sea law of the Rhodians when our own law does not conflict with it." Augustus, now deified, decided likewise.[2]

The text makes a rather broken-backed case for world sovereignty and for imperial rights over the world's oceans – presumably, the seaman had described Antoninus in the usual fulsome terms as "master of the world," hoping to get round the Rhodian laws, and the Emperor was busy disavowing any practical legal consequences to the title. Since Antoninus was indeed master of the entire Mediterranean, it was reasonable for him to assert rights that were co-extensive with the scope of the Rhodian sea laws; but we have no idea at all about how the Romans handled disputes between sailors in (say) the Indian Ocean. It is, however, worth noting (for its later significance) that the Romans did not believe that the impossibility of claiming private property in the sea – something that is repeatedly stressed in the *Digest* – was incompatible with the existence of political jurisdiction over it.

Apart from this passage, the Roman view of international relations seems on the whole to have been one of parity between independent states. This comes out most clearly in the legal theory of *postliminium*, the principle that Roman citizens taken as prisoners by an enemy were slaves in the eyes of Roman law also, until they returned to Roman jurisdiction. For example, the Roman jurist Pomponius remarked in a passage that was much cited in the Renaissance that *postliminium* could operate in peace as well as in war:

for if we have neither friendship nor *hospitium* with a particular people, nor a treaty made for the purpose of friendship, they are not precisely [*quidem*] enemies, but that which passes from us into their hands becomes their property, and a freeman of ours who is captured by them becomes their slave, and similarly if anything of theirs passes into our hands . . . [3]

This was a startling vision of an international order in which any nations who had not made explicit treaties with one another were entitled to enslave one another's citizens and in which the Romans were involved in a struggle for power with morally equal rivals. But such a vision was often expressed by Roman historians when they spoke sympathetically of the patriotic struggles of their own enemies – thus Caesar could allow that his Gallic opponents were fighting for liberty, "for which all men naturally strive" (*De Bello Gallico* 3.10.3), and Sallust could voice persuasively the anti-Roman sentiments of Mithridates, King of Pontus.[4] The countervailing idea – that the Roman Empire was established to rule morally inferior peoples – was rather seldom voiced; it is found in a fragment of Cicero's *De Republica*, but we do not fully understand its context within the dialogue. Much more popular seems to have been the view of Plutarch, that the Empire was "the anchor for a floating world."

Later European powers frequently made a distinction, as we shall see, between their equal dealings with developed or civilized states and their unequal dealings with primitive (characteristically, non-agrarian) peoples; in particular, it was often assumed that Europeans could settle and farm on the lands that aboriginal peoples used for hunting. The issue of the movement of peoples and their settlement was a familiar one in the ancient world, and of course came to be a critical matter in the last years of the Empire in the West; but there was surprisingly little theoretical discussion of it. Tacitus's *Annals* contain a striking dialogue on the subject, of great importance to Renaissance writers, in which the Ansibarii (a people displaced by their enemies in the Low Countries and seeking entry into the Empire) are represented as arguing that

As the Gods have Heaven, so the Earth was given to Mankind, and what is possessed by none, belongs to every one. And then looking up to the Sun and Stars as if present, and within hearing, they asked them, whether they could bear to look on those uninhabited lands, and whether they would not rather pour in the Sea upon those who hindered other to settle on them.[5]

According to Tacitus, the Roman legate to whom this argument was addressed "was impressed. But he replied that men must obey their betters, that the gods they invoked had empowered the Romans to decide what to give and take away and to tolerate no judges but themselves." In other words, the Romans were sovereign even over unoccupied land within their domains – just as, in Roman private law, all land was presumed to have an owner, and could not be occupied by another party against his express wishes (though there were, of course, rules about what could happen if an owner failed to express a wish). It is true that some sort of minimal requirement upon us to share our goods with the needy was widely recognized: Cicero said in the *De Officiis* that the principles of *omnibus inter omnes societas* means that we should "bestow even upon a stranger what it costs us nothing to give," while in the same work he observed that "they do wrong who would debar foreigners from enjoying the advantages of their city and would exclude them from its borders... to debar foreigners from enjoying the advantages of the city is altogether inhuman" (*De Officiis* III.xi.47). Similarly, Plutarch records a discussion at a Roman dinner table (appropriately enough) about the obligation to allow others to share our unwanted food.[6] Many ancient cities allowed settlers to have squatters' rights on public land, a practice eloquently defended by Dio Chrysostom, the Greek orator who was a contemporary of Tacitus, in his Seventh or "Euboean" Discourse[7]; but even Dio did not say clearly that waste land could simply be taken by those who need it.

We can summarize the Roman view (albeit roughly) as one that recognized distinct boundaries between what were in effect sovereign states, and that did not see any part of the world's surface, including the high seas, as in principle outside the control of the states. Rome enjoyed a practical hegemony in this world, but all states would fight to protect their liberty, if necessary by dominating their neighbors; Rome had simply enjoyed the good fortune that it had won its battles and secured its liberty in a decisive fashion. This degree of respect for the general principle of sovereignty was thus compatible with a high degree of aggression in practice, since pre-emptive strikes in defence of the state's freedom were generally acknowledged as legitimate: as Cato is recorded as saying about the destruction of Carthage, "the Carthaginians are our enemies already; for whoever is directing all his preparations against me, so that he may make war on me at the time of his own choice, is already my enemy, even if he is not yet taking armed action."[8]

2. The Relationships of Post-Roman Kingdoms: Union, Conquest, and Secession

Something like the Roman view, it must be said (contrary to the assertions of many historians), persisted throughout the rest of European history. The Roman idea of what constituted an independent *respublica* was not very precise, but it is clear that it was essentially a political entity with its own law-making power and with some notion of common citizenship: it was not simply the private property of an individual or group of individuals who could dispose of it *ad libitum*. Even under the Principate, as is well known, Rome remained technically a republic with elected Emperors; the repudiation of monarchy, and with it overt dynastic politics, was so basic to Rome's self-esteem that (at least in the Western Empire), republicanism was never formally abandoned. Even after the fall of Rome, however, genuine dynasticism (of the sort that is often casually contrasted with "modern" nationalist politics) is very hard to find. Dark Age kings were primarily kings of peoples not territories, and it was not unknown for quite complicated arrangements to be made in which each ethnic or linguistic group in a single territory would look to its own ruler and set of laws (classic cases are provided by the various treaties agreed on by the Viking kings and the rulers of their enemies in North-West Europe).

But as territoriality became more important, and (for example) the *Rex Anglorum* became the *Rex Angliae*,[9] it was still not the case that the kingdoms were seen as the straightforward property of their rulers. We can see this most clearly in the extremely careful arrangements that were made whenever the vagaries of royal succession led to the union of independent kingdoms. A particularly good early example again comes from the island of Britain, where these issues were constantly faced: when the marriage was arranged between the young Queen of Scots and the eldest son of the King of England in 1290, with a view to the union of the two crowns, the commissioners at the treaty conference agreed that after the union, Scotland would remain "separate, distinct and sovereign" [*separatum, et divisum, et liberum in se*] without subjection to the Kingdom of England; the Scottish Church would remain independent (in the sense that no one would be obliged to leave the kingdom of Scotland for his election), no one could be forced to plead outside Scotland, there would be a separate Royal Seal and Chancery, and Parliaments had to be held in Scotland to deal with anything that concerned that kingdom.[10] The arrangement envisaged in 1290 was substantially the same as the one forced on James VI by his English Parliament after the successful Union of the Crowns in 1603, in a clear demonstration of resistance to fully dynastic politics; full union, as we all know, had to wait until 1707 (though even then many important areas of public life were left separate). A similar example of repeated resistance to dynastic union comes from the other famous case of national union in the late Middle Ages, the Polish-Lithuanian union, which began as a dynastic union in 1401, and which, despite various attempts to weld the two countries into (as one proposal put it) "one nation, one people, one brotherhood and a common council," did not become a full union (that is, with, in particular, a common Sejm, or parliament) until the Union of Lublin in 1569.[11]

The same instinct to maintain separateness was also manifested even in the aftermath of wholesale conquest. The full annexation of another kingdom by conquest, without any more or less plausible claim to inherit, was in fact rather rare among the rulers of Christian Europe, though all of them were prepared to attack and conquer infidels (see Section 3); the Conquest of England in 1066 was an unusual event, and even there William both had a plausible title to the throne (indeed, more plausible than the man he defeated) and undertook to maintain the laws and customs of England separate from those of Normandy. On his death, Normandy and England were again separated under different rulers, with his eldest son (interestingly) inheriting Normandy but not England (though the king of England conquered Normandy in 1106, in a striking, and longer-lasting, reversal of 1066). This caution about full annexation was all the more significant given that it was universally believed in the Middle Ages and Early Modern period that conquest in a just war gave the conqueror full power to reconstruct the conquered territory as he saw fit.

Where independent states were linked together in these ways, they could also dissolve the unions and secede if the agreements came to be seen as violated; the most striking case of this in Early Modern times was the secession of Sweden from the Union of Kalmar, the dynastic union between Sweden, Denmark, and Norway effected in 1397, which was destroyed by the Swedish rebellion under Gustavus Vasa in 1525. It does not seem that Medieval or Early Modern theorists were particularly puzzled by these issues: on the whole, they took for granted something like national identity manifested especially through a common set of laws and a distinct representative body, and treated the nation identified in this way as a genuine agent in international affairs. The nations created in the obscure movements of peoples in the Dark Ages were in fact astonishingly resilient: testimony to this is, on the one hand, the marked unwillingness of Medieval or Early Modern authorities to accord the title of King to any ruler other than the heir to one of the Dark Age monarchies (the only new kingdoms constituted in Europe between c. 950 and 1700 were Portugal and the Kingdom of Sicily),[12] and, on the other hand, the persistence of the ancient titles and separate jurisdictions even through the vicissitudes of union and conquest.

3. Was There a World Ruler?

Thus the principal issues under debate in this period did not include the question of whether the ancient kingdoms were genuinely separate entities in their dealings with each other; that was largely a settled issue until the French Revolution. Instead, two questions divided theorists in what one might think of as the period of "natural law" thinking (that is, the long period, running from the fall of Rome until the eighteenth century, in which fundamental ethical issues tended to be couched in the language of natural law, though with many different accounts of what those "laws" were). They were, first, the question of whether above the ancient kingdoms was some sort of power that could claim a kind of *world* domination, and, second, the related but distinct question of whether non-agricultural peoples possessed full rights against agriculturalists. The former question was faced first, for the obvious reason that Europe had little to do with any non-agricultural peoples until the fifteenth century, and I shall accordingly deal with it first.

In the early Middle Ages, on the whole, the original Roman view persisted, that there was (except in some hyperbolic sense) no world ruler. A.J. Carlyle wisely observed in his history of political thought that the Carolingians claimed to be lords of "Europe" or of the *populus Christiana*, but not of any wider entity. Augustine, moreover, did not think of the Roman Empire as *global*, though he did of course believe in its world-historical significance. Even after the *Digest* was read again, and the Maecianus quotation came to be known, early glossators such as Accursius tended to treat the passage as possessing little significance. What seems to have marked a major change was the activity of the "Decretists" – the commentators on Gratian's *Decretum*, the principal early codification of canon law.[13] By the end of the twelfth century, canonists could freely say (in the words of Alanus Anglicus) that "the ancient law of nations held that there should be only one emperor in the world" and that "infidel rulers" have no right to the sword.[14] This idea gathered pace among the canonists, and became enshrined in the mid-thirteenth-century *Decretals*, the supplement to the *Decretum*. There, the gloss to a Papal Bull dealing with the "translation" of the Empire to the Germans said expressly that *regnum mundi* was translated, and that the emperor was *princeps mundi et dominus* (I VI 34, *Venerabilem*).

The reason why it was the canonists rather than the civilians who led the way was of course that unlike the Roman writers and lawyers, they already possessed a coherent account of world rule, in the form of the idea that the Pope was "Vicar of Christ" with rights of some kind over all the peoples of the Earth. The origins of this idea lay in the ninth century, when Popes such as Nicholas I could say that they were set up as princes over the whole earth,[15] and it was clearly a more plausible view than the belief that the Roman Emperor had been lord of all the world: the Emperor's claims were straighforwardly refuted by the facts of geopolitics, but the Pope's claims belonged to a different scheme of things and could not be refuted (in principle) by the existence of any number of independent principalities. Since the canonists also believed that imperial power had been conferred on the Christian Emperors by the Pope, it simply followed for them that the Emperors must possess *dominium mundi* by virtue of certain fundamental features of Christianity.

Throughout the late Middle Ages, canonists pursued these two ideas: that the Pope was in some sense lord of the world, and that he had transferred some of his powers to an Emperor who also had a global responsibility. In practice, what one might term the reserved rights of the Papacy came to be of greater significance, as Emperors proved (for example), to be broken reeds over such matters as Crusades; it came to be commonly held that the Pope could exercise his global jurisdiction by calling on any secular rulers to implement his decisions. As for the character of Papal jurisdiction over infidels (for of course his jurisdiction over Christians was much less problematic), the standard view was that put forward by Sinibaldo Fieschi, later Pope Innocent IV, in the mid-thirteenth century. Infidels were not *as such* enemies of the Christian world, nor deserving of punishment; indeed, physical punishment for unbelief violated one of the prime dogmas of Christianity, that unbelievers should not be converted by force. But the Pope as Christ's vicar had a general responsibility for ensuring that all men obeyed God's laws, and he could therefore punish infidels, as well as Christians, for breaking them. It was not part of God's law in this sense that one should be a Christian – there was no natural obligation on men to follow the gospel. But it was part of God's law (according to Innocent) not to commit sodomy or idolatry, since both these sins could be recognized as such even by natural men, and infidels could be punished by Christian arms, at the behest of the Pope, for sins of this kind.

They could also be punished for denying access by Christian missionaries to their territory: this was another aspect of their obligation to obey God's law, since it was a general requirement on men at least to listen to the truth. Unlike many later writers, Innocent actually faced up to the question of whether infidels could similarly send missionaries into Christian lands, and replied stiffly that they could not, "because they are in error and we are on the righteous path." Papal intervention to protect Christians tyrannized by infidels was also legitimate, on the same grounds as intervention by the Papacy in the affairs of any kingdom to protect its subjects was justified.[16] Though Innocent's view was undoubtedly the most authoritative within the Church, there was a more radical tradition, represented particularly by his pupil Henry of Segusio ("Hostiensis"), which held that infidels were by definition sinners who had forfeited any right to hold property or political office, and who could therefore in principle legitimately be governed directly by Christian rulers under the general direction of the Pope.[17] In the fourteenth century, this view came to be smeared with heresy, through its similarity to the heretical doctrine that *dominium* rested on grace, and the Innocentian view survived as the orthodox Papalist theory. It is accordingly found in writers such as Augustinus Triumphus, who argued that all pagans can be punished by the Pope for breach of any law that they themselves accept "and which they profess to observe," such as (he alleged) the law of nature. To meet the objection that the Pope does not in fact possess jurisdiction over pagans, Augustinus replied that "Pagans are not subject to the Pope *de facto*, but they are *de iure*, since *de iure* no rational creature can remove itself from his dominion, any more than from the dominion of God."[18] The same argument is still found in a standard Late-Medieval textbook, which was to be very influential throughout the sixteenth century, Sylvestro Mazzolini's *Summa Summarum.*[19]

Some civil lawyers were ready to incorporate the canonists' views into their own work; thus, Frederick II proclaimed that he was *dominus mundi* in an imperial constitution that became incorporated into the *Corpus Juris Civilis.* Commenting on this, and on *Digest* 14.2.9, Bartolus of Sassoferrato in the fourteenth century produced an influential formulation. Citing the same array of Biblical texts that the canonists had used, Bartolus accepted the notion that "after Christ all *imperium* was in Christ and his Vicar; and was transferred by the Pope onto the secular prince" with the result that the Emperor became *dominus mundi*[20]; indeed, "he who says the Emperor is not lord and monarch of the whole world is a heretic."[21] But he recognized the force of the argument that there are many peoples who have never accepted the rights of the Emperor, and who might even believe (as in the case of the "Grand Cham" of the Tartars) that it is their ruler who is in fact dominus mundi.[22] His solution was to employ the same distinction as Augustinus: infidels are subject to the Emperor *de iure* but not *de facto*.

Bartolus's view remained common among civilans who worked with and were sympathetic to canonists and theologians, but it came under fire from Renaissance jurists as they recovered the original Roman ideas. Andrea Alciato, the quintessential humanist jurist, expressed scorn for the idea of the *Doctores* that the whole world is subject to the Emperor *de iure*.

I do not agree with this, partly because there are many areas which do not obey the Romans, such as Scythia and Sarmatia, and all the East beyond the Euphrates ... And although some Emperors called themselves lords of the world, either that should be taken as hyperbole, or their remarks should be discounted, as being in their own interests.[23]

Alciato also dissented from the claim that the Pope could exercise jurisdiction over infidels, at least where their conduct had no effect on Christians; in doing so, he said (interestingly), he was lining up with most of the other *moderni*.[24]

Despite this, the first voyagers to the New World, who were Alciato's contemporaries, began by using medieval accounts of world *dominium* to justify their activities. Portuguese expansion in Africa and the Atlantic islands was usually accompanied by Papal Bulls legitimating the conquest of infidels in those territories along Innocentian lines, and Pope Alexander VI in 1493 issued a famous set of Bulls making the same point about Portuguese and Castilian conquests in the New World, and calling on the governments to settle a demarcation line between them (duly accomplished in the Treaty of Tordesillas the following year).[25] Though it is sometimes said that the Pope merely wished to act as an arbitrator, the text of the Bulls strongly suggests that Alexander's lawyers believed he had the right to allocate unknown lands. When the Spanish government in the first years of the new century consulted experts about the legitimacy of its conquest, it too received strong advice that Papal authority entitled Christian rulers to occupy the lands of infidels. Its advisers stressed in particular both the need to protect missionaries, and the sins of the Indians against natural law in matters of sexual morality, as justifications for Papal intervention.[26] By the 1520s, however, this was far less commonly claimed – partly because it no longer fitted Spanish policy, but partly because the views of the *moderni* had won out among the jurists who provided professional advice to the government.

The victory of the *moderni* was also no doubt the result of the fact that the most powerful group of theologians in Spain belonged to a tradition that had always been sceptical of the canonists' ideas in this area (and indeed in most areas). This was the tradition of the Dominicans, including most importantly Thomas Aquinas, who disagreed profoundly with any theory of world authority, preferring instead a vision of a world of independent and equal political communities. A powerful basis for this view was of course Aristotle's account of the proper *polis* as a relatively small unit: no Aristotelian could easily accept the idea of a world state, whether it was couched in the language of Papalism or in that of humanism (the *societas* or *respublica humana*). Aquinas himself was somewhat equivocal on the subject of infidel societies: in the *Secunda Secundae* of the *Summa*, he wrote:

Dominion or authority [*dŏminium vel praelatio*] ... is an institution of human law, whereas the distinction between the faithful and infidels is by divine law. Now divine law, which is from grace, does not do away with human law, which is from natural reason. Consequently the distinction between the faithful and infidels, considered in itself, does not cancel the dominion or authority of infidels over the faithful. However this right can be justly taken away by the sentence or ordinance of the Church which has the authority of God, for infidels by their infidelity deserve to forfeit power over the faithful.[27]

This referred only to the special case of infidels ruling over Christians; he later seemed to extend the discussion, though again in an equivocal fashion, when he remarked:

one who sins by infidelity can be sentenced to deprivation of his dominion, as also on occasion for other faults. The Church, however, is not competent to penalize unbelief in those who have never received the faith, according to St Paul's disclaimer [1 *Corinthians* 5.12]. Yet she can sentence to punishment the unbelief of those who received the faith ... [28]

But many of Aquinas's Dominican followers were more outspoken. John of Paris, for example, in his famous defence of French kingship against Boniface VIII, *De Potestate Regia et Papali* of 1302–3, argued that

there can be different ways of living and different kinds of state conforming to differences in climate, language, and the conditions of men, with what is is suitable for one nation not so for another ... Accordingly, the Philosopher shows in the *Politics* that development of individual states and kingdoms is natural, although that of an empire or [universal] monarchy is not.[29]

The fact that this was in many ways a *Dominican* rather than purely a *Thomist* tradition is illustrated by the fact that Durandus of San Porciano, who was the most anti-Thomist of the early Dominicans, agreed with this view, and applied it to infidel societies; he wrote that infidel rulers not harassing Christian subjects could not be deprived of their *dominium*, and that "pagans and infidels are outside the church and we have no right to judge them."[30]

By the time of the discovery of the New World, this view was commonplace among Dominicans: thus, Cajetan, the most authoritative Dominican writer of the late fifteenth century, who was also a loyal Thomist, declared firmly:

Some infidels do not fall under the temporal jurisdiction of Christian princes either in law or in fact (*nec de iure nec de facto*). Take as an example the case of pagans who were never subjects of the Roman Empire, and who dwell in lands where the term "Christian" was never heard. For surely the rulers of such persons are legitimate rulers, despite the fact that they are infidels and regardless of whether the government in question is a monarchical régime or a commonwealth (*politico regimine*); nor are they to be deprived of dominion over their own peoples on the ground of lack of faith . . . No king, no emperor, not even the Church of Rome, is empowered to undertake war against them for the purpose of seizing their lands or reducing them to temporal subjection. Such an attempt would be based upon no just cause of war . . . Thus I do not read in the Old Testament, in connection with the occasions on which it was necessary to seize possession by armed force, that war was ever declared against any nation of infidels on the ground that the latter did not profess the true faith. I find, instead, that the reason for such declarations of war was the unwillingness of the infidels to concede the right of passage, or the fact that they had attacked the faithful (as the Midianites did, for example), or a desire on the part of the believers to recover their own property . . . Men of integrity ought to be sent as preachers to these infidels, in order that unbelievers may be induced by teaching and by example to seek God; but men ought not to be sent with the purpose of crushing, despoiling and tempting unbelievers, bringing them into subjection, and making them twofold more the children of hell.[31]

The Dominicans of early sixteenth-century Spain continued this attack on their countrymen's American adventure. The most radical of them, Domingo de Soto, devoted a section of his unpublished *Relectio De Dominio* of 1534–35 to the question of "the temporal dominion of Christ and the Pope, and the right by which the Spaniards maintain an overseas empire." He concluded that the Pope had no kind of temporal authority, direct or indirect, over the world.

So by what right do we maintain the overseas empire which has recently been discovered? To speak truly, I do not know. In the Gospel we find: "Go ye into all the world, and preach the Gospel to every creature" (Mark 16[:15]); this gives us a right to preach everywhere in the world, and, as a consequence, we have been given a right to defend ourselves against anyone who prevents us from preaching. Therefore if we were in danger, we could defend ourselves from them at their expence; but I do not see that we have any right beyond this to take their goods or subject them to our rule... [The Lord said in Luke 9:5] "whosoever will not receive you, when ye go out of that city, shake off the very dust from your feet for a testimony against them". He did not say that we were to preach to an unwilling audience, but that we should go and leave vengeance to God. I do not say this to condemn everything that has taken place with those islanders; for God's judgements have many depths, and God perhaps wishes those people to be converted in ways unknown to us. Let this be enough for the present on these topics.[32]

De Soto's doubts about the Spanish conquest of the Americas formed the basis of the well-known discussions of the issue by his Dominican colleague Francisco de Vitoria, in his *relectiones* on dietary law (1538) and the Indies (1539), though Vitoria was characteristically more guarded in his condemnation[33]; De Soto's doubts also closely resemble the criticisms of the conquest voiced by Las Casas.

4. The Rights of Non-Agricultural Peoples

While both Thomist and humanists by the middle of the sixteenth century had thus come to the conclusion that there was no Christian *dominium mundi*, it remained an open question whether in its place the world was exhaustively divided among independent and jurisdictionally equal states. As we have just seen, the Thomist answer had always been that it was, and they applied this to the New World as much as to the Old; but among humanists, it came gradually to be thought that the New World was a special case because the rulers of the American aborigines did not possess territorial rights. By the seventeenth century, a familiar view had taken hold of mainstream liberal writers such as Locke to the effect that the land of North America was jurisdictionally like the high seas: both were common to all humans (Locke described the oceans as "the last great common of mankind"), and men roamed over both of them without possessing them. Only settled agriculture could establish property rights in a territory, and only territory with property rights could come under the full control of a state. Political relationships between the American kings and their subjects were like the relationship between an admiral at sea and the vessels under his command: they were purely personal, and did not extend to the medium over which the people concerned were voyaging. It might be supposed that this theory took a non-controversial view of the sea and controversially applied it to the land, but in fact each part of the theory was controversial, and neither was at all widely accepted until the end of the sixteenth century.

As far as the right to settle on uncultivated land against the wishes of a local ruler was concerned, the first clear statement comes, oddly enough, in More's *Utopia*.

If the population throughout the entire island exceeds the quota, they enrol citizens out of every city and plant a colony under their own laws on the mainland near them, wherever the natives have plenty of unoccupied and uncultivated land. Those natives who want to live with the Utopians are taken in. When such a merger occurs the two peoples gradually and easily blend together, sharing the same way of life and customs, much to the advantage of both. For by their policies the Utopians make the land yield an abundance for all, though previously it had seemed too barren and paltry even to support the natives. But those who refuse to live under their laws the Utopians drive out of the land they claim for themselves; and on those who resist them, they declare war. The Utopians say it's perfectly justifiable to make war on people who leave their land idle and waste yet forbid the use and possession of it to others who, by the law of nature, ought to be supported from it.[34]

The Utopians' view is close in its expression to that of the Ansibarii in Tacitus, and it was the Tacitus passage that was picked up by the next influential statement of the right to settle, in Alberico Gentili's *De Iure Belli* of 1588. Gentili was one of the greatest humanist jurists of his generation, as well as being a Protestant exile in England who was devoted to the anti-Spanish crusade of Protestant Europe at the end of the century; he was also an admirer of More. Quoting the Ansibarii, he continued:

True indeed, "God did not create the world to be empty". And therefore the seizure of vacant places is regarded as a law of nature ... And even though such lands belong to the sovereign of that territory, ... yet because of that law of nature which abhors a vacuum, they will fall to the lot of those who take them, though the sovereign will retain jurisdiction over them ... Are there today no unoccupied lands on the earth? Is it not, pray, being reduced more and more to the wilderness of primeval times? What is Greece today, and the whole of Turkey? What is Africa? What of Spain? It is the most populous country of all; yet under the rule of Spain is not almost all of the New World unoccupied? ... [35]

Gentili had some influence on the early English colonial enterprise, and already by 1609 this view was being utilized as a defence of the occupation of Virginia:

Some affirme, and it is likely to be true, that these Savages have no particular pro-prietie in any part or parcell of that Countrey, but only a general residencie there, as wild beasts have in the forest, for they range and wander up and downe the Countrey, without any law or government, being led only by their own lusts and sensualitie, there is not *meum et tuum* amongst them: so that if the whole lande should bee taken from them, there is not a man that can complaine of any particular wrong done unto him.[36]

In the next burst of English colonization, in the 1620s, the same was regularly said – for instance by John Donne in 1622:

if the inhabitants doe not in some measure fill the Land, so as the Land may bring foorth her increase for the use of men: for as a man doth not become proprietary of the Sea, because he hath two or three Boats fishing in it, so neither does a man become Lord of a maine Continent, because hee hath two or three Cottages in the Skirts thereof... [37]

By the 1630s it was taken for granted that this was the key argument for the occupation of North America by the English, as when it featured as the principal point in debate in the first and most important controversy within the colonies about the legitimacy of the settlements – that between John Cotton and Roger Williams in Massachussets during the mid1630s. This was in effect the English equivalent of the debate between Las Casas and Sepulveda. In it, Williams insisted that the settlers could have no title to their lands by royal grant, since the country "belonged to the native Indians."

It was answered to him, first, That it was neither the Kings intendement, nor the English Planters to take possession of the Countrey by murther of the Natives, or by robbery: but either to take possession of the voyd places of the Countrey by the Law of Nature, (for *Vacuum Domicilium cedit occupanti*) or if we tooke any Lands from the Natives, it was by way of purchase, and free consent.[38]

In reply, Williams made an extremely apposite and difficult point.

This answer did not satisfie Mr. Williams, who pleaded, the Natives, though they did not, nor could subdue the Countrey, (but left it *vacuum Domicilium*) yet they hunted all the Countrey over, and for the expedition of their hunting voyages, they burnt up all the underwoods in the Countrey, once or twice a yeare, and therefore as Noble men in England possessed great Parkes, and the King, great Forrests in England onely for their game, and no man might lawfully invade their Propriety: So might the Natives challenge the like Propriety of the Countrey here.[39]

The similarity between the parks of England and the landscape of parts of North America was indeed often remarked upon by the first settlers.

Cotton's reply was unavoidably rather feeble, making such observations as that the King and nobility in England "employed their Parkes, and Forrests, not for hunting onely, but for Timber, and for the nourishment of tame beasts, as well as wild, and also for habitation to sundry Tenants." The only passage in it which came from the heart was the outburst that "we did not conceive that it is a just Title to so vast a Continent, to make no other improvement of millions of Acres in it, but onely to burne it up for pastime"[40] – a passage that (as Axtell has noted about similar remarks of a later date) conveyed the deeply rooted English sense that hunting must be merely a "pastime," and that the Indian way of life was really one of incurable frivolity.[41]

But by the 1630s, this defence of settlement had already been given its most authoritative expression, in Grotius's *De Iure Belli ac Pacis* of 1625. In II.2, he listed a number of qualifications on men's right to enjoy owner-ship over terrestrial objects, which together represent a formidable set of constraints on property in land. The alleged owners of a territory must always permit free passage over it, both of persons and goods; must allow any strangers the right to build temporary accommodation on the seashore; must permit exiles to settle (all of these rights which the Spaniards and other Europeans had pleaded against native peoples); and, in particular, must allow anyone to possess things that are of no use to the owners. This is a right (he argued II.2.11) based on

innocent Profit; when I seek my own Advantage, without damaging anyone else. *Why should we not*, says Cicero, *when we can do it without any Detriment to ourselves, let others share in those Things that may be beneficial to them who receive them, and no inconvenience to us who give them.* Seneca therefore denies that it is any Favour, properly so called, to permit a Man to light a Fire by ours. And we read in Plutarch, . . . *'Tis an impious Thing for those who have eat sufficiently, to throw away the remaining Victuals; or for those who have had Water enough, to stop up or hide the Spring; or for those who themselves have had the Advantage of them, to destroy the Sea or Land Marks; but we ought to leave them for the Use and Service of them, who, after us, shall want them.*

Seneca's remark is important in Grotius's general argument, for he too wished to emphasize that it is not a *favor* – that is, it does not belong to the sphere of distributive justice and imperfect right, the *locus* of "benefits." There is no ownership in things that are of no use to their owners, and therefore other people have a *perfect* right to occupy them.

Drawing on Gentili, though characteristically without acknowledgement, Grotius argued (II.2.17) that it followed from this that

if there be any waste or barren Land within our Dominions, that also is to be given to Strangers, at their Request, or may be lawfully possessed by them, because whatever remains uncultivated, is not to be esteemed a Property, only so far as concerns Jurisdiction [*imperium*], which always continues the Right of the ancient People. And *Servius* remarks, that seven hundred Acres of bad unmanured Land were granted to the *Trojans*, by the original *Latins*: So we read in *Dion Prusaensis* [i.e. Dio Chrysostom], . . . that *They commit no Crime who cultivate and manure the untilled Part of a Country.*

And he concluded with the speech of the Ansibarii.

Grotius's ideas about cultivating land should be associated with an equally striking passage in his *De Veritate Christianis Religionis*, composed in Loevestein gaol and first published (in Dutch) in 1622, in which he praised Christianity for being the religion that most clearly recognized the moral truth that

our natural needs are satisfied with only a few things, which may be easily had without great labor or cost. As for what God has granted us in addition, we are commanded not to throw it into the sea (as some Philosophers foolishly asserted), nor to leave it unproductive (*inutile*), nor to waste it, but to use it to meet the needs (*inopiam*) of other men, either by giving it away, or by lending it to those who ask; as is appropriate for those who believe themselves to be not owners (*dominos*) of these things, but representatives or stewards (*procuratores ac dispensatores*) of God the Father . . . [42]

The theoretical basis for Grotius's defence of settlement had been worked out twenty years earlier, as part of the new account of property rights he devised to justify an attack on the ownership of the sea. As I said earlier, the defence of settlement always involved an analogy between the sea and the terrestrial wilderness, both being space that was not farmed and over which men could roam freely; but it was as difficult a job to persuade educated Europeans that the sea could not be owned by states as it was to persuade them that the wilderness was unownable by the local kings. The Romans, as we have seen, believed that while private estates could not be carved out of the sea, this did not mean that the Emperor did not have full jurisdiction over it, including such things as policing shipboard disputes and controlling entry. Their view was followed by medieval lawyers; as one gloss to the Maecianus passage said, things such as the sea and the coastline "are common with respect to use and ownership [*dominium*], but with respect to protection [*protectionem*] they are the Roman people's." A later note to this gloss explained that "protection" meant "jurisdiction," which is "Caesar's."[43]

The principal medieval dispute was between those lawyers who thought that jurisdiction over all seas remained in the hands of Caesar, and those who believed it had come to the various successor states to the Roman Empire: an anonymous early fourteenth-century English jurist remarked that the law of nature (on which Roman law was of course supposed by these writers to be based) was followed "less in England than anywhere else in the world" because the King of England claimed jurisdictional rights in the seas around his country.[44] Similar rights were claimed in the Northern Seas, even over to Greenland and beyond, by the Kings of Denmark, and in the Adriatic by the Republic of Venice. Not until 1563, it seems, did any theorist explicitly say that political authorities could not exercise jurisdiction over seas: this was Ferdinand Vazquez in his *Controversiae illustres* of that year, an idiosyncratic collection of *paradoxa* in law with an overpowering hostility to navigation *as such* – which Vazquez claimed had breached a divine law. The English, characteristically, seem to have led the way in voicing the claim in practice. In the early part of Elizabeth's reign, English lawyers had still accepted the traditional view that states can command the sea off their coasts: a dispute with Portugal about access to the African littoral in the 1560s turned (as Selden later rightly observed) on the question of how extensive Portugal's African possessions were, rather than on the issue of *dominium maris* as such.[45] But twenty years later this had changed, as the English began to think of themselves as "lords of navigation."[46] Thus the diplomat and juridical writer Robert Beale defended the Elizabethan government's incursions into Spanish waters in the following vigorous terms in a conference of 1580:

[The Queen] understood not, why hers and other Princes Subiects, should be barred from the Indies, which she could not perswade her selfe the Spaniard had any rightfull title to the the Bishop of *Romes* donation, in whom she acknowledged no prerogative, much lesse authority in such causes, that he should binde Princes which owe him no obedience . . . : nor yet by any other title than that the Spaniards had arrived here and there, built Cottages, and given names to a River or a Cape; which things cannot purchase any proprietie. So as this donation of that which is anothers, which in right is nothing worth, and this imaginary propriety, cannot let, but that other Princes may trade in those Countries, and without breach of the Law of Nations, transport Colonies thither, where the *Spaniards* inhabite not, forasmuch as prescription without possession is little worth, and may also freely navigate that vast Ocean, seeing the use of the Sea and Ayre is common to all. Neither can any title to the Ocean belong to any people, or private man; forasmuch as neither Nature, nor regard of the publicke use permitteth any possession thereof.[47]

The principal defender of the Virginian enterprise, Richard Hakluyt (who had consulted Gentili on its legitimacy) quickly realized that some jurists (though not, it should be said, Gentili himself, who continued to subscribe to the Roman view in this area) were saying things that were very similar to the English position, and by 1598, he was citing Vazquez in notes urging an American plantation on the government.[48] Almost as soon as Grotius's *Mare Liberum* appeared, in 1609, Gentili produced a manuscript translation of it.[49]

The English case turned, it should be stressed, on denying the distinction that traditional legal thinking had made between property and jurisdiction: from the point of view of people such as Beale, the fact that the seas could not be *owned* meant that no government could have rights over them. This was a hard argument to mount, and not until *Mare Liberum* was it at all persuasively put forward, as part of a new general theory of politics and ethics. *Mare Liberum* was cut out of a longer work, discovered in 1864, to which Grotius gave the title *De Indis*, but which modern historians know as *De Iure Praedae*. The book was intended to defend Dutch incursions into the waters of the Far East that the Portuguese claimed as their own, and to make this case, Grotius rewrote political theory. His central assertion came in a passage on the right to punish:

Is not the power to punish essentially a power that pertains to the state [*respublica*]? Not at all! On the contrary, just as every right of the magistrate comes to him from the state, so has the same right come to the state from private individuals; and similarly, the power of the state is the result of collective agreement . . . Therefore, since no one is able to transfer a thing that he never possessed, it is evident that the right of chastisement was held by private persons before it was held by the state. The following argument, too, has great force in this connexion: the state inflicts punishment for wrongs against itself, not only upon its own subjects but also upon foreigners; yet it derives no power over the latter from civil law, which is binding upon citizens only because they have given their consent; and therefore, the law of nature, or law of nations, is the source from which the state receives the power in question.[50]

The claim that all political rights, including the right to use violence, came only from the individuals who comprised the state was highly original: even the radical resistance theorists of the previous century had supposed that the magisterial right to use violence was a special right possessed only by rulers, though their subjects could determine how it should be used and by whom. In the case of the sea, Grotius linked this claim to his other distinctive argument, that ownership was possible only in things where individual control made practical difference to the use of the object, as in farming (where no one would plant unless he could reap). He then drew the conclusion that if something cannot become private property, it cannot come under the control of a state either:

Ownership [*Occupatio*], . . . both public and private, arises in the same way. On this point Seneca [*De Beneficiis* VII 4.3] says: "We speak in general of the land of the Athenians or the Campanians. It is the same land which again by means of private boundaries is divided among individual owners."[51]

To make clear his ideas, Grotius argued in the key passage of *Mare Liberum* that

Those who say that a certain sea belonged to the Roman people explain their statement to mean that the right of the Romans did not extend beyond protection and jurisdiction; this right they distinguish from ownership [*proprietas*]. Perchance they do not pay sufficient attention to the fact that although the Roman People were able to maintain fleets for the protection of navigation and to punish pirates captured on the sea, it was not done by private right, but by the common right which other free peoples also enjoy on the sea.[52]

Grotius acknowledged that this common right might be limited by an agreement about its exercise (so that one nation might agree not to police part of the sea that another nation was willing to patrol), but (my italics) *"this agreement does bind those who are parties to it, but it has no binding force on other nations, nor does it make the delimited area of the sea the private property of any one. It merely constitutes a personal right between contracting parties."* True property rights, on the other hand, Grotius believed, were not contractual in this sense: they arose from the practical exigencies of the situation, backed by a general recognition that the transformation of the material world is to everyone's advantage.

In the *De Indis*, Grotius was not concerned with settlement – the Dutch were not yet interested in doing more than breaking the trading monopolies of the Portuguese and their Far Eastern allies. But after the Dutch settlement in the Americas and the East Indies began, as we have seen, he recognized the appropriateness of his general theory as a defence of the Gentilian justification of expropriation. Interestingly, however, the *De Iure Belli ac Pacis* in one way does not go as far as *Mare Liberum* had done. As Grotius said in the passage on settlement I quoted earlier, while waste land must be given to anyone who needs it, "Jurisdiction [*imperium*]... always continues the Right of the ancient People" – in other words, political authority could be exercised over land, but not over sea. He explained what he now understood by the distinction between property and jurisdiction:

> as to what belongs properly to no Body, there are two Things which one may take Possession of, Jurisdiction, and the Right of Property, as it stands distinguished from Jurisdiction... Jurisdiction is commonly exercised on two Subjects, the one primary, *viz.* Persons, and that alone is sometimes sufficient, as in an Army of Men, Women, and Children, that are going in quest of some new Plantations; the other secundary [sic], *viz.* the Place, which is called *Territory*... (II.3.4)

For Grotius, the principal sense of Jurisdiction was personal – a special and stable right to police people, the kind of right exercised over the personnel of an army or a fleet at sea by a general or an admiral. He conceded that armies could come to enjoy an equally stable and effective right to command *anyone* who entered into a certain area of land, and they could then be said to possess jurisdiction over territory; this right should be distinguished from the kind of right he had allowed to the Romans over the Mediterranean in *Mare Liberum*, since that right (he had argued) was enforceable only against other nations who recognized it and had agreed to it. He continued to deny that the oceans could be under jurisdiction of this kind, as only coastal waters could be effectively policed against all comers.

> The Jurisdiction or Sovereignty over a Part of the Sea is acquired, in my Opinion, as all other Sorts of Jurisdiction; that is, as we said before, in Regard to Persons, and in Regard to Territory. In Regard to Persons, as when a Fleet, which is a Sea-Army, is kept in any Part of the Sea: In Regard to Territory, as when those that sail on the Coasts of a Country may be compelled from the Land, for then it is just the same as if they were actually upon the Land. (II.3.13)

So while the Romans could not possess jurisdiction, in this sense, over the Mediterranean, the King of the Algonquins could possess it over the New Netherlands, despite the fact that in neither case was the actual material of the earth's surface owned by anyone. This view of colonization and passage across the sea in fact fitted rather neatly into the actual Dutch practices during the 1620s: as the famous purchase of Manhattan Island illustrates, the Dutch were in general fairly anxious to ensure that what they took to be the local political authorities were agreeable to the removal of land from their jurisdiction. Indeed, the rules of the West India Company for New Netherlands, drawn up in 1629, specified that "whoever shall settle any colony out of the limits of the Manhattes' Island, shall be obliged to satisfy the Indians for the land they shall settle upon."[53]

But of course this distinction was a highly implausible one, as the colonists quickly discovered: in no sense was the King of the Algonquins more effective at controlling the Hudson Valley than the Romans had been at controlling the Mediterranean. John Selden, Grotius's first serious critic, used the discrepancy between *Mare Liberum* and *De Iure Belli ac Pacis* to argue that the oceans could be under full political control in the same way as the land, though he did not deny that sovereigns were morally obliged to permit settlement in their waste lands; this was not an issue that arose out at sea.[54] Samuel Pufendorf, the most authoritative writer on these issues for the late seventeenth century, went further, insisting that not only jurisdiction but also full property rights could be possessed by native rulers over the wilderness. Neither the sea nor the wilderness of America should be seen as free from jurisdiction *or* property: property relations were conventional, and the agreements underlying them could take account of all kinds of future possibilities. Someone could appropriate a substantial area of wholly unowned and unoccupied land, "for it is sufficient that, while he took possession physically of some portion of things, he included others in his intent, and was going to take possession of them when need of them arose; just as he who entered merely one apartment of a palace, has occupied the whole . . ."[55] Pufendorf was careful not to go too far, however, observing that

Should one Man, for Instance, be, with his Wife, cast upon a desert Island, sufficient to maintain Myriads of People; he could not, without intolerable Arrogance, challenge the whole Island to himself upon the Right of Occupancy, and endeavour to repulse those who should land on a different part of the shore. But when any number of Men jointly possess themselves of a Tract of Land, this Occupancy is wont to be made either *by the Whole*, or *by Parcels*. The former happens, when Men in an united Body seize on some desolate Region, encompassed with certain Bounds, either by Nature, or by human Appointment . . . Nor is it necessary that all things which are first occupied in this general Way, should be afterwards divided amongst particular and distinct Proprietors. Therefore, if in a Region thus possessed, any thing should be found, which is not ascertained to a private Owner, it must not presently be looked upon as *void* and *waste*, so that any one Person may seize it as his *Peculiar*, but we must suppose it to belong to the whole People.[56]

Indeed, Pufendorf delivered the most extreme attack on the colonizing enterprise found in any of the great seventeenth-century writers, attacking *inter alia* the old defence that the colonists were punishing acts of extreme immorality such as cannibalism.

My Lord *Bacon* . . . gives this a sufficient Reason for making War upon the *Americans*, which I must confess I cannot agree with him in: "That they were to be look'd upon as People proscribed by the Law of Nature, inasmuch as they had a barbarous Custom of sacrificing Men, and feeding upon Man's Flesh." For it ought to be distinctly considered, whether Christian Princes have sufficient Licence given them to invade those *Indians*, as People proscribed by Nature, only because they made Man's Flesh their common Food? Or because they eat the Bodies of Persons of their own Religion? Or, because they devoured Strangers and Foreigners? And then again it must be ask'd, whether those Strangers they are said to kill and eat, come as Enemies and Robbers, or as innocent Guests and Travellers, or as forc'd by Stress of Weather? For this last

Case only, not any of the others, can give any Prince a *Right of War* against them; and this to those Princes only, whose Subjects have been used with that Inhumanity by them.[57]

Anyone who lives in Cambridge, U.K., in the summer must be sympathetic to the idea that there is a right to eat tourists.

By the 1670s, the general tenor of European political theory was thus swinging against the Grotian or Gentilian defence of settlement, particularly as, after Grotius, its most obvious defender (though not in any great detail) was Thomas Hobbes, who had remarked in *Leviathan* that

The multitude of poor, and yet strong people still encreasing, they are to be transported into Countries not sufficiently inhabited: where neverthelesse, they are not to exterminate those they find there; but constrain them to inhabit closer together, and not range a great deal of ground, to snatch what they find; but to court each little Plot with art and labour, to give them their sustenance in due season . . . [58]

At the same time, the English colonists themselves were becoming increasingly uneasy about the critical attitude of the imperial government towards them, and the sympathy sometimes expressed by the Restoration regime to the native peoples – sympathy reflected in the famous anxiety by William Penn, the favorite of the Duke of York and pioneer of a new style of settlement, to conciliate with the aboriginal rulers.[59] The English government had also fairly thoroughly abandoned the Elizabethan idea of the free seas – this, after all, was the *casus belli* of the Dutch wars.[60] But, at least as far as the justification of settlement went, the Gentilian view was decisively rescued by John Locke, who went even further in his defence of it than Grotius had done, and eliminated the discrepancy between land and sea, to the disbenefit (it should be said) of the native peoples.

Thus, Locke argued, against Pufendorf and the other critics of Grotius, that property was *not* conventional: only labor, the transformation of the commons, gave rise to individual property rights, and neither the seas nor the wilderness could therefore currently be owned. Thus far he was of course simply restating Grotius – though that was striking enough in the 1670s and 1680s. But he went beyond Grotius in his remarks on jurisdiction: according to Locke in Chapter VIII of the *Two Treatises*, "*Of the Beginning of Political Societies*,"

every man when he first incorporates himself into any commonwealth, he, by his uniting himself thereunto, annexes also, and submits to the community those possessions, which he has, or shall acquire, that do not already belong to any other government . . . By the same act therefore, whereby anyone unites his person, which was before free, to any commonwealth; by the same he unites his possessions, which were before free, to it also; and they become, both of them, person and possession, subject to the government and dominion of that commonwealth, as long as it hath a being . . . ('120)

The implication of this argument is that government follows the ownership of land: only if land has been brought into cultivation and thereby appropriated, can a government claim jurisdiction over it. Locke was fully aware (and indeed it is an important part of his argument at this point) that once a land-owner had put his land under the jurisdiction of his political community or commonwealth, his descendants could not easily withdraw it from the commonwealth's control; but he was clear that a commonwealth could only claim jurisdiction over the territory under its control if that territory had at some point been brought into private ownership through cultivation. It followed that the kings of America could not claim jurisdiction over the waste lands (indeed, Locke was hesitant about whether they could claim to be full commonwealths at all – see his remarks at II′ 102), and that European settlers did not need to acknowledge their rights. It is not surprising that the settlers became so enthusiastic about Locke's political theory.[61]

After Locke, European views on these issues split into two camps. One, particularly powerful in North Britain and North America, continued to restate the Lockean view that native rulers had no rights and the sea could not be controlled; this is found in Gershom Carmichael's influential lectures on Pufendorf at Glasgow University, in Francis Hutcheson, and most notably in that favorite text of the American revolutionaries, Emmerich de Vattel's *Le Droit des Gens*.[62] The other, which was very influential in Germany, but which found echoes in the later eighteenth century in England (as *bien pensant* English opinion turned against the values of the settlers), continued to insist on the Pufendorfian view that settlement against the wishes of native rulers was clearly illegitimate – and often, by association, that *dominium maris* was possible. This is found in the highly important edition of Grotius produced by Jean Barbeyrac in the early eighteenth century, which, though sympathetic to Locke in many ways, clearly dissociated itself from his views on settlement[63]; it is found in Christian Wolff[64]; and in England it is found in the highly interesting lectures by the Regius Professor of Divinity at Cambridge, Thomas Rutherforth (to whose interest and importance Peter Miller has drawn our attention).[65] It is also, of course, the view taken by Kant, though on utterly different theoretical foundations from those of Pufendorf or Wolff.[66] The actual practices of states in the eighteenth and nineteenth centuries also reflected these differences, with the independent American settlers in particular continuing their occupation of aboriginal lands and their enthusiastic support for *mare liberum*,[67] while their former imperial government moved much more cautiously in much of its domains (though the occupation of Australia, unlike that of Western Canada and New Zealand, seems to have proceeded on the assumption that the aboriginal peoples had no rights over their territory). However, a full account of nineteenth-century practices, taking account of all the areas of settlement such as Siberia, Russian Central Asia, Africa, the Americas, and Australasia, has yet to be written.

There is a paradox in this story that must be pointed out at its conclusion. Though we have lost sight of this fact, the great seventeenth-century rights theorists who in most respects founded modern liberalism also originated the idea that the control of the earth's surface is not something to be divided up between responsible political organizations. Much of the surface of the globe is still (they believed) in a state of primitive communism, in the sense that there is as yet no private ownership, and unless certain quite stringent moral conditions were met, communism might legitimately re-assert itself in the territory that was privately owned. Freedom for the modern European meant, for many of these writers, the denial of freedom for any people who lived by hunting or gathering, while the *ancien régimes*, which the writers (mostly) hated, tended to respect to an equal extent the rights of all the peoples under their rule – though for someone like Locke, this was precisely what was wrong with the Duke of York, who treated Englishmen as if they were American savages, and vice versa. In the 1770s, these issues came to a head when the imperial government (among other things) accorded great rights to the aboriginal kings on whom it had relied to defeat the French, as well as extending civil rights to the defeated enemy. It thus told the English settlers that the two groups in the struggle against whom the settlers had repeatedly risked their lives – the native Americans and the French – were to be seen as broadly equivalent in status to the settlers, and we know the result.

These paradoxes of liberalism are not empty ones: there is a genuine moral dilemma about the presence of hunter-gatherers in a world of subsistence agriculture, where respect for a few native peoples might in effect condemn many other people to death by famine. And it is also true that the kind of enterprising and free-spirited agent beloved of liberalism does not fit easily into a tightly controlled world of states and estates. With his customary insight, Weber spotted the connection between the history of freedom and the destruction of barriers, and drew the appropriate tragic conclusion.

The question is: how are freedom and democracy in the long run at all possible under the domination of highly developed capitalism? ... The historical origin of modern freedom has had certain unique preconditions which will never repeat themselves. Let us enumerate the most important of these: First, the overseas expansions. In the armies of Cromwell, in the French constituent assembly, in our whole economic life even today this breeze from across the ocean is felt ... but there is no new continent at our disposal.[68]

Notes to Chapter 8

1. Paul Veyne, "Y a-t-il eu un imperialisme romain?" *Mélanges de l'Ecole française à Rome* 87 (1975), 793–855.
2. *Digest of Justinian*, Latin text, eds., Theodor Mommsen and Paul Krueger, English trans., ed., Alan Watson (Philadelphia: University of Pennsylvania Press,

1985), 14.2.9. It should be said that this is the modern translation, based on the Greek text that became available in the Renaissance. Throughout the Middle Ages, this passage was accessible only in a Latin version, which went as follows (my translation): "I am master of the world: and the law for the sea. Marine affairs are to be judged by the law of the Rhodians: the law makes no conflict between our rights and that law. Augustus, now deified, decided likewise."

3. Ibid., 48.15.5.

4. On this, and much more of the Roman view of imperialism, see P.A. Brunt, "Laus Imperii," in P.D.A. Garnsey and C.R. Whittaker, eds., *Imperialism in the Ancient World* (Cambridge: Cambridge University Press 1978), 183 and n84.

5. *The Annals of Imperial Rome*, trans. Michael Grant (Harmondsworth: Penguin,1959), 300–1 (XIII.55). I have used the translation of the Ansibarian plea found in the edition of Grotius's *De Iure Belli ac Pacis* I cite later – *The Rights of War and Peace, in Three Books... To which are added, all the large notes of Mr. J. Barbeyrac...* (London 1738), 156 (II.2.17).

6. Plutarch, *Moralia* IX, trans. Edwin L. Minaar, F.H. Sandbach, and W.C. Helmhold (Cambridge, Mass.: Loeb Classical Library, 1961), 36–7 (VII.4,703).

7. Dio Chrysostom, *Works* I (*Discourses I–IX*), trans. J.W. Cohoon (Cambridge, Mass.: Loeb Classical Library, 1971), 304–7.

8. *Oratorum Romanorum Fragmenta*, ed., H. Malcovati (Turin 1967–79), I p.78 (fr. 195); trans. P.A. Brunt, "Laus Imperii" in Garnsey and Whittaker, eds., *Imperialism in the Ancient World*, 177.

9. The formal change in the style of the Kings of England came as late as King John (1199–1216).

10. These are included in the provisions of the Treaty of Birgham; see Thomas Rymer, ed., *Foedera* I Part III (The Hague 1745, reprinted Farnborough, England, 1967), 70.

11. See Harry E. Dembkowski, *The Union of Lublin: Polish Federalism in the Golden Age* (New York: Columbia University Press, 1982), 30. The passage quoted is from a proposal for closer union in 1501.

12. And only two were created in the eighteenth century before the Revolution, Sardinia and – the first modern kind of kingdom – Prussia.

13. For both the *Decretum* and the *Decretals*, see *Corpus Iuris Canonici*, eds., E.L. Richter and E. Friedberg (Graz: Akademische Druck, 1959). The relevant *quaestiones* in the *Decretum* are II. c.23 qu.1,2 (I, 889–895).

14. See A.M. Stickler, "Alanus Anglicus als Verteidiger des Monarchischen Papsttums," *Salesianum* 21 (1959), 363, 362.

15. See, for example, Walter Ullmann, *A History of Political Thought: The Middle Ages* (Harmondsworth: Penguin Books, 1965), 78.

16. See James Muldoon, *Popes, Lawyers, and Infidels: The Church and the Non-Christian World 1250–1550* (Philadelphia: University of Pennsylvania Press, 1979), 5–15.

17. Ibid., 16–7. This seems to be similar to the remarks of Alanus Anglicus quoted in note 14.

18. Augustinus Triumphus, *De Potestate Ecclesiastica* qu. 23 (1584), 137. The same view is found later in Antonius of Florence's *Summa* III.22.5.8.

19. Sylvestro Mazzolini, "De Papa," qu. 7 (Nuremberg 1518 p. 358r).

20. *Post Christum vere omne imperium est apud Christum; &eius Vicariam: & transfertur per Papam in principem saecularem. On Extravagantes, Quomodo in laesae maiestatis* tit.1, *Ad respicium, Corpus Juris Civilis* V (Geneva 1625) sig. PP1r.

21. Bartolus, *In Digestum Novum Commentarii* (Basle 1562), 983–4 (on 49.15.24).

22. Ibid., 983–4 (on 49.15.24).

23. *sed haec ipse non probo: tum quia multa sunt provinciae quae non paruerunt Romanis, ut Scythia & Sarmatia, et ultra Euphratem fluvium universus Oriens... Et quamvis quandoque Imperatores orbis dominos se appellent, id vel per hyperbolem accipiendum est, vel eorum dictis minime credendum, quia in causa propria. Opera* III col.180.

24. *Opera*, IV 449.

25. See, for example, Muldoon, *Popes. Lawyers, and Infidels*, 137–9. For the Bulls, see Frances Gardiner Davenport, ed., *European Treaties Bearing on the History of the United States and its Dependencies to 1648* I (Washington D.C.: Carnegie Institution of Washington, 1917), 56–83.

26. The Burgos *junta* of 1512 at which these issues were first extensively discussed in Spain is dealt with in Anthony Pagden, *The Fall of Natural Man* (Cambridge, Mass.: Cambridge University Press, 1982), 47–50. The extensive treatises that were submitted to the King in the same year by two members of the *junta*, Juan López de Palacios Rubios and Matías de Paz, are translated in *De las Islas del mar Océano [and] Del dominio de los Reyes de España sobre los indios*, trans. Agustín Millares Carlo, ed., Silvio Zavala (Mexico City: Fondo de Cultura Económica,1954), and are discussed in Pagden, *The Fall of Natural Man*, 50–6 and Muldoon, *Popes, Lawyers, and Infidels*, 142. De Paz was particularly critical of the Dominican tradition as represented by Durandus – see *De las Islas del mar Océano*, 234–9.

27. St. Thomas Aquinas, *Summa Theologiae* XXXII, trans. and ed., Thomas Gilby (New York: Image Books, 1969), 68–71 (II.IIae 10.10)

28. Ibid., 100–1 (II.IIae 12.2).

29. John of Paris, *On Royal and Papal Power*, trans. Arthur P. Monahan (New York: Columbia University Press, 1974), 15.

30. Durandus of San Porciano, *De Iurisdictione Ecclesiastica* (Paris 1506) f.4r.; see also his *In Petri Lombard Sententias Theologicas Commentariorum Libri IIII* (Venice 1571), 206v. For a short account of Durandus, see *Dictionnaire de biographie française*, s.n. For a similar view from a Thomist layman, see Aquinas's pupil Pierre Dubois's opposition to a universal temporal monarchy in his *The Recovery of the Holy Land*, trans. and ed., Walther I. Brandt (New York: Columbia University Press, 1956), 121–2. (For the fact that he attended Aquinas's lectures, see 3.)

31. Cf. *Matthew* xxiii.15. On Aquinas, *Secunda Secundae*, qu.66 art.8. Aquinas, *Secunda Secundae* (Lyons 1552), 109r. The translation is taken from Grotius, *De Iure Praedae* I, trans. Gwladys L. Williams (Oxford: Oxford University Press, Publications of the Carnegie Endowment for International Peace, 1950), 225, where Grotius quotes this passage against the claims of the Portuguese and the Spaniards to rights over the Indians.

32. *Relección*, "De Dominio," ed., Jaime Brufau Prats (Granada 1964). See also Jaime Brufau Prats, *La Escuela de Salamanca ante el Descrubimento del Nuevo Mundo* (Salamanca: Editorial San Esteban, 1989), 152.

33. See Francisco de Vitoria, *Vitoria Political Writings*, eds., Anthony Pagden and Jeremy Lawrance (Cambridge: Cambridge University Press, 1991).

34. Thomas More, *Utopia*, 56.

35. Alberico Gentili, *De Iure Belli*, (1588), 80–81. Gentili was also an admirer of More; see 342.

36. Robert Gray, *A Good Speed to Virginia* (London 1609) sigg C3v-C4. Although Gray went on to say that in fact the Indians were willing to part with their land. Earlier (sig. C2) he had said that "we are warrented by this direction of *Ioshua* [*Joshua* 17.14, his text] to destroy wilfull and convicted Idolaters, rather then to let them live, if by no other meanes they can be reclaimed."

37. John Donne, *The Sermons of John Donne* IV, eds., George R. Potter and Evelyn M. Simpson (Berkeley: University of California Press, 1959), 274.

38. Roger Williams, *The Complete Writings* (New York: Russell and Russell, 1963), 46.

39. Ibid., 46–7.

40. 40. Ibid., 47.

41. See the remark on the "Gentlemanly Diversions of Hunting and Fishing" practised by the Indians. James Axtell, *The Invasion Within: The Contest of Cultures in Colonial North America* (New York: Oxford University Press, 1985), 158.

42. Hugo Grotius, *Opera Omnia Theologica* (London 1679) III, 43 (II.14) The last sentence is a reference to 1 Tim. VI. 17,18.

43. *Digest* 1.8.2, *Digestum Vetus* (Lyons 1569) col. Fenn's discussion of this passage is very unreliable: he attributes it to 43.8.3, and confuses the later *additio* (which dates from the late Middle Ages) with the original gloss. Percy Thomas Fenn, *The Origin of the Right of Fishery in Territorial Waters* (Cambridge, Mass.: Harvard University Press, 1926), 38.

44. Bracton and Azo, *Select Passages from the Works of Bracton and Azo*, ed., F.W. Maitland (London: Selden Society VIII, 1895), 125.

45. The papers for this dispute are in B.L. Cottonian MSS Nero B.I. Portuguese translations of the documents are to be found in M. de Santaren, ed., *Quadro Elementar das Relações Politicas e Diplomaticas de Portugal com as Diversas Potencias do Mundo* XV (Paris: Aillaud, 1854), 128–339. For the English position, see, for example, the Privy Council letter, at 174. The Portuguese ambassador took the view that "all the provinces of Ethiopia recognise the supremacy and sovereignty of the Crown of Portugal" (158). Selden's observation upon this material (which he will have seen in Cotton's library) is in his *Opera Omnia*, II col. 1243.

46. "We are lords of navigation, and they [the native Virginians] are not." Richard Hakluyt, in *The Original Writings & Correspondence of the Two Richard Hakluyts*, ed., E.G.R. Taylor II (London: Hakluyt Society Series II Vol. 77, 1935), 329. "We have got/The Maxim gun, and they have not" (Hilaire Belloc, *The Modern Traveller*, pt.6).

47. William Camden, *Annals, or, The Historie of the Most Renowned and Victorious Princesse Elizabeth* (London 1635), 225. For the Latin text, see Thomas Hearne's edition, *Annales Rerum Anglicarum et Hibernicarum* (n.p.1717), 359–60. It is a conjecture that this is the speech by Robert Beale referred to in *Calendar of State Papers Foreign 1579–1580*, 463, but it so fits Beale's known interests and capacities that I think there can be little doubt. For Beale, see D.N.B. *sub nomine*.

48. Richard Hakluyt, *The Original Writings & Correspondence of the Two Richard Hakluyts*, ed., E.G.R. Taylor II (London: Hakluyt Society Series II Vol. 77, 1935), 425. The "Spanish lawiers" referred to are clearly (from the examples cited) substantially Vazquez.

49. Ibid., 497–99.
50. Hugo Grotius, *De Iure Praedae Commentarius* I, trans. Gwladys L. Williams and Walter H. Zeydel (Oxford: Oxford University Press, Carnegie Endowment for International Peace, 1950), 91–2. For the Latin text, the easiest source (since the Carnegie Endowment text is a photocopy of the manuscript) is still the original edition by H.G. Hanaker (The Hague 1868), 91. See also Peter Borschberg, *Hugo Grotius: "Commentarius in Theses XI"* (Berne: P. Lang Publishers, 1994), 244–5, for an early statement of this idea, in the manuscript, which seems to be part of the working papers for the *De Indis*.
51. Hugo Grotius, *The Freedom of the Seas*, trans. R. van D. Magoffin, ed., J.B. Scott, (New York: Carnegie Endowment for International Peace, Oxford University Press, 1916), 26.
52. Ibid., 35.
53. E.B. O'Callaghan, *History of New Netherland*, 2nd ed. (New York: Appleton, 1855), 119.
54. See John Selden, *Mare Clausum*, e.g. *Opera Omnia*, ed., David Wilkins (London 1726) coll. 1197–1198.
55. Samuel Pufendorf, *Elementorum Jurisprudentiae Universalis Libri Duo*, trans. William Abbott Oldfather and Edwin H. Zeydel , ed., Hans Wehberg (New York: Carnegie Endowment for International Peace, Oxford University Press, 1931), II, 36.
56. Samuel Pufendorf, *The Law of Nature and Nations*, trans. Basil Kennet (London: 5th ed. 1749), 386–88 (IV.6.3–4).
57. Ibid., 840 (VIII.6.5). The passage from Bacon (as Barbeyrac observed) is from his dialogue *An Advertisement Touching an Holy War*. This was written at about the time Bacon was associating with Hobbes, and Hobbes may have translated it into Latin – Bacon himself arranged for its translation, though it first appeared after his death in Bacon,*Operum Moralium et Civium Tomus*, ed., W. Rawley (London 1638). See sigg A3r-A3v.
58. Thomas Hobbes, *Leviathan*, ed., Richard Tuck (Cambridge: Cambridge University Press, 1991), 239 (181, original ed.). Hobbes was himself a shareholder in the Virginia Company and active in its affairs. See Noel Malcolm, "Hobbes, Sandys and the Virginia Company," *Historical Journal* 24 (1981).
59. In October 1681, Penn wrote to the Indian kings in the area assuring them "that I am very sensible of the unkindness and injustice that has been too much exercised towards you by the people of these parts of the world", and in June 1682 he wrote to "the Emperor of Canada" that "The great God, that made thee and me and all the world, incline our hearts to love peace and justice that we may live friendly together as becomes the workmanship of the great God. The king of England, who is a great prince, has for divers reasons granted to me a large country in America which, however, I am willing to enjoy upon friendly terms with thee". The initial instructions he sent to his agents in 1681 ordered them "to buy land of the true owners, which I think is the Susquehanna people" and "to treat speedily with the Indians for land before they are furnished by others with things that please them." See Jean R. Soderlund, ed., *William Penn and the Founding of Pennsylvania, 1680–1684: A Documentary History* (Philadelphia: University of Pennsylvania Press, 1983), 88 and 156.

60. See Thomas Wemyss Fulton, *The Sovereignty of the Sea* (Edinburgh and London: Blackwood Press, 1911), 378–516. A good example of the English view in the 1670s is provided by Molloy's *De Jure Maritimo et Navali* of 1676, which strongly asserts English sovereignty over the seas from Cape Finisterre to Norway. See ibid., 513–4.

61. For more on this, see James Tully, "Redicovering America: the *Two Treatises* and aboriginal rights," in his collection of essays, *An Approach to Political Philosophy: Locke in Contexts* (Cambridge: Cambridge University Press, 1993), 137–78.

62. Gershom Carmichael, ed., Samuel Puffendorf [sic], *De Officio Hominis et Civis* (Edinburgh 1724), 212–16 and 221; see James Moore and Michael Silverthorne, "Gershoom Carmichael and the natural jurisprudence tradition in eighteenth-century Scotland," in *Wealth and Virtue*, eds., Istvan Hont and Michael Ignatieff (Cambridge: Cambridge University Press, 1983), 73–87; Francis Hutcheson, *A System of Moral Philosophy, in Three Books*, ed., Francis Hutcheson, Jr. (Glasgow 1755) I, 328 (II.7.3); Emmerich de Vattel, *Le Droit des Gens*, trans. Charles G. Fenwick and G.D. Gregory, ed., Albert de Lapradelle (Washington: Carnegie Endowment for International Peace, 1916), I.7.81, 37–8. See also 85–6 and II.7.97, 43. For the sea, see the Whig writer Philip Meadows's *Observations concerning the Dominion and Sovereignty of the Seas* (1689 – but, like Locke's *Two Treatises*, based on a manuscript of the 1670s). See Fulton, *The Sovereignty of the Sea*, 524–25.

63. Hugo Grotius, *The Rights of War and Peace, in Three Books* (London 1738),156, 147 n9. Barbeyrac drew his ideas on *dominium maris* from the Dutch jurist Bynkershoek – under the stress of the attacks on the Dutch empire, the Dutch had begun to retreat to support for controlled seas. See Cornelis van Bynkershoek, *De Dominio Maris*, trans. Ralp Van Deman Magoffin, ed., James Bell Scott (New York: Carnegie Endowment for International Peace, 1923).

64. Christian Wolff, *Jus Gentium Methodo Scientifica Pertractatum*, trans. Joseph H. Drake and Francis J. Hemelt, ed., Otfried Nippold (New York: Oxford University Press, Carnegie Endowment for International Peace, 1934) ' 310–311.

65. Thomas Rutherforth, *Defining the Common Good: Empire, Religion and Philosophy in Eighteenth-Century Britain* (Cambridge: Cambridge University Press 1994), 142–49. Rutherforth's views on settlement are in his *Institutes of Natural Law. Being the Substance of a Course of Lectures on* Grotius De Jure Belli et [sic] Pacis read in *S. Johns College Cambridge* (Cambridge, 1754–1756) II, 481. Molloy's book (note 60) was extensively reprinted in the later eighteenth century – see Fulton, *The Sovereignty of the Sea*, 514n4. See also the array of eighteenth-century jurists cited by Fulton, 580n1. Not until 1878 and the passing of the Territorial Waters Jurisdiction Act did the English formally abandon claims to *dominium maris* over the British Seas (ibid).

66. Immanuel Kant, *Kant Political Writings*, ed. Hans Reiss (Cambridge: Cambridge University Press, 1991), 106. See Kant's *The Metaphysics of Morals*, ed., Mary Gregor (Cambridge: Cambridge University Press, 1991) ' I.62, 158–59; but see also DR '15 for a characteristically more nuanced account.

67. See Fulton, *The Sovereignty of the Sea*, 573–75.

68. Max Weber, *From Max Weber*, trans. and eds., H.H. Gerth and C. Wright Mills (London: Routledge, 1948), 71–2.

9

Natural Law and the Re-making of Boundaries

John Finnis

1. Introduction

When I taught law in the University of Malawi between 1976 and 1978, I lived in houses owned by the university in succession to the government, houses formerly occupied by colonial civil servants. From my first house in Zomba, I looked over the roof of the adjacent Parliament House, across the trees hiding the university down on the plain, and on towards the mountains of Mozambique, an even more newly independent country. At night we could see, out on the plain beyond the university, the arc lights around the prison camp where several hundred prisoners were detained on Presidential orders, including the most recent holders of the offices of Registrar of the University and Principal of the university college of which the Law Faculty was part. The President's powers of detention without trial were copied from powers used sometimes by the British government of the Nyasaland Protectorate. That protectorate, or colonial administration of the territory, had been inaugurated partially and informally in 1884, formally but partially in 1889 and formally and entirely in 1891, and terminated formally in 1964 (in substance in February 1963).

The Nyasaland protectorate was inaugurated against the long-standing wishes of the Foreign and Colonial Offices of the British Government, under pressure of public opinion keen to prevent the humanitarian disaster of an immense and long-standing slave trade conducted by Arabs with the willing assistance of the tribe that dominated the southern and south-eastern shores of Lake Nyasa and preyed on peaceable but loosely organized Nyanja peoples just as the Angoni, pushed back from southern Africa by the Zulu, annually pillaged and slaughtered the Maravi on the western and northern shores of the lake. Had I been looking out over the plain from the same spot a longish lifetime earlier, I could have seen the long slave columns beginning their death march 750 miles north-east as the crow flies to Zanzibar, to the slave market on the site of the cathedral there. To humanitarian and missionary British public opinion, Cecil Rhodes and a few others added some commercial suggestions, as inducements for the parsimonious British Government. The first acts of *imperium* and jurisdiction by the new Commissioner, Harry Johnston, on his arrival in 1891 were the forcible suppression of the slave trade and the cancelling of a large number of land purchases made by enterprising Europeans from native chiefs. His stated objects in respect of land were "firstly, to protect the rights of the natives, to see that their villages and plantations are not disturbed, and that sufficient space is left for their expansion; secondly, to discourage land speculation; and thirdly, to secure the rights of the Crown in such a way that the Crown shall profit by the development of this country." His broader purposes were stated by him to his Whitehall superiors in 1893: "we do not come here necessarily to subjugate; we come to protect and instruct." The government school for Zomba children whose families speak English at home bears his name to this day.

In 1936, the Native Trust Land Order in Council confirmed and protected the position about settlement reached after forty years: Native Trust Land, administered and controlled by the Governor for the use and common benefit, direct or indirect of the natives of the Protectorate, comprised over 87 percent of the land in the Protectorate; 7.65 percent was held as forest reserves, townships, and leasehold Crown land; and 5.1 percent was alienated in freehold to European settlers – an amount much larger than the few hundred farmers and planters could cultivate. Settlement had never been a substantial motive or justification advanced for the establishing of the protectorate.

There were a number of important injustices in the Protectorate's administration and laws – the head tax, for example, designed to force the population into some kind of commercial life, the failure to institute any governmental plan for and encouragement of education (left entirely to the missionaries), the unprotected status of squatters on uncultivated freehold land, the inadequate albeit real measures to protect public health, and so forth.

But it would, in my view, be unreasonable to judge that the decisions to declare the Protectorate, to enforce its administration of justice, and to maintain it for three-score years and ten, against German attack in 1914 and the one significant act of internal subversion (the Chilembwe uprising in 1915) were unjust or unjustified decisions. They were decisions made with generally good motives and just intentions, and were in all the circumstances fair and reasonable. It would have been, it seems to me, unjust and unreasonable for persons with the opportunities open to the British authorities in 1884 to have decided to leave the peoples of the territory under the sway of local rulers quite indifferent to the rule of law and incapable of defending their people against ruthless aggression, pillage, ethnic cleansing, and slavery at the hands of other Africans, or to a languid and capricious rule of Portuguese, who had for centuries done little or nothing about those very evils, or to the generally brutal rule of the German East Africa colonial authorities.

The boundaries of Nyasaland were negotiated in the late 1880s between the British, Portuguese, and German governments, far from the scene. They make little intrinsic sense, cutting through a number of tribal areas. But it was clearly appropriate that some such boundaries should have been drawn in order to determine where a particular magistrate's jurisdiction – responsibility for maintaining peace and justice – ended or, perhaps, began. As one drives north along the highlands on the western shore of Lake Nyasa, one finds that the road itself, nothing more, marks the boundary between Malawi and Mozambique. To get, say, breakfast one must drive off a few hundred yards into Mozambique; the locals move back and forth between countries without apparent care or concern. But if a dispute arises between neighbors, or a man murders his wife or his neighbor or the shop-keeper, who is to exercise that kind of jurisdiction that only states can exercise with the prospect of due and impartial process of law? A Malawian or a Mozambiquan judge, with the help of whose police? When one gets to the outer reaches, the marches, a boundary provides a hardly dispensable service to fairness and to peace.

It would be summary but reasonable to say that British state rule in Nyasaland did not invade any state, did not transgress any state boundaries, respected existing property or quasi-property rights, and supplanted the jurisdiction only of rulers of manifest unfairness (if not always of bad faith), unwillingness to respect the boundaries of others, and incapacity to defend let alone appropriately promote the common good of their peoples. The era has now passed. But its contours remain relevant to any reflection on the justice of boundaries.

2

The principles of public reason that since Plato have been called natural law, natural justice, or natural right suggest and justify a territorial division and assumption of political/state jurisdiction for reasons closely analogous to those that suggest and justify the appropriation of land and other natural and artificial resources to private owners, individual or corporate. Those reasons can be summarised in headline form: service to common good (ultimately to the common good of all persons); responsibility for such service, and consequent authority to legislate, adjudicate, and administer (jurisdiction, *imperium* and, mutatis mutandis, *dominium*); and reciprocity.

One or two applications and illustrations. The domination of a nomadic tribe over the territory it happens to control at the present stage of its wandering, in the present balance of power with neighboring nomadic or non-nomadic tribes does not constitute it as a state, a political community organized for justice and peace, and does not constitute its boundaries to be respected by persons interested in bringing peace and justice to the area. This thought is relevant to a consideration of the justice of instituting colonial government in, say, Australia or, as I suggested, in parts of Africa.[1] Or again, a ruler's or ruling group's forcible domination of a people for the gratification of the ruling person's or group's own interests and advantage is tyrannical rule that has no title to respect by persons who intend and are equipped to protect and promote the common good of that same people. This thought, too, is relevant to reflections on Australia and some parts of Africa.

Richard Tuck says that Aquinas, like other Dominicans, "disagreed profoundly with any theory of world authority, preferring instead a vision of a world of independent and equal political communities." I doubt this. To me its seems a cardinal feature of Aquinas's treatment of political matters that he abstracts entirely from all questions about the conditions under which it is proper for political communities to be brought into being or dissolved or otherwise replaced.[2] His theory, it seems to me, is of a political community, whether it be as small as Sparta or Florence or as large as France or indeed the world. His silence about the Holy Roman Empire seems to me just that: silence – like his silence about the Crusades: a kind of abstracting from radically contingent circumstances, enterprises, and institutions, in favour of keeping the focus upon the essential principles of good government:

> ... if the good for one human being is the same good [i.e. *human good*] as the good for a whole *civitas*, still it is evidently a much greater and more perfect thing to procure and preserve the state of affairs which is the good of a whole *civitas* than the state of affairs which is the good of a single human being. For: it belongs to the love which should exist between human persons that one should seek and preserve the good of even one single human being; but how much better and more godlike that this should be shown for a whole people and *for a plurality* of *civitates*. Or: it is lovable that this be shown for one single *civitas*, but *much more godlike that it be shown for the whole people embracing many civitates.* ("More godlike" because more in the likeness of God who is the universal cause of all goods.) This good, *the good common to one or many civitates*, is what the theory, i.e. the 'art' which is called 'civil', has as its point [intendit]. And so it is this theory, above all – as the most primary [principalissima] of all practical theories – that considers the ultimate end of human life.[3]

Of course, there is no reason to think that Aquinas considered world government a desirable possibility in any concretely foreseeable circumstances. How could anyone in the world he knew claim with justice to be able to promote, and therefore be potentially responsible for, the political common good, the justice and peace, of people in India?[4]

Tuck goes further (p. 13): "the Thomist answer [to the question whether the world was exhaustively divided among independent and jurisdictionally equal states] has always been that it was." Tuck contrasts this with the rejected thesis that there was a Christian *dominium mundi.*[5] But the alternative theses do not exhaust the possibilities. A third possibility was that some parts of the world are administered as states and others are not, yet. (And a fourth possibility would question the jurisdictional equality of states.) It seems to me that Thomism was quite open to that third possibility. Certainly Aquinas seems quite relaxed when he himself writes about the responsibilities of rulers to found *civitates* or *regna* by choosing a good, temperate, fertile, beautiful (but not too beautiful) location for the realm and then, within that realm, selecting a site suitable for the building of a city – and all this somewhere where no realm or city was already established.[6]

True, Vitoria – taking up the mantle of St. Thomas in the 1530s – thinks that "after Noah the world was divided into various countries and kingdoms."[7] But he says this to refute the thesis that the whole world is or has been under the one emperor, not to refute the thesis that some parts of the world are as yet not part of the territory of any political community. True, too, Vitoria denies that the Spaniards acquired the "Indies" by discovery "just as if they had discovered a hitherto uninhabited desert." But he is concerned here to refute the thesis that the Indies were "unoccupied" or "deserted" or otherwise outside "true public and private dominion."[8] He is not concerned to deny that there are or may be regions which *are* outside such dominion, such as that "hitherto uninhabited desert." So he is not claiming that the world is exhaustively divided among states.

Moreover, at the end of his discussion of the seven or eight *just* titles the Spanish *might* have had for assuming the administration of the Indies as their territorial possessions, Vitoria states that "there are many things which they [the native peoples and rulers of the Indies] regard as uninhabited, or which are common to all who wish to appropriate them."[9] This harks back to the first of these just titles, to which he gives the headline: "natural partnership [societas] and interaction [communicatio]." The thrust of the argument is that even though the native peoples and their rulers have governmental jurisdiction and genuine ownership of their territories and of any privately or publicly owned lands within them, they nonetheless are bound by natural justice and the quasi-positive law common to all peoples (the *ius gentium*) to allow well-intentioned travellers into their territories as tourists, missionaries, and traders, and as miners, pearl-fishers, and collectors of other kinds of *communia* or *res nullius*. Unowned natural resources are to be available to peaceful and well-intentioned foreigners on essentially the same terms as they are available to citizens. The division of resources for the purposes of private appropriation is in almost all human circumstances a requirement of justice, and results in ownership, *dominium*, which is just but also is far from absolute. *Dominium* is subject to override for the prevention of criminal or harmful activities, and to outright expropriation for the satisfaction of debts (including taxes), the relief of others' urgent necessities, eminent domain for road-building, fire-prevention, and so forth. Just so, the state's or political community's jurisdiction over its boundaries is far from absolute, and the boundaries themselves are quite permeable.[10] For a state to close its borders to well-intentioned strangers, exclude them from its territories or from the fair exploitation of its natural resources or from its markets, and enforce these exclusions by force, would be unjust aggression entitling those whose rights are so violated to undertake a defensive war of conquest – a war intended, that is to say, for the purposes of establishing on a stable footing a substantially just regime of government and property.[11]

This line of thought about just titles for taking territorial possession of lands that are *not* empty *res nullius* appears in Tuck's chapter (8), but rather late – in his discussion of Grotius, nearly a century after Vitoria. (Tuck remarks parenthetically, however, that "the Spaniards and other Europeans had pleaded [these titles] against native peoples.") It is important to notice that it is a line of thought that Vitoria advances substantially as a matter of *ius gentium* rather than as a sheer implication of the principles of natural law or justice. One may think that Vitoria does not work hard enough to show that the customs of all or most peoples treat such offences of exclusion as grounds for a war not simply of satisfaction but of conquest. And one can certainly think that the international law that has supplanted the old, relatively informal *ius gentium* has set its face not only against such *casus belli* but also against the notion that boundaries are properly required to be as permeable to non-citizens as Vitoria contends or assumes.

It is not, perhaps, so clear that the modern *ius gentium* entirely excludes another title that Vitoria advances for the just suppression or overriding of boundaries: defence of the innocent against tyranny or other unjust attacks on human life.[12] We hear talk of justified resort to force to prevent a humanitarian disaster – or at least, if we cannot prevent it, or have perhaps unintentionally provoked it, to put an end to such radical injustice – and establish a more or less international protectorate for ensuring, so far as fairly possible, that injustice of that kind does not quickly resume.

The informing principle is no more and no less precise than the Golden Rule, the requirement of reciprocity, a genuine willingness to consider what one would wish for, or be content to see done to, one's closest friends if they were the ones whose possessions (with their boundaries) were in question.

Notes to Chapter 9

1. There has been a tendency to suppose that if nineteenth-century judges were using a false factual premise in treating the colonisation of Australia as occupation of a *res nullius*, it follows that that colonisation lacked moral or legal title. *Non sequitur*, as the sixteenth-century discussions mentioned at nn.9–12 here make clear.

2. See my *Aquinas: Moral, Political, and Legal Theory* (Oxford: Oxford University Press, 1998) 219–21: "Aquinas's most important treatment of political matters is perhaps his treatise on law (ST I–II qq. 90–108), a discussion shaped by a methodological decision and a theoretical thesis. The thesis is that law exists,

focally or centrally, only in complete communities (*perfectae communitates*). The methodological decision is to set aside all questions about which sorts of multi-family community are 'complete', and to consider a type, usually named *civitas*, whose completeness is simply posited. It is not a decision to regard the *civitas* as internally static or as free from external enemies. Revolutions and wars, flourishing, corruption, and decay are firmly on the agenda. But not the question which people are or are entitled to be a *civitas*.

> The methodological decision . . . has important consequences. He is well aware that in his own world, though there are some city-*states* (*civitates*), there are also many cities (*civitates*) which make no pretension to being complete communities but exist (perhaps established rather like castles to adorn a kingdom) as parts of a realm, and *civitates*, kingdoms, and realms may be politically organized in sets, perhaps as 'provinces' (of which he often speaks) or empires (about which he discreetly remains almost wholly silent). He is well aware of the idea, and the reality, of peoples (*gentes; populi*) and nations (*nationes*) and regions (*regiones*). As we have seen [see passage quoted at n2 below], Aquinas is willing to raise his eyes to relationships of friendship between states, and to the widest horizons of human community, and he envisages treaties and other binding sources of law or right even between warring states. His methodological decision allows him to abstract from all this.
>
> It also allows him to abstract from a number of deep and puzzling questions: how – and indeed by what right – any particular *civitas* comes into being (and passes away); how far the *civitas* should coincide with unities of origin or culture; and whether and what intermediate constitutional forms there are, such as federations or international organisations. Liberated from such questions, Aquinas will consider the *civitas* rather as if it were, and were to be, the only political community in the world and its people the only people. All issues of *extension* – of origins, membership, and boundaries, of amalgamations and dissolutions – are thereby set aside. The issues will all be, so to speak, intentional: the proper functions and modes and limits of government, authoritative direction, and obligatory compliance in a community whose 'completeness' is presupposed."

3. Thomas Aquinas, *In Eth.* [Commentary on Aristotle's *Ethics*] I.2 nn.11–12 [29–30].

4. See *Aquinas*, 126 n112: "Who then is my neighbour, my *proximus?* If 'people in Ethiopia or India', as Aquinas says (*Virt.* q. 2 a. 8c), can be benefited by my prayer, they are my neighbours, though he mentions them to his thirteenth-century audience as people so *remote* that we cannot and therefore morally need not seek to benefit, i.e. to love, them in any other way. As he explains in his discussion of the neighbour-as-oneself principle in *ST* II–II q. 44 a. 7c, 'neighbour' is synonymous here with 'brother' (as in 'fraternity') or 'friend' or any other term which points to the relevant affinity (*affinitas*), which consists in sharing a common human nature (*secundum naturalem Dei imaginem*). 'We ought to treat every human being as, so to speak, neighbour and brother (*omnem hominem habere quasi proximum et fratrem*)': II–II q. 78 a. 1 ad 2."

5. Note that the would-be Thomist who "completed" Aquinas's treatise *De Regno* [*De Regimine Principum*], and whose work was long accepted as Aquinas's by good Thomists (for example, Vitoria), considered that the whole world was subject to the Roman emperor at the time of, and as regent for, Christ – seeing nothing inappropriate in that. See *Reg.* 3 c. 13; cf. Vitoria, *De Indis* I q. 2 a. 1. Francisco

de Vitoria, *Vitoria Political Writings*, eds., Anthony Pagden and Jeremy Lawrance (Cambridge: Cambridge University Press, 1991) 255–6.

6. St. Thomas Aquinas, *De Regno* II cc. 2, 5–8, ed., Phelan and Eschmann, 1949, 56–7, 68, 71, 74–5, 78.

7. Vitoria, *De Indis* I q. 2 a.1, 255.

8. Ibid., I q. 2 a. 3, 264–5.

9. Ibid., I q. 3 conclusion, 291: *multa enim sunt quae ipsi pro desertis habent, vel sunt communia omnibus volentibus occupare.* (I depart in more than one respect from Pagden/Lawrance's "they have many possessions which they regard as uninhabited, which are open to anyone who wishes to occupy" and from Gwladys Williams's "there are many commodities which the natives treat as ownerless or as common to all who like to take them".)

10. Ibid., I q. 3 a. 1, 278–81.

11. Ibid., 281–4.

12. Ibid., I q. 3 a. 5, 287–8.

PART 5

THE ISLAMIC TRADITION

Political Boundaries and Moral Communities: Islamic Perspectives

Sohail H. Hashmi

From its formative years, the Islamic tradition has grappled with the tension between the existential reality of particularistic group identities and loyalties and the normative vision of a universal Muslim community; between the attachments and claims of peoples to particular places and the recognition that the world we inhabit is the common legacy of all humankind. The life of the prophet Muhammad contains ample evidence that he both recognized and used the power of tribal affinities while simultaneously working to establish the transcendent identity of membership in the community of Muslim believers, the *umma*. According to one *hadith*, the Prophet declared: "He is not of us who proclaims the cause of tribal partisanship (*'asabiyya*); and he is not of us who fights in the cause of tribal partisanship; and he is not of us who dies in the cause of tribal partisanship."[1] Seven centuries later, Ibn Khaldun argued that what the Prophet castigated was not group loyalties (*'asabiyya*) per se, only the negative consequences stemming from blind chauvinism. Group feelings are natural to human beings and, when properly motivated and channelled, are necessary to the Muslims' fulfillment of God's purpose.[2] In 1933, Rashid Rida responded in much the same way when asked if twentieth-century Muslim nationalism was merely another manifestation of *'asabiyya*. When nationalism is the patriotic expression of a people's desire to rid themselves of foreign oppression, he argued, it is quite different from the narrow tribal ethos condemned by Islam. At the same time, the Muslim patriot cannot forget that "he is a member of a body greater than his people, and his personal homeland is part of the homeland of his religious community. He must be intent on making the progress of the part a means for the progress of the whole."[3]

The Islamic tradition, therefore, has historically acknowledged the human propensity toward partial loyalties and the resulting drive to erect boundaries of one sort or another. Muslim theorists have disagreed on the moral value to assign such identities and divisions, and whether such natural propensities are to be embraced or combatted as averse to what the

Qur'an repeatedly stresses as the single community of the faithful. Yet, even for those theorists who accept the possibility of social and political divisions within the Muslim *umma*, such particularistic loyalties enjoy only a derivative, functional value in Islamic ethics, only so long as they serve as the means toward the realization of Islam's universalistic moral vision.

This chapter begins with an examination of the types of boundaries found in the two fundamental sources of Islamic ethics, the Qur'an and *sunna* (moral injunctions and example) of the Prophet. As we shall see, they offer only sparse guidance toward an Islamic view of the making and unmaking of territorial or political boundaries. The Qur'an and the *sunna* are replete with references to human boundaries. Invariably, however, the boundaries discussed are social, religious, and metaphysical, those separating human beings from one another primarily on theological or ideological differences. The Qur'an uses such terms as *qawm*, *umma*, *shi'a*, or *hizb* (or their plural forms) to designate separate religious communities, factions, or sects (for example, 6:159, 7:203, 23:53, 30:32, 43:65). The Arabic word most commonly used to connote the idea of a limit or boundary, *hadd*, appears fourteen times in its plural form *hudud*, but each reference is to the limits or ordinances established by God for one who would live a righteous life (for example, 2:229–30, where the expression *hudud Allah* occurs six times in reference to divorce).

Nevertheless, given the early and thorough incorporation of politics into Islamic morality, the issues discussed in this volume have figured prominently in Muslim discourse. The scholars who first and most systematically grappled with these issues were invariably lawyers. Beginning in the second Islamic century, these men produced a wide-ranging body of ethical-legal rulings that purported to offer all Muslims – from the common believer to the commander of the faithful – an integrated and comprehensive path (*shari'a*) through the vicissitudes of this earthly life. Though claiming ultimate sanction from the Qur'an and *sunna* for their rulings, the early jurists necessarily drew upon the much more extensive body of rulings and practice from the period of the Prophet's successors, from the first four rightly guided caliphs through Umayyad rule and up to the Abbasid period in which most of them lived and worked. This was particularly true for administrative and "international" law, the fields in which many of the moral questions discussed here fall.

The juristic tradition has historically dominated Islamic intellectual life. No survey of the Islamic ethics of social or political matters can dispense with it. I do not want, however, to make an explication of this medieval jurisprudence (*fiqh*) the sole concern of this chapter. To do so would be to neglect other intellectual and spiritual strands within Islam that have quite a bit to say on the ethics of boundaries, most importantly, for example, the Sufi tradition. It would also reduce the Islamic tradition to a rather arcane, and some would say obsolete, set of doctrines that applied to the first few Islamic centuries, but which have little relevance to the twenty-first century. Muslim philosophical engagement with the topics of this volume continues in a lively and dynamic manner. Some Muslims defer to the work of the medieval jurists as being an authoritative expression of Islamic ethics; others call for a reopening – or perhaps more accurately, continuation – of the methodology of the early jurists, so that each new generation derives for itself its conclusions from the Qur'an and *sunna*.

Social Boundaries in the Qur'an and *Sunna*

The Qur'an declares in one key verse: "O humanity! We created you from a male and a female, and made you into peoples and tribes that you may know one other. Truly the most honored among you in the sight of God is the most righteous among you" (49:13). This is one of the clearest articulations of a recurring theme in the Qur'an: recognition – even divine sanction – of particularistic human loyalties, combined with constant reminding of the essential oneness of humanity. "Peoples" (*sha'ub*) and "tribes" (*qaba'il*) have their place in God's unknown plan for humanity. They serve useful purposes, as a means of self-reference and facility of interaction. But the clear intent of the verse is to condemn such ascriptive categories as sources of value in themselves; the only truly meaningful label is that of the righteous human being.[4]

Many other qur'anic passages invoke the same idea, but in the context of a different type of human community: "If God so willed, He could make you all one nation [*umma wahida*], but He leaves straying whom He pleases, and He guides whom He pleases" (16:93; see also 11:118, 42:8). In these verses, the emphasis is clearly upon moral or religious disunity, not the ethnic, racial, or linguistic divisions suggested in Q. 49:13. The key term here is *umma*, surely one of the central ethical concepts introduced in the Qur'an. *Umma* (or its plural form *umam*) appears sixty-four times in the Qur'an. In the overwhelming majority of cases, the word evokes the idea of a moral community. The size of this community ranges from one, as in Q. 16:120, where Abraham alone is described as being an *umma*, to all of humanity as indicated in the verses cited earlier.[5] The size of the community is not significant; it is the idea that righteousness and adherence to the truth as revealed by God and as suggested by the human conscience inherently demarcates boundaries between one individual or group and another.

Most occurrences of the term *umma* emphasize the fact that human beings are fractured into a number of different *umam* on theological and moral grounds. The reason suggested by the Qur'an for the stubborn persistence of this moral diversity is again a combination of human will and divine plan. God created human beings as one community (*umma wahida*; see Q. 2:213, 10:19), and then – in what Frederick Denny calls a "characteristically Qur'anic" ambiguity – both allowed human beings to fracture this unity as well as willed it.[6] A manifestation of God's mercy is that He has sent to every community a messenger bearing the same message: "Serve God and eschew evil" (16:36). All the prophets themselves form a single *umma* (21:92, 23:52), joined together, the Qur'an suggests, by both their common mission and the way they are received by their respective audiences. All human beings are potentially members of this same community that acknowledges and submits to the divine guidance, the *umma muslima*, if they so choose. Yet, as the Qur'an makes clear, the majority of human beings will reject the message outright or distort it over time to suit their own desires (e.g., 21:93; 23:44, 53; 34:28; 40:5). Even the children of Abraham, the Jews and Christians, have "cut their affair [of unity] between them, into sects" (23:53). Thus the need for Muhammad, the messenger sent to renew the pristine monotheism preached by all the prophets (see especially Q. 7, *surat al-a'raf*).

Western students of Islam have speculated for centuries as to the Jewish or Christian "sources" for Muhammad's ideas and the various events in his prophetic career that forced his thinking to evolve. One piece of orthodoxy in the orientalist literature is that in Mecca the Prophet saw his message as essentially the same faith as that of the Jews, Christians, and other unorganized monotheists (*hanifs*), but directed specifically at a pagan Arab audience. He saw himself as the prophet sent to his particular community or *umma* just as earlier prophets had been sent to their respective communities. When he relocated to Medina in 622 C.E. (the Hijra), Muhammad broadened the *umma* concept to embrace the Jews of Medina as well, an arrangement formalized in the so-called Constitution of Medina. However, when the Jews proved adamant in their rejection of his prophetic claims, Muhammad severed his ties with them, and began to emphasize the separateness of the Muslim *umma*. He now explicitly linked himself and the message he brought to the original faith of Abraham, which preceded Jewish and Christian sectarianism (2:135, 3:65). By the time of his triumphant return to Mecca, Muhammad had clearly conceptualized the distinctiveness and universality of the Muslim *umma* in opposition to other religious or ethnic groupings.[7]

This account of the evolution of the Muslim *umma* is primarily grounded in a chronological reconstruction of the qur'anic revelation. Though this has always been an imprecise science, enough information is available to support Denny's conclusion that "not until Medina do we discover any instances of *ummah* which are exclusively Muslim in their application, although . . . many of the Meccan passages apply to the developing Muslim community as well as to other peoples and religious traditions."[8] Muslim scholars emphasize the second half of Denny's statement to argue against the orientalist suggestion of "breaks" or major reformulations of the *umma* concept over time. As Fazlur Rahman writes: "A closer study of the Qur'an reveals, rather, a gradual development, a smooth transition where the later Meccan phase has basic affinities with the earlier Medinan phase; indeed, one can 'see' the latter in the former."⁹ The idea of separate religious communities was therefore already present towards the end of the Meccan period, and although the Medinan verses reflect the changed circumstances of the Muslim community, the notion of *umma* remains rather consistent.

In Medina, once the Muslim community had acquired a degree of social cohesion and a geo-political center, the Qur'an begins to emphasize its special mission among other moral communities. The Muslim community is a "median community" (*ummatun wassatun*), one avoiding sectarian extremes and witnessing to the true faith of Abraham (2:143). It is the "best community" (*khaira ummatin*), one "enjoining what is right and forbidding what is wrong, and believing in God" (3:110). The characterization as the "best community" comes with an important caveat, for as the Qur'an had indicated in a previously revealed verse, "If you [Muslims] turn away [from the right path], He will substitute in your place another people. Then they would not be like you!" (47:38).

One significant clue to the Prophet's understanding of *umma* comes from the so-called Constitution of Medina, preserved by the Prophet's biographer Ibn Ishaq as a single document, but most likely a series of agreements forged by Muhammad among the Meccan and Medinan Muslims, and eventually the Medinan Jews as well.¹⁰ The first article of this document establishes the "believers" (*mu'minun*) and the Muslims of Quraysh and Yathrib (the original name for Medina) and "those who follow them and are attached to them" as constituting a single *umma* distinct from other people. Much later in the document (perhaps appended to the original contract a year or two later) appear a series of articles incorporating individual Jewish tribes of Medina as an *umma* along with the believers (*ma'a al-mu'minin*).¹¹

The ambiguity of the preposition has given rise to controversy over the status of the Jews in the Muslim *umma*. Some argue that Muhammad envisioned the *umma* quite expansively, to include Jews and pagans residing in Medina. The Medinan *umma* emerges in this reading as some sort of overarching, secular identity, within which are a number of separate confessional groups, joined together in a political and military alliance. The more likely reading, however, is that the Jews form a separate *umma* alongside the Muslim community. As the document itself states, the Jews "have their religion or law [*din*] and the Muslims have theirs."¹² The historical records indicate that Muhammad followed a rather consistent policy of treating the Medinan Jews as a community apart from the Muslims. Moreover, this view is supported by the Qur'an's use of *umma* in the Medinan period, which is to designate separate and clearly articulated religious communities, though not necessarily mutually incompatible or exclusive in their moral mission. As Q. 5:48 states: "If God so willed, He would have made you a single people [*umma wahida*]. But [His plan is] to test you in what He has given you. So strive as in a race in all the virtues. The goal of you all is to God. It is He who will tell you the truth as to your differences." If the traditional dating of the *sura* (chapter) containing this verse is to be believed, this is one of the final occurrences of *umma* in the Qur'an. The clear implication is that the Muslim *umma* is merely one of many *umam* necessary to fulfill God's plan.

Thus, by the end of the qur'anic revelation, the Muslim *umma* emerges as the most inclusive, universal moral community, transcending other ethnic, racial, and religious boundaries, but existing in a world in which other *ummas* persist. The question now before us is: Does the Muslim *umma* also transcend all geographical limitations?

Sacred Space in the Qur'an and *Sunna*

Very few references to spatial boundaries may be found in either the Qur'an or the *sunna*, and these relate more to sacred space than to any political borders. On the basis of these two sources, and apparently from an early period in Islamic history, three sites acquired particular sanctity in Muslim piety: Mecca, Medina, and Jerusalem.

The sanctity of Mecca stems from the presence at its heart of the sanctuary of the Ka'ba. This sacred space predates the birth of Muhammad in 570 C.E. and may very well predate the creation of the city itself.[13] The Ka'ba had evolved in the centuries prior to Muhammad's birth as a principal center of the religious life of the Arabs. Islamic tradition holds that the structure had been erected by Abraham and Ishmael as the first place of worship for the One God (Q. 2:125–29, 3:96). This belief, according to Muslim historians, was part of the pre-Islamic Arab religion as well, but by the late sixth century, the worship of Allah had been combined with polytheistic, animist worship centering on the Ka'ba.[14] An annual pilgrimage brought tribes from diverse parts of the Arabian peninsula for a series of rituals involving some 360 deities housed in the Ka'ba.

The Qur'an speaks of the Ka'ba and its environs as a sanctuary or prohibited space (*haram* or *harâm*) on some nineteen occasions. These numerous references have the general aim of "reappropriating" the sanctuary of the Ka'ba for its "original" purpose, the worship of Allah alone. When the Quraysh, the custodians of the Ka'ba, rebuff the Prophet's call by saying that their conversion would result in their expulsion from the sacred land, presumably by pagan tribes, the Qur'an reminds them that it is God – even in their own beliefs – who established the sanctuary from which they derive benefits (28:57). God made this space sacred, the Qur'an declares, when He commanded Abraham and Ishmael to build the Ka'ba there, and He reaffirmed this purpose in the revelation given to Muhammad (27:91). The "restored" Ka'ba is to be the focus of Islamic worship, the direction for prayer (*qibla*) (2:142–45, 149–50) and the pilgrimage (*hajj*) destination for all Muslims at least once during their lifetime (2:158, 196–200, 3:97,

22:26–29). In addition, the Qur'an assimilates into Islamic doctrine the ancient Arabian notions of both prohibited space and time[15]: "Allah made the Ka'ba, the sacred house, an asylum of security for men, as are also the sacred months" (5:2, 97). The reference to the sacred months is to the first, seventh, eleventh, and twelfth months of the lunar calendar, in which raiding and bloodshed were considered taboo among the Arab tribes. But the prohibition on bloodshed within the precincts of the Masjid al-Haram is perpetual and includes a ban on hunting and killing game (5:95–96). There is an important caveat, however: the ban on fighting both in the sacred months and in the sanctuary of the Ka'ba is lifted in the case of self-defense (2:191, 217; 9:36).

Given the importance of the Ka'ba to Islamic ritual, Mecca and its vicinity naturally acquired a central place in both popular and intellectual culture. Jewish and Christian legends of Jerusalem as the "navel of the earth" were adapted by Muslims eager to establish the equal if not greater sanctity of Mecca. Support for the idea that Mecca was the primordial birthplace of the earth, the point from which all other lands were stretched out, was found in the qur'anic characterization of it as the "mother of cities" (6:92, 42:7). As Muslim cosmology evolved, Mecca became not only the center of the earth, but also the axis connecting the seven earthly and seven heavenly layers, with mirror images of the earthly Ka'ba found in each of the seven firmaments.[16] The earliest Muslim geographers reflected this popular spirituality in their cartography; Mecca was frequently placed at the geographic center of the world, commonly depicted as a saucer, with the landmass of Asia, Europe, and Africa surrounded by an unbroken, circular sea.[17]

The sanctity of Mecca is firmly established by the Qur'an. The sanctity of Medina springs entirely from its role in the life of Muhammad and the earliest Muslims following the Hijra. When Muhammad and his Meccan followers relocated to the small settlement of Yathrib some 270 miles to the north, the Muslim *umma* metamorphosed from a small, persecuted sect to an organized community and state. Although Mecca capitulated within eight years to the Muslims, the Prophet chose not to return to his native city, but remained until his death in 632 C.E. in what had come to be known as *madinat al-nabi*, the "city of the Prophet," where he was buried.

The Prophet's tomb, situated in a corner of his mosque, and the graves of many of his family and closest companions in a cemetery within the confines of the town soon became assimilated in Muslim popular piety with the sanctity of Mecca. A visit to the Prophet's tomb (*ziyara*) became a meritorious addition to the obligatory pilgrimage itinerary, sanctioned on the basis of numerous *hadiths*,[18] including one stating: "One prayer at my mosque is better than one thousand at others, with the exception of the Masjid al-Haram" in Mecca.[19] Muslim poets, and particularly those with mystical or Sufi tendencies, have embellished the standing of Medina in Muslim piety over the ages by singing elegies to the beloved Messenger buried in a wondrous garden (*rawda*) that defies earthly comparison. Muhammad Iqbal, the great Urdu-Persian poet of the twentieth century, writes in one of his final verses:

> Old as I am, I am going to Medina
> To sing my song there, full of love and joy
> Just like a bird who, in the desert night
> Spreads out his wings when thinking of his nest.[20]

Occasionally, puritanical elements within Islam have challenged the elevation of Medina's status to a par nearly equal to that of Mecca. In particular, the veneration of the Prophet's tomb and the tombs of other key personages in the first Muslim generation has been attacked by those who see in such practices a dilution of the strict monotheism preached by Muhammad. When Sa'ud b. 'Abd al-'Aziz stormed Medina at the head of a Wahhabi force in 1804, he ordered his followers to strip the tomb of the Prophet bare of its treasures and to demolish the massive green dome over it. The dome survived only because two zealots tumbled to their deaths in the attempt to destroy it.[21] The Wahhabis then turned their attention to the nearby cemetery of al-Baqi', containing the graves of many of the Prophet's family and companions. John Lewis Burckhardt, who visited Medina in 1815, relates that Sa'ud "ruined, without exception, all the buildings of the public burial-ground, where many great saints repose, and destroyed even the sculptured and ornamented stones of those tombs, a simple block being thought by him quite sufficient to cover the remains of the dead."[22]

Such depredations have been decidedly rare, however. Even the most zealous guardians of the unique sanctity of Mecca would not deny the special status of Medina. As Burckhardt's account makes clear, "in prohibiting any visit to the tomb [of the Prophet], the Wahabys never entertained the idea of discontinuing the visit to the mosque. That edifice having been built by the Prophet, at the remarkable epoch of his flight from Mekka, which laid the first foundations of Islam, it is considered by them as the most holy spot upon earth, next to the Beitullah of Mekka."[23] Indeed, the twentieth-century heirs of the early Wahhabi invaders, the Saudi ruling house, have lavished millions of dollars on maintaining the tomb and expanding the mosque of the Prophet to facilitate the performance of *ziyara* by throngs of the faithful.[24]

The origins of Medina's prohibited status is more difficult to ascertain than is the case with Mecca. One indication that the city had already acquired a special status during the lifetime of the Prophet comes from the Constitution of Medina. The center of Yathrib is established as a sanctuary for "people of this document. A stranger under protection shall be as his host doing no harm and committing no crime."[25] R.B. Serjeant quotes a number of Muslim sources that support the view that Muhammad intended to establish in Medina a *haram* akin to that of Mecca. The historian al-Samhudi relates a tradition stating: "God made for his temple (at Mecca) a haram to magnify it, and he made for his Habib and the noblest of mankind to Him, that area which surrounded his place a haram, the statutes (ahkam) of which must be observed." Two more traditions, narrated by no less an authority than Ibn Hanbal, state: "Each prophet has a haram, and al-Madinah is my haram." "Mecca was Abraham's Haram and al-Madinah is my haram."[26]

According to al-Samhudi, the "haramization" of Medina occurred late in the Prophet's life, around year 6 or 7 A.H. By this time, the Muslims were relatively secure from the military threat of the Meccans, so the establishment of the sanctuary could have been, as the traditions suggest, intended to create another sacred territory. But aside from the traditions quoted earlier, there is little evidence in the Prophet's biography to support this idea. Jerusalem and Mecca were clearly the two sacred cities for the early Muslim community, as indicated in the change of the *qibla* (direction of prayer) from the former to the latter in the second year of the Hijra (Q. 2:142).

It is possible that the haramization of Yathrib occurred earlier than al-Samhudi records, when the Quraysh still posed a threat. The *haram* in this case would have served, in a pattern that Serjeant observes to be common among the Arabs, as primarily a "nucleus around which may be gathered an indefinite number of tribes."[27] The force that holds the tribes together is the presence of a charismatic or "holy" individual. Yathrib's sanctity in the constitution could simply refer to profane matters, such as the prohibition on murder, theft, and other crimes that would disturb the fragile communal solidarity forged by the Prophet. Such a reading is supported by the fact that the Medinan tribes had welcomed the Prophet into their midst and accepted his authority in part to quell the internecine blood feuds that had wracked their settlement.[28] Medina's transformation into a sacred space just below Mecca in sanctity probably did not occur until well after the Prophet's death, and the traditions purportedly comparing Medina to Mecca may be explained by the historical rivalry between the inhabitants of the two cities.

As the discussion here demonstrates, the idea of a *haram* most commonly entails restrictions on what all persons, believers or not, may do *within* the designated precincts. One qur'anic verse adds another dimension, that of prohibiting entry into the precincts to certain people: "O you who believe! Truly the pagans are unclean. So let them not after this year of theirs, approach the Masjid al-Haram" (9:28). This verse was revealed most probably after the fall of Mecca to the Muslims and after the Ka'ba had been "cleansed" of its polytheist associations. Those who are prohibited henceforth from access to the Ka'ba are the *mushrikun*, a term that the Qur'an generally employs with reference to the pagan Arabs who had rejected Muhammad's call. The reference to their "uncleanliness" could be understood as an allusion to the various pagan rituals associated with the ancient cults of the Arab bedouin. Early Muslim jurists drew conflicting conclusions as to the legal import of this verse. Abu Hanifa thought the verse prohibited the pagan Arabs from entering only the Masjid al-Haram during the annual *hajj* season, but permitted access at other times. Al-Shafi'i permitted *dhimmis* (non-Muslim subjects of the Islamic state) to visit the Hijaz for a maximum stay of three days.[29] Malik b. Anas argued that the ban not only barred access to the Masjid al-Haram, but to mosques everywhere. The latter opinion, as one modern commentator, Abu al-A'la Mawdudi, notes, is rather untenable because the Prophet allowed pagans into his own mosque in Medina on several occasions.[30]

As indicated by some of the jurists' positions, this verse over time became one of the sanctions for a far broader exclusion than its words suggest. The origins of the practice of excluding all non-Muslims from residing in these two Muslim holy sites are unclear, as have been the precise boundaries of this prohibited zone. Muslim historians record the expulsion of Jews and Christians from parts of the Arabian peninsula during the caliphate of 'Umar (634–644 C.E.). The reasons given for this action are varied. One motive commonly cited is religious: 'Umar acted on the basis of a Prophetic *hadith* that states, "Two religions shall not remain together in the peninsula of the Arabs (*jazirat al-'Arab*)."[31] A number of other *hadiths* convey a similar instruction.[32]

Not only are these reports rather vague in their wording, but their authenticity is also doubtful. Antoine Fattal argues that it is unlikely that such an important instruction of the Prophet would lie unimplemented for eight years after his death, only to be revived toward the end of the second caliph's reign.[33] Greater emphasis must therefore be placed on more pragmatic military and economic explanations for the policy, including suggestions in the Muslim sources that agreements had been violated or simply that the caliph wanted to distribute land owned by Jews and Christians to Muslims.[34]

Whatever the basis for 'Umar's actions, it is extremely unlikely that a ban of all non-Muslims from the peninsula was ever implemented. Claude Cahen notes that "only in Arabia, most strictly in the Holy Cities, was permanent residence by *dhimmis* forbidden, following measures some of which go back to 'Umar – although temporary exceptions under the Umayyads and the 'Abbasids were numerous, and indeed Jews lived in the Yemen until a few years ago [until the creation of the state of Israel]."[35] And as F.E. Peters observes, the boundaries of the prohibited area have fluctuated dramatically over time, encompassing at times western Arabia, or even the entire peninsula, and at others being confined to the Hijaz, the province containing Mecca and Medina. Since the seventeenth century, non-Muslim Europeans were permitted to establish residence in the port city of Jidda, "a mere forty-five miles west of Mecca."[36] Given this fact, the exploits of the Europeans who dared to circumvent the ban and then proceeded to publicize their derring-do seem less than remarkable.[37]

The borders have always been porous, but their continuing importance to conservative Muslim opinion is indicated by a controversy that erupted during the Gulf War of 1990–91. Following the arrival of American and other Western troops in the Arabian peninsula as part of the multinational coalition to repulse the Iraqi invasion of Kuwait, rumors that American soldiers had been invited into Mecca by the Saudi rulers spread through the Muslim world. No doubt such insinuations were part of Iraq's propaganda, but they found a receptive audience in many countries where the reputation of the Saudis and the other Gulf amirs was already quite tarnished because of their perceived subservience to the United States (among other grievances). The intense denials issued by the Saudis reflect their appreciation of the potential threat to their position as the "custodians of the two holy shrines." On August 11, 1990, Rabitat al-'Alam al-Islami (Muslim World League), an international organization based in Mecca and largely controlled by the Saudi regime, published a statement declaring that Mecca and Medina were not under foreign occupation, but were being "tended by secure hands who cherish the religion and the sanctities of all Muslims."[38] Nevertheless, the fact that American troops had been called in to protect those who were "protecting" the Islamic sanctuaries placed the anti-Iraq coalition on the defensive throughout the war.[39] The continuing presence of foreign troops in the Persian Gulf area remains a significant grievance for Islamic opponents of the Saudi regime, including most famously the group led by Usama bin Ladin. In the two most detailed statements of their grievances,the first published in 1996 and the second in 1998 (both receiving scant attention until the September 11, 2001, attacks), Bin Ladin and his supporters placed the American presence in the "holiest of places, the Arabian Peninsula," at the top of the list.[40]

Beyond the two sacred cities of the Hijaz, there is of course a third sacred space in the Islamic tradition: Jerusalem and its environs. The Qur'an alludes to the biblical "promised land" in several verses. Only one verse (5:21) describes this "holy land" (*ard muqaddasa*) as "ordained" or "assigned by God" (*kataba Allah*) to the people of Moses. A second (7:137) says that God fulfilled his promise to the Children of Israel by making them "inheritors" (*awrathna*) of the eastern and western portions of the lands that "We have blessed" (*barakna*). Q. 21:71 and 21:81 repeat the reference to the "blessed land" in contexts indicating that it is Palestine (or, as Muslim commentators frequently refer to it, al-Sham, which encompasses Syria and Palestine). In the first of these references, however, the special claim of the Children of Israel to it is negated by the phrase: "the land which We have blessed for all peoples" (*al-ard allathi barakna fiha li'l-'alamin*). Although the Qur'an never explicitly denies the Jewish claim to this territory, Muslim exegesis generally infers this result from the many charges of Jewish unfaithfulness to God's covenant (for example, 2:61, 83–86; 4:155), resulting in their loss of God's favor (for example, 2:40–44, 45:16–17) and the destruction twice of the temple in Jerusalem (17:2–8).[41] In the rise and fall of moral communities that is one of the Qur'an's central leitmotifs, the Jewish *umma* was succeeded by the Christian *umma,* and both now have been superseded by the Muslim *umma,* to which has passed the claim and the responsibility of upholding the sanctity of the "holy land." This claim, though, has never been an exclusive one. Different levels of discrimination were enforced by Muslim rulers over the centuries, but the presence of Jews and Christians in the city and their right to maintain their places of worship has been generally upheld.[42]

The sanctity of Jerusalem enters the Islamic tradition directly, Muslims believe, with the Qur'an's mention of Muhammad's mystical night journey (*isra'*), during which he was transported from the "sacred mosque" (*al-masjid al-haram*) in Mecca to the "farthest mosque" (*al-masjid al-aqsa*), whose "precincts We have blessed" (17:1). From this single verse has sprung an enormous literature, and from a very early date, this literature identified the sacred precincts (*al-haram al-sharif*) as those on and around the Rock (*al-sakhra*) in the city of Jerusalem.[43] Ibn Ishaq's biography of the Prophet (composed sometime before the middle of the second Islamic century) interprets the verse thus: "Then the apostle was carried by night from the mosque at Mecca to the Masjid al-Aqsa, which is the temple of Aelia [*al-masjid al-aqsa' wa huwa bait al-maqdis min Iliya'*] …."[44]

The earliest Islamic sources date the *isra'* to the year before the Hijra, at a time when the Prophet and the small Muslim community turned towards Jerusalem in prayer.[45] Jerusalem remained the *qibla* following the Hijra, when the first mosques were established in Medina. It was changed to Mecca some seventeen or eighteen months after the migration, and as the relevant qur'anic verses indicate, not without much controversy from the Jews and the remaining polytheist Arabs in Medina. The Jews may have seen the change as dashing their hopes of convincing Muhammad to embrace their faith; the polytheists undoubtedly used the occasion to sow further dissension in the Muslim ranks.[46] The shift in the *qibla* is commonly cited by orientalists as marking the decisive "break" from the Jews and the launching of the independent Muslim *umma* that was discussed earlier.[47] The Qur'an itself downplays the significance of this event, telling the Prophet to inform his detractors that "To God belong east and west. He guides whom He will to the straight path" (2:142). Nevertheless, there can be no doubt from three unambiguous verses that the orientation of Muslim worship is henceforward to be Mecca (2:144, 149, 150).

Some orientalists have questioned whether Jerusalem occupied any significant position in Islamic piety in the centuries before the Crusades. The problem for them stems from the limited *fada'il al-Quds* (blessings of Jerusalem) literature dating from the period before the eleventh century.[48] What little exists may be ascribed to mystics and residents of the city who sought to enhance its status as a pilgrimage site. Thus, legends of the Dome of the Rock (constructed in the late seventh century) being the site of the final judgment proliferated, along with Prophetic traditions alleging the desirability of visiting and living in al-Sham. The dissemination of such legends produced a response aimed at countering the exaltation of Jerusalem over the sacred cities of Mecca and Medina. [49]

The capture of Jerusalem by the Crusaders in July 1099 created no great alarm among Muslims, according to these scholars. Calls for jihad against the invaders were numerous, but references to Jerusalem were sparse. This situation began to change by the mid-twelfth century, largely through the efforts of 'Imad al-Din al-Zanki, who launched a campaign for the liquidation of Frankish rule in al-Sham, the principal goal being the liberation of Jerusalem. Al-Zanki's jihad was buttressed by a propaganda campaign conducted by court poets, who lauded the city's holiness. This new wave of *fada'il al-Quds* literature reached its climax in the second half of the twelfth century during Salah al-Din al-Ayyubi's (Saladin') campaigns against the Crusaders. The effectiveness of this propaganda can be measured by the widespread protests over al-Kamil al-Ayyubi's surrender of Palestine and Jerusalem in 1229 to Frederick II during the Sixth Crusade.[50]

The multiplication of the *fada'il al-Quds* literature continued well beyond the termination of a foreign military threat to the city. In the fourteenth century, Ibn Kathir characterized the legends surrounding Jerusalem as fabrications intended to attract visitors to the city.[51] Ibn Taymiyya felt compelled to compose a special treatise attacking the cult surrounding Jerusalem's holiness, a cult that threatened to overshadow the importance of Mecca and Medina in Islamic faith.[52]

The argument for the late development of Jerusalem's importance to Islam – and largely through political rather than strictly religious motives – places undue weight upon the *fada'il al-Quds* literature while neglecting or discounting the authenticity of the *hadiths* that refer to the city.[53] Numerous traditions extolling the sanctity of Jerusalem were already in wide circulation by the end of the second Islamic century, including one in which the Prophet ordered his followers to "set out [for pilgrimage] to only three mosques – the Masjid al-Haram, the Masjid al-Aqsa, and this mosque of mine [in Medina]."[54] The chain of transmitters for this and other traditions makes it implausible to suggest that they were fabricated by people who were somehow partisans of Jerusalem. Muslim disputes were never over Jerusalem's status as one of Islam's sacred sites, only its standing relative to Mecca and Medina. Neither Ibn Kathir nor Ibn Taymiyya challenged the position of Jerusalem as Islam's third holiest city, nor would they have countenanced foreign rule over it. Similarly, in the modern period, few incidents have produced as concerted and widespread a Muslim response as did the loss of the old city of Jerusalem to Israel in June 1967. Restoring the Haram al-Sharif to Muslim sovereignty is a principal tenet in the manifestoes of Islamic movements worldwide.[55] Israel's "unification" of East and West Jerusalem, and an arsonist's attack on the al-Aqsa mosque in August 1969, spurred the creation of the Organization of the Islamic Conference, an intergovernmental

Sohail H. Hashmi

body that secular Muslim states, such as Turkey and Egypt, had previously rejected.[56]

Political Boundaries in the Qur'an and *Sunna*

In comparison to the numerous references to sacred space in the Qur'an and *sunna* and the richness of the literature that such texts have spawned, profane space and political boundaries occupy a far more limited place in the two basic sources of Islamic ethics. There are, however, a few intriguing allusions that hearken back to conceptions of territoriality held by Arabs before the rise of Islam.

The dominant influence upon these views was of course the desert environment in which Arab mores had developed. Physical boundaries of any sort are hard to maintain in the desert, and the necessity of nomadism in the quest for scarce water and grazing land diminishes their value even more. Yet the territorial imperative asserted itself even in these unfavorable conditions, naturally so perhaps given the bitter struggle for scarce resources. The bedouin tribes circulated generally within a prescribed area, moving from one place to another as the depletion of water and grazing land required.[57] Physical demarcations of a tribe's boundaries were likely rare, and if present, constructed crudely of stones, stakes, or shallow ditches.[58] Powerful chieftains sometimes marked off grazing land for their private use, and this "inviolable pasture" (*hima*) was in turn assimilated into the religious concept of a *haram* through the designation of a deity that safeguarded it. Such appropriations of fertile land ran counter to the communal ethic of the bedouin, and as pre-Islamic poetry attests, ended on occasion in bloodshed among members of the same or related tribes.[59]

Raids by one tribe into the territory of another were common, but such incursions were generally aimed at snatching movable property, and not for territorial expansion. To signal their peaceful intentions in the territory of a particular tribe, an individual or a caravan would apply for protection (*jiwar*) from the tribal chieftain, who then was honor-bound to protect the lives and property of his clients until they had passed beyond his territory.[60]

Islam was born in an urban, not nomadic, milieu. At the time of Muhammad's birth, his tribe, the Quraysh, had been settled in Mecca for perhaps little over a century. Legend held that it was Qusayy b. Kilab who had seized control of the settlement for the Quraysh and had transformed a melange of habitations surrounding the sacred sanctuary of the Ka'ba into a city. Qusayy divided the land around the Ka'ba into districts, which he then allotted to the various clans comprising the tribe of Quraysh. The clans that settled in the hollow where the Ka'ba is situated emerged as the most prestigious families in Mecca because of the proximity of their territory to the sanctuary.[61]

Muhammad was born into one of these sedentarized families. The Quraysh by this time had long since left behind the uncertainties of a nomadic existence. The tribe had generally prospered on the revenues accrued from the annual pilgrimage, which it supervised, and through the caravan trade from Yemen to Syria, which Mecca was ideally placed to exploit. The Qur'an intimates in *surat al-balad* of the social position of Muhammad's family and his own emotional attachment to the the city when it describes him as *hillun* (a native freeman), whose ties to Mecca are as those of a child to a parent (90:1–3).

Yet memories of the Quraysh's desert origins lingered. Ibn Ishaq reports that in keeping with custom, Muhammad was turned over to bedouin foster-parents shortly after his birth. This period of infancy would become embellished in the earliest biographies as a period of spiritual preparation and even miraculous "cleansing" prior to his assumption of his prophetic mission. We are told that the Prophet recalled with fondness his years in the desert.[62] There is clearly an intimation in these sources that although the majority of early Muslims came from a sedentarized background, and that Islam sanctioned property rights and defined territorial boundaries, the nomadic life of unrootedness, migration, and sharing of resources remained an ideal.

The bedouin aversion to personal claims of monopoly on scarce resources, for example, is reflected in the treatment of the institution of *hima* in Islamic tradition. Although it survived into the Islamic era on a strictly secular basis – the idea of a *haram* being disentangled from it and limited to the three sacred sites discussed earlier – its validity even then was challenged by some legal scholars.[63] The Qur'an seems to be condemning *hima* when it repeatedly recounts the prophet Salih's warning to his tribe of Thamud not to harm "God's she-camel" as it grazes on "God's land," land which they – or perhaps the wealthy among them – had restricted to their own use (7:73, 17:59, 26:155–58). In addition, the *hadith* are replete with condemnations of hoarding, especially of vital resources, as in the tradition that "All Muslims own alike three things: water, forage, and fire."[64]

The ideal of being free of any territorial restrictions, of any cultural parochialisms, comes together in another central Islamic motif: *hijra*. Two examples of migration are present in the Prophet's life. The first is the sending of the poorest and most vulnerable Muslims to the protection of a Christian ruler in Abyssinia (615 C.E.) in order to escape the persecution of the Quraysh. Muhammad and those of his followers who still enjoyed the protection of their clans did not participate in this migration. The second is, of course, the migration to Medina in 622 C.E. Although the majority of the Prophet's followers accompanied him on this migration, some chose to remain in Mecca. The Qur'an hints at the psychic difficulties associated with uprooting oneself and one's family from familiar surroundings (4:100; 16:41, 110–11), while at the same time leaving no doubt that such a course is obligatory for the true believer: The angels will question those who protest that they could not escape from sin because they were weak and oppressed, "Was the earth not spacious enough for you to migrate [away from evil]?" (4:97). Beyond the change of locality, and perhaps the more difficult challenge, was the changing of one's communal identity involved in the Hijra. The emigrants severed ties to their own clans, the source of identity in this tribal culture, in exchange for allegiance to a new community, the moral community of the Muslim *umma*.[65]

Given the importance of the Prophet's migration to Islamic history, the significance of *hijra* is naturally broad and multifaceted in the Islamic tradition. For the Sufis, *hijra* is the willingness to leave behind all earthly attractions in quest of the divine beloved, the fleeing from the outward world to the depths of the interior, spiritual world.[66] We will consider later the powerful and varied political roles *hijra* has played throughout Islamic history.

The Meaning of *Dar al-Islam*

As we have seen thus far, the notion of territoriality is present in the basic sources of Islamic ethics, but hardly emphasized. With the expansion and consolidation of the Islamic empire after the death of Muhammad, the idea of frontiers separating lands under Muslim sovereignty from those under neighboring powers developed naturally. The most important frontier during the early medieval period was the marches (*thugur*) separating the Islamic caliphate from the Byzantine empire.[67] Some of the seminal works on jihad relate to the merits of manning the lonely outposts (*ribat*) and occasionally combatting the enemy in the prolonged war of attrition along this border.[68] Similar literature developed later in the *thugur* of Andalucia, the Sahara, the Balkans, and in the Caucusus and central Asia.

Territorial boundaries apparently acquire a central significance in the development of the juridical theory of international relations (*siyar*), premised as it is on the division and opposition of *dar al-Islam* and *dar al-harb* – terms that may be rendered as "territories of Islam" and "territories of war." This translation, however, is fraught with some basic problems, so fundamental as to render the territorial component virtually meaningless.[69] First, as Khaled Abou El Fadl demonstrates in Chapter 11, the terms were hardly used in a consistent manner, even by the leading, orthodox schools of jurisprudence. Disputes abounded on such basic questions as what conditions qualified territory for either designation, whether Muslims may reside outside of *dar al-Islam*,[70] and whether other *diyar* (pl. of *dar*) existed between the two.[71]

Second, the idea of defined territorial frontiers seems to have played an insignificant part in the medieval understanding of these terms. Theoretically, the limits of *dar al-Islam* could not be fixed because the goal of the caliphate was to incorporate *dar al-harb* steadily into *dar al-Islam* by expanding the area where Muslim sovereignty prevailed. In historical reality, the frontiers of *dar al-Islam* always remained extremely fluid: Muslim power periodically waxed or waned along the Syrian and Anatolian borders with the Byzantine empire; the Reconquista nibbled away at Muslim principalities in Spain over four centuries; the Ottomans withdrew piecemeal from the Balkans and the Black Sea littoral from the eighteenth through the early twentieth centuries.[72]

Moreover, the ideal of a unified Muslim community inhabiting a territory under the sway of a righteous, unitary caliphate was belied by the emergence in the second Islamic century of rival principalities, ruled often by corrupt and oppressive rulers. For some scholars, particularly those from minority Muslim communities, *hijra* within *dar al-Islam* became as much a religious duty as *hijra* to *dar al-Islam*.[73] Similarly, many radical Islamic groups today enjoin upon their followers a withdrawal from allegedly corrupt, nominally Muslim societies in preparation for jihad to reestablish the authentic Islamic order.[74]

Finally, the works of early Muslim geographers also indicate that the idea of well-defined territorial boundaries was lacking with respect to both the frontiers separating *dar al-Islam* from *dar al-harb*, as well as the internal boundaries that divided *dar al-Islam*. Ralph Brauer writes that Muslim geographers from the ninth through the fourteenth centuries generally distinguished the two types of boundaries in their terminology: *thagr* (pl. *thugur*), *'asim* (pl. *'awasim*), or *nib* (pl. *aniab*) for the first type; *hadd* for the second.[75] In both cases, however, boundaries existed "in the sense that as one progressed in a direction away from the center of a state, one would sooner or later pass from one sovereignty to another or that one's taxes would flow to different places on either side of such a division. Yet, clearly in the minds of these cartographers such boundaries were constituted not as sharply defined boundary lines but rather as transition zones of uncertain sovereignty between two states."[76]

If not principally as a territorial concept, then how was *dar al-Islam* understood by its medieval theorists? It was, I suggest, fundamentally a political, cultural, and ethical construct, a logical derivative of the moral ideal of the united Muslim *umma*. *Dar al-Islam* was simply any area in which the *umma* could realize the Islamic message. Intrinsic to this message was the notion that non-Muslim communities were constituent elements of *dar al-Islam* and that they were entitled to a degree of autonomy within it. For the jurists, this understanding required a state governed by Islamic law and led by Muslim rulers. Thus, territoriality was a functional necessity inasmuch as any state secures territory for the use and welfare of its population. But for jurists of the Shafi'i, Maliki, and Hanbali schools, territory was decidedly of secondary importance on the fundamental issue of legal jurisdiction. The *shari'a* injunctions bound Muslims whether they were in *dar al-Islam* or *dar al-harb*. Only the Hanafi school held that Islamic law was territorial, not personal in application, and thus allowed Muslims residing outside of *dar al-Islam* to follow local laws or customs – such as those relating to commerce and diet – even though they contravened Islamic law.[77]

While the theory of an internally borderless *dar al-Islam* was never quite matched by reality, there was over much of Islamic history substance to this ideal. Not only could a merchant-adventurer such as Ibn Battuta wander freely from one Muslim state to another, but he and others – including most famously Ibn Jubayr, Ibn Khaldun, and Moses Maimonides – could secure employment as roving intellectuals in Muslim capitals as distant as Cordoba, Tunis, Cairo, Baghdad, and Delhi. Even after the simultaneous consolidation of the three great modern Muslim empires – the Ottoman, Safavid, and Mughal – travel and migration across borders remained relatively unimpeded.[78]

European imperialism and the emergence of post-colonial Muslim states in the mold of the territorial "nation-state" have, of course, dramatically altered the situation. *Dar al-Islam* has today been effectively stripped of whatever little territorial or political connotation was still attached to it. Yet references to it – such as talk of the Muslim *umma* – still abound in Muslim discourse. It is tempting to dismiss them as mere rhetoric, and certainly in the language of politicians that is often precisely what they are. In the language of Islamic scholars and activists, references to *dar al-Islam* and the *umma* reflect not an attempt to resurrect medieval conceptions, but the recognition that much of Muslim international politics today does not accord with Islam's universalist vision. The work of the Syrian scholar Wahba al-Zuhayli is representative of the ambivalence toward the post-colonial territorial state in contemporary Islamic discourse. He argues that the Islamic ideal of *dar al-Islam* embraces all Muslims as the ocean embraces all fish. This ideal, however, need not require the political unity of all Muslims in a single state. *Dar al-Islam* may be divided into numerous states – with the significant proviso that each fulfill the ethical and legal requirements incumbent upon an Islamic state.[79]

The Expansion and Contraction of *Dar al-Islam*: Settlement, Conquest, and Migration

Insofar as *dar al-Islam* held some territorial content, the means by which its territory expanded or contracted became an important subject of juristic concern. Acquisition of rights to land by the state or an individual was treated in medieval jurisprudence under two broad categories: (1) open land not claimed by any state or people, and (2) land in the possession of another state or people.[80] The following discussion focuses primarily on the rules governing acquisition of territory by the Islamic state.

Unclaimed territory and dead or waste land (*mawat* or *'adi*) raised relatively few problems in medieval law. The Islamic state could claim and settle it according to its interests. A tradition of the Prophet stipulates: "The '*adi* lands belong to God and to His messenger and then to you. So whoever revives dead land has the right to it." This *hadith* is transmitted in many variations,[81] leaving the jurists in disagreement on whether private efforts (and hence legal claims) to revive dead land without prior state authorization are permitted or proscribed.[82] Nevertheless, general agreement existed that once a claim to waste land is made by establishing some physical boundaries (such as "heaping earth," according to al-Mawardi), steps must be taken to revive it and bring it under cultivation within three years. Otherwise, it reverts to the state, which should then assign it to any individual who has already taken, or is likely to take, steps to revive it.[83]

The second category was obviously much more relevant to the Muslim experience, from the consolidation of the Prophet's state in Medina to the rapid expansion of the Islamic empire following his death. The large and complex body of juristic literature on this subject may be further divided into two sub-categories according to the method by which territory was added to *dar al-Islam*. The first includes such peaceful means as cession, purchase, or bequest. *Dar al-Islam* was born out of the voluntary conversion of the Medinan tribes and their invitation to the Prophet and his Meccan followers to resettle in their town. The religio-political center of the new state – the mosque and attached apartments of the Prophet – were built on land purchased by a Medinan convert.[84] Over the next eight years, through a combination of diplomacy and missionary activity, the Prophet forged alliances with the bedouin tribes in the vicinity of Medina. They were thus incorporated into *dar al-Islam*, albeit tentatively, as we shall see in the next section.

Another method of transferring property rights – inheritance – figures prominently in medieval jurisprudence, but only in the private sphere. Islamic law makes accretion of territory to *dar al-Islam* through inheritance difficult, since generally Muslims may not inherit from unbelievers. A Muslim ruler could not therefore acquire territory as an inheritance from a related non-Muslim ruler. Theoretically, of course, a ruler in *dar al-harb* could embrace Islam and then bequeath territory to his Muslim relative. This scenario seems not to have received serious consideration by the jurists, perhaps because of its implausibility, but more importantly because the institution of hereditary rule – with its attendant territorial claims – was never fully legitimized in the *shari'a*. Dynastic rule – though the prevalent form of government throughout the Muslim world – was merely tolerated by Sunni theorists as a fait accompli.[85]

The evolution of the institution of *iqta '*demonstrates well the ambivalence with which hereditary claims to territory and rulership were treated in Muslim societies. The practice of *iqta'* varied widely in details over time and place, but it generally involved a concession of land to fighters as a reward for their service to the state. Under some rulers, and especially during periods of dynastic decline, *such a concession* became effectively synonymous with ownership and hereditary rule over provincial areas. Yet *iqta'* was most commonly understood as only a temporary grant to a specific person for the right to receive rent from small landowners within the boundaries of the concession. This right reverted to the state upon the death or fall from grace of the concessionaire.[86]

The second sub-category includes land absorbed forcefully through jihad. Conquest could occur through the enemy's capitulation by treaty or unconditional surrender (*sulhan*) or seizing through force of arms (*'anwatan*). Both cases constitute what Muslim writers dubbed the *futuhat*, the "opening" of territory to Islamic preaching, to taxation, and to settlement by Muslims.

Territorial expansion is prominently absent from all the motives presented in the Qur'an for fighting (*qital*) (e.g., 2:190–93; 9:5, 29; 22:39–40). The few verses that allude to it do so only in the context of the incidental consequences of war. And the majority of these relate to the clashes between the Muslims and two Jewish tribes originally resident in Medina, the Banu Nadir and Banu Qurayza.

The Nadir tribe was expelled from Medina in 4 A.H. after a brief siege of their fortified settlement. They withdrew to a more northern oasis named Khaybar, carrying with them as much of their property as they could move. The landed property was claimed by the Prophet alone to dispense as he saw fit because the Nadir capitulated without battle. He chose to distribute it to the poorest Meccan immigrants and to a couple of indigent Medinan Muslims on the basis of their acute need.[87] This type of land claimed in war came to be known as *fay'* from the qur'anic verse describing it as "what God has bestowed (*afa'*) on His Messenger" (59:6).

The Nadir tribe continued to instigate hostility against the Muslims from Khaybar. The following year they formed a confederacy consisting of the Quraysh, other Arab tribes, and the Banu Qurayza, who remained in Medina, to attack the Muslims. When the siege of Medina was successfully lifted, the Prophet turned to besiege the Qurayza in their strongholds. After twenty-five days, the tribe agreed to surrender on the terms of a Muslim arbitrator of their choosing. The arbitrator ruled that the adult men of the tribe be executed and the women and children enslaved. The historians provide few details on the dispensation of the Qurayza's landed property. Ibn Ishaq records only that the Prophet "divided the property, wives, and children of B. Qurayza among the Muslims, and he made known on that day the shares of horse [cavalry] and men [foot soldiers], and took out the fifth [as state property]." He adds that this dispensation provided the precedent for later raids, in which booty (*ghanima*) was dispersed among all participants.[88]

In 7 A.H., the Prophet moved to eliminate the threat from the exiled Nadir tribe in Khaybar. Following a series of encounters and a siege, the residents of Khaybar agreed to leave the settlement in exchange for safe passage. Some appealed to the Prophet, as Ibn Ishaq relates, "to employ them on the property with half share in the produce, saying, 'We know more about it than you and we are better farmers.' The apostle agreed to this arrangement on the condition that 'if we wish to expel you we will expel you.' "[89]

These three cases, each with its different outcome, demonstrate that the Prophet did not adhere dogmatically to any particular custom, but was willing to adapt to the exigencies of the situation. A similar improvisational approach is evident in the actions taken by his immediate successors. By far the most significant for the subsequent development of Islamic law was the caliph 'Umar b. al-Khattab's dispensation of the territory in southern Iraq known as the Sawad. The conquest of this area from the Sassanids was probably complete by 637 C.E., and although conversion had begun to occur, the vast majority of the peasants in this fertile valley between the Tigris and Euphrates remained non-Muslim at the time of 'Umar's decree.[90] According to some traditions, 'Umar initially apportioned parts of the Sawad to tribes that had participated in its conquest, then after two or three years requested the land be returned.[91] Other narratives mention only that he, on the advice of 'Ali b. Abu Talib and others, "declared al-Sawad and other lands fay' in trust for all Muslims, those living at that time and those to come after them, and did not distribute the land."[92] As al-Mawardi points out, however, the key difference between this *fay'* and the Prophet's actions relating to the property of Banu Nadir in Medina and Khaybar was that a fifth was not claimed by the state, nor were specific shares apportioned to individuals or tribes.[93] Instead, the inhabitants of the Sawad were to remain on their land as free tenants paying (if they remained non-Muslim) the capitation tax (*jizya*) and (Muslim or non-Muslim) the land tax (*kharaj*) directly to the state treasury.

The early sources generally emphasize the interests of contemporary and future *Muslim* generations as the basis for 'Umar's actions. One modern scholar, Fazlur Rahman offers an explanation cast in a slightly broader moral framework. Basing his argument on the account given by Abu Yusuf,[94] Rahman suggests that the caliph and those who supported him in this controversial move were motivated by a fundamental sense of socio-economic justice, which militated against the dispossession and dislocation of large numbers of people: "[H]e refused to concede the distribution of one whole country after another among the Muslim-Arab soldiery to the neglect of the world population and future generations." In his creative reinterpretation of the Prophet's precedents, 'Umar was in fact abiding by the Prophet's example.[95]

When the juristic theory of jihad was first elaborated in the eighth and ninth centuries, the expansion of *dar al-Islam* had already begun to slow following a century of remarkable expansion. By the eleventh century, *dar al-Islam* was beginning to contract as Muslim rule crumbled in northern Spain, Sicily, and in the Levant. As large Muslim populations came under non-Muslim rule, the jurists disputed over the permissibility of continued residence in the "lapsed" territories of *dar al-Islam*. For many, *hijra* away from these areas was incumbent upon the faithful; some permitted continued residence so long as Islamic practice was allowed or if emigration was impossible.[96] Given the connection between migration and return in the Prophet's life, the call for *hijra* was invariably coupled with the call for jihad to restore lost territories. In the case of the Levant, Muslim rule was eventually reestablished, but in Spain, Sicily, and later the Balkans, India, and elsewhere, it became clear over time that Muslim rule would likely not be restored. Consequently, the connection between *hijra* and jihad became increasingly ambiguous in the works of religious scholars, a tacit acknowledgement that contractions in *dar al-Islam's* frontiers may be irreversible.[97]

In modern Muslim works on international relations, the acquisition of territory through conquest is disavowed by the vast majority of Muslim writers. The *futuhat* of early Islam are generally consigned to history, an interpretation of Islamic ethics – a misguided interpretation, as some have argued – that does not bind in any way contemporary Muslim generations. The general bent of Islamic opinion today seems to agree with international law that claims to land through military conquest or forcible expulsion of existing populations is illegal.[98] The calls for jihad that resonate most among Muslim populations are those calling for defense of Muslims against military occupation, dispossession, and expulsion by others, as in Palestine, Afghanistan, Bosnia, and Chechnya, to name just a few contemporary cases.

The Fragmentation of *Dar al-Islam*: Secession

As argued earlier, the Prophet emphasized the moral and political unity of the Muslim community from an early date. Not only did he encourage the evacuation of all Muslims from Mecca to Medina, he also recalled the few remaining Muslim emigrants in Abyssinia in 7 A.H., when his position in Medina had stabilized.[99]

As for the internal politics of the Medinan community, the earliest sources record only occasional dissent with specific policies of the Prophet, but provide little indication of serious disunity among the Muslims. The most serious opposition to Muhammad seems to have come from a group of Medinans whose conversion was nominal and who continued to hope and scheme for the demise of Islam. This party of hypocrites (*munafiqun*), as the Qur'an refers to them, does not seem to have been numerically significant or well organized, but as a fifth column within the Muslim ranks, it continued to pose a danger until the final years of the Prophet's life. In one of the final chapters to be revealed, the Qur'an mentions the "mosque of dissension" (*masjid dirar*) erected by a group of hypocrites at Quba on the outskirts of Medina "by way of mischief and infidelity – to disunite the believers" (9:107).

Before the mosque could become the base of operations for his opponents, the Prophet ordered that it be destroyed.[100]

In the later Medinan period, the Qur'an also castigates the bedouins of the interior, whose commitment to Islam constantly wavered according to their own material interests. During the lifetime of the Prophet, these tribes were not considered to be fully a part of the Muslim body politic, and the Prophet exempted them from the duty to migrate to Medina.[101] Soon after his death, the majority of bedouin tribal chieftains refused to pay the alms-tax (*zakat*) that had been instituted by the Qur'an as a principal obligation of Muslim faith. It is unclear whether this refusal signified a reversion of some of the tribes to their pre-Islamic religion, or whether it constituted a political defection from the authority of the central Islamic state, now led by the first caliph, Abu Bakr. Both motives seem to have been involved among the disparate tribes of the peninsula. Yet Islamic history records Abu Bakr's campaigns to enforce the *zakat* upon the tribes as the *ridda* (apostasy) wars. Nevertheless, the true significance of these campaigns is that they constituted the first real test of the nascent Islamic state's claims of sovereignty and territoriality against would be secessionists. In the wake of the *ridda* wars, not only the recalcitrant bedouins, but all the tribes of the peninsula had been brought under Islamic rule,[102] and the principle of the political unity of the ever-growing *umma* had been forcefully asserted.

This principle would be tested and effectively destroyed within thirty years of Abu Bakr's caliphate. The threat was latent even in Abu Bakr's time. It had arisen immediately after the Prophet's death when a party of Muslims loyal to the Prophet's cousin and son-in-law 'Ali felt that the succession had passed to the wrong man when Abu Bakr was chosen by acclamation to lead the community. Though disgruntled at what they considered an injustice, the partisans of 'Ali (*shi'at 'Ali*) had upon the instructions of their leader done nothing to challenge Abu Bakr's authority.

In 656 C.E., after having been passed over twice more, 'Ali finally assumed the caliphate by consensus of the Muslims in Medina. The following five years (656–661 C.E.) of 'Ali's brief tenure were wracked by civil war. Initially, 'Ali's authority was challenged not by men who wanted to secede from the Islamic state centered in Medina, but those who would overthrow 'Ali in order to assume the caliphate themselves.

In the midst of this civil war (referred to in Islamic histories as the first great *fitna*, or "testing"), a group of secessionists known as the Khawarij (from *kharaja*, to "go outside," "depart") broke away from the camp of 'Ali in 657 C.E. This group was disgruntled with 'Ali's agreement to submit his dispute with his principal rival Mu'awiya to arbitration. Human will could not substitute for divine will, which presumably for the Khawarij could be discerned only through victory on the battlefield. Rejecting the claims of both 'Ali and Mu'awiya to the caliphate, the Khawarij pledged their allegiance to their own leader (*imam*).

When the results of the arbitration proved unfavorable to 'Ali, the Khawarij ranks swelled further. Within months, the dissenters had grown into a powerful and militant force. Fueling the movement was a sense shared by many in the Muslim camp that the civil war demonstrated the illegitimacy of the old Medinan elite that had inherited the mantle of leadership from the Prophet. The Khawarij never evolved a coherent body of political doctrine, but at the heart of what little we can discern lies a strictly egalitarian view of the community of believers. The only legitimate credential for leadership of the community was piety, not lineage or Arab descent. Such ideas naturally appealed to the recent non-Arab converts, who formed an important source of Khawarij recruits. The converse of their inclusiveness was an intense fanaticism toward any Muslim who did not share their views. These Muslims were, in the Khawarij view, apostates who could be killed and their property seized. Such views and their rather indiscriminate implementation naturally alienated many Muslims, and in the end kept the Khawarij movement confined to a small minority.

As the Khawarij rebellion intensified in central Iraq, 'Ali changed his initial policy of avoiding contact with them to suppressing the revolt. On July 17, 658, 'Ali's forces destroyed the main Khawarij camp and killed a number of the founding members of the movement, including its leader. This action, far from suppressing the rebellion, only radicalized the survivors, one of whom succeeded in assassinating 'Ali three years later.[103]

With 'Ali's death, the Shi'a began centuries of evolution as a minority community within Islam. In 680 C.E., 'Ali's second son, Husayn, was killed by an Umayyad force at Karbala as he prepared, some think, to lead a Shi'i revolt from southern Iraq. After his death, no subsequent Shi'i leader (*imam*) made any serious bid for political power against the dynastic rule of the Umayyads and later the Abbasids. What had begun as a political dispute with little theological content evolved under the leadership of the nine imams who followed Husayn (in the Twelver Imami tradition) into a separate legal school with distinct conceptions of legitimate rulership, but with few political aspirations. Shi'i political theorists accommodated to the realities of Muslim political life in which Shi'ism constituted a small and, over most of its early history, powerless community. Although Shi'ism was the true Islam and all Sunnis were therefore in error, the Shi'a were not expected to challenge the political authority of the state in which they lived. They could instead practice dissimulation (*taqiyya*) in the face of illegitimate rule.[104]

Dissimulation was in fact the general policy of most Shi'i populations throughout the medieval period. Powerful Shi'i states did arise, particularly the Fatimids who ruled Egypt in 909–1171 C.E., but these were generally established by Shi'i communities who themselves had split from the main line of Twelver Imami Shi'ism, and in the end these states were defeated by Sunni rulers. A powerful and enduring Twelver Imami state would not be established until Iran was conquered by the Safavids in 1501.

As for the Khawarij, they continued harassing the government of the Umayyads; uprisings of individual groups in Iraq are recorded throughout the Umayyad period. Some of these revolts succeeded in establishing independent Khawarij rule in parts of the empire. Although no Khawarij "state" ever managed to survive for very long or to gain substantial territory, the continuing revolts ultimately weakened Umayyad sovereignty in the eastern portions of their empire to the extent that the successful Abbasid revolt of the mid-eighth century originated in this area.

Khawarij militancy waned under Abbasid rule. The movement lost its military and political dynamism and survived only as a separate and distinctly minoritarian strand of theological and political thought. The most lasting impact of the Khawarij revolt was its decisive role in shaping the medieval attitude toward secession.

Within the four principal Sunni schools of law, the value of political stability prevailed over claims of just rule. Umayyad and Abbasid dynastic rule was acknowledged to be a departure from and even a corruption of the Islamic ideal, but in order to avoid a return to the perils of civil war, the jurists were willing to legitimate it. As Ibn Hanbal is reported to have declared:

Whoever secedes (*kharaja*) from the *imam* of the Muslims – when the people have agreed on him and acknowledged his caliphate for any reason, either satisfaction with him or compulsion – that rebel has broken the unity of the Muslims and opposed the tradition coming from God's messenger, God's blessings and peace be upon him. . . . It is not permitted for any person to kill the wielder of power (*sultan*) or to secede from him.[105]

Interestingly, the strong condemnation of secession notwithstanding, Muslim rebels were to be treated, according to the medieval law, rather leniently. The precedent for these policies was 'Ali's treatment of the Khawarij, whom he considered as errant Muslims who had to be reincorporated into the Muslim fold, not as criminals who had forfeited their rights. Thus, rebel prisoners could not be killed or their property confiscated. If rebel forces were fleeing from battle without any expectation that they were regrouping, they could not be pursued by the Muslim army. Certain types of weapons and tactics that were permissible against other targets were to be avoided when fighting rebels.[106]

Despite the significant changes in the political conditions of modern Muslims, contemporary attitudes toward secession remain largely the same, an example, I believe, of the continuing relevance of the *umma* concept. Muslim minorities seeking independence from non-Muslim rule, as in the Philippines, Bosnia, and Chechnya, have received popular and sometimes even state support for their secessionist efforts. In contrast, Muslims wanting to secede from Muslim-majority states have received much less interest and support. Bangladesh successfully seceded from Pakistan in 1971, and today Iraqi Kurdistan enjoys political autonomy only because of foreign, non-Muslim intervention and in the face of general opposition from both Muslim states and Islamist parties.[107]

Conclusion

This chapter demonstrates the great ambivalence and ambiguity characteristic of Islamic discourse on territorial boundaries. The emphasis of Islamic ethics is elsewhere, on other sorts of boundaries, on tearing boundaries down rather than on erecting them.

The Qur'an emphasizes repeatedly the common ontology of human beings as the creation of God. Human beings are all essentially the same in their common origin, condition, and fate.

Human beings establish social boundaries based on a multitude of criteria, some of which have their place, but only in a limited, functional capacity. The only truly meaningful criterion is that of *taqwa*, one of those qur'anic concepts that defies translation. *Taqwa* conveys the sense of being constantly aware of God's presence in one's life; it encapsulates both inner faith as well as outward action. Religion itself then becomes a creator of boundaries, the one separating those cultivating *taqwa* and those rejecting it.

Yet it is clear in the Qur'an that the boundary here is hardly firm, that in this earthly life there is hardly a recognizable community of saved and damned. The boundary is constantly fluctuating and will do so until God reveals the nature of His plan.

Given the primary concern of the Qur'an with spiritual boundaries, physical boundaries play a decidedly secondary role, as merely the means for attaining the spiritual goals. The Prophet stressed the practical bent of Islam's spirituality: religion has to acknowledge and serve both the physical as well as metaphysical needs of human beings. These needs include security and sustenance. Even the most other-worldly moral community, if it is to survive, needs a physical home. Territorial boundaries, therefore, are made to promote the implementation of Islamic ethics, and when they become obstacles in this path, it is the Muslims' obligation to unmake them and imagine new possibilities.

Notes to Chapter 10

1. This *hadith* (report of the Prophet's sayings and actions) is related by Abu Da'ud and cited in Muhammad Asad, *The Message of the Qur'an* (Gibraltar: Dar al-Andalus, 1993), 591,n.15.
2. Ibn Khaldun, *The Muqaddimah: An Introduction to History*, trans. Franz Rosenthal (New York: Bollingen Foundation, 1958), 1:414–17. Another *hadith* clarifies the type of *'asabiyya* condemned by the Prophet: "It means helping your

own people in an unjust cause." Related by Abu Da'ud and cited in Asad, op. cit.

3. Muhammad Rashid Rida, "al-Wataniyya wa al-qawmiyya wa al-'asabiyya wa al-Islam," *al-Manar* 33 (1933): 190–92. Cf. English translation, "Patriotism, Nationalism, and Group Spirit in Islam," in *Islam in Transition*, ed. John Esposito and John Donohue (Oxford: Oxford University Press, 1982), 57–59.

4. For a study of early Muslim interpretations of this verse, and the accommodation of ethnic identities in Islamic ethics, see Roy P. Mottahedeh, "The Shu'ubiyah Controversy and the Social History of Early Islamic Iran," *International Journal of Middle East Studies* 7 (1976):161–82.

5. See Frederick Denny, "The Meaning of *Ummah* in the Qur'an," *History of Religions* 15:1 (August 1975): 34–70.

6. Denny, "Meaning of *Ummah* in the Qur'an," 50.

7. For a succinct version of this argument, see *Encyclopaedia of Islam*, 1st ed., s.v. "Umma," by Rudi Paret.

8. Denny, "Meaning of *Ummah* in the Qur'an," 68.

9. Fazlur Rahman, *Major Themes of the Qur'an* (Minneapolis: Bibliotheca Islamica, 1980), 133.

10. Ibn Ishaq, *Sirat rasul Allah (The Life of Muhammad)*, trans. Alfred Guillaume (Karachi: Oxford University Press, 1990), 231–33. For a reconstruction of the historical circumstances surrounding the document, see R.B. Serjeant, "The *Sunnah Jami'ah*, Pacts with the Yathrib Jews, and the *tahrim* of Yathrib: Analysis and Translation of the Documents Comprised in the So-called 'Constitution of Medina'," *Bulletin of the School of Oriental and African Studies* 41 (1978): 1–42 (reprinted in R.B. Serjeant, *Studies in Arabian History and Civilisation* [London: Variorum, 1981]); and W. Montgomery Watt, *Muhammad at Medina* (Oxford: Oxford University Press, 1956), 221–49.

11. Muhammad Hamidullah, *The First Written Constitution in the World: An Important Document of the Time of the Holy Prophet*, 2nd ed. (Lahore: Sh. Muhammad Ashraf, 1968), 22–3, suggests that the Jews were not incorporated until following the first battle of Badr (2 A.H.), when they realized the growing military strength of the Muslims. Watt, *Muhammad at Medina*, 227, argues that the list of Jewish tribes in the document omits the three most important present in Medina when Muhammad arrived, the Qaynuqa', Nadir, and Qurayza. Thus, the Jewish clauses of the document may date to as late as 5 A.H. or after, when the three main tribes had been either evicted or killed following hostilities with the Muslims.

12. See Frederick Denny, "*Ummah* in the Constitution of Medina," *Journal of Near Eastern Studies* 36:1 (1977): 44.

13. F.E. Peters, *Mecca: A Literary History of the Muslim Holy Land* (Princeton: Princeton University Press, 1994), 19.

14. The vague recognition by the polytheist Arabs of their monotheist origins in the religion of Abraham and Ishmael is commonly asserted in the Muslim sources. See, for example, Ibn Ishaq, *Life of Muhammad*, 38. Western historians have challenged this view, arguing that the connection between the biblical patriarchs and the Ka'ba was invented by Muhammad in Medina as a way of asserting the independence of Islam from Judaism and its associations with Jerusalem. See, for example, Peters, *Mecca*, 19–20; Patricia Crone and Michael Cook, *Hagarism: The Making of the Islamic World* (Cambridge: Cambridge University Press, 1977),

12–4. It should be noted, however, that the first references to Abraham as the original monotheist occur in the early Meccan period of qur'anic revelation (87:18–19, 53:36–37), and that the Qur'an in this period is generally addressing the Meccan polytheists who presumably had some familiarity with him. For further evidence of pre-Islamic traditions linking Abraham to the Ka'ba, see Uri Rubin, "*Hanifiyya* and Ka'ba: An Inquiry into the Arabian Pre-Islamic Background of *Din Ibrahim*," *Jerusalem Studies in Arabic and Islam* 13 (1990): 85–112.

15. For general accounts of pre-Islamic Arabian conceptions of prohibited space, see *Encyclopaedia of Religion*, s.v. "Arabs (Ancient)," by Theodor Nöldeke. See also the *Encyclopaedia of Religion and Ethics*, s.v. "Haram and Hawtah," by R.B. Serjeant.

16. *Encyclopaedia of Islam*, 1st ed., s.v. "Ka'ba."

17. See Husayn Mu'nis, *Atlas tarikh al-Islam* (Cairo: Al-Zahra li'l-I'lam al-'Arabi, 1987), 12–28.

18. See Muhammad ibn 'Abdallah, Khatib al-Tabrizi, *Mishkat al-Masabih*, trans. Mawlana Fazlul Karim (New Delhi: Islamic Books Service, 1998), 3:652–63.

19. This tradition is related by a number of transmitters. See ibid., 3:213.

20. Muhammad Iqbal, *Armaghan-i Hijaz* in *Kulliyat-i Iqbal (Farsi)* (Lahore: Sh. Ghulam 'Ali, 1985), 906; trans. by Annemarie Schimmel, "Sacred Geography in Islam," in *Sacred Places and Profane Spaces: Essays in the Geographics of Judaism, Christianity, and Islam*, ed. Jamie Simpson and Paul Simpson-Housley (New York: Greenwood Press, 1991), 168.

21. John Lewis Burckhardt, *Travels in Arabia* (London: Frank Cass & Co., 1968), 335–36.

22. Ibid., 346. For more on the Wahhabi attack, see John Sabini, *Armies in the Sand: The Struggle for Mecca and Medina* (London: Thames and Hudson, 1981), chap. 4.

23. Burckhardt, *Travels in Arabia*, 346.

24. Greg Noakes, "The Servants of God's House," *Aramco World* (January/February 1999): 48–67.

25. Ibn Ishaq, *Life of Muhammad*, 233.

26. Cited in R.B. Serjeant, "Haram and Hawtah: The Sacred Enclave in Arabia," *Mélanges Taha Husain, publiés par Abdurrahman Badawi* (Cairo: Dar al-Ma'arif, 1962), 50 (reprinted in Serjeant, *Studies in Arabian History and Civilisation*).

27. Serjeant, "Haram and Hawtah," 50.

28. The Constitution of Medina establishes Muhammad as the ultimate arbiter of disputes among Muslims and their confederates. Ibn Ishaq, *Life of Muhammad*, 232–33. Cf. W. Montgomery Watt, *Muhammad at Mecca* (Oxford: Oxford University Press, 1960), 141–44.

29. A.S. Tritton, *The Caliphs and Their Non-Muslim Subjects* (London: Frank Cass and Co., 1970), 176.

30. See Abu al-A'la Mawdudi, *Tafhim al-Qur'an* (*Towards Understanding the Qur'an*), trans. Zafar Ishaq Ansari (Leicester, UK.: The Islamic Foundation, 1990), 3: 200–1.

31. Ibn Ishaq, *Life of Muhammad*, 525. The historian al-Tabari reports that the first caliph Abu Bakr cited this *hadith* when the people of Najran (a town of northern Yemen) petitioned for a renewal of their pact with Muhammad. Muhammad ibn Jarir al-Tabari, *Tarikh al-rusul wa al-muluk* (*The History of al-Tabari*), vol. 10, *The Conquest of Arabia*, trans. Fred M. Donner (Albany: State University of New York

Press, 1993), 163. Nevertheless, non-Muslims apparently continued to reside in Najran during Abu Bakr's reign because soon after 'Umar succeeded to the caliphate, he ordered the relocation of the Christian population of Najran, citing once again the Prophet's *hadith*. Al-Tabari, *History of al-Tabari*, vol. 11, *The Challenge to the Empires*, trans. Khalid Yahya Blankinship (Albany: State University of New York Press, 1993), 175–76. Reports of a Christian presence in Najran continued even afterwards.

32. See *Mishkat al-masabih*, 2:453–57; Antoine Fattal, *Le statut légal des non-musulmans en pays d'Islam* (Beirut: Imprimérie Catholique, 1958), 85.

33. Fattal, *Statut légal des non-musulmans*, 90–91. While the Christians of Najran apparently elicited the attention of Abu Bakr and 'Umar, the Jews of Khaybar, a settlement in the northern Hijaz, do not become a concern until late in 'Umar's reign.

34. Ibn Ishaq, *Life of Muhammad*, 525, for example, cites both the *hadith* on "two religions in the Arabian peninsula" as well as an alleged attack by the Jews of Khaybar upon a Muslim as the reason for the Jews' explusion. See also Fattal, *Statut légal des non-musulmans*, 91, for other Muslim sources.

35. *Encyclopaedia of Islam*, 2nd ed., s.v. "Dhimma," by Claude Cahen.

36. Peters, *Mecca*, xxi.

37. Arthur Jeffery, "Christians at Mecca," *Moslem World* 29:3 (July 1929): 221–35, opens his article by citing unspecified "reliable authorities [who] have told us in regard to Mecca, that hardly a pilgrimage season passes without somebody being done to death on the suspicion of being a Christian in disguise." Nevertheless, as Jeffery's list shows, numerous Christians and undoubtedly other non-Muslims have managed to breach the prohibited space around Mecca and Medina through the centuries with relative ease.

38. *Rabita*, September 1990, pp. 14–15.

39. See Sohail H. Hashmi, "But Was It *Jihad*? Islam and the Ethics of the Persian Gulf War," in *The Eagle in the Desert: Looking Back on U.S. Involvement in the Persian Gulf War*, ed. William Head and Earl Tilford (Westport, Conn.: Praeger, 1996), 47–64.

40. The two statements were published in the London-based Arabic newspaper *al-Quds al-'Arabi*. They were later translated into English and posted on the internet by Bin Ladin sympathizers. For the 1996 statement, dubbed the "Ladenese Epistle: Declaration of War against the Americans Occupying the Land of the Two Holy Places (Parts I–III)," see www.washingtonpost.com (posted Sept. 21, 2001). For the 1998 statement, "Jihad Against Jews and Crusaders," see www.washingtonpost.com (posted Sept. 21, 2001); and Bernard Lewis, "License to Kill: Usama bin Ladin's Declaration of Jihad," *Foreign Affairs* 77:6 (November/December 1998):14–19.

41. See Heribert Busse, "The Destruction of the Temple and Its Reconstruction in the Light of Muslim Exegesis of Sura 17:2–8," *Jerusalem Studies in Arabic and Islam* 20 (1996): 1–17.

42. According to the so-called Covenant of 'Umar – the terms under which Byzantine Jerusalem capitulated to Muslim forces in 638 C.E. – the Christian population was guaranteed "their persons, their goods, their churches, their crosses... No constraint will be imposed upon them in the matter of religion and no one of them will be annoyed." The Christians also demanded and

allegedly received assurance that "No Jew will be authorized to live in Jerusalem with them." The entire document may well be a Christian forgery, and certainly the stipulation regarding Jews was never implemented. Records of small Jewish communities permanently residing in Jerusalem date to immediately after the Arab conquest. See F.E. Peters, *Jerusalem: The Holy City in the Eyes of Chroniclers, Visitors, Pilgrims, and Prophets from the Days of Abraham to the Beginning of Modern Times* (Princeton: Princeton University Press, 1985), 185–86, and chaps. 5–6 passim.

43. See Abdul Aziz Duri, "Jerusalem in the Early Islamic Period: 7th–11th Centuries A.D.," in *Jerusalem in History*, ed. K.J. Asali (Essex, U.K.: Scorpion Publishing, 1989), 105–29.

44. Ibn Ishaq, *Life of Muhammad*, 181; cf. Ibn Hisham, *al-Sira al-nabawiyya* (Al-Zarqa', Jordan: Maktabat al-Manar, 1988), 2:42. Iliya' is the Arabized form of Aelia (Capitolina), the Roman name for Jerusalem that was common in the early Islamic centuries. Arabic sources also commonly used the term for the Temple, *bait al-maqdis*, to designate the city. By the tenth century, the name al-Quds had gained currency. *Encyclopaedia of Islam*, 2nd ed., s.v. "al-Kuds," by S.D. Goitein.

45. Ibn Ishaq, *Life of Muhammad*, 135, tells us that while in Mecca, the Prophet prayed in the direction of Syria (al-Sham), that is, towards Jerusalem.

46. See Ibn Ishaq, *Life of Muhammad*, 258–59.

47. See, for example, Arent Jan Wensinck, *Muhammad and the Jews of Medina*, trans. Wolfgang Behn (Freiburg: Klaus Schwarz Verlag, 1975), 95–96; Watt, *Muhammad at Medina*, 202.

48. Emmanuel Sivan, "The Beginnings of the *Fada'il al-Quds* Literature," *Israel Oriental Studies* 1 (1971): 265, writes: "The date and place of composition of the first *Fada'il al-Quds* tracts induce us to the inevitable conclusion that as a matter of fact Jerusalem did not command such a paramount place in the consciousness of the world of Islam as we might be tempted to infer from various extolling *hadiths*, dating from the eighth century onwards." Oleg Grabar, "The Umayyad Dome of the Rock in Jerusalem," *Ars Orientalis* 3 (1959): 33–62, also considers the *fada'il* literature suspect and so turns to a study of the most important Islamic monument in the city, the Dome of the Rock. The construction and architecture of the Dome, he writes, point to the religio-political motivations of its builder, the Umayyad ruler 'Abd al-Malik, against Jerusalem's preponderantly Christian population. Nevertheless, Grabar does not discount the possibility that other structures in the Haram al-Sharif, including the Masjid al-Aqsa, attest to early Islam's strictly religious connections to Jerusalem – that is, to the Prophet's night journey (pp. 61–62).

49. See S.D. Goitein, "The Sanctity of Jerusalem and Palestine in Early Islam," in *Studies in Islamic History and Institutions* (Leiden: E.J. Brill, 1966), 140–48.

50. Emmanuel Sivan, "Le caractère sacré de Jérusalem dans l'Islam aux XIIe -XIIIe siècles," *Studia Islamica* 27 (1967): 149–82.

51. Goitein, "Sanctity of Jerusalem," 141.

52. See Charles D. Matthews, "A Muslim Iconoclast (Ibn Taymiyyeh) on the 'Merits' of Jerusalem and Palestine," *Journal of the American Oriental Society* 56:1 (March 1936): 1–21.

53. See Amikam Elad, "The History and Topography of Jerusalem during the Early Islamic Period: The Historical Value of *Fada'il al-Quds* Literature: A Reconsideration," *Jerusalem Studies in Arabic and Islam* 14 (1991): 47–48.

54. Khatib al-Tabrizi, *Mishkat al-Masabih*, 3: 213.

55. See Yvonne Haddad, "Islamists and the 'Problem of Israel': The 1967 Awakening," *Middle East Journal* 46:2 (Spring 1992): 266–85; Charter of the Islamic Resistance Movement (Hamas) of Palestine, *Journal of Palestine Studies* 22:4 (Summer 1993): 126–27.

56. See Noor Ahmad Baba, *Organisation of the Islamic Conference: Theory and Practice of Pan-Islamic Cooperation* (Dhakka: University Press Ltd., 1994), 53–55.

57. De Lacy O'Leary, *Arabia Before Muhammad* (London: Kegan Paul, Trench, Trubner and Co., 1927), 14.

58. *Encyclopaedia of Islam*, 2nd ed., s.v. "Mar'a," by J. Chelhod.

59. One of the most famous stories recounted in pre-Islamic poetry was the war of al-Basus, which began when Kulaib b. Rabi'a dealt a mortal wound to a camel belonging to another tribe that had strayed upon his *hima*. See Charles Lyall, *Ancient Arabian Poetry* (New York: Columbia University Press, 1930), 6–7.

60. See O'Leary, *Arabia Before Muhammad*, 179.

61. Peters, *Mecca*, 18–19; Watt, *Muhammad at Mecca*, 5.

62. Ibn Ishaq, *Life of Muhammad*, 72.

63. *Encyclopaedia of Islam*, 2nd ed., s.v. "Hima," by J. Chelhod.

64. Narrated by Abu Da'ud and Ibn Maja. Khatib al-Tabrizi, *Mishkat al-Masabih*, 2: 311.

65. Watt, *Muhammad at Medina*, 242.

66. See Annemarie Schimmel, *Mystical Dimensions of Islam* (Chapel Hill: University of North Carolina Press, 1975), 222.

67. See Michael Bonner, "The Naming of the Frontier: 'Awasim, Thughur, and the Arab Geographers," *Bulletin of the School of Oriental and African Studies* 57:1 (1994): 17–24.

68. See Michael Bonner, *Aristocratic Violence and Holy War: Studies in the Jihad and the Arab Byzantine Frontier* (New Haven, Conn.: American Oriental Society, 1996).

69. See Manoucher Parvin and Maurie Sommer, "Dar al-Islam: The Evolution of Muslim Territoriality and Its Implications for Conflict Resolution in the Middle East," *International Journal of Middle East Studies* 11:1 (February 1980): 1–21.

70. Khaled Abou El Fadl, "Islamic Law and Muslim Minorities: The Juristic Discourse on Muslim Minorities from the Second/Eighth to the Eleventh/Seventeenth Centuries," *Islamic Law and Society* 1:2 (1994): 141–87, esp. 161.

71. The Shafi'i school interposed a third category, *dar al-sulh* or *dar al-'ahd* – territory governed by a power with whom the Muslims had treaty relations. The majority of other schools, most notably the Hanafis, rejected such a category, arguing that any territory that came to terms with the Islamic state should be considered part of *dar al-Islam*. Wahba al-Zuhayli, *Athar al-harb fi al-fiqh al-Islami: Dirasa muqarana* (Beirut: Dar al-Fikr, 1981), 175–76.

72. See Aziz Ahmad, "The Shrinking Frontiers of Islam," *International Journal of Middle East Studies* 7 (1976): 145–59.

73. Abou El Fadl, "Islamic Law and Muslim Minorities," 152.

74. See, for example, Gilles Kepel, *Muslim Extremism in Egypt: The Prophet and Pharoah* (Berkeley: University of California Press, 1985), 77–91.

75. Ralph W. Brauer, *Boundaries and Frontiers in Medieval Muslim Geography* (Philadelphia: American Philosophical Society, 1995), 12–13.

76. Ibid., 5.

77. Abou El Fadl, "Islamic Law and Muslim Minorities," 172–75.

78. The accounts of Muslim and European travelers highlight the fact that access to and travel within these empires was restricted by rival European powers, not the empires themselves.

79. Al-Zuhayli, *Athar al-harb,* 180–81. See also Abdullah al-Ahsan, *Ummah or Nation? Identity Crisis in Contemporary Muslim Society* (Leicester, U.K.: Islamic Foundation, 1992); Bahgat Korany, "Alien and Besieged Yet Here to Stay: The Contradictions of the Arab Territorial State," in *The Foundations of the Arab State,* ed., Ghassan Salamé (London: Croom Helm, 1987), 47–74; and my essay, "Sovereignty, Pan-Islamism, and International Organization," in *State Sovereignty: Change and Persistence in International Relations,* ed. Sohail H. Hashmi (University Park, Penn.: Pennsylvania State University Press, 1997), 49–80.

80. Muhammad Hamidullah, *The Muslim Conduct of State,* 7th ed. (Lahore: Sh. Muhammad Ashraf, 1977), 99.

81. See Yahya b. Adam, *Kitab al-kharaj,* trans. A. Ben Shemesh (Leiden: E.J. Brill, 1958), 65–66.

82. Abu al-Hasan al-Mawardi, *al-Ahkam al-sultaniyya wa al-wilayat al-diniyya (The Ordinances of Government),* trans. Wafaa H. Wahba (Reading, U.K.: Garnet Publishing, 1996), 194.

83. Ibid., 194, 208–9; Yahya b. Adam, *Kitab al-kharaj,* 68–70; Qudama b. Ja'far, *Kitab al-kharaj,* trans. A. Ben Shemesh (Leiden: E.J. Brill, 1965), 32–33.

84. Ibn Ishaq, *Life of Muhammad,* 228.

85. See the survey by H.A.R. Gibb, "Constitutional Organization," in *Law in the Middle East,* ed. Majid Khadduri and Herbert Liebesny (Washington, D.C.: Middle East Institute, 1955), 3–27.

86. See *Encyclopaedia of Islam,* 2nd ed., s.v. "Ikta'," by Claude Cahen; and Claude Cahen, "L'évolution de l'iqta' du IXᵉ au XIIIᵉ siècle," *Annales: économies, sociétés, civilisations* 18:1 (1953): 25–52.

87. Ibn Ishaq, *Life of Muhammad,* 438. See also Q. 59: 8–10.

88. Ibn Ishaq, *Life of Muhammad,* 466.

89. Ibn Ishaq, *Life of Muhammad,* 515. The Qur'an refers to the acquisition of landed property from B. Qurayza and from the expedition to Khaybar at 33:27.

90. See Paul G. Forand, "The Status of the Land and Inhabitants of the Sawad during the First Two Centuries of Islam," *Journal of the Economic and Social History of the Orient* 14 (1971): 25–37.

91. Yahya, *Kitab al-kharaj,* 42–43; al-Mawardi, *al-Ahkam al-sultaniyya,* 190–91.

92. Qudama, *Kitab al-kharaj,* 25.

93. Al-Mawardi, *al-Ahkam al-sultaniyya,* 191.

94. Abu Yusuf, *Kitab al-kharaj,* trans. A. Ben Shemesh (Leiden: E.J. Brill, 1969), 94–95.

95. Fazlur Rahman, *Islamic Methodology in History* (Islamabad: Islamic Research Institute, 1984), 180–81.

96. Abou El Fadl, "Islamic Law and Muslim Minorities," 149–64.

97. For a general survey of Muslim thinking on *hijra* and jihad, see Muhammad Khalid Masud, "The Obligation to Migrate: The Doctrine of *Hijra* in Islamic

Law," in *Muslim Travellers: Pilgrimage, Migration, and the Religious Imagination,* ed. Dale Eickelman and James Piscatori (Berkeley: University of California Press, 1990), 29–49. For details on two important twentieth-century cases of *hijra,* the repatriation of Turks and other Muslim groups from Russia and the Balkans as the Ottoman empire retreated, and the Khilafat Movement in India, see Kemal H. Karpat, "The *Hijra* from Russia and the Balkans: The Process of Self-Definition in the Late Ottoman State", in ibid., 131–52; and Gail Minault, *The Khilafat Movement: Religious Symbolism and Political Mobilization in India* (New York: Columbia University Press, 1982), 106–7.

98. See Sohail H. Hashmi, "Saving and Taking Life in War: Three Modern Muslim Views," *Muslim World* 89 (April 1999): 161–68.

99. Al-Tabari, *The History of al-Tabari,* vol. 6, *Muhammad at Mecca,* trans. W. Montgomery Watt and M.V. MacDonald (Albany: State University of New York Press, 1988), 114.

100. Ibn Ishaq, *Life of Muhammad,* 609–10, provides a brief account of this episode. See also Watt, *Muhammad at Medina,* 190.

101. Masud, "Obligation to Migrate," 36–37.

102. Fred Donner, *The Early Islamic Conquests* (Princeton: Princeton University Press, 1981), 82–90.

103. On the history and political ideas of the Khawarij, see *Encyclopaedia of Islam,* 2nd ed., s.v. "Kharidjites," by G. Levi Della Vida; Elie Adib Salem, *Political Theory and Institutions of the Khawarij* (Baltimore: Johns Hopkins University Press, 1956).

104. For an overview of Shi'i political doctrine, see Moojan Momen, *An Introduction to Shi'i Islam* (New Haven: Yale University Press, 1985), esp. chap. 7.

105. Ibn Abi Ya'la, *Tabaqat al-hanabila* (Beirut: Dar al-Kutub al-'Ilmiyya, 1998), 228–29.

106. See al-Mawardi, *al-Ahkam al-sultaniyya,* 65–67.

107. I have discussed this topic much more fully in "Self-Determination and Secession in Islamic Thought," in *The New World Order: Sovereignty, Human Rights, and the Self-Determination of Peoples,* ed. Mortimer Sellers (Providence, R.I.: Berg Press, 1996), 117–52.

11

The Unbounded Law of God and Territorial Boundaries

Khaled Abou El Fadl

Debates on the proper balance in Islamic theology between political bound-aries and moral communities are premised on assumptions that are rarely made exact or explicit. The issue of whether political boundaries are nec-essary to protect and safeguard moral communities is formulated in the Islamic tradition in terms of whether God's morality must necessarily be ac-tualized through a political community dedicated to fulfilling this morality. If God's morality is expressed through a set of laws, the question becomes: Does God's law need a political community and a plot of land in which it has jurisdiction and sovereignty? Is it possible to give effect to God's moral imperatives without achieving sovereignty over a piece of land that grants God's law full dominion? The problem that plagues these debates is what may be called competing comprehensive views about the nature and role of *Shari'ah* and its relation to political and moral communities.

There is no doubt, as Sohail Hashmi and Rashid Rida point out, that the Qur'an and *Sunna* exhibit considerable hostility to the ethos of blind loyalty to a tribe, clan, family, or even a piece of land.[1] The Qur'an, for instance, commands Muslims to commit themselves to justice, even if that means being forced to testify against their own families, clans or tribes.[2] It also condemns the moral corruptness of blind loyalty to ancestoral prac-tices, and calls such loyalties the "cant of ignorance (*hamiyyat al-jahiliyyah*)."[3] Significantly, Islamic theological doctrine has consistently claimed moral su-periority over normative systems that are based on loyalty to a king, to an institution (such as a church), or to ethnic or racial affiliations. The Islamic bond is founded on a moral commitment to God, to a principle, and a Book (the Qur'an).[4] The Qur'an emphasizes that the essential bond that unites the Islamic community is a conviction and belief in a particular conception of life that places God in the center of all loyalties and commitments.[5] Land or territory, other than Mecca, Medina, and Jerusalem, which are blessed and purified by an exceptional Divine act, are seen in a largely functional capacity.

The Qur'an insists that all of the earth and all lands belong to God, but that God has delegated custody of the earth to human beings, as a whole, and made all of humanity God's deputies (*khulafa'*) on earth.[6] There are over a hundred references in the Qur'an to the notion of the *ard* (land, territory, or earth), but these references do not seem to recognize formal or official boundaries. Rather, the Qur'an consistently speaks of land, in general, as a consecrated gift made available to human beings as a source of refuge or haven. The Qur'an often refers to earth as spacious or expansive, and then specifies that the full expanse of the earth was made available to human beings to inhabit (*li tu'ammiruha*), to establish safety and peace (*amn*), and to discharge the obligation of justice (*'adl*).[7] Therefore, for instance, when addressing the problem of oppression, the Qur'an poses the rhetorical question, "... wasn't God's earth spacious enough for you to migrate and move away [from oppression]?"[8] Finally, the Qur'an repeatedly condemns what it calls the act of corrupting the earth, or the spreading of corruption on the earth. Although the Qur'an is ambiguous as to what exactly are the elements of this "corruption," it does list certain acts as constituting corruption on the earth. Among the acts listed are destroying places of worship, war (presumably, unjust war), injustice, murder, and the persecution of the believers.[9] The relevant symbolic point is that corrupting the earth, or corruption on the earth, is considered a breach of God's trust, and a grave moral infraction.

This Qur'anic discourse challenges the legitimacy of formal borders – a challenge that is consistent with the notion of Islam as a universal moral message that cannot be confined or limited by territorial constraints. Arguably, the concept of corrupting the earth (*al-ifsad fi al-ard*) transcends any formal borders – political or otherwise. According to this conceptual framework, Muslims are under an obligation to fight injustice, oppression, and all forms of immorality, and if Muslims are unable to do so, they would be under an obligation to migrate in God's spacious earth. As Hashmi points out, this is consistent with the migration of a large number of Muslims to Abyssinia in response to the corruption and injustice prevailing in Mecca at the time of the Prophet. Furthermore, this is consistent with the Islamic imperative of enjoining the good and forbidding the evil (*al-amr bi al-ma'ruf wa al-nahy 'an al-munkar*) pursuant to which Muslims are under an unwavering extra-territorial duty of resisting injustice and immorality. Hence, the Qur'an repeatedly commands the Muslim community (the *ummah*) to enjoin the good and forbid the evil, and, in fact, the Qur'an indicates that this is the core virtue of the Muslim moral community. The Qur'an, for instance, states: "You are the best community (*ummah*) sent to humankind, enjoining what is good and forbidding what is wrong and believing in God."[10]

All of this invites an inquiry into the basis for the normativities that are supposed to guide the commitments and behaviors of Muslims. Put differently, how do we identify or define the constituent elements of abstract concepts such as "corruption on the earth," the good and evil that is to be enjoined or forbidden, and justice or oppression? Do these normativities mandate the existence of a system of laws that defines, articulates, and implements these moral imperatives? The crucial issue here is the importance and role of Islamic law.

The Qur'an repeatedly commands Muslims to live according to the dictates of God's law. Qur'anic discourse indicates that God's law is comprised both of general imperatives such as establishing justice and equity, and also of specific and concrete positive commands, for instance, relating to divorce or inheritance.[11] Muslim jurists have called God's law, in its ideal and abstract form, the *Shari'ah* (the Way to God), and called the attempt to understand and implement the *Shari'ah*, the *fiqh* (literally, the understanding). The *Shari'ah* encompasses the basic and core normative values of the Islamic message. The question then becomes: To what extent are territories and institutions necessary for understanding and implementing the *Shari'ah*? If Muslims are commanded to live according to the dictates of God's law, doesn't this necessarily mean that jurisdiction over a piece of land and its inhabitants is necessary for the implementation of this law? This point is crucial for all discourses on political boundaries and notions of territory in Islam.

In order to convey a sense of the centrality of the concept of law in the Islamic tradition, I will reproduce a lengthy quote by the prominent Muslim jurist Ibn Qayyim al-Jawziyyah d. 751 (A.H.)/1350–1 (C.E.). He states:

The *Shari'ah* is God's justice among His servants, and His mercy among His creatures. It is God's shadow on this earth. It is His wisdom that leads to Him in the most exact way and the most exact affirmation of the truthfulness of His Prophet. It is His light that enlightens the seekers and His guidance for the rightly-guided. It is the absolute cure for all ills and the straight path which, if followed, will lead to righteousness... It is life and nutrition, the medicine, the light, the cure, and the safeguard. Every good in this life is derived from it and achieved through it, and every deficiency in existence results from its dissipation. If it had not been for the fact that some of its rules remain [in this world], this world would become corrupted and the universe would be dissipated... If God would wish to destroy the world and dissolve existence, He would void whatever remains of its injunctions. For the *Shari'ah*, which was sent to His Prophet... is the pillar of existence and the key to success in this world and the Hereafter.[12]

Pre-modern Muslim jurists often asserted that the purpose for the existence of government in Islam is to establish justice and security, which, the jurists argued, is not possible without the implementation of *Shari'ah*. Pre-modern Muslim jurists also argued that the main distinction between an Islamic system of government and all other political systems is that an Islamic government is bound by *Shari'ah*, while all other governments are bound only by capricious whim (*hawa*).[13] By the expression "capricious whim," Muslim jurists meant that an Islamic government is bound by Divine directives while other forms of government are bound only by mundane directives based on utility or rational preference. Importantly, the notion of a society based on the Divine law is supported and reinforced by the early Islamic historical experience. As Hashmi notes, the Prophet migrated from Mecca to Medina, and became the effective ruler of an expanding city-state based in Medina. While I think it would be anachronistic to claim that the polity in Medina had a notion of well-defined political boundaries, there is little doubt that the early Muslims did have a definite concept of territorial integrity and legal jurisdiction.

The concept of a *Shari'ah*-based society is further strengthened by a Qur'anic discourse that indicates that the mandate to live according to the dictates of the Divine law is not only individual, but also collective. This discourse often occurs in the context of addressing the threat of *fitnah* (severe tribulations) that might befall an unjust society. The Qur'an emphasizes that a society that does not abide by the commands of God, becomes ungrateful towards God, or that is overcome by large-scale injustice, runs the risk of Divine collective punishment. If a people live in defiance of God and refuse to submit to the Divine dictates, the Qur'an states that God will deny such a society its security and tranquility, and inflict the people with great tribulations.[14] The Qur'an explicitly states that this *fitnah* will not afflict only the unjust classes or individuals in society, but will befall society as a whole, and will cause its destruction.[15] Interestingly, in this discourse, the Qur'an calls upon Muslims to protect their territories by fighting the unbelievers, and warns that if Muslims fail to take up arms in order to protect the city-state in Medina, a great corruption and *fitnah* will befall them as a result. Importantly, the Qur'an equates the defense of the religion with the defense of the polity in Medina, which effectively represents the religion.[16] Therefore, in this discourse, the Islamic religion is represented by a territorial polity, and the duty to defend the religion becomes inseparable from the duty to defend the territory.

However, some contemporary observers, such as Abdullahi An-Na'im, have argued that the historical experience in Medina was not essential to the basic and fundamental character of the Islamic message.[17] According to these observers, the experience in Medina was dictated by the exigencies of historical circumstances that confronted the Prophet in Mecca. The historical experience in Medina should not be given normative weight in mandating the creation of, what may be called, a *Shari'ah* state – a state with jurisdiction over a specific territory that investigates and implements the God's law. The logical effect of this argument is to conclude that Islam sets out general moral imperatives, expressed by the Prophet in Mecca, and that these moral imperatives may be pursued and enforced at a personal and individual level. The creation, however, of a territorial state that is charged with the implementing of the specific and positive rules of *Shari'ah* law, or with emulating and reproducing the Prophetic experience in Medina, is not an Islamic imperative. In effect, this position maintains that political boundaries, legal institutions, and territory need not define the Islamic moral community.

The difficulty with this Mecca-oriented position is that it dismisses the entire Medina experience as a mere technicality. Certainly, the Prophet could have preached his message in Mecca, and could have martyred himself in Mecca without establishing a full polity in Medina. From the perspective of a Muslim, however, it is difficult to think of the legalistic and territorial experience of the Prophet in Medina as an aberration, or as merely incidental to the core of the Islamic message. Significantly, this Mecca-centric, and anti-Medina, thesis would render more than half the Qur'an marginal, since most of the Qur'an was revealed in the second half of the Prophetic period while the Prophet was in Medina. Furthermore, the vast majority of the *Sunna* of the Prophet is a product of the Medina experience. The argument of scholars such as An-Na'im would a priori render the very idea of Islamic law problematic since it would deny it the basic body of precedents upon which it is founded – namely, the *Sunna* of the Prophet. Furthermore, the Mecca-centric view would arguably vitiate the need for establishing a *Shari'ah*-based polity, or the need for political boundaries that encompass this polity. Put differently, Muslims may form a moral community that transcends all political boundaries, and since *Shari'ah*, according to this thesis, is constituted of general and universal moral imperatives revealed in Mecca, Muslims are not obligated to create Islamic polities. Rather, Muslims may reside wherever they can find lands in which morality and justice prevails. Even more, *dar al-Islam* (the abode of Islam) becomes a metaphysical symbolic association, not a territorial polity, that bonds decent and moral human beings everywhere.

I have, in fact, argued elsewhere that Muslim jurists did not demand that all Muslims reside only in territory governed by *Shari'ah*.[18] Furthermore, as Hashmi notes, I have also argued that the notion of *dar al-Islam* (the abode of Islam as opposed to the abode of non-Muslims) was ill-defined and ambiguous in the pre-modern juristic discourses of Islam.[19] The juristic debate often focused on the tension between the formal character of a territory and the substantive quality of life that a specific territory is able to afford. Most jurists argued that Muslims may lawfully reside in non-Muslim lands that afford them safety and freedom to practice their religion. Furthermore, some jurists argued that regardless of the formal association of a territory, wherever safety (*amn*) and justice (*'adl*) can be found, that territory is part of *dar al-Islam*. As a result, a territory could be predominately non-Muslim and could be governed by non-Muslims, but if it offers Muslims safety and justice, it is to be considered a part of the abode of Islam. On the other hand, some jurists argued that for any territory that was once ruled by Muslims and was later conquered by non-Muslims, such territory remains forever a part of the abode of Islam, and Muslims are under a duty to liberate it.

For instance, Andalusia or Palestine, although occupied by non-Muslims, are nonetheless a part of the abode of Islam, and therefore Muslims may reside in them, but should eventually liberate these territories and re-institute the rule of *Shari'ah*.[20] The tension between the substantive moral character of a polity and the formal association of a territory is perhaps best exemplified by juristic debates that focused on the authenticity and meaning of reports attributed to the Prophet that asserted that it is better to live under a non-Muslim government that is just than to live under a Muslim government that is unjust.[21]

It is important to note, however, that these various debates were often the product of specific historical circumstances, but also presupposed agreement on a unitary and essential paradigm. Specifically, these debates do not raise doubts about the normative nature of the Prophet's historical experience in Medina, and maintain that it is unnecessary to establish a state that implements the *Shari'ah*. The material issue dealt with in these debates was whether in the absence of a just and rightful *Shari'ah*-state, Muslims could live a moral and just life in non-Muslim territories. In other words, none of these debates claimed that a just non-*Shari'ah*-state is preferable to a just *Shari'ah*-state. Rather, the issues debated by the pre-modern jurists could be summarized in two main points. The first is whether an unjust state can still be considered a *Shari'ah*-state; the second is whether formally, or nominally, a Muslim state is superior to a state that is not Muslim, but just. Nevertheless, in all cases, these juristic debates did not represent a relinquishment of the ideal of a *Shari'ah*-governed territorial state.[22]

Hashmi, however, argues that one need not be limited to what he calls "a rather arcane and . . . obsolete set of doctrines that applied to the first few Islamic centuries, but which have little relevance to the twenty-first century." By this statement, I understand Hashmi to refer to the legacy of the Islamic pre-modern juristic tradition. In addition, Hashmi stresses the need for each new generation to be able to derive for itself its own conclusions from the Qur'an and *Sunna* instead of simply relying on the pre-modern juristic heritage. I agree, in part, with Hashmi, but it is important to consider two basic points in this context. Firstly, I agree that the juristic tradition should not be determinative of any issue in the contemporary age, but that does not mean that this tradition is not authoritative. After all, it is this juristic tradition that constructed and preserved the heritage of the Qur'an and *Sunna*, and it is impossible to refer to either of these sources without invoking the symbolism and interpretive activities of the pre-modern juristic tradition. Furthermore, I believe it is fair to say that all interpretive activities function within particular communities of meaning. At this point in Muslim history, the relevant community of meaning for the Qur'an and *Sunna* is largely that of the pre-modern juristic tradition. In my view, those who have challenged or cast doubts upon the authoritativeness of the juristic community of meaning have not offered any plausible alternatives. Secondly, even if we consider the juristic tradition not to be authoritative, and attempt to derive conclusions from the Qur'an and *Sunna* directly, this does not necessarily challenge the conclusions reached by pre-modern jurists. As I am sure Hashmi recognizes, the *Sunna*, in particular, is the source for a jurisprudential system of exceeding complexity and richness. The *Sunna* contains numerous specific and detailed rules of law that form the basis for what is known as the *Shari'ah* system.

Whether the juristic tradition is relevant or not, if the *Sunna* still applies in the contemporary age, and if the Qur'anic injunctions about governing ourselves according to God's law are to be taken seriously, then we will necessarily end up with the same basic set of dilemmas. Either we will have to pretend that the Islamic moral experience is represented only by the Mecca phase of the Prophet's life, and that the Medina polity was an arrangement of historical convenience, or we will end up with a set of fairly detailed legal imperatives that invite us to give them effect through an institutional structure that is defined by political boundaries.

My point is that the functional necessity of political boundaries and territorial jurisdiction in Islam is a complex matter, and that it is intimately related to the larger issue of the existence of a *Shari'ah*-state. The issue is not resolved by setting aside the juristic tradition, or by a pristine and de novo re-interpretation from the Qur'an and *Sunna*. In fact, the complexity and diversity of the juristic tradition might act as an intellectual restraint against puritan movements, which aim to implement the *Shari'ah* through theocratically modeled states. I will explain this point in Section 2.

1. Territory as Homeland in the Qur'an

Among the issues that have not received adequate attention in contemporary discourses is the Qura'nic concept of territory as a home. Here, the main functionality of territory is not to serve as a basis for a political entity, or even as a basis for the implementation of the *Shari'ah*, but as place in which a people find shelter, security, and a livelihood. In this context, the Qur'an tends to emphasize that the main grievance against the unbelievers at the time of Prophet, and the main injustice that befell the Prophet and his followers, were that they were expelled from their homeland. The Qur'an treats this expulsion as a sin worse than murder, and commands Muslims to fight to regain their rights over their homeland. For example, the Qur'an states: "Fight in the cause of God those who fight you, but do not transgress for God does not like the transgressors. Slay them wherever you find them, and expel them from where they expelled, for oppression (*fitnah*) is worse than slaughter... But if they cease, then God is forgiving and most Merciful. Fight them until there is no more tumult or oppression, and until justice and faith in God prevails. But if they cease to fight you, let there be no hostility except towards those who practice oppression."[23] Elsewhere the Qur'an states the following: "God does not forbid you with regard to those who do not fight you for (your) faith, or those who do not drive you out of your homes, from dealing kindly and justly with them. For, God loveth those who are just. God forbids you with regard to those who fight you for (your) faith, and drive you out of your homes, and support others in expelling you out of your homes, from befriending them, and those who befriend them are transgressors."[24] Importantly, these verses were revealed in the Medina period of the Islamic message. What emerges as central in this discourse is the right of people over their homes, and their right to regain their lost homes, even if they have to use force. This lends support to the idea that territory does not simply serve as a base for the enforcement of the Divine law, but also that people acquire rights over territory by forming ties and bonds of habitation. This idea was at the core of the juristic determination that Muslims may continue to reside in territories that are not ruled by *Shari'ah*, but that constitute a homeland for Muslims. When Muslim territory was conquered by the Crusaders and Mongols, Muslim jurists were very reluctant to conclude that since these territories were no longer governed by *Shari'ah*, these conquered territories ceased to be a part of the abode of Islam. Rather, the majority of Muslim jurists argued that since these conquered territories served as a homeland for Muslims, either that the territories ought to be considered as a part of the abode of Islam, or that these conquered territories would cease to be a part of the abode of Islam but that Muslims should continue to reside in them anyway. In addition, as noted earlier, some pre-modern jurists argued that wherever Muslims are able to establish a safe and secure homeland, that territory, regardless of its formal association, becomes a part of the abode of Islam. This right or expectation of security and safety in one's homeland became a pervasive theme in Islamic juristic discourses. In some juristic discourses, this reached the point of making stability, security, and safety, core values that prevailed over competing values such as justice or the enforcement of *Shari'ah*. This type of logic motivated some jurists to prohibit all acts that might endanger these core values such as sedition or rebellion. These jurists relied on the logic of *ittiqa' al-fitnah* (the avoidance of discord) to claim that rash armed conflicts have the unfortunate tendency of causing the destruction of homes (*takhrib al-diyar*) and the obliteration of livelihoods (*inqita' al-ma'ayish*). Some modern scholars have described, unfairly in my judgment, these arguments as politically quietist.[25]

2. Territoriality and Universality of *Shari'ah*

Thus far, this chapter has explored the idea of territory as a base for the establishment of justice, as a base for the establishment of the rules of

Shari'ah, and as a base for the founding or maintenance of a homeland. Another element to consider here is the jurisdiction of *Shari'ah* law. Put simply, is the obligation to establish *Shari'ah* territorially bound or not? A related question would be: Does *Shari'ah* apply wherever a person's homeland might be, or is *Shari'ah* enforceable only in territory that is ruled by a *Shari'ah*-bound government? As discussed earlier, both the Qur'an and *Sunna* mandate a life lived according to the rules of *Shari'ah*, but the relevant issue is whether the *Shari'ah* can only survive within territorial boundaries, or whether the *Shari'ah* is extra- or supra-territorial in nature?

The Qur'an and *Sunna* do not directly address this issue, but pre-modern juristic culture dealt with the matter at length. One of the four major Sunni schools of thought, the Hanafis, held that the jurisdiction of *Shari'ah* is largely territorial in nature. In the same way that Muslim territory must apply *Shari'ah*, *Shari'ah*, for the most part, only applies within the boundaries of a Muslim state. Boundaries, according to this argument, become crucial – they define the parameters within which the law of God applies. God's law is bounded and constrained within political boundaries.

The majority of Muslim juristic schools, however, disagreed with the Hanafi position, and held that the *Shari'ah's* jurisdiction is universal. This position is well-explained by the influential Sunni jurist al-Shafi'i (d. 819–820 A.H.). He states:

There is no difference between the abode of non-Muslims and the abode of Muslims as to the laws that God has decreed to His people . . . [The Prophet] has not exempted any of his people from any of his decrees, and he did not permit them anything that was forbidden in the abode of non-Muslims. What I am saying is consistent with the Qur'an and *Sunna*, and it is what rational people can understand and agree on. What is allowed in the lands of Islam is allowed in the lands of non-Muslims, and what is forbidden in the land of Islam is forbidden in the lands of non-Muslims. So whoever commits an infraction is subject to the punishment that God has decreed and [his presence in] the lands of non-Muslims does not exempt him from anything."[26]

If the duties of *Shari'ah*, figuratively speaking, accompany a Muslim wherever he/she may go, and if political boundaries are not the only means of discharging the obligations of the *Shari'ah*, this would seem to lend support to the conclusion that moral communities are more essential to the Islamic message than territorial boundaries. It is possible to comply with the Qur'anic command of living according to the dictates of *Shari'ah* without necessarily establishing a full-fledged state dedicated for that purpose. To avoid any misunderstandings, this statement does not mean that I am expressing opposition to the idea of a territorially bound state that enforces *Shari'ah* law, it only means that territorially bound states are not the only possible mechanism for the enforcement of *Shari'ah*. *Shari'ah* may be enforced individually and personally, as well as collectively and communally. This would include, but need not be limited to, enforcement through formally organized states.

3. Rebellion and Secession

Hashmi has done a thoughtful job of addressing the various issues raised by territorial boundaries, and I have little to add to his thorough discussion. I would like, however, to briefly comment on the issues of secession and spatial boundaries. Hashmi accurately notes that pre-modern jurists argued that rebels should be treated leniently. The majority of pre-modern jurists argued that such rebels should not be treated as unbelievers or even criminals. The implications of these arguments are significant, and so I will comment briefly on the law of secession and rebellion. In order for Muslim secessionists or rebels to be treated leniently, pre-modern jurists argued that their rebellion or secession must be based on a *ta'wil* (an ideology, cause, or principled reason that motivates the rebels or secessionists). If their rebellion was, in fact, based on a *ta'wil*, they acquired the protected status known as the *bughah*, and they became entitled to lenient treatment. Pre-modern jurists were exceedingly hostile to rebellions or secessionist movements that were based on tribal, ethnic, or nationalistic causes – pre-modern jurists considered these motivations to be illegitimate and reprehensible. Those who rebelled or attempted to secede because of tribal, ethnic, or nationalistic reasons were denied the status of *bughah*. In contrast, those who rebelled or seceded because of a principled interpretation of *Shari'ah*, or because of an injustice inflicted upon them, were not equated, at a moral and legal level, with common criminals, or with those who rebelled because of capricious whim (*hawa*). Importantly, the pre-modern jurists went further and argued that if the rebels or secessionists establish a government and enforce *Shari'ah*, their legal acts and adjudications must be recognized and enforced by all Muslims.[27]

The significance of this discourse is that it underlines the prevalence of principle, or moral communities, over territorial associations. Muslim jurists did not argue that there is a single comprehensive view that represents the "true" *Shari'ah*. Rather, these jurists accepted the legitimacy of divergent comprehensive views of *Shari'ah*, and also accepted the notion of the transformability of territory. In other words, a particular territory may be governed according to a certain comprehensive view of *Shari'ah*, but a competing view of *Shari'ah*, or justice, may challenge the prevailing view, and may even motivate its adherents to secede with a particular piece of territory in order to give effect to their own *Shari'ah* conceptions and priorities. What is notable in this discourse is that *Shari'ah* remained the core value worthy of deference and consideration, and not territory or allegiance to political boundaries. This point is further underscored by the fact that pre-modern jurists did not consider secession, per se, or the control of rebels over a plot of land, to be determinative in invoking leniency. Rather, whether the rebels had a territorial base or not, they were entitled to leniency because of the simple fact that they relied on a *ta'wil.* Put differently, rebels did not need to achieve control over a territorial base in order for their *Shari'ah*-view to be entitled to deference or tolerance. Rebels needed to espouse a cause that was *Shari'ah*-based or, at least a cause that was consistent with *Shari'ah.* If they did so, the rights of the rebels prevailed over the rights of the state in maintaining its territorial integrity or unity. This is consistent with the secondary importance of territorial boundaries as compared to moral communities. Importantly, many pre-modern jurists argued that if the rebels slaughtered Muslims indiscriminately or terrorized Muslims by expelling them from their homes, these rebels should lose their protected status as *bughah* and, instead, be treated as bandits (*muharibun*).

4. Spatial Boundaries

As discussed earlier, a prominent exception to the relative lack of centrality of territorial boundaries in the Islamic juristic tradition is the idea of homeland or the land that constitutes a Muslim's home. Nonetheless, other than the homeland exception, the other prominent exception is the notion of holy land (*al-ard al-muqaddasah*). There is no question that Islam treats certain locations as sanctified, or made-holy by God. The general vicinity of these territories become sanctified and inviolable, and all acts of bloodshed or desecration are considered blasphemous. For instance, the Qur'an instructs Muslims not to shed blood in the vicinity of the Ka'bah in Mecca unless Muslims are acting in self-defense.[28] In the Qur'an, this status is recognized for two locations: the vicinity of the mosque in Mecca and the vicinity of the mosque in Jerusalem. As Hashmi notes, historically speaking, Muslims tended to sanctify the vicinity of the Prophet's mosque in Medina as well. Hashmi spends an admirable amount of effort in discussing recent orientalist works that have tried to prove that, historically, Muslims have not revered, and have not been very interested in, Jerusalem. According to these orientalists, Jerusalem entered Muslim consciousness only after the commencement of the Crusades, and so Muslim interest in Jerusalem was largely politically motivated. I think it is important to note that the emergence of this recent orientalist scholarship is itself politically motivated, and has tended to be offensively selective about the historical, legal, and theological evidence. As Hashmi explains, this scholarship has argued that Muslims invented Prophetic traditions that extolled and praised the position of Jerusalem, largely in response to the Crusades. Suffice it to say that these traditions, if invented, must have been invented well before the age of the Crusaders since they are documented in *hadith* books that were in circulation more than a century before Jerusalem fell to the Crusaders in the fifth (A.H.)/eleventh (C.E.) century.

Even more, these orientalist works ignore the significance of Jerusalem in Islamic theology. In Islamic theology, Jerusalem represents the essential unity of the Abrahamic religions, while Mecca represents the uniqueness of the Islamic message. The spiritual connection between Jerusalem and Mecca is well-represented by the Qur'anic narrative that asserts that the Ka'bah was founded by the Prophet Abraham and his son Ishmael as God's promise of the coming of the seal of the Prophets (that is, Muhammad).[29] In Islamic theology, the Prophet and the early Muslims prayed in the direction of Jerusalem for the first half of the Islamic message in order to affirm the essential unity between Islam and the messages of Abraham, Moses, and Jesus. The spiritual connection comes full circle, so to speak, when Muslims direct their prayers to the structure constructed by the father of the prophets, Abraham, thereby, signifying the distinctiveness of the Islamic message, but also its commonality with the Abrahamic faiths.[30] Of course, the truth of this theology is not the issue – the issue is that if one wishes to assess the importance of spatial boundaries in any normative tradition, it is necessary to try to understand that tradition in terms of its own alleged normativities, and not in terms of what an outside observer believes makes historical sense for that tradition. In essence, I think it is appropriate to try to understand the spatial and moral boundaries of a particular creed, but unlike political boundaries, they tend to defy functionality and negotiability. Put simply, if Muslims believe that the Qur'an is the Divine Word, and the Qur'an tells Muslims that the Aqsa Mosque and its vicinity in Jerusalem have been sanctified, and was the site of the miraculous journey of Muhammad to Jerusalem, orientalist attempts to inform Muslims that they have misunderstood their proper spatial boundaries must be regarded with much suspicion.

5. Conclusion

If one can imagine that moral communities are akin to an open text whose significance and meaning are constantly being explored and developed, then the risk is that political and territorial boundaries would be akin to artificial constraints that close the text and stun the evolvement of meaning. Political and territorial boundaries might make good functional sense, but they also threaten to lock up moral communities within the confines of superficial dividers that prevent the development and enrichment of these moral communities. As the Qur'an states: "O' humankind! We created you from a man and woman and made you into nations and tribes so that you may come to know each other. The most honored of you in the sight of God is the most righteous of you."[31] Arguably, artificial territorial dividers are not consistent with the need for mutual exploration and edification.

This Qur'anic passage highlights a very real concern when one considers the possibility of an Islamic message that is enclosed within and defined by political boundaries. These political boundaries threaten to transform the moral communities of Islam to political entities, and to transform the universality and transcendentalism of the Islamic message into a closed determined and parochial reality. These same concerns exist in the case of *Shari'ah*. If *Shari'ah* can only be given effect within the confines of territories and boundaries, Muslims run the risk of transforming the *Shari'ah* from an open, ethereal, and transcendental ideal to a closed, mundane, limited, and territorially based reality. Put differently, Muslims run the risk of numbing the moral and universal voice of *Shari'ah* and replacing it with a set of territorially specific legal adjudications and rules. The fear is that the adjudications generated within the confines of a territorially bounded locality, with the passage of time, would come to fully represent or embody the vastness and magnanimity of the *Shari'ah*. If this takes place, there is no doubt that the successes of the territorially bounded locality will come to represent the successes of the *Shari'ah*, but so will the failures. The holy sites in Mecca, Medina, and Jerusalem are at the very heart of any Islamic territorial claim. However, beyond the holy sites, it seems to me that every other territorial boundary is secondary in importance to the universal moral imperative of *Shari'ah*.

Notes to Chapter 11

1. For further analysis of Rashid Rida's position on this issue see Khaled Abou El Fadl, "Striking a Balance: Islamic Legal Discourse on Muslim Minorities," in Yvonne Yazbeck Haddad and John L. Esposito, eds., *Muslims on the Americanization Path?* (Oxford: Oxford University Press, 2000), 47–62.
2. Qur'an, 4:135.
3. Qur'an, 48:26.
4. For the idea that what distinguishes the Islamic system from other systems is loyalty to *Shari'ah*, see W. Montgomery Watt, *Islamic Political Thought* (Edinburgh: Edinburgh University Press, 1968), 102; Ann K. S. Lambton, *State and Government in Medieval Islam: An Introduction to the Study of Islamic Political Theory: The Jurists* (Oxford: Oxford University Press, 1981), 13–20; H.A.R. Gibb, "Constitutional Organization," in Majid Khadduri and Herbert J. Liebesny, eds., *Origin and Development of Islamic Law,* vol. 1 of *Law in the Middle East,* (Washington, D.C.: The Middle East Institute, 1955), 2–27.
5. Qur'an, 21:92; 23:52; 2:143.
6. Qur'an, 35:39; 27:62; 6:12.
7. Qur'an, 7:10; 11:61; 16:112; 106:4.
8. Qur'an, 4:97.
9. For instance, see Qur'an, 5:32–3; 5:64; 7:56; 7:74; 7:85; 7:127; 8:73; 2:251; 23:71; 27:34; 2:27; 2:30; 2:205; 89:12; 11:85; 26:183; 28:77; 29:36.

10. Qur'an, 3:110. Also see Qur'an, 3:104; 3:114; 9:67; 9:71; 22:41.
11. For instance see, Qur'an, 5:42; 4:58–9; 4:105; 2:213; 3:23; 5:44–7; 38:26; 6:57; 42:10.
12. Khaled Abou El Fadl, "Muslim Minorities and Self-Restraint in Liberal Democracies," *Loyola International and Comparative Law Journal* 29 (1996), 1526.
13. See, for example, Watt, *Islamic Political Thought*, 102; Lambton, *State and Government*, 13–20; Gibb, "Constitutional Organization," 3–6, 14.
14. Qur'an, 65:8; 28:58; 22:45; 22:48; 16:112;
15. Qur'an, 8:25.
16. Qur'an, 8:39; 8:73.
17. See, for instance, Abdullahi Ahmad An-Na'im, *Toward an Islamic Reformation: Civil Liberties, Human Rights, and International Law* (Syracuse: Syracuse University Press, 1990); Ali Abd al-Raziq, *al-Islam wa Usul al-Hukm: Bahth fi al-Khilafah wa al-Hukumah fi al-Islam* (Beirut: Dar Maktabat al-Hayah).
18. Abou El Fadl, "Islamic Law and Muslim Minorities: The Juristic Discourse on Muslim Minorities from the Second/Eighth to the Eleventh/Seventeenth Centuries," *Islamic Law and Society* 1/2 (1994), 141–87.
19. Abou El Fadl, "Islamic Law and Muslim Minorities, " 161.
20. I discuss these various positions in greater detail in Abou El Fadl, "Islamic Law and Muslim Minorities," 153–64, and Abou El Fadl, "Striking a Balance," 58–63.
21. Abou El Fadl, "Legal Debates on Muslim Minorities: Between Rejection and Accommodation," *Journal of Religious Ethics* 22/1 (1994), 131–2.
22. Interestingly, some jurists argued that if people would be able to fulfill their *Shari'ah* obligations without a central institutional power, a government would not be necessary. Abu Hamid al-Ghazali, "al-Iqtisad fi al-I'tiqad," in Nusus al-Fikr al-Siyasi al-Islami: al-Imamah 'inda al-Sunna, ed. Yusuf Aybash (Beirut: Dar al-Tali'ah, 1966), 363; Qamar al-Din Khan, Ibn Taymiyyah, trans. Mubarak al-Baghdadi (Kuwait: Maktabat al-Falah, 1973, 59–61.
23. Qur'an, 2:190–3.
24. Qur'an, 60:8–9. Also see, Qur'an, 2:246; 3:195; 22:40; 59:8.
25. Abou El Fadl, "The Islamic Law of Rebellion," Ph.D. diss., Princeton University, 1999, 309–39.
26. Abu 'Abd Allah Muhammad b. Idris al-Shafi'i, in Muhammad al-Najjar, ed., *al-Umm* (Beirut: Dar al-Ma'rifah, n.d.), 7:354–355; Abou El Fadl, "Striking the Balance," 68–9. For greater details, see Abou El Fadl, "Islamic Law and Muslim Minorities," 172–81.
27. For details, see Abou El Fadl, "Islamic Law of Rebellion," 178–79, 203–04, 210, 214; Abou El Fadl, "Political Crime in Islamic Jurisprudence and Western Legal History," *UC Davis Journal of International Law and Policy* 4/1 (1998), 2–28; Abou El Fadl, "*Ahkam al-Bughat*: Irregular Warfare and the Law of Rebellion in Islam," in James T. Johnson and John Kelsay, eds., *Cross, Crescent, & Sword: The Justification and Limitation of War in Western and Islamic Tradition* (New York: Greenwood Press, 1990), 149–76.
28. Qur'an, 2:191.
29. Qur'an, 2:125–30.
30. For the Qur'anic discourse on this issue, see Qur'an, 2:140–152.
31. Qur'an, 49:13

PART 6

THE LIBERAL TRADITION

12

The Making and Unmaking of Boundaries: What Liberalism Has to Say

Allen Buchanan

1. The Ethical Issues

How to Ignore Them

The making and unmaking of boundaries raises ethical issues because which side of a boundary people find themselves on can have profound consequences for their freedom, their welfare, their identity, and even their survival. Yet existing political theory, including liberal political theory, has remarkably little to say about the ethics of creating and changing boundaries. This deficiency stems from two shamelessly convenient simplifying assumptions. The first, which I call the *congruence assumption*, is that the membership boundaries of primary political communities and the geographical boundaries of primary political units (call them "states") coincide. The second, which I call the *perpetuity assumption*, is that primary political units remain intact over time, that the only form of exit from existing states is by emigration (departure of people) rather than by fragmentation of the states themselves. Given these two assumptions, most of the more difficult ethical issues concerning the creation and changing of borders simply do not arise.[1]

Liberalism, which at least in its contemporary forms prides itself on accommodating pluralism, does not assume that the populations of existing states are homogeneous in all respects. But at least until very recently, liberal theorists have tended to assume that whatever pluralism exists within states can be accommodated within states – that is, without changing their boundaries.[2] Classical liberalism tended to assume that a regime of universal rights, including preeminently freedom of association, religion, and expression, and rights to private property, is sufficient to accommodate pluralism within the boundaries of the state.

Some contemporary liberals are less sanguine about exclusive reliance on the same set of individual rights for all citizens. They propose instead a regime of internal political differentiation in which minority rights – and not necessarily the same minority rights for all groups – have a prominent place.[3] Increasingly, contemporary political theorists, whether they qualify as liberal or not, are beginning to appreciate the enormous limitations imposed by the congruence and perpetuity assumptions. And many are beginning to doubt the adequacy of attempting to accommodate pluralism within existing states by reliance on universal liberal rights even when combined with rights of internal political differentiation.

In other words, political theorists are beginning to take the ethical issues of state-breaking seriously.[4] But at present, systematic liberal thinking about the making and unmaking of boundaries is in its infancy (or perhaps gestation). Hence there is no characteristic liberal view on the topic.

Liberalism comes in many forms; there is no single liberal theory or even a single liberal tradition of thought. Accordingly, there is no reason to believe that there is only one way of developing a liberal account of the making and unmaking of boundaries. The attempt to assess the resources of liberal thinking for dealing with the problem of boundaries that follows will inevitably be selective and to some extent partisan: More consideration will be given to what I take to be the more defensible and promising strands of liberal thought and to the most fundamental principles held by all or most liberal thinkers.

Confusing Property in Land with Territory

Among the questions an ethical theory of the making and changing of boundaries would have to answer is this: under what conditions is the incorporation of new land within the boundaries of a state ethically permissible? It might be thought that at least one important strand of the liberal tradition – Lockean theories of initial acquisition – provides an answer to this question. This is not the case, however, and understanding why proves instructive.

Lockean theories attempt to provide an account of the just initial acquisition of property in land. But property in land is conceptually and morally distinct from the right to territory, for two reasons: first, because land is not the same as territory, and second, because the right to territory is not reducible to a property right, although territories contain property regimes in which individuals and groups have property rights.

By "territory" I shall mean the area that is circumscribed by boundaries of political units. Land is a geographical concept; territory is a political and, more specifically, a juridical concept. A territory, in simplest terms, is a geographical jurisdiction. The qualifier "geographical" is important: not all jurisdictional domains are geographical; some may be personal. A religious court, for example, may have jurisdiction over persons regardless of where they reside. Similarly, a special legislature for the members of a minority group (such as the Sami Parliament in Finland) may serve as the vehicle for exercising rights of the group in question to control certain activities that members of the group engage in, such as education, regardless of where those activities occur. Here too the jurisdiction is personal, not geographical. Or, more precisely, jurisdiction over persons is not achieved by way of jurisdiction over the area in which they are found.

2. Toward an Analytical Framework for the Ethics of Boundary Changes

The Concept of a Jurisdiction
A jurisdiction, whether geographical or personal, is a domain of legal rules and, derivatively, a sphere of authority for the agency or agencies that make, adjudicate, and enforce those rules. The Lockean story of initial acquisition is an account of how appropriation of land creates property rights in land, not an account of how jurisdictions and hence boundaries are created. The key to developing a liberal theory of boundaries, I shall argue, is to distinguish clearly between (1) jurisdictional authority (the right to make, adjudicate, and enforce legal rules within a domain), (2) meta-jurisdictional authority (the right to create or alter jurisdictions, including geographical jurisdictions), and (3) the property rights of individuals and groups within jurisdictions. Because jurisdictional authority includes the right to make legal rules that define property rights, no account of how property in land may be acquired can carry us far toward a comprehensive moral theory of boundaries.[5]

What is more, it can be argued that it is not possible to develop a freestanding specification of what the regime of property rights should be – that is, one that is independent of a prior account of jurisdictional authority. It is true that some in the liberal tradition have believed that there are natural rights to property in what might be called the strong sense: that revelation or abstract and entirely universal reasoning can by themselves provide a specification of a regime of property rights, without reliance upon political processes or authoritative conventions to flesh out the general liberal principle that a just society will include a prominent role for private property. However, a convincing case for the strong natural property-rights thesis has never been made, nor is it likely to be.[6] A more plausible view, and one that is probably at present the dominant liberal position, is that even if it can be shown that any just society will have a prominent place for private property, there is no one, uniquely optimal or morally required substantive and concrete specification of a regime of private property rights that is appropriate for all societies at all times.

Without attempting here to argue for the latter position, let me simply note that the Lockean view itself appears to require some kind of political process or other means of specifying the abstract notion of acquisition by "mixing one's labor" with things in the natural condition in order to yield substantive and concrete property rights.[7] Even if we accept Locke's mysterious idea that "mixing one's labor" with objects somehow transforms them into something like an extension of one's body (understood as one's original property), we still need an account of what counts as "mixing one's labor." (Does simply walking through a piece of land and perhaps touching objects on it, or enclosing it in a fence, or tidying up the landscape a bit count?[8]) To move from the abstract claim that "mixing of labor" generates an entitlement, the specification of a regime of property rights that plays the fundamental coordinating and liberty-protecting role liberalism assigns to the institution of private property, authoritative conventions presumably will be needed. But if this is so, then it appears that the question of jurisdictional authority must be answered, at least in broad outlines, before we can determine what constitutes property rights in land.

In other words, we must first know who has the rightful authority to promulgate the needed conventions. To assume that a Lockean theory of property rights in land can provide the basis for a liberal theory of jurisdictional authority is to put the cart before the horse. To think that a Lockean theory of property in land can yield an account of meta-jurisdictional authority – a theory of who has the right to change the boundaries that determine geographical jurisdictions – is even less plausible.

Liberal Democratic Theory: The Peoples' Territory
The gospel of liberalism, at least in its democratic variants, included the message that the state, including its territorial dimension, is not the property of a dynasty, an aristocracy, or any other political elite, but rather "belongs" to the people. Yet liberalism in all its variants, as I have already noted, also gives a prominent place to private property. Therefore, liberal theory must somehow distinguish the sense in which the state's territory belongs to the people as a whole from the relationship of particular individuals or groups to the property they own within the boundaries of the state. If the state territory as a whole belongs to the whole people, but if some of the land within the state is owned by some people but not others, then the relationship of the people to the state territory cannot be that of the owner of land to the land owned.

It is true of course that all existing liberal states include some public land. But the fact that not all land is public only highlights the need to distinguish between property and territory. The people as a whole stand in a special relationship to the whole area within the boundaries of the state; this much is conveyed by the idea of popular sovereignty. But whatever this relationship is, it cannot be reduced to property in land, since this would render unintelligible the distinction between the people's relationship to public land (a relationship of property ownership) and their relationship to the whole territory of the state (which includes private as well as public land).

In simplest terms, the relationship of the people to the area enclosed by the state's boundaries is this: at least in *democratic* liberal theory, the people are supposed to be both (1) the ultimate beneficiaries of the exercise of jurisdictional authority, and (2) the possessors of jurisdictional authority, the ultimate authors, through democratic processes, of the legal rules that are created by the exercise of that authority and that are to be applied within those boundaries.

The people, through democratic legislation or constitutional rules, may or may not decide to include a place for public property in land in the property rights regime they author. So, although popular (legislative) sovereignty includes, within the scope of jurisdictional authority, the right to define legal property rights in land (as well as in other things), it is not reducible to a property right in the land that comprises the geographical domain of their jurisdiction.

Distinguishing Rights to Make Rules Within a Jurisdiction from Rights to Create or Alter Jurisdictions

Among liberals, it is uncontroversial that popular sovereignty encompasses the right of the people as a whole, through representative processes, to make the most basic legal rules to be applied within the territory of the state (the geographical domain of jurisdiction).[9] But from the fact that the people have ultimate jurisdictional authority it does not follow that the people as a whole have meta-jurisdictional authority, the right (unilaterally) to change boundaries. For one thing, changing the state's boundaries may violate the rights of other individuals and states, as when one state expands its borders by conquest of another. In addition, there may be some cases in which it would be unfair to leave to the people of the state as a whole the decision as to whether to alter the boundaries of the state by allowing a subregion of the state to secede.

The clearest example of the latter situation is where the people of a subregion seek to secede to escape serious and persistent violations of their basic rights at the hands of the state through the application of discriminatory laws supported by a majority of the population as a whole. It would be unfair to insist that they be allowed to escape these injustices by separation only if those who are inflicting the injustices consent to separation.[10] For this reason, no appeal to popular sovereignty of the people of the state as a whole can provide a comprehensive theory of the ethics of boundary changes, which must include an account of meta-jurisdictional authority.

I shall also argue later that the attempt to ground the right to change boundaries by secession on a principle of popular sovereignty for the population of the seceding subregion also fails. Democratic principles, I will show, turn out to shed very limited light on the ethics of making and changing boundaries. More generally, I will argue that none of the usual liberal suspects – principles of popular sovereignty or democracy, freedom of association, and consent, as well as the more recent liberal commitment to accommodating pluralism – is adequate to ground a theory of boundary changes. The ethics of boundary changes proves to be an integral part of a much more complex liberal theory, in which a number of principles must be appropriately ordered and balanced.

A Major Complication

Following all too common practice, I have proceeded thus far as if the boundaries we are talking about when we ponder the ethics of creating and changing boundaries are *state* borders. This tack would be unobjectionable if two assumptions held: first, that it is only the making and changing of those boundaries that are borders between states that raises moral issues, and second, that the concept of a state is sufficiently definite and fixed as to allow a clear distinction between those boundaries that are the borders of states and boundaries of other sorts. Unfortunately, neither assumption holds.

The first assumption overlooks the need for an ethical theory of intrastate political differentiation. Such a theory would address a wide range of issues from rights of national minorities, to indigenous peoples' rights, to the choice among centralized, unitary states and various forms of federalism and consociationalism. At present, neither liberalism, nor any other theory, offers a systematic normative theory of intrastate political differentiation. The second assumption equates "state" with "sovereign political unit," and then makes the mistake of thinking that sovereignty is an all-or-nothing affair – that a state is a political unit that has (or whose people have) the unlimited right to make legal rules within its geographical area. This is a mistake because there are no such political entities. Sovereignty is a matter of degree. Some political units have more independent control over the making, application, and enforcement of legal rules than others.

To make matters even more complex, in many cases there is no neat hierarchy of spheres of control. A political unit can have much control over some matters but lesser control over others, and there may be no plausible way of summing up all the disparate dimensions of control and lack of control to derive a net "sovereignty score" by which all different units may be compared.[11]

As what we now call states come to have more international legal and economic limitations on their abilities to conduct not only their external relations but also their internal affairs, and as more spheres of political differentiation appear within states, it will become more difficult to determine which boundaries are interstate boundaries. Or at least states, and with them interstate boundaries, will become less important, not only economically and politically, but also morally. Indeed, the very concept of a state may become, not just problematic, but unserviceable.

Nevertheless, states at present are still important, especially from the perspective of international legal institutions. So, for the foreseeable future, one important dimension of an ethical theory of boundaries is an account of how international legal institutions should regard the creation of states and the changing of boundaries of existing states. For this reason, I will indulge in the simplifying assumption that the boundaries we are most concerned about in this volume are the borders of states.

So, in the remainder of this chapter I shall plumb the resources of liberal theory for answers to the central moral questions concerning the making and changing of boundaries, understood chiefly as borders between states. Under what conditions if any does *settlement* of land justify incorporation within existing state borders? Does *conquest* ever justify incorporation? Under what conditions, if any, may a part of the territory of a state be *alienated* through sale, exchange, or gift? Under what conditions, if any, is *secession* of a part of a state's territory justifiable? For reasons I hope will become clear as I proceed, my main focus will be on the last question. Nevertheless, the analytic framework sketched here, which will be fleshed out in what follows, should shed light on all of the questions just listed.

3. Settlement as a Mode of Incorporation

To my knowledge, there is nothing that warrants the title of a liberal theory of the acquisition of territory by settlement. There are, as noted earlier, Lockean views about how property rights to land may be acquired, but for reasons already indicated, these should not be confused with theories of the incorporation of land into the territories of states or the creation of new states. Nevertheless, Lockean theories were sometimes used to justify such incorporation, especially in the case of colonial incursions into aboriginal lands in the new world.

I have already explained why it is implausible to think that a Lockean theory of property rights could be developed independently of a theory of jurisdictional authority. Though I cannot argue the point here in the detail it deserves, I would now like to suggest that the well-known flaws of Lockean theories of acquisition of property in land and the resources land contains also afflict any attempt to harness these theories for the task of justifying settlement as a mode of justly incorporating land into the territory of existing states.

The chief flaw of Lockean theories of initial acquisition can be framed as a dilemma: either (1) they are to be understood as requiring, but not achieving, an account of what it is for land or other natural resources to be in the natural condition – that is, not to be the subject of pre-existing claims of property by others, in which case they presuppose, rather than provide, a theory of property rights; or (2) they assume, quite implausibly, that the only basis for pre-existing claims that could limit just acquisition is that those who make these claims are already using the land or resources in question in an optimally efficient manner. Let us consider each of the horns of the dilemma in turn.[12]

According to interpretation (1), the Lockean account of initial acquisition merely claims that the productive appropriation of land and other resources ("mixing one's labor," and so on) creates an entitlement *when* there are no valid prior claims to the land or resources in question – but the Lockean account itself does not purport to provide an exhaustive explanation of all the ways that valid prior claims may originate. In other words, the Lockean account merely says: "If land or other resources are not the subject of valid claims by others, then one can come to have an entitlement to them by using them productively." But this is remarkably uninformative – and in no way justifies colonial expropriation of native lands – unless accompanied by an account of the ways that valid prior claims can originate according to which native occupation and use does not generate valid claims. Simply to assume that the ways native peoples utilized land and other natural resources did not serve as a basis for valid claims is simply to beg the questions a theory of property rights is supposed to answer. So, on the first interpretation, the Lockean account does not provide a justification for entitlement to land but at most a justification for entitlement to land that is the subject of no prior claims, and this is so regardless of whether what is sought is a justification for assertions of property rights by individuals or groups or for sovereignty over territory asserted by states or peoples.

The second interpretation of the Lockean account avoids the fatal flaw of the first, but only by explicitly committing itself to a very implausible view about what alone generates claims to land – namely, optimally productive use. Notoriously, Lockean views about initial acquisition were marshaled to defend colonialism in the new world by coupling them with a scurrilous interpretation of the idea of *terra nullius*. Native peoples (read "savages") were said to have no prior claims to the land they occupied because they were not using it productively by cultivating it in European fashion. Strictly speaking, this was not the view that *settlement* by Europeans justified their claims to the land, but rather that these claims were justified because Europeans made formerly "waste lands" productive. Although native lands were not literally unoccupied, they were not productively occupied, to European eyes.

Taken literally, the claim about productivity is, of course, quite false. Native peoples did use natural resources productively – they succeeded in securing shelter, food, clothing, and various amenities (not to mention rich and complex forms of culture that depended on the creative use of natural resources). So the Lockean initial acquisition argument for dispossessing native peoples must rest on a thesis about *relative* productivity: that Europeans were entitled to lands occupied by native peoples because the latter failed to use them as productively as the Europeans would. In other words, only the most productive users gain entitlements.

There are two major objections to the Lockean view thus interpreted. First, it is question-begging to assume that all that counts from the standpoint of productivity is the ratio of material inputs to material outputs or, even more narrowly, the yield of agricultural products per acre. People use material resources to produce not just material goods that can be weighed and measured (as can bushels of corn per acre or calories gained per calories expended), but also to produce what might be broadly called cultural goods. Thus the judgment that native peoples were less productive not only assumes commensurability of the various goods produced by them and by Europeans respectively (not a trivial assumption, to put it mildly), but also that gross measures of material productivity provide an adequate surrogate for productivity overall.

Second, and more important, the principle that simply being a more productive user of resources generates an entitlement is not so much a principle of property acquisition as a denial that there is such a thing as property rights as ordinarily understood. Especially in a market system in which techniques for greater productivity are supposed to emerge continuously, it would be absurd to say that entitlement depends upon relative productivity. Entitlements would be radically insecure and ephemeral. Moreover, the ordinary understanding of a property right is that it confers a sphere of discretion; one may choose to use one's property in less than the most productive manner.

Understood as a theory of what generates entitlements to territory rather than property in land, the greater-productivity criterion is no less absurd. It would commit liberals to the view that one state is justified in forcibly annexing another's territory whenever it could use the resources therein more productively.

The difficulty for the second interpretation of the Lockean account lies not in the idea that there is some connection between productivity and the justification of property rights but rather in the much more specific and implausible thesis that greater productivity itself creates entitlements. A property rights system ought to enhance productivity, other things being equal, at least to the extent that the inequalities the system inevitably generates should work to produce a greater social surplus that will benefit even the worse off. But this is not to say that conflicting claims to entitlements within the system ought to be adjudicated by direct application of the criterion of greater productivity.

To summarize: attempts to utilize the Lockean justification for property rights to develop an account of how settlement and use of land can create an entitlement to territory, fail, regardless of whether we regard it as (1) a theory of how a state could come to have a claim to land to which there are no valid prior claims, but which presupposes, but does not supply, a theory of the various ways that such prior claims could originate, or as (2) a less radically incomplete but wildly implausible theory according to which the only way valid claims to land can arise is by using the land more productively than any one else can. And these two flaws are quite independent of the more profound error of any such endeavor: the confusion of land with territory and property rights with jurisdictional authority.

Given the poor prospects for converting the Lockean account of initial acquisition of property rights into a theory of acquisition of territory by states, what *does* the liberal tradition offer? What I would like to suggest here, but do not pretend to demonstrate, is that although there is nothing that could qualify as a liberal theory of acquisition of territory by settlement (or by use), there is some recent work in the liberal theory of justice that bears on the project. I refer here, to liberal theorizing about international distributive justice by Thomas Pogge, Charles Beitz, Onora O'Neill and others.[13]

This work does not engage directly with the question of acquisition of territory by settlement for the simple reason that there is virtually no land on Earth that is not already claimed by one (or more) states, with the exception of the polar regions that have been reserved as a kind of international scientific commons by international agreement.

However, the liberal principles of egalitarian international distributive justice these theorists defend have implications for the acquisition of new land if this becomes possible through the discovery of other planets that humans are capable of reaching and settling. Whether or not various liberal theories of international distributive justice would impose conditions on the claims states could make to genuinely uninhabited land on other planets is perhaps unclear. What is clear is that such theories, at least the more egalitarian of them, would include the productive assets states would gain from extraterrestrial settlement within the domain of distributive justice.

There are two quite distinct ways a liberal egalitarian theory of international distributive justice might accommodate entitlements to previously unclaimed lands: (1) by making the case that such lands be treated as an international commons (as the polar regions have been), or (2) by allowing individual states to appropriate new land and then extending to these new assets the same principles of redistributive justice that the theories now apply to the productive assets already contained within existing state borders. The contrast, roughly, is between efforts to achieve a more egalitarian global distribution of resources by regarding new resources as literally common property for all humanity and efforts to tax new lands or the resources they contain while allowing them to become part of the territory of particular states (or the "offshore" property of its citizens). It seems very unlikely that which of these strategies for egalitarian distributive justice is best can be determined by liberal *theory*, properly speaking. Instead, this appears to be a question of how best to apply whatever egalitarian distributive principles the best liberal theory would contain.

Settlement and Customary Rights to Land
The recent proliferation of litigation over land tenure rights of indigenous peoples provides an important challenge to liberal thinking about the role of settlement in establishing claims to land. Increasingly, indigenous groups are pressing claims to land before both domestic courts and international

judicial or quasi-judicial entities (such as the Inter-American Commission on Human Rights). In some cases, the basis for the indigenous claim is a treaty that the state has violated. But in other cases, the problem is that under the property rules of the states within whose borders they were forcibly incorporated during the process of colonization, indigenous peoples have no clear entitlement to the lands, in spite of the fact that they have occupied them for centuries and utilized their resources under stable systems of customary rights rooted in their own cultures and forms of government. Moreover, these groups may have a vital interest in securing their tenure, both because their livelihood depends upon it and because the particular land in question is bound up with their cultural and religious identities.

The conventional doctrine of human rights, which is generally regarded as liberal in its foundation, may not provide adequate support for such claims. A common diagnosis of the deficiency is that as liberal rights, human rights are exclusively individual, while the valid claims of indigenous peoples rights can only be fully protected by recognition of group rights. However, the difficulty may not be so much that human rights are thought to be exclusively individual, as distinct from group rights, but that human rights as commonly understood include neither (1) rights of rectificatory justice regarding land (which could be appealed to in order to address violations of treaties that involved unjust taking of land), nor (2) a proper recognition of the validity of customary rights to land that existed prior to the imposition of alien property rights regimes on indigenous peoples. There appears to be nothing in the standard lists of human rights that unambiguously and effectively speaks either to the rectification of past unjust takings or the protection of customary rights not recognized by the dominant formal legal system.

It is worth noting that liberal political and legal theory, to the extent that it accords great importance to contracts broadly conceived, is in no way unreceptive to the idea of rights of rectificatory justice regarding unjust taking of lands by the violation of treaties or other agreements. Here, the lack of protection for indigenous rights has been a failure of practice to measure up to theory, not a deficiency of theory.

Liberalism's theoretical resources for providing secure protection for claims to land based on customary law that existed prior to the imposition of formal property rights systems are far more questionable. Yet there is something at the heart of liberalism that could supply a rationale for developing a theory of claims to land based on customary rights – namely, the emphasis on the need to secure reasonable expectations that is the basis for liberalism's commitment to the rule of law, along with liberalism's insistence on the importance of property rights for liberty and well being.

Liberalism champions the rule of law as a necessary condition for persons to be able to plan their projects and pursuits with reasonable assurance as to the likely outcome of their actions. Given the reliance that indigenous peoples and others have placed on access to land based on long-standing custom, any political theory that takes the stability of reasonable expectations seriously and recognizes the importance of property rights for human flourishing cannot simply dismiss such claims because they are not unambiguously valid under existing formal property rights regimes. My suggestion, then, is that even though it is true that liberal theory, including the conventional liberal theory of human rights, is deficient regarding land claims based on "settlement", understood as generating customary rights, this deficiency may not be irremediable.

Nevertheless, it is a deficiency in liberal theory, and one that has facilitated gross injustices in practice. Indeed, it can be argued that the failure of liberal theory to provide a coherent basis for the current claims of indigenous peoples to land is simply a repetition of its failure to take customary land-tenure rights seriously three centuries ago when the forces of the market first gave the landed aristocracy in Great Britain incentives to expel tenants from their land and enclose their commons.

4. Conquest

Given a reasonable conception of what distinguishes conquest properly speaking from other modes of acquiring territory, it is hard to see how a genuinely liberal theory could justify conquest as a legitimate mode of acquisition. By "conquest" I mean the forcible incorporation of territory – that is, land already within the geographical jurisdiction of another state. Conquest is thus to be distinguished from mere military occupation, which might be undertaken, as may have been the case in the international intervention in Somalia, for humanitarian reasons rather than for the purpose of incorporation.

Understood in this way, conquest would by its very nature seems to involve a violation of rights – not just the rights of sovereignty of the state whose territory is invaded, but more important, the rights of the individual citizens of that state upon whom force is inflicted. But liberal theories by their nature take the problem of justifying the use of force very seriously. And among the justifications for the use of force that liberal theories countenance, the expansion of state territory is not to be found.

There is, however, one possible exception to the general principle that conquest is not a legitimate mode of acquiring territory according to liberal theory. Pre-emptive self-defense might under certain highly constrained circumstances justify the forcible taking of territory for the purpose of incorporation. What I have in mind can be made clearer by modifying two actual historical examples – the first involving the South Tyrol, the second, the Rhineland region of Germany.

In 1919, as a part of the various agreements collectively known as the Versailles Treaty, the victorious allies awarded Italy the South Tyrol region, which was at that time part of Austria. The official justification for doing so was that Italian security required control over the passes in the region, which constituted the traditional invasion route from Austria to Italy, most recently utilized in the war that had just ended.

Imagine the following hypothetical modification of the South Tyrol case. Country X has repeatedly been the innocent victim of aggression by its neighbor to the North, country Y. There is good reason to believe that if country X's border with country Y were pushed forward sixty miles, to coincide with a formidable natural boundary such as a mountain range or major river, the threat of future successful invasions by Y would be greatly diminished. Under these conditions, would X be justified, according to liberal principles, in seeking to expand its territory sixty miles northward, by force if necessary?

The attraction of an affirmative answer lies in the moral propriety of justified self-defense, a well-established principle in the common law of liberal societies. Given the long-standing pattern of aggression by Y, may X not act pre-emptively? Why must X wait until it is actually attacked again?

Analogy with the liberal common law principle of justified self-defense must proceed cautiously, however. In general, no right to pre-emptive self-defense is allowed in the common law, except where a reasonable person would judge that an attack is literally imminent. Moreover, the dangers of affirming a more permissive general principle of pre-emptive conquest as a matter of international law or morality are manifest. Such a principle would be eminently abusable (and has been abused often in the past). It is therefore worth noting that there may be other ways that X can gain reasonable assurance that it will not be invaded by Y without the drastic step of pre-emptive conquest.

First, much will depend upon whether X can rely on allies or international organizations to control Y's aggression. Second, there may be reasonable alternatives short of incorporating the invasion corridor into X's territory. For example, out of similar concerns, the Allies agreed at Versailles that France could occupy (not incorporate) the Rhineland region of Germany. The French eventually agreed to an even less drastic measure, the exclusion of German troops and military construction in the region. At least from a liberal standpoint, there is a very strong, if not absolute, presumption against pre-emptive conquest and in favor of other, less restrictive strategies for self-defense, in all cases other than that of literally imminent aggression.

At the end of the day, whether or not a liberal theory would countenance a more permissive right of pre-emptive conquest that allowed armed border crossings in circumstances in which aggression was not literally imminent depends upon whether that theory incorporates a Realist view of international relations. Liberals who hold that the international scene is close to anarchical will generally be more sympathetic to the Hobbesian view that transforms a narrowly circumscribed right of self-defense into a much broader principle of pre-emptive conquest. Liberals who have more confidence in the effectiveness of international institutions will tend to adhere more closely to the collective analog of the narrower common law right to act in self-defense only in the face of a literally imminent threat.[14]

5. Alienation of Territory (exchange, sale, gift)

Contemporary liberal theories are silent on the morality of alienating territory. This is perhaps not surprising, given that states rarely voluntarily give up territory nowadays. However, prior to the rise of liberalism, state territory was often exchanged, and sometimes sold, by monarchs and political elites.

Both in their emphasis on popular sovereignty and in their insistence that the property of citizens may not be appropriated for state use without compensation and due process of law within representative institutions, classical liberal theorists roundly rejected the assumption that rulers may treat state territory as if it were their own property. In the early twentieth century, Woodrow Wilson was the most passionate proponent of this classical liberal position.

Thus the key distinction of the analytical framework sketched in Section 2, between jurisdictional authority, meta-jurisdictional authority, and rights to land as property within a jurisdiction, is again relevant. In democratic liberal theory, it is the people, ultimately, for whom and by whom jurisdictional authority is to be exercised, but in such a way as to give proper weight to private property rights within the jurisdiction. And while the people as a whole have no right of conquest to expand their territory by aggressive war (except perhaps in some cases of pre-emptive self-defense), no one other than the people as a whole have the ultimate authority to alienate state territory.

In any theory that can be called liberal, there will be at least three major sources of constraint on the right of the people as a whole to alienate territory. First, there is the need to give private-property right holders within the territory to be alienated their due. As already noted, alienation of territory that includes private property may only take place according to due process of law and with appropriate compensation. Appropriate respect for private property rights would also presumably require that the justification for alienating the territory would rise to an appropriate threshold of importance – something like the notion of a compelling state interest, to be fleshed out ultimately by reference to important interests of the people as a whole.

Second, the "people" here is to be understood as an *intergenerational* community. Hence, it would be impermissible for the current citizenry, even if it voted directly and unanimously to do so, to alienate state territory solely for the purpose of benefit to themselves, without regard for the interests of future generations of citizens.

Whether or not all liberal theories are committed to recognizing significant obligations to preserve resources for future generations of mankind generally, including those who will not be fellow citizens, is perhaps less clear. For here we come to what I have argued elsewhere is a great divide among liberal theories: the distinction between those that understand the state primarily or even exclusively as a cooperative venture for the mutual benefit of *its* citizens (present and future generations of citizens included) and those that understand the state as an important resource for contributing to the fulfillment of a moral obligation to help ensure that all persons (whether they are our fellow citizens or not) have access to institutions that protect their basic rights.[15]

According to the first type of view, our obligations to those who are not our fellow citizens (whether of the present or future generations) include, at most, a negative duty not to harm, but no duties to benefit. And if we have no obligations to benefit future generations of persons who are not citizens of our states, then the right to alienate territory is correspondingly less constrained. For example, there might be no moral barrier to the present generation of citizens voting to sell land containing valuable natural resources to another state that would deplete them without regard to conservation for future generations, so long as those selling the resources and their own future fellow citizens derived sufficient benefit from the bargain. According to the view that the state is merely a cooperative venture for the benefit of its own citizens, there would be nothing wrong with such a sale of territory, unless it could be shown that future generations of persons who are not citizens of the state selling the territory would be wrongfully harmed (as opposed to being merely not benefited) by the sale.

In contrast, the second type of view of the state allows for the possibility that the citizens of a state have obligations of justice, including obligations to benefit, that are owed to persons who will not be members of their state in the future. And the possibility of such obligations represents a further constraint on a liberal theory of the alienation of territory, beyond those supplied by a proper acknowledgment that the territory of the state "belongs" to its own people as an intergenerational community. However, existing normative political theories, including liberal theories, are notoriously uninformative about the nature and extent of obligations to future generations generally, in addition to lacking a coherent account of the distinction between the special obligations that the present generation of citizens owe to their future co-citizens and what is owed to future humanity at large.[16]

The third source of constraint on the right of the (current) people of a state to alienate territory does not depend upon the assumption that there are obligations to future generations, whether of fellow citizens or humanity at large. Another historical example, suitably modified, will illustrate. Throughout World War II, Sweden continued to sell iron to Nazi Germany – iron that was used to produce weapons and other materials used to commit millions of unjustified killings. Suppose that instead of selling iron to the Nazis, Sweden had chosen to sell them the part of its territory in which iron ore deposits were concentrated, knowing that these resources would be used to violate basic human rights.

Presumably any liberal theory worthy of consideration would include a presumption against the permissibility of alienating territory in such a case. Whether that presumption could be overridden in some circumstances – for example, if the Nazis threatened to conquer the whole of Sweden and annihilate its citizens if the territory containing iron deposits were not sold to them – is another matter.

6. Secession

As already noted, liberal theorists have recently begun to develop explicit views concerning one process by which state borders can change and new state territories can be created – namely, secession.[17]

Types of Secession, Theories of the Right to Secede

To understand the options, within liberalism, for a theory of secession, two crucial distinctions are needed. The first is between two ways in which secession may occur: unilaterally, without the consent of the state, and consensually; the second is between two basic types of theories of the right to secede unilaterally, what I call remedial right-only theories and primary right theories.[18] Most secessions (unlike the secession of Norway from Sweden) are nonconsensual, and the response of the state is usually not just refusal to agree to the separation, but violent suppression of it. Thus it is not surprising that in most cases, when theorists ponder the existence or nature of a "right to secede," they are concerned with unilateral secession.

Liberal theory can, without much difficulty, accommodate consensual secession. So far as liberalism includes an emphasis on the rule of law and on constitutionalism broadly conceived, consensual secession should be a constitionalized process or at least a rule-governed, procedurally just one. Constitutionalizing a process of secession could occur in either of two ways: by exercise of a right to secede specified in the constitution, or, in the absence of a specific constitutional right to secede, by structuring the process of secession by general constitutional principles, perhaps in combination with constitutional amendments to achieve the separation. The 1993 constitution of Ethiopia, as well as the constitutions of the Soviet Union and Yugoslavia, all include or included a right to secede. Although Canada's constitution does not include a specific right to secede, the Supreme Court of Canada has recently ruled that if secession of Quebec is to occur, it must be according to four fundamental constitutional principles (democracy, federalism, constitutionalism and the rule of law, and protection of minority rights), and that constitutional amendments will be needed.[19]

Both of these modes of constitutionalizing the process of consensual secession will be structured by features of the particular constitution in question. Therefore, we should not expect a single universal substantive theory of the precise conditions under which consensual secession is justified. The main point, however, is that a broad range of liberal theories can agree that consensual secession is an option, especially if constitutionalizing the process of secession achieves the liberal values of the rule of law and procedural fairness.[20]

This is not to say that developing a liberal account of how consensual secession ought to proceed, even in a particular country under a particular constitution, will be easy or uncontroversial. As the Canadian case clearly illustrates, many difficult issues will have to be resolved – from the fair division of the national debt to the protection of minority rights.

Moreover, no straightforward appeal to familiar liberal principles, such as the rule of law, procedural fairness, or democracy, will do the job. For example, does a commitment to democracy in the process of consensual secession require only a simple majority in favor of secession in the seceding area, or more (and if so, how much more)? And should a majority decision in the region in question suffice (however what counts as a majority is specified), or are there cases in which the preferences of a minority (such as the Native peoples of Quebec, who appear to reject secession) should have special weight? Liberal thinking about consensual secession is at present so undeveloped that differing liberal positions have not yet emerged.

Unilateral secession is another matter. Here, theorists who all call themselves liberals have developed quite different views as to when secession is justified. To appreciate the full range of theoretical options within liberalism, a second distinction is needed: that between remedial right-only theories and primary right theories of (unilateral) secession.

Remedial Right-Only Theories
This first type of theory of unilateral secession construes the right to secede without consent as a close relative to the right of revolution as understood in the mainstream of the liberal tradition. According to the latter, the right to revolution is not a primary right, but rather a remedial one: it comes to exist when its exercise provides a remedy of last resort to escape injustices – understood as violations of other more basic rights. Similarly, according to the remedial right-only theory of the right to (unilateral) secession, a group comes to have the right to secede (unilaterally) only when secession is the remedy of last resort in conditions in which that group is the victim of persistent violations of important rights of its members.[21]

According to the version of remedial right-only theory that I have developed in some detail elsewhere, the rights in question are primarily individual human rights. However, a group may also come to have the (unilateral) right to secede under two other circumstances: first, if the state has granted it autonomous status or other special rights and then defaults on this commitment; second, if the territory in question was that of an independent state and was unjustly annexed, in which case secession can be viewed as the remedying of an injustice also.

In its most plausible forms, the remedial right-only theory of the unilateral right to secede is combined with an unequivocal commitment to the permissibility of consensual secession. Thus the remedial right-only position is not that secession is only justified as a remedy for injustices, but rather that unilateral secession is only thus justified. For this reason, the remedial right-only view is not as restrictive, nor as supportive of the preservation of existing state boundaries, as might first appear.

Primary Right Theories
The second type of theory asserts that unilateral secession can be justified in the absence of serious injustices perpetrated against the seceding group, and indeed even when the state is acting in a perfectly just manner. Note that primary right theories are *not* primary right-*only* theories; they acknowledge that injustices can justify unilateral secession, holding only that this is not the only sound justification.

Primary right theories can be divided into two main types, and both types have been endorsed by theorists who claim the title of liberal. The first is what I have called *plebiscitary* right theories; the second, *ascriptive* right theories. The former hold that a right to secede (unilaterally) exists whenever a majority in the region in question chooses to secede, regardless of whether that majority shares any characteristics other than this preference for separation. The latter attributes the right to secede (unilaterally) to groups that are defined by what might be called ascriptive characteristics.

At present, at least, those who subscribe to the ascriptivist variant of primary right theory identify *nations* as the particular sort of group that has the right of unilateral secession.[22] Just what constitutes a nation is a matter of dispute, but the most widely accepted definition invoked by ascriptive right theorists runs roughly as follows: a nation is a group united by an "encompassing" common culture, membership in which is chiefly a matter of belonging, rather than achievement, where the group in question feels an attachment to a particular area (understood as its homeland), and where the group (or a substantial proportion of its members) aspires for some form of political organization (though not necessarily full independent statehood).[23]

It is important to understand that the position described here is not just that nations may have a right to secede (unilaterally), but that nations – by virtue of their characteristics as nations – have this right. A remedial right-only theorist can readily embrace the former claim. For example, she can include among the grievances that justify unilateral secession the unjust taking of the territory of sovereign states, including nation-states that are sovereign. Under such circumstances, the nation whose territory had been unjustly taken by another state would have the right to secede from the latter unilaterally, as a remedy for the injustice of the taking.

To my knowledge, no contemporary theorist who is considered or considers herself to be liberal endorses the thesis that all nations, in every, or even in most, circumstances, have the right to secede if this is necessary in order to have its own state. Instead, they hold the weaker, more plausible thesis that there is a (unilateral) right of *national self-determination*, which only sometimes, not always, may rightly be exercised by attempting unilateral secession.

This softened nationalist view recognizes that there are forms of self-determination short of full independence, and that giving due weight to competing moral considerations may require something less than full independence. Among the most obvious of these competing considerations is the fact that in many cases, more than one group that qualifies as a nation will claim the same area as its homeland, with the result that it is impossible to act consistently on the general principle that every nation is entitled to its own state. David Miller holds the even weaker view that nations "have a strong claim [not a right] to self-determination" in some form or other, though not necessarily secession.[24]

At present, no liberal theorist of national self-determination has provided a detailed account of precisely when nationhood grounds a right to secede, and when it falls short of this. Consequently, the appeal to national self-determination is far short of providing a theory of the ethics of border changes by secession.

To understand the ways in which the notion of a right of national self-determination might be integrated into a liberal "theory" of boundaries, another distinction is required, this time between two quite different types of arguments that are given to show why nations, as Miller puts it, have a strong claim to self-determination, where this means some form of political organization of their own. Interestingly enough, those who invoke these two types of arguments typically present them as arguments for the stronger conclusion that nations have at least a strong claim to having their own states.[25] Presumably the idea is that in themselves these arguments provide a case for the stronger conclusion, but that the right to secede they support must be regarded as only prima facie because in some, perhaps many, circumstances, there are countervailing moral considerations that require weakening the claim to independent statehood to a claim, if not a right, to some lesser form of self-determination. Nevertheless, both types of arguments hold that there are some cases in which divisions between nations can provide decisive reasons for creating or changing state boundaries.

The first type of argument may be called *the cultural goods argument*. It appeals to the importance of nationality for individuals. According to Margalit and Raz, the most basic interests of the individual are strongly influenced by how the nation to which she belongs fares and the most reliable way to ensure that the nation, and hence its members, flourish is for the nation to have its own state.[26] For Kymlicka, the "societal culture" that is a nation provides a context for meaningful choice for the individual, and security for that culture is likely to require that it have its own state. The credentials of this first type of argument appear to be impeccably liberal because the case for the importance of nations – and for their self-determination – is rooted in moral individualism, the position that ultimately it is individuals and only individuals that matter morally.[27]

The chief difficulty with the cultural goods argument is that it fails to distinguish nations from other types of cultural groups. At least in the modern world, individuals have diverse sources of identity, among which nationality is only one, and not the most important one. Religion, political ideologies, even professional commitments, can and do provide important contexts for meaningful choice for some individuals, and how well an individual fares will in some cases be more dependent upon the success of these identity-conferring groups than upon the flourishing of her nation, if she can even be said to belong to a nation.[28] This criticism can be deflected, of course, if the proponent of the national self-determination thesis is willing to broaden the notion of a nation to encompass whatever cultural group happens to be most crucial for an individual's identity and interests. The price of this move, however, is exorbitant: it saps the notion of a "nation" of its distinctive content (obliterating the distinction between nations and ethnic, political, and religious groups) and thereby robs the national self-determination thesis of any distinctive interest. In addition, expanding the concept of a nation in this way only makes more apparent the fact that for different individuals, different groups will be most important from the standpoint of the individual's identity and interests. What appeared to be a distinctive claim about nations then becomes merely a vague prescription that political boundaries should somehow take into account the many sources of identity for individuals and the way they affect individuals' interests.

In response to this criticism, some advocates of the cultural goods argument for national self-determination have replied that the point of the argument is not that nations are unique as sources of identity or of cultural goods that depend upon identity, but are merely one important source.[29] This reply, however, robs the argument of much, if not all, of its significance. Once again, all that remains is the admittedly liberal sounding but rather vague thesis that among the many sources of identity and cultural goods, nationality is one. We are left with no inkling as to the circumstances in which this one form of identity, as opposed to the others, ought to be politically empowered. Initially, the interest of the national self-determination view was supposed to lie in its providing an account of why nationality, rather than religion, gender identification, political ideology, or any number of other sources of identity, is especially appropriate as a criterion for creating and altering state boundaries. But now it seems that the claim of privilege has been abandoned, and what is left is a kind of toothless liberal pluralism, the unexceptionable, assertion that, other things being equal, the determination of boundaries should reflect the importance for individuals of membership in nations, among other sources of identity.

The second type of argument for the conclusion that nations ought to have their own states I shall call the *instrumental argument*. It relies on the idea that in order for states to be successful in doing what liberalism says states ought to do, it is important for the citizens to be members of one nation. Two variants of this type of argument are found in liberal writings. The first, which goes back at least to John Stuart Mill's presentation of it, is that mononational states are necessary if democratic institutions are to function properly.[30] The second is that mononational states are either necessary for achieving the goals of distributive justice or at least more likely to achieve them than those in which there is more than one national group.[31]

Each variant faces serious objections. The main problem with the *democratic institutions* variant is that the premise that multinational states cannot function democratically is a rather sweeping and, one can argue, prematurely pessimistic empirical generalization. The sample on the basis of which the generalization is made is disturbingly small, for the simple reason that until quite recently there have been very few states that could be called democratic. (When attempting to answer the question of whether multinational democratic states are possible, one would do well to recall Chou En Lai's response to the question "What was the greatest effect of the French Revolution?": "It is too soon to tell.")

The argument might of course be retrenched to the weaker conclusion that mononationality, though not necessary for democracy, allows for the democratic ideal to be satisfied more fully. But if so, then it is far from clear what the practical implications of the argument really are, since the obvious disadvantages of trying to achieve a redrawing of boundaries so as to create mononational states may well outweigh the relative gains for democracy of doing so. Liberalism, at least in its modern forms, does include a commitment to democracy; but there is no absolute commitment to maximal democracy.

The other variant of the instrumental argument for mononational states, according to which the latter are necessary for achieving the goals of *distributive justice*, or at least for optimally approximating their achievement, is subject to a similar objection. The main premise of the argument is that the degree of redistribution that distributive justice requires can only be achieved, or best approximated, if citizens are motivated by the distinctive sense of solidarity that only co-nationality supplies. But this premise is far from self-evident, and the empirical backing it requires is probably not available. It is one thing to say that the more redistribution is required, the greater the sense of solidarity that is needed to achieve it – indeed this approaches tautology. But it is quite another to establish that the needed solidarity must be nationalist in any interesting sense. In addition, it is simply not the case that nationalism is inherently, or even in most cases support-ive of, egalitarian redistribution. Some forms of nationalism are extremely inegalitarian. (Examples include National Socialism in Germany and, some would argue, contemporary Hindu Nationalism so far as it does not chal-lenge, and perhaps even endorses, the caste system).

Another objection to both forms of the instrumental argument for na-tional self-determination is worth mentioning. Even if it were true that nationalism provides a valuable source of the solidarity needed for achieving distributive justice or for democracy, it may carry other baggage that is un-acceptable from a moral point of view. Nationalism in the real world, as opposed to the highly sanitized nationalism of liberal political theory, is typically chauvinistic or exclusionary and provides a powerful tool for dis-criminatory and even aggressive policies toward non-nationals both at home and abroad. One cannot assume, then, that the motivating power of nation-alist solidarity will always or even usually be harnessed to the engine of justice or democracy, rather than to other, less attractive conveyances.

And finally, liberals should be suspicious about attempts to motivate jus-tice by appeal to co-nationality. At least from a liberal standpoint, justice in its most basic aspect is supposed to rest on universal considerations. As Arthur Ripstein has suggested, even if nationalism is potentially a powerful motivator, it does not follow that it is a suitable motivator for justice, so far as justice has fundamentally to do with impartiality, granted that impartiality must reflect, ultimately, respect for universal characteristics that all human beings possess. Nationalism, in contrast, is by its nature highly particularis-tic, and to that extent partial.[32] Perhaps even more important, an account of justice that relies very heavily on the motivating power of co-nationality will have a hard time indeed in making the case that any substantial requirement of international distributive justice is at all practicable.[33]

Arguments for the Plebiscitary Right View

Perhaps in part because they are impressed with the foregoing objections to the ascriptive right version of the primary right theory of unilateral se-cession, some liberal thinkers have argued for a nonremedial plebiscitary right to secede.[34] Indeed, liberalism would seem to have an affinity for the plebiscitary view, so far as the right of a majority in a region to decide to form its own state might be viewed either (1) as being necessary for satisfac-tion of the very liberal-sounding requirement that government must be by consent, (2) as being a direct implication of the right of freedom of associ-ation, or (3) as being a direct implication of commitment to the principle of democracy. As hinted earlier, however, it can be argued that neither con-sent, nor freedom of association, nor democracy provides a principled basis for a liberal theory of secession by plebiscite.

Consent

Most liberal theorists find unexceptionable the assertion that government requires consent. However, liberal thinking divides as to whether representative institutions suffice to satisfy this requirement or whether consent in some more literal and full-bodied sense is necessary. Harry Beran subscribes to the latter view, and then argues that to satisfy the requirement of consent, it is necessary to recognize a plebiscitary right to secede.[35] In other words, Beran bases a plebiscitary right theory of border changes by unilateral secession on a particular view of what makes government legitimate – namely, consent of the governed.

The notion of legitimacy, however, is ambiguous. According to the stronger notion of legitimacy, government is legitimate if and only if the government enjoys political authority in this sense: not only is it morally justified in enforcing laws, but also the citizens have an obligation to it to obey.[36] According to a weaker notion of legitimacy, all that is required is that the government be morally justified in enforcing laws; it is not necessary in addition that the citizens have an obligation to obey it. The weaker notion of legitimacy allows for the possibility that citizens can be morally obligated to obey the laws even though they have no obligation to the government to obey it. In particular, citizens may be morally obligated to obey the law to the extent that the law codifies valid moral principles, such as the prohibitions against murder and theft. And, of course, citizens may also have prudential reasons for obeying the law.

If one assumes that the fundamental task of political theory is to establish the conditions under which government is legitimate in the *strong* sense, then one will find the requirement of consent (strictly speaking, representative institutions) very attractive. For presumably if one consents to government enforcing the laws, then one thereby obligates oneself to obey it. But the chief concern is legitimacy in the *weak* sense; then the consent requirement is not so compelling, since it may be possible to provide a convincing account of what makes government's enforcement of laws morally justifiable without thereby showing that citizens have an obligation to the government to obey it. At least from a liberal standpoint, such an account would presumably emphasize that in order to be legitimate in the weak sense, government must do a decent job of respecting the basic rights liberalism champions, and must do so according to the strictures of the rule of law.[37]

Much of the literature on the consent requirement simply assumes that the strong notion of legitimacy is the correct one for political theory, and then either argues that the requirement is not and cannot be met in the case of most if not all governments (with the implication that virtually no governments are legitimate), or attempts to rebut these criticisms.[38]

The arguments against fulfillment of the consent requirement by any governments that now exist or are likely to are, in my opinion, conclusive. The chief difficulties are these: first, it would be immoral for anyone to agree to obey any government, for the simple reason that all governments are likely sometimes to require unethical behavior on the part of their citizens. If the response to this objection is that what one consents to is to obey only those laws that are morally sound, then the question arises as to whether the consent requirement, thus watered down, adds much of substance to the weaker notion of legitimacy, according to which what is important is that government be morally justified in enforcing the law and that citizens, generally speaking, have moral and prudential reasons for obeying the law. Second, given the extreme dependency of almost all citizens upon the state (compounded by the high costs of exiting one's own state and the lack of better alternatives), the idea that consent could be freely given is highly dubious.

Given these and other well-known objections, we should question the assumption that an adequate liberal theory must include a consent requirement for government. However, without the assumption that consent is required for government, the consent-based theory of the plebiscitary right to unilateral secession collapses. Recall that Beran argues that secession by majority vote in a plebiscite must be allowed if the requirement of consent is to be met.

There is another, equally serious objection to the proposal that a liberal theory of boundary change by unilateral secession must include a plebiscitary right. Either the requirement of consent is taken at face value and applied consistently to the secessionist plebiscite itself, in which case the view is of no practical consequence because secession will virtually always be blocked by dissenting votes, or the requirement of unanimous consent is relaxed for the population of the subregion though not for the population of the state as a whole, but without any explanation of why this is so. For, remember, the attraction of the consent approach to government legitimacy was that consent puts the one who consents under an obligation to the one to whom he gives consent. But if anyone votes "no" in the plebiscite (as virtually always occurs), then she will not have consented to government in the new state created by secession. Yet if lack of consent is acceptable here, why not also in the original state? To summarize, the variant of the primary right theory of unilateral secession that relies on a consent requirement seems unpromising, because the consent theory of government on which it is based faces well-known objections, and because it simultaneously endorses and violates the requirement of consent itself.

Freedom of Association

On the face of it, liberalism's commitment to freedom of association might seem to provide a principled basis for a theory of border changes by unilateral secession.[39] There are, however, two powerful objections to this strategy. First, in virtually every actual case of secession, there will be some within the area in question who oppose secession. Yet it is hard to see how the right to freedom of association of those who wish to secede can justify the forcible inclusion of others who do not wish to be associated with them. Second, it is one thing to say that persons within a polity have the right to associate together for political or religious purposes; it is another to say that this same right includes the right to take *territory* that is claimed by others. The freedom to associate refers to the right of persons to choose to relate themselves to other persons for various purposes (religious, political, commercial, and so on). But the right to secede is the right to territory. Granted that this is so, it is hard to see how the exercise of the right to relate to other persons can itself generate the required relationship between persons and territory, especially when that territory is claimed by others.

To say that the right to freedom of association includes the right to alter jurisdictional boundaries (meta-jurisdictional authority) by taking territory, is to trade on the uncontroversial liberal credentials of this right, but only by stretching its meaning unconscionably. When liberals say that the right to freedom of association is unquestionably among the rights any political order ought to respect, they have in mind the freedom of persons to associate with each other within a jurisdiction, not the right to take territory to form a new jurisdiction unilaterally.

The deficiencies of the attempt to base a plebiscitary right to unilateral secession on the right to freedom of association can be approached from another angle. Why should we assume that the people who happen to be in a certain region of the state's territory have the right to create a new state out of it if a majority of them vote to do so? According to liberal theory, as it is ordinarily understood, the citizens of the state as a whole enjoy extensive freedom of movement and occupation, as well as the right to acquire property, throughout the extent of the state's territory. And according to the analytical framework sketched at the outset of this chapter, popular sovereignty implies that in some sense, the territory of the whole state "belongs" to the people as a whole.

Whatever it is supposed to be that entitles a majority of those in the region unilaterally to take that part of the territory and to alter the fundamental citizenship status of all those within it, it cannot be the mere fact that they happen to be in the territory. Being in the territory does not mean owning it, and in any case, ownership of land does not imply meta-jurisdictional authority over the territory in which the land is contained. Moreover, even if it were plausible to say that ownership of land is what entitles people to this exercise of meta-jurisdictional authority, there will virtually always be some anti-secessionists who own land in the area, whether they reside in the area or not. The most fundamental flaw, then, of the freedom-of-association approach to a liberal theory of border changes by unilateral secession is that it fails to explain why a majority of those who happen to be in a region of the state have the right not only to associate together for political or other purposes, but to make unilateral changes of borders that involve the taking of territory.

Democracy

Some recent theorists who credibly regard themselves as liberal have proposed to ground a unilateral plebiscitary right to secede in the principle of democracy.[40] There appear to be two variants of this strategy. The first, developed in greatest detail by Daniel Philpott, argues that the same liberal value – namely, individual autonomy – that grounds the commitment to democracy also requires acknowledgment of a plebiscitary right to unilateral secession.[41] This approach, however, seems unpromising, for two reasons. First, contrary to Philpott's claim, democracy (understood primarily as majority rule) is *not* individual self-determination, but rather determination of political decisions by the majority. It is simply a fallacy, stirring rhetoric though it may be, to say that when one exercises one's right of democratic participation one is ruled by oneself; on the contrary, one is ruled by the majority. It is true, of course, that there is a connection between individual autonomy and democracy: it can be argued that democratic government is the most reliable guarantor of basic liberal rights, and that where these rights are respected, individual autonomy is more likely to flourish. But this connection does nothing to establish that a proper respect for individual autonomy requires recognition of a plebiscitary right to unilateral secession, because the standard liberal rights that promote individual autonomy can and do exist without a plebiscitary right to secede (indeed they do so exist in every major liberal-democratic state).[42]

The second strategy for enlisting the notion of democracy in support of a plebiscitary right of unilateral secession has been advanced by David Copp.[43] He asserts that the same equal respect and concern for persons that requires democracy also requires a plebiscitary right to unilateral secession. The familiar idea here is that at least part of what justifies democracy is that it is required by a fundamental commitment to the moral equality of persons. Showing equal respect and concern for persons, according to Copp, requires that they should have an equal say over important political decisions, and this, in turn, requires a right to unilateral secession by plebiscite.

This approach to a liberal theory of border changes by unilateral secession suffers two flaws. First, the premise that equal concern and respect requires that each person have an equal say over important political decisions does not single out the persons who live in the seceding region as the ones who alone ought to have a say. Why not have a state-wide plebiscite, or better yet a global one? (The latter alone would show equal concern and respect for all persons). Second, and more important, to be at all plausible, the sweeping thesis that equal respect and concern requires having a say in political decisions requires considerable qualification. If by a political decision is meant simply any decision that has political consequences or that affects political relations or the political status of persons, then liberal theory vehemently denies that equal concern and respect require that all have an equal say in all political decisions. After all, liberalism includes the view that the scope of democratic decision-making must be constrained, above all, by individual rights. More generally, which decisions ought to be subjected to democratic decision-making is a question that divides liberals from one another, especially when it comes to the problem of drawing the proper boundary between what political processes should do and what should be left to the market or other institutions in the private sphere. But if this is so, then we cannot simply assume, as Copp does, that because the decision to alter boundaries is a political decision, equal concern and respect for persons requires that this decision is to be made unilaterally by majority vote, whether by those in the area in question or by the population as a whole.

The gap between the abstract principle of equal concern and respect and the particular device of secession by regional plebiscite is simply too great. There is no reason to assume that the same principle of majority rule that is generally appropriate for making political decisions within a given jurisdiction is also appropriate for making the fundamental decision to create a new jurisdiction unilaterally out of a part of an old one.[44]

Reflection on the difference between what is usually at stake in political decisions within a jurisdiction taken as given and relatively fixed and the decision to take part of an existing jurisdiction to form a new one leads to another, more basic reason to doubt that a liberal theory of border changes will include the very direct and simple move from a commitment to democracy to a plebiscitary right of unilateral secession endorsed by Philpott and Copp. As has often been pointed out (not least of all by Abraham Lincoln, but also by Albert Hirschman[45]), the connection between democracy and secession cannot be so simple and straightforward as these theorists believe, if only for the simple reason that secession, or even the credible threat of secession, can undermine democracy. If the "exit" option of secession is too easy, then a regionally concentrated minority may use the threat of exit as a de facto veto over majority decisions, thus undermining democratic rule. Just as important, constitutional measures that require something more than or other than a regional majority plebiscite may be valuable to all citizens, so far as they create the right incentives for a sustained commitment to the hard work of deliberative democracy, for working out differences within the polity rather than by trying to eliminate differences by redrawing boundaries.[46]

I have argued that a plausible liberal theory of border changes by unilateral secession will at least include a right to secession as a remedy of last resort for serious injustices. In exploring the possibility that a liberal theory will also include a primary right to unilateral secession, I have taken a more skeptical stance, arguing that none of the usual liberal suspects – consent, democracy, freedom of association – is likely to provide a basis for a unilateral primary right. I have also raised what I believe are serious difficulties for attempts to incorporate a principle of national self-determination into a liberal theory of border changes, at least so far as the latter are made unilaterally through secession. These conclusions, as well as others advanced in this chapter concerning border changes by settlement, conquest, and alienation, must be taken as quite tentative. Liberal theorizing about the morality of boundaries is regrettably, though not uniquely, undeveloped. My aim here has been the limited one of offering some distinctions and arguments that I hope will contribute to the task of remedying this deficiency.

Notes to Chapter 12

1. Allen Buchanan, "Rawls's Law of Peoples: Rules for a Vanished Westphalian World," *Ethics* 110/4 (2000), 697–721.
2. Rawls in his later work makes the convenient but implausible assumption that what might be called deep pluralism exists only across state boundaries, not within the liberal state. John Rawls, *The Law of Peoples* (Cambridge, MA: Harvard University Press, 1999).
3. Will Kymlicka, *Multicultural Citizenship: A Liberal Theory of Minority Rights* (Oxford: Clarendon Press, 1995); Kymlicka, ed., *The Rights of Minority Cultures* (Oxford: Oxford University Press, 1995); Judith Baker, ed., *Group Rights* (Toronto: University of Toronto Press, 1994).
4. Allen Buchanan, *Secession: The Morality of Political Divorce from Fort Sumter to Lithuania and Quebec* (Boulder: Westview Press, 1991), and "Theories of Secession," *Philosophy and Public Affairs* 26/1 (1997), 31–61; P. Lehning, ed., *Theories of Secession* (London: Routledge, 1998); R. McKim and J. McMahan, eds., *The Morality of Nationalism* (New York: Oxford University Press, 1997); Margaret Moore, ed., *National Self-Determination and Secession* (Oxford: Oxford University Press, 1998); J. Couture, K. Nielsen, and M. Seymour, eds., *Rethinking Nationalism* (Calgary: University of Calgary Press, 1998).
5. Avery Kolers, "Locke, Property and Territory," unpublished dissertation, University of Arizona, 2000.
6. See Stephen Munzer, *A Theory of Property* (New York: Cambridge University Press, 1990), and Allen Buchanan, *Ethics, Efficiency, and the Market* (Totowa, N.J.: Rowman & Allanheld, 1985).
7. Robert Nozick, *Anarchy, State, and Utopia* (New York: Basic Books, 1974); Kolers, "Locke, Property and Territory," unpublished paper.
8. Nozick, *Anarchy, State, and Utopia*, 174–5.
9. Under "representative processes" here I include processes for Constitutional Amendment.
10. Buchanan, *Secession: The Morality of Political Divorce*, and Buchanan, "Theories of Secession."
11. Will Kymlicka, "*Secession: The Morality of Political Divorce from Fort Sumter to Lithuania and Quebec*, by Allen Buchanan" (book review), *Political Theory* 20/3 (August 1992), 527–32.

12. My criticisms of the Lockean theory in what follows draw upon Kolers' "Locke, Property, and Territory," unpublished manuscript.

13. Thomas Pogge, "An Egalitarian Law of Peoples," *Philosophy and Public Affairs* 23/3 (Summer 1994), 195–224; Charles Beitz, *Political Theory and International Relations* (Princeton, NJ: Princeton University Press, 1979); Onora O'Neill, "Justice, Gender, and International Boundaries," in Martha Nussbaum and Amartya Sen, eds., *Quality of Life* (Oxford: Clarendon Press, 1993), 303–23.

14. For valuable critiques of the Realist position, see Charles Beitz, *Political Theory and Moral Obligation*, Part 1, 13–66; Ann-Marie Slaughter, "International Law in a World of Liberal States," *European Journal of International Law* 6 (1995), 503–38; Andrew Moravscik, "Taking Preferences Seriously: A Liberal Theory of International Politics," *International Organization* 51/4 (Autumn 1997), 513–53.

15. Allen Buchanan, "The Internal Legitimacy of Humanitarian Intervention," *Journal of Political Philosophy* 7/1 (1999), 71–87.

16. Derek Parfit, "Future Generations: Further Problems," *Philosophy and Public Affairs* 11 (1982), 113–72; Clark Wolf, "Contemporary Property Rights, Lockean Provisos, and the Interests of Future Generations," *Ethics* 105/4 (1995), 791–818.

17. By "secession" I shall mean the separation of a part of the territory of an existing state to form an independent state. Admittedly, this definition suffers from at least two limitations. First, separation in some cases leads and is intended to lead, not to independent statehood, but to incorporation of the territory in question into an already-existing neighboring state. For simplicity I will set aside such cases of irredentist separation. Second, some are reluctant to call cases of decolonization (for example, American independence from Britain, or liberation of Congo from Belgian rule) instances of secession. A distinction between decolonization and secession could be captured by sticking with the definition of "secession" proposed earlier while denying that the relationship between a colonial power and its colony is the same as that between a state and a region of its territory – by insisting that a colony is not "part" of the colonizing state. This move might appear to be more plausible in cases of so-called "saltwater colonialism," where the colonizing state and the colony are not geographically contiguous, but comes at the price of a denial that there can be geographically contiguous colonization.

18. Wayne Norman prefers to capture the same distinction as that between just cause theories and choice theories. Both he and Margaret Moore use a tripartite distinction between just cause theories, choice theories, and national self-determination theories. Margaret Moore, "Introduction," in Margaret Moore, ed., *National Self-Determination and Secession* (New York: Oxford University Press, 1998); Wayne Norman, "The Ethics of Secession as the Regulation of Secessionist Politics," in Moore, ed., *National Self-Determination and Secession*, Chapter 3.

19. Supreme Court of Canada, *Reference re Secession of Quebec* (1998) 2 S.C.R. See also Allen Buchanan, "The Quebec Secession Issue: Democracy, the Rule of Law, and Minority Rights," paper prepared for Department of Intergovernmental Affairs, Office of the Privy Council, Government of Canada, 2000.

20. Norman, "The Ethics of Secession as the Regulation of Secessionist Politics," in Moore, ed., *National Self-Determination and Secession*.

21. Buchanan, *Secession: The Morality of Political Divorce*; Buchanan, "Theories of Secession"; Buchanan, "Recognitional Legitimacy and the State System," *Philosophy and Public Affairs* 28/1 (1999), 46–78.

22. Avishai Margalit and Joseph Raz, "National Self-Determination," *Journal of Philosophy* 87/9 (1990); David Miller, *On Nationality* (Oxford: Clarendon Press, 1995).

23. Margalit and Raz, "National Self-Determination"; Miller, *On Nationality*.

24. Miller, *On Nationality*, Chapter 4, "National Self-Determination."

25. Ibid.

26. Margalit and Raz, "National Self-Determination."

27. Kymlicka, *Multicultural Citizenship*.

28. Harry Brighouse, "Against Nationalism," and Allen Buchanan, "What's So Special About Nations?" both in Couture, Nielsen, and Seymour, eds., *Rethinking Nationalism*.

29. David Miller, panel discussion, American Political Science Association Meetings, September 1998.

30. J.S. Mill, *Considerations on Representative Government*, Ch. XVI, "Of Nationality as Connected with Representative Government"; Miller, *On Nationality*, 89–90.

31. Miller, *On Nationality*, 83–5.

32. Arthur Ripstein, "Context, Continuity, and Fairness," in Robert McKim and Jeffrey McMahan, eds., *The Morality of Nationalism* (New York: Oxford University Press, 1997), 209–26.

33. The great liberal thinker Lord Acton drew a precisely opposite conclusion from the shared premise of the two instrumentalist arguments for national self-determination. According to Acton, mononational states are to be avoided because they will tend to be characterized by such a high degree of solidarity as to encourage the state to overreach its proper bounds of action and in so doing infringe individual liberty. Lord Acton, "Nationality," in John Figgis and Reginald Laurence, eds., *History of Freedom and Other Essays* (London: Macmillan and Co., 1907), 270–300.

34. Christopher Wellman, "In Defense of Self-Determination and Secession," *Philosophy and Public Affairs* 24/2 (1995), 142–71; Harry Beran, "A democratic theory of political self-determination for a new world order," in Lehning, ed., *Theories of Secession*; Harry Beran, "A Liberal Theory of Secession," *Political Studies* 32/1 (March 1984), 21–31; Daniel Philpott, "In Defense of Self-Determination," *Ethics* 105/2 (1995), 352–85; David Copp, "Democracy and Communal Self-Determination," in McKim and MacMahan, eds., *The Morality of Nationalism*.

35. Beran, "A democratic theory of political self-determination," and Beran, "A Liberal Theory of Secession."

36. John Simmons, *Moral Theory and Political Obligation* (Princeton, NJ: Princeton University Press, 1979), 38–45, 195–6.

37. For a detailed account of this sort of liberal theory of (weak) government legitimacy, see Allen Buchanan, "Recognitional Legitimacy and the State System," *Philosophy and Public Affairs* 28/1 (1999), 46–78.

38. For a valuable critical overview of this debate, see Simmons, *Moral Theory and Political Obligation*.

39. See J.S. Mill, *Considerations on Representative Government*.

40. Daniel Philpott, "In Defense of Self-Determination,"; David Copp, "Democracy and Communal Self-Determination."

41. Philpott, "In Defense of Self-Determination."

42. For a more detailed criticism of Philpott's democratic approach to a plebiscitary right to secede, see Allen Buchanan, "Democracy and Secession," in Moore, ed., *Secession and National Self-Determination*.

43. See Copp, "Democracy and Communal Self-Determination."

44. This criticism of Copp's position is elaborated in Buchanan, "Democracy and Secession," 16–21.

45. Albert O. Hirschman, *Exit, Voice, and Loyalty: Responses to Decline in Firms, Organizations, and States* (Cambridge, MA: Harvard University Press, 1970).

46. Cass Sunstein, "Constitutionalism and Secession," *University of Chicago Law Review* 58 (1991), 633; Buchanan, *Secession: The Morality of Political Divorce*, Chapter 4, "A Constitutional Right to Secede?"; Norman, "The Ethics of Secession as the Regulation of Secessionist Politics."

13

Liberalism and Boundaries: A Response
to Allen Buchanan

David Miller

It is not easy to give a clear account of what liberalism has to say about the making and unmaking of boundaries. This is not because liberal political philosophers, taken individually, have not developed clear positions, but because liberalism itself is so protean a phenomenon that any general statement one makes is likely to bring counter-examples instantly to mind. So a first step might be to find a way of classifying different versions of liberalism. One familiar contrast is the political division between classical (minimal-state, free market) and modern (welfare-state, interventionist) forms of liberalism. Another is the philosophical division between rights-based, contractarian, utilitarian, perfectionist, and other modes of justifying liberal principles. However, for present purposes, I believe that a third kind of distinction may prove to be more illuminating. One could call this a methodological distinction, a contrast in the way liberals see the whole enterprise of constructing a liberal political theory. The contrast I want to draw here is between forms of liberalism that are essentially individualistic and those that we might like to call sociological.[1]

Individualistic liberals see their task as one of designing a social order that respects the free agency of individuals. They begin with persons viewed as having certain capacities, notably the capacity for autonomous choice, and ask what kind of social and political relations will show proper respect for such persons. Very often this involves endowing individuals with inalienable rights that protect their capacities, though it is not essential to this view that it be rights-based. When it comes to justifying political authority, the question that liberals of this stripe ask is 'What can make such authority legitimate? Given that political authority involves the exercise of coercion, under what circumstances may individuals rightfully be subject to it?' The answer that comes most naturally is some version of the social contract. Individuals are rightfully subject to political authority when they have agreed to it, either in the sense that they have actually given their consent, or in the sense that as rational agents, they would have consented given the opportunity. The best social order is one that comes closest to the ideal of free association, one where people choose whom to associate with and on what terms, so that their independence is compromised as little as possible.

Liberals of a more sociological cast of mind approach their task differently. They begin with liberal values – values such as personal freedom, equality, and self-determination – and then ask what kind of social and political order is likely to realize these values to the greatest extent. In other words, their approach is more empirical. They do not simply elaborate principles starting from some fundamental intuition about, say, the nature and value of autonomy, but they look at actual societies, both liberal and non-liberal, and ask what conditions favour liberalism in some places and what obstacles it faces in others. They look, for instance, at levels of economic development, at class divisions, at cultural cleavages, and so forth, and try to reach conclusions about which array of sociological factors is most likely to make for a successful liberal society. Then they may suggest how societies that are already liberal can consolidate their liberal institutions, and how societies that are not can move in a liberal direction.

You might think that these two forms of liberalism are simply complementary. The first approach elaborates liberal principles in a purely normative fashion. The second looks at how liberal principles can best be implemented, given the world as it is. It seems as though the two approaches can easily be combined. But I believe that this underestimates the difference between them. I believe in fact that the two approaches are likely to produce quite different answers to disputed political questions. Let me illustrate briefly by taking the question of immigration – how far states should allow free immigration into their jurisdictions, and how far they are justified in imposing immigration controls. Individualistic liberals will answer this by considering, for instance, whether the right of free movement includes the right to move and settle anywhere in the world, and whether freedom of association entails being able to exclude others from the territory you currently occupy. Sociological liberals will focus on the likely consequences of different immigration policies. They may ask, for instance, to what extent effective democracy requires a body of citizens whose membership is largely stable, or they may ask whether immigration is likely to enhance cultural pluralism and thereby expand the range of options open to everyone, or whether it will threaten the secure identities of the natives and thereby provoke illiberal responses on their part. It seems clear enough in this example that the way one goes about posing and answering the question will have a significant effect on the substantive answer that one finally gives.

I have taken this distinction as my starting point because I believe that the second, sociological, version of liberalism has a good deal to tell us about the various aspects of the boundaries question, while the first version has rather little. Although Allen Buchanan does not frame it in this way, I think he has a similar view: I shall record some concrete points of agreement in a moment, though I shall also suggest that in some places he does not go far enough down the sociological path.

In individualistic versions of liberalism, particularly those standing at the extreme end of the spectrum, such as Robert Nozick's, the boundaries question disappears almost completely from view.[2] Nozick's thesis is that territory is assigned to individuals, who acquire full property rights to pieces of land by exercising their rights of acquisition and exchange. These individuals may then contract with protective agencies whose job it is to enforce rights and punish rights-violators. A protective agency may evolve over time into something that resembles a minimal state, but this is contingent, and relies upon the fact that people will generally have an incentive to sign up with the protective agency that has become dominant in the region where they live. In principle, there is nothing in Nozick's argument to rule out protective agencies competing for clients on a non-territorial basis. So there are no jurisdictional boundaries in a Nozickian world, except in the sense that one may pass from a region where most people have signed up with agency A to a region where most people have signed up with agency B. The only firm boundaries are those that demarcate individuals' holdings of property.

Buchanan has shown very effectively what is wrong with this picture. It relies on giving an account of property rights prior to an account of territorial jurisdiction, and it collapses as soon as we observe that there is no "natural" system of property, but instead property entitlements depend upon the positive laws of the state. Equally, the notion that we can settle the jurisdiction of a political authority by looking at what individuals have consented to runs into two kinds of problem. First, the idea that state S has rightful jurisdiction over piece of territory T because T's owner O has consented to its authority depends upon first establishing that O has a (property) right to T. But if the only way in which we can demonstrate that O has a right to T is by referring to the law of S, then clearly our account becomes circular. So unless it can be shown that O has a pre-political, natural right to T, then S's jurisdiction over T cannot be established by referring to O's consent. Second, we run into problems whenever territorially intermingled individuals prefer to contract with different political authorities. Either we say that jurisdiction should be personal, rather than territorial, and abandon the idea of political authority residing in a state in Weber's sense of an institution that successfully claims a monopoly of the legitimate use of force in a given territorial area,[3] or else we have to abandon the idea of individual consent, and say, for example, that *majority* consent in any given territory is sufficient to establish legitimate authority. But this creates problems of its own, and in any case is inconsistent with the original belief, of individualistic liberals, that political authority should be constituted on the model of free association, with everyone having a choice about who he is engaged with politically.[4]

Liberals of a sociological cast will approach boundaries issues by asking about the consequences, for well-functioning liberal political communities, of different ways of deciding the issues. Take first the question of *settlement*. I agree with Buchanan that there is nothing that strictly deserves the name of a liberal theory of settlement, once one abandons trying to use the Lockean theory of property acquisition for this purpose. However, it is not difficult to see, on general liberal grounds, why people who settle a territory have a good claim to continuing control of that territory, a claim that can be set aside only in fairly extreme circumstances. People who occupy a territory, cultivate it, build houses, schools, churches, and so forth also form a close attachment to that territory. It acquires a significance for them that goes beyond the material advantage they derive from it. Furthermore, over time, their culture is likely to adapt to the demands of their physical situation; their social norms and practices will tend to be those that work best in the environment they inhabit. This is borne out by the dislocation we nearly always observe when people are forcibly removed from the territory they have come to regard as their own, or indeed even when they have chosen to leave.[5] We think of ethnic cleansing as one of the worst horrors of the modern age, not just because people are being discriminated against on ethnic grounds and subjected to the threat of violence, but because they are being cut off from places they have come to identify as 'home.'

The claim to territory via settlement is very strong, but not absolute. One limit has to do with the amount of territory a group of people can lay claim to by virtue of settlement, in the face of competing claims, say claims of simple necessity.[6] The argument sketched in the last paragraph presupposes a fairly close link between land and people, and it will generally be hard to establish such a link with territories of vast extent.[7] The other limit has to do with the successful functioning of liberal states. There may be cases – hopefully very few – in which it turns out to be impossible for two or more peoples to live in close proximity to one another under a liberal regime. Ethnic groups with a history of deep mutual antagonism may not be able co-exist in the absence of forms of coercion that liberal states will rightly be reluctant to impose. So there may be circumstances in which liberals should support a division of territory involving some movement of population to create political units that can then operate according to liberal principles. Those required to move will still suffer a substantial loss, but in the long term they may be better off living in circumstances where their rights and liberties are more secure.[8]

Turning next to *conquest*, it is important to bear in mind that historically speaking, most liberals have endorsed the form of conquest involved in the building of empires by liberal states. Buchanan in his chapter (12) focuses on the case of one state's attempting to take over a second, but this is not the situation envisaged by liberal imperialists. Colonisation involved either the creation of forms of political authority in places where no such authority was deemed to exist (this was broadly the picture presented in the case of the English colonisation of America), or the replacement of manifestly deficient systems of authority by good government (this was the picture presented in the case of India, for example). The justification for imperialism was that in the long term this provided the best way of bringing 'civilisation,' including the liberal form of government, to people who presently lacked the economic, cultural, and political resources to acquire it. In other words, the immediate establishment of self-governing liberal states in the colonised territories was not seen as an option. The preconditions for liberalism were not met, and in those circumstances, liberals had no hesitation in prescribing benign but authoritarian government from the outside. According to J.S. Mill, for instance, 'subjection to a foreign government [by rulers superior in civilisation to those over whom they rule] notwithstanding its inevitable evils, is often of the greatest advantage to a people, carrying them rapidly through several stages of progress, and clearing away obstacles to improvement which might have lasted indefinitely if the subject population had been left unassisted to its native tendencies and chances.'9

Such views are of course no longer expressed by liberals, partly because they are now likely to rate the 'inevitable evils' of empire as greater than its likely benefits, partly because they no longer rank cultures as 'superior' and 'inferior' with Mill's unhesitating confidence. Yet unless liberals cleave to the principle of national self-determination – an issue I shall return to later – it is not clear why they should rule out conquest in principle as a way of determining boundaries, so long as conquest can be shown to have good effects, measured in terms of the underlying aims of liberalism. Indeed, recent events in Rwanda, Bosnia, Kosovo, and elsewhere have led some to recommend the resurrection of a mild version of liberal imperialism, in the form of a system of trusteeship, undertaken by liberal states in combination, whose aim is to avert humanitarian disasters, and in the longer term, create viable political institutions of self-government in countries such as these.[10] This is not exactly 'conquest' as traditionally conceived, but it does serve as a reminder that on liberal principles, political boundaries must be regarded as violable whenever internal forces put human rights and other core liberal values at risk.[11]

I do not dissent from anything that Buchanan says about *alienation* of territory. I agree with him that it is an issue little discussed in liberal political philosophy. There is one aspect of the issue that may deserve further exploration – the obligations political communities have towards those of their members who inhabit territory to which, for one reason or another, it is difficult or expensive to supply the normal range of services – say, because the territory is very remote. Under what circumstances might it be legitimate to cast the inhabitants adrift, requiring them either to form their own self-governing state, or to affiliate themselves to some neighboring state that can more easily supply protection and other services? This issue arose in practical form at the time of the Falklands conflict between Britain and Argentina, when it was pointed out by some observers that the cost of defending the Falkland islanders against Argentinean aggression far exceeded the amount required to settle each Falkland islander comfortably in a congenial spot in Britain (such as the rural areas of Scotland, where conditions of life are not so different from the Falklands). Would it have been reasonable to ask the islanders to leave on these terms, and then hand the islands over to the Argentinean state? Generalising the issue, how far may citizens of a liberal state insist that the government protect the territorial integrity of the state despite the cost, in circumstances where it would be possible to move them on to territory that is easier to defend or easier to service?

This question connects to a debate within liberal political philosophy about where to draw the line between citizens' preferences and their essential interests – the principle being that the state need not alter its policies to take account of mere preferences, but ought to do so where essential interests are threatened. So if I should choose to remove myself to a small uninhabited island off the Scottish coast, building a cabin in the woods and so on, the state has no reason to do anything special on my account: it need not set up a postal service, or lay on an electricity cable, much as I might wish for these conveniences. My choice to live in this inconvenient place is just that – a choice. By contrast, liberals will believe that the state has an obligation to fund education for children living in established communities on remote islands, even where the cost per head is considerably greater than the average. Here, education is treated as an essential interest and island-dwelling is not regarded as a choice but as a circumstance. The problem is how, within this framework, to treat communities who live in 'expensive' places and are reluctant to move. For the reasons given in my discussion of settlement, liberals are likely to regard historic attachment to land as something more than a mere preference, and therefore to go some considerable way to accommodate those who live in communities rooted in such places. So the justified alienation of *occupied* land would be a rare occurrence, on liberal principles, since the fact of occupation over time generates essential interests that cannot be ignored by casting the occupants adrift.

Let me turn finally to the issue of *secession*, where my disagreements with Buchanan are more far-reaching. He identifies three leading families of theories: remedial right-only theories, plebiscitary right theories, and ascriptive right theories. He favours a theory of the first kind, and is strongly critical of the others. Remedial right theories justify secession in three circumstances: when it is necessary in order to allow the population in question to escape serious injustices, especially in the form of violations of human rights; when it grants self-determination to a territory that was previously an independent state, and has been unjustly annexed, or that is owed autonomy by previous agreement; and when the secession is consensual.

Every liberal is likely to acknowledge the first of these three reasons for secession, though it is important not to be mesmerised by the belief that secession will ever be a complete remedy for serious injustice. Recent events in Kosovo remind us that secession is likely at best to mean *fewer* rights violations, not *no* rights violations (more injustices were committed by Serbs against Kosovo Albanians than have so far been committed by Albanians against Serbs, if prematurely we treat what has happened in Kosovo as a secession). But liberals of a realistic disposition will accept this.

Buchanan's second condition poses more problems. In order for us to say that a secession is a remedy for the unjust annexation of territory, we have to be able to say that what existed before the annexation was a legitimate state, and we have to be able to do this without helping ourselves to one of the primary right theories that Buchanan rejects. So if we are to treat the Soviet annexation of the Baltic states (for example) as an injustice that warranted secession as a remedy, we have to be able to show that the political regimes that existed in Lithuania and the other states in 1940 were legitimate without, in particular, referring to the fact that the Lithuanians formed a nation and the regime was recognised by them as a vehicle of national self-determination. It is not clear from Buchanan's chapter what positive account of legitimacy he favours, other than that a legitimate state must be one that respects liberal principles. But what if a liberal state annexes a second liberal state, or indeed a non-liberal state? Would the remedial right-only theory apply to such a case, and if so how?

Liberals will again probably share Buchanan's favourable disposition towards consensual secessions. The problem here, I think, is going to be one of finding conditions for consent that are consistent with the sharply critical things he has to say about plebiscitary right theories – criticisms I very largely share. The central problem with plebiscitary theories is that if one takes literally the idea that a legitimate political order must win the consent of everyone who is subject to it, one quickly runs into insoluble difficulties; but if one dilutes the condition by allowing *majorities* to give consent on behalf of individuals, then the problem is to know which majority is to count. But this problem applies to consensual secession, too. What we describe as consensual secessions (Norway and Sweden, the Czech Republic and Slovakia) are actually deals brokered by the political elites in the countries concerned, and accepted by most of their followers; there is no requirement of unanimous consent. When we regard such secessions as relatively un-problematic, in the back of our minds there is surely the thought that these really are separate *nations* and therefore that individual Swedes, say, who in 1905 might have opposed the secession of Norway, *lacked sufficient reason* to oppose it. Sweden's claim to sovereignty over the territory of Norway was defeated by the overwhelming and reasonable wish of Norwegians to become fully autonomous (they already enjoyed a large measure of effective autonomy through having their own parliament). But these thoughts again invoke a *substantive* theory of political legitimacy without which, I have suggested, even the idea of consensual secession becomes problematic.

So here I must turn to Buchanan's critique of ascriptive right theories, principally nationalist theories that hold that secessions are justified when they allow nations that cannot enjoy self-determination within existing states to do so. What is principally at stake here is the claim that national self-determination is something that liberals should value, either because it protects valuable cultures or because it contributes to ends that liberals support, such as democracy and social justice.

The cultural argument is certainly one that needs some clarification. If a culture is regarded simply as a vehicle for individual autonomy, as it sometimes seems to be by Will Kymlicka,[12] then it does appear arbitrary to single out *national* cultures for special protection, given that the cultural goods out of which individuals can fashion autonomous lives may stem from a whole variety of ethnic, religious, regional, and other sources. It is more illuminating here to look at different types of culture, and see what each of them actually requires for its realisation. For instance, if someone is to participate in a religious culture, then this requires a range of conditions, such as religious toleration, the opportunity to build churches, synagogues, and so on, access to important religious sites, and so forth. These conditions are internal to the idea of religion as a cultural form. If we turn to national culture, and look at what *that* requires, then two essential features are territorial control and collective self-determination. To think of oneself as belonging to a nation just *is* to think of oneself as belonging to a community that has the right to occupy its homeland, and has the right to determine its future way of life through internal debate and decision-making. It follows that someone's interest in the flourishing of the culture to which he or she belongs takes the form, in the case of national cultures, of an interest in political self-determination. That is the sense in which nations are 'special.' They are not special in the sense of being the strongest or most important cultural affiliation that people everywhere have; they are special because they generate political demands that are qualitatively different from the demands generated by cultures of other kinds, such as religious cultures.

Liberals vary in the weight they attach to the interest just described. So it is probably more compelling, from a liberal perspective, to develop instrumental arguments for self-determination that appeal to the values of democracy and social justice. Clearly these arguments rest upon a large empirical claim: that states are more likely to be democratically governed, and to implement socially just policies, when their citizens are bound together by the common identity that nationality provides. Perhaps this claim is better formulated as the conjunction of two others: first, that common nationality is a precondition for effective democracy and the pursuit of social justice; second, that although some national identities contain elements that are hostile to these values – particularly national identities that are ethnically exclusive – it is always possible to move in the desired liberal direction, either by broadening the definition of nationality so that more citizens are included, or by altering political arrangements to form units within which identities are less antagonistic. In other words, the liberal nationalist project of forming political communities whose members share an overarching national identity that supports the practice of democracy and the pursuit of justice is nearly always feasible,[13] even if existing national identities have some of the malign properties that Buchanan has identified.

As I have noted, this argument involves an empirical claim, and so it will find favour with liberals whose approach is sociological in the sense explained earlier – liberals who are not content simply to enunciate political principles, but try to reflect seriously on the conditions under which these principles are likely to be put into effect. The evidence backing the claim is of two kinds: on the one hand, simple observation of the circumstances of liberal states that have already gone furthest towards realising the values in question (the Scandinavian states, for instance); on the other hand, more experimental work on the mechanisms that encourage people to use democratic methods for reaching decisions, or that favour the use of egalitarian principles to allocate resources within social groups.[14] This evidence will never be conclusive, but if our aim is to give guidance of some sort when practical questions concerning boundaries are at stake, we have to follow the balance of probabilities. On my reading, the evidence supports the proposition that liberal principles are most likely to be followed in states whose populations share a common national identity. It follows that when liberals think about a proposed act of secession, a key concern should be whether the political units that would be formed following the secession fulfil this condition more or less closely than the existing state. This is not the only question that needs to be asked, but it is a central question.

To conclude, Buchanan rightly steers away from versions of liberalism that try to model the state as a kind of giant joint-stock company, and to apply the idea of free association not only to groupings within the political community but to the political community itself. Like many others in the liberal tradition, he has a more realistic view of the conditions of political legitimacy, and therefore of when boundaries can rightfully be altered in the name of legitimacy. My mild complaint is that he does not go quite far enough in pursuit of the conditions under which liberal principles can most successfully be implemented, and that had he done so, he would have given nationality a larger role in the setting of political boundaries. J.S. Mill may have overstated the point a little in his well-known remark that 'free institutions are next to impossible in a country made up of different nationalities,'[15] but the arguments he deployed to justify that remark should still be taken seriously by any liberal who wants to think about boundaries in a clear-headed and empirically informed way.

Notes to Chapter 13

1. A similar contrast has been applied to the history of liberalism by Larry Siedentop, "Two Liberal Traditions," in A. Ryan, ed., *The Idea of Freedom* (Oxford: Oxford University Press, 1979).
2. Robert Nozick, *Anarchy, State, and Utopia* (Oxford: Blackwell, 1974), especially Part I.
3. Max Weber, *The Theory of Social and Economic Organization*, ed., T. Parsons (New York: Free Press, 1964), 154–6.
4. I have explored the problems with Nozick's attempted justification of political authority in greater depth in David Miller, "The Justification of Political Authority", in D. Schmidtz, ed., *Robert Nozick* (Cambridge: Cambridge University Press, 2002).
5. A moving example of this is provided by the voluntary evacuation of the remote Scottish islands of St. Kilda by the last remaining families in 1930. The St. Kildans had evolved a distinctive, strongly communitarian, form of social life to cope with the harsh conditions prevailing on the islands, and although they agreed to move to the mainland to escape increasingly extreme poverty, they found it difficult to adjust to their new, materially much better, circumstances, and many continued to hanker after a return to St. Kilda. See T. Steel, *The Life and Death of St. Kilda* (London: Harper Collins, 1994).
6. See Michael Walzer, *Spheres of Justice* (Oxford: Martin Robertson, 1983), 46–8, for the argument that the quantity of land a people can claim as their territorial home may be limited by 'the claims of necessitous strangers.'
7. It is difficult, therefore, to say what kind of claim nomadic peoples have to the large territories they may travel across. They do not mark and transform territory in the way that settled peoples do; on the other hand, the land may have symbolic significance for them, as in the case of Australian aborigines. *Access* and *protection* seem to matter more here than *control.*
8. The best-known case of a large scale population movement engineered in order to create more homogeneous political communities is the exchange of populations between Greece and Turkey in the 1920s. I have discussed this briefly (with references) in "Secession and the Principle of Nationality," in J. Couture, K. Nielsen, and M. Seymour, eds., *Rethinking Nationalism* (Calgary: University of Calgary Press, 1998), 276–7 (reprinted in M. Moore, ed., *National Self-Determination and Secession* (Oxford: Oxford University Press, 1998), 77–8.
9. J.S. Mill, *Considerations on Representative Government* in *Utilitarianism; On Liberty; Representative Government*, ed., H.B. Acton (London: Everyman, 1972), 224.
10. "Our choice at the millennium seems to boil down to imperialism or barbarism. Half-measures of the type we have seen in various humanitarian interventions, and in Kosovo, represent the worst of both worlds. Better to grasp the nettle and accept that liberal imperialism may be the best we can do in these callous times." David Rieff, "Imperialism or Barbarism," *Prospect* 43 (July 1999), 40.
11. Did the NATO take-over of Kosovo amount to "conquest"? I do not think a clear answer can be given to this interesting question.
12. See Will Kymlicka, *Multicultural Citizenship* (Oxford: Clarendon Press, 1995), Chapter 5.

13. "Nearly always" because there are hard cases in which mutually antagonistic populations are intermingled in such a way that the project I am describing becomes impossible, in the short term at least. These are the cases that have led some liberals to call for a return to the moderate form of imperialism described in note 10. I have set out a framework for distinguishing these hard cases from other kinds of intra-state cleavage in "Nationality in Divided Societies," in D. Miller, *Citizenship and National Identity* (Cambridge: Polity Press, 2000).

14. I have looked at some of the evidence that relates to social justice in my *Principles of Social Justice* (Cambridge: Harvard University Press, 1999), Chapters 3 and 4.

15. Mill, *Considerations on Representative Government*, 361.

PART 7

THE INTERNATIONAL LAW TRADITION

14

International Law and the Making and Unmaking of Boundaries

Andrew Hurrell

It is no doubt the case that all of the ethical traditions included in this volume contain within them deep tensions and fissures. Yet the difficulty of isolating the ethical perspectives that are contained within, or that lie behind and around, international law presents a particular challenge. One major – perhaps *the* major – line of thought has insisted that the international legal order should be separated from both the political order on the one side and the moral order on the other, and that the law as it is should be distinguished from the law as it ought to be. At most, international law is viewed as a vehicle, or a container, or an instrument for the realization of particular ethical goals or commitments that are themselves beyond the scope of legal analysis. So an international legal perspective on ethics and territorial boundaries must begin by addressing, if only briefly, the relationship between ethics and international law.

There is a further important reason for beginning at a general level – namely, that the issue of boundaries and the questions of how, when, and why boundaries may be changed have to be understood within the context of the meta-rules of the legal order as a whole. A state or political grouping may unilaterally assert that a boundary exists, or it may succeed in establishing a boundary unilaterally. Such assertions or actions do not necessarily imply acceptance or agreement by any other party. Equally – and surely a common experience across many different periods, places, and cultures – boundaries may be agreed amongst neighboring states or communities, or groups of states and communities. And yet in the modern state system, this agreement has taken on a distinctive and historically unique form: questions such as the nature and demarcation of boundaries, the varieties of title to territory, the issues of when and how both boundaries may be changed and title to territory transferred have all come to be regulated by specific, but interlinked, sets of systemic rules. These rules grew out of the European state system, but now apply globally, and can be said to represent a core element of the institutional structure of international society. These specific rules are, in turn, deeply shaped by the evolution of the primary norms of the legal order – norms relating to the changing character of sovereignty, to the use of force, and to self-determination.

This chapter will therefore begin by looking at the relationship between law and ethics. It will then sketch out three images of international law, examine what each image implies for the acquisition of territory and the making and unmaking of boundaries, and explore the deep tensions that exist between them. The remaining sections will consider the specific topics that run through this volume, placing particular emphasis on the impact of ideas about self-determination and giving particular attention to the questions of conquest and secession.

1. Law as an Ethical System

The ethical dimension of international law involves two sets of dialectical relations and patterns of mediation: between fact and value and between process and substance. There has been a tremendous variety of mediation strategies, and evaluation of their success has always been highly contested. But it is very hard to think about international law as an ethical perspective without returning to them.

First, then, there is the dialectic between fact and law, between norms rooted in the conventions and practices of states and other actors, on the one hand, and international law as an integrated normative structure by which those practices and conventions can be evaluated and judged, on the other. International law represents a particular form of practice, of reasoning, and of argumentation in which this dialogue between fact and value is carried out. This form of reasoning is socially contrived and historically constructed, but it is based on a remarkably broad consensus and is relatively well institutionalized. But both its strength and its fragility derive from the need to maintain connections with murky practice as well as normative aspiration. The procedural and substantive rules of international law must remain connected to concrete institutions, to power-political structures, and to the often very rough trade of international politics. A very great deal of classical international law is, after all, self-created and self-imposed out of both self-interest and common interests and, more or less directly, reflects the practice of states. Moving too far away from hard reality and international law courts ineffectiveness and irrelevance. And yet, to have any normative bite, these rules must be counterfactually valid and involve intersubjectively shared and institutionalized normative reflection on the often illegal practices of states and other actors. Moreover, in an ever-changing world, international law can never remain static. Lawyers (and those seeking to use legal instruments) cannot avoid trying to keep pushing out the normative boat. This is, after all, what having a normative agenda is all about.

International law also involves a dialogue between process and substance, between the value of substantive norms and the legitimacy of the process by which they are arrived at. This dialogue is especially important because international law seeks both to identify, promote, and institutionalize universal values and also to mediate amongst different and often conflicting ethical traditions. Much of international law has to do with the creation of a framework of shared understandings, institutions, and practices by which substantive rules can be created and through which clashes of interest and conflicting values can be mediated. Many legal rules are constitutive of actors – not least those concerning sovereignty, jurisdiction, and territorial boundaries. Such norms determine who are legitimate actors, and structure the processes by which those actors interact and by which other norms are developed. Other sets of process rules determine what law is and how both political facts and moral claims are received into law.

In a very important sense, the ethical claims of international law rest on the contention that it is the *only* set of globally institutionalized processes by which norms can be negotiated on the basis of dialogue and consent, rather than being simply imposed by the most powerful. And yet process can never be the whole story for four reasons. First, our own ethical commitments demand that we engage politically on the basis of our own values, and seek to promote and uphold them. Second, even the most open process will always presuppose certain kinds of implied normative assumptions about who should be there and how the process should be conducted. Third, even on grounds of efficiency, some commitment to equity and fairness may be necessary to secure the effectiveness and legitimacy of cooperative endeavors and shared institutions. And fourth, the density, scope, and complexity of the agreements, norms, and rules in which states and societies are already enmeshed provide some basis for positing a community interest or an agreed set of purposes and values against which new substantive norms may be judged – the idea of an objective community interest or of the common interest of global society.

But – and it is a tremendously important "but" – the ease with which this putative international or global public interest may be captured or contaminated by the power and special interests of particular states; the utter unobviousness of what substantive norms ought to be once we move down from high-minded sloganizing (the importance of peace and security, of sustainability, of democracy and human rights, of global economic justice); the extent to which understandings of these issues do in fact diverge so substantially as a result of cultural heterogeneity but, more importantly, vastly different historical experiences and material circumstances – all of these factors underpin the importance of a commitment to legal processes and to taming the political order within which that process is embedded. The unavoidability of process again separates law as an ethical enterprise from other forms of normative enquiry and debate.

2. Three Images of International Law

Pluralist Statist

As is well known, the international law developed within the classical European state system was largely concerned with elaborating limited rules of coexistence. This *pluralist* conception of international law was built around the goal of coexistence, and reflected an ethic of difference. It was to be constructed around the mutual recognition of sovereignty, and aimed at the creation of certain minimalist rules, understandings, and institutions designed to limit the inevitable conflict that was to be expected within such a fragmented political system. These rules were built around the mutual recognition of states as independent and legally equal members of society, the unavoidable reliance on self-preservation and self-help, and the freedom of states to promote their own moral (or immoral) purposes subject to minimal external constraints.

Boundaries were, of course, fundamental to the European state system within which these pluralist understandings developed. It is here that we find much elaborate discussion of the core character of boundaries – places or zones where different societies or communities encounter one another or come together. It is here that we find the basic distinctions that arise in all analyses of boundaries: distinctions between boundaries as lines and boundaries as zones[1]; distinctions between strategic, economic, national, cultural or linguistic, and historic boundaries and the extent to which conflict has continually arisen from the lack of congruence between them; distinctions between natural and artificial boundaries; distinctions between questions of title to territory, on the one hand, and issues relating more directly to the determination of frontiers and boundaries, on the other – a distinction mirrored on the other side by the difference between frontier disputes and territorial disputes. It is also in this world that we find analysis of the ideologies of boundaries and the powerful role that they have played in the foreign policies of individual states (for example, the drive to establish the "natural" boundaries of France); of regions (for example, the concept of moving frontiers and the mythology of the frontier in post-colonial North and South America); and of empires (for example, the importance of frontier policy within the British Empire).

For some, boundaries themselves lay at the heart of conflict. As Curzon put it in his classic study: "Frontiers are, indeed, the razor's edge on which hang suspended the modern issues of war and peace, of life or death to nations."[2] Boundaries and frontiers may indeed have been a direct cause of conflict. More often they have served either as a pretext for conflict (as in the Mukden incident of 1931), or as symptoms of deeper problems (as with many of the major tensions of the post-1945 period, for example between Russia/USSR and China; China and India; India and Pakistan; Israel and its neighbors; Greece and Turkey).

But whilst boundaries were central to the problem of international relations, they were also fundamental to the pluralist conception of international law as a means of managing that problem. By establishing the limits to the authority of states over territory they formed – and still form – an essential part of the structure of rules and institutions that enable separate political communities to coexist. Again, to quote Curzon, they represented "a prevention of misunderstanding, a check to territorial cupidity, and an agency of peace."[3]

First, they helped secure a basis for coexistence and cooperation through the precise allocation of the jurisdiction and authority over territory as between one political community and another. In a fundamental sense, boundaries lay at the heart of the classical international legal order. As Jennings puts it: "This mission and purpose of traditional international law has been the delimitation of the exercise of sovereign power on a territorial basis."[4] Second, international law elaborated a complex system of shared rules as to what boundaries were and how they should be agreed upon – distinctions between the allocation of frontiers (general political agreement), their delimitation (marking out on maps), and then their demarcation (marking out on the ground). Third, law developed rules regulating title to territory and the conditions under which title could be transferred (occupation, prescription, cession, accession, subjugation), and mechanisms for the peaceful settlement of disputes (by bilateral negotiation, multilateral decision-making, political mediation, or legal adjudication or arbitration). Finally, moving beyond the strictly legal, boundaries might be manipulated to promote security: the strategic values of defensible frontiers; the idea of a buffer zone to prevent friction (an artificially-maintained frontier zone that should be denied to hostile power, such as the system of buffer states surrounding British India); or the related concept of agreed spheres of influence as a basic norm of conflict-management amongst the Great Powers before World War I.

The defects, including obviously the ethical limitations, of this image of international law were, in Robert Tucker's words "little short of monumental."[5] It was a system of law that faithfully mapped the contours of power: hence the special role and status of Great Powers as the managers of international security; hence the extent to which international lawyers had to reconcile themselves to the centrality of the balance of power; and hence the dominant role of major states in establishing by their practice or agreement the rules of international law. International law imposed few restrictions on the use of force and resort to war. War was, as Hall expressed it, "a permitted mode of giving effect to decisions"; conquest and subjugation were permitted modes of acquiring territory – mechanisms "by which the successful deployment of armed force might serve not only to wrest the territory from the rightful sovereign but also to invest the conqueror with a superior title."[6] More commonly, territory was transferred by coercive cession. In other words a peace treaty duly solemnized the transfer of territory imposed on the vanquished following defeat in war. There was no place for notions of self-determination, and the dominant powers determined the criteria by which non-European political communities could be admitted to membership of international society.

The dominant values of this society of states were, to quote Vattel, "the maintenance of order and the preservation of liberty." As that remark suggests, the ethical claims of this image of international law rest on two sets of arguments: first, the extent to which the state (but not necessarily any particular state) and the apparatus of state sovereignty provides a container for pluralism and for the protection of diversity; and second, the idea that this limited form of international society provides a morally significant means of promoting coexistence and limiting conflict in a world in which consensus for more elaborate forms of cooperation does not exist.

This did not mean that further moral evaluation was impossible. Writing as this conception of international law was emerging, Vattel, for example, continued to uphold the importance of natural law, but argued that to try and act directly upon its injunctions within the legal (as opposed to the moral) order "would be to prescribe a medicine far more troublesome and dangerous than the disease." Unless law reconciled itself with the realities of the power-political order, it would, to quote Julius Stone, "have a moth-like existence, fluttering inevitably and precariously year by year into the destructive flame of power."

To avoid so shiftless an existence, the international legal order takes the extraordinary course of providing by its own rules for its collision with overwhelming power. It allows the military victor through the imposed treaty of peace to incorporate his dictated terms into the body of international law, thus preserving at any rate the rest of the rules and its own continued existence. By this built-in device it incorporates into the legal order the net result of what otherwise would be an extra-legal, or even illegal, revolution.[7]

The law of the jungle may not be deflected by very much, but for the pluralist, in the absence of any firm reason for believing in the viability of a transformed international society, this will always remain morally highly significant.

Solidarist Statist

This pluralist image has always had its critics, and obviously came under tremendous challenge in the course of the twentieth century. Four dimensions of change are especially important. The first has to do with the *content* of norms. In contrast to mere coexistence, the norms of this more solidarist law involve more extensive schemes of cooperation to safeguard peace and security (for example, prohibiting aggression or broadening understandings of what constitutes threats to peace and security); to solve common problems (such as tackling environmental challenges or managing the global economy in the interests of greater stability or equity); and to sustain common values (such as the promotion of self-determination, human rights, or political democracy). This expansion has been driven both by moral change but also by material and pragmatic imperatives. The second dimension concerns the *source* of these norms. In a traditional pluralist conception, the dominant norms are created by states and depend directly on the consent of states. In a solidarist conception, the process of norm creation is opened to a wider range of actors, both states and non-state groups, and there is an easing of the degree to which states can only be bound by rules to which they have given their explicit consent – a move from consent to consensus.

The third dimension has to do with the *justification and evaluation* of norms. Alongside the old idea that actors create and uphold law because it provides them with functional benefits, the post-1945 period has seen the emergence of a range of internationally agreed core principles – respect for fundamental human rights, prohibition of aggression, self-determination – that may underpin some notion of a world common good and some broader basis for evaluating specific rules. This may be viewed in terms of the surreptitious return of natural law ideas or of a philosophically-anchorless, but nevertheless reasonably solid, pragmatic consensus. The fourth dimension has to do with moves towards the more effective *implementation* of these norms and the variety of attempts to move beyond the traditionally very "soft" compliance mechanisms and to give more effective teeth to the norms of this more ambitious society.

Within the hugely increased normative aspiration of this model of international law and society, two clusters of norms emerge as central to the analysis of boundaries. The first cluster has to do with the elaboration of those rules that restrict the resort to force and that delegitimize the use of force to seize territory and to alter boundaries. The reentry into the international legal order of rules governing the right to resort to force in the post-1919 and especially post-1945 period is well known. Equally well known are the ambiguities of the apparently clear-cut proscription on aggressive use of force. These follow from both the internal open-endedness of the concepts of aggression and self-defence, and from the unsteady relationship between the normative order and its political underpinnings. These ambiguities have led to an expanded category of "justified intervention" and "legitimate self-defence." Moreover, as will be discussed later, even the end of the "right of conquest" is not itself wholly without ambiguity. Nevertheless the basic line appears clear enough: the increasing illegality of the acquisition of territory and the changing of inter-state boundaries as a result of the illegal use of force.

The second cluster of norms revolves around national self-determination.[8] This remains an extremely difficult subject to deal with because it has meant so many different things to so many different people, and continues to do so. It is, first of all, a *political ideology* asserting that the nation can be distinguished from the state (note that even civic or voluntarist nationalism must posit the nation as an entity separate from the state if it is to be distinguished from patriotism); that nations and states should be coextensive in their boundaries; that every nation should have a state corresponding to it; and that any state that does not express a nation or national idea is potentially illegitimate. This ideology clearly represented a major challenge to the earlier (if always rather stylized) image of international relations as the relations of ruling princes and their houses – a world in which sovereignty over people and territory belonged to rulers; in which people or territory were exchanged from one ruler to another on the basis of inheritance, marriage, or conquest without the consent of the people or any attention to issues of nationality or ethnicity; and in which political loyalties were assumed to be to dynastic rulers and states.

National self-determination can be also be seen as *an international political norm* that confers political and moral rights on national groups (or on those speaking in their name) and that encourages and legitimizes demands for the redrawing of state boundaries. As a norm influencing political action, this was already well established by the mid-nineteenth century. This was a period that saw the emergence of national liberation groups commanding loyalty and able to challenge the state's monopoly of legitimate force, the ascription to such movements of moral rights, and the development of a doctrine of national liberation. As a norm shaping the institutional structure of international society, 1918/19 and the roles of Lenin and Wilson remain crucial despite the simplifications.[9] Its application as a political norm has always been uneven and highly selective for all of the well-known reasons: the difficulties of identifying the "self" given incompatible definitions and conflicting claims; the importance of other criteria in redrawing boundaries (economic/strategic viability, and so on); and, above all, the intrusion of political imperatives and the special interests of the powerful. Nevertheless, despite the ambiguities, (national) self-determination has been implicated in almost all of the great redrawing of maps of the past 150 years – the four great waves of decolonization, the unification of Germany, the end of Yugoslavia, and so on.

International lawyers have always treated self-determination extremely cautiously, and its emergence as an *international legal norm* has been gradual and highly qualified. For a long time, it was common to see it only as a political principle that might have some legal implications. As this strategy of denial gave way to a strategy of limitation, it came to be seen, first as a general principle against which individual rules and state actions could be judged, and then as a set of more specific rules that sought to contain the concept of self-determination along two crucial dimensions: to narrow as far as possible the "units" to which self-determination may be held to apply, and to limit understandings of the meaning of self-determination so as to inflict as little damage as possible to the core features of the pluralist order: state sovereignty and territorial integrity.

What matters for this chapter is the dual impact of self-determination as an ideology, a political norm, and a set of legal rules. On the one hand, of course, national self-determination represents a destabilizing force: it provides both a criterion and a moral imperative by which the boundaries of states should be redrawn to reflect the aspirations of national groups, and it empowers and legitimizes national groups as actors in their own right. On the other hand, national self-determination has added powerful justification for the existence of separate nation-states and for obligations owed to them rather than to humankind in general. States, now nation-states in aspiration and in the ideology of the system, are deemed legitimate because they embody the exercise of political self-determination; because they allow groups of individuals to give expression to their values, their culture, their sense of themselves; and because they offer protection to groups who would otherwise be extremely vulnerable.

So state boundaries become both politically and morally far more important. They are, after all, the lines that demarcate not just abstract units of administration but communities that are supposed to share both an identity and a legitimate political purpose. Within this solidarist image, there is a consolidation and hardening of the boundary that separates political communities from each other and citizens from non-citizens. It is very important to underline the degree to which this image of international law is statist and to which national self-determination reinforces, as well as challenges, that statism. There may be a degree of greater space for other arrangements (protectorates, confederations, condominia, not-quite federal unions), but territorial states remain central. The statism of this model also narrows the range of options through which self-determination can be pursued – if not through one's own state, then through the structure of rights and institutions created by, and around, states.

But what emerged in the course of the twentieth century has been a deep structural tension between the imperatives of stable boundaries, stable identities, and the legal structures of the older pluralist world, on the one hand, and the dynamic character of self-determination as both a political and legal norm, on the other. The difficulties in the interpretation and application of self-determination have meant that whilst unable to deny the power of newer normative claims, the instinct of many international lawyers and the direction of so much international practice has been to revert to the assumptions and management techniques of the older pluralist order. So international society and international law navigate constantly between the by-now undoubted legitimacy of the principle and its disintegrative potential.

This persistence of pluralism is given further impetus by the weakness of the political order on the back of which these normative ambitions are supposed to be achieved. This is most obviously visible in terms of what Cassese calls "the end of a magnificent illusion" – namely that the UN Charter system could provide an effective answer to the use of aggressive force and an effective instrument for the management of other conflicts (which in so many cases involve claims for self-determination or secession). Equally illusory is the idea that this failure was somehow due to the Cold War, and that the end of the Cold War would open up a new age of international cooperation.

Although the 1990s witnessed a remarkable expansion in the role of the United Nations in the management of international security, the old obstacles to a full-blown collective security system remain all too visible. Moreover, as in the past, where collective action has been possible (as in the Persian Gulf, Bosnia, Haiti, or Somalia), it has depended to an uncomfortable extent, on the political interests of the United States and its allies and on the military capabilities built up in the course of the Cold War. An effective *system* of collective security has therefore remained out of reach, although the collective *element* in security management has expanded (as in the role of regional alliances or coalitions, international peacekeeping forces, and UN authorizations of the use of force). More generally, the promotion of many solidarist norms has taken place on the back of a political order in which hierarchy, even hegemony, has reassumed a central role.

This is not, very definitely, to say that the increased aspirations of this solidarist law do not matter. It is impossible to think seriously about boundaries today without reference to norms against conquest or in favor of self-determination. There is a political as well as a moral reality, and even on purely pragmatic grounds, states need to justify their actions in terms of those norms and to seek the legitimacy from those international bodies that are the repositories of those norms. But it is to say, first, that the aspirations of this normatively ambitious international society remain deeply contaminated by power and that the normative theorist can only ignore the persistence of this structural contamination at the cost of idealization; second, that where solidarist cooperation is weak or breaks down, the older imperatives of pluralist law continue to flourish; third, that even when genuinely consensual, the promotion of solidarist values both depends on, and reinforces, the power and privileges of the dominant state or states; and finally, that international law remains deeply influenced by the distribution of power: in the Cold War world, the problem often lay in the intensity of bipolar confrontation; in the post-Cold War world, the problem lies in the inequality of power distribution and the temptations to unilateralism to which hegemony naturally gives rise.

The Law of a Transnational Society

If one kind of legal progressivism looks to an improved society of states united by a far higher degree of solidarity, another looks beyond the state, or at least comes to view the state within the context of a broader legal order. This image builds on many of the trends already visible in the contemporary international legal system: the pluralism of the norm-creating processes; the role of private market actors and civil society groups in articulating values that are then assimilated in inter-state institutions; and the increased range of informal, yet norm-governed, governance mechanisms often built around complex networks, both transnational and trans-governmental. Tied closely to processes of social and economic globalization, this view sees traditional inter-state law as increasingly subsumed within a broader process in which old distinctions between public and private international law and between municipal and international law are being steadily eroded. The state loses its place as the privileged sovereign institution, and instead becomes one of many actors and one participant in a broader and more complex social process.

One element of change is the rise in the number of international institutions and the exponential increase in the number and scope of internationally-agreed norms. Even if many individual institutions are weak, it is the cumulative extent of this institutional enmeshing that is crucial. But, more importantly, this image of law emphasizes the emergence of transnational rule and authority systems involving a wide range of actors. Thus, important sets of rules and norms are made by a wide variety of actors (states, international organizations, multinational enterprises, nongovernmental organizations, and private individuals) in a wide variety of public and private, domestic, and international fora. The interpretative community involved in law creation and implementation is broadened very significantly, and norms and rules are created, diffused, internalized, and enforced through a variety of material and symbolic incentives. What does this law of a transnational community imply for boundaries? There are three strands to the argument.

The first can be seen in much on the writing of the 1990s on "global governance," and is resolutely technocratic. It stresses the extent to which international law and institutions are to be seen above all as a response to the governance problems created by high and rising levels of globalization. States may still be useful answers to the problem of governance, but not necessarily so: they may "fail," in which case their functions may need to be transferred up to international bodies or down to local administrations or civil society groups. And, in any case, "optimum governance areas" will vary according to the particular problem involved. Boundaries, then, are a matter of pragmatic judgement and utilitarian calculation. For the good governance-minded technocrat, it may well make sense to press a government to devolve power, or to recognize the autonomy of a particular group, or to move towards supranational management in a particular issue area. This is not because the resulting change in boundaries or effective territorial control has any moral significance in itself.

The second strand pays more attention to transnational civil society as a key political arena in a globalized world. On this view, groups within civil society provide a framework for a broader and more inclusive transcultural dialogue through which global moral values can be established and greater human solidarity promoted and fostered. There are two sets of implications for boundaries. First, transnational civil society might be viewed as a realm of political practice within which new forms of non-territorial identity can be established and existing boundaries between citizens and aliens transcended. Second, and more modestly, it might be understood as providing a set of additional political processes by which questions of contested boundaries could be debated and negotiated.

The third strand takes the rights of individuals and groups that have already been developed within the solidarist legal order, but pushes them harder and further. In part, this involves an expanded range of international norms seeking to govern the domestic arrangements of states (from human rights to rights to democratic government). But it gives higher priority to the rights and identity claims of peoples. These rights should not be constrained by the concepts and clusters of rules that states have developed, and often manipulated for their own purposes. Self-determination should not be understood solely in terms of a right to form a territorially-defined state or to enjoy individual political rights within such a state. Rather, such arrangements should be open to reassessment and reevaluation, particularly on the part of those groups (such as refugees or indigenous peoples) that have found it hard to find a secure place within the traditional inter-state order.

Many of these developments may be viewed simply as taking further values, rights, and principles that have already been collectively endorsed by an increasingly solidarist society of states. With good reason they may also be seen as helping to stabilize the statist order. Thus, successfully addressing the numerous governance failures may shore up the legitimacy of states as the primary form of political arrangement. Equally, groups within transnational civil society may play both a direct role in conflicts over territories and borders, as well as providing sorely-needed legitimacy to inter-state institutions. But this transnational law stands in deep tension with the inherited statism of the legal order – by suggesting that state legitimacy should be far more directly dependent on the degree to which states reflect the wishes and interests of people and peoples, and by placing still higher demands on its weak political institutions. In addition to the previously noted weakness of solidarist institutions such as the UN, it is important to underline the degree to which both markets and civil society are themselves characterized by unequal power and political conflict. Indeed, alternative systems of multilayered governance may be just as subject to direct manipulation by powerful actors (states, but also firms and NGOs), as is the current system of states.

Despite the rhetoric of a "borderless world" and the "end of geography," globalization has not reduced the political significance of borders and boundaries. Traditional border disputes persist in many parts of the world (Peru/Ecuador, Eritrea/Ethiopia, Spratly Islands, Greece and Turkey, Israel and its neighbors). Thousands are prepared to die for the creation of new state borders even in the supposed post-Westphalian heartland of Europe. What globalization has done is to intensify the many conflicts that arise from the disjuncture between the dynamism of economic and societal interdependence and the rigidity of political boundaries. The three images of law sketched here each suggest different ways of framing the many problems associated with boundaries and territoriality and seeking to manage them. Yet they press in different directions, and are often in tension with each other. Thus, if moves towards a more solidarist society of states are constrained on one side by the still-powerful imperatives of pluralism, they are challenged on the other by the powerful claims promoted within and on the basis of an aspired-to transnational or cosmopolitan legal order.

3. Settlement, Inheritance, and Sale/Purchase

These three concepts were central to questions of boundaries and territory within the classical pluralist legal order. Thus the extension of settlement and the incorporation of previously remote regions was a basic element in the process of state formation (as in the United States and Canada in the nineteenth century or Brazil, India, China, and Indonesia in the twentieth). It also created the preconditions for border disputes as cartographically contiguous states came into meaningful contact for the first time. Effective settlement also represented one of the principal criteria by which legal title to territory might be established and by which disputes over borders and border zones might be legally settled. Finally, the notion of settlement as a particular kind of territorial occupation creating effective control was crucial to the juridical framework of European colonial expansion. The transfer of territory on the basis of inheritance was common within a patrimonial and dynastic conception of international relations, and formed an accepted part of the pluralist legal order. The same was true of sale/purchase, which survived quite late as one motive that might encourage states to transfer territory via treaty (for example, the purchase of Alaska by the United States from Russia in 1867, or the sale by Denmark to the United States of its territories in the West Indies in 1916).

All of these concepts have been profoundly affected by the emergence of ideas about self-determination. In the case of settlement, the drive of states to settle their territories often disrupted the autonomy of previously isolated communities and stimulated demands for self-determination. Settlement has also been central to the various ways in which states and other groups have sought to manipulate self-determination to their own advantage – for example, in the case of Israeli settlement policy, or the Western Sahara and the so-called Green March, in which 350.000 unarmed Moroccans entered the disputed territory.

In the case of the sale or purchase of territory, any such action would now clearly be subject to the general principle of self-determination and to some expression of the consent of the people affected. The same is true of inheritance, although legacies of the older order continue to shape on-going self-determination conflicts, as, for example, in Kashmir, where the Hindu ruling dynasty was, under the terms of the partition settlement, permitted to opt for India despite the fact that the majority of the population was Muslim.

Inherited historical claims to territory are also very common either on the basis of previous population movements, or other sorts of claims to title (Israel and the frontiers of Eretz Israel; Argentina and idea of nineteenth century territorial dispossession; Spain and Gibraltar; China's claims to its historical and "natural" borders, including Hong Kong, Taiwan, Tibet). Whatever their legal or moral status, these claims are often politically very powerful. Such cases highlight the central difficulty of identifying the "self" to which self-determination is deemed to apply. This is true of those classic cases where essentialist national claims clash with the rights of the majority of people who happen to live in the territory concerned (France and Alsace Lorraine; Serbia and Kosovo). But it is also true of those cases where the parties accept the notion of consent, but argue over who should qualify – as in the case of Western Sahara, where the MINURSO Identification Commission has had to deal with the clash between Morocco's demand that all Saharans be eligible to participate in the referendum and the Polisario's demand that the relevant electorate should consist of those who lived in the territory in 1974.

In general, the traditional view is that existing titles must be valid either because they were in themselves legitimate or because prescription and continued occupation has served to cure any defect in the title. Where the historical claims to territory clash with the wishes of present inhabitants, international law most commonly argues that the rights (but sometimes just interests) of the people affected should trump the territorial claims of outsiders. But it has also pressed for inclusive rights of citizenship where population movements have undermined the position of those who consider themselves the historically-entitled nation (as with the movement of Russians into the Baltic states).

Finally, each of these concepts can be unpacked in ways that raise difficult questions for statist international law. Thus the idea of sale/purchase may legitimately raise issues about the private/public divide – for example, where a legitimate government decides to sell to private economic agents the territory that constitute the "public" lands of a group or community within its borders. The idea of settlement may well involve a complex set of moral and legal issues that arise from the internal movement of settlers or from the enforced displacement of particular groups within a state. Strong claims concerning the right of peoples would call into question title established in the course of unjust colonial expansion and settlement. And historic patterns of settlement and strongly-felt inherited identities may form one element of the claim for special status made by, or on behalf of, indigenous peoples despite subsequent population movements (in or out of the territory concerned).

4. Conquest

The basic line is reasonably clear-cut. Conquest in terms of forcible seizure of territory by one state from another and its subsequent incorporation has become both illegal and illegitimate. "So perhaps we have properly no alternative but to begin from the premise that neither conquest nor a cession imposed by illegal force of themselves confer title."[10] In addition, for all the uncertainties, one of the areas where external self-determination applies as a legal rule beyond situations of European colonialism is in the case of peoples subjected to foreign military domination or occupation.

All recent clear-cut attempts at "conquest" have been met with a reassertion of this norm (as in the Falklands/Malvinas and Kuwait). In the latter case, the UN sought to deny all legal effects of the illegal use of force: "the annexation of Kuwait by Iraq under any form and whatever pretext has no legal validity and is considered null and void." Equally, the UNSC in the case of the former Yugoslavia has repeatedly reaffirmed that the taking of any territory by force was unlawful and unacceptable, called on all parties to respect the territorial integrity of Bosnia-Herzegovina, and stated that "any entities unilaterally declared or arrangements imposed in contravention thereof will be not be accepted."

But this does not mean that ambiguities have gone away or that problems do not arise. In the first place, when there is at least a degree of factual or legal murkiness (as in cases of the use of force in the context of decolonization) and where political interests press powerfully against international action, the clarity of the norm against conquest looks less secure (as in the case of Western Sahara, where Morocco annexed the Mauritanian sector in 1979 and then consolidated its military control over the territory, or the example of Indonesia and East Timor).

A second area of debate concerns the redrawing of boundaries as a result of the legal use of force and the notion of "punitive conquest." After all, concurrent with the negotiation of the UN Charter, the World War II allied powers engaged in a classical exercise of redrawing maps and transferring both peoples and territory. This formalized in treaty form the horsetrading

done at Teheran and Yalta, and included the redrawing of the frontiers
of Germany and Poland, the annexation by USSR of territories it had
demanded as its price for declaring war on Japan, and the seizure by the
United States of those Pacific territories that it deemed to be "strategically
necessary." Has all of this disappeared? Much legal argument seems to say
"yes." And yet the doctrine of collective security and the tradition of the just
war on which that doctrine has in part relied has always involved the notion
of punishment. Thus there were demands for the breaking-up of Iraq after
what was widely viewed as a just war, first in order to punish aggression,
but also to promote the interests and self-determination of minority groups
within the country. That such thinking was resisted attests to the strength of
the pluralist impulse to uphold territorial integrity and the legal argument
that even collective action under Chapter VII of the UN Charter should not
threaten the territorial integrity of states.

Third, where conquest is both illegitimate and costly, powerful states have
found alternative mechanisms of indirect external control; have intervened
to change domestic arrangements in ways that further their interests; or
have developed an expanded category of "occupation" – different forms of
domination or authority over inhabited territories by a state or group of
state outside its/their accepted international boundaries. Although success
is far from guaranteed, such strategies have been an important feature of
international relations in the post-1945 period.[11]

Such developments pose serious political, legal, and moral problems.
Military victory and even successful conquest did, at least sometimes, settle
matters. One way of ending protracted political disputes is by the clear victory of one side over the other, by establishing a clear-cut result, which is
then stabilized via collective recognition by the major states. Has the illegality of conquest and the rise of the norm of self-determination not given rise
to the messy, intermediate status of protracted occupation (as in the case of
northern Cyprus or the Israeli occupied territories). Is this not a case of un-
fulfilled solidarist ambition working against the older pluralist imperatives
of stable coexistence?

When we come to civil wars, the issue appears still more open. Civil wars
matter morally because of the monstrous numbers killed. For example, in
the twenty-years from 1970 to 1990 [that is, before the end of the Cold War]
there were sixty-three civil wars claiming around eight million lives. Civil
wars are also the wars in which most modern-day "conquest" takes place –
the forcible seizure and subsequent control of territory by one political
group from either another such group or a recognized central government.
Some 30 percent of Colombia has been "conquered" by the FARC and ELN
guerrillas, and is administered by them. Armenian forces control Karabakh
and six autonomous districts of Azerbaijan, and in the conflicts in Abkhazia,
South Ossetia, and Chechnya, the central state lost control of significant
areas of territory.

Traditionally, in international law, the existence of civil war with a clear breakdown of governmental authority both eases the legal constraints on outside intervention and allows outside parties to recognize the belligerent parties. The dominant legal line in the post-1945 period has been to try and extend the ambit of humanitarian law and the proscription of genocide to such conflicts. More generally, it has highlighted the need for humanitarian protection and political settlement. The closest that international institutions and international law have come to territorial rearrangement has been the development of the concept of "safe areas" – in other words, the protection of individuals or groups on a territorial basis but without directly raising the issue of title to territory or sovereignty.

It is certainly the case that outside parties and international bodies have often been forced to take a view on the justice of the actions of one side or the other – most notably in denunciations of attempts to change boundaries in the former Yugoslavia. But it is striking just how powerful the traditional criterion of effectiveness remains. Whatever the justice or injustice of actions taken in a civil war, there appears little alternative but to accept the outcome of armed force. Thus, for example, the Dayton peace settlement (as with the previous Owen and Vance plans) was built around lines of effective control as they emerged from the fighting. These were to be the basis for the political settlement, and there was no attempt to reverse or alter these lines, either because of some evaluation of the justice of the respective cause or because of some criteria of ethnic distribution. Equally, outside parties and international institutions have consistently recognized that successful conquest and effective control create a legitimate claim to participate in a political settlement, however unsavoury the previous actions of the group concerned (for example, the UN's decision to work with Renamo in Mozambique in 1992). Or, again, outside parties (including the German churches, which sponsored the March 1999 peace negotiations) have raised few questions about the legitimate status of the ELN in Colombia.

5. Secession

Despite its calm and authoritative tone, legal writing on the subject of secession exposes all too clearly the fault-lines between law and politics and the tensions amongst the three images of international law. It provides one of the purest examples of where returning to a world of old-fashioned pluralism is impossible for both moral and pragmatic reasons, but where there is insufficient consensus either to agree on clear rules as to when and how secession will be permitted or to secure the solidarist forms of international political involvement necessary for the effective management of secessionist conflicts.

Within the pluralist-statist model of international law, there was no right of self-determination, but states were free to recognize new states that resulted either from an agreed process of devolution of power (Canada, Brazil) or from successful revolt and revolution (United States, Spanish America). As ideas about self-determination gathered political momentum, the dominant legal response was to stress the threat that any implied or actual right of secession would pose. As one of the classic statements put it:

To concede to minorities, either of language or religion, or to any fractions of a population the right of withdrawing from the community to which they belong, because it is their wish or their good pleasure, would be to destroy order and stability within States and to inaugurate anarchy in international life; it would be to uphold a theory incompatible with the very idea of the State as a territorial and political unity.[12]

Equally, there has been a very powerful political presumption against secession (Katanga, Cyprus), with only three clear-cut exceptions (Bangladesh, Singapore, and Eritrea in 1993 after a long war and UN-supervised referendum). This pattern continues. For example, in the secessionist struggles in the former Soviet Union, and its erstwhile sphere of influence, international bodies such as the UN and OSCE have consistently stated that no recognition will be given to any attempt to change international borders by force. So if secession is not to be accepted, what then? The answer has been an expanding range of strategies aimed either at limiting the disruptive potential of self-determination or at meeting aspirations for self-determination in ways that would hopefully undercut secessionist demands. Five such strategies can be noted.

The first was to restrict the range of "units" to which self-determination should apply. Thus, self-determination after World War I was to apply to (at least parts of) the defeated European empires and, very indirectly, to mandated territories. After World War II, it would apply to peoples under European colonial domination; and then to peoples under alien occupation (Israeli occupied territories) or under racist regimes (South Africa under apartheid). In each case, law followed and adjusted to political developments and reflected powerful pluralist imperatives at the obvious cost of normative coherence. The idea that self-determination applied only to place separated by water from the mother country, while depending on a manifestly unjustified distinction, at least had a certain clarity. It also served a policy that was easy to understand – namely, that it was time to stop breaking up larger state entities into ever smaller ones.[13]

Second, within the context of decolonization, international law generally took the UN Charter idea of the "equal rights and self-determination of peoples" to mean the peoples of established territories who should enjoy a one-off choice (although not necessarily to form an independent state). So many state borders derived either from boundaries between imperial powers, or from domestic boundaries within imperial polities. Those boundaries were to remain sacrosanct unless all of the people within those boundaries agreed to alter them by dividing the state or integrating with another. And, after this one-off moment of self-determination had passed, the principle of territorial integrity would be resolutely upheld and, of course, all further secessionist claims would be resisted. Hence the continued importance in all four waves of decolonisation of the principle of *uti possidetis*. Once more the pluralist impulse persisted and, whenever there was any doubt, the default position leaned towards territorial integrity.

These first two strategies are reflected in the double-talk of the classic decolonization statements on self-determination: statements that seek to uphold both self-determination as a basic norm of the system and the territorial integrity of states. They reflect the tremendously powerful impulse towards stable frontiers and the finality of borders. The strength of this impulse can be seen in the degree to which the boundaries of even deeply fragile and unstable states have been stable. As Christopher Clapham puts it:

Second, and more basically, African rulers overwhelmingly shared a common 'idea of the state', which removed many potential sources of conflict between them, and made it possible for them to devise generally agreed principles by which to regulate their relations with one another. One important expression of this was...that the artificiality of their boundaries normally created a shared interest in boundary maintenance, rather than a mass of boundary conflicts.[14]

This instinct persists, as for example, in the former Yugoslavia, where all of the Western states decided from 1991 that the former internal borders of constituent republics would remain sacrosanct.

A third strategy is to try and distinguish between different types of nationalism. There is a long tradition of seeking to make such distinctions (for example, Western vs. Eastern European nationalisms; European vs. Third World nationalisms; civic nationalism vs. ethnic nationalism; statist nationalism vs. anti-statist nationalism) and to use these to justify support for one category against another. There are undoubtedly distinctions (most usefully between voluntarist and objectivist nationalism), and there is good reason to believe that voluntarist nationalisms are more amenable to political resolution or at least containment. And yet such distinctions are in practice slippery and very hard to operationalize in the form of agreed international rules. All too often, denunciations of particular kinds of nationalist claims serve polemical or political purposes. Or they rely on dubious historical distinctions, as, for instance, in the claim that the state-forming, and at least potentially liberal, nationalist movements of the European past have given way to a contemporary explosion of "post-modern neo-tribalism."

The fourth strategy is to seek to undercut the problem via the promotion of internal self-determination. Basically, if we can get internal self-determination right and if we can provide an alternative framework for self-determination, then we can reduce the demands for external self-determination and the redrawing of boundaries. This tendency is reflected in the move to reinterpret self-determination from the mid-1960s as part of the international human rights regime, and more recently in attempts to revive mechanisms for the international protection of minorities. For some, the logic of this position leads inexorably to the idea of an internationally-agreed right to democratic governance. For others it leads to an expanded agenda of internationally-supported group rights, even those that cut across territorial divisions. Whilst carrying no guarantee of success, there is no doubt that this represents the morally most appealing and politically most realistic solution to the dilemmas of self-determination.

Building on these strategies, a final strategy is to seek to avoid the problem by unpacking sovereignty. Inside the state, this obviously involves a wide variety of federal, consociational, non-territorial rights and protections, and power-sharing models. But it may also involve rethinking the international position of the state. The reasoning runs as follows: The problems of self-determination has at least as much to do with the triumph of the sovereignty model as it does with nationalism. In any case nationalism is obdurate despite the prophecies of the modernists and anti-essentialists. So let us seek a solution in which we unpack and unravel sovereignty and promote multilevel governance in which "state" responsibilities are dispatched to various sites of power and the diversification of human loyalties is encouraged. One aspect might be involve the construction of regional systems of multi-layered governance (as in the image of constitutionally-structured neo-medieval order in Europe). Another involves a return of semi-sovereign territories and internationally-administered de facto protectorates (as in Bosnia and Kosovo).

There is clearly a great deal of good sense in these kinds of arguments. But there is also a good deal of romanticization of the possibilities of such a post-Westphalian order. It assumes that the fundamental problem of legitimate political order remains intact whilst sovereignty is reparcelled in this way. Where it breaks down, force and coercion may be required, and it is states that alone still possess the capacity to exercise legitimate force. Put more generally, the fundamental problem with models of dispersed sovereignty is that whilst they correctly acknowledge the dangers of centralized power, they fail to acknowledge the necessity of such power for social order and the promotion of common moral purposes. It is instructive that this should be the case even in the very favorable conditions of Europe.

If these strategies do not work, then international law has little more to say. There is no legal right of secession, but states are free to recognize secession either if it is agreed by the parties (as in the velvet Czech/Slovak divorce of 1993 or many of the post-Soviet successor states), or if it is contested but successful and does not involve illegal use of force by outside parties. So international law accepts the political power of secessionist movements but grants no legal entitlement. There is a great deal of discussion as to how rules might be taken forward. But in almost every case, such proposals involve real difficulties, and there is little sign of consensus on what the new rules might be or on how they might be applied and by whom.

One strand in the debate stresses the conditionality of secession. Thus, secessionist movements could be recognized where a secessionist movement can demonstrate its legitimacy. But how, prior to the creation of a state or some stable political order, is this to be done, especially in conditions of conflict? Since nations are understood to be separate from states or from any particular administrative structure, then there can *never* be a secure answer as to the legitimacy of those who claim to speak on its behalf. A secessionist movement might also be recognized where the putative new state is willing to sign up to international human or minority rights agreements. This is deeply seductive as a way of squaring the circle. But there has, in practice, been little willingness to follow up on the conditionality of recognition; even in Europe, the human rights machinery to secure such compliance is weak, and as the inter-war period suggests, partial and selective conditionality is likely to prove illegitimate and unsustainable. Making secession conditional may sound good and may make outsiders feel better, but it does not necessarily offer any secure protection to those at risk.

Perhaps the most widely-agreed condition would apply in cases where continued membership of a state would perpetuate extreme denial of individual rights or of the rights of a group or national minority. But it is worth noting that it has not been possible to turn this into an operational legal rule and that it is not necessarily politically persuasive – after all, even following NATO's involvement, Kosovo remains part of Serbia.

As this example also shows, it is hard to imagine politicians or lawyers giving up the deep-rooted instinct to apply self-determination only within some preexisting set of boundaries and to continue giving significant weight to the effective control of territory. One possible exception may occur where there is a general regional or sub-regional dissolution of boundaries and loss of control by existing states. If there is no possibility of outside involvement, then there may well be a realistic case for allowing the lines of military confrontation to stabilize and new political entities to emerge, and then to re-legalize the outcome on the basis of the fall-back legal option of collective recognition. This may be realistic, but it is not normatively very appealing.

If clear rules are hard to identify, then management becomes crucial. One possibility is management by the "Great Powers." Although sounding archaic, the continued prevalence of such management is striking, and reflects both inequalities of effective power and the weakness of international institutions. But although politically still powerful, the idea that "joint disposition by the principal powers" could have any firm legal basis in a solidarist or transnational legal order must be questionable. This one of the chief reasons why even the United States cannot afford to escape the UN.

What of management by international organizations? This is normatively most appealing, and lies at the heart of solidarist aspirations. And yet recent experience has been sobering. International appetite to manage secessionist crises, even those involving high casualties, remains limited. The continued capacity of many conflicts to remain internationally invisible is just as striking as the media attention devoted to particular cases. Cross-cutting political interests (including those related to de facto understandings of spheres of influence) mean that the selectivity of involvement may well be unavoidable and the only way of ever achieving anything in practice. And yet it must work to strain the normative coherence of the legal order and the legitimacy of its solidarist aspirations.

The conjuncture of legal and moral norms that shape contemporary international politics with a particular set of political circumstances should leave us deeply troubled. *If* international society is unwilling to accept the forcible redrawing of boundaries; *if* it is also unwilling to sanction the movement of peoples into ethnically more homogeneous entities[15]; and *if* it also unwilling to accept the denial of self-determination and the atrocities that denial may often lead to, then there can be logically no other route except to deeper and deeper involvement in the restructuring and internal administration of states. Yet, as is often remarked, we live in an age of hesitant internationalists and still more reluctant imperialists. The result is surely a significant element of moral delinquency on the part of an international order that upholds the right to self-determination but can do so little to provide for its consistent or effective implementation.

Notes to Chapter 14

1. For some, this is the basis of distinguishing between frontier as zones and boundaries as lines. See C.B. Fawcett, *Frontiers* (Oxford: Clarendon Press, 1918), Chapter 2.
2. Lord Curzon, *Frontiers* (Oxford: Clarendon Press, 1907), 7.
3. Ibid., 48.
4. R.Y. Jennings, *The Acquisition of Territory in International Law* (Manchester: Manchester University Press, 1963), 2. But note that states could be recognized without clear or agreed boundaries, as with Poland in 1918 or Israel after 1948.
5. Robert W. Tucker, *The Inequality of Nations* (New York: Basic Books, 1977), 12.
6. Jennings, *The Acquisition of Territory*, 3–4. It was never quite solely a matter of force establishing valid title. See Sharon Korman, *The Right of Conquest* (Oxford: Clarendon Press, 1996), Chapter 4.
7. Julius Stone, "Approaches to the Notion of International Justice," in C.E. Black and Richard Falk, eds., *The Future of the International Legal Order* (Princeton: Princeton University Press, 1969), 386. See also J.L. Brierly, who writes that "The truth is that international law can no more refuse to recognize that a finally successful conquest does change the title to territory than municipal law can a

change of regime brought about by successful revolution." J.L. Brierly, *The Law of Nations*, 6th ed. (Oxford: Clarendon Press, 1963), 172–3.

8. These two clusters of norms are related. Self-determination played a major role in changing attitudes to the use of force, but was not the only factor. Also to be taken into account were the escalating costs of military force in an age of total war, the declining importance of control over territory as a source of power, and the decreased tolerance of casualties in many societies. Although self-determination generally reinforces restraints on use of force, this is not always the case – most obviously in the legitimacy given to national liberation movements and in the encouragement of assistance to such movements.

9. See Woodrow Wilson's Four Principles speech: "There shall be no annexations, no contributions, no punitive damages. Peoples are not to be handed about from one sovereignty to another by an international conference or an understanding between rivals and antagonists. National aspirations must be respected: peoples may now be dominated and governed only by their own consent." R.S. Baker and W.E Dodd, eds., *The Public Papers of Woodrow Wilson, Volume I. War and Peace: Presidential Messages, Addresses and Public Papers 1917–1924* (London and New York: Harper and Brothers, 1927), 180. That peoples and provinces were "not to be bartered from sovereignty to sovereignty as if they were mere chattels and pawns in a game" was clear to Wilson (182). But note that he rarely spoke of national determination directly, and that he usually referred to the "interests" and "benefits" of peoples rather than their wishes, and to "autonomous development" rather than any right to statehood.

10. Jennings, *The Acquisition of Territory*, 61.

11. Adam Roberts has identified seventeen different categories of occupation. See his "What is a military occupation?" *British Yearbook of International Law* (Oxford: Clarendon Press, 1984), 249–305.

12. *The Aaland Islands Question. Report presented to the Council of the League by the Commission of Rapporteurs*, League of Nations Doc.B.7.21/68/106, 1921, 28.

13. Thomas M. Franck, *Fairness in International Law and Institutions* (Oxford: Clarendon Press, 1995), 155.

14. Christopher Clapham, *Africa and the International System: The Politics of State Survival* (Cambridge: Cambridge University Press, 1996), p. 107.

15. But note the gap between rhetoric and reality. Despite paper commitments, little serious effort has been made to enforce the return of refugees under the Dayton Agreement. And Dayton itself was in part made possible by the Croatian seizure of Krajina and the expulsion of 200,000 Serbs – an action in which the West was complicit but that has arguably stabilized Croatia as an ethnic state. Together with the "softer" ethnic cleansing of Eastern Slovonia, Croatia went from 14–15 percent Serb before the war to 1–2 percent today.

People and Boundaries: An "Internationalized Public Law" Approach

Benedict Kingsbury[1]

The editors of this volume regard international law as an ethical tradition to be appraised alongside Confucianism or liberalism. Certainly it is a tradition of thought – its adherents are conscious of carrying on a shared enterprise, recognize canonical texts and modes of argument, identify a common (if changing) set of problems, and have a defined professional identity of mutual recognition and mutual defense. But is it an ethical tradition? Three features of the international law tradition muddy comparison with archetypal ethical traditions.

First, international law is almost bound to aspire to universality: its normative propositions thus appeal to universalist ethical justifications, but seemingly-universal justifications often prove to be particularist when probed in hard cases. Ethical justifications in international law thus move between universals stated very abstractly – the ethic of peace and effectiveness has been preponderant among international lawyers since 1945 – and a plethora of unreconciled and often contested specific ethical structures. These can endure unreconciled because international law holds itself out not only as an ethical tradition, but as a means of bridging traditions and establishing widely-accepted criteria under which those from different ethical traditions can agree together on practical action. The discipline is thus in internal tension between this pull toward ecumenical neutrality and competing pulls of specific ethical traditions, above all the pull of the liberal ethical systems in which many of the dominant voices in international law are socialized.

Second, international law is to some extent validated by practice, and continuous movement between theory and practice is essential to the argumentative pattern of international law. The concept of law involves both texts and behavior. Thus the internal criteria of the mainstream of the international law discipline require that it be explicated and evaluated not as pure theory or pure practice, but as a web spun between these poles.

Third, the tradition has never quite successfully integrated the view of international law as being about rights and duties of states with a view of international law as being expressly and directly concerned with people. It thus contains both an ethic of order between states associated since the sixteenth century with European statecraft and since the nineteenth century with positivism, and an ethic of rights of individuals and collectivities associated with Enlightenment rationalism, the American and French Revolutions, socialism, anti-colonialism, and human rights. The lack of resolution between these ethical strands is evident in much of the law concerning boundaries and territory.

Rather than ruminate in detached and abstract terms on these three tensions in international law as an ethical tradition, I will make a specific argument from within the tradition, and develop this argument by reference to illustrative subject matter in which these tensions are acutely evident. The argument I will make – a non-standard one, to be explained in Section 2 – is for an internationalized public law approach, and the subject matter I will explore to illustrate it in Sections 3–7 is the relation between people and boundaries.

1. The Pluralism/Solidarism/Transnationalism Heuristic

In his contribution to this volume, Andrew Hurrell (Chapter 14) employs the distinctive approach of the English school of international relations, represented especially in the work of Hedley Bull, to establish an understanding of the main currents of the international law tradition. Hurrell frames his discussion of the international law of boundaries in terms of the layering of three broad approaches to international society and its law: pluralist, solidarist, and transnationalist. This is a valuable starting point. Rather than reexamining it *in extenso*, I will comment briefly in this section on aspects that lead me to regard it as an illuminating but unduly limited template for appreciating the full range of relevant material. In the remainder of the chapter, I will propose a different, cross-cutting approach as a necessary (albeit incomplete) supplement to this framework for understanding the international law tradition.

The pluralism that became one axis of international law orthodoxy in the period from Vattel's *Droit des gens* (1758) to the exemplary first edition of Lassa Oppenheim's *International Law* (1905–1906) still represents the point of departure in the professional practice of international law. Its precepts in relation to boundaries raise immediate ethical questions. For example, it is a liberal ethical intuition that any boundary that has real meaning – a boundary that truly divides, that limits transborder political representation or moral entitlements of people on one side of the border as against people on the other – is not morally justified where it entrenches vast inequality. Yet pluralist international law has long taken, and continues strongly to take, the opposite position. The general principle is that once boundaries are legally delimited, there is almost no basis for altering them except genuine agreement between the parties. Neither a fundamental change of circumstances[2] nor the emergence of a new rule such as the prohibition of acquisition of territory by aggressive force in itself displaces a prior valid boundary treaty. What are the ethics of this position? The short answer is that pluralism gives normative priority to the maintenance of the stability and basic institutions of the international system on the ground that attempting to do much more is disastrous idealism.[3]

Standard legal texts such as Oppenheim's first edition take a pluralist view of boundaries as divisions between territorially-defined states, and trace intricate bodies of doctrine on such practical matters as the legal implications of a sudden shift in the course of a boundary river, or the techniques for delimiting a boundary in a mountain range by reference to the watershed. Pluralism of this sort focuses on managing rather than preventing coerced territorial change as power shifts, and gives little credence to the claims of groups and entities not deemed members of the "family of nations." As a practical matter, legal rules and institutions understood in this pluralist mode have had, and still have, a significant role in assisting resolution of disputes between states as territorial units, and in fixing and maintaining their common boundaries, thereby ameliorating some causes of war and instability. Thus, potentially dangerous land boundary disputes between Thailand and Cambodia, Burkina Faso and Mali, El Salvador and Honduras, and Libya and Chad have been resolved pursuant to reasoned decisions of the International Court of Justice.[4] Boundary or territorial disputes between India and Pakistan, Dubai and Sharjah, and Egypt and Israel have been resolved by binding legal arbitration.[5] Many more boundary problems have been addressed by negotiations leading to the conclusion of a treaty, such as that between Ecuador and Peru. All of this is important, but it does not represent all that is important even about inter-state boundaries; hence the demand for more far-reaching solidarist approaches.

Solidarism places greater weight on morality and justice, although still within a statist framework, in which a majority of states may deploy their power for the "common good." It is not clear that solidarism has in fact had a great impact in bringing the ethics of the traditional pluralist international law of boundaries closer to the liberal intuition about the ethical problems of boundaries as structures of inequality. Indeed, a paradox of statist solidarism is that the more far-reaching and enforceable international law becomes, the more it depends on heightened inequalities between states for its effectiveness – inequalities that are facilitated and intensified by boundaries. Nevertheless, on other ethical issues, solidarism has had a shaping impact on the international law tradition, as Hurrell shows. Whereas Bull treated solidarism as a kind of overlay, which episodically breaks down to reveal the hard floor of pluralist law beneath, Hurrell suggests that solidarism has wrought an enduring transformation in the old system of pluralist international law, above all in embracing self-determination and its underpinning notion of the nation as a legally and politically significant concept separate from the state. It is difficult to weigh fairly the importance of solidarism within the "English school" heuristic because of the way in which Bull's early work structured the pluralist/solidarist divide to weight the debate in favor of pluralism. This weighting reflected Bull's strong initial normative commitment to order: he associated the rise of solidarism with the international lawyers' weakening grasp of their true responsibilities as they became captivated by the utopian projects of the League of Nations and the United Nations.[6] Solidarism is not an independent quantum: its meaning and importance for different writers are a function of their more fundamental views on the primacy of order, justice, or other values in the international system.

How far is this pluralist/solidarist analytical dichotomy (bracketing transnationalism for the moment) helpful in the specific project of integrating the rules and practices of international law with international politics in relation to ethical aspects of interstate interactions concerning boundaries? The statist pluralism that has been the bedrock of an international law tradition over at least the past 150 years purports to rest many of its rules on state consent. The establishment of general principles of the international law of boundaries has thus been a perplexing exercise within the traditional consent-based sources of international law. Many individual boundaries have been fixed by consent, often by treaty between the states involved. But there have been remarkably few efforts to codify the principles of the international law of boundaries in general treaties. By contrast, codificatory treaties have been adopted on other institutions of international society that are central to the pluralist account, including diplomatic relations, war, and treaty-making, as well as sources of potential conflict such as the use and allocation of the oceans, the airwaves, or air transport. Pluralist lawyers often anchor the law of boundaries in custom, but as a practical matter, much of the articulation and development of general rules has depended on judges or arbitrators, buttressed by diplomats and text writers, drawing in some cases on Roman law, in others on state practice, in others on common sense or newly enunciated principles. Resolving boundary disputes has been one of the major functions of public international adjudication for more than a century, but the task of the adjudicators has often been to find a politically and practically workable solution and persuade the parties to accept it, rather than to find and apply general principles clearly established by the consent of states. By contrast, solidarist principles, although decried by pluralists for moving away from consent, have often rested on greater state participation.

The UN Charter principles of non-use of force, peaceful settlement of disputes, and self-determination have been elaborated in formally non-binding General Assembly resolutions. Other fundamental legal principles, such as the application in Africa of *uti possidetis juris*, rest not on formally binding instruments but on conference diplomacy and consensus statements of government leaders. Thus, in relation to boundaries, the pluralist/solidarist dichotomy does not correspond with a consensual/non-consensual dichotomy as to sources of law, or with a clear rules/vague aspirations dichotomy as to the substance of law, in the way pluralists assert and expect. Doubts therefore arise about the validity of the initial dichotomy as the basic analytical structure of the international law of boundaries. This discordance, combined with the weighting of the analysis in favor of pluralism, has led to an undervaluing in standard texts of the kinds of public law approaches to boundaries described later in this chapter.

The incompleteness of the pluralist/solidarist structure, with its focus on the interactions of states, is well recognized in the English school. Bull's solution, which Hurrell endorses, was to identify a third, transnational approach, whose advocates believe international law has been, or at least should be, transformed from pluralist or solidarist inter-state law into the law of a transnational society.[7] Such a view has much current support as a repudiation of statism and as the basis for an emancipatory project focused on people. Hurrell's account of the third approach is a catch-all for a variety of non-statecentric ideas relevant to the ethics of a law of boundaries, extending from functionalist arguments for multiple levels of governance, through economic arguments for the globalization of markets, to liberal advocacy of a globalized transnational civil society. These have in common advocacy of a diminution in the importance of existing inter-state boundaries. But reflection on the legal programs that actually result from these ideas suggests that in some cases they involve the intensification of existing boundaries for certain purposes – for example, free movement within the European Union has spurred more rigorous patrolling of its perimeter. In other cases, these programs call, in effect, for the establishment of new types of boundaries, which state power is called upon to police. For instance, the balance between religious freedom, cultural autonomy, and institutional power leads some to advocate a rough allocation of territorially-bounded spheres of influence among major world religions: Hindu nationalists seek restrictions on Christian evangelism in India, some Islamic states apply legal sanctions to Muslim apostasy, strong demands are made in Russia and Greece for anti-proselytism measures favoring the established Orthodox churches, the authorities in China maintain control on papal authority over Catholics in China, and sharp criticisms continue to be leveled at missionary activity by "foreign" churches in Africa. Transnational activity is important in relation to boundaries, but its mosaic of legal effects does not by any means correspond to the ideology of a borderless world. I will integrate elements of the interaction between statist and transnationalist dimensions into the cross-cutting argument that follows.

2. Internationalized Public Law

While the three-fold "English school" division is helpful as a way of understanding some important lines of division in the international law tradition with regard to boundaries, it does not capture an important dimension of legal thinking about boundaries, which I term "internationalized public law." Public law is here understood as the law that empowers the state and that regulates state power. National public law usually has its locus within the state, but it is internationalized insofar as it is shaped by, and shapes, traditional international legal rules, international public policy, and transnational ethical norms.[8] The interaction between intra-state and international law and politics has the result that principles developed within the state spill out and become principles shaping what the state is, what the relevant interpretive communities are, and what roles extra-state actors play. In that respect, the account I propose might be regarded as constructivist, although this label often adds more confusion than clarity. Internationalized public law differs from traditional pluralist public international law in that it is not dependent on true inter-state agreement, whether explicit or implicit. This body of internationalized public law derives its impetus from norms, practices, and decisions taken within state institutions, so it has more in common with statist solidarism than with the most frequently advocated varieties of transnational or global law. But it is not simply solidarist. An internationalized public law approach cuts across the inside/outside distinction that has structured traditional public international law analysis, and in doing so moves outside the standard parameters of pluralism and solidarism – but it does not correspond with approaches that locate the impetus for law in transnational interactions or global civil society.

I argue that this approach brings into focus substantial bodies of ethically-significant practice on aspects of the relations between people and boundaries in established states that are obscured from view, let alone analysis, by the pluralist/solidarist dichotomy, and are outside the purview of contemporary transnationalism. These bodies of practice are taken into consideration by traditional international law only in very circumscribed ways. In relation to boundaries, the internationalized public law approach is well established with regard to boundaries within federations; federal courts often draw upon international law principles in resolving boundary disputes between constituent units, and such federal decisions are sometime referred to in inter-state cases. But the argument here is that this form of internationalized public law is of much wider importance.

The sections that follow explore the implications of an internationalized public law approach for the relations between people and boundaries under the five headings prescribed as the organizing scheme for this volume: settlement, inheritance, voluntary transfer, conquest, and secession. In the first of these sections, on settlement, I will briefly sketch ways in which the pluralist, solidarist, and transnational approaches to international law have dealt with specific issues of people and boundaries, then highlight features of legal thought and practice that become more fully evident when an internationalized public law approach is adopted. Because of limits of space, subsequent sections will be confined to features of legal thought and practice that are identified and illuminated in a distinctive way under the internationalized public law approach.

3. Settlement

In standard pluralist texts, settlement is treated primarily as an effective way for a state to demonstrate occupation and control of territory, thereby consolidating a claim in an area where the boundary with a neighboring state has not been definitively established; the legal implications of this process are reflected in the notion of historic consolidation of title.[9] Weak claims may be somewhat strengthened de facto by settlement. Even established boundaries are sometimes successfully contested by transforming the facts on the ground through settlement. For example, United States non-compliance with the 1911 arbitration award in the Chamizal case – non-compliance that rested on dubious legal grounds but was the result of strong pressure from local political interests – was buttressed by subsequent settlement. Some 8,000 homes had been built for U.S. settlers on the relevant portion of the Chamizal contiguous to El Paso, Texas, by the time a solution involving allocation of compensating territory to Mexico was finally reached in 1963.[10]

Yet international law cannot sustain an ostrich-like effort to confine its treatment of settlement to claims of this sort between legally-recognized states or states-in-waiting. International law as an ethical tradition is beset by doubts about its dealings with colonialism, doubts that have perhaps intensified in the recent wave of efforts to face past wrongs through apologies, truth commissions, and restitutionary payments. Many of the early texts of international law deal with the European expansion, and many of the fragments of practice relevant to territory and boundaries arise specifically from colonialism or its aftermath. Colonialism is not foreign to the tradition that has made modern international law, but a part of it.[11] In dealing with the past, therefore, international law deals not only with facts, but with itself. This is acutely so in relation to settlement.

Settlement, colonialism, and state formation are intertwined. The formal proclamation by a European state of colonial authority in a territory was frequently preceded, and sometimes initiated, by deliberate encouragement of settlement, as with Charters issued to English mercantile ventures such as the Virginia company to establish colonies in North America, and was often followed by planned settlement, as with the New Zealand Company. Unplanned settlement of nationals often generated demand among them for colonialism, justified by the need to keep order among these subjects and to bring the area within the pale of the "rule of law." Substantial European settlement in areas of the extra-European world was accompanied by formation of state structures that followed European models and internalized established traditions, albeit with local systems of authority or social and economic organization incorporated to varying degrees. Settlement (under the juridical name "occupation") regularly provided a basis for claiming title to vastly larger areas that were not "settled" by Europeans, or in many cases by anyone, and in countries such as Brazil and Bolivia the state was only transformed from a series of islands of authority into a truly encompassing territorial entity in the first decades of the twentieth century.[12]

From a solidarist perspective, "settlement" is a term that joins a debate rather than merely identifying one. In the canonical history of modern state formation, "settlement" connotes particular ways of living and of using land. People without permanent dwellings may be occupants, but they are not settlers. Many state governments continue to pursue policies of trying to "settle" nomads. "Settlement" has often been associated with Lockean values: proper use of the land is to inhabit, enclose, and develop it as an individual family unit, whereas improper use (or at least inferior use) is to "wander" over it in "hordes."[13] One of the many ironies of the Lockean system as applied in practice, however, was that sparse European settlement might underpin vast claims to imperium and dominium over lands the Europeans did not use, while systematic use of lands by indigenous peoples was thought by Europeans to justify at most a weak, defeasible usufruct. "Settlement" has thus operated as part of a concept of property: "settlers" have the full panoply of perfected land rights in the state legal system; "squatters" or "encroachers" do not. More recently, perceptions of justice have led to a solidarist reassessment. Whereas "settler" has been a privileged term in state formation and consolidation, it now sometimes appears as a term of denigration: a "settler" is the antithesis of an indigene, and settlement connotes migration and incursion on the rights of those who were there already.

Accompanying and spurring this solidarist shift has been the rise of a transnational indigenous peoples movement, which asserts the entitlement of groups to self-determination as against past or future settlers, or at least to reparations from the settlers' descendants. If liberalism tends to value present lives, the indigenous movement has to some extent sought to construct as a counter a continuous entity comprising past, present, and future human generations, the land and territory, and the spirits. This transnational movement has had an impact on political discourse and ideas. It has begun to shape a distinct status for indigenous peoples and others who have lost out in the process of settlement and state formation. But while such movements have added a dimension to the ethical tradition of international law, their impact on the pluralist, and even the solidarist, dimensions of the discipline has remained modest.

Within established states, settlement has frequently been used to consolidate state power and subdue distinct groups that might challenge the existing power distribution or even press for autonomy or secession. Settlement schemes have also been used – often overlapping with the political and security motives already mentioned – to make available land to very populous groups in overcrowded areas, to increase the tax base, and to increase production of certain kinds of crops and commodities. Population transfers to alter demographics are clearly impermissible where the territory in question is under military occupation as defined by international law, and they have been denounced by the UN General Assembly and other bodies in certain specific cases where the demography of a unit of self-determination was being altered in politically significant ways. Outside these contexts, however, international law has traditionally left internal settlement arrangements to the discretion of the state responsible. Some principles limiting this discretion may nevertheless be emerging – an internationalized public law approach provides a useful prism for identifying these.

First, freedom of movement of persons within states is a standard liberal-legal principle, and restrictions on this freedom may in certain circumstances be unjustified.[14] The prohibition of racial discrimination (and discrimination on other specified grounds) rendered clearly unlawful the settlement system, centered in South Africa on the creation of bantustans and restrictions on internal freedom of movement and residence through pass laws, established by the apartheid government. On grounds of individual rights, courts in Hong Kong ruled in 1999 that substantial numbers of people from mainland China with family connections to Hong Kong had a right to cross the internal boundary to settle and reside there. The difficulty of establishing a universal principle of free movement within the state is indicated by the aftermath of this case: the Hong Kong authorities, with considerable public support, requested Beijing authorities to amend the Basic Law with the aim of nullifying the effect of the court decision and tightening the internal boundaries between Hong Kong and China. Non-ethnic internal controls on movement and residence in China have received only muted criticism from outside, even though significant human rights questions arise.[15] By contrast, a proposal to alleviate poverty and environmental degradation in overcrowded hills in western China by moving an ethnically mixed group into an area with a substantial Tibetan presence was rejected by the World Bank Board in 2000.[16] Although this project was probably less disruptive of individual people's lives and prospects than other problematic resettlement projects the Bank has decided to finance, the fact that Tibetans were involved transformed the international political dynamic. From the standpoint of individual welfare, cases of this kind raise a challenging ethical problem: does a very poor person hoping to resettle somewhere else to have a better life have the same moral claim as a better-off person who is already there and whose living standard or cultural integrity will be reduced by new arrivals? The justification given for the project in China is that it improves the economic possibilities of poor migrants and upholds their basic economic and social rights. Opponents argue that the rights of the existing populations of the colonized territories are violated, as they lose land, means of livelihood, cultural integrity, and some of their ability to shape their communities. Such opposition can be understood as drawing upon a second principle, one that limits internal freedom of the government to rely on the freedom of movement principle in certain cases.

The second principle is that public law may uphold, or even require, some types of intra-state boundaries in order to achieve values of group maintenance and autonomy, even where these boundaries have adverse implications for full enjoyment of some human rights. Belgian constitutional arrangements illustrate some of the dilemmas. The division of the country into linguistic regions, in each of which the public schools operate only in the official language of that region regardless of how many people speaking the other main national language might live in a particular town, is premised on protecting each language community in its traditional territory from threats to its own future. When French-speaking parents living in the Flemish region argued that they suffered discrimination because if their children wished to attend local public schools they would have to study in Flemish, the European Court of Human Rights held that there was no discrimination.[17] This decision was doubtless influenced by the careful set of compromises Belgian constitutional arrangements require to keep the country together, as well as by the parallel structure operating in the French unilingual area, and the practical alternatives available to the complainant parents. For similar reasons, the Court rejected a subsequent challenge to the complex communally-based system of voting arrangements, which, although designed to be broadly fair, had the effect that some 100,000 Walloons were in practice rendered unable to vote for a French-speaking parliamentarian.[18] In effect, the court upheld in these cases linguistic and communal boundaries that in a carefully qualified way constrained internal settlement and helped preserve the status quo on the ground. For similar reasons, autonomy arrangements for particular regions in several states include a power to regulate internal settlement that is secured by constitutional provisions or, more rarely, by international guarantee. For example, restrictions on the right of non-Aaland Islanders to settle in the islands have been adopted under the Constitution of Finland and pursuant to international law arrangements for the autonomous status of the islands established under League of Nations auspices.

Third, the expulsion of the population of a discrete territory within the state to another part of the state is restricted in certain circumstances. The forced easterly resettlement of Crimean Tartars and numerous other groups in the USSR under Stalin, the westward deportation of Cherokee and other groups in the United States under Andrew Jackson, and the massive expulsions in the states of the former Yugoslavia in the 1990s have all been strongly condemned, and in each case some modest ameliorative measures were counseled under subsequent public law regimes.

4. Inheritance

That inheritance is no longer a current concept in the pluralist international law of boundaries is a reflection of the position of states as ontological givens, sharply distinguished from the inter-generational human descent groups with which inheritance is commonly associated. The continuity of states is almost axiomatic in pluralist international law, making clear for example that the Soviet government was legally responsible for unpaid Czarist bonds issued in the name of Russia, that the post-Soviet Russian government was entitled to continue to occupy the seat of the defunct USSR on the UN Security Council, and that boundary treaties between Czarist Russia and Imperial China are presumed to be inherited on both sides.[19] Such legal continuity is a way of organizing inheritance that makes it scarcely noticeable (even less so perhaps than the similar achievement of corporate bodies in national law.) National public law (particularly constitutional law) may limit the state's ability to acquire or shed territory or modify boundaries, in effect maintaining not only the legal but the physical identity of the state intact, and thus protecting or shaping the inheritance of future generations.[20]

If continuity of a single entity makes inheritance invisible, discontinuities raise acute questions. These are addressed by international law provisions for succession between entities whose status the law recognizes, above all state succession. The much-invoked stabilizing principle of *uti possidetis juris* is in part one of state succession with respect to territory and boundaries – it has been repeatedly upheld as against other kinds of justice claims.

Pluralist attempts to circumscribe international law within the confines of official inter-state interactions have not succeeded so comprehensively as to entirely exclude the intervening concepts of "the nation" or "the people."[21] Succession questions thus appear in traditional international law not simply in relation to states, but also in relation to other possible moral claimants to territory, especially peoples. Historically, the territorial extent of many states depended on relationships of persons rather than simple territoriality, and modern international law may have to take account of this history, as with Morocco's attempt to show that nomadic groups in Western Sahara had been within the authority of the Sherifian state.[22] Canada has made comparable use of Inuit history in bolstering its northern claims.

Even apart from this connection with states, a people may function (like a state) as a unit of disguised inheritance. The problem of the legal identity of a people involves the ancient question of whether an entity (the ship of Theseus, or Hume's sock) retains its identity despite every component part's having been replaced over time.[23]

This question has been largely skirted in pluralist and solidarist international law, even though it seems to demand attention as international lawyers grapple with the meaning of "peoples" in the major human rights treaties that provide: "All peoples have the right of self-determination." Questions of group identity over time arise frequently in national public law, however, often in cases involving indigenous peoples. United States federal authorities, for instance, follow a somewhat variable policy: they formally insist that there be clear evidence of continuity from earlier persons to the present claimants when dealing with a claim by Indians to land or to be recognized as an Indian tribe, but incline to find such continuity between past and present where pre-Columbian burial remains are found and returned to the current Indian occupants of the territory. National public law takes on an increasingly internationalized aspect in the growing number of group reparations claims, when pressed to face the question: "Should the modern successors of victims of historical injustice inherit the injustice or a claim against the injustice?" To take one example, French public law has confronted in relation to New Caledonia the question of criteria of eligibility to vote in decisions on the political future of the territory. After an armed conflict in New Caledonia between an indigenous Kanak independence movement and the French authorities supported mainly by settlers, a compromise was reached in the 1988 Matignon accord, under which eligibility to vote in the referendum to be held in 1998 would be restricted to people who lived in the territory in 1988. Kanaks were accorded special rights in determining the future of the territory, although the interests of settlers were also protected, and the arrangements eventually embodied in the Noumea Accord received the support of the UN General Assembly.

5. Voluntary Transfer (Sale and Purchase)

The imagery of sale and purchase suggests that the transfers of Alaska from Russia to the United States or the Chagos from Mauritius to the United Kingdom are comparable to the conveyance of a house. In practice, many of the real problems are public law questions: who has the power to decide on such a transfer, what are the conditions for the valid exercise of this power, what are the consequences of a purported transfer? The notion of cession, involving the transfer and renunciation of rights to exercise public power, more expressly encompasses these public law elements, although in practice the law has not necessarily been an effective constraint on abusive transactions dignified as "cessions."

In situations where a transfer of territory between two existing sovereign states is proposed, public international law encompasses a venerable history of plebiscites,[24] extending from the French Revolutionary wars and the Second Empire through a raft of European reconfigurations under the League of Nations, a few contested cases (especially Tacna-Arica) in Latin America, and an assortment of special situations connected with decolonization since 1945, such as the complex questions as to whether part or all of northern Cameroon should join Nigeria or Cameroon.²⁵ In many such situations, plebiscites have been of value in expressing popular will, shaping emerging politics, or shoring up the legitimacy of contested transactions. One strand of international law thinking holds that plebiscites are required by principles of self-determination and democracy. But a long line of liberal thought, running from Locke and Constant to J.S. Mill, has contested the wisdom of always requiring plebiscites, and international legal practice seems to cleave more to this view. Some of the arguments made against plebiscites are the same as those against plebiscitary democracy; others relate to the higher needs of statecraft, or to the dangers of plebiscites in particular cases. Public law has often followed this strand of argument. Finland gave up its claims to Eastern Karelia, Pesamo, and other parts of its territory to the USSR without plebiscites, seeing no practical alternative and much danger for the locals if they voted no and ended up under Stalin anyhow. British authorities gave no serious thought to holding a plebiscite before transferring Hong Kong to China. This reflected longstanding British hesitancy about self-determination generally, and the lack of democratic institutions in Hong Kong until after 1984, but one factor was concern that a plebiscite would encourage an independence movement that might lead to calamitous confrontation with China.

As these episodes indicate, internationalized public law has been slow to develop process standards, let alone substantive standards, requiring the involvement, protection, or consent of the people of a territory prior to its transfer. Similarly, internationalized public law has not built very fully on the background international law principle that when a transfer of territory between sovereigns occurs, the law of state succession broadly supposes the continuity of private rights, but the transference or termination of public powers. In situations where the transfer will in practice result in the abnegation of private rights, national governments and even some national courts dealing with indigenous peoples or other colonized groups (unlike situations where large corporations of the state might suffer) have often taken the view that little can be done. When Finland under the threat of Soviet demands proposed to transfer the Pesamo area, with its strategic nickel mines, to the USSR in the 1940s, should the Sami who had lived there for many generations have had a say in the decision? Their private rights were certain to be jeopardized by Stalin (other Sami already in that area of Russia were forcibly moved thousands of miles east), and in fact they opted to move to Finland at the time of the transfer. But the question was viewed as one of public law, and at the time they had no public law right to insist on Finland's securing effective guarantees for their future in their ancestral land. British courts similarly were not willing to require very strong assurances of protection for First Nations as a condition of the patriation of the Canadian constitution – the transfer and termination of U.K. public law authority.[26] In establishing conditions for any negotiated transfer of authority from Canada to an independent Quebec, however, Canadian public law may be moving to a requirement of negotiation with the indigenous peoples in the area involved, alongside some possible requirement that the consent of the wider public or their legislative representatives be obtained. This suggests that the development of more robust public law within states may in the future be a promising basis to protect the interests of distinct groups living in territory the transfer of which is proposed.

In certain circumstances, however, internationalized public law imposes potential constraints on the evolution of such public policy – for example, in cases where land is to be restored to a particular group to rectify a historic injustice. In *Gerhardy v. Brown*, a very large tract of land that in Australia had been classified as state land was transferred by legislation to a Pitjantjatjara incorporation comprising Aboriginal people described as the "traditional owners."[27] The majority on the High Court of Australia held that the right of the traditional owners to exclude others from their lands was a public law right, and hence subject to challenge by disgruntled non-Pitjantjatjara under the Racial Discrimination Act. Had this challenge succeeded (it failed because special measures for the advancement of disadvantaged groups are expressly permitted in the Racial Discrimination Act), everyone would have had the same right of access to the land as do the Pitjantjatjara. The court's logic entails treating the boundary of the Pitjantjatjara lands as a public law boundary, and subject therefore to the usual restrictions on state power, rather than as the type of boundary that defines private land under Australian law. A public/private distinction is constructed differently here than in other property cases, with little explanation. The court did not make clear why it did not think the Pitjantjatjara ownership was analogous to the private law situation of a white farmer owning a very large sheep station, beyond a reference to the tract's being 10 percent of the state of South Australia. Passages in the judgement suggest the court was worried about the entrenchment of apartheid, and anxious to assert the kind of judicial power over public law necessary to ensure that something akin to the South African Group Areas Act could not be upheld in Australia. While the court's holding that returning Pitjantjatjara land to Pitjantjatjara was prima facie discrimination seems misplaced here, internationalized public law policies of human rights and equality in harder cases do potentially conflict with the internationalized public law logic of group-based claims.

6. Conquest

As Andrew Hurrell points out, the internationalist ethic against conquest as a means for establishing title to territory has underpinned a regime of legal prohibition that may have fostered both hazardous surrogate devices for control and unrealistic attempts to evade legal recognition of change that has already happened on the ground. Comparable problems arise when the legal implications of conquest are considered in the public law of the conqueror. The conqueror may erect internal boundaries in the expanded realm, so that the new subjects do not become full citizens. This was the approach finally adopted by the United States Supreme Court in the Insular cases, holding (as pro-imperialists hoped it would) that the guarantees of the U.S. Constitution need not necessarily apply in territories acquired after the victorious war with Spain in 1898.[28] More fundamentally, if conquest itself is no longer thought to be a sufficient basis of legitimacy, the conqueror's courts confront the problem of the validity of public law and the authority of the courts themselves. The U.S. Supreme Court in the era of Chief Justice Marshall faced this problem. In a series of decisions in the 1820s and 1830s dealing with the legal rights of Indian tribes, he sought to craft an approach under U.S. law that made some sense of prevailing international or natural law ideas on title to territory, colonization, and indigenous entitlements. Unsurprisingly, he held that the conqueror's title is not open to challenge in the conqueror's courts, and he sought to protect the wider interests of the settler states and their Union. But he concocted an ameliorative doctrine under which Indian groups existed as "domestic dependent nations," with a set of legal competencies, especially within the boundaries of the reservation, that is often termed residual sovereignty. Aspects of this jurisprudence have been influential in other states, and in international law. In *Mabo*,[29] the High Court of Australia faced at the beginning of the 1990s the failure of the public law system earlier to grapple with the conundrums that had occupied Chief Justice Marshall. Both imperium and dominium in Australia rested on the extraordinary theory that Australia was a land belonging to no one until the Europeans arrived. While refusing to put Australian sovereignty into question, the High Court concluded both that developments in international law made it almost impossible to persist with this orthodoxy with regard to land rights, and that international law militated strongly against a public law that violated the fundamental rights of Aboriginal people to equality. Its decision led to a general process under which Aboriginal people could obtain recognition of "native title" to particular lands, erecting new, if porous, boundaries that public law had not hitherto recognized.

7. Secession

Andrew Hurrell's chapter (14) implies that international law cannot be an ideal ethical system – that its universalism and engagement with practice necessarily channel its ethical possibilities. He draws attention to the interdependence of theory and practice in current legal policy on secession, arguing that any generally-applicable criteria for lawful secession that international law might establish would become self-fulfilling. This is also a case in which the very abstract ethical principles that might be called universal are too limited to establish criteria for justified secession, leaving international law either to embrace particularist ethics for specific situations – a dangerous strategy that most prefer to eschew – or to fall back on agreed political values of order and stability.

As might be expected, national public law has historically been hostile to claims of secessionists within the state's territory. Yet there are glimmers of change. In the final stages of its dissolution, the Soviet Union adopted a law defining conditions for secession of Union Republics from the USSR, requiring the approval of the populace of the secessionist entity in two referenda held five years apart. More recently, the Supreme Court of Canada has defined conditions under which the secession of Quebec from Canada might take place. This is a graphic example of the phenomenon of internationalized public law: an opinion given by a national court referring primarily to its assessment of fundamental principles of Canadian constitutionalism, but informed in its assessment of these principles by trends it expressly discerned in international law, in turn has an effect on international law and on public law in other states.[30]

8. Conclusion

The pluralist/solidarist/transnationalist trifurcation honed by the English school of international relations theorists provides a useful basis for understanding the international law tradition with regard to boundaries, as Andrew Hurrell has convincingly shown. But other, cross-cutting ways of examining relevant legal materials bring into focus important elements that are blurred or neglected in this trifurcated analysis. I have sought in this chapter to bring into focus some neglected aspects of the legal relationships between people and boundaries by developing an internationalized public law approach. Many other approaches also find significant support within the broad tradition of international law. This chapter is thus representative of a widely-felt caution within the discipline about totalization and certitude with regard to the relationship of international law and ethics in many areas of practical activity. This caution is not so much a function of ethical ambivalence, or agnosticism, or pragmatism, as it is an inherent characteristic of a discipline that is defined by the ceaseless, if uneasy, integration of universal and particular, international and national, norms and power, and above all, theory and practice.

Notes to Chapter 15

1. The research assistance of Stephen Ostrowski, the comments of Andrew Hurrell, and the support of the Filomen D'Agostino and Max E. Greenberg

Research Fund at New York University Law School are all gratefully acknowledged.

2. See the Vienna Convention on the Law of Treaties 1969, Article 62.

3. Hedley Bull, "The Grotian Conception of International Society," in Herbert Butterfield and Martin Wight, eds., *Diplomatic Investigations* (London: Allen and Unwin, 1966).

4. Temple of Preah Vihear (Thailand v. Cambodia), 1962 International Court of Justice, Rep. 6; Frontier Dispute (Burkina Faso/Mali), 1986 International Court of Justice, Rep. 554; Land, Island and Maritime Frontier Dispute (El Salvador/Honduras, Nicaragua Intervening), 1992 International Court of Justice, Rep. 351; Territorial Dispute (Chad/Libya), 1994 International Court of Justice, Rep. 6.

5. Rann of Kutch (India/Pakistan) (1968), 50 ILR 2; Dubai/Sharjah Border Arbitration (1981), 91 ILR 543; Taba (Egypt/Israel) (1988), 80 ILR 244.

6. Hedley Bull, "International Law and International Order," *International Organization* (1972), 583–88.

7. On this category, see Hedley Bull, "International Relations as an Academic Pursuit," *Australian Outlook* 26/3, (1972) [reprinted in Kai Alderson and Andrew Hurrell, eds., *Hedley Bull on International Society* (Basingstoke, U.K.: Macmillan, 2000), 246–64].

8. A different meaning of internationalized public law refers to the complex set of principles and rules of public law, with multiple formal sources including analogies from national law, that apply to the operational activities of international institutions, but I will not consider this here as it not as important in relation to boundaries as it is on other issues.

9. Charles de Visscher, *Theory and Reality of Public International Law*, 2nd ed. (Princeton: Princeton University Press, 1968), 209.

10. A. Oye Cukwurah, *The Settlement of Boundary Disputes in International Law* (Manchester: Manchester University Press, 1967).

11. See Richard Tuck, *The Rights of War and Peace: Political Thought and International Order from Grotius to Kant* (Oxford: Oxford University Press, 1999); and the chapters by Richard Tuck (8) and Anthony Pagden (6) in this volume.

12. See Laurence Whitehead's contribution to Leslie Bethell, ed., *Latin America Since 1930: Economy, Science, Politics*, vol. 6 (Cambridge: Cambridge University Press, 1994).

13. Barbara Arneil, *John Locke and America: The Defence of English Colonialism* (Oxford: Oxford University Press, 1996).

14. See generally Article 12 of the International Covenant on Civil and Political Rights, and the Human Rights Committee's General Comment on this; Brian Barry and Robert Goodin, eds., *Free Movement: Ethical Issues in the Transnational Migration of People and Money* (London: Harvester, 1992); Henry Schermers, ed., *Free Movement of Persons in Europe: Legal Problems and Experiences* (Dordrecht: Nijhoff, 1993).

15. Dorothy Solinger, "Human Rights Issues in China's Internal Migration: Insights from Comparisons with Germany and Japan," in Joanne Bauer and Daniel Bell, eds., *The East Asian Challenge for Human Rights* (Cambridge: Cambridge University Press, 1999), 285–312.

16. Materials on the China Western Poverty Reduction Project appear on the Internet at www.worldbank.org.

17. See *Belgian Linguistic* case, European Court of Human Rights (1968), 1 EHRR 252.

18. See *Mathieu-Mohin and Clerfayt v. Belgium,* European Court of Human Rights (1987), 10 EHRR 1.

19. The weight of state continuity is evident in the acceptance by the People's Republic of China of nineteenth century "unequal treaties" as the basis for modern negotiations on demarcation of frontiers. China was dissatisfied with the ethics of this, even while accepting it in practice, and insisted on the inclusion in post-1949 boundary agreements of a statement that the earlier treaties had been unjust.

20. The U.S. Constitution provides in Article IV, section 3, that Congress (and, it is usually held, *only* Congress) has the power to dispose of United States territory. This provision was invoked in the 1790s to challenge the authority of the President and Senate to conclude the provisions of the Jay Treaty with Britain dealing with boundary issues.

21. Lassa Oppenheim conceded as much in his *International Law* (London: Longmans, 1905), commenting with some regret that the principle of nationalities had so much political vitality that international law could not disregard it.

22. See also Michael Reisman's discussion of the El Salvador-Honduras case in his "Protecting Indigenous Rights in International Adjudication," *American Journal of International Law* 89 (1995), 350–62.

23. Hugo Grotius framed the question in this way in his *De Jure Belli ac Pacis* (1625), Book II, Chapter 9.

24. Anne Peters, *Das Gebietsreferendum im Völkerrecht: seine Bedeutung im Licht der Staatenpraxis nach 1989* (Baden-Baden: Nomos, 1995); Sarah Wambaugh, *The Doctrine of National Self-Determination: A Monograph on Plebiscites* (New York: Oxford University Press, 1920); Sarah Wambaugh, *Plebiscites Since the World War,* 2 volumes, (Washington: Carnegie Endowment for International Peace,1933).

25. This discussion leaves aside the cases of territories likely to choose independence, where a plebiscite or at least a post-independence popular ratification is almost universal practice as a basis for the legitimacy of the new state.

26. *Indian Association of Alberta v. Secretary of State for Foreign Affairs,* (1982) 2 WLR 641.

27. High Court of Australia, (1985) 57 ALR 472.

28. The line of cases runs from *DeLima v. Bidwell* (1901), 182 US 1, to *Balzac v. Porto Rico* (1922), 288 US 298.

29. *Mabo v. Queensland* (No. 2), (1992) 175 CLR 1.

30. See the use of the Supreme Court of Canada's opinion in an argument about the position of Taiwan, in Jonathan I. Charney and J. R. V. Prescott, "Resolving Cross-Strait Relations Between China and Taiwan," *American Journal of International Law* 94 (2000), 453–77.

16

Conclusion and Overview

Margaret Moore

The unique insight of this volume is that regardless of whether boundaries are viewed as mere administrative conveniences or as having some intrinsic moral value in our non-ideal world of sovereign, bounded political jurisdictions, people have had to consider the appropriateness of the methods by which boundaries are made or unmade.

This comparative overview is designed to facilitate this comparison by focusing on the typology of boundary-alteration – conquest, settlement, sales/purchase, inheritance, and secession – rather than the principles of each of the traditions.

1. Conquest

Conquest, in the sense of the forcible annexation and incorporation of territory that is already within the geographical jurisdiction of another state, is viewed by most of the traditions in this volume as a wholly unacceptable means of acquiring territory. However, many of these same traditions, particularly those with a religious basis, accept the legitimacy of territory conquered in a just war (variously defined). The two modern ethical traditions – liberal theory and international law – also condemn conquest as a means of altering territory, and have strongly resisted it, when it has occurred in clear-cut cases. However, beyond the clear-cut cases, international law, and especially liberal theory, have been prepared to countenance external intervention in the affairs of another state, although supporters of the intervention would never describe it as a "conquest."

The approach to conquest taken in Jewish political and ethical thought is both complicated and contested. One interpretation of the Jewish tradition (Lorberbaum's Chapter 2) focusses on the certain piece of land or territory that is defined in the Bible as the land to which the Jewish people are entitled, as part of a covenant between God and the His People. Lorberbaum argues that the covenant is central to the legitimacy of Joshua's conquest of this

317

land. He also notes that there is a second discourse in the Bible, which places Joshua's conquest in the context of a crusade against idolatry. The two discourses press in somewhat different directions, since the first implies that the promise of the land to the Israelites justifies the conquest and is the necessary precondition for the legitimacy of the possession, while the second suggests a different ground for legitimizing the conquest.

A rival interpretation (Statman's Chapter 3) argues that God's covenant with the Jewish people is not important to the issue of the legitimacy of the conquest: it is the conquest itself that establishes legitimate possession. On this view, the central question is the morality of the war in which the land was acquired (for example, was it a defensive war?). According to this view, it is the conquest of the territory that fixes the political boundaries, and this in turn fixes the sacred boundaries in the sense that the laws of God are upheld within the territory in which the Israelites live.

The other religious-based approaches also tend to be critical of state aggrandizement for its own sake, but view it as justified when territory is acquired in a just war. Confucianism, for example, is critical of rulers who seek to launch wars of conquest to expand their territory, but argue that conquest can be legitimate, and territory acquired through conquest legitimately held. According to Confucianism, a war is just only if the aim of the war is to secure peace, and the war is waged under the following conditions: (1) the conquered people are liberated from tyranny; (2) the people welcome their conquerors; and (3) the war is relatively clean, and stands a good chance of success.

The two main proselytizing monotheistic religions – Christianity and Islam – were historically quite prepared to attack and conquer infidels, and this was entirely consistent with their view that conquest was unacceptable unless the territory was acquired in a just war. The Islamic tradition defined a war as just – as consistent with *jihad* – if the conquest was in order to expand the territory in which Islamic law prevailed, but not if the primary purpose of the conquest was simple territorial gain. This meant that there was a general acceptance, indeed encouragement of, conquest for the purpose of extending the Islamic *umma*, but not conquest directed against fellow Muslim territories. There is now, however, very little expansionist connotation connected to the term *jihad*, which is now primarily directed to the defence of existing Muslim communities from aggression. Both the Christian and the Islamic traditions now share the prevailing view in international law that military conquest is illegal. Interestingly, this far more negative view of conquest seems to coincide with the loss of Muslim territory (especially in Palestine) through conquest.

The Christian and natural law traditions both accepted a "just war" doctrine, developed from the Roman period through the work of Cicero, Augustine, and Vitoria. The main component of the just war doctrine is that war is legitimate if it is defensive in nature, or if it is in pursuit of compensation for an alleged act of aggression. Historically, conquest was quite rare among the rulers of medieval Christian Europe, although they were quite prepared to attack and conquer non-Christians. Wars against infidels (non-Christians) were common, and were justified by the constraints outlined initially in Book 3 of Cicero's *De Republica,* which described as legitimate those wars waged "in defence of faith." War "in defense of faith" did not justify wars waged against principalities where the current prince was not a good Christian, but was mainly interpreted to mean that a Christian prince could go to war to defend the Christian *civita,* and it was easy to argue that infidels constituted just such a threat.Moreover, while infidels could not be punished for their disbelief in the tenets of Christianity, they sometimes engaged in practices that Christians viewed as contrary to God's laws, which was viewed as a legitimate concern of Christians.

Within Europe, full conquest and annexation of the territory of another was quite rare in the Middle Ages. As Tuck argues in his chapter (8), the conquest of England by Normandy in 1066 was quite unusual, and even then William had a plausible title to the throne, and undertook to maintain the laws and customs of England separate from those of Normandy. This was so, even though it was widely believed at that time that conquest in a just war gave the conqueror the power to reconstruct the conquered territory as he saw fit.

There was also some debate about whether it might be legitimate to engage in war "on account of the personal tyranny of the barbarians' masters towards their subjects." This defence, most famously put forward by Vitoria, suggests that a just war might be extended beyond a defensive war to involve a conception of humanitarian war. Such a conception needed to specify what constitutes an "offence against the innocent" – Vitoria put forward this idea in the context of allegations of human sacrifice and cannibalism among natives in the Americas. Logically, this defence would seem to require an express request to the external power to intervene by a legally recognized representative body of the state, or, at the minimum, a version of the principle employed in Confucianism that the new legal and political authority would have to be welcomed by the people. Unfortunately, those who put forward this defence did not develop the implications of this position.

The two modern political and legal theories – liberalism and international law – oppose conquest as a means of acquiring territory, and, in clear-cut cases, have vigorously resisted it. Conquest of the territory of another state is illegal under international law, and all recent clear-cut attempts at conquest have been met by the international community by a reassertion of the unacceptability of conquest. In Kuwait, the Malvinas/Falkland Islands, and in Bosnia-Herzegovina, the UN has tried to deny all legal effects of the illegal use of force.[1]

However, in cases where there is factual or legal unclarity, intervention (never called conquest by its perpetrators) may be justified on international law principles. Hurrell (Chapter 14) argues that it would not have been wholly implausible for the international community to accede to the break-up of Iraq as a means of punishing the aggressor in a just war. This view is, after all , consistent with most Christian and natural law thinking on the subject, and the West, which was influenced by this line of thinking, was the leading protagonist in the war. Intervention is also thinkable in cases of civil wars, where there is a clear breakdown in governmental authority, for this helps to redefine outside intervention not as a conquest but as humanitarian intervention – necessary to get aid to those in need and/or to assist a political settlement. It is also implicit in this justification that the outside intervener cannot remain on the territory once the humanitarian crisis is over, or a political settlement is achieved. In some cases, the international law stricture against the forcible seizure of territory, and the defense of the territorial integrity of states, has meant that the international community has been engaged in unrealistic attempts to evade the issue of legal recognition, and to ignore what is happening on the ground. This is true of the UN safe areas, which aim to protect groups on a territorial basis, but to evade the issue of legal title to the territory.

Liberalism, too, clearly opposes any attempt to change boundaries or to acquire territory through conquest, but has been willing to countenance external intervention in defence of liberal principles or in situations of un-clear or ineffective governmental authority. One reason why liberal theory is hostile to the idea of conquest is that conquest by its very nature violates the rights of sovereignty of that state whose territory is invaded – a point of particular concern in international law – but also relevant to liberal theory, insofar as liberalism places great value on due process and the rule of law. In addition, conquest constitutes a violation of the rights of individual citizens of the state against whom force is used. Liberal theory is primarily a theory about the appropriate line between individual autonomy and state action, which it seeks to draw in a way that will protect individual freedom. Unsur-prisingly, coercion is not viewed positively, and cannot be justified simply to acquire more territory.[2]

While it is difficult to justify conquest using liberal principles, it is impor-tant to distinguish between theory and practice, especially when principles are being appealed to in a non-ideal world. In practice, liberals have his-torically used something resembling conquest in the building of empires by liberal states. As Miller argues, this was not conquest in the clear, inter-national law sense of one state attempting to take over the territory of an-other state by force. It more typically involved the creation of forms of polit-ical authority where no such authority existed, or where political authority was either deficient or extremely weak. John Stuart Mill, probably the most famous liberal thinker, presented liberal imperialism as necessary to bring about net improvements in the lives of those people who were currently living under barbaric regimes, and as a stepping-stone to full liberal rights and representative government, which were not yet possible in these areas, given the stage of culture and political development of these communities. Contemporary liberals rarely speak in these ways nowadays, but it is important to note that liberal imperialism was a central plank in the European empires, and is still implied in some of the current literature on group rights, particularly as that discusses the appropriate balance to be struck between the protection of liberal-democratic values and the value of collective self-government.[3] The clear implication of this literature is the same as the nineteenth-century literature justifying liberal imperialism: that sometimes a benign liberal external government is preferable to an illiberal government established by the subjected people themselves.

2. Settlement

Settlement was one of the primary methods by which European civilizations achieved control over the Americas, Australia, and New Zealand, and was commonly justified, either in terms quite specific to settlement or in terms of bringing a true religion or superior culture to the native inhabitants. It has been a central plank in achieving the Zionist quest for a national homeland for Jews. And, in the course of history, many different peoples, with different cultures and different traditions, moved and settled in different places, sometimes displacing the current inhabitants, sometimes mixing with them, and sometimes at their invitation.

The word "settlement" is nowadays typically used as a derogatory term. The Jewish settlements west of the Jordan river are usually referred to in the context of being a primary obstacle to peace in the region, as well as viewed as immoral, in and of themselves.[4] The conquest and settlement of the Americas, which occurred with such devastating cost to the indigenous inhabitants, is generally regarded as a moral blot on the history of these societies. This is partly because the justificatory arguments employed, especially those based on the superior culture or religion of the settlers, or the idea that there were no significant aboriginal populations, are no longer taken seriously, but also because it is clear that the settlement was enormously destructive to the indigenous communities.

This examination of the normative basis of settlement does not question the contemporary view that settlement is generally immoral, and has caused grave hardship to the indigenous inhabitants of areas settled by rival cultures and traditions. But I will examine the kinds of distinctions and justifications proffered by the ethical traditions explored in this book, in order to determine if, and under what conditions, settlement is justified.

Many of the ethical traditions discussed in this volume justify settlement under specific, carefully circumscribed conditions, which can be explored fruitfully through distinguishing between two distinct senses of "settlement." One sense of the term "settlement" is the idea that humans should be able to live in or travel in an area, or, in stronger language, have a natural right to travel and live in an area, as long as they conform to the existing political authority. The second question is whether a group of people can move, wholesale, to another territory, and try to reproduce their culture and institutions, including their political institutions, in land occupied by another group. The two kinds of settlement are obviously connected in that, if enough individuals move into an area, they will have the demographic strength and institutional capacity to reproduce their cultural institutions.

Justificatory arguments in favor of "settlement" in the first sense are quite common, especially if the settlement occurs on land not currently occupied. It was commonly assumed, in the Islamic tradition, that vacant land could be claimed by the Islamic state and distributed in any manner deemed appropriate or in the interests of the state. Both the natural law and Christian traditions appealed to an ancient customary principle of hospitality, and extended it to argue that people have a general right to travel freely and seek sustenance from the land. A prominent Catholic thinker, Vitoria, argued: "In the beginning of the world, when all things were held in common, everyone was allowed to visit and travel through any land he wished. This right was clearly not taken away by the division of property; it was never the intention of nations to prevent men's free mutual intercourse with one another by its division."[5] The right of individuals to settle was viewed as an extension of a right to travel and seek sustenance from the earth. This extension is clearly made when Vitoria argues that the French cannot lawfully "prevent the Spaniards from travelling to or even living in France and vice versa."[6]

None of the traditions explored in this volume see any problem with settling on waste land or vacant land. The natural law tradition, and subsequently the liberal tradition that developed out of it, thought that vacant land could and should be appropriated by individuals to become individual private property holdings. The Catholic theorists, too, accepted the principle that unoccupied land (*terra nullius*) became the possession of whoever first occupied it. They also tended to distinguish between public jurisdictional authority and private ownership. This meant that the appropriation of small plots of land should be regulated by the local public authority, or the local sovereign. If a whole land is unoccupied, either by individuals and by any governing authority, settlement would indeed confer entitlement to the land. This follows from the Roman law of presumption, which suggested that the de facto occupation of a thing could, over time, confer retrospective rights to it. This is relevant to the issue of settlement, since it suggests that people settled in an area have more rights, greater entitlement, to that land, both in the sense of private property and in the sense of jurisdictional territory, than any other group.

Another line of argument – implicit in the Jewish, Christian, and Islamic traditions – viewed the legitimacy of settlement as derivative on a prior conception of justice or of legitimate rule. This pattern of argument is clearest in the Jewish tradition, which endorses settlement as a legitimate practice, although it is not the settlement of the land that confers entitlement to it. The principal normative justification in the Bible for settlement occurs at Numbers 33:53, when God grants land to the Patriarch Abraham and urges him to settle the land. The verse reads: "And you shall take possession of the land and settle in it, for I have assigned the land to you to possess (my italics)." This formulation makes it clear that settlement is sometimes legitimate, but it does not give settlement a foundational normative role, in the sense that it does not seem that the fact of settlement confers entitlement to the land: the entitlement follows from the fact that God explicitly granted the land to the Israelites.

The Confucian tradition also tended to regard the legitimacy of the political or jurisdictional authority as central to the question of settlement. Accordingly, Confucius argued that common people may choose to leave their homelands if they are governed tyrannically. It is assumed that people will tend to gravitate towards more just, better run states. This line of argument considers the issue of individuals settling on land, but not the issue of settling in areas where there is no jurisdictional authority whatsoever. This is probably because in the Confucian world order of rival, jurisdictionally equal political powers, the issue of land untilled or unclaimed by any person or political authority was of purely theoretical significance. Nevertheless, this formulation seems to suggest that people can settle on waste land, or otherwise acquire land by just procedures, and so live out their lives in peace, and in conformity with Confucian principles.

Of course, in many cases, the view of settlement depended on whether the exponents of the particular tradition were imagining their members settling on other people's land, or other people settling on their lands. The Christian doctrine applied initially to Christians wandering throughout Europe, which was conceived, at least prior to the Reformation, as all part of Christendom, and did not seem to apply, with any kind of force, to non-Christians travelling freely within Christian Europe. When asked whether proselytizing non-Christians could be accepted in Christian lands, since Christians were sending missionaries to non-Christian lands, Pope Innocent IV argued that of course the reverse did not hold, "because they are in error and we are on the righteous path."[7] One suspects that the same lack of reciprocity would have characterized the Christian acceptance of large settlements of non-Christians within Christian Europe, especially given the periodic attempts to drive Muslims from Spain and south-east Europe, and the expulsion of Jews from Spain and periodic persecution and expulsion in other parts of Europe.

The Confucian view, too, applies to those who accept fundamental Confucian values: the question of resettlement arises when people live under an oppressive and unjust ruler (defined in Confucian terms) and seek to leave that area of rule and live in accordance with Confucian values. It is not clear that the Confucian doctrine would apply to those who seek to live in accordance with some other values or doctrines .

In the Jewish case, settlement was viewed as legitimate for Jews, because it was in accordance with God's will, but the question of whether other peoples could settle in the Land of Israel was far more problematic, first, because this was obviously not in accordance with the will of God, and second, because the people, by their practices, would not treat the land in a holy fashion. The uneven treatment of the two situations was evident in the intense debate, discussed by Lorberbaum, over whether Jews should be permitted to sell land to gentiles.

In the case of all these ethical theories, there are some striking commonalities: waste land, is relatively unproblematic. This is especially true of land that is bereft, not only of people but also political authority (surely, a rare case), but also not particularly problematic if the local rulers permit settlement, and there was a sense, at least amongst natural law theorists, Confucians, and Catholic Christians that they should.

What about land that is already occupied? This much more common case posed many more difficulties, and raised the question of whether settlement in this context can be justified, and what the terms of the relationship should be between settlers and the indigenous population.

In its early years, the Islamic tradition regarded settlement of frontier regions – termed "relocation" in Hashmi's Chapter 10 – as a duty. Muslims had an obligation to ensure that the land remained part of dar-al-Islam, and that the people were part of the Muslim community, or *umma*. There was also a practical side to this policy: land was distributed as war booty to those who had risked their life in the *jihad*, and this had the additional function of providing (individual self-interest) motivation for soldiers. However, over time, Muslim scholars began to distinguish between aggressive non-Muslims who were oppressive to Muslims, and who may justifiably be removed from the territory, and those non-Muslims who were not acting in oppressive ways. This distinction was deployed to suggest that wholesale confiscation of the land and resettlement would not be in accordance with justice. Confiscation and subsequent resettlement was only justified against those non-Muslims who engaged in unjust, oppressive, and aggressive practices. In line with this, it became commonplace to permit the local peasantry, who lacked the power or means to oppress anyone, to remain on their land, in return for payment of a land tax.

Both Christian and natural law theorists tended to view the world as divided into independent and jurisdictionally equal states. Settlement required the consent of the local sovereign power. But there remained the question of whether this principle applied with equal force to the New World. Locke had an argument, discussed by Tuck (Chapter 8) and Finnis (Chapter 9), and by Buchanan in Chapter 12 (because Locke is also a foundational theorist in the liberal tradition), to the effect that the American natives did not possess territorial rights. Only settled agriculture can establish property rights, and only property gives rise to territorial jurisdiction. (This argument is flawed in a number of ways, as Buchanan points out in his chapter, not least because it reverses the real order: jurisdictional authority is necessary to establish property rights, in contrast to mere possession.)

This meant that in the case of the New World, natives could not be said to be occupying the land in the relevant sense, so that land could be treated as unoccupied or waste land. In that context, settlement is justified, even against the wishes of the local population, because the native people were unjustifiably trying to prevent the productive use of land that was going to waste anyway.

The Christian view of settlement was somewhat different, since Christians accepted the view that first occupancy conferred entitlement, and were more receptive to the view that indigenous people were rightful owners of the land. However, the papal donation argument – which establish the jurisdictional authority of the Spanish and Portuguese crowns over large parts of the New World – meant that the European monarchies had public dominium over these areas, and it was entirely within their purview to treat natives in ways similar to the those of European descent. This conceptual framework did not distinguish between settlers and natives, or see any particular problem in the relations between the two, since both those of native and European origin were viewed as legitimate subjects of the Spanish (or Portuguese) crowns. The injustice of settler appropriation of the land and the displacement of indigenous population disappeared on this conceptual framework – although it could never disappear entirely, since it was in clear tension with the idea that first occupancy generates entitlements.

Settlement, as this survey has indicated, is rarely a straightforward, benign process of 'settling a people without land on a land without people,'[8] but typically involves either the removal or "swamping" of the indigenous population by the settlers, who are acting either individually, or as agents of state-directed policy.[9] This suggests that international law, at least in so far as it institutionalizes norms, should have a great deal to say about the terms and conditions under which settlement can justifiably take place. In fact, international law employs a number of distinctions relevant to the legitimacy of settlement policies, but many of these are only indirectly related to the harm caused by the policy, and are more closely dictated by the status of the actors in international law.

On the one hand, one of the dominant norms of international law is the principle of national self-determination, both in the period following the First World War and then, in a somewhat altered form, in the decolonization period. Implicit in this appeal to the democratic will of the people living in the disputed area is the view that patterns of settlement are relevant to the making of boundaries. One of the methods for resolving disputes over borders and border zones, especially in the post-First World War period, was through determining the preferences of those who are settled in the disputed region. Plebiscites were held in the disputed areas in Carinthia (1920), and Saarland (1935 and again in 1955) to determine which states these areas should be part of.[10] This seems to indicate that patterns of settlement, and the preferences of the people ensconced in these areas, should be regarded as an important moral basis for carving out state boundaries, although it does not address the question of which settlement policies are legitimate, according to international law.

One obvious problem with policies such as this is that it raises the possibility of creating perverse incentives. If demographic facts "on the ground" are relevant to the creation of boundaries, then one way in which groups can help to create or force boundary change in their favor is through attempting to change the demographic "facts on the ground." This charge was, of course, raised during the course of the Bosnian war, although that example is complicated by the fact that a principal method for achieving the desired boundary changes seemed also to be military force. A clearer example of an attempt to alter demographic facts through settlement policies, and to do so prior to the holding of a UN-supervised referendum on the issue, is the Green March of an estimated 350,000 unarmed Moroccan "settlers" into the Western Sahara. This served to dilute the claims of the nomadic groups in the area, and so consolidate Moroccan control over the area. It also helped to de-legitimize the proposed UN referendum on the question by raising the thorny problem of who should be able to vote in the proposed referendum deciding the fate of the Western Sahara.

Indeed, to the extent that international law considers as relevant the de facto possession of political power, it provides an incentive for political authorities to engage in settlement policies, because this is an effective way for a state to demonstrate control of a territory, and consolidate its authority. In his chapter (15), Kingsbury outlines the transformation of countries like Brazil and Bolivia from a series of islands of authority into encompassing territorial states through the strategic settlement of Europeans or Europeanized Brazilians and Bolivars in the country. Similarly, Israeli settlement policies in the West Bank can also be seen as a response to the internal security-driven needs of the Israeli state and an attempt to consolidate its control over the occupied territory. It is, however, clearly impermissible under international law, because the territory that is being settled by Jews is under military occupation, as defined by international law.

On the other hand, while historically it has been a central tenet of international law to regard states as the principal actor in international law, and settlement policies within states as a purely internal matter, there has been a changing focus in favor of the defence of human rights, and an increased willingness to contemplate intervention for humanitarian reasons or in defence of certain moral norms. Instances of forced deportation and "internal" settlement are extremely numerous: from the westward deportation of the

Cherokees under U.S. President Jackson to the deportation of the Chechens, Kalmyks, Volga Germans, Crimean Tatars, and other minorities under Stalin in the former Soviet Union.[11] Although these were all in violation of standard liberal principles, and did invoke some condemnation in international circles, it was also clear that these actions were within the sovereign jurisdiction of the state in question. More recently, policies of ethnic cleansing or forced deportation targeted at a particular ethnic group in Bosnia and in Kosovo has led to NATO intervention there, aimed at altering the balance of power (in Bosnia), or to enable the displaced Kosovars to return to their homes.

While these interventions suggest that the role of morality in international affairs cannot be ignored, they have, as Hurrell writes in his chapter (14), relied to an uncomfortable extent on the support of the United States. Moreover, the institutions of the international community are not organized to play this kind of role – in both Bosnia and Kosovo, NATO's military intervention was in violation of international law. It is hard to see how that could have been different, because the Security Council, whose members exercise a veto over any UN-authorized intervention, includes countries with dubious records on human rights and the illiberal treatment of their own minorities.

Further, the Westphalian view of international law as establishing the minimum rules by which sovereign states can regulate their interaction and the internal policies of the state as entirely within their sovereign authority is not only historically fundamental to the inter-state system, but is still a dominant norm today. It might be increasingly subject to criticism, and occasional violations, as in Kosovo or Bosnia, but it is upheld when the human rights violator is a major political actor. The West, or the international community as a whole, might be prepared to force the Baltic states (Latvia, Lithuania, Estonia) to treat its Russian settlers fairly, and extend citizenship to them, but is less willing to force Russia to behave appropriately with regard to Chechnya or force China to respect the human collective rights of its Tibetan or Mongolian minorities.

Moreover, the fact of jurisdictional control enables the state to act in ways that do not distinguish appropriately between groups of citizens within the state. As with the Christian justification of settlement in the New World, which appealed to the idea of appropriate jurisdictional authority, so current norms in international law view it as acceptable that rules are made in the public domain, and these rules should apply equally to all those subject to it. The question of the differential impact of policies on the different cultural or identity groups in the population is hidden from view. The international community may be moved to action in the context of gross violations of human rights on the part of a small political actor in the south east of Europe, but settlement policies can also proceed with less flagrant violations of human rights and in areas where the international community either has less clout, or is not willing to exercise it. Various internal settlement policies, involving economic development, housing permits, and a wide range of policies with the purported aim of leading to the advancement of the Chinese population as a whole, has had the effect of leading to the massive influx of Han Chinese into areas previously populated by the indigenous Tibetan, Uighur, or Mongolian groups.[12] These policies, as well as gerrymandering of political districts, are designed to lead to the displacement of the local inhabitants, and their swamping by the demographically more numerous Han Chinese. The current empowering of the state authority, and the derivation of its jurisdictional authority, makes it difficult, conceptually, to distinguish between groups within the state, and to condemn general policies of economic development simply on the grounds that they are unwanted by minority cultural groups.

3. Sales/Purchase and   4. Inheritance

Most of the ethical traditions surveyed in this volume do not deal directly with the issue of the sale or purchase of territory. This is because they distinguish between public jurisdictional authority and private property.

The voluntary alienation of private property by either selling it or bequeathing it to another is generally accepted by most ethical traditions. Of course, most communities had certain restrictions on the autonomy of the owner, who was somewhat constrained by the moral vision of the community. The Islamic tradition, for example, permitted inheritance, but there was a rule, stemming from basic social justice concerns, that the wealth should be as widely distributed as possible to the heirs. The Jewish tradition also viewed sales and inheritance as legitimate modes for the transfer of private property, although there were important constraints: Jews were not allowed to sell houses and fields in the land of Israel to non-Jews, although, as Statman points out in Chapter 3, this prohibition is not absolute.

Territory, unlike property, is the land on which a community dwells, and it is not clear that it can be transferred as a commodity, since it is constitutive of the community's identity, and the community does not properly "own" it. Rather, territory refers to the area or domain of jurisdictional authority of a ruler (in monarchical systems) or of the people who are conceived of as sovereign (in democratic systems). Private property and territory are not analogous because private property can be acquired through rules, which are established by the appropriate governing authority, whereas territory refers to the area in which the rules apply.

There are two exceptions to this general tendency to distinguish between the two: Confucianism and the natural law tradition. Confucianism, like the other traditions, permitted the buying and selling of land in the sense of private property, but, unlike many of the other ethical traditions, did not explicitly distinguish between land and territory. This suggest that sale may be a legitimate mode to transfer territory. However, there are three basic principles constraining the sale (and bequest) of territory, and, because they are primarily political in nature, they do point to an implicit distinction between the treatment of land and territory. The constraining principles are that any sale (or inheritance) must promote (1) peace, (2) unity, and (3) virtuous rule.

The constraint that any sale of territory must promote unity makes it difficult to imagine cases where sale would be justified – especially if the baseline by which unity is measured is the state prior to the selling off of one of its bits. In fact, the Confucian state in Imperial China did not engage in the selling of territory, and the apparent counter-example (Hong Kong) was not really transferred to Britain by way of free exchange, but, as Bell points out in his Chapter, was part of the price that China had to pay Britain following its loss of the Opium War. The subsequent lease of the New Territories in 1894–95 also followed from its defeat by Japan, and was never regarded by the Chinese government, or Chinese popular opinion, as a voluntary exchange, but as a source of humiliation.

The natural law tradition is somewhat unique in that it has a long practice, and a theoretical justificatory argument underlying the practice, of permitting the sale and purchase of territory. Catholic countries did enter into treaties or leased territory in non-Christian lands: the Portuguese, for example, leased, or acquired through treaty with native rulers, territory in Asia and coastal west Africa, as did the French in North America. However, these practices were not supported by much justificatory argument, or debate, and both Tuck (8) and Pagden (6) argue in their chapters that these practices were essentially borrowed from the English and the Dutch. The natural law tradition, which was expressed clearly in both English and Dutch political practice, viewed sales primarily as a means to eliminate the presence of any indigenous inhabitants. By purchasing the land (not the persons) and by ensuring that the native inhabitants withdrew from the area, the occupying power avoided the unpleasant, and clearly unethical, practice of forcibly displacing people. Conceptualized in this way, it also meant that the settling power had no authority over the native groups in their area.

In his chapter on the natural law tradition, Tuck details how both the English and the Dutch viewed purchase as an important means for extending their power in the New World. As Tuck cites in his chapter, the rules governing the West Indies Company of the New Netherlands, drawn up in 1629, specified that whoever shall settle any colony out of the limits of the Manhattes' Island, shall be obliged to satisfy the Indians for the land they shall settle upon.[13] Dutch practice during the 1620s, most famously manifested in the purchase of Manhattan Island, typically involved a treaty by which the natives ceded both land and jurisdictional control over a specified area of land, or withdrew their claims to the area. This made possible the uncontested settlement of that area by the European power, which could then give rise to jurisdictional control over the territory. The natural law view of sales or purchase dovetails with the natural law view of settlement, such that it amounts to agreement with the local authority on what constitutes waste land. The natives agreed to remove land from their jurisdiction, or remove themselves from that area of land (which amounted to the same thing), and this allowed the settlers to legitimately move in to the area, and establish their own properties and their own jurisdictional authority.

It is possible to conceptualize this practice in different ways: some might claim that the decision to cede jurisdiction over a territory to a different political community or to its inhabitants should not properly be described as selling the land, but only vacating that area of one's authority. However, since the treaties typically involved the exchange of money or goods, the distinction seems a bit fine: the process could also be described accurately as selling the territory.

Inheritance was, interestingly, a somewhat different matter from sale or purchase, at least as far as monarchies were concerned. In the pre-modern period, states were subsumed into the person of their ruler. This meant that individual subjects had some right over and against their rulers, but these did not extend to questions related to the extent of the ruler's territory. The jurisdictional territory of the sovereign could be carried with him or her into marriage, just as private property could be. Indeed, many dynastic marriages were designed to gain or secure territory for the realm, just as aristocratic marriages were often decided on the basis of the lands that the marriage partners brought with them. Many of the current boundaries of European states have developed through dynastic marriage: modern-day Spain is largely a product of the marriage of Ferdinand of Aragon with Isabella of Castile. The Union of England and Scotland was facilitated by the ascension of James VI, King of Scotland, to the English throne.[14] Since jurisdictional territory was attached to the crown, it was inherited through clear rules of male primogeniture. Interestingly, voluntary alienation of the territory worked quite differently from inheritance: while territorial jurisdictions can be inherited, at least under monarchical systems, they are subject to quite different rules than other forms of inheritances. In short, if states are subsumed into the person of their ruler, as they were conceptualized in European political thought, it is not at all clear that the ruler can simply dispense with parts of the territory.

Of course, in the modern period, the view of the relationship of jurisdictional authority to the people has altered: no longer is the state contained in the person of the sovereign, and so transferred through marriage or bequest. The state is viewed as belonging in some sense to the whole people. This democratic notion has become so embedded in contemporary liberal political philosophy and international law that it has undercut, or is at least in tension with, earlier views that regarded sale as a legitimate mode of acquiring territory.

Liberal political philosophy's emphasis on autonomy and free exchange suggests that both property and territory can be purchased. Early liberal political thinkers, like John Locke, operating within the natural law tradition, assumed that sale of territory was entirely legitimate. Similarly, in international law, the juridical framework of European colonial expansion permitted the sale and purchase of territory – and indeed as late as 1867 the United States bought Alaska from Russia, and Denmark sold its territories in the West Indies to the United States in 1916. In some sense, this seemed a legitimate mode by which territory is transferred, since it seems to involve the consent of the parties.

However, it has becoming increasingly problematic in both liberal ethics and international law to accept sale as a straightforwardly legitimate mode to transfer territory, mainly because it ignores the interests of those people who live on the territory in question.

The most pressing questions in the transfer of territory are quite unlike those involved in the transfer of property. As Kingsbury argues in his chapter (15), there are important question of who has the power to decide on such a transfer, what are the conditions for the valid exercise of such a transfer, and what are the consequences of this transfer. The first question is importantly bound up with modern democratic notions of the sovereignty of the people, and whether political authorities can legitimately transfer territory without considering the views of the people living on the territory.[15]

There are no current examples of territory being offered for sale, but a related and recently pressing issue is whether the state can voluntarily dispense with bits of its territory. One does not have to imagine that these bits have been offered for sale: the question here concerns the power of jurisdictional authority to shed bits of territory that it no longer wants. This issue is relevant today in Northern Ireland, where there is clear asymmetry between the desires of the (Protestant) majority to remain part of the United Kingdom and the desire of those on the British mainland for a settlement in Northern Ireland, which may indeed involve dispensing with, or changing the political (sovereign) status of the territory. This issue also arises with respect to very expensive outposts, such as the Falkland Islands, which may prefer to remain British, but which it is extremely expensive for the British to maintain, not only in terms of the economic subvention, but also in terms of military costs (given the dispute over the islands with Argentina).

5. Secession

The term "secession" generally refers to the separation of a part of the territory of an existing state either to form an independent state, or, possibly, join the territory with an already-existing neighboring state. Most of the contributions to this volume confine themselves to considering the first type of secession, mainly because irredentist secession is (1) much rarer, and (2) mainly motivated by nationalism, which was not a factor prior to the modern era.

Secessions are viewed somewhat differently in the pre-modern period and the modern period. This is primarily because, while both liberal theory and international law are concerned about the instability that would result from a permissive right to secede, they also value democratic norms and "the will of the people," and this makes the legitimacy of (democratically-mandated) secessions hard to ignore, both conceptually or practically. In the pre-modern period, by contrast, there was little concern for the democratic will of the people, although there was a general expectation that there would be temporal authorities and political boundaries. In this context, secessions themselves raised very little debate. The central normative issue seemed to be concerned with the legitimacy of the previous governing authority, or the seceding unit, and whether the secessionists suffered unjust treatment at the hands of the previous governing authority. All the pre-modern political and ethical traditions surveyed in this volume seemed to regard secession as a remedy for injustice in a non-ideal world, and, in the case of Christian and natural law tradition – which placed less emphasis on unity than either Judaism, Islam, or Confucianism – as a normal part of the general practice of unity and division within the temporal order.

In both natural law and Christian political thought, boundaries were assumed to be the creation of the civil or human law. There is no *de jure* right of a people to secede from a legitimately constituted state. Indeed, the people were not consulted at all, but were always conceived of as one with the person of their prince. While there was no right of secession residing in the will of the people, it was assumed that different titles and jurisdictions created as the result of human law, and that many of these historic rights and privileges would survive, and did survive, even the vicissitudes of conquest and union. There was very little consideration or debate given to the changes which resulted when one crown united or separated from another. As Tuck explains in his chapter (8), there was almost no debate surrounding Sweden's secession from the Union of Kalmar (a dynastic union between Sweden, Denmark, and Norway, effected in 1397) when Sweden seceded in 1527.

In other ethical traditions, unity tends to be strongly valued, but this runs alongside recognition of the fact that political rule might be unjust or unwise. For example, in an ideal Confucian world, as Bell (Chapter 4) and Ling (Chapter 5) relate, one sage-king would rule peacefully and justly over the whole world. Unity is valued, and secession in this context would be viewed harshly. The Islamic tradition also values unity: the Prophet repeatedly emphasized the moral and political unity of the Muslim community.

In practice, however, political power might not be used for good ends, and both traditions were aware of the possibility of dissension from the central political body, and the possibility that this dissension might have justice on its side. Although the many different possible contexts in which secession might occur are not discussed directly, Confucius put forward the view that states that have been conquered unjustly have a right to secede. This suggests (1) that injustice provides a ground for secession, and (2) that the historic rights and privileges and autonomy of political units should be respected. This latter point is consistent with the Confucian emphasis on pluralism.

In the Islamic tradition, some of the dissension during the Prophet's lifetime was condemned on the grounds that these secessionists and rebels (these are not clearly distinguished by pre-modern jurists) were not full converts to the Islamic world, and were merely trying to wrest political power for their own ends. Ethnic or linguistic bases for political communities are viewed within Islamic political thought as inadequate and non-moral grounds for the constitution of a just political community. Those rebels or secessionists who sought political power for its own sake or to improve the position of their tribe or ethnic group were regarded as akin to common criminals. However, the Islamic tradition recognizes that in a non-ideal world, there is the possibility that the central authority might not cleave fully to the Islamic faith, or that the secessionists might be making claims of justice. Thus, unlike earlier attempts by certain tribal leaders to assume the caliphate for themselves, the group of secessionists that emerged in 657, known as the Kharaij, justified their actions by a particular brand of Islam, and believed themselves to constitute a community of believers. The general view taken within Islam is that people motivated by a principled regard for Islam, and acting out of justice, should receive some legal protection or leniency. If they succeeded in implementing the *Shariah*, their legal enactments and adjudications should be recognized and enforced by Muslims.

The Jewish tradition bears many strong similarities with the other pre-modern traditions, insofar as it also entertained the possibility of a legitimate secession from an unjust or oppressive political power, especially along the lines of already legitimate constitutive units (in this case, the ten tribes of Israel), but valued unity under one rule and centered on one city (Jerusalem). The view of secession was mainly informed by the fact that the ancient Kingdom of Israel, independent from the Kingdom of Judah, was the result of the secession of the northern tribes, led by Jeroboam, from the rule of the House of David. This was regarded as legitimate, because of the oppression to which the tribes were subject under that particular ruler and the dominance within the political structure of the tribe of Judah. Nevertheless, there is a strong emphasis on unity in Jewish political thought, which is evident in the imaginative focus on the House of David for messianic hopes of future generations and on Jerusalem as the center of the Jewish people.

The liberal and international law traditions have much more contradictory impulses on the issue of secession than pre-modern theories. This seems to be partly due to the fact that the issue reveals a tension between universal principles based on justice and democratic governance, which are hegemonic in the modern period, and the difficulties attached to institutionalizing a permissive right to secede.

While liberal theory has historically ignored issues related to boundaries and membership, state break-ups since 1989 have forced liberal political theorists to examine their own assumptions and arguments, and articulate a principled theory of the justifiability of secession. Because liberal theory values individual autonomy, individual freedom of choice, democratic governance, and rules of justice, it would seem sympathetic to the view that people should be permitted to choose the conditions of their existence, including the state that they belong to. In fact, these principles do come into play to permit consensual secession, and, as Buchanan argues in his chapter (12), unilateral secessions as a remedy of last resort for serious injustices. It is possible, on liberal-democratic grounds, to support a right of secession when territorially-concentrated majorities are in favor of it, but there are also serious difficulties with this, from a liberal perspective. Most of these concerns highlight the perverse consequences that would attach to any attempt to institutionalize the view that secession should be part of the democratic agenda. Too easy a right of secession might undermine the conditions that make democracy stable and the sustained commitment that democratic voice requires. Further, there is the danger that a regional minority, empowered by a right of secession, might use that as an effective veto and so undermine democratic rule.

International legal writings on secession tends to be fairly united in their condemnation of unilateral secession, but, like liberal theory, this masks a number of tensions within international law and between its normative and political power components. Like liberalism, international law has to consider the strong institutional constraints, and the possibility of erecting perverse incentives, which might attach to a permissive right to secede. The traditional Westphalian model of territorially bounded sovereign political units rests on two planks: (1) the territorial integrity of states, and (2) the view that the internal affairs of states are the sole concern of that state. This lineage, combined with the fact that international law is made by territorially intact states, which may be concerned about their own minorities, and the possibility of their own break-up, has led to an extreme reluctance to sanction unilateral secession in international law. On the other hand, the normative power of the idea of self-determination, the universal approbation that accompanied decolonization, the close relationship between decolonization and secessionist forms of self-determination in actual cases, as well as the practical reality on the ground that some states are brutally oppressive towards their minorities and/or lack legitimacy in the eyes of the minority population all suggest that the international community cannot simply ignore secessionist mobilization. It cannot ignore these particularly when they are made by beleaguered minorities who have no alterative within their own states, or when there is a clear sense of overwhelming support for secession.

This tension between these two issues – the normative force of some of the secessionist's demands, on the one hand, and the extreme reluctance to sanction secession in international law, on the other – has resulted in a number of strategies, detailed in Hurrell's chapter (14), to reconcile these two positions. These strategies include attempting to restrict the range of units entitled to self-determination, and defining self-determination as entirely "internal" (that is, democratic) self-determination. However, it is unclear that the basic idea that government should serve the interests of the governed, and the violations of minority rights and democratic will of the people in these nationally mobilized areas, can be contained in this way. Indeed, Hurrell suggests in his chapter, that it is with the issue of secession, in particular, that the normative basis of international law, as the only global set of institutionalized norms, and the basic normative concepts of self-determination, human rights, democratic governance and minority rights, conflict with rival conceptions of international law, shaped by *realpolitik* and considerations of security and power.

Conclusion

Ethical theories, by their very nature, are universal theories, and tend to be somewhat suspicious of boundaries. This is particularly true of liberalism and Confucianism: liberalism's emphasis on the equal freedom of all seems to apply to everyone, not merely citizens of liberal-democratic states, and Confucianism is explicit about its contempt for boundaries and limited political jurisdictions. The other religious traditions examined in this volume are also less than enthusiastic about temporal political authority and the kind of limited obligations that go with it. Christianity and natural law accept a kind of division between spiritual and temporal authority; but even they share with Judaism and Islam the view that political boundaries as justified ultimately in spiritual or higher terms – either because they are consistent with a particular religion, or political authority – as delegated power from a higher, religious order, or that the rules implemented in the political sphere are justified when they help to instill the right values and ethics.

Despite these varying views of political jurisdictions and boundaries – positive and negative – all the traditions examined in this volume have had to cope with and address a wide variety of circumstances. In these various contexts, they have developed subtle and nuanced views about particular kinds of boundary changes that follow from their principles, as the authors of the various chapters have explained. The most striking element in this comparison of ethical traditions is the broad agreement on certain questions – on the undesirability of conquest, except in a just war (although this conception was variously defined); the general problems that many traditions identified attached to moving from the sales and inheritance of property to these questions as they apply to territory; and the problem of indigenous populations in the case of settlement. This overview has tried to capture the main elements in each of the traditions' responses to the five methods of boundary-change discussed in this volume.

Notes to Chapter 16

1. However, some of the peace plans drawn up seemed more strongly related to the military capabilities of the ground, while of course denying that this was relevant.
2. Buchanan argues that there is a possible exception to this general prohibition against conquest, which suggests that the liberal common law principle of justified self-defence could be extended to include or acquire territory that is needed for security against a proven aggressor. Buchanan employs the example of the Tyrol region of Austria, given to Italy following the First World War, and the Saar region of Germany, given to France following the Second World War. However, this possible justification would also run up against resistance to the idea of conquest and liberal norms of collective self-determination and autonomy.
3. See Susan Moller Okin, "Feminism and Multiculturalism: Some Tensions," *Ethics* 108/4 (July 1998), 661–84.
4. Settlement was a central plank in the creation of the Jewish state as a whole. However, that was typically justified in terms of the need to create some state, somewhere on earth, where Jews were in the majority, given the vulnerability to which their minority status conferred on them, and its devastating consequences during the Holocaust. Other arguments, similar to the ones supporting European settlement of the New World, were also employed, but this argument has the greatest relevance and validity. It is doubtful, however, that it confers legitimacy on settlement beyond the borders of pre-1967 Israel.
5. Francisco de Vitoria, "On the Law of War," 1.2., in Anthony Pagden and Jeremy Lawrance, eds., *Vitoria Political Writings* (Cambridge: Cambridge University Press, 1991), 299.
6. Cited in Pagden's contribution to this volume. The reference is Vitoria "On the American Indians," Ibid., 3.
7. Cited in note 16 in Tuck's contribution to this volume.
8. Edward Said discusses three pillars of (Hess's and Eliot's) Zionism: the first two are the nonexistence of the Arab inhabitant, and a positive attitude towards the "empty" territory. These make Zionism seem like a restorative project. Edward Said, *The Question of Palestine* (New York: Vintage Books, 1992, 2nd edition), 68.
9. In many cases, state policies simply provide incentives for individuals to move, as was the case with Russian policy in the Baltics in the post-Second World War period, and makes this distinction difficult to figure out, in practice. See John McGarry, "Demographic Engineering: The State-Directed Movement of Ethnic

Groups as a Technique of Conflict-Regulation," *Ethnic and Racial Studies*, 21/4 (July, 1998), 613–38.

10. Carinthian Slovenes voted in a referendum in 1920 whether to join Austria or the newly-created SHS-state (which later became Yugoslavia). They opted to remain in Austria.

11. Details in John McGarry, "Demographic Engineering: The State-Directed Movement of Ethnic Groups as a Technique of Conflict Resolution," *Ethnic and Racial Studies* 21/4 (July 1998), 613–38.

12. See "China's Uighurs: a train of concern," *The Economist*, 12 Feb. 2000, 40.

13. E.B. O'Callaghan, *History of New Netherland*, 2nd ed. (New York: Appleton, 1855), 119. Quoted in Tuck's contribution to this volume.

14. However, in many cases, the sovereign king was not an absolute monarch, but one whose power was limited in various ways, most notably the historic privileges of the nobles and regions of the country. The full Union of Scotland and England required the Scottish nobles to vote in favor of union with England with the Act of Union, 1707.

15. If the people no longer seek to belong to the overholding state, that constitutes secession or secession, and is no longer a case of straightforward sale.

Index